Born in Denver on 8 April 1909, John Fante migrated to Los Angeles in his early twenties. He began writing in 1930 and had numerous short stories published in American magazines, the likes of *American Mercury*, *Harper's Bazaar*, *Esquire*, *Saturday Evening Post* and the *Atlantic Monthly*. Fante also wrote several collections of short stories and numerous screenplays, including *Full of Life* and *Walk on the Wild Side*.

His first published novel, *Wait Until Spring, Bandini*, appeared in 1938 and was followed in 1939 by *Ask the Dust*. Though he made his living as a screenwriter, Fante was often out of place in a town built on celluloid dreams, and was not truly discovered as a great fiction writer until many years later.

Stricken with diabetes in the '50s, Fante lost his sight in 1978, but continued to write by dictation to his wife, Joyce. *Dreams From Bunker Hill*, his final book, was published in 1982. He died the following year at the age of 74.

Discovered posthumously among his papers was *The Road to Los Angeles*. Written in 1933, it was the first book he produced as part of the Arturo Bandini cycle of novels. *Wait Until Spring, Bandini*, though written later, was in effect a prequel that introduced us to a brash young Bandini, whom many believed to be Fante's alter ego.

John Fante was recognised in 1987 with a Lifetime Achievement Award by PEN, Los Angeles. He is now regard... ...tion.

Also by John Fante

Dago Red (later published as *The Wine of Youth: Selected Stories of John Fante*)
Full of Life
The Brotherhood of the Grape
1933 Was a Bad Year
West of Rome

The Big Hunger: Stories 1932–1959
Selected Letters: 1932–1981

JOHN FANTE

The Bandini Quartet

Wait Until Spring, Bandini
The Road to Los Angeles
Ask the Dust
Dreams From Bunker Hill

With Introductions by
Charles Bukowski
and
Dan Fante

CANONGATE
Edinburgh · New York · Melbourne

WAIT UNTIL SPRING, BANDINI.
Copyright © 1938, 1983, John Fante
THE ROAD TO LOS ANGELES. First published in
the United States of America in 1985 by Black Sparrow Press.
Copyright © Joyce Fante, 1985
ASK THE DUST. Copyright © John Fante, 1939, 1980
DREAMS FROM BUNKER HILL. Copyright © John Fante, 1982

9

Introduction Copyright © Charles Bukowski, 1980
Introduction Copyright © Dan Fante, 2003

British Library Cataloguing-in-Publication Data
A catalogue record for this book is available on
request from the British Library

ISBN 978 1 84195 497 4

Book Design by Jim Hutcheson
Typeset by Palimpsest Book Production Limited,
Polmont, Stirlingshire
Printed and bound in Great Britain by Clays Ltd, St Ives plc

www.canongate.tv

Contents

Introduction to *Ask the Dust*

I was a young man, starving and drinking and trying to be a writer. I did most of my reading at the downtown L.A. Public Library, and nothing that I read related to me or to the streets or to the people about me. It seemed as if everybody was playing word-tricks, that those who said almost nothing at all were considered excellent writers. Their writing was an admixture of subtlety, craft and form, and it was read and it was taught and it was ingested and it was passed on. It was a comfortable contrivance, a very slick and careful Word-Culture. One had to go back to the pre-Revolution writers of Russia to find any gamble, any passion. There were exceptions but those exceptions were so few that reading them was quickly done, and you were left staring at rows and rows of exceedingly dull books. With centuries to look back on, with all their advantages, the moderns just weren't very good.

I pulled book after book from the shelves. Why didn't anybody say something? Why didn't anybody scream out?

I tried other rooms in the library. The section on Religion was just a vast bog – to me. I got into Philosophy. I found a couple of bitter Germans who cheered me for a while, then that was over. I tried Mathematics but upper Maths was just like Religion: it ran right off me. What *I* needed seemed to be absent everywhere.

I tried Geology and found it curious but, finally, non-sustaining.

I found some books on Surgery and I liked the books on Surgery: the words were new and the illustrations were wonderful. I particularly liked and memorized the operation on the mesocolon.

Then I dropped out of Surgery and I was back in the big room with the novelists and short story writers. (When I had enough cheap wine to drink I never went to the library. A library was a good place to be when you had nothing to drink or to eat, and the landlady was looking for you and for the back rent money. In the library at least you had the use of the toilet facilities.) I saw quite a number of other bums in there, most of them asleep on top of their books.

I kept on walking around the big room, pulling the books off the shelves, reading a few lines, a few pages, then putting them back.

Then one day I pulled a book down and opened it, and there it was. I stood for a moment, reading. Then like a man who had found gold in the city dump, I carried the book to a table. The lines rolled easily across the page, there was a flow. Each line had its own energy and was followed by another like it. The very substance of each line gave the page a form, a feeling of something *carved* into it. And here, at last, was a man who was not afraid of emotion. The humour and the pain were intermixed with a superb simplicity. The beginning of that book was a wild and enormous miracle to me.

I had a library card. I checked the book out, took it to my room, climbed into my bed and read it, and I knew long before I had finished that here was a man who had evolved a distinct way of writing. The book was *Ask the Dust* and the author was John Fante. He was to be a lifetime influence on my writing. I finished *Ask the Dust* and looked for other books of Fante's in the library. I found two: *Dago Red* and *Wait Until Spring, Bandini*. They were of the same order, written of and from the gut and the heart.

Yes, Fante had a mighty effect upon me. Not long after reading these books I began living with a woman. She was a worse drunk than I was and we had some violent arguments, and often I would scream at her, 'Don't call me a son of a bitch! *I am Bandini, Arturo Bandini!*'

Fante was my god and I knew that the gods should be left alone, one didn't bang at their door. Yet I liked to guess about where he had lived on Angel's Flight and I imagined it possible that he still lived there. Almost every day I walked by and I thought, is that the window Camilla crawled through? And, is that the hotel door? Is that the lobby? I never knew.

Thirty-nine years later I reread *Ask the Dust*. That is to say, I reread it this year and it still stands, as do Fante's other works, but this one is my favourite because it was my first discovery of the *magic*. There are other books beside *Dago Red* and *Wait Until Spring, Bandini*. They are *Full of Life* and *The Brotherhood of the Grape*. And, at the moment, Fante has a novel in progress, *A Dream of Bunker Hill*.

Through other circumstances, I finally met the author this year [1979]. There is much more to the story of John Fante. It is a story of terrible luck and a terrible fate and of a rare and natural courage. Some day it will be told but I feel that he doesn't want me to tell it here. But let me say that the way of his words and the way of his way are the same: strong and good and warm.

That's enough. Now this book is yours.

Charles Bukowski

The End of Arturo Bandini

In 1979, my father, John Fante, suddenly went blind from the complications of diabetes. The year before that both of his legs were amputated and, as a result, he became marooned in a stinking wheel-chair and dependent entirely upon my mother. Disease was killing Pops off an inch at a time. It was a brutal, unforgiving journey to the boneyard.

At that time my father was virtually unknown as a writer. All of his books were out of print and his last novel, *Brotherhood of the Grape* (1977), had sold a scant 3,000 copies in America. His once-promising career as an author had been replaced by forty years of cranking out fix-it hack screenplays for an industry that cared more about the price of popcorn than a line of prose. Hollywood had changed my Dad, then broken his heart and his spirit. Years of boozing and fast-money success gave way to failed health and bleak cynicism. Now, even his best friends kept their distance, lest they should feel the sting of John Fante's notoriously unkind tongue.

By all rights the story should have ended there: *Forgotten writer sells his soul to the Hollywood movie machine then dies, embittered and alone.*

Everyone, it seemed, had given up on John Fante. His ability to earn a living was gone. The family bank accounts had been drained by his long illness and the expense of five terrible surgeries. His doctors, depending on which dogmatic sawbones was pontificating that day, now calculated my Pop's lifespan on one calendar page. For those of us left waiting there was little to be optimistic about. Soon we would walk together single file out his front door, across the road to the high Malibu cliffs overlooking the Pacific Ocean, then fling his ashes to the winds.

Everyone had given up except John Fante. On his own this stubborn, angry artist, whose roots came from the hard cold mountains of Abruzzi in Italy, had come to a decision: He would not die. Not yet. Instead he would write one more book.

In fact, the rest of what you will read here will have the echo of a cheap Hollywood script, like a World War II tear-jerker starring Spencer Tracy and Lana Turner. Even my old man himself would have turned down the insipid re-write, or at least asked Jack Warner for more fix-it money.

But each morning for the next year John Fante would get himself up, and with the help of my mother, shave and get dressed. Mom would wheel the old man into the dining room where he would smoke his cigarettes and drink his coffee and listen to the news and sports scores on the radio, never missing an opportunity to heap curses on the luckless L.A. Dodgers for failing him again on the baseball field.

Then my mother would roll the old man into his den, beneath his tall wall of books, where the morning sun filled the room and warmed his skin.

Once there and comfortable, something inexplicable began to take place. A transformation. It was as if my father had consumed an artist's potion instead of five cups of black espresso and half a pack of cigarettes. Maybe it was his stubborn courage or maybe it was a visitation from the Blessed Virgin of his childhood, but in those days John Fante became possessed by magic. He was himself. A writer of books. The result was dazzling.

My father would turn in the direction of his wife and say, 'Okay, where are we?' And Mom would read aloud the last paragraph or page of what he had dictated to her the day before. The story would later be named *Dreams from Bunker Hill*, the last installment in the saga of Arturo Bandini.

That entire novel was spoken to my mother line for line, written down by her on yellow notebooks exactly as dictated. Not a comma or a phrase of what came from my father was changed. John Fante was able to *see* an entire book in his mind, word-for-word. He knew he was dying. He knew his career was over. The years of grudges and battles with agents and a thousand film-business antagonists no longer mattered. My Dad's unrelenting, ruminative mind was finally silent. The ghosts were gone. His skill as an artist was now, remarkably, better than ever. All that remained for my father was his passion for words.

During the months that my Dad wrote the last of the Arturo Bandini books I was unemployed from my phone sales career. Unemployable is more the truth. I was a drunk, a failed poet, and no credit to the capitalist work ethic that had possessed my father for half a century. Yet, twice a week, I made myself get behind the wheel of my sputtering old Pontiac, leaving a dingy one-room apartment in Venice to drive twenty miles up the Coast Highway to his home above the sea.

We didn't like each other very much and the only reason I

made those trips was because of my mother and because he'd asked me to come. I told myself it was for the free whiskey. My phone would ring and wake me up and it would be him, demanding my presence.

Several years of more boozing and insanity passed for me before I came to understand the meaning of those hours and days we'd spent together. John Fante had chosen me as his witness. My father was teaching me his trade. I was his son and he was showing me how to write the way his own father from Torricella Peligna had shown him, as a boy, how to work a wall of stone or lay a row of brick. I was learning how to build books. Watching a master at work. Those would be the most important days of my life.

John Fante's gift to the world was his pure writer's heart. Christ, what a writer! What an honor to have been his son.

For the record, Wait Until Spring, Bandini, *my father's second novel, was actually his first published novel – the year was 1938. Here we meet the Bandini family from Abruzzi Italy and young Arturo himself, a kid of fourteen. A year later came* Ask the Dust, *where Arturo is 'a young man, starving and drinking and trying to be a writer'.*

Several years after my father's death, while looking through a filing cabinet, my mother and I discovered The Road to Los Angeles *in a box among some early forgotten screenplays. This is John Fante's first book in the saga of Arturo Bandini. It took an accident and over fifty years for* The Road to Los Angeles *to find its way to a publisher. At the time it was written (1935) no one would touch it.*

Of the four Bandini books, The Road to Los Angeles *and* Ask the Dust *are certainly the most autobiographical. Was*

Arturo Bandini John Fante's alter-ego in those two novels? You decide.

I recommend that you read any of the novels in this anthology in the order you wish. Each book stands by itself and does not rely on another.

Now the saga of Arturo Bandini is yours.

Dan Fante
Los Angeles
December, 2003

Wait Until Spring, Bandini

This book is dedicated to my mother,
Mary Fante, with love and devotion;
and to my father, Nick Fante, with
love and admiration.

Author's Note

Now that I am an old man I cannot look back upon *Wait Until Spring, Bandini* without losing its trail in the past. Sometimes, lying in bed at night, a phrase or a paragraph or a character from that early work will mesmerize me and in a half dream I will entwine it in phrases and draw from it a kind of melodious memory of an old bedroom in Colorado, or my mother, or my father, or my brothers and sister. I cannot imagine that what I wrote so long ago will soothe me as does this half dream, and yet I cannot bring myself to look back, to open this first novel and read it again. I am fearful, I cannot bear being exposed by my own work. I am sure I shall never read this book again. But of this I am sure: all of the people of my writing life, all of my characters are to be found in this early work. Nothing of myself is there any more, only the memory of old bedrooms, and the sound of my mother's slippers walking to the kitchen.

John Fante

Chapter One

He came along, kicking the deep snow. Here was a disgusted man. His name was Svevo Bandini, and he lived three blocks down that street. He was cold and there were holes in his shoes. That morning he had patched the holes on the inside with pieces of cardboard from a macaroni box. The macaroni in that box was not paid for. He had thought of that as he placed the cardboard inside of his shoes.

He hated the snow. He was a bricklayer, and the snow froze the mortar between the brick he laid. He was on his way home, but what was the sense in going home? When he was a boy in Italy, in Abruzzi, he hated the snow too. No sunshine, no work. He was in America now, in the town of Rocklin, Colorado. He had just been in the Imperial Poolhall. In Italy there were mountains, too, like those white mountains a few miles west of him. The mountains were a huge white dress dropped plumb-like to the earth. Twenty years before, when he was twenty years old, he had starved for a full week in the folds of that savage white dress. He had been building a fireplace in a mountain lodge. It was dangerous up there in the winter. He had said the devil with the danger, because he was only twenty then, and he had a girl in Rocklin, and he needed money. But the roof of the lodge had caved beneath the suffocating snow.

It harassed him always, that beautiful snow. He could never understand why he didn't go to California. Yet he stayed in Colorado, in the deep snow, because it was too late now. The beautiful white snow was like the beautiful white wife of Svevo Bandini, so white, so fertile, lying in a white bed in a house up the street. 456 Walnut Street, Rocklin, Colorado.

Svevo Bandini's eyes watered in the cold air. They were brown, they were soft, they were a woman's eyes. At birth he had stolen them from his mother – for after the birth of Svevo Bandini, his mother was never quite the same, always ill, always with sickly eyes after his birth, and then she died and it was Svevo's turn to carry soft brown eyes.

A hundred and fifty pounds was the weight of Svevo Bandini, and he had a son named Arturo who loved to touch his round shoulders and feel for the snakes inside. He was a fine man, Svevo Bandini, all muscles, and he had a wife named Maria who had only to think of the muscle in his loins and her body and her mind melted like the spring snows. She was so white, that Maria, and looking at her was seeing her through a film of olive oil.

Dio cane. Dio cane. It means God is a dog, and Svevo Bandini was saying it to the snow. Why did Svevo lose ten dollars in a poker game tonight at the Imperial Poolhall? He was such a poor man, and he had three children, and the macaroni was not paid, nor was the house in which the three children and the macaroni were kept. God is a dog.

Svevo Bandini had a wife who never said: give me money for food for the children, but he had a wife with large black eyes, sickly bright from love, and those eyes had a way about them, a sly way of peering into his mouth, into his ears, into his stomach, and into his pockets. Those eyes were so clever in a sad way, for they always knew when the Imperial Poolhall had done a good business. Such eyes for a wife! They saw all he was and all he hoped to be, but they never saw his soul.

That was an odd thing, because Maria Bandini was a woman who looked upon all the living and the dead as souls. Maria knew what a soul was. A soul was an immortal thing she knew about. A soul was an immortal thing she would not argue about. A soul was an immortal thing. Well, whatever it was, a soul was immortal.

Maria had a white rosary, so white you could drop it in the snow and lose it forever, and she prayed for the soul of Svevo Bandini and her children. And because there was no time, she hoped that somewhere in this world someone, a nun in some quiet convent, someone, anyone, found time to pray for the soul of Maria Bandini.

He had a white bed waiting for him, in which his wife lay, warm and waiting, and he was kicking the snow and thinking of something he was going to invent some day. Just an idea he had in his head: a snow plow. He had made a miniature of it out of cigar boxes. He had an idea there. And then he shuddered as you do when cold metal touches your flank, and he was suddenly remembering the many times he had got into the warm bed beside Maria, and the tiny cold cross on her rosary touched his flesh on winter nights like a tittering little cold serpent, and how he withdrew quickly to an even colder part of the bed, and then he thought of the bedroom, of the house that was not paid for, of the white wife endlessly waiting for passion, and he could not endure it, and straightway in his fury he plunged into deeper snow off the sidewalk, letting his anger fight it out with the snow. *Dio cane. Dio cane.*

He had a son named Arturo, and Arturo was fourteen and owned a sled. As he turned into the yard of his house that was not paid for, his feet suddenly raced for the tops of the trees, and he was lying on his back, and Arturo's sled was still in motion, sliding into a clump of snow-weary lilac bushes. *Dio cane!* He had told that boy, that little bastard, to keep his sled out of the front walk. Svevo Bandini felt the snow's cold attacking his hands like frantic ants. He got to his feet, raised his eyes to the sky, shook his fist at God, and nearly collapsed with fury. That Arturo. That little bastard! He dragged the sled from beneath the lilac bush and with systematic fiendishness tore the runners off. Only when the destruction was complete did he remember that the sled had cost seven-fifty. He stood brushing the snow from his clothes, that strange hot feeling in his ankles, where the snow had entered from the tops of his shoes. Seven dollars and fifty cents torn to pieces. *Diavolo!* Let the boy buy another sled. He preferred a new one anyway.

The house was not paid for. It was his enemy, that house. It had a voice, and it was always talking to him, parrot-like, forever chattering the same thing. Whenever his feet made the porch floor creak, the house said insolently: you do not own me, Svevo Bandini, and I will never belong to you. Whenever he touched the front doorknob it was the same. For fifteen years that house had heckled him and exasperated him with its idiotic independence. There were times when he wanted to set dynamite under it, and blow it to pieces. Once it had been a challenge, that house so like a woman, taunting him to possess her. But in thirteen years he had wearied and weakened, and the house had gained in its arrogance. Svevo Bandini no longer cared.

The banker who owned that house was one of his worst enemies. The mental image of that banker's face made his heart pound with a hunger to consume itself in violence. Helmer, the banker. The dirt of the earth. Time and again he had been forced to stand before Helmer and say that he had not enough money to feed his family. Helmer, with the neatly parted gray hair, with the soft hands, the banker eyes that looked like oysters when Svevo Bandini said he had no money to pay the installment on his house. He had had to do that many times, and the soft hands of Helmer unnerved him. He could not talk to that kind of a man. He hated Helmer. He would like to break Helmer's neck, to tear out Helmer's heart and jump on it with both feet. Of Helmer he would think and mutter: the day is coming! the day is coming! It was not his house, and he had but to touch the knob to remember it did not belong to him.

Her name was Maria, and the darkness was light before her black eyes. He tiptoed to the corner and a chair there, near the window with the green shade down. When he seated himself both knees clicked. It was like the tinkling of two bells to Maria, and he thought how foolish for a wife to love a man so much. The room was so cold. Funnels of vapor tumbled from his breathing lips. He grunted like a wrestler with his shoe laces. Always trouble with his shoe laces. *Diavolo!* Would he be an old man on his death bed before he ever learned to tie his shoe laces like other men?

'Svevo?'

'Yes.'

'Don't break them, Svevo. Turn on the light and I'll untie them. Don't get mad and break them.'

God in heaven! Sweet Mother Mary! Wasn't that just like a woman? Get mad? What was there to get mad about? Oh God, he felt like smashing his fist through that window! He gnawed with his fingernails at the knot of his shoe laces. Shoe laces! Why did there have to be shoe laces? Unnh. Unnh. Unnh.

'Svevo.'

'Yes.'

'I'll do it. Turn on the light.'

When the cold has hypnotized your fingers, a knotted thread is as obstinate as barbed wire. With the might of his arm and shoulder he vented his impatience. The lace broke with a cluck sound, and Svevo Bandini almost fell out of the chair. He sighed, and so did his wife.

'Ah, Svevo. You've broken them again.'

'Bah,' he said. 'Do you expect me to go to bed with my shoes on?'

He slept naked, he despised underclothing, but once a year, with the first flurry of snow, he always found long underwear laid out for him on the chair in the corner. Once he had sneered at this protection: that was the year he had almost died of influenza and pneumonia; that was the winter when he had risen from a death bed, delirious with fever, disgusted with pills and syrups, and staggered to the pantry, choked down his throat a half dozen garlic bulbs, and returned to bed to sweat it out with death. Maria believed her prayers had cured him, and thereafter his religion of cures was garlic, but Maria maintained that garlic came from God, and that was too pointless for Svevo Bandini to dispute.

He was a man, and he hated the sight of himself in long underwear. She was Maria, and every blemish on his underwear, every button and every thread, every odor and every touch, made the points of her breasts ache with a joy that came out of the middle of the earth. They had been married fifteen years, and he had a tongue and spoke well and often of this and that, but rarely had he ever said, I love you. She was his wife, and she spoke rarely, but she tired him often with her constant, I love you.

He walked to the bedside, pushed his hands beneath the covers, and groped for that wandering rosary. Then he slipped between the blankets and seized her frantically, his arms pinioned around hers, his legs locked around hers. It was not passion, it was only the cold of a winter night, and she was a small stove of a woman whose sadness and warmth had attracted him from the first. Fifteen winters, night upon night, and a woman warm and welcoming to her body feet like ice, hands and arms like ice; he thought of such love and sighed.

And a little while ago the Imperial Poolhall had taken his last ten dollars. If only this woman had some fault to cast a hiding shadow upon his own weaknesses. Take Teresa DeRenzo. He would have married Teresa DeRenzo, except that she was extravagant, she talked too much, and her breath smelled like a sewer, and she – a strong, muscular woman – liked to pretend watery weakness in his arms: to think of it! And Teresa DeRenzo was taller than he! Well, with a wife like Teresa he could enjoy giving the Imperial Poolhall ten dollars in a poker game. He could think of that breath, that chattering mouth, and he could thank God for a chance to waste his hard-earned money. But not Maria.

'Arturo broke the kitchen window,' she said.

'Broke it? How?'

'He pushed Federico's head through it.'

'The son of a bitch.'

'He didn't mean it. He was only playing.'

'And what did you do? Nothing, I suppose.'

'I put iodine on Federico's head. A little cut. Nothing serious.'

'Nothing serious! Whaddya mean, nothing serious! What'd you do to Arturo?'

'He was mad. He wanted to go to the show.'

'And he went.'

'Kids like shows.'

'The dirty little son of a bitch.'

'Svevo, why talk like that? Your own son.'

'You've spoiled him. You've spoiled them all.'

'He's like you, Svevo. You were a bad boy too.'

'I was – like hell! You didn't catch me pushing my brother's head through a window.'

'You didn't have any brothers, Svevo. But you pushed your father down the steps and broke his arm.'

'Could I help it if my father . . . Oh, forget it.'

He wriggled closer and pushed his face into her braided hair. Ever since the birth of August, their second son, his wife's right ear had an odor of chloroform. She had brought it home from the hospital with her ten years ago: or was it his imagination? He had quarreled with her about this for years, for she always denied there was a chloroform odor in her right ear. Even the children had experimented, and they had failed to smell it. Yet it was there, always there, just as it was that night in the ward, when he bent down to kiss her, after she had come out of it, so near death, yet alive.

'What if I did push my father down the steps? What's that got to do with it?'

'Did it spoil you? Are you spoiled?'

'How do I know?'

'You're not spoiled.'

What the hell kind of thinking was that? Of course he was spoiled! Teresa DeRenzo had always told him he was vicious and selfish and spoiled. It used to delight him. And that girl – what was her name – Carmela, Carmela Ricci, the friend of Rocco Saccone, she thought he was a devil, and she was wise, she had been through college, the University of Colorado, a college graduate, and she had said he was a wonderful scoundrel, cruel, dangerous, a menace to young women. But Maria – oh Maria, she thought he was an angel, pure as bread. Bah. What did Maria know about it? She had had no college education, why she had not even finished high school.

Not even high school. Her name was Maria Bandini, but before she married him her name was Maria Toscana, and she never finished high school. She was the youngest daughter in a family of two girls and a boy. Tony and Teresa – both high school graduates. But Maria? The family curse was upon her, this lowest of all the Toscanas, this girl who wanted things her own way and refused to graduate from high school. The ignorant Toscana. The one without a high school diploma – almost a diploma, three and one-half years, but still, no diploma. Tony and Teresa had them, and Carmela Ricci, the friend of Rocco, had even gone to the University of Colorado. God was against him. Of them all, why had he fallen in love with this woman at his side, this woman without a high school diploma?

'Christmas will soon be here, Svevo,' she said. 'Say a prayer. Ask God to make it a happy Christmas.'

Her name was Maria, and she was always telling him something he already knew. Didn't he know without being told that Christmas would soon be here? Here it was, the night of December fifth. When a man goes to sleep beside his wife on a Thursday night, is it necessary for her to tell him the next day would be Friday? And that boy Arturo – why was he cursed with a son who played with a sled? *Ah, povera America!* And he should pray for a happy Christmas. Bah.

'Are you warm enough, Svevo?'

There she was, always wanting to know if he was warm enough. She was a little over five feet tall, and he never knew whether she was sleeping or waking, she was that quiet. A wife like a ghost, always content in her little half of the bed, saying the rosary and praying for a merry Christmas. Was it any wonder that he couldn't pay for this house, this madhouse occupied by a wife who was a religious fanatic? A man needed a wife to goad him on, inspire him, and make him work hard. But Maria? *Ah, povera America!*

She slipped from her side of the bed, her toes with sure precision found the slippers on the rug in the darkness, and he knew she was going to the bathroom first, and to inspect the boys afterward, the final inspection before she returned to bed for the rest of the night. A wife who was always slipping out of bed to look at her three sons. Ah, such a life! *Io sono fregato!*

How could a man get any sleep in this house, always in a turmoil, his wife always getting out of bed without a word?

Goddamn the Imperial Poolhall! A full house, queens on deuces, and he had lost. *Madonna!* And he should pray for a happy Christmas! With that kind of luck he should even talk to God! *Jesu Christi*, if God really existed, let Him answer – why!

As quietly as she had gone, she was beside him again.

'Federico has a cold,' she said.

He too had a cold – in his soul. His son Federico could have a snivel and Maria would rub menthol on his chest, and lie there half the night talking about it, but Svevo Bandini suffered alone – not with an aching body: worse, with an aching soul. Where upon the earth was the pain greater than in your own soul? Did Maria help him? Did she ever ask him if he suffered from the hard times? Did she ever say, Svevo, my beloved, how is your soul these days? Are you happy, Svevo? Is there any chance for work this winter, Svevo? *Dio maledetto!* And she wanted a merry Christmas! How can you have a merry Christmas when you are alone among three sons and a wife? Holes in your shoes, bad luck at cards, no work, break your neck on a goddamn sled – and you want a merry Christmas! Was he a millionaire? He might have been, if he had married the right kind of woman. Heh: he was too stupid though.

Her name was Maria, and he felt the softness of the bed recede beneath him, and he had to smile for he knew she was coming nearer, and his lips opened a little to receive them – three fingers of a small hand, touching his lips, lifting him to a warm land inside the sun, and then she was blowing her breath faintly into his nostrils from pouted lips.

'*Cara sposa,*' he said. 'Dear wife.'

Her lips were wet and she rubbed them against his eyes. He laughed softly.

'I'll kill you,' he whispered.

She laughed, then listened, poised, listened for a sound of the boys awake in the next room.

'*Che sara, sara*,' she said. 'What must be, must be.'

Her name was Maria, and she was so patient, waiting for him, touching the muscle at his loins, so patient, kissing him here and there, and then the great heat he loved consumed him and she lay back.

'Ah, Svevo. So wonderful!'

He loved her with such gentle fierceness, so proud of himself, thinking all the time: she is not so foolish, this Maria, she knows what is good. The big bubble they chased toward the sun exploded between them, and he groaned with joyous release, groaned like a man glad he had been able to forget for a little while so many things, and Maria, very quiet in her little half of the bed, listened to the pounding of her heart and wondered how much he had lost at the Imperial Poolhall. A great deal, no doubt; possibly ten dollars, for Maria had no high school diploma but she could read that man's misery in meter of his passion.

'Svevo,' she whispered.

But he was sound asleep.

Bandini, hater of snow. He leaped out of bed at five that morning, like a skyrocket out of bed, making ugly faces at the cold morning, sneering at it: bah, this Colorado, the rear end of God's creation, always frozen, no place for an Italian bricklayer; ah, he was cursed with this life. On the sides of his feet he walked to the chair and snatched his pants and shoved his legs through them, thinking he was losing twelve dollars a day, union scale, eight hours hard work, and all because of that! He jerked the curtain string; it shot up and rattled like a machine gun, and the white naked morning dove into the room, splashing brightly over him. He growled at it. *Sporca chone*: dirty face, he called it. *Sporcaccione ubriaco*: drunken dirty face.

Maria slept with the drowsy awareness of a kitten, and that curtain brought her awake quickly, her eyes in nimble terror.

'Svevo. It's too early.'

'Go to sleep. Who's asking you? Go to sleep.'

'What time is it?'

'Time for a man to get up. Time for a woman to go to sleep. Shut up.'

She had never got used to this early morning rising. Seven was her hour, not counting the times in the hospital, and once, she had stayed in bed until nine, and got a headache because of it, but this man she had married always shot out of bed at five in winter, and at six in summer. She knew his torment in the white prison of winter; she knew that when she arose in two hours he would have shoveled every clod of snow from every path in and around the yard, half a block down the street, under the clothes lines, far down the alley, piling it high, moving it around, cutting it viciously with his flat shovel.

And it was so. When she got up and slipped her feet inside of slippers, the toes aburst like frayed flowers, she looked through the kitchen window and saw where he was, out there in the alley, beyond the high fence. A giant of a man, a dwarfed giant hidden on the other side of a six-foot fence, his shovel peering over the top now and then, throwing puffs of snow back to the sky.

But he had not built a fire in the kitchen stove. Oh no, he never built a fire in the kitchen stove. What was he – a woman, that he should build a fire? Sometimes though. Once he had taken them into the mountains for a beefsteak fry, and absolutely no one but himself was permitted to build that fire. But a kitchen stove! What was he – a woman?

It was so cold that morning, so cold. Her jaw chattered and ran away from her. The dark green linoleum might have been a sheet of ice under her feet, the stove itself a block of ice. What a stove that was! a despot, untamed and ill-tempered. She always coaxed it, soothed it, cajoled it, a black bear of a stove subject to fits of rebellion, defying Maria to make him glow; a cantankerous stove that, once warm and pouring sweet heat, suddenly went berserk and got yellow hot and threatened to destroy the very house. Only Maria could handle that black block of sulking iron, and she did it a twig at a time, caressing the shy flame, adding a slab of wood, then another and another, until it purred beneath her care, the iron heating up, the oven expanding and the heat thumping it until it grunted and groaned in content, like an idiot. She was Maria, and the stove loved only her. Let Arturo or August drop a lump of coal into its greedy mouth and it went mad with its own fever, burning and blistering the paint on the walls, turning a frightful yellow, a chunk of hell hissing for Maria, who came frowning and capable, a cloth in her hand as she twitted it here and there, shutting the vents deftly, shaking its bowels until it resumed its stupid normalcy. Maria, with hands no larger than frayed roses, but that black devil was her slave, and she really was very fond of it. She kept it shining and flashily vicious, its nickel-plated trade name grinning evilly like a mouth too proud of its beautiful teeth.

When at length the flames rose and it groaned good morning, she put water on for coffee and returned to the window. Svevo was in the chicken yard, panting as he leaned on his shovel. The hens had come out of the shed, clucking as they eyed him, this man who could lift the fallen white heavens off the ground and throw them over the fence. But from the window she saw that the hens did not saunter too close to him. She knew why. They were her hens; they ate from her hands, but they hated him; they remembered him as the one who sometimes came of a Saturday night to kill. This was all right; they were very grateful he had shoveled the snow away so they could scratch the earth, they appreciated it, but they could never trust him as they did the woman who came with corn dripping from her small hands. And spaghetti too, in a dish; they kissed her with their beaks when she brought them spaghetti; but beware of this man.

Their names were Arturo, August, and Federico. They were awake now, their eyes all brown and bathed brightly in the black river of sleep. They were all in one bed, Arturo twelve, August ten, and Federico eight. Italian boys, fooling around, three in a bed, laughing the quick peculiar laugh of obscenity. Arturo, he knew plenty. He was telling them now what he knew, the words coming from his mouth in hot white vapor in the cold room. He knew plenty. He had seen plenty. He knew plenty. You guys don't know what I saw. She was sitting on the porch steps. I was about this far from her. I saw plenty.

Federico, eight years old.

'What'ya see, Arturo?'

'Shut yer mouth, ya little sap. We ain't talkin' to you!'

'I won't tell, Arturo.'

'Ah, shut yer mouth. You're too little!'

'I'll tell, then.'

They joined forces then, and threw him out of bed. He bumped against the floor, whimpering. The cold air seized him with a sudden fury and pricked him with ten thousand needles. He screamed and tried to get under the covers again, but they were stronger than he and he dashed around the bed and into his mother's room. She was pulling on her cotton stockings. He was screaming with dismay.

'They kicked me out! Arturo did. August did!'

'Snitcher!' yelled from the next room.

He was so beautiful to her, that Federico; his skin was so beautiful to her. She took him into her arms and rubbed her hands into his back, pinching his beautiful little bottom, squeezing him hard, pushing heat into him, and he thought of the odor of her, wondering what it was and how good it was in the morning.

'Sleep in Mamma's bed,' she said.

He climbed in quickly, and she clamped the covers around him, shaking him with delight, and he was so glad he was on Mamma's side of the bed, with his head in the nest Mamma's hair made, because he didn't like Papa's pillow; it was kind of sour and strong, but Mamma's smelt sweet and made him warm all over.

'I know somethin' else,' Arturo said. 'But I ain't telling.'

August was ten; he didn't know much. Of course he knew more than his punk brother Federico, but not half so much as the brother beside him, Arturo, who knew plenty about women and stuff.

'What'll ya give me if I tell ya?' Arturo said.

'Give you a milk nickel.'

'Milk nickel! What the heck! Who wants a milk nickel in winter?'

'Give it to you next summer.'

'Nuts to you. What'll ya give me now?'

'Give you anything I got.'

'It's a bet. Whatcha got?'

'Ain't got nothing.'

'Okay. I ain't telling nothing, then.'

'You ain't got anything to tell.'

'Like hell I haven't!'

'Tell me for nothing.'

'Nothing doing.'

'You're lying, that's why. You're a liar.'

'Don't call me a liar!'

'You're a liar if you don't tell. Liar!'

He was Arturo, and he was fourteen. He was a miniature of his father, without the mustache. His upper lip curled with such gentle cruelty. Freckles swarmed over his face like ants over a piece of cake. He was the oldest, and he thought he was pretty tough, and no sap kid brother could call him a liar and get away with it. In five seconds August was writhing. Arturo was under the covers at his brother's feet.

'That's my toe hold,' he said.

'Ow! Leggo!'

'Who's a liar!'

'Nobody!'

Their mother was Maria, but they called her Mamma,

and she was beside them now, still frightened at the duty of motherhood, still mystified by it. There was August now; it was easy to be his mother. He had yellow hair, and a hundred times a day, out of nowhere at all, there came that thought, that her second son had yellow hair. She could kiss August at will, lean down and taste the yellow hair and press her mouth on his face and eyes. He was a good boy, August was. Of course, she had had a lot of trouble with him. Weak kidneys, Doctor Hewson had said, but that was over now, and the mattress was never wet anymore in the mornings. August would grow up to be a fine man now, never wetting the bed. A hundred nights she had spent on her knees at his side while he slept, her rosary beads clicking in the dark as she prayed God, please Blessed Lord, don't let my son wet the bed anymore. A hundred, two hundred nights. The doctor had called it weak kidneys; she had called it God's will; and Svevo Bandini had called it goddamn carelessness and was in favor of making August sleep in the chicken yard, yellow hair or no yellow hair. There had been all sorts of suggestions for cure. The doctor kept prescribing pills. Svevo was in favor of the razor strap, but she had always tricked him out of the idea; and her own mother, Donna Toscana had insisted that August drink his own urine. But her name was Maria, and so was the Savior's mother, and she had gone to that other Maria over miles and miles of rosary beads. Well, August had stopped, hadn't he? When she slipped her hand under him in the early hours of the morning, wasn't he dry and warm? And why? Maria knew why. Nobody else could explain it. Bandini had said, by God it's about time; the doctor had said it was the pills had done it, and Donna Toscana insisted it would have stopped a long time ago had they followed her suggestion.

Even August was amazed and delighted on those mornings when he wakened to find himself dry and clean. He could remember those nights when he woke up to find his mother on her knees beside him, her face against his, the beads ticking, her breath in his nostrils and the whispered little words, Hail Mary, Hail Mary, poured into his nose and eyes until he felt an eerie melancholy as he lay between these two women, a helplessness that choked him and made him determined to please them both. He simply *wouldn't* pee the bed again.

It was easy to be the mother of August. She could play with the yellow hair whenever she pleased because he was filled with the wonder and mystery of her. She had done so much for him, that Maria. She had made him grow up. She had made him feel like a real boy, and no longer could Arturo tease him and hurt him because of his weak kidneys. When she came on whispering feet to his bedside each night he had only to feel the warm fingers caressing his hair, and he was reminded again that she and another Maria had changed him from a sissy to a real guy. No wonder she smelled so good. And Maria never forgot the wonder of that yellow hair. Where it came from God only knew, and she was so proud of it.

Breakfast for three boys and a man. His name was Arturo, but he hated it and wanted to be called John. His last name was Bandini, and he wanted it to be Jones. His mother and father were Italians, but he wanted to be an American. His father was a bricklayer, but he wanted to be a pitcher for the Chicago Cubs. They lived in Rocklin, Colorado, population ten thousand, but he wanted to live in Denver, thirty miles away. His face was freckled, but he wanted it to be clear. He went to a Catholic school, but he wanted to go to a public school. He had a girl named Rosa, but she hated him. He was an altar boy, but he was a devil and hated altar boys. He wanted to be a good boy, but he was afraid to be a good boy because he was afraid his friends would call him a good boy. He was Arturo and he loved his father, but he lived in dread of the day when he would grow up and be able to lick his father. He worshipped his father, but he thought his mother was a sissy and a fool.

Why was his mother unlike other mothers? She was that, and everyday he saw it again. Jack Hawley's mother excited him: she had a way of handing him cookies that made his heart purr. Jim Toland's mother had bright legs. Carl Molla's mother never wore anything but a gingham dress; when she swept the floor of the Molla kitchen he stood on the back porch in an ecstasy, watching Mrs Molla sweep, his hot eyes gulping the movement of her hips. He was twelve, and the realization that his mother did not excite him made him hate her secretly. Always out of the corner of his eye he watched his mother. He loved his mother, but he hated her.

Why did his mother permit Bandini to boss her? Why was she afraid of him? When they were in bed and he lay awake sweating in hatred, why did his mother let Bandini do that to her? When she left the bathroom and came into the boys' bedroom, why did she smile in the darkness? He could not see her smile, but he knew it was upon her face, that content of the night, so much in love with the darkness and hidden lights warming her face. Then he hated them both, but his hatred of her was greatest. He felt like spitting on her, and long after she had returned to bed the hatred was upon his face, the muscles in his cheeks weary with it.

Breakfast was ready. He could hear his father asking for

coffee. Why did his father have to yell all the time? Couldn't he talk in a low voice? Everybody in the neighborhood knew everything that went on in their house on account of his father constantly shouting. The Moreys next door – you never heard a peep out of them, never; quiet, American people. But his father wasn't satisfied with being an Italian, he had to be a noisy Italian.

'Arturo,' his mother called. 'Breakfast.'

As if he didn't know breakfast was ready! As if everybody in Colorado didn't know by this time that the Bandini family was having breakfast!

He hated soap and water, and he could never understand why you had to wash your face every morning. He hated the bathroom because there was no bathtub in it. He hated toothbrushes. He hated the toothpaste his mother bought. He hated the family comb, always clogged with mortar from his father's hair, and he loathed his own hair because it never stayed down. Above all, he hated his own face spotted with freckles like ten thousand pennies poured over a rug. The only thing about the bathroom he liked was the loose floorboard in the corner. Here he hid *Scarlet Crime* and *Terror Tales*.

'Arturo! Your eggs are getting cold.'

Eggs. Oh Lord, how he hated eggs.

They were cold, all right; but no colder than the eyes of his father, who glared at him as he sat down. Then he remembered, and a glance told him that his mother had snitched. Oh Jesus! To think that his own mother should rat on him! Bandini nodded to the window with eight panes across the room, one pane gone, the opening covered with a dish towel.

'So you pushed your brother's head through the window?'

It was too much for Federico. All over again he saw it: Arturo angry, Arturo pushing him into the window, the crash of glass. Suddenly Federico began to cry. He had not cried last night, but now he remembered: blood coming out of his hair, his mother washing the wound, telling him to be brave. It was awful. Why hadn't he cried last night? He couldn't remember, but he was crying now, the knuckle of his fist twisting tears out of his eyes.

'Shut up!' Bandini said.

'Let somebody push *your* head through a window,' Federico sobbed. 'See if *you* don't cry!'

Arturo loathed him. Why did he have to have a little brother? Why had he stood in front of the window? What kind of people were these wops? Look at his father, there. Look at him smashing eggs with his fork to show how angry he was. Look at the egg yellow on his father's chin! And on his mustache. Oh sure, he was a dago wop, so he had to have a mustache, but did he have to pour those eggs through his ears? Couldn't he find his mouth? Oh God, these Italians!

But Federico was quiet now. His martyrdom of last night no longer interested him; he had found a crumb of bread in his milk, and it reminded him of a boat floating on the ocean; *Drrrrrr*, said the motor boat, *drrrrrr*. What if the ocean was made out of real milk – could you get ice cream at the North Pole? *Drrrrrr*, *drrrrrr*. Suddenly he was thinking of last night again. A gusher of tears filled his eyes and he sobbed. But the bread crumb was sinking. *Drrrrr*, *drrrrr*. Don't sink, motor boat! don't sink! Bandini was watching him.

'For Christ's sake!' he said. 'Will you drink that milk and quit fooling around?'

To use the name of Christ carelessly was like slapping

Maria across the mouth. When she married Bandini it had not occurred to her that he swore. She never quite got used to it. But Bandini swore at everything. The first English words he learned were God damn it. He was very proud of his swear words. When he was furious he always relieved himself in two languages.

'Well,' he said. 'Why did you push your brother's head through the window?'

'How do I know?' Arturo said. 'I just did it, that's all.'

Bandini rolled his eyes in horror.

'And how do you know I won't knock your goddamn block off?'

'Svevo,' Maria said. 'Svevo. Please.'

'What do *you* want?' he said.

'He didn't mean it, Svevo,' she smiled. 'It was an accident. Boys will be boys.'

He put down his napkin with a bang. He clinched his teeth and seized the hair on his head with both hands. There he swayed in his chair, back and forth, back and forth.

'Boys will be boys!' he jibed. 'That little bastard pushes his brother's head through the window, and boys will be boys! Who's gonna pay for that window? Who's gonna pay the doctor bills when he pushes his brother off a cliff? Who's gonna pay the lawyer when they send him to jail for murdering his brother? A murderer in the family! *Oh Deo uta me!* Oh God help me!'

Maria shook her head and smiled. Arturo screwed his lips in a murderous sneer: so his own father was against him too, already accusing him of murder. August's head racked sadly, but he was very happy that he wasn't going to turn out to be a murderer like his brother Arturo; as for August he was going to be a priest; maybe he would be there to deliver the last sacraments before they sent Arturo to the electric chair. As for Federico, he saw himself the victim of his brother's passion, saw himself lying stretched out at the funeral; all his friends from St Catherine were there, kneeling and crying; oh, it was awful. His eyes floated once more, and he sobbed bitterly, wondering if he could have another glass of milk.

'Kin I have a motor boat for Christmas?' he said.

Bandini glared at him, astonished.

'That's all we need in this family,' he said. Then his tongue flitted sarcastically: 'Do you want a real motor boat, Federico? One that goes put put put put?'

'That's what I want!' Federico laughed. 'One that goes puttedy puttedy put put!' He was already in it, steering it over the kitchen table and across Blue Lake up in the mountains. Bandini's leer caused him to kill the motor and drop anchor. He was very quiet now. Bandini's leer was steady, straight through him. Federico wanted to cry again, but he didn't dare. He dropped his eyes to the empty milk glass, saw a drop or two at the bottom of the glass, and drained them carefully, his eyes stealing a glance at his father over the top of the glass. There sat Svevo Bandini – leering. Federico felt goose flesh creeping over him.

'Gee whiz,' he whimpered. 'What did *I* do?'

It broke the silence. They all relaxed, even Bandini, who had held the scene long enough. Quietly he spoke.

'No motor boats, understand? Absolutely no motor boats.'

Was that all? Federico sighed happily. And all the time he believed his father had discovered that it was he who had stolen the pennies out of his work pants, broken the street lamp on the corner, drawn that picture of Sister Mary Constance on the blackboard, hit Stella Colombo in the eye with a snowball, and spat in the holy water font at St Catherine's.

Sweetly he said, 'I don't want a motor boat, Papa. If you don't want me to have one, I don't want one, Papa.'

Bandini nodded self-approvingly to his wife: here was the way to raise children, his nod said. When you want a kid to do something, just stare at him; that's the way to raise a boy. Arturo cleaned the last of his egg from the plate and sneered: Jesus, what a sap his old man was! He knew that Federico, Arturo did; he knew what a dirty little crook Federico was; that sweet face stuff wasn't fooling him by a long shot, and suddenly he wished he had shoved not only Federico's head but his whole body, head and feet and all, through that window.

'When I was a boy,' Bandini began. 'When I was a boy back in the Old Country –'

At once Federico and Arturo left the table. This was old stuff to them. They knew he was going to tell them for the ten thousandth time that he made four cents a day carrying stone on his back, when he was a boy, back in the Old Country, carrying stone on his back, when he was a boy. The story hypnotized Svevo Bandini. It was dream stuff that suffocated and blurred Helmer the banker, holes in his shoes, a house that was not paid for, and children that must be fed. When I was a boy: dream stuff. The progression of years, the crossing of an ocean, the accumulation of mouths to feed, the heaping of trouble upon trouble, year upon year, was something to boast about too, like the gathering of great wealth. He could not buy shoes with it, but it had happened to him. When I was a boy —. Maria, listening once more, wondered why he always put it that way, always deferring to the years, making himself old.

A letter from Donna Toscana arrived, Maria's mother. Donna Toscana with the big red tongue, not big enough to check the flow of angry saliva at the very thought of her daughter married to Svevo Bandini. Maria turned the letter over and over. The flap gushed glue thickly where Donna's huge tongue had mopped it. Maria Toscana, 345 Walnut Street, Rocklin, Colorado, for Donna refused to use the married name of her daughter. The heavy, savage writing might have been streaks from a hawk's bleeding beak, the script of a peasant woman who had just slit a goat's throat. Maria did not open the letter; she knew its substance.

Bandini entered from the back yard. In his hands he carried a heavy lump of bright coal. He dropped it into the coal bucket behind the stove. His hands were smeared with black dust. He frowned; to carry coal disgusted him; it was a woman's work. He looked irritably at Maria. She nodded to the letter propped against a battered salt cellar on the yellow oilcloth. The heavy writing of his mother-in-law writhed like tiny serpents before his eyes. He hated Donna Toscana with a fury that amounted to fear. They clashed like male and female animals whenever they met. It gave him pleasure to seize that letter in his blackened, grimy hands. It delighted him to tear it open raggedly, with no care for the message inside. Before he read the script he lifted piercing eyes to his wife, to let her know once more how deeply he hated the woman who had given her life. Maria was helpless; this was not her quarrel, all of her married life she had ignored it, and she would have destroyed the letter had not Bandini forbidden her even to open messages from her mother. He got a vicious pleasure out of her mother's letters that was quite horrifying to Maria; there was something black and terrible about it, like peering under a damp stone. It was the diseased pleasure of a martyr, of a man who got an almost exotic joy out of the castigation of a mother-in-law who enjoyed his misery now that he had come upon hard times. Bandini loved it, that persecution, for it gave him a wild impetus to drunkenness. He rarely drank to excess because it sickened him, but a letter from Donna Toscana had a blinding effect upon him. It served him with a pretext that prescribed oblivion, for when he was drunk he could hate his mother-in-law to the point of hysteria, and he could forget, he could forget his house that remained unpaid, his bills, the pressing monotony of marriage. It meant escape: a day, two days, a week of hypnosis – and Maria could remember periods when he was drunk for two weeks. There was no concealing of Donna's letters from him. They came rarely, but they meant only one thing; that Donna would spend an afternoon with them. If she came without his seeing a letter, Bandini knew his wife had hidden the letter. The last time she did that, Svevo lost his temper and gave Arturo a terrible beating for putting too much salt on his macaroni, a meaningless offense, and, of course, one he would not have noticed under ordinary circumstances. But the letter had been concealed, and someone had to suffer for it.

This latest letter was dated the day before, December eighth, the feast of the Immaculate Conception. As Bandini read the lines, the flesh upon his face whitened and his blood disappeared like sand swallowing the ebb tide. The letter read:

My Dear Maria:

Today is the glorious feast day of our Blessed Mother, and I go to Church to pray for you in your misery. My heart goes out to you and the poor children, cursed as they are by the tragic condition in which you live. I have asked the Blessed Mother to have mercy on you, and to bring happiness to those little ones who do not deserve their fate. I will be in Rocklin Sunday afternoon, and will leave by the eight o'clock bus. All love and sympathy to you and the children.

Donna Toscana.

Without looking at his wife, Bandini put the letter down and began gnawing at an already ravaged thumb nail. His fingers plucked his lower lip. His fury began somewhere outside of him. She could feel it rising from the corners of the room, from the walls and the floor, an odor moving in a whirlpool completely outside of herself. Simply to distract herself, she straightened her blouse.

Feebly she said, 'Now, Svevo –'

He arose, chucked her under the chin, his lips smiling fiendishly to inform her that this show of affection was not sincere, and walked out of the room.

'Oh Marie!' he sang, no music in his voice, only hatred pushing a lyrical love song out of his throat. 'Oh Marie. Oh Marie! *Quanto sonna perdato per te! Fa me dor me! Fa me dor me!* Oh Marie, Oh Marie! How much sleep I have lost because of you! Oh let me sleep, my darling Marie!'

There was no stopping him. She listened to his feet on thin soles as they flecked the floor like drops of water spitting on a stove. She heard the swish of his patched and sewed overcoat as he flung himself into it. Then silence for a moment, until she heard a match strike, and she knew he was lighting a cigar. His fury was too great for her. To interfere would have been to give him the temptation of knocking her down. As his steps approached the front door, she held her breath: there was a glass panel in that front door. But no – he closed it quietly and was gone. In a little while now he would meet his good friend, Rocco Saccone, the stonecutter, the only human being she really hated. Rocco Saccone, the boyhood friend of Svevo Bandini, the whiskey-drinking bachelor who had tried to prevent Bandini's marriage; Rocco Saccone, who wore white flannels in all seasons and boasted disgustingly of his Saturday night seductions of married American women at the Old-time dances up in the Odd Fellows Hall. She could trust Svevo. He would float his brains on a sea of whiskey, but he would not be unfaithful to her. She knew that. But could she? With a gasp she threw herself into the chair by the table and wept as she buried her face in her hands.

Chapter Two

It was a quarter to three in the eighth-grade room at St Catherine's. Sister Mary Celia, her glass eye aching in its socket, was in a dangerous mood. The left eyelid kept twitching, completely out of control. Twenty eighth graders, eleven boys and nine girls, watched the twitching eyelid. A quarter to three: fifteen minutes to go. Nellie Doyle, her thin dress caught between her buttocks, was reciting the economic effects of Eli Whitney's cotton gin, and two boys behind her, Jim Lacey and Eddie Holm, were laughing like hell, only not out loud, at the dress caught in Nellie's buttocks. They had been told time and time again to watch out, if the lid over Old Celia's glass eye started jumping, but would you look at Doyle there!

'The economic effects of Eli Whitney's cotton gin were unprecedented in the history of cotton,' Nellie said.

Sister Mary Celia rose to her feet.

'Holm and Lacey!' she demanded. 'Stand up!'

Nellie sat down in confusion, and the two boys got to their feet. Lacey's knees cracked, and the class tittered, Lacey grinned, then blushed. Holm coughed, keeping his head down as he studied the trade lettering on the side of his pencil. It was the first time in his life he had ever read such writing, and he was rather surprised to learn it said simply, Walter Pencil Co.

'Holm and Lacey,' Sister Celia said. 'I'm bored with grinning goons in my classes. Sit down!' Then she addressed the whole group, but she was really speaking to the boys alone, for the girls rarely gave her trouble: 'And the next scoundrel I catch not paying attention to recitation has to stay until six o'clock. Carry on, Nellie.'

Nellie stood up again. Lacey and Holm, amazed that they had got off so easy, kept their heads turned toward the other side of the classroom, both afraid they might laugh again if Nellie's dress was still stuck.

'The economic effects of Eli Whitney's cotton gin were unprecedented in the history of cotton,' Nellie said.

In a whisper, Lacey spoke to the boy in front of him.

'Hey, Holm. Give the Bandini a gander.'

Arturo sat in the opposite side of the room, three desks from the front. His head was low, his chest against the desk, and propped against the ink-stand was a small hand mirror into which he stared as he worked the point of a pencil along the line of his nose. He was counting his freckles. Last night he had slept with his face smeared with lemon juice: it was supposed to be wonderful for the wiping out of freckles. He counted, ninety-three, ninety-four, ninety-five . . . A sense of life's futility occupied him. Here it was, the dead of winter, with the sun showing itself only a moment in the late afternoons, and the count around his nose and cheeks had jumped nine freckles to the grand total of ninety-five. What was the good of living? And last night he had used lemon juice, too. Who was that liar of a woman who had written on the Home Page of yesterday's *Denver Post* that freckles 'fled like the wind' from lemon juice? To be freckled was bad enough, but as far as he knew, he was the only freckle-faced

Wop on earth. Where had he got these freckles? From what side of the family had he inherited those little copper marks of the beast? Grimly he began to poll around his left ear. The faint report of the economic effects of Eli Whitney's cotton gin came to him vaguely. Josephine Perlotta was reciting: who the hell cared what Perlotta had to say about the cotton gin? She was a Dago – how could she possibly know anything about cotton gins? In June, thank God for that, he would graduate from this dump of a Catholic school, and enroll in a public high school, where the wops were few and far between. The count on his left ear was already seventeen, two more than yesterday. God damn these freckles! Now a new voice spoke of the cotton gin, a voice like a soft violin, sending vibrations through his flesh, catching his breath. He put down his pencil and gaped. There she stood in front of him – his beautiful Rosa Pinelli, his love, his girl. Oh you cotton gin! Oh you wonderful Eli Whitney! Oh Rosa, how wonderful you are. I love you, Rosa, I love you, love you, love you!

She was an Italian, sure; but could she help that? Was it her fault anymore than it was his? Oh look at her hair! Look at her shoulders! Look at that pretty green dress! Listen to that voice! Oh you Rosa! Tell 'em Rosa. Tell 'em about that cotton gin! I know you hate me, Rosa. But I love you, Rosa. I love you, and some day you'll see me playing center field for the New York Yanks, Rosa. I'll be out there in center field, Honey, and you'll be my girl, sitting in a box seat off third base, and I'll come in, and it'll be the last half of the ninth, and the Yanks'll be three runs behind. But don't you worry, Rosa! I'll get up there with three men on base, and I'll look at you, and you'll throw me a kiss, and I'll bust that old apple right over the center field wall. I'll make history, Honey. You kiss me and I'll make history!

'*Arturo Bandini!*'

I won't have any freckles then, either, Rosa. They'll be gone – they always leave when you grow up.

'*Arturo Bandini!*'

I'll change my name too, Rosa. They'll call me Banning, the Banning Bambino; Art, the Battering Bandit . . .

'*Arturo Bandini!*'

That time he heard it. The roar of the World Series crowd was gone. He looked up to find Sister Mary Celia looming over her desk, her fist pounding it, her left eye twitching. They were staring at him, all of them, even his Rosa laughing at him, and his stomach rolled out from under him as he realized he had been whispering his fancy aloud. The others could laugh if they pleased, but Rosa – ah Rosa, and her laughter was more poignant than all others, and he felt it hurting him, and he hated her: this dago girl, daughter of a wop coal miner who worked in that guinea-town Louisville: a goddamn lousy coal miner. Salvatore was his name; Salvatore Pinelli, so low down he had to work in a coal mine. Could he put up a wall that lasted years and years, a hundred, two hundred years? Nah – the dago fool, he had a coal pick and a lamp on his cap, and he had to go down under the ground and make his living like a lousy damn dago rat. His name was Arturo Bandini, and if there was anybody in this school who wanted to make something out of it, let him speak up and get his nose broke.

'*Arturo Bandini!*'

'Okay,' he drawled. 'Okay, Sister Celia. I heard you.' Then he stood up. The class watched him. Rosa whispered something to the girl behind her, smiling behind her hand. He saw the gesture and he was ready to scream at her, thinking she had made some remark about his freckles, or the big patch on the knee of his pants, or the fact that he needed a hair cut, or the cut-down and remodeled shirt his father once wore that never fit him smartly.

'Bandini,' Sister Celia said. 'You are unquestionably a moron. I warned you about not paying attention. Such stupidity must be rewarded. You're to stay after school until six o'clock.'

He sat down, and the three o'clock bell sounded hysterically through the halls.

He was alone, with Sister Celia at her desk, correcting papers. She worked oblivious of him, the left eyelid twitching irritably. In the southwest the pale sun appeared, sickly, more like a weary moon on that winter afternoon. He sat with his chin resting in one hand, watching the cold sun. Beyond the windows the line of fir trees seemed to grow even colder beneath their sad white burdens. Somewhere in the street he heard the shout of a boy, and then the clanking of tire chains. He hated the winter. He could picture the baseball diamond behind the school, buried in snow, the backstop behind home plate cluttered with fantastic heaviness – the whole scene so lonely, so sad. What was there to do in winter? He was almost satisfied to sit there, and his punishment amused him. After all, this was as good a place to sit as anywhere.

'Do you want me to do anything, Sister?' he asked.

Without looking up from her work, she answered, 'I want you to sit still and keep quiet – if that's possible.'

He smiled and drawled, 'Okay, Sister.'

He was both still and quiet for all of ten minutes.

'Sister,' he said. 'Want me to do the blackboards?'

'We pay a man for doing that,' she said. 'Rather, I should say we overpay a man for that.'

'Sister,' he said. 'Do you like baseball?'

'Football's my game,' she said. 'I hate baseball. It bores me.'

'That's because you don't understand the finer side of the game.'

'Quiet, Bandini,' she said. 'If you please.'

He changed his position, resting his chin on his arms and watching her closely. The left eyelid twitched incessantly. He wondered how she had got a glass eye. He had always suspected that someone had hit her with a baseball; now he was almost sure of it. She had come to St Catherine's from Fort Dodge, Iowa. He wondered what kind of baseball they played in Iowa, and if there were very many Italians there.

'How's your mother?' she asked.

'I don't know. Swell, I guess.'

She raised her face from her work for the first time and looked at him. 'What do you mean, you *guess?* Don't you know? Your mother's a dear person, a beautiful person. She has the soul of an angel.'

As far as he knew, he and his brothers were the only nonpaying students at that Catholic school. The tuition was only two dollars a month for each child, but that meant six a month for him and his two brothers, and it was never paid. It was a distinction of great torment to him, this feeling that others paid and he did not. Once in a while his mother would put a dollar or two in an envelope and ask him to deliver it to the Sister Superior, on account. This was even more hateful.

He always refused violently. August, however, didn't mind delivering the rare envelopes; indeed, he looked forward to the opportunity. He hated August for it, for making an issue of their poverty, for his willingness to remind the nuns that they were poor people. He had never wanted to go to Sister School anyway. The only thing that made it tolerable was baseball. When Sister Celia told him his mother had a beautiful soul, he knew she meant his mother was brave to sacrifice and deny for those little envelopes. But there was no bravery in it to him. It was awful, it was hateful, it made him and his brothers different from the others. Why, he did not know for certain – but it was there, a feeling that made them different to all the others in his eyes. It was somehow a part of the pattern that included his freckles, his need for a haircut, the patch on his knee, and being an Italian.

'Does your father go to Mass on Sunday, Arturo?'

'Sure,' he said.

It choked in his throat. Why did he have to lie? His father only went to Mass on Christmas morning, and sometimes on Easter Sunday. Lie or not, it pleased him that his father scorned the Mass. He did not know why, but it pleased him. He remembered that argument of his father's. Svevo had said, if God is everywhere, why do I have to go to church on Sunday? Why can't I go down to the Imperial Poolhall? Isn't God down there, too? His mother always shuddered in horror at this piece of theology, but he remembered how feeble her reply to it was, the same reply he had learned in his catechism, and one his mother had learned out of the same catechism years before. It was our duty as Christians, the catechism said. As for himself, sometimes he went to Mass and sometimes not. Those times he did not go, a great fear clutched him, and he was miserable and frightened until he had got it off his chest in the confessional.

At four thirty, Sister Celia finished correcting her papers. He sat there wearily, exhausted and bruised by his own impatience to do something, anything. The room was almost dark. The moon had staggered out of the dreary eastern sky, and it was going to be a white moon if it ever got free. The room saddened him in the half light. It was a room for nuns to walk in, on quiet thick shoes. The empty desks spoke sadly of the children who had gone, and his own desk seemed to sympathize, its warm intimacy telling him to go home that it might be alone with the others. Scratched and marked with his initials, blurred and spotted with ink, the desk was as tired of him as he was of the desk. Now they almost hated one another, yet each so patient with the other.

Sister Celia stood up, gathering her papers.

'At five you may leave,' she said. 'But on one condition –'

His lethargy consumed any curiosity as to what that condition might be. Sprawled out with his feet twined around the desk in front of him, he could do no more than stew in his own disgust.

'I want you to leave here at five and go to the Blessed Sacrament, and I want you to ask the Virgin Mary to bless your mother and bring her all the happiness she deserves – the poor thing.'

Then she left. The poor thing. His mother – the poor thing. It worked a despair in him that made his eyes fill up. Everywhere it was the same, always his mother – the poor thing, always poor and poor, always that, that word, always in him and around him, and suddenly he let go in that half darkened room and wept, sobbing the poor out of him, crying and choking, not for that, not for her, for his mother, but for Svevo Bandini, for his father, that look of his father's, those gnarled hands of his father's, for his father's mason tools, for the walls his father had built, the steps, the cornices, the ashpits and the cathedrals, and they were all so very beautiful, for that feeling in him when his father sang of Italy, of an Italian sky, of a Neapolitan bay.

At a quarter to five his misery had spent itself. The room was almost completely dark. He pulled his sleeve across his nose and felt a contentment rising in his heart, a good feeling, a restfulness that made the next fifteen minutes a mere nothing. He wanted to turn on the lights, but Rosa's house was beyond the empty lot across the street, and the school windows were visible from her back porch. She might see the light burning, and that would remind her that he was still in the classroom.

Rosa, his girl. She hated him, but she was his girl. Did she know that he loved her? Was that why she hated him? Could she see the mysterious things that went on inside him, and was that why she laughed at him? He crossed to the window and saw the light in the kitchen of Rosa's house. Somewhere under that light Rosa walked and breathed. Perhaps she was studying her lessons now, for Rosa was very studious and got the best grades in class.

Turning from the window, he moved to her desk. It was like no other in that room: it was cleaner, more girlish, the surface brighter and more varnished. He sat in her seat and the sensation thrilled him. His hands groped over the wood, inside the little shelf where she kept her books. His fingers found a pencil. He examined it closely: it was faintly marked with the imprint of Rosa's teeth. He kissed it. He kissed the books he found there, all of them so neatly bound with clean-smelling white oilcloth.

At five o'clock, his senses reeling with love and Rosa, Rosa, Rosa pouring from his lips, he walked down the stairs and into the winter evening. St Catherine's Church was directly next to the school. Rosa, I love you!

In a trance he walked down the gloom-shrouded middle aisle, the holy water still cold on the tips of his fingers and forehead, his feet echoing in the choir, the smell of incense, the smell of a thousand funerals and a thousand baptisms, the sweet odor of death and the tart odor of the living mingled in his nostrils, the hushed gasp of burning candles, the echo of himself walking on tiptoe down and down the long aisle, and in his heart, Rosa.

He knelt before the Blessed Sacrament and tried to pray as he had been told, but his mind shimmered and floated with the reverie of her name, and all at once he realized he was committing a sin, a great and horrible sin there in the presence of the Blessed Sacrament, for he was thinking of Rosa evilly, thinking of her in a way that the catechism forbade. He squeezed his eyes tightly and tried to blot out the evil, but it returned stronger, and now his mind turned over the scene of unparalleled sinfulness, something he had never thought of before in his whole life, and he was gasping not only at the horror of his soul in the sight of God, but at the startling ecstasy of that new thought. He could not bear it. He might die for this: God might strike him dead instantly. He got up, blessed himself, and fled, running out of the church, terrified, the sinful thought coming after him as if on wings. Even as he reached the freezing street, he wondered that he had ever made it alive, for the flight down that long aisle over which so many dead had been wheeled seemed endless. There was no trace of the evil thought in his mind once he reached the street and saw the evening's first stars. It was too cold for that. In a moment he was shivering, for though he wore three sweaters he possessed no mackinaw or gloves, and he slapped his hands to keep them warm. It was a block out of his way, but he wanted to pass Rosa's house. The Pinelli bungalow nestled beneath cottonwoods, thirty yards from the sidewalk. The blinds over the two front windows were down. Standing in the front path with his arms crossed and his hands squeezed under his armpits to keep them warm, he watched for a sign of Rosa, her silhouette as she crossed the line of vision through the window. He stamped his feet, his breath spouting white clouds. No Rosa. Then in the deep snow off the path his cold face bent to study the small footprint of a girl. Rosa's – who's else but Rosa, in this yard. His cold fingers grubbed the snow from around the print, and with both hands he scooped it up and carried it away with him down the street . . .

He got home to find his two brothers eating dinner in the kitchen. Eggs again. His lips contorted as he stood over the stove, warming his hands. August's mouth was gorged with bread as he spoke.

'I got the wood, Arturo. You got to get the coal.'

'Where's Mamma?'

'In bed,' Federico said. 'Grandma Donna's coming.'

'Papa drunk yet?'

'He ain't home.'

'Why does Grandma keep coming?' Federico said. 'Papa always gets drunk.'

'Ah, the old bitch!' Arturo said.

Federico loved swear words. He laughed. 'The old bitchy bitch,' he said.

'That's a sin,' August said. 'It's two sins.'

Arturo sneered. 'Whaddya mean, *two* sins?'

'One for using a bad word, the other for not honoring thy father and mother.'

'Grandma Donna's no mother of mine.'

'She's your grandmother.'

'Screw her.'

'That's a sin too.'

'Aw, shut your trap.'

When his hands tingled, he seized the big bucket and the little bucket behind the stove and kicked open the back door. Swinging the buckets gingerly, he walked down the accurately cut path to the coal shed. The supply of coal was running low. It meant his mother would catch hell from Bandini, who never understood why so much coal was burned. The Big 4 Coal Company had, he knew, refused his father any more credit. He filled the buckets and marveled at his father's ingenuity at getting things without money. No wonder his father got drunk. He would get drunk too if he had to keep buying things without money.

The sound of coal striking the tin buckets roused Maria's hens in the coop across the path. They staggered sleepily into the moon-sodden yard and gaped hungrily at the boy as he stooped in the doorway of the shed. They clucked their greeting, their absurd heads pushed through the holes in the chicken wire. He heard them, and standing up he watched them hatefully.

'Eggs,' he said. 'Eggs for breakfast, eggs for dinner, eggs for supper.'

He found a lump of coal the size of his fist, stood back and measured his distance. The old brown hen nearest him got the blow in the neck as the whizzing lump all but tore her head loose and caromed off the chicken shed. She staggered, fell, rose weakly and fell again as the others screamed their fear and disappeared into the shed. The old brown hen was on her feet again, dancing giddily into the snow-covered section of the yard, a zig-zag of brilliant red painting weird patterns in the snow. She died slowly, dragging her bleeding head after her in a drift of snow that ascended toward the top of the fence. He watched the bird suffer with cold satisfaction. When it shuddered for the last time, he grunted and carried the buckets of coal to the kitchen. A moment later he returned and picked up the dead hen.

'What'd you do *that* for?' August said. 'It's a sin.'

'Aw, shut your mouth,' he said, raising his fist.

Chapter Three

Maria was sick. Federico and August tiptoed into the dark bedroom where she lay, so cold with winter, so warm with the fragrance of things on the dresser, the thin odor of Mamma's hair coming through, the strong odor of Bandini, of his clothes somewhere in the room. Maria opened her eyes. Federico was about to sob. August looked annoyed.

'We're hungry,' he said. 'Where does it hurt?'

'I'll get up,' she said.

They heard the crack of her joints, saw the blood seep back into the white side of her face, sensed the staleness of her lips and the misery of her being. August hated it. Suddenly his own breath had that stale taste.

'Where does it hurt, Mamma?'

Federico said: 'Why the heck does Grandma Donna have to come to our house?'

She sat up, nausea crawling over her. She clinched her teeth to check a sudden retch. She had always been ill, but hers was ever sickness without symptom, pain without blood or bruise. The room reeled with her dismay. Together the brothers felt a desire to flee into the kitchen, where it was bright and warm. They left guiltily.

Arturo sat with his feet in the oven, supported on blocks of wood. The dead chicken lay in the corner, a trickle of red slipping from her beak. When Maria entered she saw it without surprise. Arturo watched Federico and August, who watched their mother. They were disappointed that the dead chicken had not annoyed her.

'Everybody has to take a bath right after supper,' she said. 'Grandma's coming tomorrow.'

The brothers set up a groaning and wailing. There was no bathtub. Bathing meant pails of water into a washtub on the kitchen floor, an increasingly hateful task to Arturo, since he was growing now and could no longer sit in the tub with any freedom.

For more than fourteen years Svevo Bandini had reiterated his promise to install a bathtub. Maria could remember the first day she walked into that house with him. When he showed her what he flatteringly termed the bathroom, he had quickly added that next week he would have a bathtub installed. After fourteen years he was still affirming it that way.

'Next week,' he would say, 'I'll see about that bathtub.'

The promise had become family folklore. The boys enjoyed it. Year after year Federico or Arturo asked, 'Papa, when we gonna have a bathtub?' and Bandini would answer in profound determination, 'Next week,' or, 'The first of the week.'

When they laughed to hear him say it over and over again, he glared at them, demanded silence and shouted, 'What the hell's so funny?' Even he, when he bathed, grumbled and cursed the washtub in the kitchen. The boys could hear him deprecating his lot with life, and his violent avowals.

'Next week, by God, next week!'

While Maria dressed the chicken for dinner, Federico shouted: 'I get the leg!' and disappeared behind the stove with a pocket knife. Squatting on the kindling wood box, he carved boats to sail as he took his bath. He carved and stacked them, a dozen boats, big and small, enough wood indeed to fill the tub by half, to say nothing of water displacement by his own body. But the more the better: he could have a sea-battle, even if he did have to sit on some of his craft.

August was hunched in the corner studying the Latin liturgy of the altar boy at Mass. Father Andrew had given him the prayer-book as a reward for outstanding piety during the Holy Sacrifice, such piety being a triumph of sheer physical endurance, for whereas Arturo, who was also an altar boy, was always lifting his weight from one knee to the other as he knelt through the long services of High Mass, or scratching himself, or yawning, or forgetting to respond to the priest's words, August was never guilty of such impiety. Indeed, August was very proud of a more or less unofficial record he now held in the Altar Boy Society. To wit: He could kneel up straight with his hands reverently folded for a longer period of time than any other acolyte. The other altar boys freely acknowledged August's supremacy in this field, and not one of the forty members of the organization saw any sense in challenging him. That his talent as an endurance-kneeler went unchallenged often annoyed the champion.

August's great show of piety, his masterful efficiency as an altar boy, was a matter of everlasting satisfaction to Maria. Whenever the nuns or members of the parish mentioned August's ritualistic proclivities, it made her glow happily. She never missed a Sunday Mass at which August served. Kneeling in the first pew, at the foot of the main altar, the sight of her second son in his cassock and surplice lifted her to fulfillment. The flow of his robes as he walked, the precision of his service, the silence of his feet on lush red carpet, was reverie and dream, paradise on earth. Some day August would be a priest; all else became meaningless; she could suffer and slave; she could die and die again, but her womb had given God a priest, sanctifying her, a chosen one, mother of a priest, kindred of the Blessed Virgin . . .

With Bandini it was different. August was very pious and desired to become a priest – *si*. But *Chi copro!* What the hell, he would get over that. The spectacle of his sons as altar boys gave him more amusement than spiritual satisfaction. The rare times he went to Mass and saw them, usually Christmas morning when the tremendous ceremony of Catholicism reached its most elaborate expression, it was not without chuckling that he watched his three sons in the solemn procession down the center aisle. Then he saw them not as consecrated children cloaked in expensive lace and deeply in communion with the Almighty; rather, such habiliments served to heighten the contrast, and he saw them simply and more vividly, as they really were, not only his sons but also the other boys – savages, irreverent kids uncomfortable and itching in their heavy cassocks. The sight of Arturo, choking with a tight celluloid collar against his ears, his freckled face red and bloated, his withering hatred of the whole ceremony made Bandini titter aloud. As for little Federico, he was the same, a devil for all his trappings. The seraphic sighs of women to the contrary notwithstanding, Bandini knew the embarrassment, the discomfort, the awful annoyance of the boys. August wanted to be a priest; oh, he would get over that. He would grow up and forget all about it. He would grow up and be a man, or he, Svevo Bandini, would knock his goddamn block off.

Maria picked up the dead chicken by the legs. The boys held their noses and fled from the kitchen when she opened and dressed it.

'I get the leg,' Federico said.

'We heard you the first time,' Arturo said.

He was in a black mood, his conscience shouting questions about the murdered hen. Had he committed a mortal sin, or was the killing of the hen only a venial sin? Lying on the floor in the living room, the heat of the pot-bellied stove scorching one side of his body, he reflected darkly upon the three elements which, according to the catechism, constituted a mortal sin. first, grievous matter; second, sufficient reflection; third, full consent of the will.

His mind spiralled in gloomy productions. He recalled that story of Sister Justinus about the murderer who, all of his waking and sleeping hours, saw before his eyes the contorted face of the man he had murdered; the apparition taunting him, accusing him, until the murderer had gone in terror to confession and poured out his black crime to God.

Was it possible that he too would suffer like that? That happy, unsuspecting chicken. An hour ago the bird was alive, at peace with the earth. Now she was dead, killed in cold blood by his own hand. Would his life be haunted to the end by the face of a chicken? He stared at the wall, blinked his eyes, and gasped. It was there – the dead chicken was staring him in the face, clucking fiendishly! He leaped to his feet, hurried to the bedroom, locked the door:

'Oh Virgin Mary, give me a break! I didn't mean it! I swear to God I don't know why I done it! Oh please, dear chicken! Dear chicken, I'm sorry I killed you!'

He launched into a fusillade of Hail Marys and Our Fathers

until his knees ached, until having kept accurate record of each prayer, he concluded that forty-five Hail Marys and nineteen Our Fathers were enough for true contrition. But a superstition about the number nineteen forced him to whisper one more Our Father that it might come out an even twenty. Then, his mind still fretting about possible stinginess he heaped on two more Hail Marys and two more Our Fathers just to prove beyond a doubt that he was not superstitious and had no faith in numbers, for the catechism emphatically denounced any species of superstition whatever.

He might have prayed on, except that his mother called him to dinner. In the center of the kitchen table she had placed a plate piled high with brown fried chicken. Federico squealed and hammered his dish with a fork. The pious August bent his head and whispered grace before meals. Long after he had said the prayer he kept his aching neck bent, wondering why his mother made no comment. Federico nudged Arturo, then thumbed his nose at the devout August. Maria faced the stove. She turned around, the gravy pitcher in her hand, and saw August, his golden head so reverently tipped.

'Good boy, August,' she smiled. 'Good boy. God bless you!'

August raised his head and blessed himself. But by that time Federico had already raided the chicken dish and both legs were gone. One of them Federico gnawed; the other he had hidden between his legs. August's eyes searched the table in annoyance. He suspected Arturo, who sat with zestless appetite. Then Maria seated herself. In silence she spread margarine over a slice of bread.

Arturo's lips were locked in a grimace as he stared at the crisp, dismembered chicken. An hour ago that chicken had been happy, unaware of the murder that would befall it. He glanced at Federico, whose mouth dripped as he tore into the luscious flesh. It nauseated Arturo. Maria pushed the plate toward him.

'Arturo – you're not eating.'

The tip of his fork searched with insincere perspicacity. He found a lonely piece, a miserable piece that looked even worse when he lifted it to his own plate – the gizzard. God, please don't let me be unkind to animals anymore. He nibbled cautiously. Not bad. It had a delicious taste. He took another bite. He grinned. He reached for more. He ate with gusto, rummaging for white meat. He remembered where Federico had hidden that other leg. His hand slipped under the table and he filched it without anyone noticing the act, took it from Federico's lap. When he had finished the leg, he laughed and tossed the bone into his little brother's plate. Federico stared at it, pawing his lap in alarm:

'Damn you,' he said. 'Damn you, Arturo. You crook.'

August looked at his little brother reproachfully, shaking his yellow head. Damn was a sinful word; possibly not a mortal sin; probably only a venial sin, but a sin for all that. He was very sad about it and was so glad he didn't use cuss words like his brothers.

It was not a large chicken. They cleaned the plate in the center of the table, and when only bones lay before them Arturo and Federico gnawed them open and sucked the marrow.

'Good thing Papa ain't coming home,' Federico said. 'We'd have to save some for him.'

Maria smiled at them, gravy plastered over their faces, crumbs of chicken even in Federico's hair. She brushed them aside and warned about bad manners in front of Grandma Donna.

'If you eat the way you did tonight, she won't give you a Christmas present.'

A futile threat. Christmas presents from Grandma Donna! Arturo grunted. 'All she ever gives us is pajamas. Who the heck wants pajamas?'

'Betcha Papa's drunk by now,' Federico said. 'Him and Rocco Saccone.'

Maria's fist went white and tight. 'That beast,' she said. 'Don't mention him at this table!'

Arturo understood his mother's hatred for Rocco. Maria was so afraid of him, so revolted when he came near. Her hatred of his lifelong friendship with Bandini was tireless. They had been boys together in Abruzzi. In the early days before her marriage they had known women together, and when Rocco came to the house, he and Svevo had a way of drinking and laughing together without speaking, of muttering provincial Italian dialect and then laughing uproariously, a violent language of grunts and memories, teeming with implication, yet meaningless and always of a world in which she had never belonged and could never belong. What Bandini had done before his marriage she pretended not to care, but this Rocco Saccone with his dirty laughter which Bandini enjoyed and shared was a secret out of the past that she longed to capture, to lay open once and for all, for she seemed to know that, once the secrets of those early days were revealed to her, the private language of Svevo Bandini and Rocco Saccone would become extinct forever.

With Bandini gone, the house was not the same. After supper the boys, stupid with food, lay on the floor in the living room, enjoying the friendly stove in the corner. Arturo fed it coal, and it wheezed and chuckled happily, laughing softly as they sprawled around it, their appetites sodden.

In the kitchen Maria washed the dishes, conscious of one less dish to put away, one less cup. When she returned them to the pantry, Bandini's heavy battered cup, larger and clumsier than the others, seemed to convey an injured pride that it had remained unused throughout the meal. In the drawer where she kept the cutlery Bandini's knife, his favorite, the sharpest and most vicious table knife in the set, glistened in the light.

The house lost its identity now. A loose shingle whispered caustically to the wind; the electric light wires rubbed the gabled back porch, sneering. The world of inanimate things found voice, conversed with the old house, and the house chattered with cronish delight of the discontent within its walls. The boards under her feet squealed their miserable pleasure.

Bandini would not be home tonight.

The realization that he would not come home, the knowledge that he was probably drunk somewhere in the town, deliberately staying away, was terrifying. All that was hideous and destructive upon the earth seemed privy to the information. Already she sensed the forces of blackness and terror gathering around her, creeping in macabre formation upon the house.

Once the supper dishes were out of the way, the sink cleaned, the floor swept, her day abruptly died. Now nothing remained to occupy her. She had done so much sewing and patching over fourteen years under yellow light that her eyes resisted violently whenever she attempted it; headaches seized her, and she had to give it up until the daytime.

Sometimes she opened the pages of a woman's magazine

whenever one came her way; those sleek bright magazines that shrieked of an American paradise for women: beautiful furniture, beautiful gowns: of fair women who found romance in yeast: of smart women discussing toilet paper. These magazines, these pictures represented that vague category: 'American women.' Always she spoke in awe of what 'the American women' were doing.

She believed those pictures. By the hour she could sit in the old rocker beside the window in the living room, ever turning the pages of a woman's magazine, methodically licking the tip of her finger and turning the page. She came away drugged with the conviction of her separation from that world of 'American women.'

Here was a side of her Bandini bitterly derided. He, for example, was a pure Italian, of peasant stock that went back deeply into the generations. Yet he, now that he had citizenship papers, never regarded himself as an Italian. No, he was an American; sometimes sentiment buzzed in his head and he liked to yell his pride of heritage; but for all sensible purposes he was an American, and when Maria spoke to him of what 'the American women' were doing and wearing, when she mentioned the activity of a neighbor, 'that American woman down the street,' it infuriated him. For he was highly sensitive to the distinction of class and race, to the suffering it entailed, and he was bitterly against it.

He was a bricklayer, and to him there was not a more sacred calling upon the face of the earth. You could be a king; you could be a conqueror, but no matter what you were you had to have a house; and if you had any sense at all it would be a brickhouse; and, of course, built by a union man, on the union scale. That was important.

But Maria, lost in the fairyland of a woman's magazine, gazing with sighs at electric irons and vacuum cleaners and automatic washing machines and electric ranges, had but to close the pages of that land of fantasy and look about her: the hard chairs, the worn carpets, the cold rooms. She had but to turn her hand and examine the palm, calloused from a washboard, to realize that she was not, after all, an American woman. Nothing about her, neither her complexion, nor her hands, nor her feet; neither the food she ate nor the teeth that chewed it – nothing about her, nothing, gave her kinship with 'the American women.'

She had no need in her heart for either book or magazine. She had her own way of escape, her own passage into contentment: her rosary. That string of white beads, the tiny links worn in a dozen places and held together by strands of white thread which in turn broke regularly, was, bead for bead, her quiet flight out of the world. Hail Mary, full of grace, the Lord is with thee. And Maria began to climb. Bead for bead, life and living fell away. Hail Mary, Hail Mary. Dream without sleep encompassed her. Passion without flesh lulled her. Love without death crooned the melody of belief. She was away: she was free; she was no longer Maria, American or Italian, poor or rich, with or without electric washing machines and vacuum cleaners; here was the land of all-possessing. Hail Mary, Hail Mary, over and over, a thousand and a hundred thousand times, prayer upon prayer, the sleep of the body, the escape of the mind, the death of memory, the slipping away of pain, the deep silent reverie of belief. Hail Mary and Hail Mary. It was for this that she lived.

* * *

Tonight the beaded passage into escape, the sense of joy the rosary brought her, was in her mind long before she turned out the kitchen light and walked into the living room, where her grunting, groggy sons were sprawled over the floor. The meal had been too much for Federico. Already he was heavily asleep. He lay with his face turned aside, his mouth wide open. August, flat on his stomach, stared blankly into Federico's mouth and reflected that, after he was ordained a priest, he would certainly get a rich parish and have chicken dinner every night.

Maria sank into the rocking chair by the window. The familiar crack of her knees caused Arturo to flinch in annoyance. She drew the beads from the pocket of her apron. Her dark eyes closed and the tired lips moved, a whispering audible and intense.

Arturo rolled over and studied his mother's face. His mind worked fast. Should he interrupt her and ask her for a dime for the movies, or should he save time and trouble by going into the bedroom and stealing it? There was no danger of being caught. Once his mother began her rosary she never opened her eyes. Federico was asleep, and as for August, he was too dumb and holy to know what was going on in the world anyway. He stood up and stretched himself.

'Ho hum. Guess I'll get me a book.'

In the chilling darkness of his mother's bedroom he lifted the mattress at the foot of the bed. His fingers pawed the meager coins in the ragged purse, pennies and nickels, but so far no dimes. Then they closed around the familiar thin smallness of a ten-cent piece. He returned the purse to its place within the coil spring and listened for suspicious sounds. Then with a flourish of noisy footsteps and loud whistling he walked into his own room and seized the first book his hand touched on the dresser.

He returned to the living room and dropped on the floor beside August and Federico. Disgust pulled at his face when he saw the book. It was the life of St Teresa of the Little Flower of Jesus. He read the first line of the first page. 'I will spend my heaven doing good on Earth.' He closed the book and pushed it toward August.

'Fooey,' he said. 'I don't feel like reading. Guess I'll go out and see if any of the kids are on the hill coasting.'

Maria's eyes remained closed, but she turned her lips faintly to denote that she had heard and approved of his plan. Then her head shook slowly from side to side. That was her way of telling him not to stay out late.

'I won't,' he said.

Warm and eager under his tight sweaters, he sometimes ran, sometimes walked down Walnut Street, past the railroad tracks to Twelfth, where he cut through the filling station property on the corner, crossed the bridge, ran at a dead sprint through the park because the dark shadows of cottonwood scared him, and in less than ten minutes he was panting under the marquee of the Isis Theater. As always in front of small town theatres, a crowd of boys his own age loafed about, penniless, meekly waiting the benevolence of the head usher who might, or might not, depending upon his mood, let them in free after the second show of the night was well under way. Often he too had stood out there, but tonight he had a dime, and with a good-natured smile for the hangers-on, he bought a ticket and swaggered inside.

He spurned the military usher who wagged a finger at

him, and found his own way through the blackness. First he selected a seat in the very last row. Five minutes later he moved down two rows. A moment later he moved again. Little by little, two and three rows at a time, he edged his way toward the bright screen, until at last he was in the very first row and could go no farther. There he sat, his throat tight, his Adam's apple protruding as he squinted almost straight into the ceiling as Gloria Borden and Robert Powell performed in *Love On The River*.

At once he was under the spell of that celluloid drug. He was positive that his own face bore a striking resemblance to that of Robert Powell, and he was equally sure that the face of Gloria Borden bore an amazing resemblance to his wonderful Rosa: thus he found himself perfectly at home, laughing uproariously at Robert Powell's witty comments, and shuddering with voluptuous delight whenever Gloria Borden looked passionate. Gradually Robert Powell lost his identity and became Arturo Bandini, and gradually Gloria Borden metamorphosed into Rosa Pinelli. After the big airplane crackup, with Rosa lying on the operating table, and none other than Arturo Bandini performing a precarious operation to save her life, the boy in the front seat broke into a sweat. Poor Rosa! The tears streamed down his face and he wiped his drooling nose with an impatient pull of his sweater sleeve across his face.

But he knew, he had a feeling all along, that young Doctor Arturo Bandini would achieve a medical miracle, and sure enough, it happened! Before he knew it, the handsome doctor was kissing Rosa; it was springtime and the world was beautiful. Suddenly, without a word of warning, the picture was over, and Arturo Bandini, sniffling and crying, sat in the front row of the Isis Theater, horribly embarrassed and utterly disgusted with his chicken-hearted sentiment. Everybody in the Isis was staring at him. He was sure of it, since he bore so striking a resemblance to Robert Powell.

The effects of the drugged enchantment left him slowly. Now that the lights were on and reality returned, he looked about. No one sat within ten rows of him. He looked over his shoulder at the mass of pasty, bloodless faces in the center and rear of the theater. He felt a streak of electricity in his stomach. He caught his breath in ecstatic fright. Out of that small sea of drabness, one countenance sparkled diamond-like, the eyes ablaze with beauty. It was the face of Rosa! And only a moment ago he had saved her on the operating table! But it was all such a miserable lie. He was here, the sole occupant of ten rows of seats. Lowering himself until the top of his head almost disappeared, he felt like a thief, a criminal, as he stole one more glance at that dazzling face. Rosa Pinelli! She sat between her mother and father, two extremely fat, double-chinned Italians, far toward the rear of the theater. She could not see him; he was sure she was too far away to recognize him, yet his own eyes leaped the distance between them and he saw her miscroscopically, saw the loose curls peeking from under her bonnet, the dark beads around her neck, the starry sparkle of her teeth. So she had seen the picture too! Those black and laughing eyes of Rosa, they had seen it all. Was it possible that she had noticed the resemblance between himself and Robert Powell?

But no: there really wasn't any resemblance at all; not really. It was just a movie, and he was down front, and he felt hot and perspiring beneath his sweaters. He was afraid to touch his hair, afraid to lift his hand up there and smooth back his hair. He knew it grew upward and unkempt like weeds. People were always recognizing him because his hair was never combed and he always needed a haircut. Perhaps Rosa had already discovered him. Ah – why hadn't he combed his hair down? Why was he always forgetting things like that? Deeper and deeper he sank into the seat, his eyes rolling backward to see if his hair showed over the chair-back. Cautiously, inch by inch, he lifted his hand to smooth down his hair. But he couldn't make it. He was afraid she might see his hand.

When the lights went out again, he was panting with relief. But as the second show began, he realized he would have to leave. A vague shame strangled him, a consciousness of his old sweaters, of his clothes, a memory of Rosa laughing at him, a fear that, unless he slipped away now, he might meet her in the foyer as she left the theater with her parents. He could not bear the thought of confronting them. Their eyes would look upon him; the eyes of Rosa would dance with laughter. Rosa knew all about him; every thought and deed. Rosa knew that he had stolen a dime from his mother, who needed it. She would look at him, and she would know. He had to beat it; or had to get out of there; something might happen; the lights might go on again and she would see him; there might be a fire; anything might happen; he simply had to get up and get out of there. He could be in a classroom with Rosa, or on the school-grounds; but this was the Isis Theater, and he looked like a lousy bum in these lousy clothes, different from everybody else, and he had stolen the money: he had no right to be there. If Rosa saw him she could read in his face that he had stolen the money. Only a dime, only a venial sin, but it was a sin any way you looked at it. He arose and took long, quick, silent steps up the aisle, his face turned aside, his hand shielding his nose and eyes. When he reached the street the huge cold of the night leaped as though with whips upon him, and he started to run, the wind in his face stinging him, flecking him with fresh, new thoughts.

As he turned into the walk that led to the porch of his home, the sight of his mother silhouetted in the window released the tension of his soul; he felt his skin breaking like a wave, and in a rush of feeling he was crying, the guilt pouring from him, inundating him, washing him away. He opened the door and found himself in his home, in the warmth of his home, and it felt deep and wonderful. His brothers had gone to bed, but Maria had not moved, and he knew her eyes had not opened, her fingers ever moving with blind conviction around the endless circle of beads. Oh boy, she looked swell, his mother, she looked keen. Oh kill me God because I'm a dirty dog and she's a beauty and I ought to die. Oh Mamma, look at me because I stole a dime and you keep on praying. Oh Mamma kill me with your hands.

He fell on his knees and clung to her in fright and joy and guilt. The rocker jerked to his sobs, the beads rattling in her hands. She opened her eyes and smiled down at him, her thin fingers gently raking his hair, telling herself he needed a haircut. His sobs pleased her like caresses, gave her a sense of tenderness toward her beads, a feeling of unity of beads and sobs.

'Mamma,' he groped. 'I did something.'

'It's all right,' she said. 'I knew.'

That surprised him. How could she have possibly known? He had swiped that dime with consummate perfection. He had fooled her, and August, and everyone. He had fooled them all.

'You were saying the rosary, and I didn't want to bother you,' he lied. 'I didn't want to interrupt you right in the middle of the rosary.'

She smiled. 'How much did you take?'

'A dime. I coulda taken all of it, but I only took a dime.'

'I know.'

That annoyed him. 'But *how* do you know? Did you see me take it?'

'The water's hot in the tank,' she said. 'Go take your bath.'

He arose and began to pull off his sweaters.

'But how did you know? Did you look? Did you peek? I thought you always closed your eyes when you said the rosary.'

'Why shouldn't I know?' she smiled. 'You're always taking dimes out of my pocketbook. You're the only one who ever does. I know it every time. Why, I can tell by the sound of your feet!'

He untied his shoes and kicked them off. His mother was a pretty darned smart woman after all. But what if next time he should take off his shoes and slip into the bedroom barefoot? He was giving the plan deep consideration as he walked naked into the kitchen for his bath.

He was disgusted to find the kitchen floor soaked and cold. His two brothers had raised havoc with the room. Their clothes were scattered about, and one washtub was full of grayish soapy water and pieces of water-soaked wood: Federico's battleships.

It was too darn cold for a bath that night. He decided to fake it. Filling a washtub, he locked the kitchen door, produced a copy of *Scarlet Crime*, and settled down to reading *Murder For Nothing* as he sat naked upon the warm oven door, his feet and ankles thawing in the washtub. After he had read for what he thought was the normal length of time it took really to have a bath, he hid *Scarlet Crime* on the back porch, cautiously wet his hair with the palm of one hand, rubbed his dry body with a towel until it glowed a savage pink, and ran shivering to the living room. Maria watched him crouch near the stove as he rubbed the towel into his hair, grumbling all the while of his detestation of taking baths in the dead of winter. As he strode off to bed, he was pleased with himself at such a masterful piece of deception. Maria smiled too. Around his neck as he disappeared for the night, she saw a ring of dirt that stood out like a black collar. But she said nothing. The night was indeed too cold for bathing.

Alone now, she turned out the lights and continued with her prayers. Occasionally through the reverie she listened to the house. The stove sobbed and moaned for fuel. In the street a man smoking a pipe walked by. She watched him, knowing he could not see her in the darkness. She compared him with Bandini; he was taller, but he had none of Svevo's gusto in his step. From the bedroom came the voice of Federico, talking in his sleep. Then Arturo, mumbling sleepily: 'Aw, shut up!' Another man passed in the street. He was fat, the steam pouring from his mouth and into the cold air. Svevo was a much finer-looking man than he; thank God Svevo was not fat. But these were distractions. It was sacrilegious to allow stray thoughts to interfere with prayer. She closed her eyes tightly and made a mental checklist of items for the Blessed Virgin's consideration.

She prayed for Svevo Bandini, prayed that he would not get too drunk and fall into the hands of the police, as he had done on one occasion before their marriage. She prayed that he would stay away from Rocco Saccone, and that Rocco Saccone would stay away from him. She prayed for the quickening of time, that the snow might melt and spring hurry to Colorado, that Svevo could go back to work again. She prayed for a happy Christmas and for money. She prayed for Arturo, that he would stop stealing dimes, and for August, that he might become a priest, and for Federico, that he might be a good boy. She prayed for clothes for them all, for money for the grocer, for the souls of the dead, for the souls of the living, for the world, for the sick and the dying, for the poor and the rich, for courage, for strength to carry on, for forgiveness in the error of her ways.

She prayed a long, fervent prayer that the visit of Donna Toscana would be a short one, that it would not bring too much misery all around, and that some day Svevo Bandini and her mother might enjoy a peaceful relationship. That last prayer was almost hopeless, and she knew it. How even the mother of Christ could arrange a cessation of hostilities between Svevo Bandini and Donna Toscana was a problem that only Heaven could solve. It always embarrassed her to bring this matter to the Blessed Virgin's attention. It was like asking for the moon on a silver brooch. After all, the Virgin Mother had already interceded to the extent of a splendid husband, three fine children, a good home, lasting health, and faith in God's mercy. But peace between Svevo and his mother-in-law, well, there were requests that taxed even the generosity of the Almighty and the Blessed Virgin Mary.

Donna Toscana arrived at noon Sunday. Maria and the children were in the kitchen. The agonized moan of the porch beneath her weight told them it was Grandma. An iciness settled in Maria's throat. Without knocking, Donna opened the door and poked her head inside. She spoke only Italian.

'Is he here – the Abruzzian dog?'

Maria hurried from the kitchen and threw her arms around her mother. Donna Toscana was now a huge woman, always dressed in black since the death of her husband. Beneath the outer black silk were petticoats, four of them, all brightly colored. Her bloated ankles looked like goiters. Her tiny shoes seemed ready to burst beneath the pressure of her two hundred and fifty pounds. Not two but a dozen breasts seemed crushed into her bosom. She was constructed like a pyramid, without hips. There was so much flesh in her arms that they hung not downward but at an angle, her puffed fingers dangling like sausages. She had virtually no neck at all. When she turned her head the drooping flesh moved with the melancholy of melting wax. A pink scalp showed beneath her thin white hair. Her nose was thin and exquisite, but her eyes were like trampled concord grapes. Whenever she spoke her false teeth chattered obliviously a language all their own.

Maria took her coat and Donna stood in the middle of the room, smelling it, the fat crinkling in her neck as she conveyed to her daughter and grandsons the impression that the odor in her nostrils was definitely a nasty one, a very filthy one. The boys sniffed suspiciously. Suddenly the house *did* possess an odor they had never noticed before. August thought about his kidney trouble two years before, wondering if, after two years, the odor of it was still in existence.

'Hi ya, Grandma,' Federico said.

'Your teeth look black,' she said. 'Did you wash them this morning?'

Federico's smile vanished and the back of his hand covered his lips as he lowered his eyes. He tightened his mouth and resolved to slip into the bathroom and look in the mirror as soon as he could. Funny how his teeth *did* taste black.

Grandma kept sniffing.

'What *is* this malevolent odor?' she asked. 'Surely your father is not at home.'

The boys understood Italian, for Bandini and Maria often used it.

'No, Grandma,' Arturo said. 'He isn't home.'

Donna Toscana reached into the folds of her breasts and drew out her purse. She opened it and produced a ten-cent piece at the tips of her fingers, holding it out.

'Now,' she smiled. 'Who of my three grandsons is the most honest? To the one who is, I will give this *deci soldi*. Tell me quickly: is your father drunk?'

'Ah, *Mamma mio*,' Maria said. 'Why do you ask that?'

Without looking at her, Grandma answered, 'Be still, woman. This is a game for the children.'

The boys consulted one another with their eyes: they were silent, anxious to betray their father but not anxious enough. Grandma was so stingy, yet they knew her purse was filled with dimes, each coin the reward for a piece of information about Papa. Should they let this question pass and wait for another – one not quite so unfavorable to Papa – or should one of them answer before the other? It was not a question of answering truthfully: even if Papa *wasn't* drunk. The only way to get the dime was in answering to suit Grandma.

Maria stood by helplessly. Donna Toscana wielded a tongue like a serpent, ever ready to strike out in the presence of the children: half-forgotten episodes from Maria's childhood and youth, things Maria preferred that her boys not know lest the information encroach upon her dignity: little things the boys might use against her. Donna Toscana had used them before. The boys knew that their Mamma was stupid in school, for Grandma had told them. They knew that Mamma had played house with nigger children and got a licking for it. That Mamma had vomited in the choir of St Dominic's at a hot High Mass. That Mamma, like August, had wet the bed, but, unlike August, had been forced to wash out her own nighties. That Mamma had run away from home and the police had brought her back (not *really* run away, only strayed away, but Grandma insisted she had run away). And they knew other things about Mamma. She refused to work as a little girl and had been locked in the cellar by the hour. She never was and never would be a good cook. She screamed like a hyena when her children were born. She was a fool or she would never have married a scoundrel like Svevo Bandini . . . and she had no self-respect, otherwise why did she always dress in rags? They knew that Mamma was a weakling, dominated by her dog of a husband. That Mamma was a coward who should have sent Svevo Bandini to jail a long time ago. So it was better not to antagonize her mother. Better to remember the Fourth Commandment, to be respectful toward her mother so that her own children by example would be respectful toward her.

'Well,' Grandma repeated. 'Is he drunk?'

A long silence.

Then Federico: 'Maybe he is, Grandma. We don't know.'

'*Mamma mio*,' Maria said. 'Svevo is not drunk. He is away on business. He will be back any minute now.'

'Listen to your mother,' Donna said. 'Even when she was old enough to know better she never flushed the toilet. And now she tries to tell me your vagabond father is not drunk! But he *is drunk!* Is he not, Arturo? Quick – for *deci soldi*!'

'I dunno, Grandma. Honest.'

'Bah!' she snorted. 'Stupid children of a stupid parent!'

She threw a few coins at their feet. They pounced upon them like savages, fighting and tumbling over the floor. Maria watched the squirming mass of arms and legs. Donna Toscana's head shook miserably.

'And you smile,' she said. 'Like animals they claw themselves to pieces, and their mother smiles her approval. Ah, poor America! Ah, America, thy children shall tear out one another's throats and die like bloodthirsty beasts!'

'But *Mamma mio*, they are boys. They do no harm.'

'Ah, poor America!' Donna said. 'Poor, hopeless America!'

She began her inspection of the house. Maria had prepared for this: carpets and floors swept, furniture dusted, the stoves polished. But a dust rag will not remove stains from a leaking ceiling; a broom will not sweep away the worn places on a carpet; soap and water will not disturb the omnipresence of the marks of children: the dark stains around door knobs, here and there a grease spot that was born suddenly; a child's name crudely articulate; random designs of tic-tac-toe games that always ended without a winner; toe marks at the bottom of doors, calendar pictures that sprouted mustaches overnight; a shoe that Maria had put away in the closet not ten minutes before; a sock; a towel; a slice of bread and jam in the rocking chair.

For hours Maria had worked and warned – and this was her reward. Donna Toscana walked from room to room, her face a crust of dismay. She saw the boys' room: the bed carefully made, a blue spread smelling of mothballs neatly completing it; she noticed the freshly ironed curtains, the shining mirror over the dresser, the rag rug at the bedside so precisely in order, everything so monastically impersonal, and under the chair in the corner – a pair of Arturo's dirty shorts, kicked there, and sprawled out like the section of a boy's body sawed in half.

The old woman raised her hands and wailed.

'No hope,' she said. 'Ah, woman! Ah, America!'

'Well, how did *that* get there?' Maria said. 'The boys are always so careful.'

She picked up the garment and hastily shoved it under her apron, Donna Toscana's cold eyes upon her for a full minute after the pair of shorts had disappeared.

'Blighted woman. Blighted, defenseless woman.'

All afternoon it was the same, Donna Toscana's relentless cynicism wearing her down. The boys had fled with their dimes to the candy store. When they did not return after an hour Donna lamented the weakness of Maria's authority. When they did return, Federico's face smeared with chocolate, she wailed again. After they had been back an hour, she complained that they were to noisy, so Maria sent them outside. After they were gone she prophesied that they would probably die of influenza out there in the snow. Maria made her tea. Donna clucked her tongue and concluded that it was too weak. Patiently Maria watched the clock on the stove. In two hours, at seven o'clock, her mother would leave. The time halted and limped and crawled in agony.

'You look bad,' Donna said. 'What has happened to the color in your face?'

With one hand Maria smoothed her hair.

'I feel fine,' she said. 'All of us are well.'

'Where is he?' Donna said. 'That vagabond.'

'Svevo is working, *Mamma mio*. He is figuring a new job.'

'On Sunday?' she sneered. 'How do you know he is not out with some *puttana*?'

'Why do you say such things? Svevo is not that kind of a man.'

'The man you married is a brutal animal. But he married a stupid woman, and so I suppose he will never be exposed. Ah, America! Only in this corrupt land could such things happen.'

While Maria prepared dinner she sat with her elbows on the table, her chin in her hands. The fare was to be spaghetti and meatballs. She made Maria scour the spaghetti kettle with soap and water. She ordered the long box of spaghetti brought to her, and she examined it carefully for evidences of mice. There was no icebox in the house, the meat being kept in a cupboard on the back porch. It was round steak, ground for meatballs.

'Bring it here,' Donna said.

Maria placed it before her. She tasted it with the tip of her finger. 'I thought so,' she frowned. 'It is spoiled.'

'But that is impossible!' Maria said. 'Only last night I bought it.'

'A butcher will always cheat a fool,' she said.

Dinner was delayed a half hour because Donna insisted that Maria wash and dry the already clean plates. The kids came in, ravenously hungry. She ordered them to wash their hands and faces, to put on clean shirts and wear neckties. They growled and Arturo muttered 'The old bitch,' as he fastened a hated necktie. By the time all was ready the dinner was cold. The boys ate it anyhow. The old woman ate listlessly, a few strands of spaghetti before her. Even these displeased her, and she pushed her plate away.

'The dinner is badly prepared,' she said. 'This spaghetti tastes like dung.'

Federico laughed.

'It's good, though.'

'Can I get you something else, *Mamma mio*?'

'No!'

After dinner she sent Arturo to the filling station to phone for a cab. Then she left, arguing with the cab driver, trying to bargain the fare to the depot from twenty-five to twenty cents. After she was gone Arturo stuffed a pillow into his shirt, wound an apron around it, and waddled around the house, sniffing contemptuously. But no one laughed. No one cared.

Chapter Four

No Bandini, no money, no food. If Bandini were home, he would say, 'Charge it.'

Monday afternoon, and still no Bandini, and that grocery bill! She could never forget it. Like a tireless ghost it filled the winter days with dread.

Next door to the Bandini house was Mr Craik's grocery store. In the early years of his marriage Bandini had opened a credit business with Mr Craik. At first he managed to keep the bills paid. But as the children grew older and hungrier, as bad year followed bad year, the grocery bill whizzed into crazy figures. Every year since his marriage things got worse for Svevo Bandini. Money! After fifteen years of marriage Bandini had so many bills that even Federico knew he had no intention or opportunity to pay them.

But the grocery bill harassed him. Owing Mr Craik a hundred dollars, he paid fifty – if he had it. Owing two hundred, he paid seventy-five – if he had it. So it was with all the debts of Svevo Bandini. There was no mystery about them. There were no hidden motives, no desire to cheat in their non-payment. No budget could solve them. No planned economy could alter them. It was very simple: the Bandini family used up more money than he earned. He knew his only escape lay in a streak of good luck. His tireless presumption that such good luck was coming forestalled his complete desertion and kept him from blowing out his brains. He constantly threatened both, but did neither. Maria did not know how to threaten. It was not in her nature.

But Mr Craik the grocer complained unceasingly. He never quite trusted Bandini. If the Bandini family had not lived next door to his store, where he could keep his eye on it, and if he had not felt that ultimately he would receive at least most of the money owed him, he would not have allowed further credit. He sympathized with Maria and pitied her with that cold pity small businessmen show to the poor as a class, and with that frigid self-defensive apathy toward individual members of it. Christ, he had bills to pay too.

Now that the Bandini account was so high – and it rose by leaps throughout each winter – he abused Maria, even insulted her. He knew that she herself was honest to the point of childish innocence, but that did not seem relevant when she came to the store to increase the account. Just like she owned the place! He was there to sell groceries, not give them away. He dealt in merchandise, not feelings. Money was owed him. He was allowing her additional credit. His demands for money were in vain. The only thing to do was keep after her until he got it. Under the circumstances, his attitude was the best he could possibly muster.

Maria had to coax herself to a pitch of inspired audacity in order to face him each day. Bandini paid no attention to her mortification at the hands of Mr Craik.

Charge it, Mr Craik. Charge it.

All afternoon and until an hour before dinner Maria walked the house, waiting for that desperate inspiration so necessary for a trip to the store. She went to the window and sat with hands in her apron pockets, one fist around her rosary – waiting. She had done it before, only two days ago, Saturday, and the day before that, all the days before that, spring, summer, winter, year in, year out. But now her courage slept from overuse and would not rise. She couldn't go to that store again, face that man.

From the window, through the pale winter evening, she saw Arturo across the street with a gang of neighborhood kids. They were involved in a snowball fight in the empty lot. She opened the door.

'Arturo!'

She called him because he was the oldest. He saw her standing in the doorway. It was a white darkness. Deep shadows crept fast across the milky snow. The street lamps burned coldly, a cold glow in a colder haze. An automobile passed, its tire chains clanging dismally.

'Arturo!'

He knew what she wanted. In disgust he clinched his teeth. He *knew* she wanted him to go to the store. She was a yellow-belly, just plain yellow, passing the buck to him, afraid of Craik. Her voice had that peculiar tremor that came with grocery-store time. He tried to get out of it by pretending that he hadn't heard, but she kept calling until he was ready to scream and the rest of the kids, hypnotized by that tremor in her voice, stopped throwing snowballs and looked at him, as though begging him to do something.

He tossed one more snowball, watched it splatter, and then trudged through the snow and across the icy pavement. Now he could see her plainly. Her jaws quivered from the twilight cold. She stood with arms squeezing her thin body, tapping her toes to keep them warm.

'Whaddya want?' he said.

'It's cold,' she said. 'Come inside, and I'll tell you.'

'What *is* it, Ma? I'm in a hurry.'

'I want you to go to the store.'

'The store? No! I know why you want me to go – because you're afraid on account of the bill. Well, I ain't going. Never.'

'Please go,' she said. 'You're big enough to understand. You know how Mr Craik is.'

Of course he knew. He hated Craik, that skunk, always asking him if his father was drunk or sober, and what did his father *do* with his money, and how do you wops live without a cent, and how does it happen that your old man never stays home at night, what's he got – a woman on the side, eating up his money? He knew Mr Craik and he hated him.

'Why can't August go?' he said. 'Heck sakes, I do all the work around here. Who gets the coal and wood? I do. Every time. Make August go.'

'But August won't go. He's afraid.'

'Blah. The coward. What's there to be afraid of? Well, I'm not going.'

He turned and tramped back to the boys. The snowball fight was resumed. On the opposition side was Bobby Craik, the grocer's son. I'll get you, you dog. On the porch Maria called again. Arturo did not answer. He shouted so that her voice might be drowned out. Now it was darkness, and Mr Craik's windows bloomed in the night. Arturo kicked a stone from the frozen earth and shaped it within a snowball. The Craik boy was fifty feet away, behind a tree. He threw with a frenzy that strained his whole body, but it missed – sailing a foot out of line.

Mr Craik was whacking a bone with his cleaver on the chopping block when Maria entered. As the door squealed he looked up and saw her – a small insignificant figure in an old black coat with a high fur collar, most of the fur shed so that white hide spots appeared in the dark mass. A weary brown hat covered her forehead – the face of a very old little child hiding beneath it. The faded gloss from her rayon stockings made them a yellowish tan, accentuating the small bones and white skin beneath them, and making her old shoes seem even more damp and ancient. She walked like a child, fearfully, on tiptoe, awed, to that familiar place from which she invariably made her purchases, farthest away from Mr Craik's chopping block, where the counter met the wall.

In the earlier years she used to greet him. But now she felt that perhaps he would not relish such familiarity, and she stood quietly in her corner, waiting until he was ready to wait on her.

Seeing who it was, he paid no attention, and she tried to be an interested and smiling spectator as he swung his cleaver. He was of middle height, partially bald, wearing celluloid glasses – a man of forty-five. A thick pencil rested behind one ear, and a cigarette behind the other. His white apron hung to his shoe tops, a blue butcher string wound many times around his waist. He was hacking a bone inside a red and juicy rump.

She said: 'It looks good, doesn't it?'

He flipped the steak over and over, swished a square of paper from the roll, spread it over the scales, and tossed the steak upon it. His quick, soft fingers wrapped it expertly. She estimated that it was close to two dollars' worth, and she wondered who had purchased it – possibly one of Mr Craik's rich American women customers up on University Hill.

Mr Craik heaved the rest of the rump upon his shoulder and disappeared inside the icebox, closing the door behind him. It seemed he stayed a long time in that icebox. Then he emerged, acted surprised to see her, cleared his throat, clicked the icebox door shut, padlocked it for the night, and disappeared into the back room.

She supposed he was going to the washroom to wash his hands, and that made her wonder if she was out of Gold Dust Cleanser, and then, all at once, everything she needed for the house crashed through her memory, and a weakness like fainting overcame her as quantities of soap, margarine, meat, potatoes, and so many other things seemed to bury her in an avalanche.

Craik reappeared with a broom and began to sweep the sawdust around the chopping block. She lifted her eyes to the clock: ten minutes to six. Poor Mr Craik! He looked tired. He was like all men, probably starved for a hot meal.

Mr Craik finished his sweeping and paused to light a cigarette. Svevo smoked only cigars, but almost all American men smoked cigarettes. Mr Craik looked at her, exhaled, and went on sweeping.

She said, 'It is cold weather we're having.'

But he coughed, and she supposed he hadn't heard, for he disappeared into the back room and returned with a dust pan and a paper box. Sighing as he bent down, he swept the sawdust into the pan and poured it into the paper box.

'I don't like this cold weather,' she said. 'We are waiting for spring, especially Svevo.'

He coughed again, and before she knew it he was carrying the box back to the rear of the store. She heard the splash of running water. He returned, drying his hands on his apron, that nice white apron. At the cash register, very loudly, he rang up NO SALE. She changed her position, moving her weight from one foot to the other. The big clock ticked away. One of those electric clocks with the strange ticks. Now it was exactly six o'clock.

Mr Craik scooped the coins from the cash box and spread them on the counter. He tore a slip of paper from the roll and reached for his pencil. Then he leaned over and counted the day's receipts. Was it possible that he was not aware of her presence in the store? Surely he had seen her come in and stand there! He wet the pencil on the tip of his pink tongue and began adding up the figures. She raised her eyebrows and strolled to the front window to look at the fruits and vegetables. Oranges sixty cents a dozen. Asparagus fifteen cents a pound. Oh my, oh my. Apples two pounds for a quarter.

'Strawberries!' she said. 'And in winter, too! Are they California strawberries, Mr Craik?'

He swept the coins into a bank sack and went to the safe, where he squatted and fingered the combination lock. The big clock ticked. It was ten minutes after six when he closed the safe. Immediately he disappeared into the rear of the store again.

Now she no longer faced him. Shamed, exhausted, her feet had tired, and with hands clasped in her lap she sat on an empty box and stared at the frosted front windows. Mr Craik took off his apron and threw it over the chopping block. He lifted the cigarette from his lips, dropped it to the floor and crushed it deliberately. Then he went to the back room again, returning with his coat. As he straightened his collar, he spoke to her for the first time.

'Come on, Mrs Bandini. My God, I can't hang around here all night long.'

At the sound of his voice she lost her balance. She smiled to conceal her embarrassment, but her face was purplish and her eyes lowered. Her hands fluttered at her throat.

'Oh!' she said. 'I was – waiting for you!'

'What'll it be, Mrs Bandini – shoulder steak?'

She stood in the corner and pursed her lips. Her heart beat so fast she could think of nothing at all to say now.

She said: 'I think I want –'

'Hurry up, Mrs Bandini. My God, you been here about a half hour now, and you ain't made up your mind yet.'

'I thought –'

'Do you want shoulder steak?'

'How much is shoulder steak, Mr Craik?'

'Same price. My God, Mrs Bandini. You been buying it for years. Same price. Same price all the time.'

'I'll take fifty cents' worth.'

'Why didn't you tell me before?' he said. 'Here I went and put all that meat in the icebox.'

'Oh, I'm sorry, Mr Craik.'

'I'll get it this time. But after this, Mrs Bandini, if you want my business, come early. My God, I got to get home sometime tonight.'

He brought out a cut of shoulder and stood sharpening his knife.

'Say,' he said. 'What's Svevo doing these days?'

In the fifteen-odd years that Bandini and Mr Craik knew one another, the grocer always referred to him by his first name. Maria always felt that Craik was afraid of her husband. It was a belief that secretly made her very proud. Now they talked of Bandini, and she told him again the monotonous tale of a bricklayer's misfortunes in the Colorado winters.

'I seen Svevo last night,' Craik said. 'Seen him up around Effie Hildegarde's house. Know her?'

No – she didn't know her.

'Better watch that Svevo,' he said with insinuating humor. 'Better keep your eye on him. Effie Hildegarde's got lots of money.'

'She's a widow too,' Craik said, studying the meat scale. 'Own's the street car company.'

Maria watched his face closely. He wrapped and tied the meat, slapped it before her on the counter. 'Owns lots of real estate in this town too. Fine-looking woman, Mrs Bandini.'

Real estate? Maria sighed with relief.

'Oh, Svevo knows lots of real estate people. He's probably figuring some job for her.'

She was biting her thumbnail when Craik spoke again.

'What else, Mrs Bandini?'

She ordered the rest: flour, potatoes, soap, margarine, sugar. 'I almost forgot!' she said. 'I want some fruit too, a half dozen of those apples. The children like fruit.'

Mr Craik swore under his breath as he whipped a sack open and dropped apples into it. He did not approve of fruit for the Bandini account: he could see no reason for poor people indulging in luxury. Meat and flour – yes. But why should they eat fruit when they owed him so much money?

'Good God,' he said. 'This charging business has got to stop, Mrs Bandini! I tell you it can't go on like this. I ain't had a penny on that bill since September.'

'I'll tell him!' she said, retreating. 'I'll tell him, Mr Craik.'

'Ack! A lot of good that does!'

She gathered her packages.

'I'll tell him, Mr Craik! I'll tell him tonight.'

Such a relief to step into the street! How tired she was. Her body ached. Yet she smiled as she breathed the cold night air, hugging her packages lovingly, as though they were life itself.

Mr Craik was mistaken. Svevo Bandini was a family man. And why shouldn't he talk to a woman who owned real estate?

Chapter Five

Arturo Bandini was pretty sure that he wouldn't go to hell when he died. The way to hell was the committing of mortal sin. He had committed many, he believed, but the confessional had saved him. He always got to confession on time – that is, before he died. And he knocked on wood whenever he thought of it – he always would get there on time – before he died. So Arturo was pretty sure he wouldn't go to hell when he died. For two reasons. The confessional, and the fact that he was a fast runner.

But purgatory, that midway place between hell and heaven, disturbed him. In explicit terms the catechism stated the requirements for heaven: a soul had to be absolutely clean, without the slightest blemish of sin. If the soul at death was not clean enough for heaven, and not befouled enough for hell, there remained that middle region, that purgatory where the soul burned and burned until it was purged of its blemishes.

In purgatory there was one consolation: soon or late you were a cinch for heaven. But when Arturo realized that his stay in purgatory might be seventy million trillion billion years, burning and burning and burning, there was little consolation in ultimate heaven. After all, a hundred years was a long time. And a hundred and fifty million years was incredible.

No: Arturo was sure he would never go straight to heaven. Much as he dreaded the prospect, he knew that he was in for a long session in purgatory. But wasn't there something a man could do to lessen the purgatory ordeal of fire? In his catechism he found the answer to this problem.

The way to shorten the awful period in purgatory, the catechism stated, was by good works, by prayer, by fasting and abstinence, and by piling up indulgences. Good works were out, as far as he was concerned. He had never visited the sick, because he knew no such people. He had never clothed the naked because he had never seen any naked people. He had never buried the dead because they had undertakers for that. He had never given alms to the poor because he had none to give; besides, 'alms' always sounded to him like a loaf of bread, and where could he get loaves of bread? He had never harbored the injured because − well, he didn't know − it sounded like something people did on seacoast towns, going out and rescuing sailors injured in shipwrecks. He had never instructed the ignorant because after all, he was ignorant himself, otherwise he wouldn't be forced to go to this lousy school. He had never enlightened the darkness because that was a tough one he never did understand. He had never comforted the afflicted because it sounded dangerous and he knew none of them anyway: most cases of measles and smallpox had quarantine signs on the doors.

As for the Ten Commandments he broke practically all of them, and yet he was sure that not all of these infringements were mortal sins. Sometimes he carried a rabbit's foot, which was superstition, and therefore a sin against the First Commandment. But was it a mortal sin? That always bothered him. A mortal sin was a serious offense. A venial sin was a slight offense. Sometimes, playing baseball, he crossed bats with a fellow player: this was supposed to be a sure way to get a two-base hit. And yet he knew it was superstition. Was it a sin? And was it a mortal sin or a venial sin? One Sunday he had deliberately missed mass to listen to the broadcast of the world series, and particularly to hear of his god, Jimmy Foxx of the Athletics. Walking home after the game it suddenly occurred to him that he had broken the First Commandment: thou shalt not have strange gods before me. Well, he had committed a mortal sin in missing Mass, but was it another mortal sin to prefer Jimmy Foxx to God Almighty during the world series? He had gone to confession, and there the matter grew more complicated. Father Andrew had said, 'If you think it's a mortal sin, my son, then it is a mortal sin.' Well, heck. At first he had thought it was only a venial sin, but he had to admit that, after considering the offense for three days before confession, it had indeed become a mortal sin.

The Second Commandment. It was no use even thinking about that, for Arturo said 'God damn it' on an average of four times a day. Nor was that counting the variations: God damn this and God damn that. And so, going to confession each week, he was forced to make wide generalizations after a futile examination of his conscience for accuracy. The best he could do was confess to the priest, 'I took the name of the Lord in vain about sixty-eight or seventy times.' Sixty-eight mortal sins in one week, from the Second Commandment alone. Wow! Sometimes, kneeling in the cold church awaiting confessional, he listened in alarm to the beat of his heart, wondering if it would stop and he drop dead before he got those things off his chest. It exasperated him, that wild beating of his heart. It compelled him not to run but often to walk, and very slowly, to confessional, lest he overdo the organ and drop in the street.

'Honor thy father and thy mother.' Of course he honored his father and his mother! Of course. But there was a catch in it: the catechism went on to say that any disobedience of thy father and thy mother was dishonor. Once more he was out of luck. For though he did indeed honor his mother and father, he was rarely obedient. Venial sins? Mortal sins? The classifications pestered him. The number of sins against that commandment exhausted him; he would count them to the hundreds as he examined his days hour by hour. Finally he came to the conclusion that they were only venial sins, not serious enough to merit hell. Even so, he was very careful not to analyze this conclusion too deeply.

He had never killed a man, and for a long time he was sure that he would never sin against the Fifth Commandment. But one day the class in catechism took up the study of the Fifth Commandment, and he discovered to his disgust that it was practically impossible to avoid sins against it. Killing a man was not the only thing: the by-products of the commandment included cruelty, injury, fighting, and all forms of viciousness to man, bird, beast, and insect alike.

Goodnight, what was the use? He enjoyed killing blue-bottle flies. He got a big kick out of killing muskrats, and birds. He loved to fight. He hated those chickens. He had had a lot of dogs in his life, and he had been severe and often harsh with them. And what of the prairie dogs he had killed, the pigeons, the pheasants, the jackrabbits? Well, the only thing to do was to make the best of it. Worse, it was a sin to even think of killing or injuring a human being. That sealed his doom. No matter how he tried, he could not resist expressing the wish of violent death against some people: like Sister Mary Corta, and Craik the grocer, and the freshmen at the university, who beat the kids off with clubs and forbade them to sneak into the big games at the stadium. He realized that, if he wasn't actually a murderer, he was the equivalent in the eyes of God.

One sin against that Fifth Commandment that always seethed in his conscience was an incident the summer before, when he and Paulie Hood, another Catholic boy, had captured a rat alive and crucified it to a small cross with tacks, and mounted it on an anthill. It was a ghastly and horrible thing that he never forgot. But the awful part of it was, they had done this evil thing on Good Friday, and right after saying the Stations of the Cross! He had confessed that sin shamefully, weeping as he told it, with true contrition, but he knew it had piled up many years in purgatory, and it was almost six months before he even dared kill another rat.

Thou shalt not commit adultery; thou shalt not think about Rosa Pinelli, Joan Crawford, Norma Shearer, and Clara Bow. Oh gosh, oh Rosa, oh the sins, the sins, the sins. It began when he was four, no sin then because he was ignorant. It began when he sat in a hammock one day when he was four, rocking back and forth, and the next day he came back to the hammock between the plum tree and the apple tree in the back yard, rocking back and forth.

What did he know about adultery, evil thoughts, evil actions? Nothing. It was fun in the hammock. Then he learned to read, and the first of many things he read were the Commandments. When he was eight he made his first confession, and when he was nine he had to take the Commandments apart and find out what they meant.

Adultery. They didn't talk about it in the fourth grade catechism class. Sister Mary Anna skipped it and spent most of the time talking about Honor thy Father and Mother and Thou Shalt Not Steal. And so it was, for vague reasons he never could understand, that to him adultery always has had something to do with bank robbery. From his eighth year to his tenth, examining his conscience before confession, he would pass over 'Thou shalt not commit adultery' because he had never robbed a bank.

The man who told him about adultery wasn't Father Andrew, and it wasn't one of the nuns, but Art Montgomery at the Standard Station on the corner of Arapahoe and Twelfth. From that day on his loins were a thousand angry hornets buzzing in a nest. The nuns never talked about adultery. They only talked about evil thoughts, evil words, evil actions. That catechism! Every secret of his heart, every sly delight in his mind was already known to that catechism. He could not beat it, no matter how cautiously he tiptoed through the pinpoints of its code. He couldn't go to the movies anymore because he only went to the movies to see the shapes of his heroines. He liked 'love' pictures. He liked following girls up the stairs. He liked girls' arms, legs, hands, feet, their shoes and stockings and dresses, their smell and their presence. After his twelfth year the only things in life that mattered were baseball and girls, only he called them women. He liked the sound of the word. Women, women, women. He said it over and over because it was a secret sensation. Even at Mass, when there were fifty or a hundred of them around him, he reveled in the secrecy of his delights.

And it was all a sin — the whole thing had the sticky sensation of evil. Even the sound of some words was a sin.

Ripple. Supple. Nipple. All sins. Carnal. The flesh. Scarlet. Lips. All sins. When he said the Hail Mary. Hail Mary full of grace, the Lord is with thee and blessed art thou among women, and blessed is the fruit of thy womb. The word shook him like thunder. Fruit of thy womb. Another sin was born.

Every week he staggered into the church of a Saturday afternoon, weighted down by the sins of adultery. Fear drove him there, fear that he would die and then live on forever in eternal torture. He did not dare lie to his confessor. Fear tore his sins out by the roots. He would confess it all fast, gushing with his uncleanliness, trembling to be pure. I committed a bad action I mean two bad actions and I thought about a girl's legs and about touching her in a bad place and I went to the show and thought bad things and I was walking along and a girl was getting out of a car and it was bad and I listened to a bad joke and laughed and a bunch of us kids were watching a couple of dogs and I said something bad, it was my fault, they didn't say anything, I did, I did it all, I made them laugh with a bad idea and I tore a picture out of a magazine and she was naked and I knew it was bad but did it anyway. I thought a bad thing about Sister Mary Agnes; it was bad and I kept on thinking. I also thought bad things about some girls who were laying on the grass and one of them had her dress up high and I kept on looking and knowing it was bad. But I'm sorry. It was my fault, all my fault, and I'm sorry, sorry.

He would leave the confessional, and say his penance, his teeth gritted, his fist tightened, his neck rigid, vowing with body and soul to be clean forevermore. A sweetness would at last pervade him, a soothing lull him, a breeze cool him, a loveliness caress him. He would walk out of the church in a dream, and in a dream he would walk, and if no one was looking he'd kiss a tree, eat a blade of grass, blow kisses at the sky, touch the cold stones of the church wall with fingers of magic, the peace in his heart like nothing save a chocolate malted, a three-base hit, a shining window to be broken, the hypnosis of that moment that comes before sleep.

No, he wouldn't go to hell when he died. He was a fast runner, always getting to confession on time. But purgatory awaited him. Not for him the direct, pure route to eternal bliss. He would get there the hard way, by detour. That was one reason why Arturo was an altar boy. Some piety on this earth was bound to lessen the purgatory period.

He was an altar boy for two other reasons. In the first place, despite his ceaseless howls of protests, his mother insisted on it. In the second place, every Christmas season the girls in the Holy Name Society feted the altar boys with a banquet.

Rosa, I love you.

She was in the auditorium with the Holy Name Girls, decorating the tree for the altar boy banquet. He watched from the door, feasting his eyes upon the triumph of her tiptoed loveliness. Rosa: tinfoil and chocolate bars, the smell of a new football, goalposts with bunting, a home run with the bases full. I am an Italian too, Rosa. Look, and my eyes are like yours. Rosa, I love you.

Sister Mary Ethelbert passed.

'Come, come, Arturo. Don't dawdle there.'

She was in charge of the altar boys. He followed her black flowing robes to the 'little auditorium' where some seventy boys who comprised the male student body awaited her. She mounted the rostrum and clapped her hands for silence.

'All right boys, do take your places.'

They lined up, thirty-five couples. The short boys were in front, the tall boys in the rear. Arturo's partner was Wally O'Brien, the kid who sold the *Denver Post*s in front of the First National Bank. They were twenty-fifth from the front, the tenth from the rear. Arturo detested this fact. For eight years he and Wally had been partners, ever since kindergarten. Each year found them moved back farther, and yet they had never made it, never grown tall enough to make it back to the last three rows where the big guys stood, where the wisecracks came from. Here it was, their last year in this lousy school, and they were still stymied around a bunch of sixth- and seventh-grade punks. They concealed their humiliation by an exceedingly tough and blasphemous exterior, shocking the sixth-grade punks into a grudging and awful respect for their brutal sophistication.

But Wally O'Brien was lucky. He didn't have any kid brothers in the line to bother him. Each year, with increasing alarm, Arturo had watched his brothers August and Federico moving toward him from the front rows. Federico was now tenth from the front. Arturo was relieved to know that this youngest of his brothers would never pass him in the line-up. For next June, thank God, Arturo graduated, to be through forever as an altar boy.

But the real menace was the blond head in front of him, his brother August. Already August suspected his impending triumph. Whenever the line was called to order he seemed to measure off Arturo's height with a contemptuous sneer. For indeed, August was the taller by an eighth of an inch, but Arturo, usually slouched over, always managed to straighten himself enough to pass Sister Mary Ethelbert's supervision.

It was an exhausting process. He had to crane his neck and walk on the balls of his feet, his heels a half inch off the floor. Meanwhile he kept August in complete submission by administering smashing kicks with his knee whenever Sister Mary Ethelbert wasn't looking.

They did not wear vestments, for this was only practice. Sister Mary Ethelbert led them out of the little auditorium and down the hall, past the big auditorium, where Arturo caught a glance of Rosa sprinkling tinsel on the Christmas tree. He kicked August and sighed.

Rosa, me and you: a couple of Italians.

They marched down three flights of stairs and across the yard to the front doors of the church. The holy water fonts were frozen hard. In unison, they genuflected; Wally O'Brien's finger spearing the boys in front of him. For two hours they practiced, mumbling Latin responses, genuflecting, marching in miltary piousness. *Ad deum qui loctificat, juventutem meum.*

At five o'clock, bored and exhausted, they were finished. Sister Mary Ethelbert lined them up for final inspection. Arturo's toes ached from bearing his full weight. In weariness he rested himself on his heels. It was a moment of carelessness for which he paid dearly. Sister Mary Ethelbert's keen eye just then observed a bend in the line, beginning and ending at the top of Arturo Bandini's head. He could read her thoughts, his weary toes rising in vain to the effort. Too late, too late. At her suggestion he and August changed places.

His new partner was a kid named Wilkins, fourth-grader who wore celluloid glasses and picked his nose. Behind him, triumphantly sanctified, stood August, his lips sneering implacably, no word coming from him. Wally O'Brien looked at his erstwhile partner in crestfallen sadness, for Wally too had been humiliated by the intrusion of this upstart sixth-grader. It was the end for Arturo. Out of the corner of his mouth he whispered to August.

'You dirty –' he said. 'Wait'll I get you outside.'

Arturo was waiting after practice. They met at the corner. August walked fast, as if he hadn't seen his brother. Arturo quickened his pace.

'What's your hurry, Tall Man?'

'I'm not hurrying, Shorty.'

'Yes you are, Tall Man. And how would you like some snow rubbed in your face?'

'I wouldn't like it. And you leave me alone – Shorty.'

'I'm not bothering you, Tall Man. I just want to walk home with you.'

'Don't you try anything now.'

'I wouldn't lay a hand on you, Tall Man. What makes you think I would?'

They approached the alley between the Methodist church and the Colorado Hotel. Once beyond that alley, August was safe in the view of the loungers at the hotel window. He sprang forward to run, but Arturo's fist seized his sweater.

'What's the hurry, Tall Man?'

'If you touch me, I'll call a cop.'

'Oh, I wouldn't do that.'

A coupe passed, moving slowly. Arturo followed his brother's sudden open-mouthed stare at the occupants, a man and a woman. The woman was driving, and the man had his arm at her back.

'Look!'

But Arturo had seen. He felt like laughing. It was such a

strange thing. Effie Hildegarde drove the car, and the man was Svevo Bandini.

The boys examined one another's faces. So that was why Mamma had asked all those questions about Effie Hildegarde! If Effie Hildegarde was good looking. If Effie Hildegarde was a 'bad' woman.

Arturo's mouth softened to a laugh. The situation pleased him. That father of his! That Svevo Bandini! Oh boy – and Effie Hildegarde was a swell-looking dame too!

'Did they see us?'

Arturo grinned. 'No.'

'Are you sure?'

'He had his arm around her, didn't he?'

August frowned.

'That's bad. That's going out with another woman. The Ninth Commandment.'

They turned into the alley. It was a short cut. Darkness came fast. Water puddles at their feet were frozen in the growing darkness. They walked along, Arturo smiling. August was bitter.

'It's a sin. Mamma's a swell mother. It's a sin.'

'Shut up.'

They turned from the alley on Twelfth Street. The Christmas shopping crowd in the business district separated them now and then, but they stayed together, waiting as one another picked his way through the crowd. The street lamps went on.

'Poor Mamma. She's better than that Effie Hildegarde.'

'Shut up.'

'It's a sin.'

'What do you know about it? Shut up.'

'Just because Mamma hasn't got good clothes . . .'

'Shut up, August.'

'It's a mortal sin.'

'You're dumb. You're too little. You don't know anything.'

'I know a sin. Mamma wouldn't do that.'

The way his father's arm rested on her shoulder. He had seen her many times. She had charge of the girls' activities at the Fourth of July celebration in the Courthouse Park. He had seen her standing on the courthouse steps the summer before, beckoning with her arms, calling the girls together for the big parade. He remembered her teeth, her pretty teeth, her red mouth, her fine plump body. He had left his friends to stand in the shadows and watch as she talked to the girls. Effie Hildegarde. Oh boy, his father was a wonder!

And he was like his father. A day would come when he and Rosa Pinelli would be doing it too. Rosa, let's get into the car and drive out in the country, Rosa. Me and you, out in the country, Rosa. You drive the car and we'll kiss, but you drive, Rosa.

'I bet the whole town knows it,' August said.

'Why shouldn't they? You're like everybody else. Just because Papa's poor, just because he's an Italian.'

'It's a sin,' he said, kicking viciously at frozen chunks of snow. 'I don't care what he is – or how poor, either. It's a sin.'

'You're dumb. A saphead. You don't savvy anything.'

August did not answer him. They took the short path over the trestle bridge that spanned the creek. They walked in single file, heads down, careful of the limitations of the deep path through the snow. They took the trestle bridge on tiptoe, from railroad tie to tie, the frozen creek thirty feet below them. The quiet evening spoke to them, whispering of a man riding in a car somewhere in the same twilight, a woman not his own riding with him. They descended the crest of the railroad line and followed a faint trail which they themselves had made all that winter in the comings and goings to and from school, through the Alzi pasture, with great sweeps of white on either side of the path, untouched for months, deep and glittering in the evening's birth. Home was a quarter of a mile away, only a block beyond the fences of the Alzi pasture. Here in this great pasture they had spent a great part of their lives. It stretched from the backyards of the very last row of houses in the town, weary frozen cottonwoods strangled in the death pose of long winters on one side, and a creek that no longer laughed on the other. Beneath that snow was white sand once very hot and excellent after swimming in the creek. Each tree held memories. Each fence post measured a dream, enclosing it for fulfillment with each new spring. Beyond that pile of stones, between those two tall cottonwoods, was the graveyard of their dogs and Suzie, a cat who had hated the dogs but lay now beside them. Prince, killed by an automobile; Jerry, who ate the poison meat; Pancho the fighter, who crawled off and died after his last fight. Here they had killed snakes, shot birds, speared frogs, scalped Indians, robbed banks, completed wars, reveled in peace. But in that twilight their father rode with Effie Hildegarde, and the silent white sweep of the pasture land was only a place for walking on a strange road to home.

'I'm going to tell her,' August said.

Arturo was ahead of him, three paces away. He turned

around quickly. 'You keep still,' he said. 'Mamma's got enough trouble.'

'I'll tell her. She'll fix him.'

'You shut up about this.'

'It's against the Ninth Commandment. Mamma's our mother, and I'm going to tell.'

Arturo spread his legs and blocked the path. August tried to step around him, the snow two feet deep on either side of the path. His head was down, his face set with disgust and pain. Arturo took both lapels of his mackinaw and held him.

'You keep still about this.'

August shook himself loose.

'Why should I? He's our father, ain't he? Why does he have to do that?'

'Do you want Mamma to get sick?'

'Then what did he do it for?'

'Shut up! Answer my question. Do you want Mamma to be sick? She will if she hears about it.'

'She won't get sick.'

'I know she won't – because you're not telling.'

'I am too.'

The back of his hand caught August across the eyes.

'I said you're not going to tell!'

August's lips quivered like jelly.

'I'm telling.'

Arturo's fist tightened under his nose.

'You see this? You get it if you tell.'

Why should August want to tell? What if his father *was* with another woman? What difference did it make, so long as his mother didn't know? And besides, this wasn't another woman: this was Effie Hildegarde, one of the richest women in town. Pretty good for his father; pretty swell. She wasn't as good as his mother – no: but that didn't have anything to do with it.

'Go ahead and hit me. I'm telling.'

The hard fist pushed into August's cheek. August turned his head away contemptuously. 'Go ahead. Hit me. I'm telling.'

'Promise not to tell or I'll knock your face in.'

'Pooh. Go ahead. I'm telling.'

He tilted his chin forward, ready for any blow. It infuriated Arturo. Why did August have to be such a damn fool? He didn't want to hit him. Sometimes he really enjoyed knocking August around, but not now. He opened his fist and clapped his hands on his hips in exasperation.

'But look, August,' he argued. 'Can't you see that it won't help to tell Mamma? Can't you just see her crying? And right now, at Christmas time too. It'll hurt her. It'll hurt her like hell. You don't want to hurt Mamma, you don't want to hurt your own mother, do you? You mean to tell me you'd go up to your own mother and say something that would hurt the hell out of her? Ain't that a sin, to do that?'

August's cold eyes blinked their conviction. The vapors of his breath flooded Arturo's face as he answered sharply. 'But what about him? I suppose he isn't committing a sin. A worse sin than any I commit.'

Arturo gritted his teeth. He pulled off his cap and threw it into the snow. He beseeched his brother with both fists. 'God damn you! You're not telling.'

'I am too.'

With one blow he cut August down, a left to the side of his head. The boy staggered backward, lost his balance in the snow, and floundered on his back. Arturo was on him, the two buried in the fluffy snow beneath the hardened crust. His hands encircled August's throat. He squeezed hard.

'You gonna tell?'

The cold eyes were the same.

He lay motionless. Arturo had never known him that way before. What should he do? Hit him? Without relaxing his grip on August's neck he looked off toward the trees beneath which lay his dead dogs. He bit his lip and sought vainly within himself the anger that would make him strike.

Weakly he said, 'Please, August. Don't tell.'

'I'm telling.'

So he swung. It seemed that the blood poured from his brother's nose almost instantly. It horrified him. He sat straddling August, his knees pinning down August's arms. He could not bear the sight of August's face. Beneath the mask of blood and snow August smiled defiantly, the red stream filling his smile.

Arturo knelt beside him. He was crying, sobbing with his head on August's chest, digging his hands into the snow and repeating: 'Please August. Please! You can have anything I got. You can sleep on any side of the bed you want. You can have all my picture show money.'

August was silent, smiling.

Again he was furious. Again he struck, smashing his fist blindly into the cold eyes. Instantly he regretted it, crawling in the snow around the quiet, limp figure.

Defeated at last, he rose to his feet. He brushed the snow from his clothes, pulled his cap down and sucked his hands to warm them. Still August lay there, blood still pouring from his nose: August the triumphant, stretched out like one dead, yet bleeding, buried in the snow, his cold eyes sparkling their serene victory.

Arturo was too tired. He no longer cared.

'Okay, August.'

Still August lay there.

'Get up, August.'

Without accepting Arturo's arm he crawled to his feet. He stood quietly in the snow, wiping his face with a handkerchief, fluffing the snow from his blond hair. It was five minutes before the bleeding stopped. They said nothing. August touched his swollen face gently. Arturo watched him.

'You all right now?'

He did not answer as he stepped into the path and walked toward the row of houses. Arturo followed, shame silencing him: shame and hopelessness. In the moonlight he noticed that August limped. And yet it was not a limp so much as a caricature of one limping, like the pained embarrassed gait of the tenderfoot who had just finished his first ride on a horse. Arturo studied it closely. Where had he seen that before? It seemed so natural to August. Then he remembered: that was the way August used to walk out of the bedroom two years before, on those mornings after he had wet the bed.

'August,' he said. 'If you tell Mamma, I'll tell everybody that you pee the bed.'

He had not expected more than a sneer, but to his surprise August turned around and looked him squarely in the face. It was a look of incredulity, a taint of doubt crossing the once cold eyes. Instantly Arturo sprang to the kill, his senses excited by the impending victory.

'Yes, sir!' he shouted. 'I'll tell everybody. I'll tell the whole world. I'll tell every kid in the school. I'll write notes to every kid in the school. I'll tell everybody I see. I'll tell it and tell it to the whole town. I'll tell them August Bandini pees the bed. I'll tell 'em!'

'No!' August choked. 'No, Arturo!'

He shouted at the top of his voice.

'Yes sir, all you people of Rocklin, Colorado! Listen to this: August Bandini pees the bed! He's twelve years old and he pees the bed. Did you ever hear of anything like that? Yipee! Everybody listen!'

'Please, Arturo! Don't yell. I won't tell. Honest I won't, Arturo. I won't say a word! Only don't yell like that. I don't pee the bed, Arturo. I used to, but I don't now.'

'Promise not to tell Mamma?'

August gulped as he crossed his heart and hoped to die.

'Okay,' Arturo said. 'Okay.'

Arturo helped him to his feet and they walked home.

Chapter Six

No question about it: Papa's absence had its advantages. If he were home the scrambled eggs for dinner would have had onions in them. If he were home they wouldn't have been permitted to gouge out the white of the bread and eat only the crust. If he were home they wouldn't have got so much sugar.

Even so, they missed him. Maria was so listless. All day she swished in carpet slippers, walking slowly. Sometimes they had to speak twice before she heard them. Afternoons she sat drinking tea, staring into the cup. She let the dishes go. One afternoon an incredible thing happened: a fly appeared. A fly! And in winter! They watched it soaring near the ceiling. It seemed to move with great difficulty, as though its wings were frozen. Federico climbed a chair and killed the fly with a rolled newspaper. It fell to the floor. They got down on their knees and examined it. Federico held it between his fingers. Maria knocked it from his hand. She ordered him to the sink, and to use soap and water. He refused. She seized him by the hair and dragged him to his feet.

'You do what I tell you!'

They were astonished: Mamma had never touched them, had never said an unkind thing to them. Now she was listless again, deep in the ennui of a teacup. Federico washed and dried his hands. Then he did a surprising thing. Arturo and August were convinced that something was wrong, for Federico bent over and kissed his mother in the depths of her hair. She hardly noticed it. Absently she smiled. Federico slipped to his knees and put his head in her lap. Her fingers slid over the outlines of his nose and lips. But they knew that she hardly noticed Federico. Without a word she got up, and Federico looked after her in disappointment as she walked to the rocking chair by the window in the front room. There she remained, never moving, her elbow on the window sill, her chin in her hand as she watched the cold deserted street.

Strange times. The dishes remained unwashed. Sometimes they went to bed and the bed wasn't made. It didn't matter but they thought about it, of her in the front room by the window. Mornings she lay in bed and did not get up to see them off to school. They dressed in alarm, peeking at her from the bedroom door. She lay like one dead, the rosary in her hand. In the kitchen the dishes had been washed sometime during the night. They were surprised again, and disappointed: for they had awakened to expect a dirty kitchen. It made a difference. They enjoyed the change from a clean to a dirty kitchen. But there it was, clean again, their breakfast in the oven. They looked in before leaving for school. Only her lips moved.

Strange times.

Arturo and August walked to school.

'Remember, August. Remember your promise.'

'Huh. I don't have to tell. She knows it already.'

'No, she doesn't.'

'Then why does she act like that?'

'Because she thinks it. But she doesn't really know it.'

'It's the same.'

'No it isn't.'

Strange times. Christmas coming, the town full of Christmas trees, and the Santa Claus men from the Salvation Army ringing bells. Only three more shopping days before Christmas. They stood with famine-stricken eyes before shop windows. They sighed and walked on. They thought the same: it was going to be a lousy Christmas, and Arturo hated it, because he could forget he was poor if they didn't remind him of it: every Christmas was the same, always unhappy, always wanting things he never thought about and having them denied. Always lying to the kids: telling them he was going to get things he could never possibly own. The rich kids had their day at Christmas. They could spread it on, and he had to believe them.

Wintertime, the time for standing around radiators in the cloak rooms, just standing there and telling lies. Ah, for spring! Ah, for the crack of the bat, the sting of a ball on soft palms! Wintertime, Christmas time, rich kid time: they had high-top boots and bright mufflers and fur-lined gloves. But it didn't worry him very much. His time was the springtime. No high-top boots and fancy mufflers on the playing field! Can't get to first base because you got a classy necktie. But he lied with the rest of them. What was he getting for Christmas? Oh, a new watch, a new suit, a lot of shirts and ties, a new bicycle, and a dozen Spalding Official National League Baseballs.

But what of Rosa?

I love you, Rosa. She had a way about her. She was poor too, a coal miner's daughter, but they flocked around her and listened to her talk, and it didn't matter, and he envied her and was proud of her, wondering if those who listened ever considered that he was an Italian too, like Rosa Pinelli.

Speak to me, Rosa. Look this way just once, over here Rosa, where I am watching.

He had to get her a Christmas present, and he walked the streets and peered into windows and bought her jewels and gowns. You're welcome, Rosa. And here is a ring I bought you. Let me put it on your finger. There. Oh, it's nothing, Rosa. I was walking along Pearl Street, and I came to Cherry's Jewelry Shop, and I went in and bought it. Expensive? Naaaw. Three hundred, is all. I got plenty of money, Rosa. Haven't you heard about my father? We're rich. My father's uncle in Italy. He left us everything. We come from fine people back there. We didn't know about it, but come to find out, we were second cousins of the Duke of Abruzzi. Distantly related to the King of Italy. It doesn't matter, though. I've always loved you, Rosa, and just because I come from royal blood never will make any difference.

Strange times. One night he got home earlier than usual. He found the house empty, the back door wide open. He called his mother but got no answer. Then he noticed that both stoves had gone out. He searched every room in the house. His mother's coat and hat were in the bedroom. Then where could she be?

He walked into the back yard and called her.

'Ma! Oh, Ma! Where are you?'

He returned to the house and built a fire in the front room. Where could she be without her hat and coat in this weather? God damn his father! He shook his fist at his father's hat hanging in the kitchen. God damn you, why don't you come home! Look what you're doing to Mamma! Darkness came suddenly and he was frightened. Somewhere in that cold house he could smell his mother, in every room, but she was not there. He went to the back door and yelled again.

'Ma! Oh, Ma! Where are you?'

The fire went out. There was no more coal or wood. He was glad. It gave him an excuse to leave the house and fetch more fuel. He seized a coal bucket and started down the path.

In the coal shed he found her, his mother, seated in the darkness in the corner, seated on a mortar board. He jumped when he saw her, it was so dark and her face so white, numb with cold, seated in her thin dress, staring at his face and not speaking, like a dead woman, his mother frozen in the corner. She sat away from the meager pile of coal in the part of the shed where Bandini kept his mason's tools, his cement and sacks of lime. He rubbed his eyes to free them from the blinding light of snow, the coal bucket dropped at his side as he squinted and watched her form gradually assume clarity, his mother sitting on a mortar board in the darkness of the coal shed. Was she crazy? And what was that she held in her hand?

'Mamma!' he demanded. 'What're you *doing* in here?'

No answer, but her hand opened and he saw what it was: a trowel, a mason's trowel, his father's. The clamor and protest of his body and mind took hold of him. His mother in the darkness of the coal shed with his father's trowel. It was an intrusion upon the intimacy of a scene that belonged to him alone. His mother had no right in this place. It was as though she had discovered him there, committing a boy-sin, that place, identically where he had sat those times; and she was there, angering him with his memories and he hated it, she there, holding his father's trowel. What good did that do? Why did she have to go around reminding herself of him, fooling with his clothes, touching his chair? Oh, he had seen her plenty of times – looking at his empty place at the table; and now, here she was, holding his trowel in the coal shed, freezing to death and not caring, like a dead woman. In his anger he kicked the coal bucket and began to cry.

'Mamma!' he demanded. 'What're you doing! Why are you out here? You'll die out here, Mamma! You'll freeze!'

She arose and staggered toward the door with white hands stretched ahead of her, the face stamped with cold, the blood gone from it as she walked past him and into the semi-darkness of the evening. How long she had been there he did not know, possibly an hour, possibly more, but he knew she must be half dead with cold. She walked in a daze, staring here and there as if she had never known that place before.

He filled the coal bucket. The shed smelled tartly of lime and cement. Over one rafter hung a pair of Bandini's overalls. He grabbed at them and ripped the overalls in two. It was all right to go around with Effie Hildegarde, he liked that all right, but why should his mother suffer so much, making him suffer? He hated his mother too; she was a fool, killing herself on purpose, not caring about the rest of them, him and August and Federico. They were all fools. The only person with any sense in the whole family was himself.

Maria was in bed when he got back to the house. Fully clothed she lay shivering beneath the covers. He looked at her and made grimaces of impatience. Well, it was her own fault: why did she want to go out like that? Yet he felt he should be sympathetic.

'You all right, Mamma?'

'Leave me alone,' her trembling mouth said. 'Just leave me alone, Arturo.'

'Want the hot water bottle?'

She did not reply. Her eyes glanced at him out of their corners, quickly, in exasperation. It was a look he took for hatred, as if she wanted him out of her sight forever, as though he had something to do with the whole thing. He whistled in surprise: gosh, his mother was a strange woman; she was taking this too seriously.

He left the bedroom on tiptoe, not afraid of her but of what his presence might do to her. After August and Federico got home, she arose and cooked dinner: poached eggs, toast, fried potatoes, and an apple apiece. She did not touch the food herself. After dinner they found her at the same place, the front window, staring at the white street, her rosary clicking against the rocker.

Strange times. It was an evening of only living and breathing. They sat around the stove and waited for something to happen. Federico crawled to her chair and placed his hand on her knee. Still in prayer, she shook her head like one hypnotized. It was her way of telling Federico not to interrupt her, or to touch her, to leave her alone.

The next morning she was her old self, tender and smiling through breakfast. The eggs had been prepared 'Mamma's way,' a special treat, the yolks filmed by the whites. And would you look at her! Hair combed tightly, her eyes big and bright. When Federico dumped his third spoonful of sugar into his coffee cup, she remonstrated with mock sternness.

'Not that way, Federico! Let me show you.'

She emptied the cup into the sink.

'If you want a sweet cup of coffee, I'll give it to you.' She placed the sugar bowl instead of the coffee cup on Federico's saucer. The bowl was half full of sugar. She filled it the rest of the way with coffee. Even August laughed, though he had to admit there might be a sin in it – wastefulness.

Federico tasted it suspiciously.

'Swell,' he said. 'Only there's no room for the cream.'

She laughed, clutching her throat, and they were glad to see her happy, but she kept on laughing, pushing her chair away and bending over with laughter. It wasn't that funny; it couldn't be. They watched her miserably, her laughter not ending even though their blank faces stared at her. They saw her eyes fill with tears, her face swelling to purple. She got up, one hand over her mouth, and staggered to the sink. She drank a glass of water until it sputtered in her throat and she could not go on, and finally she staggered into the bedroom and lay on the bed, where she laughed.

Now she was quiet again.

They arose from the table and looked in at her on the bed. She was rigid, her eyes like buttons in a doll, a funnel of vapors pouring from her panting mouth and into the cold air.

'You kids go to school,' Arturo said. 'I'm staying home.'

After they were gone, he went to the bedside.

'Can I get you something, Ma?'

'Go away, Arturo. Leave me alone.'

'Should I call Dr Hastings?'

'No. Leave me alone. Go away. Go to school. You'll be late.'

'Should I try to find Papa?'

'Don't you dare.'

Suddenly that seemed the right thing to do.

'I'm going to,' he said. 'That's just what I'm going to do.' He hurried for his coat.

'Arturo!'

She was out of bed like a cat. When he turned around in the clothes closet, one of his arms inside a sweater, he gasped to see her beside him so quickly. 'Don't you go to your father! You hear me – don't you dare!' She bent so close to his face that hot spittle from her lips sprinkled it. He backed away to the corner and turned his back, afraid of her, afraid to even look at her. With strength that amazed him she took him by the shoulder and swung him around.

'You've seen him, haven't you? He's with that woman.'

'What woman?' He jerked himself away and fussed with his sweater. She tore his hands loose and took him by the shoulders, her finger-nails pinching the flesh.

'Arturo, look at me! You saw him, didn't you?'

'No.'

But he smiled; not because he wished to torment her, but because he believed he had succeeded in the lie. Too quickly he smiled. Her mouth closed and her face softened in defeat. She smiled weakly, hating to know yet vaguely pleased that he had tried to shield her from the news.

'I see,' she said. 'I see.'

'You don't see anything, you're talking crazy.'

'When did you see him, Arturo?'

'I tell you I didn't.'

She straightened herself and drew back her shoulders.

'Go to school, Arturo. I'm all right here. I don't need anybody.'

Even so, he remained home, wandering about the house, keeping the stoves fueled, now and then looking into her room, where she lay as always, her glazed eyes studying the ceiling, her beads rattling. She did not urge him to school again, and he felt he was of some use, that she was comforted with his presence. After a while he pulled a copy of *Horror Crimes* from his hiding place under the floor and sat reading in the kitchen, his feet on a block of wood in the oven.

Always he had wanted his mother to be pretty, to be beautiful. Now it obsessed him, the thought filtering beyond the pages of *Horror Crimes* and shaping itself into the misery of the woman lying on the bed. He put the magazine away and sat biting his lip. Sixteen years ago his mother had been beautiful, for he had seen her picture. Oh that picture! Many times, coming home from school and finding his mother weary and worried and not beautiful, he had gone to the trunk and taken it out – a picture of a large-eyed girl in a wide hat, smiling with so many small teeth, a beauty of a girl standing under the apple tree in Grandma Toscana's backyard. Oh Mamma, to kiss you then! Oh Mamma, why did you change?

Suddenly he wanted to look at that picture again. He did the pulp and opened the door of the empty room off the kitchen, where his mother's trunk was kept stored. He locked the door from the inside. Huh, and why did he do that? He unlocked it. The room was like an icebox. He crossed to the window where the trunk stood. Then he returned and locked the door again. Vaguely he felt he should not be doing this, yet why not: couldn't he even look at a picture of his mother without a sense of evil degrading him? Well, suppose it wasn't his mother, really: it used to be, so what was the difference?

Beneath layers of linen and curtains that his mother was saving until 'we get a better house,' beneath ribbons and baby clothes once worn by himself and his brothers, he found the picture. Ah, man! He held it up and stared at the wonder of that lovely face: here was the mother he had always dreamed about, this girl, no more than twenty, whose eyes he knew resembled his own. Not that weary woman in the other part of the house, she with the thin tortured face, the long bony hands. To have known her then, to have remembered everything from the beginning, to have felt the cradle of that beautiful womb, to have lived remembering from the beginning, and yet he remembered nothing of that time, and always she had been as she was now, weary and with that wistfulness of pain, the great eyes those of someone else, the mouth softer as if from much crying. He traced with his finger the line of her face, kissing it, sighing and murmuring of a past he had never known.

As he put the picture away, his eye fell upon something in one corner of the trunk. It was a tiny jewel box of purple velvet. He had never seen it before. Its presence surprised him, for he had gone through the trunk many times. The little purple box opened when he pressed the spring lock. Inside it, nestling in a silk couch was a black cameo on a gold chain. The dim writing on a card under the silk told him what it was. 'For Maria, married one year today. Svevo.'

His mind worked fast as he shoved the little box into his pocket and locked the trunk. Rosa, Merry Christmas. A little gift. I bought it, Rosa. I've been saving up for it a long time. For you, Rosa. Merry Christmas.

He was waiting for Rosa next morning at eight o'clock, standing at the water fountain in the hall. It was the last day of classes before Christmas vacation. He knew Rosa always got to school early. Usually he barely made the last bell, running the final two blocks to school. He was sure the nuns who passed regarded him suspiciously, despite their kindly smiles and greetings for a Merry Christmas. In his right coat pocket he felt the snug importance of his gift for Rosa.

By eight fifteen the kids began to arrive: girls, of course, but no Rosa. He watched the electric clock on the wall. Eight thirty, and still no Rosa. He frowned with displeasure: a whole half hour spent in school, and for what? For nothing. Sister Celia, her glass eye brighter than the other, swooped downstairs from the convent quarters. Seeing him there on one foot, Arturo who was usually late, she glanced at the watch on her wrist.

'Good heavens! Is my watch stopped?'

She checked with the electric clock on the wall.

'Didn't you go home last night, Arturo?'

'Sure, Sister Celia.'

'You mean you deliberately arrived a half hour early this morning?'

'I came to study. Behind in my algebra.'

She smiled her doubt. 'With Christmas vacation beginning tomorrow?'

'That's right.'

But he knew it didn't make sense.

'Merry Christmas, Arturo.'

'Ditto, Sister Celia.'

Twenty to nine, and no Rosa. Everyone seemed to stare at him, even his brothers, who gaped as though he was in the wrong school, the wrong town.

'Look who's here!'

'Beat it, punk.' He bent over to drink some ice water.

At ten of nine she opened the big front door. There she was, red hat, camel's hair coat, zipper overshoes, her face, her whole body lighted up with the cold flame of the winter morning. Nearer and nearer she came, her arms draped lovingly around a great bundle of books. She nodded this way and that to friends, her smile like a melody in that hall: Rosa, president of the Holy Name Girls, everybody's sweetheart coming nearer and nearer in little galoshes that flapped with joy, as though they loved her too.

He tightened the grip around the jewel box. A sudden gusher of blood thundered through his throat. The vivacious sweep of her eyes centered for a fleeting moment upon his tortured ecstatic face, his mouth open, his eyes bulging as he swallowed down his excitement.

He was speechless.

'Rosa . . . I . . . here's . . .'

Her gaze went past him. The frown became a smile as a classmate rushed up and swept her away. They walked into the cloak room, chattering excitedly. His chest sank. Nuts. He bent over and gulped ice water. Nuts. He spat the water out, hating it, his whole mouth aching. Nuts.

He spent the morning writing notes to Rosa, and tearing them up. Sister Celia had the class read Van Dyke's *The Other Wise Man*. He sat there bored, his mind attuned to the healthier writings found in the pulps.

But when it was Rosa's turn to read he listened as she enunciated with a kind of reverence. Only then did the Van Dyke trash have significance. He knew it was a sin, but he had absolutely no respect for the story of the birth of the infant Jesus, the flight into Egypt, and the narrative of the child in the manger. But this line of thought was a sin.

During the noon hour, he stalked after her; but she was never alone, always with friends. Once she looked over the shoulders of a girl as a group of them stood in a circle and saw him, as if with a prescience of being followed. He gave up, then, ashamed, and pretended to swagger down the hall. The bell rang and afternoon class began. While Sister Celia talked mysteriously of the Virgin Birth, he wrote more notes to Rosa, tearing them up and writing others. Now he realized he was unequal to the task of presenting the gift to her in person. Someone else would have to do that. The note that satisfied him was:

> *Dear Rosa:*
> *Here is a Merry Xmas*
> *from*
> *Guess Who*

It hurt him when he realized that she would not accept the gift if she recognized the handwriting. With clumsy patience he rewrote it with his left hand, scrawling it in a wild, awkward script. But who would deliver the gift? He studied the faces of classmates around him. None of them, he realized, could possibly keep a secret. He solved the matter by raising two fingers. With the saccharine benevolence of the Christmas season, Sister Celia nodded her permission for him to leave the room. He tiptoed down the side aisle toward the cloak room.

He recognized Rosa's coat at once, for he was familiar with it, having touched and smelled it on similar occasions.

He slipped the note inside the box and dropped the box inside the coat pocket. He embraced the coat, inhaling the fragrance. In the side pocket he found a tiny pair of kid gloves. They were well worn, the little fingers showing holes.

Aw, jiminy: cute little holes. He kissed them tenderly. Dear little holes in the fingers. Sweet little holes. Don't you cry, cute little holes, you just be brave and keep her fingers warm, her cunning little fingers.

He returned to the classroom, down the side aisle to his seat, his eyes as far away from Rosa as possible, for she must not know, or ever suspect him.

When the dismissal bell rang, he was the first out of the big front doors, running down the street. Tonight he would know if she cared at all, for tonight was the Holy Name banquet for the altar boys. Passing through town, he kept his eyes open for sight of his father, but his watchfulness was unrewarded. He knew he should have remained at school for altar boy practice, but that duty had become unbearable with his brother August behind him and the boy across from him, his partner, a miserable fourth-grade shrimp.

Reaching home, he was astonished to find a Christmas tree, a small spruce, standing in the corner by the window in the front room. Sipping tea in the kitchen, his mother was apathetic about it.

'I don't know who it was,' she said. 'A man in a truck.'

'What kind of a man, Mamma?'

'A man.'

'What kind of a truck?'

'Just a truck.'

'What did it say on the truck?'

'I don't know. I didn't pay any attention.'

He knew she was lying. He loathed her for this martyr-like acceptance of their plight. She should have thrown the tree back into the man's face. Charity! What did they think his family was – poor? He suspected the Bledsoe family next door: Mrs Bledsoe, who wouldn't let her Danny and Phillip play with that Bandini boy because he was (1) an Italian, (2) a Catholic, and (3) a bad boy leader of a gang of hoodlums who dumped garbage on her front porch every Hallowe'en. Well, hadn't she sent Danny with a Thanksgiving basket last Thanksgiving, when they didn't need it, and hadn't Bandini ordered Danny to take it back?

'Was it a Salvation Army truck?'

'I don't know.'

'Was the man wearing a soldier hat?'

'I don't remember.'

'It was the Salvation Army, wasn't it? I bet Mrs Bledsoe called them up.'

'What if it was?' Her voice came through her teeth. 'I want your father to see that tree. I want him to look at it and see what he's done to us. Even the neighbors know about it. Ah, shame, shame on him.'

'To heck with the neighbors.'

He walked toward the tree with his fists doubled pugnaciously. 'To heck with the neighbors.' The tree was about his own height, five feet. He rushed into its prickly fullness and tore at the branches. They had a tender willowy strength, bending and cracking but not breaking. When he had disfigured it to his satisfaction, he threw it into the snow in the front yard. His mother made no protest, staring always into the teacup, her dark eyes brooding.

'I hope the Bledsoes see it,' he said. 'That'll teach them.'

'God'll punish him,' Maria said. 'He will pay for this.'

But he was thinking of Rosa, and of what he would wear to the altar boy banquet. He and August and his father always fought about that favorite gray tie, Bandini insisting it was too old for boys, and he and August answering it was too young for a man. Yet somehow it had always remained 'Papa's tie,' for it had that good father-feeling about it, the front of it showing faint wine-spots and smelling vaguely of Toscanelli cigars. He loved that tie, and he always resented it if he had to wear it immediately after August, for then the mysterious quality of his father was somehow absent from it. He liked his father's handkerchiefs too. They were so much bigger than his own, and they possessed a softness and a mellowness from being washed and ironed so many times by his mother, and in them he had a vague feeling of his mother and father at the same time. They were unlike the necktie, which was all father, and when he used one of his father's handkerchiefs there came to him dimly a sense of his father and mother together, part of a picture, of a scheme of things.

For a long time he stood before the mirror in his room talking to Rosa, rehearsing his acknowledgment of her thanks. Now he was sure the gift would automatically betray his love. The way he had looked at her that morning, the way he had followed her during the noon hour – she would undoubtedly associate those preliminaries with the jewel. He was glad. He wanted his feelings in the open. He imagined her saying, I knew it was you all the time, Arturo. Standing at the mirror he answered, 'Oh well, Rosa, you know how it is, a fellow likes to give his girl a Christmas present.'

When his brothers got home at four thirty he was already dressed. He did not own a complete suit, but Maria always kept his 'new' pants and 'new' coat neatly pressed. They did not match, but they came pretty close to it, the pants of blue serge and the coat an oxford gray.

The change into his 'new' clothes transformed him into a picture of frustration and misery as he sat in the rocking chair, his hands folded in his lap. The only thing he ever did when he got into his 'new' clothes, and he always did it badly, was simply to sit and wait out the period to the bitter end. Now he had four hours to wait before the banquet began, but there was some consolation in the fact that tonight, at least, he would not eat eggs.

When August and Federico let loose a barrage of questions about the broken Christmas tree in the front yard, his 'new' clothes seemed tighter than ever. The night was going to be warm and clear, so he pulled on one sweater over his gray coat instead of two and left, glad to be away from the gloom of home.

Walking down the street in that shadow-world of black and white he felt the serenity of impending victory: the smile of Rosa tonight, his gift around her neck as she waited on the altar boys in the auditorium, her smiles for him and for him alone.

Ah, what a night!

He talked to himself as he walked, breathing the thin mountain air, reeling in the glory of his possessions, Rosa my girl, Rosa for me and for nobody else. Only one thing disturbed him, and that vaguely: he was hungry, but the emptiness in his stomach was dissipated by the overflow of his joy. These altar boy banquets, and he had attended seven of them in his life, were supreme achievements in food. He could see it all before him, huge plates of fried chicken and turkey, hot buns, sweet potatoes, cranberry sauce, and all the chocolate ice cream he could eat, and beyond it all, Rosa with a cameo around her neck, his gift, smiling as he gorged himself, serving him with bright black eyes and teeth so white they were good enough to eat.

What a night! He bent down and snatched at the white snow, letting it melt in his mouth, the cold liquid trickling down his throat. He did this many times, sucking the sweet snow and enjoying the cold effect in his throat.

The intestinal reaction to the cold liquid on his empty stomach was a faint purring somewhere in the middle of him and rising toward the cardiac area. He was crossing the trestle bridge, in the very middle of it, when everything before his eyes melted suddenly into blackness. His feet lost all sensory response. His breath came in frantic jerks. He found himself flat on his back. He had fallen over limply. Deep within his chest his heart hammered for movement. He clutched it with both hands, terror gripping him. He was dying: oh God, he was going to die! The very bridge seemed to shake with the violence of his heartbeat.

But five, ten, twenty seconds later he was still alive. The terror of that moment still burned in his heart. What had happened? Why had he fallen? He got up and hurried across the trestle bridge, shivering in fear. What had he done? It was his heart, he knew his heart had stopped beating and started again – but why?

Mea culpa, mea culpa, mea maxima culpa! The mysterious universe loomed around him, and he was alone on the railroad tracks, hurrying to the street where men and women walked, where it was not so lonely, and as he ran it came to him like piercing daggers that this was God's warning, this was

His way of letting him know that God knew his crime: he, the thief, filcher of his mother's cameo, sinner against the decalogue. Thief, thief, outcast of God, hell's child with a black mark across the book of his soul.

It might happen again. Now, five minutes from now. Ten minutes. Hail Mary full of grace I'm sorry. He no longer ran but walked now, briskly, almost running dreading over-excitation of his heart. Goodbye to Rosa and thoughts of love, goodbye and goodbye, and hello to sorrow and remorse.

Ah, the cleverness of God! Ah, how good the Lord was to him, giving him another chance, warning him yet not killing him.

Look! See how I walk. I breathe. I am alive. I am walking to God. My soul is black. God will clean my soul. He is good to me. My feet touch the ground, one two, one two. I'll call Father Andrew. I'll tell him everything.

He rang the bell on the confessional wall. Five minutes later Father Andrew appeared through the side door of the church. The tall, semi-bald priest raised his eyebrows in surprise to find but one soul in that Christmas-decorated church – and that soul a boy, his eyes tightly closed, his jaws gritted, his lips moving in prayer. The priest smiled, removed the toothpick from his mouth, genuflected, and walked toward the confessional. Arturo opened his eyes and saw him advancing like a thing of beautiful black, and there was comfort in his presence, and warmth in his black cassock.

'What now, Arturo?' he said in a whisper that was pleasant. He laid his hand on Arturo's shoulder. It was like the touch of God. His agony broke beneath it. The vagueness of nascent peace stirred within depths, ten million miles within him.

'I gotta go to confession, Father.'

'Sure, Arturo.'

Father Andrew adjusted his sash and entered the confessional door. He followed, kneeling in the penitent's booth, the wooden screen separating him from the priest. After the prescribed ritual, he said: 'Yesterday, Father Andrew, I was going through my mother's trunk, and I found a cameo with a gold chain, and I swiped it, Father. I put it in my pocket, and it didn't belong to me, it belonged to my mother, my father gave it to her, and it musta been worth a lot of money, but I swiped it anyhow, and today I gave it to a girl in our school. I gave stolen property for a Christmas present.'

'You say it was valuable?' the priest asked.

'It looked it,' he answered.

'How valuable, Arturo?'

'It looked plenty valuable, Father. I'm awfully sorry, Father. I'll never steal again as long as I live.'

'Tell you what, Arturo,' the priest said. 'I'll give you absolution if you'll promise to go to your mother and tell her you stole the cameo. Tell her just as you've told me. If she prizes it, and wants it back, you've got to promise me you'll get it from the girl, and return it to your mother. Now if you can't do that, you've got to promise me you'll buy your mother another one. Isn't that fair, Arturo? I think God'll agree that you're getting a square deal.'

'I'll get it back. I'll try.'

He bowed his head while the priest mumbled the Latin of absolution. That was all. Easy as pie. He left the confessional and knelt in the church, his hands pressed over his heart. It thumped serenely. He was saved. It was a swell world after all. For a long time he knelt, reveling in the sweetness of escape. They were pals, he and God, and God was a good sport. But he took no chances. For two hours, until the clock struck eight, he prayed every prayer he knew. Everything was coming out fine. The priest's advice was a cinch. Tonight after the banquet he would tell his mother the truth – that he had stolen her cameo and given it to Rosa. She would protest at first. But not for long. He knew his mother, and how to get things out of her.

He crossed the schoolyard and climbed the stairs to the auditorium. In the hall the first person he saw was Rosa. She walked directly to him.

'I want to talk to you,' she said.

'Sure, Rosa.'

He followed her downstairs, fearful that something awful was about to happen. At the bottom of the stairs she waited for him to open the door, her jaw set, her camel's hair coat wrapped tightly around her.

'I'm sure hungry,' he said.

'Are you?' Her voice was cold, supercilious.

They stood on the stairs outside the door, at the edge of the concrete platform. She held out her hand.

'Here,' she said. 'I don't want this.'

It was the cameo.

'I can't accept stolen property,' she said. 'My mother says you probably stole this.'

'I didn't!' he lied. 'I did not!'

'Take it,' she said. 'I don't want it.'

He put it in his pocket. Without a word she turned to enter the building.

'But Rosa!'

At the door she turned around and smiled sweetly.

'You shouldn't steal, Arturo.'

'I *didn't* steal!' He sprang at her, dragged her out of the doorway and pushed her. She backed to the edge of the platform and toppled into the snow, after swaying and waving her arms in a futile effort to get her balance. As she landed her mouth opened wide and let out a scream.

'I'm *not* a thief,' he said looking down at her.

He jumped from the platform to the sidewalk and hurried away as fast as he could. At the corner he looked at the cameo for a moment, and then tossed it with all his might over the roof of the two-storey house bordering the street. Then he walked on again. To hell with the altar boy banquet. He wasn't hungry anyway.

Chapter Seven

Christmas Eve. Svevo Bandini was coming home, new shoes on his feet, defiance in his jaw, guilt in his heart. Fine shoes, Bandini; where'd you get them? None of your business. He had money in his pocket. His fist squeezed it. Where'd you get that money, Bandini? Playing poker. I've been playing it for ten days.

Indeed!

But that was his story, and if his wife didn't believe, what of it? His black shoes smashed the snow, the sharp new heels chopping it.

They were expecting him: somehow they knew he would arrive. The very house had a feeling for it. Things were in order. Maria by the window spoke her rosary very fast, as though there was so little time: a few more prayers before he arrived.

Merry Christmas. The boys had opened their gifts. They each had one gift. Pajamas from Grandma Toscana. They sat around in their pajamas – waiting. For what? The suspense was good: something was going to happen. Pajamas of blue and green. They had put them on because there was nothing else to do. But something was going to happen. In the silence of waiting it was wonderful to think that Papa was coming home, and not speak of it.

Federico had to spoil it.

'I bet Papa's coming home tonight.'

A break in the spell. It was a private thought belonging to each. Silence. Federico regretted his words and fell to wondering why they had not answered.

A footstep on the porch. All the men and women on earth could have mounted that step, yet none would have made a sound like that. They looked at Maria. She held her breath, hurrying through one more prayer. The door opened and he came inside. He closed the door carefully, as though his whole life had been spent in the exact science of closing doors.

'Hello.'

He was no boy caught stealing marbles, nor a dog punished for tearing up a shoe. This was Svevo Bandini, a full-grown man with a wife and three sons.

'Where's Mamma?' he said, looking right at her, like a drunken man who wanted to prove he could ask a serious question. Over in the corner he saw her, exactly where he knew she was, for he had been frightened by her silhouette from the street.

'Ah, there she is.'

I hate you, she thought. With my fingers I want to tear out your eyes and blind you. You are a beast, you have hurt me and I shall not rest until I have hurt you.

Papa with new shoes. They squeaked with his step as though tiny mice ran around in them. He crossed the room to the bathroom. Strange sound – old Papa home again.

I hope you die. You will never touch me again. I hate you, God what have you done to me, my husband, I hate you so.

He came back and stood in the middle of the room, his

back to his wife. From his pocket he extracted the money. And to his sons he said, 'Suppose we all go downtown before the stores close, you and me and Mamma, all of us, and go down and buy some Christmas presents for everybody.'

'I want a bicycle!' from Federico.

'Sure. You get a bicycle!'

Arturo didn't know what he wanted, nor did August. The evil he had done twisted inside Bandini, but he smiled and said they would find something for all. A big Christmas. The biggest of all.

I can see that other woman in his arms, I can smell her in his clothes, her lips have roamed his face, her hands have explored his chest. He disgusts me, and I want him hurt to death.

'And what'll we get Mamma?'

He turned around and faced her, his eyes on the money as he unrolled the bills.

'Look at all the money! Better give it all to Mamma, huh? All the money Papa won playing cards. Pretty good card-player, Papa.'

He raised his eyes and looked at her, she with her hands gripped in the sides of the chair, as though ready to spring at him, and he realized he was afraid of her, and he smiled not in amusement but fear, the evil he had done weakening his courage. Fan-wise he held the money out: there were fives and tens, a hundred even, and like a condemned man going to his punishment he kept the silly smile on his lips as he bent over and made to hand her the bills, trying to think of the old words, their words, his and hers, their language. She clung to the chair in horror forcing herself not to shrink back from the serpent of guilt that wound itself into the ghastly figure of his face. Closer than ever he bent, only inches from her hair, utterly ridiculous in his ameliorations, until she could not bear it, could not refrain from it, and with a suddenness that surprised her too, her ten long fingers were at his eyes, tearing down, a singing strength in her ten long fingers that laid streaks of blood down his face as he screamed and backed away, the front of his shirt, his neck and collar gathering the fast-falling red drops. But it was his eyes, my God my eyes, my eyes! And he backed away and covered them with his cupped hands, standing against the wall, his face reeking with pain, afraid to lift his hands, afraid that he was blind.

'Maria,' he sobbed. 'Oh God, what have you done to me?'

He could see; dimly through a curtain of red he could see, and he staggered around.

'Ah Maria, what have you done? What have you done?'

Around the room he staggered. He heard the weeping of his children, the words of Arturo: 'Oh God.' Around and round he staggered, blood and tears in his eyes.

'*Jesus Christi*, what has happened to me?'

At his feet lay the green bills and he staggered through them and upon them in his new shoes, little red drops splattered over the shining black toes, round and round, moaning and groping his way to the door and outside into the cold night, into the snow, deep into the drift in the yard moaning all the time, his big hands scooping snow like water and pressing it to his burning face. Again and again the white snow from his hands fell back to the earth, red and sodden. In the house his sons stood petrified, in their new pajamas, the front door open, the light in the middle of the room blinding their view of Svevo Bandini as he blotted his face with the linen of the sky. In the chair sat Maria. She did not move as she stared at the blood and the money strewn about the room.

Damn her, Arturo thought. Damn her to hell.

He was crying, hurt by the humiliation of his father; his father, that man, always so solid and powerful, and he had seen him floundering and hurt and crying, his father who never cried and never floundered. He wanted to be with his father, and he put on his shoes and hurried outside, where Bandini was bent over, choked and quivering. But it was good to hear something over and above the choking – to hear his anger, his curses. It thrilled him when he heard his father vowing vengeance. I'll kill her, by God, I'll kill her. He was gaining control of himself now. The snow had checked the flow of blood. He stood panting, examining his bloody clothes, his hands spattered crimson.

'Somebody's got to pay for this,' he said. '*Sangue de la Madonna!* It shall not be forgotten.'

'Papa –'

'What do you want?'

'Nothing.'

'Then get in the house. Get in there with that crazy mother of yours.'

That was all. He broke his way through the snow to the sidewalk and strode down the street. The boy watched him go, his face high to the night. It was the way he walked, stumbling despite his determination. But no – after a few feet he turned, 'You kids have a happy Christmas. Take that money and go down and buy what you want.'

He went on again, his chin out, coasting into the cold air, bearing up under a deep wound that was not bleeding.

The boy went back to the house. The money was not on the floor. One look at Federico, who choked bitterly as he held out a torn section of a five-dollar bill told him what had happened. He opened the stove. The black embers of burnt paper smoked faintly. He closed the stove and examined the floor, bare except for drying blood spots. In hatred he glared at his mother. She did not move or even heed with her eyes, but her lips opened and shut, for she had resumed her rosary.

'Merry Christmas!' he sneered.

Federico wailed. August was too shocked to speak.

Yeah: a Merry Chistmas. Ah, give it to her, Papa! Me and you, Papa, because I know how you feel, because it happened to me too, but you should have done what I did, Papa, knocked her down like I did, and you'd feel better. Because you're killing me, Papa, you with your bloody face walking around all by yourself, you're killing me.

He went out on the porch and sat down. The night was full of his father. He saw the red spots in the snow where Bandini had floundered and bent to lift it to his face. Papa's blood, my blood. He stepped off the porch and kicked clean snow over the place until it disappeared. Nobody should see this: nobody. Then he returned to the house.

His mother had not moved. How he hated her! With one grasp he tore the rosary out of her hands and pulled it to pieces. She watched him, martyr-like. She got up and followed him outside, the broken rosary in his fist. He threw it far out into the snow, scattering it like seeds. She walked past him into the snow.

In astonishment he watched her wade knee-deep into the whiteness, gazing around like one dazed. Here and there she found a bead, her hand cupping fistfuls of snow. It disgusted him. She was pawing the very spot where his father's blood had colored the snow.

Hell with her. He was leaving. He wanted his father. He dressed and walked down the street. Merry Christmas. The town was painted green and white with it. A hundred dollars in the stove – but what about him, his brothers? You could be holy and firm, but why must they all suffer? His mother had too much God in her.

Where now? He didn't know, but not at home with her. He could understand his father. A man had to do something: never having anything was too monotonous. He had to admit it: if *he* could choose between Maria and Effie Hildegarde, it would be Effie every time. When Italian women got to a certain age their legs thinned and their bellies widened, their breasts fell and they lost sparkle. He tried to imagine Rosa Pinelli at forty. Her legs would thin like his mother's; she would be fat in the stomach. But he could not imagine it. That Rosa, so lovely! He wished instead that she would die. He pictured disease wasting her away until there had to be a funeral. It would make him happy. He would go to her death-bed and stand over it. She would weakly take his hand in her hot fingers and tell him she was going to die, and he would answer, too bad Rosa; you had your chance, but I'll always remember you Rosa. Then the funeral, the weeping, and Rosa lowered into the earth. But he would be cold to it all, stand there and smile a little with his great dreams. Years later in the Yankee stadium, over the yells of the crowd he'd remember a dying girl who held his hand and begged forgiveness; only for a few seconds would he linger with that memory, and then he would turn to the women in the crowd and nod, his women, not an Italian among them; blondes they'd be, tall and smiling, dozens of them, like Effie Hildegarde, and not an Italian in the lot.

So give it to her, Papa! I'm for you, old boy. Some day I'll be doing it too, I'll be right in there some day with a honey like her, and she won't be the kind that scratches my face, and she won't be the kind that calls me a little thief.

And yet, how did he know that Rosa *wasn't* dying? Of course she was, just as all people moved minute by minute nearer the grave. But just suppose, just for the heck of it, that Rosa really was dying! What about his friend Joe Tanner last year? Killed riding a bicycle; one day he was alive, the next he wasn't. And what about Nellie Frazier? A little stone in her shoe; she didn't take it out; blood-poison, and all at once she was dead and they had a funeral.

How did he know that Rosa hadn't been run over by an automobile since he saw her that last awful time? There was a chance. How did he know she wasn't dead by electrocution? That happened a lot. Why couldn't it happen to her? Of course he really didn't want her to die, not really and truly cross my heart and hope to die, but still and all there was a chance. Poor Rosa, so young and pretty – and dead.

He was downtown, walking around, nothing there, only people hurrying with packages. He was in front of Wilkes Hardware Company, staring at the sports display. It began to snow. He looked to the mountains. They were blotted by black clouds. An odd premonition took hold of him: Rosa Pinelli was dead. He was positive she was dead. All he had to do was walk three blocks down Pearl Street and two blocks east on Twelfth Street and it would be proven. He could walk there and on the front door of the Pinelli house there would be a funeral wreath. He was so sure of it that he walked in that direction at once. Rosa was dead. He was a prophet, given to understanding weird things. And so it had finally happened: what he wished had come true, and she was gone.

Well, well, funny world. He lifted his eyes to the sky, to the millions of snowflakes floating earthward. The end of Rosa Pinelli. He spoke aloud, addressing imagined listeners. I was standing in front of Wilkes Hardware, and all of a sudden I had that hunch. Then I walked up to her house, and sure enough, there was a wreath on the door. A swell kid, Rosa. Sure hate to see her die. He hurried now, the premonition weakening, and he walked faster, speeding to outlast it. He was crying: Oh Rosa, please don't die, Rosa. Be alive when I get there! Here I come Rosa, my love. All the way from the Yankee stadium in a chartered airplane. I made a landing right on the courthouse lawn – nearly killed three hundred people out there watching me. But I made it, Rosa. I got here all right, and here I am at your bedside, just in time, and the doctor says you'll live now, and so I must go away, never to return. Back to the Yanks, Rosa. To Florida, Rosa. Spring training. The Yanks need me too; but you'll know where I am, Rosa, just read the papers and you'll know.

There was no funeral wreath on the Pinelli door. What he saw there, and he gasped in horror until his vision cleared through the blinding snow, was a Christmas wreath instead. He was glad, hurrying away in the storm. Sure I'm glad! Who wants to see anybody die? But he wasn't glad, he wasn't glad at all. He wasn't a star for the Yankees. He hadn't come by chartered plane. He wasn't going to Florida. This was Christmas Eve in Rocklin, Colorado. It was snowing like the devil, and his father was living with a woman named Effie

Hildegarde. His father's face was torn open by his mother's fingers and at that moment he knew his mother was praying, his brothers were crying, and the embers in the front-room stove had once been a hundred dollars.

Merry Christmas, Arturo!

Chapter Eight

A lonely road at the West End of Rocklin, thin and dwindling, the falling snow strangling it. Now the snow falls heavily. The road creeps westward and upward, a steep road. Beyond are the mountains. The snow! It chokes the world, and there is a pale void ahead, only the thin road dwindling fast. A tricky road, full of surprising twists and dips as it eludes the dwarfed pines standing with hungry white arms to capture it.

Maria, what have you done to Svevo Bandini? What have you done to my face?

A square-built man stumbling along, his shoulders and arms covered by the snow. In this place the road is steep; he breasts his way, the deep snow pulling at his legs, a man wading through water that has not melted.

Where now, Bandini?

A little while ago, not more than forty-five minutes, he had come rushing down this road, convinced that, as God was his judge, he would never return again. Forty-five minutes – not even an hour, and much had happened, and he was returning along a road that he had hoped might be forgotten.

Maria, what have you done?

Svevo Bandini, a blood-tinted handkerchief concealing his face, and the wrath of winter concealing Svevo Bandini as he climbed the road back to the Widow Hildegarde's, talking to the snowflakes as he climbed. So tell the snowflakes, Bandini; tell them as you wave your cold hands. Bandini sobbed — a grown man, forty-two years old, weeping because it was Christmas Eve and he was returning to his sin, because he would rather be with his children.

Maria, what have you done?

It was like this, Maria: ten days ago your mother wrote that letter, and I got mad and left the house, because I can't stand the woman. I must go away when she comes. And so I went away. I got lots of troubles, Maria. The kids. The house. The snow: look at the snow tonight, Maria. Can I set a brick down in it? And I'm worried, and your mother is coming, and I say to myself, I say, I think I'll go downtown and have a few drinks. Because I got troubles. Because I got kids.

Ah, Maria.

He had gone downtown to the Imperial Poolhall, and there he had met his friend Rocco Saccone, and Rocco had said they should go to his room and have a drink, smoke a cigar, talk. Old friends, he and Rocco: two men in a room filled with cigar smoke drinking whiskey on a cold day, talking. Christmas time: a few drinks. Happy Christmas, Svevo. Gratia, Rocco. A happy Christmas.

Rocco had looked at the face of his friend and asked what troubled him, and Bandini had told him: no money, Rocco, the kids and Christmas time. And the mother-in-law — damn her. Rocco was a poor man too, not so poor as Bandini, though, and he offered ten dollars. How could Bandini accept it? Already he had borrowed so much from his friend, and now this. No thanks, Rocco. I drink your liquor, that's enough. And so, *a la salute!* for old times' sake . . .

One drink and then another, two men in a room with their

feet on the steaming radiator. Then the buzzer above Rocco's hotel-room door sounded. Once, and then once more: the telephone. Rocco jumped up and hurried down the hall to the phone. After a while he returned, his face soft and pleasant. Rocco got many phone calls in the hotel, for he ran an advertisement in the *Rocklin Herald:*

> Rocco Saccone, bricklayer and
> stonemason. All kinds of repair
> work. Concrete work a specialty.
> Call R.M. Hotel.

That was it, Maria. A woman named Hildegarde had called Rocco and told him that her fireplace was out of order. Would Rocco come and fix it right away?

Rocco, his friend.

'You go, Svevo,' he said. 'Maybe you can make a few dollars before Xmas.'

That was how it started. With Rocco's tool sack on his back, he left the hotel, crossed the town to the West End, took this very road on a late afternoon ten days ago. Up this very road, and he remembered a chipmunk standing under that very tree over there, watching him as he passed. A few dollars to fix a fireplace; maybe three hours' work, maybe more – a few dollars.

The Widow Hildegarde? Of course he knew who she was, but who in Rocklin did not? A town of ten thousand people, and one woman owning most of the land – who among those ten thousand could avoid knowing her? But who had never known her well enough to say hello, and that was the truth.

This very road, ten days ago, with a bit of cement and seventy pounds of mason's tools on his back. That was the first time he saw the Hildegarde cottage, a famous place around Rocklin because the stone work was so fine. Coming upon it in the late afternoon, that low house built of white flagstone and set among tall pine trees seemed a place out of his dreams: an irresistible place, the kind he would some day have, if he could afford it. For a long time he stood gazing and gazing upon it, wishing he might have had some hand in its construction, the delight of masonry, of handling those long white stones, so soft beneath a mason's hands, yet strong enough to outlast a civilization.

What does a man think about when he approaches the white door to such a house and reaches for the polished foxhead brass knocker?

Wrong, Maria.

He had never talked to the woman until that moment she opened the door. A woman taller than himself, round and large. Aye: fine-looking woman. Not like Maria, but still a fine-looking woman. Dark hair, blue eyes, a woman who looked as though she had money.

His sack of tools gave him away.

So he was Rocco Saccone, the mason. How do you do?

No, but he was Rocco's friend. Rocco was ill.

It didn't matter who he was, so long as he could fix a fireplace. Come in Mr Bandini, the fireplace is over there. And so he entered, his hat in one hand, the sack of tools in the other. A beautiful house, Indian rugs over the floor, large beams across the ceiling, the woodwork done in bright yellow lacquer. It might have cost twenty – even thirty thousand dollars.

There are things a man cannot tell his wife. Would Maria understand that surge of humility as he crossed the handsome room, the embarrassment as he staggered when his worn shoes, wet with snow, failed to grip the shining yellow floor? Could he tell Maria that the attractive woman felt a sudden pity for him? It was true: even though his back was turned, he felt the Widow's quick embarrassment for him, for his awkward strangeness.

'Pretty slippery, ain't it?'

The Widow laughed. 'I'm always falling.'

But that was to help him cover his embarrassment. A little thing, a courtesy to make him feel at home.

Nothing seriously wrong with the fireplace, a few loose brick in the flue-lining, a matter of an hour's work. But there are tricks to the trade, and the Widow was wealthy. Drawing himself up after the inspection, he told her the work would amount to fifteen dollars, including the price of materials. She did not object. Then it came to him as a sickening afterthought that the reason for her liberality was the condition of his shoes: she had seen the worn soles as he knelt to examine the fireplace. Her way of looking at him, up and down, that pitying smile, possessed an understanding that had sent the winter through his flesh. He could not tell Maria that.

Sit down, Mr Bandini.

He found the deep reading chair voluptuously comfortable, a chair from the Widow's world, and he stretched out in it and surveyed the bright room cluttered neatly with books and bric-a-brac. An educated woman ensconced in the luxury of her education. She was seated on the divan, her plump legs in their sheer silk cases, rich legs that swished of silk when she crossed them before his wondering eyes. She asked him to sit and talk with her. He was so grateful that he could not speak, could only utter happy grunts at whatever she said, her rich precise words flowing from her deep luxurious throat. He fell to wondering about her, his eyes bulging with curiosity for her protected world, so sleek and bright, like the rich silk that defined the round luxury of her handsome legs.

Maria would scoff if she knew what the Widow talked about, for he found his throat too tight, too choked with the strangeness of the scene: she, over there, the wealthy Mrs Hildegarde, worth a hundred, maybe two hundred thousand dollars, and not more than four feet away – so close that he might have leaned over and touched her.

So he was an Italian? Splendid. Only last year she had traveled in Italy. Beautiful. He must be so proud of his heritage. Did he know that the cradle of western civilization was Italy? Had he ever seen the Campo Santo, the Cathedral of St Peter's, the paintings of Michelangelo, the blue Mediterranean? The Italian Riviera?

No, he had seen none of these. In simple words he told her that he was from Abruzzi, that he had never been that far north, never to Rome. He had worked hard as a boy. There had been no time for anything else.

Abruzzi! The Widow knew everything. Then surely he had read the works of D'Annunzio – he, too, was an Abruzzian.

No, he had not read D'Annunzio. He had heard of him, but he had never read him. Yes, he knew the great man was from his own province. It pleased him. It made him grateful to D'Annunzio. Now they had something in common, but to his dismay he found himself unable to say more on the subject. For a full minute the Widow watched him, her blue eyes expressionless as they centered on his lips. He turned his head in confusion, his gaze following the heavy beams across the room, the frilled curtains, the nicknacks spread in careful profusion everywhere.

A kind woman, Maria: a good woman who came to his rescue and made conversation easy. Did he like to lay brick? Did he have a family? Three children? Wonderful. She, too, had wanted children. Was his wife an Italian, too? Had he lived in Rocklin long?

The weather. She spoke of the weather. Ah. He spoke then tumbling out his torment at the weather. Almost whining he lamented his stagnation, his fierce hatred of cold sunless days. Until, frightened by his bitter torrent, she glanced at her watch and told him to come back tomorrow morning to begin work on the fireplace. At the door, hat in hand, he stood waiting for her parting words.

'Put on your hat, Mr Bandini,' she smiled. 'You'll catch cold.' Grinning, his armpits and neck flooded with nervous sweat, he pulled his hat down, confused and at a loss for words.

He stayed with Rocco that night. With Rocco, Maria, not with the Widow. The next day, after ordering firebrick at the lumber yard, he went back to the Widow's cottage to repair the fireplace. Spreading a canvas over the carpet, he mixed his mortar in a bucket, tore out the loose brick in the flue-lining, and laid new brick in their place. Determined that the job should last a full day, he pulled out all the firebrick. He might have finished in an hour, might have pulled out only two or three, but at noon he was only half through. Then the Widow appeared, coming quietly from one of the sweet-scented rooms. Again the flutter in his throat. Again he could do no more than smile. How was he getting along with the work? He had done a careful job: not a speck of mortar smeared the faces of the brick he had laid. Even the canvas was clean, the old brick piled neatly at the side. She noticed this, and it pleased him. No passion lured him as she stooped to examine the new brick inside the fireplace, her sleek girdled bottom so rounded as she sank to her haunches. No Maria, not even her high heels, her thin blouse, the fragrance of the perfume in her dark hair, moved him to a stray thought of infidelity. As before he watched her in wonder and curiosity: this woman with a hundred, maybe two hundred thousand in the bank.

His plan to go downtown for lunch was unthinkable. As soon as she heard it she insisted that he remain as her guest. His eyes could not meet the cold blue of hers. He bowed his head, pawed the canvas with one toe, and begged to be excused. Eat lunch with the Widow Hildegarde? Sit across the table from her and put food in his mouth while this woman sat opposite him? He could scarcely breathe his refusal.

'No, no. Please, Mrs Hildegarde, thank you. Thank you so much. Please, no. Thank you.'

But he stayed, not daring to offend her. Smiling as he held out his mortar-caked hands, he asked her if he might wash them, and she led him through the white, spotless hall to the bathroom. The room was like a jewel box: shining yellow tile, the yellow washbowl, lavender organdie curtains over the tall window, a bowl of purple flowers on the mirrored dressing table, yellow-handled perfume bottles, yellow comb-and-brush set. He turned quickly and all but bolted away. He could not have been more shocked had she stood naked before him. Those grimy hands of his were unworthy of this. He preferred the kitchen sink, just as he did at home. But her ease reassured him, and he entered fearfully, on the balls of his feet, and stood before the washbowl with tortured indecision. With his elbow he turned the water spout, afraid to mark it with his fingers. The scented green soap was out of the question: he did the best he could with water alone. When he finished, he dried his hands on the tail of his shirt, ignoring the soft green towels that hung from the wall. The experience left him fearful of what might take place at lunch. Before leaving the bathroom, he got down on his knees and blotted up a spot or two of splashed water with his shirt sleeve . . .

A lunch of lettuce leaves, pineapple and cottage cheese. Seated in the breakfast nook, a pink napkin across his knees, he ate with a suspicion that it was a joke, that the Widow was making fun of him. But she ate it too, and with such gusto that it might have been palatable. If Maria had served him such food, he would have thrown it out the window. Then the Widow brought tea in a thin china cup. There were two white cookies in the saucer, no larger than the end of his thumb. Tea and cookies. *Diavolo!* He had always identified tea with effeminacy and weakness, and he had no liking for sweets. But the Widow, munching a cookie between two fingers, smiled graciously as he tossed the cakes in his mouth like one putting away unpleasant pills.

Long before she finished her second cookie he was done, had drained the teacup, and leaned back on the two rear legs of his chair, his stomach mewing and crowing its protest at such strange visitors. They had not spoken throughout the lunch, not a word. It made him conscious that there was nothing to say between them. Now and then she smiled, once over the rim of her teacup. It left him embarrassed and sad: the life of the rich, he concluded, was not for him. At home he would have eaten fried eggs, a chunk of bread, and washed it down with a glass of wine.

When she finished, touching the corners of her carmine lips with the tip of her napkin, she asked if there was anything else he would like. His impulse was to answer, 'What else you got?' but he patted his stomach instead, puffing it out and caressing it.

'No, thank you, Mrs Hildegarde. I'm full – full clean up to the ears.'

It made her smile. With red knotted fists at his belt, he remained leaning backward in his chair, sucking his teeth and craving a cigar.

A fine woman, Maria. One who sensed his every desire.

'Do you smoke?' she asked, producing a pack of cigarettes from the table drawer. From his shirt pocket he pulled the butt of a twisted Toscanelli cigar, bit off the end and spat it across the floor, lighted a match and puffed away. She insisted that he remain where he was, comfortable and at ease, while she gathered the dishes, the cigarette dangling from the corner of her mouth. The cigar eased his tension. Crossing his arms, he watched her more frankly, studying the sleek hips, the soft white arms. Even then his thought was clean, no vagabond sensuality clouding his mind. She was a rich woman and he was near her, seated in her kitchen; he was grateful for the proximity: for that and for nothing more, as God was his judge.

Finishing his cigar, he went back to his work. By four thirty he was finished. Gathering his tools, he waited for her to come into the room again. All afternoon he had heard her in another part of the house. For some time he waited, clearing his throat loudly, dropping his trowel, singing a tune with the words, 'It's finished, oh it's all done, all finished, all finished.' The commotion at last brought her to the room. She came with a book in her hand, wearing reading glasses. He expected to be paid immediately. Instead he was surprised when she asked him to sit down for a moment. She did not even glance at the work he had done.

'You're a splendid worker, Mr Bandini. Splendid. I'm very pleased.'

Maria might sneer, but those words almost pinched a tear from his eyes. 'I do my best, Mrs Hildegarde. I do the best I can.'

But she showed no desire to pay him. Once more the whitish-blue eyes. Their clear appraisal caused him to shift his glance to the fireplace. The eyes remained upon him, studying him vaguely, trance-like, as if she had lapsed into a reverie of other things. He walked to the fireplace and put his eye along the mantelpiece, as if to gauge its angle, pursing his lips with that look of mathematical computation. When he had done this until it could no longer seem sensible, he returned to the deep chair and seated himself once more. The Widow's gaze followed him mechanically. He wanted to speak, but what was there to say?

At last she broke the silence: she had other work for him. There was a house of hers in town, on Windsor Street. There, too, the fireplace was not functioning. Would he go there tomorrow and examine it? She arose, crossed the room to the writing desk by the window, and wrote down the address. Her back was to him, her body bent at the waist, her round hips blooming sensuously, and though Maria might tear out his very eyes and spit into their empty sockets, he could swear that no evil had darkened his glance, no lust had lurked in his heart.

That night, lying in the darkness beside Rocco Saccone, the wailing snores of his friend keeping him awake, there was yet another reason why Svevo Bandini did not sleep, and that was the promise of tomorrow. He lay grunting contentedly in the darkness. *Mannaggia*, he was no fool; he was wise enough to realize he had made his mark with the Widow Hildegarde. She might pity him, she might have given him this new job only because she felt that he needed it, but whatever it was, there was no question of his ability; she had called him a splendid worker, and rewarded him with more work.

Let the winter blow! Let the temperature drop to freezing. Let the snow pile up and bury the town! He didn't care: tomorrow there was work. And after that, there would always be work. The Widow Hildegarde liked him; she respected his ability. With her money and his ability there would always be work enough to laugh at the winter.

At seven the next morning he entered the house on Windsor Street. No one lived in the house; the front door was open when he tried it. No furniture: only bare rooms. Nor could he find anything wrong with the fireplace. It was not so elaborate as the one at the Widow's but it was well made. The mortar had not cracked, and the brick responded solidly to the tapping of his hammer. Then what was it? He found wood in the shed in the rear and built a fire. The flue sucked the flame voraciously. Heat filled the room. Nothing wrong.

Eight o'clock, and he was at the Widow's again. In a blue dressing gown he found her, fresh and smiling her good morning. Mr Bandini! But you mustn't stand out there in the cold. Come inside and have a cup of coffee! The protests died on his lips. He kicked the snow from his wet shoes and followed the flowing blue gown to the kitchen. Standing against the sink, he drank the coffee, pouring it into a saucer and then blowing on it to cool it. He did not look at her below the shoulders. He dared not. Maria would never believe that. Nervous and without speech, he behaved like a man.

He told her that he could find no trouble with the Windsor Street fireplace. His honesty pleased him, coming as it did after the exaggerated work of the day before. The Widow seemed surprised. She was certain there was something wrong with the Windsor Street fireplace. She asked him to wait while she dressed. She would drive him back to Windsor Street and show him the trouble. Now she was staring at his wet feet.

'Mr Bandini, don't you wear a size nine shoe?'

The blood rose to his face, and he sputtered in his coffee. Quickly she apologized. It was the outstanding bad habit of her life – this obsession she had of asking people what size shoe they wore. It was a sort of guessing game she played with herself. Would he forgive her?

The episode shook him deeply. To hide his shame he quickly seated himself at the table, his wet shoes beneath it, out of view. But the Widow smiled and persisted. Had she guessed right? Was size nine correct?

'Sure is, Mrs Hildegarde.'

Waiting for her to dress, Svevo Bandini felt that he was getting somewhere in the world. From now on Helmer the banker and all his creditors had better be careful. Bandini had powerful friends too.

But what had he to hide of that day? No – he was proud of that day. Beside the Widow, in her car, he rode through the middle of town, down Pearl Street, the Widow at the wheel in a seal-skin coat. Had Maria and his children seen him chatting easily with her, they would have been proud of him. They might have proudly raised their chins and said, there goes our papa! But Maria had torn the flesh from his face.

What happened in the vacant house on Windsor Street? Did he lead the Widow to a vacant room and violate her? Did he kiss her? Then go to that house, Maria. Speak to the cold rooms. Scoop the cobwebs from the corners and ask them questions; ask the naked floors, ask the frosted window panes; ask them if Svevo Bandini had done wrong.

The Widow stood before the fireplace.

'You see,' he said. 'The fire I built is still going. Nothing wrong. It works fine.'

She was not satisfied.

That black stuff, she said. It didn't look well in a fireplace. She wanted it to look clean and unused; she was expecting a prospective tenant, and everything had to be satisfactory.

But he was an honorable man with no desire to cheat this woman.

'All fireplaces get black, Mrs Hildegarde. It's the smoke. They all get that way. You can't help it.'

No, it didn't look well.

He told her about muriatic acid. A solution of muriatic acid and water. Apply it with a brush: that would remove the blackness. Not more than two hours' work –

Two hours? That would never do. No, Mr Bandini. She wanted all the firebrick taken out and new brick put in. He shook his head at the extravagance.

'That'll take a day and a half, Mrs Hildegarde. Cost you twenty-five dollars, material included.'

She pulled the coat around her, shivering in the cold room.

'Never mind the cost, Mr Bandini,' she said. 'It has to be done. Nothing is too good for my tenants.'

What could he say to that? Did Maria expect him to stalk off the job, refuse to do it? He acted like a sensible man, glad for this opportunity to make more money. The Widow drove him to the lumber yard.

'It's so cold in that house,' she said. 'You should have some kind of a heater.'

His answer was an artless confusion out of which he made it clear that if there is work there is warmth, that when a man has freedom of movement it is enough, for then his blood is hot too. But her concern left him hot and choking beside her in the car, her perfumed presence teasing him as his nostrils pulled steadily at the lush fragrance of her skin and garments. Her gloved hands swung the car to the curbing in front of the Gage Lumber Company.

Old Man Gage was standing at the window when Bandini got out and bowed goodbye to the Widow. She crippled him with a relentless smile that shook his knees, but he was strutting like a defiant rooster when he stepped inside the office, slammed the door with an air of bravado, pulled out a cigar, scratched a match across the face of the counter, puffed the weed thoughtfully, blowing a burst of smoke into the face of Old Man Gage, who blinked his eyes and looked away after Bandini's brutal stare had penetrated his skull. Bandini grunted with satisfaction. Did he owe the Gage Lumber Company money? Then let Old Man Gage take cognizance of the facts. Let him remember that with his own eyes he had seen Bandini among people of power. He gave the order for a hundred face brick, a sack of cement, and a yard of sand, to be delivered at the Windsor Street address.

'And hurry it up,' he said over his shoulder. 'I got to have it inside half an hour.'

He swaggered back to the Windsor Street house, his chin in the air, the blue strong smoke from his Toscanelli tumbling over his shoulder. Maria should have seen the whipped-dog expression on Old Man Gage's face, the obsequious alacrity with which he wrote down Bandini's order.

The materials were being delivered even as he arrived at the empty house, the Gage Lumber Co. truck backed against the front curb. Peeling off his coat, he plunged to the task. This, he vowed, would be one of the finest little bricklaying jobs in the state of Colorado. Fifty years from now, a hundred years from now, two hundred, the fireplace would still be standing. For when Svevo Bandini did a job, he did it well.

He sang as he worked, a song of spring: 'Come Back to Sorrento.' The empty house sighed with echo, the cold rooms filling with the ring of his voice, the crack of his hammer and the plink of his trowel. Gala day: the time passed quickly. The room grew warm with the heat of his energy, the window panes wept for joy as the frost melted and the street became visible.

Now a truck drew up to the curb. Bandini paused in his work to watch the green-mackinawed driver lift a shining object and carry it toward the house. A red truck from the Watson Hardware Company. Bandini put down his trowel. He had made no delivery order with the Watson Hardware Company. No – he would never order anything from the Watson people. They had garnisheed his wages once for a bill he could not pay. He hated the Watson Hardware Company, one of his worst enemies.

'Your name Bandini?'

'What do you care?'

'I don't. Sign this.'

An oil heater from Mrs Hildegarde to Svevo Bandini. He signed the paper and the driver left. Bandini stood before the heater as though it was the Widow herself. He whistled in astonishment. This was too much for any man – too much.

'A fine woman,' he said, shaking his head. 'Very fine woman.'

Suddenly there were tears in his eyes. The trowel fell from his hands as he dropped to his knees to examine the shining, nickel-plated heater. 'You're the finest woman in this town, Mrs Hildegarde, and when I get through with this fireplace you'll be damn proud of it!'

Once more he returned to his work, now and then smiling at the heater over his shoulder, speaking to it as though it were his companion. 'Hello there, Mrs Hildegarde! You still there? Watching me, eh? Got your eye on Svevo Bandini, have you? Well, you're looking at the best bricklayer in Colorado, lady.'

The work advanced faster than he imagined. He carried on until it was too dark to see. By noon the next day he would be finished. He gathered his tools, washed his trowel, and prepared to leave. It was not until that late hour, standing in the murky light that came from the street lamp, that he realized he had forgotten to light the heater. His hands shrieked with cold. Setting the heater inside the fireplace, he lighted it and adjusted the flame to a dim glow. It was safe there: it could burn all night and prevent the fresh mortar from freezing.

He did not go home to his wife and children. He stayed with Rocco again that night. With Rocco, Maria; not with a woman, but with Rocco Saccone, a man. And he slept well; no falling into black bottomless pits, no green-eyed serpents slithering after him through his dreams.

Maria might have asked why he didn't come home. That was his business. *Dio rospo!* Did he have to explain everything?

The next afternoon at four he was before the Widow with a bill for the work. He had written it on stationery from the Rocky Mountain Hotel. He was not a good speller and he knew it. He had simply put it this way: Work 40.00. And signed it. Half of that amount would go for materials. He had made twenty dollars. The Widow did not even look at the statement. She removed her reading glasses and insisted that he make himself at home. He thanked her for the heater. He was glad to be in her house. His joints were not so frozen as before. His feet had mastered the shining floor. He could anticipate the soft divan before he sat in it. The Widow depreciated the heater with a smile.

'That house was like an icebox, Svevo.'

Svevo. She had called him by his first name. He laughed outright. He had not meant to laugh, but the excitement of her mouth making his name got away from him. The blaze in the fireplace was hot. His wet shoes were close to it. Bitter-smelling steam rose from them. The Widow was behind him, moving about; he dared not look. Once more he had lost the use of his voice. That icicle in his mouth – that was his tongue: it would not move. That hot throbbing in his temples, making his hair seem on fire: that was the pounding of his brain: it would not give him words. The pretty Widow with two hundred thousand dollars in the bank had called him by his first name. The pine logs in the fire sputtered their sizzling mirth. He sat staring into the flame, his face set in a smile as he worked his big hands together, the bones cracking for joy. He did not move, transfixed with worry and delight, tormented by the loss of his voice. At last he was able to speak.

'Good fire,' he said. 'Good.'

No answer. He looked over his shoulder. She was not there, but he heard her coming from the hall and he turned and fixed his bright excited eyes on the flame. She came with a tray bearing glasses and a bottle. She put it on the mantelpiece and poured two drinks. He saw the flash of diamonds on her fingers. He saw her solid hips, the streamline, the curve of her womanly back, the plump grace of her arm as she poured the liquor from the gurgling bottle.

'Here you are, Svevo. Do you mind if I call you that?'

He took the brownish red liquor and stared at it, wondering what it was, this drink the color of his eyes, this drink rich women put into their throats. Then he remembered that she had spoken to him about his name. His blood ran wild, bulging at the hot flushed limits of his face.

'I don't care, Mrs Hildegarde, what you call me.'

That made him laugh and he was happy that at last he had said something funny in the American style, even though he had not meant to do so. The liquor was Malaga, sweet, hot, powerful Spanish wine. He sipped it carefully, then tossed it away with vigorous peasant aplomb. It was sweet and hot in his stomach. He smacked his lips, pulled the big muscles of his forearm across his lips.

'By God, that's good.'

She poured him another glassful. He made the conventional protests, his eyes popping with delight as the wine laughed its way into his outstretched glass.

'I have a surprise for you, Svevo.'

She walked to the desk and returned with a package wrapped in Christmas paper. Her smile became a wince as she broke the red strings with her jeweled fingers and he watched in a suffocation of pleasure. She got it open and the tissue inside wrinkled as though little animals thrived in it. The gift was a pair of shoes. She held them out, a shoe in each hand, and watched the play of flame in his seething eyes. He could not bear it. His mouth formed a twist of incredulous torture, that she should know he needed shoes. He made grunts of protest, he swayed in the divan, he ran his gnarled fingers through his hair, he panted through a difficult smile, and then his eyes disappeared into a pool of tears. Again his forearm went up, streaked across his face, and pulled the wetness from his eyes. He fumbled through his pocket, produced a crackling red polka-dot handkerchief, and cleared his nostrils with a rapid fire of snorts.

'You're being very silly, Svevo,' she smiled. 'I should think you'd be glad.'

'No,' he said. 'No. Mrs Hildegarde. I buy my own shoes.'

He put his hand over his heart.

'You give me work, and I buy my own.'

She swept it aside as absurd sentiment. The glass of wine offered distraction. He drained it, got up and filled it and drained it again. She came over to him and put her hand on his arm. He looked into her face that smiled sympathetically, and once more a gusher of tears rose out of him and overflowed to his cheeks. Self-pity lashed him. That he should be subjected to such embarrassment! He sat down again, his fists clamped at his chin, his eyes closed. That this should happen to Svevo Bandini!

But, even as he wept he bent over to unlace his old soggy shoes. The right shoe came off with a sucking sound, exposing a gray sock with holes in the toes, the big toe red and naked. For some reason he wiggled it. The Widow laughed. Her amusement was his cure. His mortification vanished. Eagerly he went at the business of removing the other shoe. The Widow sipped wine and watched him.

The shoes were kangaroo, she told him, they were expensive. He pulled them on, felt their cool softness. God in heaven, what shoes! He laced them and stood up. He might have stepped barefoot into a deep carpet so soft they were, such friendly things at his feet. He walked across the room, trying them.

'Just right,' he said. 'Pretty good, Mrs Hildegarde!'

What now? She turned her back and sat down. He walked to the fireplace.

'I'll pay you, Mrs Hildegarde. What they cost you I'll take off the bill.' It was inappropriate. Upon her face was an expectancy and a disappointment he could not fathom.

'The best shoes I ever had,' he said, sitting down and stretching them before him. She threw herself at the opposite end of the divan. In a tired voice she asked him to pour her a drink. He gave it to her and she accepted it without thanks, saying nothing as she sipped the wine, sighing with faint exasperation. He sensed her uneasiness. Perhaps he had stayed too long. He got up to go. Vaguely he felt her smouldering silence. Her jaw was set, her lips a thin thread. Maybe she was sick, wanting to be alone. He picked up his old shoes and bundled them under his arms.

'I think maybe I'll go now, Mrs Hildegarde.

She stared into the flames.

'Thank you Mrs Hildegarde. If you have some more work sometime . . .'

'Of course, Svevo.' She looked up and smiled. 'You're a superb worker, Svevo. I'm well satisfied.'

'Thank you, Mrs Hildegarde.'

What about his wages for the work? He crossed the room and hesitated at the door. She did not see him go. He took the knob in his hand and twisted it.

'Goodbye, Mrs Hildegarde.'

She sprang to her feet. Just a moment. There was something she had meant to ask him. That pile of stones in the back yard, left over from the house. Would he look at it before he went away? Perhaps he could tell her what to do with them. He followed the rounded hips through the hall to the back porch where he looked at the stones from the window, two tons of flagstone under snow. He thought a moment and made suggestions: she could do many things with that stone – lay down a sidewalk with it; build a low wall around the garden; erect a sundial and garden benches, a fountain, an incinerator. Her face was chalky and frightened as he turned from the window, his arm gently brushing her chin. She had been leaning over his shoulder, not quite touching it. He apologized. She smiled.

'We'll talk of it later,' she said. 'In the spring.'

She did not move, barring the path back to the hall.

'I want you to do all my work, Svevo.'

Her eyes wandered over him. The new shoes attracted her. She smiled again. 'How are they?'

'Best I ever had.'

Still there was something else. Would he wait just a moment, until she thought of it? There was something – something – something – and she kept snapping her fingers and biting her lip thoughtfully. They went back through the narrow hallway. At the first door she stopped. Her hand fumbled at the knob. It was dim in the hall. She pushed the door open.

'This is my room,' she said.

He saw the pounding of her heart in her throat. Her face was gray, her eyes bright with quick shame. Her jeweled hand covered the fluttering in her throat. Over her shoulder he saw the room, the white bed, the dressing table, the chest of drawers. She entered the room, switched on the light, and made a circle in the middle of the carpet.

'It's a pleasant room, don't you think?'

He watched her, not the room. He watched her, his eyes shifting to the bed and back to her again. He felt his mind warming, seeking the fruits of imagery; that woman and this room. She walked to the bed, her hips weaving like a cluster of serpents as she fell on the bed and lay there, her hand in an empty gesture.

'It's so pleasant here.'

A wanton gesture, careless as wine. The fragrance of the place fed his heartbeat. Her eyes were feverish, her lips parted in an agonized expression that showed her teeth. He could not be sure of himself. He squinted his eyes as he watched her. No – she could not mean it. This woman had too much money. Her wealth impeded the imagery. Such things did not happen.

She lay facing him, her head on her outstretched arm. The loose smile must have been painful, for it seemed to come with frightened uneasiness. His throat responded with a clamor of blood; he swallowed, and looked away, toward the door through the hall. What he had been thinking had best be forgotten. This woman was not interested in a poor man.

'I think I better go now, Mrs Hildegarde.'

'Fool,' she smiled.

He grinned his confusion, the chaos of his blood and brain. The evening air would clear that up. He turned and walked down the hall to the front door.

'You fool!' he heard her say. 'You ignorant peasant.'

Mannaggia! And she had not paid him, either. His lips screwed into a sneer. She could call Svevo Bandini a fool! She arose from the bed to meet him, her hands outstretched to embrace him. A moment later she was struggling to tear herself away. She winced in terrible joy as he stepped back, her ripped blouse streaming from his two fists.

He had torn her blouse away even as Maria had torn the flesh from his face. Remembering it now, that night in the Widow's bedroom was even yet worth a great deal to him. No other living being was in that house, only himself and the woman against him, crying with ecstatic pain, weeping that he have mercy, her weeping a pretense, a beseechment for mercilessness. He laughed the triumph of his poverty and peasantry. This Widow! She with her wealth and deep plump warmth, slave and victim of her own challenge, sobbing in the joyful abandonment of her defeat, each gasp his victory. He could have done away with her had he desired, reduced her scream to a whisper, but he arose and walked into the room where the fireplace glowed lazily in the quick winter darkness, leaving her weeping and choking on the bed. Then she came to him there at the fireplace and fell on her knees before him, her face sodden with tears, and he smiled and lent himself once more to her delicious torment. And when he left her sobbing in her fulfillment, he walked down the road with deep content that came from the conviction he was master of the earth.

So be it. Tell Maria? This was the business of his own soul. Not telling, he had done Maria a favor – she with her rosaries and prayers, her commandments and indulgences. Had she asked, he would have lied. But she had not asked. Like a cat she had leaped to the conclusions written on his lacerated face. Thou shalt not commit adultery. Bah. It was the Widow's doing. He was her victim.

She had committed adultery. A willing victim.

Every day he was at her house during the Christmas week. Sometimes he whistled as he sounded the foxhead knocker. Sometimes he was silent. Always the door swung open after a moment and a welcome smile met his eyes. He could not shake loose from his embarrassment. Always that house was a place where he did not belong, exciting and unattainable. She greeted him in blue dresses and red dresses, yellow and green. She bought him cigars, Chancellors in a Christmas box. They were on the mantelpiece before his eyes; he knew they were his but he always waited for her invitation to take one.

A strange rendezvous. No kisses and no embraces. She would take his hand as he entered and shake it warmly. She was so glad he had come – wouldn't he like to sit down for a while? He thanked her and crossed the room to the fireplace.

A few words about the weather; a polite enquiry about his health. Silence as she returned to her book.

Five minutes, ten.

No sound save the swish of book pages. She would look up and smile. He always sat with his elbows on his knees, his thick neck bloated, staring at the flames, thinking his own thoughts: of his home, his children, of the woman beside him, of her wealth, wondering about her past. The swish of pages, the clucking and hissing of pine logs. Then she would look up again. Why didn't he smoke a cigar? They were his; help yourself. Thank you, Mrs Hildegarde. And he would light up, pulling at the fragrant leaf, watching the white smoke tumble from his cheeks, thinking his own thoughts.

In the decanter on the low table was whiskey, with glasses and soda beside it. Did he desire a drink? Then he would wait, the minutes passing, the pages swishing, until she glanced at him once more, her smile a courtesy to let him know she remembered he was there.

'Won't you have a drink, Svevo?'

Protests, the moving about in his chair, flicking away his cigar ash, jerking at his collar. No thank you, Mrs Hildegarde: he was not what you'd call a drinking man. Once in a while – yes. But not today. She listened with that parlor smile, peering at him over her reading glasses, not really listening at all.

'If you feel that you'd like one, don't hesitate.'

Then he poured a tumblerful, disposing of it with a professional jerk. His stomach took it like ether, blotting it away and creating the desire for more. The ice was broken. He poured another and another; expensive whiskey out of a bottle from Scotland, forty cents a shot down at the Imperial Poolhall. But there was always some little prelude of uneasiness, a whistling in the dark, before he poured one; a cough, or he might rub his hands together and stand up to let her know he was about to drink again, or the humming of a shapeless nameless tune. After that it was easier, the liquor freeing him, and he tossed them down without hesitancy. The whiskey, like the cigars, was for him. When he left, the decanter was emptied and when he returned it was full again.

It was ever the same, a waiting for evening shadows, the Widow reading and he smoking and drinking. It could not last. Christmas Eve, and it would be over. There was something about that time and season – Christmas coming, the old year dying – that told him it would be for only a few days, and he felt that she knew it, too.

Down the hill and at the other end of town was his family, his wife and children. Christmas time was the time for wife and children. He would leave, never to return. In his pockets would be money. Meantime, he liked it here. He liked the fine whiskey, the fragrant cigars. He liked this pleasant room and the rich woman who lived in it. She was not far from him, reading her book, and in a little while she would walk into the bedroom and he would follow. She would gasp and weep and then he would leave in the twilight, triumph giving zest to his legs. The leave-taking he loved most of all. That surge of satisfaction, that vague chauvinism telling him no people on earth equalled the Italian people, that joy in his peasantry. The Widow had money – yes. But back there she lay, crushed, and Bandini was a better man than she, by God.

He might have gone home those nights had there been that feeling that it was over. But it was no time for thinking of his family. A few days more and his worries would begin again.

Let those days be spent in a world apart from his own. No one knew save his friend Rocco Saccone.

Rocco was happy for him, lending him shirts and ties, throwing open his big wardrobe of suits. Lying in the darkness before sleep, he would wait for Bandini's account of that day. Concerning other matters, they spoke in English, but of the Widow it was always in Italian, whispered and secretive.

'She wants to marry me,' Bandini would say. 'She was on her knees, begging me to divorce Maria.'

'*Si*,' Rocco answered. 'Indeed!'

'Not only that, but she promised to settle a hundred thousand dollars on me.'

'And what did you say?'

'I am considering it,' he lied.

Rocco gasped, swung around in the darkness.

'Considering it! *Sangue de la Madonna!* Have you lost your mind? Take it! Take fifty thousand! Ten thousand! Take anything – do it for nothing!'

No, Bandini told him, the proposition was out of the question. A hundred thousand would certainly go a long way toward solving his problems, but Rocco seemed to forget that there was a question of honor here, and Bandini had no desire to dishonor his wife and children for mere gold. Rocco groaned and tore his hair, muttering curses.

'Jackass!' he said. 'Ah *Dio!* What a jackass!'

It shocked Bandini. Did Rocco mean to tell him that he would actually sell his honor for money – for a hundred thousand dollars? Exasperated, Rocco snapped the light switch above the bed. Then he sat up, his face livid, his eyes protruding, his red fists clinching the collar of his winter underwear. 'You wish to know if I would sell my honor for a hundred thousand dollars?' he demanded. 'Then look here!' With that he gave his arm a jerk, tearing open his underwear in front, the buttons flying and scattering over the floor. He sat pounding his naked chest savagely over his heart. 'I would not only sell my honor,' he shouted. 'I would sell myself body and soul, for at least fifteen hundred dollars!'

There was the night when Rocco asked Bandini to introduce him to the Widow Hildegarde. Bandini shook his head doubtfully. 'You would not understand her, Rocco. She is a woman of great learning, a college graduate.'

'Pooh!' Rocco said indignantly. 'Who the hell are you?'

Bandini pointed out that the Widow Hildegarde was a constant reader of books, whereas Rocco could neither read nor write in English. Furthermore, Rocco still spoke English poorly. His presence would only do harm to the rest of the Italian people.

Rocco sneered. 'What of that?' he said. 'There are other things besides reading and writing.' He crossed the room to the clothes closet and flung open the door. 'Reading and writing!' he sneered. 'And what good has it done you? Do you have as many suits of clothes as I? As many neckties? I have more clothes than the president of the University of Colorado – what good have reading and writing done him?'

He smiled that Rocco should reason thus, but Rocco had the right idea. Bricklayers and college presidents, they were all the same. A matter of where and why.

'I will speak to the Widow on your behalf,' he promised. 'But she is not interested in what a man wears. *Dio cane*, it is just the other way around.'

Rocco nodded sagely.

'Then I have nothing to worry about.'

His last hours with the Widow were like the first. Hello and goodbye, they added up to the same thing. They were strangers, with passion alone to bridge the chasm of their differences, and there was no passion that afternoon.

'My friend Rocco Saccone,' Bandini said. 'He's a good bricklayer too.'

She lowered her book and looked at him over the rim of her gold reading glasses.

'Indeed,' she murmured.

He twirled his whiskey glass.

'He's a good man, all right.'

'Indeed,' she said again. For some minutes she continued to read. Perhaps he should not have said that. The obvious implication startled him.

He sat laboring in the muddle he had made of it, the sweat breaking out, an absurd grin plastered across the sickly convolutions of his face. More silence. He looked out the window. Already the night was at work, rolling shadowy carpets across the snow. Soon it would be time to go.

It was bitterly disappointing. If only something beside the beast stalked between himself and this woman. If he could but tear away that curtain the fact of her wealth spread before him. Then he might talk as he did to any woman. She made him so stupid. *Jesu Christi!* He was no fool. He could talk. He had a mind which reasoned and fought through hardships far greater than hers. Of books, no. There had been no time in his driven, worried life for books. But he had read deeper into the language of life than she, despite her ubiquitous books. He brimmed with a world of things of speak about.

As he sat there, staring at her for what he believed to be the last time, he realized that he was not afraid of this woman.

That he had never been afraid of her, that it was she who feared him. The truth angered him, his mind shuddering at the prostitution to which he had subjected his flesh. She did not look up from her book. She did not see the brooding insolence twisting one side of his face. Suddenly he was glad it was the end. With an unhurried swagger he rose and crossed to the window.

'Getting dark,' he said. 'Pretty soon I'll go away and won't come back no more.'

The book came down automatically.

'Did you say something, Svevo?'

'Pretty soon I won't come back no more.'

'It *has* been delightful, hasn't it?'

'You don't understand nothing,' he said. 'Nothing.'

'What do you mean?'

He did not know. It was there, yet not there. He opened his mouth to speak, opened his hands and spread them out.

'A woman like you . . .'

He could say no more. If he succeeded, it would be crude and badly phrased, defeating the thing he wanted to explain. He shrugged futilely.

Let it go, Bandini; forget it.

She was glad to see him sit down again, smiling her satisfaction and returning to her book. He looked at her bitterly. This woman – she did not belong to the race of human beings. She was so cold, a parasite upon his vitality. He resented her politeness: it was a lie. He despised her complacency, he loathed her good breeding. Surely, now that it was over and he was going away, she could put down that book and talk to him. Perhaps they would say nothing important, but he was willing to try, and she was not.

'I musn't forget to pay you,' she said.

A hundred dollars. He counted it, shoved it into his back pocket.

'Is it enough?' she asked.

He smiled; 'If I did not need this money a million dollars would not be enough.'

'Then you want more. Two hundred?'

Better not to quarrel. Better to leave and be gone forever, without bitterness. He pushed his fists through his coat sleeves and chewed the end of his cigar.

'You'll come to see me, won't you?'

'To be sure, Mrs Hildegarde.'

But he was certain he would never return.

'Goodbye, Mr Bandini.'

'Goodbye, Mrs Hildegarde.'

'A merry Christmas.'

'The same to you, Mrs Hildegarde.'

Goodbye and hello again in less than an hour.

The Widow opened the door to his knocking and saw the dotted handkerchief masking all but his bloodshot eyes. Her breath shot back in horror.

'God in heaven!'

He stamped the snow from his feet and brushed the front of his coat with one hand. She could not see the bitter pleasure in the smile behind the handkerchief, nor hear the muffled Italian curses. Someone was to blame for this, and it was not Svevo Bandini. His eyes accused her as he stepped inside, snow from his shoes melting in a pool on the carpet.

She retreated to the bookcase, watching him speechlessly. The heat from the fireplace stung his face. With a groan of rage he hurried to the bathroom. She followed, standing at the open door as he blubbered into fistfuls of cold water. Her cheeks crept with pity as he gasped. When he looked into the mirror he saw the twisted, torn image of himself and it repulsed him, and he shook his head in a rage of denial.

'Ah, poor Svevo!'

What was it? What had happened?

'What do you suppose?'

'Your wife?'

He dabbed the cuts with salve.

'But this is impossible!'

'Bah.'

She stiffened, lifting her chin proudly.

'I tell you it's impossible. Who could have told her?'

'How do I know who told her?'

He found a bandage kit in the cabinet and began tearing strips of gauze and adhesive. The tape was tough. He shrieked a volley of curses at its obstinacy, breaking it against his knee with a violence that staggered him backward toward the bathtub. In triumph he held the strip of tape before his eyes and leered at it.

'Don't get tough with *me*!' he said to the tape.

Her hand was raised to help him.

'No,' he growled. 'No piece of tape can get the best of Svevo Bandini.'

She turned away. When she came back he was applying gauze and tape. There were four long strips on either cheek, reaching from his eyeballs to his chin. He saw her and was startled. She was dressed to go out: fur coat, blue scarf, hat, and galoshes. That quiet elegance of her appeal, that rich simplicity of her tiny hat tipped jauntily to the side, the bright wool scarf spilling from the luxurious collar of her fur, the gray galoshes with their neat buckles and the long gray driving gloves, stamped her again for what she was, a rich woman subtly proclaiming her difference. He was awed.

'The door at the end of the hall is an extra bedroom,' she said. 'I should be back around midnight.'

'You're going someplace?'

'It's Christmas Eve.' She said it as though, had it been any other day, she would have stayed home.

She was gone, the sound of her car drifting to nothing down the mountain road. Now a strange impulse seized him. He was alone in the house, all alone. He walked to her room and groped and searched through her effects. He opened drawers, examined old letters and papers. At the dressing table he lifted the cork from every perfume bottle, sniffed it, and returned it exactly to where he had found it. Here was a desire he had long felt, bursting out of control now that he was alone, this desire to touch and smell and fondle and examine at leisure everything that was her possession. He caressed her lingerie, pressed her cold jewels between his palms. He opened inviting little drawers in her writing desk, studied the fountain pens and pencils, the bottles and boxes therein. He peered into shelves, searched through trunks, removing each item of apparel, every nicknack and jewel and souvenir, studied each with care, evaluated it, and returned it to the place whence it had come. Was he a thief groping for plunder? Did he seek the mystery of this woman's past? No and no again. Here was a new world and he wished to know it well. That and no more.

It was after eleven when he sank into the deep bed in the

extra room. Here was a bed the like of which his bones had never known. It seemed that he sank miles before dropping to sweet rest. Around his ears the satin eiderdown blankets pressed their gentle warm weight. He sighed with something like a sob. This night at least, there would be peace. He lay talking to himself softly in the language of his nativity.

'All will be well – a few days and all will be forgotten. She needs me. My children need me. A few more days and she will get over it.'

From afar he heard the tolling of bells, the call for midnight Mass at the Church of the Sacred Heart. He rose to one elbow and listened. Christmas morning. He saw his wife kneeling at Mass, his three sons in pious procession down the main altar as the choir sang 'Adeste Fideles.' His wife, his pitiful Maria. Tonight she would be wearing that battered old hat, as old as their marriage, remade year after year to meet as far as possible the new styles. Tonight – nay, at that very moment – he knew she knelt on wearied knees, her trembling lips moving in prayer for himself and his children. Oh star of Bethlehem! Oh birth of the infant Jesus!

Through the window he saw the tumbling flakes of snow, Svevo Bandini in another woman's bed as his wife prayed for his immortal soul. He lay back, sucking the big tears that streamed down his bandaged face. Tomorrow he would go home again. It had to be done. On his knees he would sue for forgiveness and peace. On his knees, after the kids were gone and his wife was alone. He could never do it in their presence. The kids would laugh and spoil it all.

One glance at the mirror next morning killed his determination. There was the hideous image of his ravaged face, now purple and swollen, black puffs under the eyes. He could meet no man with those telltale scars. His own sons would flinch in horror. Growling and cursing, he threw himself into a chair and tore at his hair. *Jesu Christi!* He dared not even walk the streets. No man, seeing him, could fail to read the language of violence scrawled upon his countenance. For all the lies he might tell – that he had fallen on the ice, that he had fought a man over a card game – there could be no doubt that a woman's hands had torn his cheeks.

He dressed, and tiptoed past the Widow's closed door to the kitchen, where he ate a breakfast of bread and butter and black coffee. After washing the dishes he returned to his room. Out of the corner of his eye he caught sight of himself on the dresser mirror. The reflection angered him so that he clinched his fists, and controlled the desire to smash the mirror. Moaning and cursing, he threw himself on the bed, his head rolling from side to side as he realized it might be a week before the scratches would heal and the swelling subside so that his face was fit for the gaze of human society.

A sunless Christmas Day. The snowing had stopped. He lay listening to the patter of melting icicles. Toward noon he heard the cautious knocking of the Widow's knuckles on the door. He knew it was she, yet he leaped out of bed like a criminal pursued by the police.

'Are you there?' she asked.

He could not face her.

'One moment!' he said.

Quickly he opened the top dresser drawer, whipped out a hand towel, and bound it over his face, masking all but his eyes. Then he opened the door. If she was startled by his appearance, she did not show it. Her hair was pulled up in a thin net, her plump figure wrapped in a frilled pink dressing gown.

'Merry Christmas,' she smiled.

'My face,' he apologized, pointing to it. 'The towel keeps it warm. Makes it get well quick.'

'Did you sleep well?'

'Best bed I ever slept in. Fine bed, very soft.'

She crossed the room and sat on the edge of the bed, bouncing herself experimentally. 'Why,' she said, 'it's softer than mine.'

'Pretty good bed, all right.'

She hesitated, then stood up. Her eyes met his frankly.

'You know you're welcome,' she said. 'I hope you'll stay.'

What should he say? He stood in silence, his mind searching about until he came upon a suitable reply. 'I'll pay you board and room,' he said. 'Whatever you charge, I'll pay.'

'Why, the idea!' she answered. 'Don't you dare suggest such a thing! You're my guest. This is no boarding house – this is my home!'

'You're a good woman, Mrs Hildegarde. Fine woman.'

'Nonsense!'

Just the same, he made up his mind to pay her. Two or three days, until his face healed . . . Two dollars a day . . . No more of the other thing.

There was something else:

'We'll have to be very careful,' she said. 'You know how people talk.'

'I know, all right,' he answered.

Still there was something more. She dug her fingers into

the pocket of the dressing gown. A key with a beaded chain attached.

'It's for the side door,' she said.

She dropped it into his open palm and he examined it, pretending it was a most extraordinary thing, but it was only a key and after a while he shoved it into his pocket.

One more matter:

She hoped he didn't mind, but this was Christmas Day, this afternoon she expected guests. Christmas gifts and such things.

'So perhaps it would be best.'

'Sure,' he interrupted. 'I know.'

'There's no great hurry. An hour or so.'

Then she left. Pulling the towel from his face, he sat on the bed and rubbed the back of his neck in bewilderment. Again his glance caught the hideous image in the mirror. *Dio Christo!* If anything, he looked even worse. What was he to do now?

Suddenly he saw himself in another light. The stupidity of his position revolted him. What manner of jackass was he, that he could be led away by the nose because people were coming to this house? He was no criminal; he was a man, a good man too. He had a trade. He belonged to the union. He was an American citizen. He was a father, with sons. Not far away was his home; perhaps it did not belong to him, but it was his home, a roof of his own. What had come over him, that he should skulk and hide like a murderer? He had done wrong – *certamente* – but where upon the earth was a man who hadn't?

His face – bah!

He stood before the mirror and sneered. One by one

he peeled off the bandages. There were other things more important than his face. Besides, in a few days it would be as good as new. He was no coward; he was Svevo Bandini; above all, a man – a brave man. Like a man he would stand before Maria and ask her to forgive him. Not to beg. Not to plead. Forgive me, he would say. Forgive me. I done wrong. It won't happen again.

The determination sent a chill of satisfaction through him. He grabbed his coat, pulled his hat down over his eyes, and walked quietly out of the house without a word to the Widow.

Christmas Day! He threw his chest into it, dragged deep breaths of it down. What a Christmas this would be! How fine to bear out the courage of his convictions. The splendor of being a brave and an honorable man! Reaching the first street within the city limits, he saw a woman in a red hat approaching him. Here was the test for his face. He threw back his shoulders, tilted his chin. To his delight, the woman did not even look at him after her first quick glance. The rest of the way home, he whistled 'Adeste Fideles.'

Maria, here I come!

The snow in the front walk had not been shoveled. Ho, and so the kids were loafing on the job during his absence. Well, he would put a stop to that immediately. From now on, things would be run differently. Not only himself, but the whole family would turn over a new leaf, beginning this day.

Strange, but the front door was locked, the curtains pulled down. Not so strange at that: he remembered that on Christmas Day there were five Masses at the church, the last Mass at twelve noon. The boys would be there. Maria, however, always went to midnight Mass on Christmas Eve.

Then she must be home. He pounded the screen without success. Then he went around to the back door and it was locked too. He peered into the kitchen window. A funnel of steam coming from the tea-kettle on the stove told him that someone was certainly there. He pounded again, this time with both fists. No answer.

'What the devil,' he grumbled, continuing around the house to the window of his own bedroom. Here the shades were down, but the window was open. He scratched it with his nails, calling her name.

'Maria. Oh, Maria.'

'Who is it?' The voice was sleepy, tired.

'It's me, Maria. Open up.'

'What do you want?'

He heard her rising from bed and the movement of a chair, as though bumped in the darkness. The curtain opened from the side and he saw her face, thick with sleep, her eyes uncertain and retreating from the blinding white snow. He choked, laughed a little in joy and fear.

'Maria.'

'Go away,' she said. 'I don't want you.'

The curtain closed again.

'But Maria. Listen!'

Her voice was tense, excited.

'I don't want you near me. Go away. I can't stand the sight of you!'

He pressed the screen with the palms of his hand and laid his head against it, beseeching her. 'Maria, please. I have something to say to you. Open the door Maria, let me talk.'

'Oh God!' she screamed. 'Get away, get away! I hate you,

I hate you!' Then there was a crash of something through the green curtain, a flash as he jerked his head aside, and the harsh tearing of screen-wire so close to his ear that he felt he had been struck. From within he heard her sobbing and choking. He drew back and examined the broken curtain and screen. Buried in the screen, pierced through to the handle, was a long pair of sewing scissors. He was sweating in every pore as he walked back to the street, and his heart was working like a sledgehammer. Reaching into his pocket for a handkerchief, his fingers touched something cold and metallic. It was the key the Widow had given him.

Good, then. So be it.

Chapter Nine

Christmas vacation was over, and on January sixth school reopened. It had been a disastrous vacation, ever unhappy and full of strife. Two hours before the first bell August and Federico sat on the front steps of St Catherine's, waiting for the janitor to open the door. It wasn't a good idea to go around saying it openly, but school was a lot better than home.

Not so with Arturo.

Anything was better than facing Rosa again. He left home a few minutes before class, walking slowly, preferring to be late and avoiding any chance meeting with her in the hall. He arrived fifteen minutes after bell-time, dragging himself up the stairs as though his legs were broken. His manner changed the moment his hand touched the doorknob of the classroom. Brisk and alert, panting as though after a hard run, he turned the knob, whisked inside, and tiptoed hurriedly to his seat.

Sister Mary Celia was at the blackboard, at the opposite side of the room from Rosa's desk. He was glad, for it spared him any stray encounter with Rosa's soft eyes. Sister Celia was explaining the square of a right triangle, and with some violence, bits of chalk spattering as she lashed the blackboard with big defiant figures, her glass eye brighter than ever as it shot in his direction and back to the blackboard. He recalled the rumor among the kids about the eye: that when she slept at night, the eye glowed on her dresser, staring intently, becoming more luminous if burglars were about. She finished at the blackboard, slapping her hands clean of chalk.

'Bandini,' she said. 'You've begun the new year true to form. An explanation please.'

He stood up.

'This is going to be good,' someone whispered.

'I went over to the church and said the rosary,' Arturo said. 'I wanted to offer up the new year to the Blessed Virgin.'

That was always incontestible.

'Boloney,' someone whispered.

'I want to believe you,' Sister Celia said. 'Even though I can't. Sit down.'

He bent to his seat, shielding the left side of his face with his cupped hands. The geometry discussion droned on. He opened his text and spread it out, both hands hiding his face. But he had to have one look at her. Opening his fingers, he peeked through. Then he sat erect.

Rosa's desk was empty. He swung his head around the room. She was not there. Rosa wasn't in school. For ten minutes he tried to be relieved and glad. Then he saw blondie Gertie Williams across the aisle. Gertie and Rosa were friends.

Pssssssssst, Gertie.

She looked at him.

'Hey Gertie, where's Rosa?'

'She isn't here.'

'I know that, stupid. Where is she?'

'I don't know. Home, I guess.'

He hated Gertie. He had always hated her and that pale pointed jaw of hers, always moving with chewing gum. Gertie always got Bs, thanks to Rosa who helped her. But Gertie was so transparent, you could almost see through her white eyes to the back of her head, where there was nothing, nothing at all except her hunger for boys, and not a boy like himself, because he was the kind with dirty nails, because Gertie had that aloof air of making him feel her dislike.

'Have you seen her lately?'

'Not lately.'

'When did you see her last?'

'Quite a while ago.'

'When? You lunkhead!'

'New Year's Day,' Gertie smiled superciliously.

'Is she quitting here? Is she going to another school?'

'I don't think so.'

'How can you be so dumb?'

'Don't you like it?'

'What do *you* think?'

'Then please don't talk to me, Arturo Bandini, because I certainly don't want to talk to you.'

Nuts. His day was ruined. All these years he and Rosa had been in the same class. Two of those years he had been in love with her; day after day, seven and a half years of Rosa in the same room with him, and now her desk was empty. The only thing on earth he cared for, next to baseball, and she was gone, only thin air around the place that once blossomed with her black hair. That and a little red desk with a film of dust upon it.

Sister Mary Celia's voice became rasping and impossible. The geometry lesson faded into English composition. He pulled out his Spalding Yearbook of Organized Baseball and studied the batting and fielding averages of Wally Ames, third baseman for the Toledo Mudhens, up in the American Association.

Agnes Hobson, that phony little apple-polishing screwball with the crooked front teeth spliced with copper wire, was reading aloud from Sir Walter Scott's *Lady of the Lake*.

Fooey, what bunk. To fight off boredom, he figured the lifetime career average of Wally Ames and compared it with that of Nick Cullop, mighty fencebuster with the Atlanta Crackers way down there in the Southern Association. Cullop's average, after an hour of intricate mathematics spread over five sheets of paper, was ten points higher than Wally Ames'.

He sighed with pleasure. There was something about that name – Nick Cullop – a thump and a wallop about it, that pleased him more than the prosaic Wally Ames. He ended with a hatred of Ames and fell to musing about Cullop, what he looked like, what he talked about, what he would do if Arturo asked him in a letter for his autograph. The day was exhausting. His thighs ached and his eyes watered sleepily. He yawned and sneered without discrimination at everything Sister Celia discussed. He spent the afternoon bitterly regretting the things he had not done, the temptations he had resisted, during the vacation period which was passed now and gone forever.

The deep days, the sad days.

He was on time the next morning, pacing his approach to the school to coincide with the bell just as his feet crossed the front threshold. He hurried up the stairs and was looking toward Rosa's desk before he could see it through the cloak-room wall. The desk was empty. Sister Mary Celia called the roll.

Payne. Present.

Penigle. Present.

Pinelli.

Silence.

He watched the nun inscribe an X in the roll book. She slipped the book in the desk drawer and called the class to order for morning prayers. The ordeal had begun again.

'Take out your geometry texts.'

Go jump in the lake, he thought.

Psssssssst. Gertie.

'Seen Rosa?'

'No.'

'Is she in town?'

'I don't know.'

'She's your friend. Why don't you find out?'

'Maybe I will. And maybe I won't.'

'Nice girl.'

'Don't cha like it?'

'I'd like to punch that gum down your throat.'

'Wouldn't you, though!'

At noon he strolled to the baseball diamond. Since Christmas no snow had fallen. The sun was furious, yellow with rage in the sky, avenging himself upon a mountain world that had slept and frozen in his absence. Dabs of snow tumbled from the naked cottonwoods around the ball field, falling to the ground and surviving for yet a moment as that yellow mouth in the sky lapped them into oblivion. Steam oozed from the earth, misty stuff oozing out of the earth and slinking away. In the west the storm clouds galloped off in riotous retreat, leaving off their attack on the mountains, the huge innocent peaks lifting their pointed lips thankfully toward the sun.

A warm day, but too wet for baseball. His feet sank in the sighing black mud around the pitcher's box. Tomorrow, perhaps. Or the next day. But where was Rosa? He leaned against one of the cottonwoods. This was Rosa's land. This was Rosa's tree. Because you've looked at it, because maybe you've touched it. And those are Rosa's mountains, and maybe she's looking at them now. Whatever she looked upon was hers, and whatever he looked upon was hers.

He passed her house after school, walking on the opposite side of the street. Cut Plug Wiggins, who delivered the *Denver Post*, moved by on his bike, nonchalantly flipping evening papers on every front porch. Arturo whistled and caught up with him.

'You know Rosa Pinelli?'

Cut Plug spewed a gusher of tobacco juice across the snow. 'You mean that Eyetalian dame three houses down the street? Sure, I know her, why?'

'Seen her lately?'

'Nah.'

'When did you see her last, Cut Plug?'

Cut Plug leaned over the handlebars, wiped sweat from his face, spewed tobacco juice again, and lapsed into a careful checkup. Arturo stood by patiently, hoping for good news.

'The last time I seen her was three years ago,' Cut Plug said at last. 'Why?'

'Nothing,' he said. 'Forget it.'

Three years ago! And the fool had said it as though it didn't matter.

The deep days, the sad days.

Home was chaos. Arriving from school, they found the

doors open, the cold evening air in possession. The stoves were dead, their bins spilling ashes. Where is she? And they searched. She was never far away, sometimes down in the pasture in the old stone barn, seated on a box or leaning against the wall, her lips moving. Once they looked for her until long after dark, covering the neighborhood, peeking into barns and sheds, seeking her footsteps along the banks of the little creek that had grown overnight to a brownish, blasphemous bully, eating the earth and the trees as it roared defiance. They stood on the bank and watched the snarling current. They did not speak. They scattered and searched upstream and down. An hour later they returned to the house. Arturo built the fire. August and Federico huddled over it.

'She'll be home pretty soon.'

'Sure.'

'Maybe she went to church.'

'Maybe.'

Beneath their feet they heard her. There they found her, down in the cellar, kneeling over that barrel of wine Papa had vowed not to open until it was ten years old. She paid no attention to their entreaties. She looked coldly at August's tear-swept eyes. They knew they did not matter. Arturo took her arm gently, to raise her up. Quickly the back of her hand slapped him across the face. Silly. He laughed, a bit self-conscious, standing with his hand touching his red cheek.

'Leave her alone,' he told them. 'She wants to be alone.'

He ordered Federico to get her a blanket. He pulled one from the bed and came down with it, stepping up and dropping it over her shoulders. She raised herself up, the blanket slipping away and covering her legs and feet.

There was nothing more to do. They went upstairs and waited.

A long time afterward she appeared. They were around the kitchen table, fooling with their books, trying to be industrious, trying to be good boys. They saw her purple lips. They heard her gray voice.

'Have you had supper?'

Sure, they had supper. A swell supper too. They cooked it themselves.

'What did you have?'

They were afraid to answer.

Until Arturo spoke up: 'Bread and butter.'

'There isn't any butter,' she said. 'There hasn't been any butter in this house for three weeks.'

That made Federico cry.

She was asleep in the morning when they left for school. August wanted to go in and kiss her goodbye. So did Federico. They wanted to say something about their lunches, but she was asleep, that strange woman on the bed who didn't like them.

'Better leave her alone.'

They sighed and walked away. To school. August and Federico together, and in a little while Arturo, after lowering the fire and taking a last look around. Should he waken her? No, let her sleep. He filled a glass of water and put it at the bedside. Then to school, tiptoeing away.

Pssssssst. Gertie.

'What do you want?'

'Seen Rosa?'

'No.'

'What's happening to her, anyway?'

'I don't know.'

'Is she sick?'

'I don't think so.'

'You *can't* think. You're too dumb.'

'Then don't talk to me.'

At noon he walked out to the field again. The sun was still angry. The mound around the infield had dried, and most of the snow was gone. There was one spot against the right field fence in the shadows where the wind had banked the snow and thrown a dirty lace over it. But it was dry enough otherwise, perfect weather for practice. He spent the rest of the noon hour sounding out the members of the team. How about a workout tonight? – the ground's perfect. They listened to him with strange faces, even Rodriquez, the catcher, the one kid in all the school who loved baseball as fanatically as himself. Wait, they told him. Wait until spring, Bandini. He argued with them about it. He won the argument. But after school, after sitting alone for an hour under the cottonwoods bordering the field, he knew they would not come, and he walked home slowly, past Rosa's house, on the same side of the street, right up to Rosa's front lawn. The grass was so green and bright he could taste it in his mouth. A woman came out of the house next door, got her paper, scanned the headlines, and stared at him suspiciously. I'm not doing anything: I'm just passing by. Whistling a hymn, he walked on down the street.

The deep days, the sad days.

His mother had done the washing that day. He arrived home through the alley and saw it hanging on the line. It had grown dark and suddenly cold. The washing hung stiff and frozen. He touched each stiffened garment as he walked up the path, brushing his hand against them to the end of the line. A queer time to wash clothes, for Monday had always been wash day. Today was Wednesday, maybe Thursday; certainly it was not Monday. A queer washing too. He stopped on the back porch to unravel the queerness. Then he saw what it was: every garment hanging there, clean and stiff, belonged to his father. Nothing of his own or his brothers, not even a pair of socks.

Chicken for dinner. He stood in the door and reeled as the fragrance of roast chicken filled his nostrils. Chicken, but how come? The only fowl left in the pen was Tony, the big rooster. His mother would never kill Tony. His mother loved that Tony with his jaunty thick comb and his fine strutting plumes. She had put red celluloid anklets on his spurred legs and laughed at his mighty swagger. But Tony it was: on the drainboard he saw the anklets broken in half like two red fingernails.

In a little while they tore him to pieces, tough though he was. But Maria did not touch him. She sat dipping bread into a yellow film of olive oil spread across her plate. Reminiscences of Tony: what a rooster he had been! They mused over his long reign in the chicken yard: they remembered him *when*. Maria dipped her bread in olive oil and stared.

'Something happens but you can't tell,' she said. 'Because if you have faith in God you have to pray, but I don't go around saying it.'

Their jaws ceased and they looked at her.

Silence.

'What'd you say, Mamma?'

'I didn't say a word.'

Federico and August glanced at one another and tried to smile. Then August's face turned white and he got up and left the table. Federico grabbed a piece of white meat and followed. Arturo put his fists under the table and squeezed them until the pain in his palms drove back the desire to cry.

'What chicken!' he said. 'You ought to try it, Mamma. Just a taste.'

'No matter what happens, you have to have faith,' she said. 'I don't have fine dresses and I don't go to dances with him, but I have faith, and they don't know it. But God knows it, and the Virgin Mary, and no matter what happens they know it. Sometimes I sit here all day, and no matter what happens they know because God died on the cross.'

'Sure they know it,' he said.

He got up and put his arms around her and kissed her. He saw into her bosom: the white drooping breasts, and he thought of little children, of Federico in infancy.

'Sure they know it,' he said again. But he felt it coming from his toes, and he could not bear it. 'Sure they know it, Mamma.'

He threw back his shoulders and strolled out of the kitchen to the clothes closet in his own room. He took the half-filled laundry bag from the hook behind the door and crushed it around his face and mouth. Then he let it go, howling and crying until his sides ached. When he was finished, dry and clean inside, no pain except the sting in his eyes as he stepped into the living-room light, he knew that he had to find his father.

'Watch her,' he said to his brothers. She had gone back

to bed and they could see her through the open door, her face turned away.

'What'll we do if she does something?' August said.

'She won't do anything. Be quiet, and nice.'

Moonlight. Bright enough to play ball. He took the short-cut across the trestle bridge. Below him, under the bridge, transients huddled over a red and yellow fire. At midnight they would grab the fast freight for Denver, thirty miles away. He found himself scanning the faces, seeking that of his father. But Bandini would not be down there; the place to find his father was at the Imperial Poolhall, or up in Rocco Saccone's room. His father belonged to the union. He wouldn't be down there.

Nor was he in the cardroom at the Imperial.

Jim the bartender.

'He left about two hours ago with that wop stonecutter.'

'You mean Rocco Saccone?'

'That's him – that good-looking Eyetalian.'

He found Rocco in his room, seated at a table radio by the window, eating walnuts and listening to the jazz come out. A newspaper was spread at his feet to catch the walnut shells. He stood at the door, the soft darkness of Rocco's eyes letting him know he was not welcome. But his father was not in the room, not a sign of him.

'Where's my father, Rocco?'

'How do I know? He'sa your fodder. He'sa not my fodder.'

But he had a boy's instinct for the truth.

'I thought he was living here with you.'

'He'sa live by hisself.'

Arturo checked it: a lie.

'Where does he live, Rocco?'

Rocco tossed his hands.

'I canna say. I no see him no more.'

Another lie.

'Jim the bartender says you were with him tonight.'

Rocco jumped to his feet and waved his fist.

'That Jeem, she'sa lyin' bastard! He'sa come along stick hissa nose where she'sa got no business. You fodder, he'sa man. He know what he'sa doing.'

Now he knew.

'Rocco,' he said. 'Do you know a woman, Effie Hildegarde?'

Rocco looked puzzled. 'Affie Hildegarde?' He scanned the ceiling. 'Who ees thees womans? For why you wanna know?'

'It's nothing.'

He was sure of it. Rocco hurried after him down the hall, shouting at him from the top of the stairs. 'Hey you keed! Where you go now?'

'Home.'

'Good,' Rocco said. 'Home, she'sa good place for keeds.'

He did not belong here. Halfway up Hildegarde Road he knew he dared not confront his father. He had no right here. His presence was intrusive, impudent. How could he tell his father to come home? Suppose his father answered: you get the hell out of here? And that, he knew, was exactly what his father would say. He had best turn around and go home for he was moving in a sphere beyond his experience. Up there with his father was a woman. That made it different. Now he remembered something: once when he was younger he sought his father at the poolhall. His father rose from the table and followed him outside. Then he put his fingers around my throat not hard but meaning it, and he said: don't do that again.

He was afraid of his father, scared to death of his father. In his life he had got but three beatings. Only three, but they had been violent, terrifying, unforgettable.

No thank you: never again.

He stood in the shadows of the deep pines that grew down to the circular driveway, where an expanse of lawn spread itself to the stone cottage. There was a light behind the Venetian blinds in the two front windows, but the blinds served their purpose. The sight of that cottage, so clear in moonlight and the glare of the white mountains towering in the west, such a beautiful place, made him very proud of his father. No use talking: this was pretty swell. His father was a lowdown dog and all those things, but he was in that cottage now, and it certainly proved something. You couldn't be very lowdown if you could move in on something like that. You're quite a guy, Papa. You're killing Mamma, but you're wonderful. You and me both. Because someday I'll be doing it too, and her name is Rosa Pinelli.

He tiptoed across the gravel driveway to a strip of soggy lawn moving in the direction of the garage and the garden behind the house. A disarray of cut stone, planks, mortar boxes, and a sand screen in the garden told him that his father was working here. On tiptoe, he made his way to the place. The thing he was building, whatever it was, stood out like a black mound, straw and canvas covering it to prevent the mortar from freezing.

Suddenly he was bitterly disappointed. Perhaps his father wasn't living here at all. Maybe he was just a common ordinary bricklayer who went away every night and came back in the morning. He lifted the canvas. It was a stone bench or something; he didn't care. The whole thing was a hoax. His father wasn't living with the richest woman in town. Hell, he was only working for her. In disgust he walked back to the road, down the middle of the gravel path, too disillusioned to bother about the crunch and squeal of gravel under his feet.

As he reached the pines, he heard the click of a latch. Immediately he was flat on his face in a bed of wet pine needles, a bar of light from the cottage door spearing the bright night. A man came through the door and stood on the edge of the short porch, the red tip of a lighted cigar like a red marble near his mouth. It was Bandini. He looked into the sky and took deep breaths of the cold air. Arturo shuddered with delight. Holy Jumping Judas, but he looked swell! He wore bright red bedroom slippers, blue pajamas, and a red lounging robe that had white tassels on the sash ends. Holy Jumping Jiminy, he looked like Helmer the banker and President Roosevelt. He looked like the King of England. O boy, what a man! After his father went inside and closed the door behind him he hugged the earth with delight, digging his teeth into acrid pine needles. To think that he had come up here to bring his father home! How crazy he had been. Not for anything would he ever disturb that picture of his father in the splendor of that new world. His mother would have to suffer; he and his brothers would have to go hungry. But it was worth it. Ah, how wonderful he had looked! As he hurried down the hill, skipping, sometimes tossing a stone into the ravine, his mind fed itself voraciously upon the scene he had just left.

But one look at the wasted, sunken face of his mother sleeping the sleep that brought no rest, and he hated his father again.

He shook her.

'I saw him,' he said.

She opened her eyes and wet her lips.

'Where is he?'

'He lives down in the Rocky Mountain Hotel. He's in the same room with Rocco, just him and Rocco together.'

She closed her eyes and turned away from him, pulling her shoulder away from the light touch of his hand. He undressed, darkened the house, and crawled into bed, pressing himself against August's hot back until the chill of the sheets had worn away.

Sometime during the night he was aroused, and he opened his sticky eyes to find her sitting at his side, shaking him awake. He could scarcely see her face, for she had not switched on the light.

'What did he say?' she whispered.

'Who?' But he remembered quickly and sat up. 'He said he wanted to come home. He said you won't let him. He said you'll kick him out. He was afraid to come home.'

She sat up proudly.

'He deserves it,' she said. 'He can't do that to me.'

'He looked awfully blue and sad. He looked sick.'

'Huh!' she said.

'He wants to come home. He feels lousy.'

'It's good for him,' she said, arching her back. 'Maybe he'll learn what a home means after this. Let him stay away a few more days. He'll come crawling on his knees. I know that man.'

He was so tired, asleep even as she spoke.

The deep days, the sad days.

When he awoke the next morning, he found August wide-eyed too, and they listened to the noise that had awakened them. It was Mamma in the front room, pushing the carpet sweeper back and forth, the carpet sweeper that went squeakedy-bump, squeakedy-bump. Breakfast was bread and coffee. While they ate she made their lunches out of what remained of yesterday's chicken. They were very pleased: she wore her nice blue housedress, and her hair was tightly combed, tighter than they had ever seen it, rolled in a coil on the top of her head. Never before had they seen her ears so plainly. Her hair was usually loose, hiding them. Pretty ears, small and pink.

August talking:

'Today's Friday. We have to eat fish.'

'Shut your holy face!' Arturo said.

'I didn't know it was Friday,' Federico said. 'Why did you have to tell us, August.'

'Because he's a holy fool,' Arturo said.

'It's no sin to eat chicken on Friday, if you can't afford fish,' Maria said.

Right. Hurray for Mamma. They yah-yah-yahed August, who snorted his contempt. 'Just the same, I'm not going to eat chicken today.'

'Okay, sucker.'

But he was adamant. Maria made him a lunch of bread dipped in olive oil and sprinkled with salt. His share of the chicken went to his two brothers.

*   *   *

Friday. Test day. No Rosa.

Pssssst, Gertie. She popped her gum and looked his way.

No, she hadn't see Rosa.

No, she didn't know if Rosa was in town.

No, she hadn't heard anything. Even if she did, she wouldn't tell him. Because, to be very honest about it, she would rather not talk to him.

'You cow,' he said. 'You milk cow always chewing your cud.'

'Dago!'

He purpled, half rose out of his desk.

'You dirty little blond bitch!'

She gasped, buried her face in horror.

Test day. By ten thirty he knew he had flunked geometry. At the noon bell he was still fighting the English composition quiz. He was the last person in the room, he and Gertie Williams. Anything to get through before Gertie. He ignored the last three questions, scooped up his papers, and turned them in. At the cloak-room door, he looked over his shoulder and sneered triumphantly at Gertie, her blond hair awry, her small teeth feverishly gnawing the end of her pencil. She returned his glance with one of unspeakable hatred, with eyes that said, I'll get you for this, Arturo Bandini: I'll get you.

At two o'clock that afternoon she had her revenge.

Pssssssst, Arturo.

The note she had written fell on his history book. That glittering smile on Gertie's face, the wild look in her eyes, and her jaws that had stopped moving, told him not to read the note. But he was curious.

Dear Arturo Bandini:

Some people are too smart for their own good, and some people are just plain foreigners who can't help it. You may think you are very clever, but a lot of people in this school hate you, Arturo Bandini. But the person who hates you most is Rosa Pinelli. She hates you more than I do, because I know you are a poor Italian boy and if you look dirty all the time I do not care. I happen to know that some people who haven't got anything will steal, so I was not surprised when someone (guess who?) told me you stole jewelry and gave it to her daughter. But she was too honest to keep it, and I think she showed character in giving it back. Please don't ask me about Rosa Pinelli anymore, Arturo Bandini, because she can't stand you. Last night Rosa told me you made her shiver because you were so terrible. You are a foreigner, so maybe that's the reason.

GUESS WHO????

He felt his stomach floating away from him, and a sickly smile played with his trembling lips. He turned slowly and looked at Gertie, his face stupid and smiling sickly. In her pale eyes was an expression of delight and regret and horror. He crushed the note, slumped down as far as his legs would reach, and hid his face. Save for the roar of his heart, he was dead, neither hearing, seeing, nor feeling.

In a little while he was conscious of a whispered hubbub about him, of a restlessness and excitement flitting through the room. Something had happened, the air fluttered with it. Sister Superior turned away and Sister Celia came back to her desk on the rostrum.

'The class will rise and kneel.'

They arose, and in the hush no one looked away from the nun's calm eyes. 'We have just received tragic news from the university hospital,' she said. 'We must be brave, and we must pray. Our beloved classmate, our beloved Rosa Pinelli, died of pneumonia at two o'clock this afternoon.'

There was fish for dinner because Grandma Donna had sent five dollars in the mail. A late dinner: it was not until eight o'clock that they sat down. Nor was there any reason for it. The fish was baked and finished long before that, but Maria kept it in the oven. When they gathered at the table there was some confusion, August and Federico fighting for places. Then they saw what it was. Mamma had set up Papa's place again.

'Is he coming?' August said.

'Of course he's coming,' Maria said. 'Where else would your father eat?'

Queer talk. August studied her. She was wearing another clean housedress, this time the green one, and she ate a lot. Federico gobbled his milk and wiped his mouth.

'Hey Arturo. Your girl died. We had to pray for her.'

He was not eating, dabbing the fish in his plate with the end of his fork. For two years he had bragged to his parents and brothers that Rosa was his girl. Now he had to eat his words.

'She wasn't my girl. She was just a friend.'

But he bowed his head, averting the gaze of his mother, her sympathy coming across the table to him, suffocating him.

'Rosa Pinelli, dead?' she asked. 'When?'

And while his brothers supplied the answers the crush and warmth of her sympathy poured upon him, and he was afraid to raise his eyes. He pushed back his chair and arose.

'I'm not very hungry.'

He kept his eyes away from her as he entered the kitchen and passed through to the back yard. He wanted to be alone so he could let go and release the constriction in his chest, because she hated me and I made her shiver, but his mother wouldn't let him, she was coming from the dining room, he could hear her footsteps, and he got up and hurried through the back yard and down the alley.

'Arturo!'

He walked down the pasture where his dogs were buried, where it was dark and he couldn't be seen, and then he cried and panted, sitting with his back against the black willow, because she hated me, because I was a thief, but Oh hell, Rosa, I stole it from my mother and that isn't really stealing, but a Christmas present, and I cleared it up too, I went to confessional and got it all cleared up.

From the alley he heard his mother calling him, calling out to tell her where he was. 'I'm coming,' he answered, making sure his eyes were dry, licking the taste of tears from his lips. He climbed the barbed-wire fence at the corner of the pasture, and she came toward him in the middle of the alley, wearing a shawl and peering secretively over her shoulder in the direction of the house. Quickly she pried open his tight fist.

'Shhhhhhh. Don't say a word to August or Federico.'

He opened his palm and found a fifty-cent piece.

'Go to the show,' she whispered. 'Buy yourself some ice cream with the rest. Shhhhhhh. Not a word to your brothers.'

He turned away indifferently, walking down the alley, the coin meaningless in his fist. She called him after a few yards, and he returned.

'Shhhhhhh. Not a word to your father. Try to get home before he does.'

He walked down to the drugstore across from the filling station and sucked up a milkshake without tasting it. A crowd of collegians came in and took up all seats at the soda-fountain. A tall girl in her early twenties sat beside him. She loosened her scarf and threw back the collar of her leather jacket. He watched her in the mirror behind the soda-fountain, the pink cheeks flushed and alive from the cold night air, the gray eyes huge and spilling excitement. She saw him staring at her through the glass and she turned and gave him a smile, her teeth even and sparkling.

'Hello there!' she said, her smile the sort reserved for younger boys. He answered, 'Hi,' and she said nothing more to him and became absorbed in the collegian on the other side of her, a grim fellow wearing a silver and gold 'C' on his chest. The girl had a vigor and radiance that made him forget his grief. Over the ethereal odor of drugs and patent medicines he scented the fragrance of lilac perfume. He watched the long, tapering hands and the fresh thickness of her strong lips as she sipped her coke, her pinkish throat pulsing as the liquid went down. He paid for his drink and lifted himself off the fountain stool. The girl turned to see him go, that thrilling smile her way of saying goodbye. No more than that, but when he stood outside the drugstore he was convinced that Rosa Pinelli was not dead, that it had been a false report, that she was alive and breathing and laughing like the college girl in the store, like all the girls in the world.

Five minutes later, standing under the street lamp in front of Rosa's darkened house, he gazed in horror and misery at the white and ghastly thing gleaming in the night, the long silk ribbons swaying as a gust of wind caressed them: the mark of the dead, a funeral wreath. Suddenly his mouth was full of dust-like spittle. He turned and walked down the street. The trees, the sighing trees! He quickened his pace. The wind, the cold and lonely wind! He began to run. The dead, the awful dead! They were upon him, thundering upon him out of the night sky, calling him and moaning to him, tumbling and rolling to seize him. Like mad he ran, the streets shrieking with the echo of his pattering feet, a cold and haunting clamminess in the middle of his back. He took the short cut over the trestle bridge. He fell, stumbling over a railroad tie, sprawling hands first into the cold, freezing embankment. He was running again even before he crawled to his feet, and he stumbled and went down and rose up again and rushed away. When he reached his own street, he trotted, and when he was only a few yards from his own home, he slowed down to an easy walk, brushing the dirt from his clothes.

Home.

There it was, a light in the front window. Home, where nothing ever happened, where it was warm and where there was no death.

'Arturo . . .'

His mother was standing in the door. He walked past her and into the warm front room, smelling it, feeling it, revelling in it. August and Federico were already in bed. He undressed quickly, frantically, in the semi-darkness. Then the light from the front room went out and the house was dark.

'Arturo?'

He walked to her bedside.

'Yes?'

She threw back the covers and tugged at his arm.

'In here, Arturo. With me.'

His very fingers seemed to burst into tears as he slipped beside her and lost himself in the soothing warmth of her arms.

The rosary for Rosa.

He was there that Sunday afternoon, kneeling with his classmates at the Blessed Virgin's altar. Far down in front, their dark heads raised to the waxen Madonna, were Rosa's parents. They were such big people, there was so much of them to be shaken and convulsed as the priest's dry intonation floated through the cold church like a tired bird doomed to lift its wings once more on a journey that had no end. This was what happened when you died: someday he would be dead and somewhere on the earth this would happen again. He would not be there but it was not necessary to be there, for this would already be a memory. He would be dead, and yet the living would not be unknown to him, for this would happen again, a memory out of life before it had been lived.

Rosa, my Rosa, I cannot believe that you hated me, for there is no hate where you are now, here among us and yet far away. I am only a boy, Rosa, and the mystery of where you are is no mystery when I think of the beauty of your face and the laughter of your galoshes when you walked down the hall. Because you were such a honey, Rosa, you were such a good girl, and I wanted you, and a fellow can't be so bad if he loves a girl so good as you. And if you hate me now, Rosa, and I cannot believe that you hate me now, then look upon my grief and believe that I want you here, for that is good too. I know that you cannot come back, Rosa my true love, but there is in this cold church this afternoon a dream of your presence, a comfort in your forgiveness, a sadness that I cannot touch you, because I love you and I will love you forever, and when they gather on some tomorrow for me, then I shall have known it even before they gather, and it will not be strange to us . . .

After the services they gathered for a moment in the vestibule. Sister Celia, sniffling into a tiny handkerchief, called for quiet. Her glass eye, they noticed, had rolled around considerably, the pupil barely visible.

'The funeral will be at nine tomorrow,' she said. 'The eighth-grade class will be dismissed for the day.'

'Hot dog – what a break!'

The nun speared him with her glass eye. It was Gonzalez, the class moron. He backed to the wall and pulled his neck far into his shoulders, grinning his embarrassment.

'You!' the nun said. 'It *would* be you!'

He grinned helplessly.

'The eighth-grade boys will please gather in the class-room immediately after we leave the church. The girls are excused.'

They crossed the churchyard in silence, Rodriguez, Morgan, Kilroy, Heilman, Bandini, O'Brien, O'Leary, Harrington, and all the others. No one spoke as they climbed the stairs and walked to their desks on the first floor. Mutely they stared at Rosa's dust-covered desk, her books still in the shelf. Then Sister Celia entered.

'Rosa's parents have asked that you boys of her class act

as pallbearers tomorrow. Those who wish to do so will please raise their hands.'

Seven hands reached for the ceiling. The nun considered them all, calling them by name to step forward. Harrington, Kilroy, O'Brien, O'Leary. Bandini. Arturo stood among those chosen, next to Harrington and Kilroy. She pondered the case of Arturo Bandini.

'No Arturo,' she said. 'I'm afraid you're not strong enough.'

'But I am!' he insisted, glaring at Kilroy, at O'Brien, at Heilman. Strong enough! They were a head taller than himself, but at one time or another he had licked them all. Nay, he could lick any two of them, at any time, day or night.

'No Arturo. Please be seated. Morgan, please step up.'

He sat down, sneering at the irony of it. Ah, Rosa! He could have carried her in his arms for a thousand miles, in his own two arms to a hundred graves and back again, and yet in the eyes of Sister Celia he was not strong enough. These nuns! They were so sweet and so gentle – and so stupid. They were all like Sister Celia: they saw from one good eye, and the other was blind and worthless. In that hour he knew that he should hate no one, but he couldn't help it: he hated Sister Celia.

Cynical and disgusted, he walked down the front steps and into the wintry afternoon that was growing cold. Head down and hands shoved in his pockets, he started for home. When he reached the corner and looked up he saw Gertie Williams across the street, her thin shoulder blades moving under her red woollen coat. She moved slowly, her hands in the pockets of her coat that outlined her thin hips. He gritted his teeth as he thought again of Gertie's note. Rosa hates you and you make her shiver. Then Gertie heard his footstep as he mounted the curbing. She saw him and began walking fast. He had no desire to speak to her or to follow her, but the moment she quickened her steps the impulse to pursue her took him, and he was walking fast too. Suddenly, somewhere in the middle of Gertie's thin shoulder blades, he saw the truth. Rosa *hadn't* said that. Rosa *wouldn't* say that. Not about anyone. It was a lie. Gertie had written that she saw Rosa 'yesterday.' But that was impossible because on that yesterday Rosa was very sick and had died in the hospital the next afternoon.

He broke into a run and so did Gertie, but she was no match for his quickness. When he caught up with her, standing in front of her and spreading his arms to prevent her from passing, she stood in the middle of the sidewalk, her hands on her hips, defiance in her pale eyes.

'If you dare lay a hand on me, Arturo Bandini, I'll scream.'

'Gertie,' he said. 'If you don't tell me the truth about that note I'm going to smack you right in the jaw.'

'Oh, that!' she said haughtily. 'A lot you know about *that*!'

'Gertie,' he said. 'Rosa never said she hated me, and you know it.'

Gertie brushed past his arm, tossed her blond curls into the air, and said, 'Well, even if she *didn't* say it, I have an idea she *thought* it.'

He stood there and watched her primping down the street, throwing her head like a Shetland pony. Then he started to laugh.

Chapter Ten

The funeral on Monday morning was an epilogue. He had no desire to attend; he had had enough of sadness. After August and Federico left for school, he sat on the steps of the front porch and opened his chest to the warm January sun. A little while and it would be spring: two or three weeks more and the big-league clubs would head south for spring training. He pulled off his shirt and lay face down on the dry brown lawn. Nothing like a good tan, nothing like having one before any other kid in town.

Pretty day, a day like a girl. He rolled to his back and watched the clouds tumble toward the south. Up there was the big wind; he had heard that it came all the way from Alaska, from Russia, but the high mountains protected the town. He thought of Rosa's books, how they were bound in blue oilcloth the color of that morning sky. Easy day, a couple of dogs wandering by, making quick stops at every tree. He pressed his ear to the earth. Over on the north side of town, in Highland Cemetery they were lowering Rosa into a grave. He blew gently into the ground, kissed it, tasted it with the end of his tongue. Some day he would get his father to cut a stone for Rosa's grave.

The mailman stepped off the Gleason porch across the street and approached the Bandini house. Arturo arose and took the letter he offered. It was from Grandma Toscana. He brought it inside and watched his mother tear it open. There was a short message and a five-dollar bill. She pushed the five-dollar bill into her pocket and burned the message. He returned to the lawn and stretched out again.

In a little while Maria came out of the house carrying her downtown purse. He did not lift his cheek from the dry lawn, nor answer when she told him that she would return in an hour. One of the dogs crossed the lawn and sniffed his hair. He was brown and black, with huge white paws. He smiled when the big warm tongue licked his ears. He made a crook in his arm, and the dog nestled his head in it. Soon the beast was asleep. He put his ear to the furry chest and counted the heartbeat. The dog opened one eye, leaped to his feet, and licked his face with overwhelming affection. Two more dogs appeared, hurrying along, very busy along the line of trees bordering the street. The brown and black dog lifted his ears, announced himself with a cautious bark, and ran after them. They stopped and snarled, ordering him to leave them alone. Sadly the brown and black dog returned to Arturo. His heart went out to the animal.

'You stay here with me,' he said. 'You're my dog. Your name's Jumbo. Good old Jumbo.'

Jumbo romped joyfully and attacked his face again.

He was giving Jumbo a bath in the kitchen sink when Maria returned from downtown. She shrieked, dropped her packages, and fled into the bedroom, barring the door behind her.

'Take him away!' she screamed. 'Get him out of here.'

Jumbo shook himself loose and rushed panic-stricken out of the house, sprinkling water and soap suds everywhere.

Arturo pursued him, pleading with him to come back. Jumbo made running dives at the earth, whizzing in a wide circle, rolling on his back, and shaking himself dry. He finally disappeared into the coal shed. A cloud of coal dust rolled from the door. Arturo stood on the back porch and groaned. His mother's shrieks from the bedroom still pierced the house. He hurried to the door and quieted her, but she refused to come out until he had locked both front and back doors.

'It's only Jumbo,' he soothed. 'It's only my dog, Jumbo.'

She went back to the kitchen and peeked through the window. Jumbo, black with coal dust, was still rushing wildly in a circle, throwing himself on his back and rushing off to do it again.

'He looks like a wolf,' she said.

'He's half wolf, but he's friendly.'

'I won't have him around here,' she said.

That, he knew, was the beginning of a controversy lasting for at least two weeks. It was so with all his dogs. In the end Jumbo, like his predecessors, would follow her around devotedly, with no regard for anyone else in the family.

He watched her unwrap her purchases.

Spaghetti, tomato sauce, Roman cheese. But they never had spaghetti on weekdays. It was exclusively for Sunday dinner.

'How come?'

'It's a little surprise for your father.'

'Is he coming home?'

'He'll be home today.'

'How do you know? Did you see him?'

'Don't ask me. I just know he'll be home today.'

He cut a piece of cheese for Jumbo and went out and called him. Jumbo, he discovered, could sit up. He was delighted: here was an intelligent dog, and not a mere hound dog. No doubt it was part of his wolf heritage. With Jumbo running along, his nose to the ground, sniffing and marking every tree on both sides of the street, now a block ahead of him, now a half behind him, now rushing up and barking at him, he walked westward toward the low foothills, the white peaks towering beyond.

At the city limits, where Hildegarde Road turned sharply to the south, Jumbo growled like a wolf, surveyed the pines and underbrush on both sides of him, and disappeared into the ravine, his menacing growl a warning to whatever wild creatures that might confront him. A bloodhound! Arturo watched him weave into the brush, his belly close to the earth. What a dog! Part wolf, and part bloodhound.

A hundred yards from the crest of the hill, he heard a sound that was warm and familiar from the earliest memories of his childhood: the plinking of his father's stone mallet when it struck the dressing chisel and split the stone asunder. He was glad: it meant that his father would be in work clothes, and he liked his father in work clothes, he was easy to approach when in work clothes.

There was a crashing of thickets at his left and Jumbo rushed back to the road. Between his teeth was a dead rabbit, dead many weeks, reeking the stench of decomposition. Jumbo loped up the road a dozen yards, dropped his prey, and settled down to watching it, his chin flat on the ground, his hind quarters in the air, his eyes shifting from the rabbit to Arturo and back again. There was a savage rumble in his throat as Arturo approached . . . The stench was revolting. He rushed up and tried to kick the rabbit off the road, but Jumbo snatched it up before his foot, found the mark, and the dog dashed away, galloping triumphantly. Despite the stench Arturo watched him in admiration. Man, what a dog! Part wolf, part bloodhound, and part retriever.

But he forgot Jumbo, forgot everything, even forgot what he had planned to say as the top of his head rose above the hill and he saw his father watching him approach, the hammer in one hand, the chisel in the other. He stood on the crest of the hill and waited motionless. For a long minute Bandini stared straight into his face. Then he raised his hammer, poised the chisel, and struck the stone again. Arturo knew then that he was not unwelcome. He crossed the gravel path to the heavy bench over which Bandini worked. He had to wait a long time, blinking his eyes to avoid the flying stone chips, before his father spoke.

'Why ain't you in school?'

'No school. They had a funeral.'

'Who died?'

'Rosa Pinelli.'

'Mike Pinelli's girl?'

'Yes.'

'He's no good, that Mike Pinelli. He scabs in the coal mine. He's a good-for-nothing.'

He went on working. He was dressing the stone, shaping it to lay along the seat of a stone bench near the place where he worked. His face still showed the marks of Christmas Eve, three long scratches traveling down his cheek like the marks of a brown pencil.

'How's Federico?' he asked.

'He's okay.'

'How's August?'

'He's all right.'

Silence but for the plink of the hammer.

'How's Federico getting along in school?'

'Okay, I guess.'

'What about August?'

'He's doing all right.'

'What about you, you getting good marks?'

'They're okay.'

Silence.

'Is Federico a good boy?'

'Sure.'

'And August?'

'He's all right.'

'And you?'

'I guess so.'

Silence. To the north he could see the clouds gathering,
the mistiness creeping upon the high peaks. He looked about
for Jumbo but found no sign of him.

'Everything all right at home?'

'Everything's swell.'

'Nobody sick?'

'No. We're all fine.'

'Federico sleep all right at night?'

'Sure. Every night.'

'And August?'

'Yep.'

'And you?'

'Sure.'

Finally he said it. He had to turn his back to do it,

turn his back, pick up a heavy stone that called for all the strength in his neck and back and arms, so that it came with a quick gasp.

'How's Mamma?'

'She wants you to come home,' he said. 'She's got spaghetti cooking. She wants you at home. She told me.'

He picked up another stone, larger this time, a mighty effort, his face purpling. Then he stood over it, breathing hard. His hand went to his eye, the finger brushing away a trickle at the side of his nose.

'Something in my eye,' he said. 'A little piece of stone.'

'I know. I've had them.'

'How's Mamma?'

'All right. Swell.'

'She's not mad anymore?'

'Naw. She wants you home. She told me. Spaghetti for dinner. That isn't being mad.'

'I don't want no more trouble,' Bandini said.

'She don't even know you're here. She thinks you live with Rocco Saccone.'

Bandini searched his face.

'But I *do* live with Rocco,' he said. 'I been there all the time, ever since she kicked me out.'

A cold-blooded lie.

'I know it,' he said. 'I told her.'

'You told her.' Bandini put down his hammer. 'How do you know?'

'Rocco told me.'

Suspiciously: 'I see.'

'Papa, when you coming home?'

He whistled absently, some tune without a melody, just a

whistle without meaning. 'I may never come home,' he said. 'How do you like that?'

'Mamma wants you. She expects you. She misses you.'

He hitched up his belt.

'So she misses me! And what of that?'

Arturo shrugged.

'All I know is that she wants you home.'

'Maybe I'll come – and maybe I won't.'

Then his face writhed, his nostrils quivering. Arturo smelled it too. Behind him squatted Jumbo, the carcass between his front paws, his big tongue dripping saliva as he looked toward Bandini and Arturo and made them know he wanted to play tag again.

'Beat it, Jumbo!' Arturo said. 'Take that out of here!'

Jumbo showed his teeth, the rumble emerged from his throat, and he laid his chin over the body of the rabbit. It was a gesture of defiance. Bandini held his nose.

'Whose dog?' he twanged.

'He's mine. His name's Jumbo.'

'Get him out of here.'

But Jumbo refused to budge. He showed his long fangs when Arturo came near, rising on his hind legs as if ready to spring, the savage guttural muttering in his throat sounding murderously. Arturo watched with fascination and admiration.

'You see,' he said. 'I can't go near him. He'll tear me to ribbons.'

Jumbo must have understood. The gurgle in his throat rose to a terrifying steadiness. Then he slapped the rabbit with his paw, picked it up, and walked away serenely, his tail wagging ... He reached the edge of the pines when the side door opened and the Widow Hildegarde emerged, sniffing precariously.

'Good heavens, Svevo! What *is* that awful smell?'

Over his shoulder Jumbo saw her. His glance shifted to the pines and then back again. He dropped the rabbit, picked it up with a firmer grip, and strolled sensuously across the lawn toward the Widow Hildegarde. She was in no mood to caper. Seizing a broom, she walked out to meet him. Jumbo raised his lips, peeling them back until his huge white teeth glistened in the sun, strings of saliva dripping from his jaws. He released his gurgle, savage, blood-curdling, a warning that was both a hiss and a growl. The Widow stopped in her tracks, composed herself, studied the dog's mouth, and tossed her head in annoyance. Jumbo dropped his burden and unrolled his long tongue in satisfaction. He had mastered them all. Closing his eyes, he pretended to be asleep.

'Get that goddam dog outa here!' Bandini said.

'Is that your dog?' the Widow asked.

Arturo nodded with subdued pride.

The Widow searched his face, then Bandini's.

'Who is this young man?' she asked.

'He's my oldest boy,' Bandini said.

The Widow said: 'Get that horrible thing off my grounds.'

Ho, so she was that kind of a person! So that was the kind of a person she was! Immediately he made up his mind to do nothing about Jumbo, for he knew the dog was playing. And yet he like to believe that Jumbo was as ferocious as he pretended. He started toward the dog, walking deliberately, slowly. Bandini stopped him.

'Wait,' he said. 'Let me handle this.'

He seized the hammer and studied his pace toward Jumbo,

who wagged his tail and vibrated as he panted. Bandini was within ten feet of him before he rose to his hind legs, stretched out his chin, and commenced his warning growl. That look on his father's face, that determination to kill which rose out of bravado and pride because the Widow was standing there, sent him across the grass and with both arms he seized the short hammer and knocked it from Bandini's tight fist. At once Jumbo sprang to action, leaving his prey and prowling steadily toward Bandini, who backed away. Arturo dropped to his knees and held Jumbo. The dog licked his face, growled at Bandini, and licked his face again. Every movement of Bandini's arm brought an answering snarl from the dog. Jumbo wasn't playing anymore. He was ready to fight.

'Young man,' the Widow said. 'Are you going to take that dog out of here, or shall I call the police and have him shot?'

It infuriated him.

'Don't you dare, damn you!'

Jumbo leered at the Widow and showed his teeth.

'Arturo!' Bandini remonstrated. 'That's no way to talk to Mrs Hildegarde.'

Jumbo turned to Bandini and silenced him with a snarl.

'You contemptible little monster,' the Widow said. 'Svevo Bandini, are you going to allow this vicious boy to carry on like this?'

'Arturo!' Bandini snapped.

'You peasants!' the Widow said. 'You foreigners! You're all alike, you and your dogs and all of you.'

Svevo crossed the lawn toward the Widow Hildegarde. His lips parted. His hands were folded before him.

'Mrs Hildegarde,' he said. 'That's my boy. You can't talk to him like that. That boy's an American. He is no foreigner.'

'I'm talking to you too!' the Widow said.

'*Bruta animale!*' he said. '*Puttana!*'

He spattered her face with spittle.

'Animal that you are!' he said. '*Animal!*'

He turned to Arturo.

'Come on,' he said. 'Let's go home.'

The Widow stood motionless. Even Jumbo sensed her fury and slunk away, leaving his noisome booty before her on the lawn. At the gravel path where the pines opened to the road down the hill, Bandini stopped to look back. His face was purple. He raised his fist.

'*Animal!*' he said.

Arturo waited a few yards down the road. Together they descended the hard reddish trail. They said nothing, Bandini still panting from rage. Somewhere in the ravine Jumbo roamed, the thicket crackling as he plunged through. The clouds had banked at the peaks, and though the sun still shone, there was a touch of cold in the air.

'What about your tools?' Arturo said.

'They're not my tools. They're Rocco's. Let him finish the job. That's what he wanted anyway.'

Out of the thicket rushed Jumbo. He held a dead bird in his mouth, a very dead bird, dead many days now.

'That damn dog!' Bandini said.

'He's a good dog, Papa. He's part bird dog.'

Bandini looked at a patch of blue in the east.

'Pretty soon we'll have spring,' he said.

'We sure will!'

Even as he spoke something tiny and cold touched the back of his hand. He saw it melt, a small star-shaped snowflake . . .

The Road to Los Angeles

Chapter One

I had a lot of jobs in Los Angeles Harbor because our family was poor and my father was dead. My first job was ditchdigging a short time after I graduated from high school. Every night I couldn't sleep from the pain in my back. We were digging an excavation in an empty lot, there wasn't any shade, the sun came straight from a cloudless sky, and I was down in that hole digging with two huskies who dug with a love for it, always laughing and telling jokes, laughing and smoking bitter tobacco.

I started with a fury and they laughed and said I'd learn a thing or two after a while. Then the pick and shovel got heavy. I sucked broken blisters and hated those men. One noon I was tired and sat down and looked at my hands. I said to myself, why don't you quit this job before it kills you?

I got up and speared my shovel into the ground.

'Boys,' I said. 'I'm through. I've decided to accept a job with the Harbor Commission.'

Next I was a dishwasher. Every day I looked out a hole of a window, and through it I saw heaps of garbage day after day, with flies droning, and I was like a housewife over a pile of dishes, my hands revolting when I looked down at them swimming like dead fish in the bluish water. The fat cook was the boss. He banged pans and made me work. It made me happy when a fly landed on his big cheek and refused to leave. I had that job four weeks. Arturo, I said, the future of this job is very limited; why don't you quit tonight? Why don't you tell that cook to screw himself?

I couldn't wait until night. In the middle of that August afternoon, with a mountain of unwashed dishes before me, I took off my apron. I had to smile.

'What's funny?' the cook said.

'I'm through. Finished. That's what's funny.'

I went out the back door, a bell tinkling. He stood scratching his head in the midst of garbage and dirty dishes. When I thought of all those dishes I laughed, it always seemed so funny.

I became a flunkie on a truck. All we did was move boxes of toilet tissue from the warehouse to the harbor grocery stores in San Pedro and Wilmington. Big boxes, three feet square and weighing fifty pounds apiece. At night I lay in bed thinking about it and tossing.

My boss drove the truck. His arms were tattooed. He wore tight yellow polo shirts. His muscles bulged. He caressed them like a girl's hair. I wanted to say things that would make him writhe. The boxes were piled in the warehouse, fifty feet to the ceiling. The boss folded his arms and had me bring boxes down to the truck. He stacked them. Arturo, I said, you've got to make a decision; he looks tough, but what do you care?

That day I fell down and a box bashed me in the stomach. The boss grunted and shook his head. He made me think of a college football player, and lying on the ground I wondered why he didn't wear a monogram on his chest. I got up smiling. At noon I ate lunch slowly, with a pain where the box bashed me. It was cool under the trailer and I was lying there. The lunch hour passed quickly. The boss came out of the warehouse and saw my teeth inside a sandwich, the peach for dessert untouched at my side.

'I ain't paying you to sit in the shade,' he said.

I crawled out and stood up. The words were there, ready. 'I'm quitting,' I said. 'You and your stupid muscles can go to hell. I'm through.'

'Good,' he said. 'I hope so.'

'I'm through.'

'Thank God for that.'

'There's one other thing.'

'What?'

'In my opinion you're an overgrown sonofabitch.'

He didn't catch me.

After that I wondered what had happened to the peach. I wondered if he had stepped on it with his heel. Three days passed and I went down to find out. The peach lay untouched at the side of the road, a hundred ants feasting upon it.

Then I got a job as a grocery clerk. The man who ran the store was an Italian with a belly like a bushel basket. When Tony Romero was not busy he stood over the cheese bin breaking off little pieces with his fingers. He had a good business. The harbor people traded at his store when they wanted imported food.

One morning he waddled in and saw me with a pad and pencil. I was taking inventory.

'Inventory,' he said. 'What's that?'

I told him, but he didn't like it. He looked around. 'Get to work,' he said. 'I thought I told you to sweep the floor the first thing every morning.'

'You mean you don't want me to take inventory?'

'No. Get to work. No inventory.'

Every day at three there was a great rush of customers. It was too much work for one man. Tony Romero worked hard but he waddled, his neck floated in sweat, and people went away because they couldn't waste time waiting. Tony couldn't find me. He hurried to the rear of the store and pounded the bathroom door. I was reading Nietzsche, memorizing a long passage about voluptuousness. I heard the banging on the door but ignored it. Tony Romero put an egg crate in front of the door. and stood on it. His big jaw pushed over the top and looking down he saw me on the other side.

'*Mannaggia Jesu Christi!*' he yelled. 'Come out!'

I told him I'd come out immediately. He went away roaring. But I wasn't fired for that.

One night he was checking the day's receipts at the cash register. It was late, almost nine o'clock. I wanted to get to the library before it closed. He cursed under his breath and called me. I walked over.

'I'm short ten dollars.'

I said, 'That's funny.'

'It's not here.'

I checked his figures carefully three times. The ten was indeed missing. We examined the floor, kicking sawdust around. Then we looked through the cash drawer again, finally taking it out and looking inside the shaft. We couldn't find it. I told him maybe he had given it to somebody by mistake. He was certain he hadn't. He ran his fingers in and out the pockets of his shirt. They were like frankfurters. He patted his pockets.

'Gimme a cigarette.'

I pulled a pack from my back pocket, and with it came the ten dollar bill. I had wadded it inside the cigarette pack, but it had worked itself loose. It fell on the floor between us. Tony crushed his pencil until it splintered. His face purpled, his cheeks puffed in and out. He drew back his neck and spat in my face.

'You dirty rat! Get out!'

'Okay,' I said. 'Suit yourself about that.'

I got my Nietzsche book from under the counter and started for the door. Nietzsche! What did he know about Friedrich Nietzsche? He wadded the ten dollar bill and threw it at me. 'Your wages for three days, you thief!' I shrugged. Nietzsche in a place like this!

'I'm leaving,' I said. 'Don't get excited.'

'Get out of here!'

He was a good fifty feet away.

'Listen,' I said. 'I'm tickled to be leaving. I'm sick of your drooling, elephantine hypocrisy. I've been wanting to abandon this preposterous job for a week. So go straight to hell, you Dago fraud!'

I stopped running when I reached the library. It was a branch of the Los Angeles Public Library. Miss Hopkins was on duty. Her blonde hair was long and combed tightly. I always thought of putting my face in it for the scent. I wanted to feel it in my fists. But she was so beautiful I could hardly talk to her. She smiled. I was out of breath and I glanced at the clock.

'I didn't think I'd make it,' I said.

She told me I still had a few minutes. I glanced over the desk and was glad she wore a loose dress. If I could get her to walk across the room on some pretext I might be lucky and see her legs moving in silhouette. I always wondered what her legs were like under glistening hose. She wasn't busy. Only two old people were there, reading newspapers. She checked in the Nietzsche while I got my breath.

'Will you show me the history section?' I said.

She smiled that she would, and I followed. It was a disappointment. The dress was the wrong kind, a light blue; the light didn't penetrate. I watched the curve of her heels. I felt like kissing them. At History she turned and sensed I'd been thinking of her deeply. I felt the cold go through her. She went back to the desk. I pulled out books and put them back again. She still felt my thoughts, but I didn't want to think of anything else. Her legs were crossed under the desk. They were wonderful. I wanted to hug them.

Our eyes met and she smiled, with a smile that said: go ahead and look if you like; there's nothing I can do about it, although I'd like to slap your face. I wanted to talk to her. I could quote her some swell things from Nietzsche; that passage from Zarathustra on voluptuousness. Ah! But I could never quote that one.

She rang the bell at nine. I hurried over to Philosophy and grabbed anything. It was another Nietzsche: *Man and Superman*. I knew that would get her. Before stamping it, she flipped a few pages.

'My!' she said. 'What books you read!'

I said, 'Haw. That's nothing. I never read folderol.'

She smiled good night and I said, 'It's a magnificent night, ethereally magnificent.'

'Is it?' she said.

She gave me an odd look, the pencil point in her hair. I backed out, falling through the door and catching myself. I felt worse outside because it wasn't a magnificent night but cold and foggy, the street lamps hazy in the mist. A car with a man at the wheel and the engine running was at the curb. He was waiting to take Miss Hopkins back to Los Angeles. I thought he looked like a moron. Had he read Spengler? Did he know the West was declining? What was he doing about it? Nothing! He was a boob and a bounder. Nuts to him.

The fog wove around me, soaking into me as I walked along with a cigarette burning. I stopped at Jim's Place on Anaheim. A man was eating at the counter. I had seen him often on the docks. He was a stevedore named Hayes. I sat near him and ordered dinner. While it was cooking I went to the bookstand and looked over the books. They were dollar reprints. I pulled out five. Then I went to the magazine stand and looked at *Artists and Models*. I found two in which the women wore the least clothes and when Jim brought my dinner I told him to wrap them up. He saw the Nietzsche under my arm: *Man and Superman*.

'No,' I said. 'I'll carry it as it is.'

I put it on the counter with a bang. Hayes glanced at the book and read the title: *Man and Superman*. I could see him looking at me through the plate mirror. I was eating my steak. Jim was watching my jaws to find out if the steak was tender. Hayes still stared at the book.

I said, 'Jim, this pabulum is indeed antediluvian.'

Jim asked what I meant and Hayes stopped eating to listen. 'The steak,' I said. 'It's archaic, primeval, paleoanthropic, and antique. In short, it is senile and aged.'

Jim smiled that he didn't understand and the stevedore stopped chewing he was so interested.

'What's that?' Jim said.

'The meat, my friend. The meat. This pabulum before me. It's tougher than a bitch wolf.'

When I glanced at Hayes he ducked his head away quickly. Jim was upset about the steak and leaned forward on the counter and whispered he would be glad to cook me another.

I said, 'Zounds! Let it go, man! It supersedes my most vaunted aspirations.'

I could see Hayes studying me through the mirror. He occupied himself between me and the book. *Man and Superman*. I chewed and stared straight ahead, not paying any attention. All through the meal he watched me intently. Once he stared fixedly at the book for a long time. *Man and Superman*.

When Hayes finished he went to the front to pay his bill. He and Jim stood whispering at the cash register. Hayes nodded. Jim grinned and they whispered again. Hayes smiled and said goodnight, taking a last look at me over his shoulder. Jim came back.

He said, 'That fellow wanted to know all about you.'

'Indeed!'

'He said you talked like a pretty smart fellow.'

'Indeed! Who is he, and what does he do?'

Jim said he was Joe Hayes, the stevedore.

'A poltroonish profession,' I said. 'Infested by donkeys and boobs. We live in a world of polecats and anthropoids.'

I pulled out the ten dollar bill. He brought back the change. I offered him a twenty-five cent tip but he wouldn't take it. 'A haphazard gesture,' I said. 'A mere symbol of fellowship. I like the way you do things, Jim. It strikes an approving note.'

'I try to please everybody.'

'Well, I'm devoid of complaints, as Chekhov might say.'

'What kind of cigarettes do you smoke?'

I told him. He got me two packages.

'On me,' he said.

I put them in my pocket.

But he wouldn't take a tip.

'Take it!' I said. 'It's just a gesture.'

He refused. We said goodnight. He walked to the kitchen with the dirty plates and I started for the front. At the door I reached out and grabbed two candy bars from the rack and shoved them under my shirt. The fog swallowed me. I ate the candy walking home. I was glad of the fog because Mr Hutchins didn't see me. He was standing in the door of his little radio shop. He was looking for me. I owed him four installments on our radio. He could have reached out and touched me but he didn't see me at all.

Chapter Two

We lived in an apartment house next door to a place where a lot of Filipinos lived. The Filipino influx was seasonal. They came south for the fishing season and went back north for the fruit and lettuce seasons around Salinas. There was one family of Filipinos in our house, directly below us. It was a two story pink stucco place with big slabs of stucco wiped from the walls by earthquakes. Every night the stucco absorbed the fog like a blotter. In the mornings the walls were a damp red instead of pink. I liked the red best.

The stairs squealed like a nest of mice. Our apartment was the last on the second floor. As soon as I touched the door knob I felt low. Home always did that to me. Even when my father was alive and we lived in a real house I didn't like it. I always wanted to get away from it, or change it. I used to wonder what home would be like if it was different, but I never could figure out what to do to make it different.

I opened the door. It was dark, the darkness smelling of home, the place where I lived. I turned on the lights. My mother was lying on the divan and the light was waking her up. She rubbed her eyes and got up to her elbows. Every time I saw her half awake it made me think of the times when I was a kid and used to go to her bed in the mornings and smell her asleep until I grew older and couldn't go to her in the mornings because it reminded me too much that she was my mother. It was a salty oily odor. I couldn't even think about her getting older. It burned me up. She sat up and smiled at me, her hair mussed from sleep. Everything she did reminded me of the days when I lived in a real house.

'I thought you'd never get here,' she said.

I said, 'Where's Mona?'

My mother said she was at church and I said, 'My own sister reduced to the superstition of prayer! My own flesh and blood. A nun, a god-lover! What barbarism!'

'Don't start that again,' she said. 'You're nothing but a boy who's read too many books.'

'That's what you think,' I said. 'It's quite evident that you have a fixation complex.'

Her face whitened.

'A what?'

I said, 'Forget it. No use talking to yokels, clodhoppers and imbeciles. The intelligent man makes certain reservations as to the choice of his listeners.'

She pushed back her hair with long fingers like Miss Hopkins's but they were worn with knobs and wrinkles at the joints, and she wore a wedding ring.

'Are you aware of the fact,' I said, 'that a wedding ring is not only vulgarly phallic but also the vestigial remains of a primitive savagery anomalous to this age of so-called enlightenment and intelligence?'

She said, 'What?'

'Never mind. The feminine mind would not grasp it, even if I explained.'

I told her to laugh if she felt like it but some day she would change her tune, and I took my new books and magazines to my private study, which was the clothes closet. There was no electric light in it, so I used candles. There was a feeling in the air that someone or something had been in the study while I was away. I looked around, and I was right, for my sister's little pink sweater hung from one of the clothes hooks.

I lifted it off the hook and said to it, 'What do you mean by hanging there? By what authority? Don't you realize you have invaded the sanctity of the house of love?' I opened the door and threw the sweater on the divan.

'No clothes allowed in this room!' I yelled.

My mother came in a hurry. I closed the door and flipped the lock. I could hear her footsteps. The door knob rattled. I started unwrapping the package. The pictures in *Artists and Models* were honeys. I picked my favorite. She was lying on a white rug, holding a red rose to her cheek. I set the picture between the candles on the floor and got down on my knees. 'Chloe,' I said, 'I worship you. Thy teeth are like a flock of sheep on Mount Gilead, and thy cheeks are comely. I am thy humble servant, and I bringeth love everlasting.'

'Arturo!' my mother said. 'Open up.'

'What do you want?'

'What're you doing?'

'Reading. Perusing! Am I denied even that in my own home?'

She rattled the buttons of the sweater against the door. 'I don't know what to do with this,' she said. 'You've got to let me have this clothes closet.'

'Impossible.'

'What're you doing?'

'Reading.'

'Reading what?'

'Literature!'

She wouldn't go away. I could see her toes under the door crack. I couldn't talk to the girl with her standing out there. I put the magazine aside and waited for her to go away. She wouldn't. She didn't even move. Five minutes passed. The candle spluttered. The smoke was filling the place again. She hadn't moved an inch. Finally I set the magazine on the floor and covered it with a box. I felt like yelling at my mother. She could at least move, make a noise, lift her foot, whistle. I picked up a fiction book and stuck my finger in it, as if marking the place. When I opened the door she glared at my face. I had a feeling she knew all about me. She put her hands on her hips and sniffed at the air. Her eyes looked everywhere, the corners, the ceiling, the floor.

'What on earth are you doing in there?'

'Reading! Improving my mind. Do you forbid even that?'

'There's something awfully strange about this,' she said. 'Are you reading those nasty picture books again?'

'I'll have no Methodists, prudes, or pruriency in my house. I'm sick of this polecat wowserism. The awful truth is that my own mother is a smut hound of the worst type.'

'They make me sick,' she said.

I said, 'Don't blame the pictures. You're a Christian, an Epworth Leaguer, a Bible-Belter. You're frustrated by your brummagem Christianity. You're at heart a scoundrel and a jackass, a bounder and an ass.'

She pushed me aside and walked into the closet. Inside was the odor of burning wax and brief passions spent on the floor. She knew what the darkness held. Then she ran out.

'God in heaven!' she said. 'Let me out of here.' She pushed me aside and slammed the door. I heard her banging pots and pans in the kitchen. Then the kitchen door slammed. I locked the door and went back to the picture and lit the candles. After a while my mother knocked and told me supper was ready. I told her I had eaten. She hovered at the door. She was getting annoyed again. I could feel it coming on. There was a chair at the door. I heard her drag it into position and sit down. I knew she sat with folded arms, looking at her shoes, her feet straight out in that characteristic way she had of sitting and waiting. I closed the magazine and waited. If she could stand it I could too. Her toe beat a tap on the carpet. The chair squeaked. The beat increased. All at once she jumped up and started hammering the door. I opened it in a hurry.

'Come out of there!' she screamed.

I got out as fast as I could. She smiled, tired but relieved. She had small teeth. One below was out of line like a soldier out of step. She wasn't more than five three but she looked tall when she had on high heels. Her aged showed most in her skin. She was forty-five. Her skin sagged some under the ears. I was glad her hair wasn't grey. I always looked for grey hairs but didn't find any. I pushed her and tickled her and she laughed and fell into the chair. Then I went to the divan and stretched out and slept awhile.

Chapter Three

My sister woke me up when she got home. I had a headache and there was a pain like a sore muscle in my back and I knew what that was from – thinking too much about naked women. It was eleven o'clock by the clock on the radio. My sister took off her coat and started for the clothes closet. I told her to stay out of there or get killed. She smiled superciliously and carried her coat to the bedroom. I rolled over and threw my feet on the floor. I asked her where she'd been but she didn't answer. She always got my goat because she seldom paid any attention to me. I didn't hate her but sometimes I wished I did. She was a pretty kid, sixteen years old. She was a little taller than me, with black hair and eyes. Once she won a contest in high school for having the best teeth. Her rear end was like a loaf of Italian bread, round and just right. I used to see fellows looking at it and I know it got them. But she was cold and the way she walked was deceptive. She didn't like a fellow to look at her. She thought it was sinful; anyhow she said so. She said it was nasty and shameful.

When she left the bedroom door open I used to watch her, and sometimes I peeked through the keyhole or hid under the bed. She would stand with her back to the mirror and examine her bottom, running her hands over it and pulling her dress around it tightly. She wouldn't wear a dress that didn't fit her tightly around the waist and hips and she was always brushing off the chair before she sat down. Then she sat down primly but in a cold way. I tried to get her to smoke cigarettes but she wouldn't. I also tried to advise her on life and sex but she thought I was crazy. She was like my father had been, very clean and a hard worker at school and home. She bossed my mother. She was smarter than my mother, but I didn't think she could ever approach my mind for sheer brilliance. She bossed everybody but me. After my father died she tried to boss me too. I wouldn't think of it, my own sister, and so she decided I wasn't worth bossing anyhow. Once in a while I let her boss me though, but it was only to exhibit my flexible personality. She was as clean as ice. We fought like cats and dogs.

I had something she didn't like. It repulsed her. I guess she suspected the clothes-closet women. Once in a while, I teased her by patting her rear. She got insanely mad. Once I did it and she got a butcher knife and chased me out of the apartment. She didn't speak for two weeks and she told my mother she'd never speak to me again, or even eat with me at the same table. Finally she got over it, but I never did forget how mad she got. She would have butchered me that time if she had caught me.

She had the same thing my father had, but it was not in my mother or me. I mean cleanliness. Once when I was a kid I saw a rattlesnake fighting three Scotch terriers. The dogs snatched him from a rock where he was sunning himself, and they tore him to pieces. The snake fought hard, never losing his temper, he knew he was finished, and each of the dogs carried off a dripping hunk of his body. They left only the tail and three rattles, and that part of him still moved.

Even after he was in pieces I thought he was a wonder. I went over to the rock, which had some blood on it. I put my finger in the blood and tasted it. I cried like a child. I never forgot him. And yet had he been alive I wouldn't have gone near him. It was something like that with my sister and my father.

I thought as long as my sister was so good-looking and bossy she would make a swell wife. But she was too cold and too religious. Whenever a man came to our house for a date with her, she wouldn't accept. She would stand in the door and not even invite him to come in. She wanted to be a nun, that was the trouble. What kept her from it was my mother. She was waiting a few more years. She said the only man she loved was the Son of Man, and the only bridegroom for her was Christ. It sounded like stuff from the nuns. Mona couldn't think things like that without outside help.

Her grade school days were spent with the nuns in San Pedro. When she graduated my father couldn't afford sending her to a Catholic high school, so she went to Wilmington High. As soon as it was over she started going back to San Pedro to visit the nuns. She stayed all day, helping them correct papers, giving kindergarten lessons and things like that. In the evenings she fooled around the Church on the Wilmington side of the harbor, decorating the altars with all kinds of flowers. She'd been doing that tonight.

She came out of the bedroom in her robe.

I said, 'How's Jehovah tonight? What does He think of the quantum theory?'

She went into the kitchen and started talking to my mother about the church. They argued about flowers, which was best for the altar, red or white roses.

I said, 'Yahweh. Next time you see Yahweh tell him I have a few questions to ask.'

They kept on talking.

'Oh Lord Holy Jehovah, behond your sanctimonious and worshipful Mona at your feet, drooling idiotic persiflage. Oh Jesus, she's holy. Sweet jumping Jesus Christ, she's sacred.'

My mother said, 'Arturo, stop that. Your sister's tired.'

'Oh Holy Ghost, Oh holy inflated triple ego, get us out of the Depression. Elect Roosevelt. Keep us on the gold standard. Take France off, but for Christ's sake keep us on!'

'Arturo, stop that.'

'Oh Jehovah, in your infinite mutability see if you can't scrape up some coin for the Bandini family.'

My mother said, 'Shame, Arturo. Shame.'

I got up on the divan and yelled, 'I reject the hypothesis of God! Down with the decadence of a fraudulent Christianity! Religion is the opium of the people! All that we are or ever hope to be we owe to the devil and his bootleg apples!'

My mother came after me with the broom. She almost stumbled over it, threatening me with the straw end in my face. I pushed the broom aside and jumped down on the floor. Then I pulled off my shirt in front of her and stood naked from the waist up. I bent my neck toward her.

'Vent your intolerance,' I said. 'Persecute me! Put me on the rack! Express your Christianity! Let the Church Militant display its bloody soul! Gibbet me! Stick hot pokers in my eyes. Burn me at the stake, you Christian dogs!'

Mona came in with a glass of water. She took the broom away from my mother and gave her the water. My mother drank it and calmed down a bit. Then she spluttered and coughed into the glass and was ready to cry.

'Mother!' Mona said. 'Don't cry. He's nutty.'

She looked at me with a waxy, expressionless face. I turned my back and walked to the window. When I turned around she was still staring.

'Christian dogs,' I said. 'Bucolic rainspouts! Boobus Americanus! Jackals, weasels, polecats, and donkeys – the whole stupid lot of you. I alone of the entire family have been unmarked by the scourge of cretinism.'

'You fool,' she said.

They walked into the bedroom.

'Don't call me a fool,' I said. 'You neurosis! You frustrated, inhibited, driveling, drooling, half-nun!'

My mother said, 'Did you hear that! How awful!'

They went to bed. I had the divan and they had the bedroom. When their door closed I got out the magazines and piled into bed. I was glad to be able to look at the girls under the lights of the big room. It was a lot better than that smelly closet. I talked to them about an hour, went into the mountains with Elaine, and to the South Seas with Rosa, and finally in a group meeting with all of them spread around me, I told them I played no favorites and that each in her turn would get her chance. But after a while I got awfully tired of it, for I got to feeling more and more like an idiot until I began to hate the idea that they were only pictures, flat and single-faced and so alike in color and smile. And they all smiled like whores. It all got very hateful and I thought, Look at yourself! Sitting here and talking to a lot of prostitutes. A fine superman *you* turned out to be! What if Nietzsche could see you now? And Schopenhauer – what would he think? And Spengler! Oh, would Spengler roar at you! You fool, you idiot, you swine, you beast, you rat, you filthy, contemptible, disgusting little swine! Suddenly I grabbed the pictures up in a batch and tore them to pieces and threw them down the bowl in the bathroom. Then I crawled back to bed and kicked the covers off. I hated myself so much that I sat up in bed thinking the worst possible things about myself. Finally I was so despicable there was nothing left to do but sleep. It was hours before I dozed off. The fog was thinning in the east and the west was black and grey. It must have been three o'clock. From the bedroom I heard my mother's soft snores. By then I was ready to commit suicide, and so thinking I fell asleep.

Chapter Four

At six my mother got up and called me. I rolled around and didn't want to get up. She took the bedclothes and tossed them back. It left me naked on the sheet because I didn't sleep wearing anything. That was all right, but it was morning and I wasn't prepared for it, and she could see it, and I didn't mind her seeing me naked but not the way a fellow will be some times in the morning. I put my hand over the place and tried to hide it, but she saw anyway. It seemed she was deliberately looking for something to embarrass me – my own mother, too.

She said, 'Shame on you, early in the morning.'

'Shame on me?' I said. 'How come?'

'Shame on you.'

'Oh God, what'll you Christians think of next! Now it's shameful to even be asleep!'

'You know what I mean,' she said. 'Shame on you, a boy your age. Shame on you. Shame. Shame.'

'Well, shame on you too, for that matter. And shame on Christianity.'

She went back to bed.

'Shame on him,' she said to Mona.

'What'd he do now?'

'Shame on him.'

'What did he do?'

'Nothing, but shame on him anyway. Shame.'

I fell asleep. After a while she called again.

'I'm not going to work this morning,' I said.

'Why not?'

'I lost my job.'

A dead silence. Then she and Mona sat up in bed. My job meant everything. We still had Uncle Frank, but they figured my earnings before that. I had to think of something good, because they both knew I was a liar. I could fool my mother but Mona never believed anything, not even the truth if I spoke it.

I said, 'Mr Romero's nephew just arrived from the old country. He got my job.'

'I hope you don't expect us to believe *that*!' Mona said.

'My expectations scarcely concern imbeciles,' I said.

My mother came to the bed. The story wasn't very convincing but she was willing to give me the breaks. If Mona hadn't been there it would have been a cinch. She told Mona to keep still and listened for more. Mona was messing it up by talking. I yelled at her to shut up.

My mother said, 'Are you telling the truth?'

I put my hand over my heart and closed my eyes and said, 'Before Almighty God and his heavenly court I solemnly swear that I am neither lying or elaborating. If I am, I hope He strikes me dead this very minute. Get the clock.'

She got the clock off the radio. She believed in miracles, any kind of miracles. I closed my eyes and felt my heart pounding. I held my breath. The moments passed. After a minute I let the air out of my lungs. My mother smiled and kissed me on the forehead. But now she blamed Romero.

'He can't do this to you,' she said. 'I won't let him. I'm going down and give him a piece of my mind.'

I jumped out of bed. I was naked but I didn't care. I said, 'God Almighty! Haven't you any pride, any sense of human dignity? Why should you see him after he treated me with such levantine scurrilousness? Do you want to disgrace the family name too?'

She was dressing in the bedroom. Mona laughed and fingered her hair. I went in and pulled off my mother's stockings and tied them in knots before she could stop me. Mona shook her head and tittered. I put my fist under her nose and gave her a final warning not to butt in. My mother didn't know what to do next. I put my hands on her shoulders and looked into her eyes. 'I am a man of deep pride,' I said. 'Does that strike an approving chord in your sense of judgment? Pride! My first and last utterance rises from the soul of that stratum I call Pride. Without it my life is a lusty disillusionment. In short, I am delivering you an ultimatum. If you go down to Romero's I'll kill myself.'

That scared the devil out of her, but Mona rolled over and laughed and laughed. I didn't say more but went back to bed and pretty soon I fell asleep.

When I woke up it was around noon and they were gone somewhere. I got out the picture of an old girl of mine I called Marcella and we went to Egypt and made love in a slave-driven boat on the Nile. I drank wine from her sandals and milk from her breasts and then we had the slaves paddle us to the river bank and I fed her hearts of hummingbirds seasoned in sweetened pigeon milk. When it was over I felt like the devil. I felt like hitting myself in the nose, knocking myself unconscious. I wanted to cut myself, to feel my bones cracking. I tore the picture of Marcella to pieces and got rid of it and then I went to the medicine cabinet and got a razor blade, and before I knew it I slit my arm below the elbow, but not deeply so that it was only blood and no pain. I sucked the slit but there was still no pain, so I got some salt and rubbed it in and felt it bite my flesh, hurting me and making me come out of it and feel alive again, and I rubbed it until I couldn't stand it any longer. Then I bandaged my arm.

They had left a note for me on the table. It said they had gone to Uncle Frank's and that there was food in the pantry for my breakfast. I decided to eat at Jim's Place, because I still had some money. I crossed the schoolyard which was across the street from the apartment and went over to Jim's. I ordered ham and eggs. While I ate Jim talked.

He said, 'You read a lot. Did you ever try writing a book?'

That did it. From then on I wanted to be a writer. 'I'm writing a book right now,' I said.

He wanted to know what kind of a book.

I said, 'My prose is not for sale. I write for posterity.'

He said, 'I didn't know that. What do you write? Stories? Or plain fiction?'

'Both. I'm ambidextrous.'

'Oh. I didn't know that.'

I went over to the other side of the place and bought a pencil and a notebook. He wanted to know what I was writing now. I said, 'Nothing. Merely taking random notes for a future work on foreign trade. The subject interests me curiously, a sort of dynamic hobby I've picked up.'

When I left he was staring at me with his mouth open. I took it easy down to the harbor. It was June down there, the best time of all. The mackerel were running off the south coast and the canneries were going full blast, night and day, and all the time at that time of the year there was a stink in the air of putrefaction and fish oil. Some people considered it a stink and some got sick from it, but it was not a stink to me, except the fish smell which was bad, but to me it was great. I liked it down there. It wasn't one smell but a lot of them weaving in and out, so every step you took brought a different odor. It made me dreamy and I did a lot of thinking about far-away places, the mystery of what the bottom of the sea contained, and all the books I'd read came alive at once and I saw better people out of books, like Philip Carey, Eugene Witla, and the fellows Dreiser made.

I liked the odor of bilge water from old tankers, the odor of crude oil in barrels bound for distant places, the odor of oil on the water turned slimy and yellow and gold, the odor of rotting lumber and the refuse of the sea blackened by oil and tar, of decayed fruit, of little Japanese fishing sloops, of banana boats and old rope, of tugboats and scrap iron and the brooding mysterious smell of the sea at low tide.

I stopped at the white bridge that crossed the channel to the left of the Pacific Coast Fisheries on the Wilmington side. A tanker was unloading at the gasoline docks. Up the street Jap fishermen were repairing their nets, stretched for blocks along the water's edge. At the American-Hawaiian stevedores were loading a ship for Honolulu. They worked in their bare backs. They looked like something great to write about. I flattened the new notebook against the rail, dipped the pencil on my tongue and started to write a treatise on the stevedore: 'A Psychological Interpretation of the Stevedore Today and Yesterday, by Arturo Gabriel Bandini.'

It turned out a tough subject. I tried four or five times but gave up. Anyhow, the subject took years of research; there wasn't any need for prose yet. The first thing to do was get my facts together. Maybe it would take two years, three, even four; in fact it was the job of a lifetime, a magnum opus. It was too tough. I gave it up. I figured philosophy was easier.

'A Moral and Philosophical Dissertation on Man and Woman, by Arturo Gabriel Bandini.' Evil is for the weak man, so why be weak. It is better to be strong than to be weak, for to be weak is to lack strength. Be strong, my brothers, for I say unless ye be strong the forces of evil shall get ye. All strength is a form of power. All lack of strength is a form of evil. All evil is a form of weakness. Be strong, lest ye be weak. Avoid weakness that ye might become strong. Weakness eateth the heart of woman. Strength feedeth the heart of man. Do ye wish to become females? Aye, then grow weak. Do ye wish to become men? Aye, aye. Then grow strong. Down with Evil! Up with Strength! Oh Zarathustra, endow thy women with plenty of weakness! Oh Zarathustra, endow thy men with plenty of strength! Down with woman! Hail Man!

Then I got tired of the whole thing. I decided maybe I wasn't a writer after all but a painter. Maybe my genius lay in art. I turned a page in the book and figured on doing some sketching just for the practice, but I couldn't find anything worth drawing, only ships and stevedores and docks, and they didn't interest me. I drew cats-on-the-fence, faces, triangles and squares. Then I got the idea I wasn't an artist or a writer but an architect, for my father had been a carpenter and maybe the building trade was more in keeping with my heritage. I drew a few houses. They were about the same, square places with a chimney out of which smoke poured. I put the notebook away.

It was hot on the bridge, the heat stinging the back of my neck. I crawled through the rail to some jagged rocks tumbled about at the edge of the water. They were big rocks, black as coal from immersions at high tide, some of them big as a house. Under the bridge they were scattered in crazy disorder like a field of icebergs, and yet they looked contented and undisturbed.

I crawled under the bridge and I had a feeling I was the only one who had ever done it. The small harbor waves lapped at the rocks and left little pools of green water here and there. Some of the rocks were draped in moss, and others had pretty spots of bird dung. The ponderous odor of the sea came up. Under the girders it was so cold and so dark I couldn't see much. From above I heard the traffic pounding, horns honking, men yelling, and big trucks battering the timber crosspieces. It was such a terrible din that it hammered my ears and when I yelled my voice went out a few feet and rushed back as if fastened to a rubber band. I crawled along the stones until I got out of the range of the sunlight. It was a strange place. For a while I was scared. Farther on there was a great stone, bigger than the rest, its crest ringed with the white dung of gulls. It was the king of all those stones with a crown of white. I started for it.

All of a sudden everything at my feet began to move. It was the quick slimy moving of things that crawled. I caught my breath, hung on, and tried to fix my gaze. They were crabs! The stones were alive and swarming with them. I was so scared I couldn't move and the noise from above was nothing compared to the thunder of my heart.

I leaned against a stone and put my face in my hands until I wasn't afraid. When I took my hands away I could see through the blackness and it was grey and cold, like a world under the earth, a grey, solitary place. For the first time I got a good look at the things living down there. The big crabs were the size of house bricks, silent and cruel as they held forth on top the large stones, their menacing antennae moving sensuously like the arms of a hula dancer, their little eyes mean and ugly. There were a lot more of the smaller crabs, about the size of my hand, and they swam around in the little black pools at the base of the rocks, crawling over one another, pulling one another into the lapping blackness as they fought for positions on the stones. They were having a good time.

There was a nest of even smaller crabs at my feet, each the size of a dollar, a big chunk of squirming legs jumbled together. One of them grabbed my pants cuff. I pulled him off and held him while he clawed helplessly and tried to bite me. I had him though and he was helpless. I pulled back my arm and threw him against a stone. He crackled, smashed to death, stuck for a moment upon the stone, then falling with blood and water exuding. I picked up the smashed shell and tasted the yellow fluid coming from it, which was salty as sea water and I didn't like it. I threw him out to deep water. He floated until a jack smelt swam around him and examined him, and then began to bite him viciously and finally dragged him out of sight, the smelt slithering away. My hands were bloody and sticky and the smell of the sea was on them. All at once I felt a swelling in me to kill these crabs, every one of them.

The small ones didn't interest me, it was the big ones

I wanted to kill and kill. The big fellows were strong and ferocious with powerful incisors. They were worthy adversaries for the great Bandini, the conquering Arturo. I looked around but couldn't find a switch or a stick. On the bank against the concrete there was a pile of stones. I rolled up my sleeves and started throwing them at the largest crab I could see, one asleep on a stone twenty feet away. The stones landed all around him, within an inch of him, sparks and chips flying, but he didn't even open his eyes to find out what was going on. I threw about twenty times before I got him. It was a triumph. The stone crushed his back with the sound of a breaking soda cracker. It went clear through him, pinning him to the stone. Then he fell into the water, the foamy green bubbles at the edge swallowing him. I watched him disappear and shook my fist at him, waving angry farewells as he floated to the bottom. Goodbye, goodbye! We will doubtless meet again in another world; you will not forget me, Crab. You will remember me forever and forever as your conqueror!

Killing them with stones was too tough. The stones were so sharp they cut my fingers when I heaved them. I washed the blood and slime off my hands and made my way to the edge again. Then I climbed onto the bridge and walked down the street to a ship chandler's shop three blocks away, where they sold guns and ammunition.

I told the white-faced clerk I wanted to buy an air gun. He showed me a high powered one and I laid the money down and bought it without questions. I spent the rest of the ten on ammunition – BB shot. I was anxious to get back to the battlefield so I told white face not to wrap the ammunition but give it to me like that. He thought that was strange and he looked me over while I scooped the cylinders off the counter and left the shop as fast as I could but not running. When I got outside I started to run, and then I sensed somebody was watching me and I looked around, and sure enough white face was standing in the door and peering after me through the hot afternoon air. I slowed down to a fast walk until I got to the corner and then I started to run again.

I shot crabs all that afternoon, until my shoulder hurt behind the gun and my eyes ached behind the gunsight. I was Dictator Bandini, Ironman of Crabland. This was another Blood Purge for the good of the Fatherland. They had tried to unseat me, those damned crabs, they had had the guts to try to foment a revolution, and I was getting revenge. To think of it! It infuriated me. These goddamned crabs had actually questioned the might of Superman Bandini! What had got into them to be so stupidly presumptuous? Well, they were going to get a lesson they would never forget. This was going to be the last revolution they'd ever attempt, by Christ. I gnashed my teeth when I thought of it – a nation of revolting crabs. What guts! God, I was mad.

I pumped shot until my shoulder ached and a blister rose on my trigger finger. I killed over five hundred and wounded twice as many. They were alive to the attack, insanely angry and frightened as the dead and wounded dropped from the ranks. The siege was on. They swarmed toward me. Others came out of the sea, still others from behind rocks, moving in vast numbers across the plain of stones toward death who sat on a high rock out of their reach.

I gathered some of the wounded into a pool and had a military conference and decided to courtmartial them. I drew them out of the pool one at a time, sitting each over the mouth of the rifle and pulling the trigger. There was one crab, bright colored and full of life who reminded me of a woman: doubtless a princess among the renegades, a brave crabess seriously injured, one of her legs shot away, an arm dangling pitifully. It broke my heart. I had another conference and decided that, due to the extreme urgency of the situation, there must not be any sexual discrimination. Even the princess had to die. It was unpleasant but it had to be done.

With a sad heart I knelt among the dead and dying and invoked God in a prayer, asking that he forgive me for this most beastly of the crimes of a superman – the execution of a woman. And yet, after all, duty was duty, the old order must be preserved, revolution must be stamped out, the regime had to go on, the renegades must perish. For some time I talked to the princess in private, formally extending to her the apologies of the Bandini government, and abiding by her last request – it was that I permit her to hear La Paloma – I whistled it to her with great feeling so that I was crying when finished. I raised my gun to her beautiful face and pulled the trigger. She died instantly, gloriously, a flaming mass of shell and yellowed blood.

Out of sheer reverence and admiration I ordered a stone placed where she had fallen, this ravishing heroine of one of the world's unforgettable revolutions, who had perished during the bloody June days of the Bandini government. History was written that day. I made the sign of the cross over the stone, kissed it reverently, even with a touch of passion, and held my head low in a momentary cessation of attack. It was an ironic moment. For in a flash I realized I had loved that woman. But, on Bandini! The attack began again. Shortly after, I shot down another woman. She was not so seriously injured, she suffered from shock. Taken prisoner, she offered herself to me body and soul. She begged me to spare her life. I laughed fiendishly. She was an exquisite creature, reddish and pink, and only a foregone conclusion as to my destiny made me accept her touching offer. There beneath the bridge in the darkness I ravaged her while she pleaded for mercy. Still laughing I took her out and shot her to pieces, apologizing for my brutality.

The slaughter finally stopped when my head ached from eye strain. Before leaving I took another last look around. The miniature cliffs were smeared with blood. It was a triumph, a very great victory for me. I went among the dead and spoke to them consolingly, for even though they were my enemies I was for all that a man of nobility and I respected them and admired them for the valiant struggle they had offered my legions. 'Death has arrived for you,' I said. 'Goodbye, dear enemies. You were brave in fighting and braver in death, and Führer Bandini has not forgotten. He overtly praises, even in death.' To others I said, 'Goodbye, thou coward. I spit on thee in disgust. Thy cowardice is repugnant to the Führer. He hateth cowards as he hateth the plague. He will not be reconciled. May the tides of the sea wash thy cowardly crime from the earth, thou knave.'

I climbed back to the road just as the six o'clock whistles were blowing, and started for home. There were some kids playing ball in an empty lot up the street, and I gave them the gun and ammunition in exchange for a pocket knife which one kid claimed was worth three dollars, but he didn't fool me, because I knew the knife wasn't worth more than fifty cents. I wanted to get rid of the gun though, so I made the deal. The kids figured I was a sap, but I let them.

Chapter Five

The apartment smelled of a steak cooking, and in the kitchen I heard them talking. Uncle Frank was there. I looked in and said hello and he said the same. He was sitting with my sister in the breakfast nook. My mother was at the stove. He was my mother's brother, a man of forty-five with grey temples and big eyes and little hairs growing out of his nostrils. He had fine teeth. He was gentle. He lived alone in a cottage across town. He was very fond of Mona and wanted to do things for her all the time but she rarely accepted. He always helped us with money, and after my father died he practically supported us for months. He wanted us to live with him, but I was against it because he could be bossy. When my father died he paid the funeral bill and even bought a stone for the grave, which was unusual because he never thought much of my father for a brother-in-law.

The kitchen overflowed with food. There was a bushel basket of groceries on the floor and the sink board was covered with vegetables. We had a big dinner. They did all the talking. I felt crabs all over me, and in my food. I thought of those living crabs under the bridge, groping in the darkness after their dead. There was that crab Goliath. He had been a great fighter. I remembered his wonderful personality; undoubtedly he had been the leader of his people. Now he was dead. I wondered if his father and mother searched for his body in the darkness and thought of the sadness of his lover, and whether she was dead too. Goliath had fought with slits of hatred in his eyes. It had taken a lot of BB shot to kill him. He was a great crab – the greatest of all contemporary crabs, including the Princess. The Crab People ought to build him a monument. But was he greater than me? No sir. I was his conqueror. To think of it! That mighty crab, hero of his people, and I was his conqueror. The Princess too – the most ravishing crab ever known – and I had killed her too. Those crabs wouldn't forget me for a long time to come. If they wrote history I would get a lot of space in their records. They might even call me the Black Killer of the Pacific Coast. Little crabs would hear about me from their forebears and I would strike terror in their memories. By fear I would rule, even though I was not present, changing the course of their existences. Some day I would become a legend in their world. And there might even be romantic female crabs fascinated by my cruel execution of the Princess. They would make me a god, and some of them would secretly worship me and have a passion for me.

Uncle Frank and my mother and Mona kept on talking. It looked like a plot. Once Mona glanced at me, and her glance said: We are ignoring you deliberately because we want you to be uncomfortable; furthermore, you'll have your hands full with Uncle Frank after the meal. Then Uncle Frank gave me a loose smile. I knew then it meant trouble.

After the dessert the women got up and left. My mother closed the door. The whole thing looked premeditated. Uncle Frank got down to business by lighting his pipe, pushing some dishes out of the way, and leaning toward me. He took the pipe out of his mouth and shook the stem under my nose.

He said, 'Look here, you little sonofabitch; I didn't know you were a thief too. I knew you were lazy, but by God I didn't know you were a thieving little thief.'

I said, 'I'm not a sonofabitch, either.'

'I talked to Romero,' he said. 'I know what you did.'

'I warn you,' I said. 'In no uncertain terms I warn you to desist from calling me a sonofabitch again.'

'You stole ten dollars from Romero.'

'Your presumption is colossal, unvaunted. I fail to see why you permit yourself the liberty of insulting me by calling me a sonofabitch.'

He said, 'Stealing from your employer! That's a fine thing.'

'I tell you again, and with utmost candor that, despite your seniority and our blood-relationship, I positively forbid you to use such opprobious names as sonofabitch in reference to me.'

'A loafer and a thief for a nephew! It's disgusting.'

'Please be advised, my dear uncle, that since you choose to vilify me with sonofabitch I have no alternative but to point out the blood-fact of your own scurrilousness. In short, if I am a sonofabitch it so happens that you're the brother of a bitch. Laugh that off.'

'Romero could've had you arrested. I'm sorry he didn't.'

'Romero is a monster, a gigantic fraud, a looming lug. His charges of piracy amuse me. I fail to be moved by his sterile accusations. But I must remind you once more to curb the glibness of your obscenities. I am not in the habit of being insulted, even by relatives.'

He said, 'Shut up, you little fool! I'm talking about something else. What'll you do now?'

'There are myriad possibilities.'

He sneered, 'Myriad possibilities! That's a good one! What the devil are you talking about? Myriad possibilities!'

I took some puffs on my cigarette and said, 'I presume I'll embark on my literary career now that I have had done with the Romero breed of proletarian.'

'Your *what?*'

'My literary plans. My prose. I shall continue with my literary efforts. I'm a writer, you know.'

'A writer! Since when did you become a writer? This is a new one. Go on, I've never heard this one before.'

I told him, 'The writing instinct has always lain dormant in me. Now it is in the process of metamorphosis. The era of transition has passed. I am on the threshold of expression.'

He said, 'Balls.'

I took the new notebook out of my pocket and flipped the pages with my thumb. I flipped them so fast he couldn't read anything but he could see some writing in it. 'These are notes,' I said. 'Atmospheric notes. I'm writing a Socratic symposium on Los Angeles Harbor since the days of the Spanish Conquest.'

'Let's see them,' he said.

'Nothing doing. Not until after publication.'

'After publication! What talk!'

I put the notebook back in my pocket. It smelled of crabs.

'Why don't you buck up and be a man?' he said. 'It would make your father happy up there.'

'Up where?' I said.

'In afterlife.'

I'd been waiting for that.

'There is no afterlife,' I said. 'The celestial hypothesis is sheer propaganda formulated by the haves to delude the have-nots. I dispute the immortal soul. It is the persistent delusion of an hoodwinked mankind. I reject in no uncertain terms the hypothesis of God. Religion is the opium of the people. The churches should be converted to hospitals and public works. All we are or ever hope to be we owe to the devil and his bootleg apples. There are 78,000 contradictions in the bible. Is it God's word? No! I reject God! I denounce him with savage and relentless imprecations! I accept the universe godless. I am a monist!'

'You're crazy,' he said. 'You're a maniac.'

'You don't understand me,' I smiled. 'But that's all right. I anticipate misunderstanding; nay, I look forward to the worst persecutions along the way. It's quite all right.'

He emptied his pipe and shook his finger under my nose. 'The thing for you to do is stop reading all these damn books, stop stealing, make a man out of yourself, and go to work.'

I smashed out my cigarette. 'Books!' I said. 'And what do *you* know about books! You! An ignoramus, a Boobus Americanus, a donkey, a clod-hopping poltroon with no more sense than a polecat.'

He kept still and filled his pipe. I didn't say anything because it was his turn. He studied me awhile while he thought of something.

'I've got a job for you,' he said.

'What doing?'

'I don't know yet. I'll see.'

'It has to fit my talents. Don't forget that I'm a writer. I've metamorphosed.'

'I don't care what's happened to you. You're going to work. Maybe the fish canneries.'

'I don't know anything about fish canneries.'

'Good,' he said. 'The less you know the better. All it takes is a strong back and a weak mind. You've got both.'

'The job doesn't interest me,' I told him. 'I'd rather write prose.'

'Prose – what's prose?'

'You're a bourgeois Babbitt. You'll never know good prose as long as you live.'

'I ought to knock your block off.'

'Try it.'

'You little bastard.'

'You American boor.'

He got up and left the table with his eyes flashing. Then he went into the next room and talked to Mother and Mona, telling them we had had an understanding and from now on I was turning over a new leaf. He gave them some money and told my mother not to worry about anything. I went to the door and nodded goodnight when he left. My mother and Mona looked at my eyes. They thought I'd come out of the kitchen with tears streaming down my face. My mother put her hands on my shoulders. She was sweet and soothing, thinking Uncle Frank had made me feel miserable.

'He hurt your feelings,' she said. 'Didn't he, my poor boy.'

I pulled her arms off.

'Who?' I said. 'That cretin? Hell, no!'

'You look like you've been crying.'

I walked into the bedroom and looked at my eyes in the mirror. They were as dry as ever. My mother followed and started to pat them with her handkerchief. I thought, what the heck.

'May I ask what you're doing?' I said.

'You poor boy! It's all right. You're embarrassed. I understand. Mother understands everything.'

'But I'm *not* crying!'

She was disappointed and turned away.

Chapter Six

It's morning, time to get up, so get up, Arturo, and look for a job. Get out there and look for what you'll never find. You're a thief and you're a crab-killer and a lover of women in clothes closets. *You'll* never find a job!

Every morning I got up feeling like that. Now I've got to find a job, damn it to hell. I ate breakfast, put a book under my arm, pencils in my pocket, and started out. Down the stairs I went, down the street, sometimes hot and sometimes cold, sometimes foggy and sometimes clear. It never mattered, with a book under my arm, looking for a job.

What job, Arturo? Ho ho! A job for you? Think of what you are, my boy! A crab-killer. A thief. You look at naked women in clothes closets. And *you* expect to get a job! How funny! But there he goes, the idiot, with a big book. Where the devil are you going, Arturo? Why do you go up this street and not that? Why go east – why not go west? Answer me, you thief! Who'll give you a job, you swine – who? But there's a park across town, Arturo. It's called Banning Park. There are a lot of beautiful eucalyptus trees in it, and green lawns. What a place to read! Go there, Arturo. Read Nietzsche. Read Schopenhauer. Get into the company of the mighty. A job? fooey! Go sit under an eucalyptus tree reading a book looking for a job.

And still a few times I did look for a job. There was the fifteen cents store. For a long time I stood out in front looking at a pile of peanut brittle in the window. Then I walked in.

'The manager, please.'

The girl said, 'He's downstairs.'

I knew him. His name was Tracey. I walked down the hard stairs, wondering why they were so hard, and at the bottom I saw Mr Tracey. He was fixing his yellow tie at a mirror. A nice man, that Mr Tracey. Admirable taste. A beautiful tie, white shoes, blue shirt. A fine man, a privilege to work for a man like that. He had something; he had *élan vital*. Ah, Bergson! Another great writer was Bergson.

'Hello, Mr Tracey.'

'Eh, what do you want?'

'I was going to ask you –'

'We have application blanks for that. But it won't do any good. We're all filled up.'

I went back up the hard stairs. What curious stairs! So hard, so precise! Possibly a new invention in stair-making. Ah, mankind! What'll you think of next! Progress. I believe in the reality of Progress. That Tracey. That lowdown, filthy, no-good sonofabitch! Him and his stupid yellow necktie standing in front of a mirror like a goddamn ape: that bourgeois Babbitt scoundrel. A yellow necktie! Imagine it. Oh, he didn't fool me. I knew a thing or two about that fellow. One night I was there, down at the harbor, and I saw him. I hadn't said anything, but I guess I'd seen him down there in his car, potbellied as a pig, with a girl at his side. I saw his fat teeth in the moonlight. He sat there under his belly, a thirty dollar a week moron of a fat Babbitt bastard with a hanging gut and a girl at his side, a slut, a bitch, a whore beside him, a scummy female. Between his fat fingers he held the girl's hand. He seemed ardent in his piggish way, that fat bastard, that stinking, nauseating, thirty dollar a week moron of a rat, with his fat teeth looming in the moonlight, his big pouch squashed against the steering wheel, his dirty eyes fat and ardent with fat ideas of a fat love affair. He wasn't fooling me; he could never fool me. He might fool that girl, but not Arturo Bandini, and under no circumstances would Arturo Bandini ever consent to work for him. Some day there would be a reckoning. He might plead, with his yellow necktie dragging in the dust, he might plead with Arturo Bandini, begging the great Arturo to accept a job, and Arturo Bandini would proudly kick him in the belly and watch him writhe in the dust. He'd pay, he'd pay!

I went out to the Ford plant. And why not? Ford needs men. Bandini at the Ford Motor Company. A week in one department, three weeks in another, a month in another, six months in another. Two years, and I would be director in chief of the Western Division.

The pavement wound through white sand, a new road heavy with monoxide gas. In the sand were brown weeds and grasshoppers. Bits of sea shell sparkled through the weeds. It was man-made land, flat and in disorder, shacks unpainted, piles of lumber, piles of tin cans, oil derricks and hot dog stands, fruit stands and old men on all sides of the road selling popcorn. Overhead the heavy telephone wires gave off a humming sound whenever there was a lull in the traffic noise. Out of the muddy channel bed came the rich stench of oil and scum and strange cargo.

I walked along the road with others. They flagged rides with their thumbs. They were beggars with jerking thumbs and pitiful smiles, begging crumbs-on-wheels. No pride. But not I – not Arturo Bandini, with his mighty legs. Not for him this mooching. Let them pass me by! Let them go ninety miles an hour and fill my nose with their exhausts. Some day it would all be different. You will pay for this, all of you, every driver along this road. I will not ride in your automobiles even if you get out and plead with me, and offer me the car to keep as my own, free and without further obligation. I will die on the road first. But my time will come, and then you will see my name in the sky. Then you shall see, every one of you! I am not waving like the others, with a crooked thumb, so don't stop. Never! But you'll pay, nevertheless.

They wouldn't give me a ride. He killed crabs, that fellow up there ahead. Why give him a ride? He loves paper ladies in clothes closets. Think of it! So don't give him a ride, that Frankenstein, that toad in the road, that black spider, snake, dog, rat, fool, monster, idiot. They wouldn't give me a ride; all right – so what! And see if I care! To hell with all of you! It suits me fine. I love to walk on these God-given legs, and by God I'll walk. Like Nietzsche. Like Kant. Immanuel Kant. What do you know about Immanuel Kant? You fools in your V-8's and Chevrolets!

When I got to the plant I stood among the others. They moved about in a thick clot before a green platform. The tight faces, the cold faces. Then a man came out. No work today, fellows. And yet there was a job or two, if you could paint, if you knew about transmissions, if you had experience, if you had worked in the Detroit plant.

But there was no work for Arturo Bandini. I saw it at a glance, and so I wouldn't let them refuse me. I was amused. This spectacle, this scene of men before a platform amused me. I'm here for a special reason, sir: a confidential mission, if I may say so, merely checking conditions for my report. The president of the United States of America sent me. Franklin Delano Roosevelt, he sent me. Frank and I – we're like that! Let me know the state of things on the Pacific Coast, Arturo; send me firsthand facts and figures; let me know in your own words what the masses are thinking out there.

And so I was a spectator. Life is a stage. Here is drama, Franklin old Kid, old Pal, old Sock; here is stark drama in the hearts of men. I'll notify the White House immediately. A telegram in code for Franklin. Frank: unrest on the Pacific Coast. Advise send twenty thousand men and guns. Population in terror. Perilous situation. Ford plant in ruins. Shall take charge personally. My word is law here. Your old buddy, Arturo.

There was an old man leaning against the wall. His nose was running clear to the tip of his chin, but he was blissful and didn't know it. It amused me. Very amusing, this old man. I'll have to make a note of this for Franklin; he loves anecdotes. Dear Frank: you'd have died if you'd have seen this old man! How Franklin will love this, chuckling as he repeats it to members of his cabinet. Say boys, did you hear the latest from my pal Arturo out on the Pacific Coast? I strolled up and down, a student of mankind, a philosopher, past the old man with the riotous nose. The philosopher out of the West contemplates the human scene.

The old man smiled his way and I smiled mine. I looked at him and he looked at me. Smile. Evidently he didn't know who I was. No doubt he confused me with the rest of the herd. Very amusing this, great sport to travel incognito. Two philosophers smiling wistfully at one another over the fate of man. He was genuinely amused, his old nose running, his blue eyes twinkling with quiet laughter. He wore blue overalls that covered him completely. Around his waist was a belt that had no purpose whatever, a useless appendage, merely a belt supporting nothing, not even his belly, for he was thin. Possibly a whim of his, something to make him laugh when he dressed in the morning.

His face beamed with a larger smile, inviting me to come forward and deliver an opinion if I liked; we were kindred souls, he and I, and no doubt he saw through my disguise and recognized a person of depth and importance, one who stood out from the herd.

'Not much today,' I said. 'The situation, as I see it, grows more acute daily.'

He shook his head with delight, his old nose running blissfully, a Plato with a cold. A very old man, maybe eighty, with false teeth, skin like old shoes, a meaningless belt and a philosophic smile. The dark mass of men moved around us.

'Sheep!' I said. 'Alas, they are sheep! Victims of Comstockery and the American system, bastard slaves of the Robber Barons. Slaves, I tell you! I wouldn't take a job at this plant if it was offered me on a golden platter! Work for this system and lose your soul. No thanks. And what does it profit a man if he gain the whole world and lose his own soul?'

He nodded, smiled, agreed, nodded for more. I warmed up. My favorite subject. Labor conditions in the machine age, a topic for a future work.

'Sheep, I tell you! A lot of gutless sheep!'

His eyes brightened. He brought out a pipe and lit it. The

pipe stunk. When he took it from his mouth the goo from his nose strung after it. He wiped it off with his thumb and wiped his thumb against his leg. He didn't bother to wipe his nose. No time for that when Bandini speaks.

'It amuses me,' I said. 'The spectacle is priceless. Sheep getting their souls sheared. A Rabelaisian spectacle. I have to laugh.' And I laughed until there wasn't anymore. He did too, slapping his thighs and shrieking to a high note until his eyes were filled with tears. Here was a man after my own heart, a man of universal humors, no doubt a well-read man despite his overalls and useless belt. From his pocket he took a pad and pencil and wrote on the pad. Now I knew: he was a writer too, of course! The secret was out. He finished writing and handed me the note.

It read: Please write it down. I am stone deaf.

No, there was no work for Arturo Bandini. I left feeling better, glad of it. I walked back wishing I had an aeroplane, a million dollars, wishing the sea shells were diamonds. I will go to the park. I am not yet a sheep. Read Nietzsche. Be a superman. *Thus Spake Zarathustra.* Oh that Nietzsche! Don't be a sheep, Bandini. Preserve the sanctity of your mind. Go to the park and read the master under the eucalyptus trees.

Chapter Seven

One morning I awoke with an idea. A fine idea, big as a house. My greatest idea ever, a masterpiece. I would find a job as a night clerk in a hotel – that was the idea. This would give me a chance to read and work at the same time. I leaped out of bed, swallowed breakfast and took the stairs six at a time. On the sidewalk I stood a moment and mulled over my idea. The sun scorched the street, burning my eyes to wakefulness. Strange. Now I was wide awake and the idea didn't seem so good, one of those which comes in half-sleep. A dream, a mere dream, a triviality. I couldn't get a job as a night clerk in this harbor town for the simple reason that no hotel in this harbor town used night clerks. A mathematical deduction – simple enough. I went back up the stairs to the apartment and sat down.

'Why did you run like that?' my mother asked.

'To get exercise. For my legs.'

The days came with fog. The nights were nights and nothing else. The days didn't change from one to the other, the golden sun blasting away and then dying out. I was always alone. It was hard to remember such monotony. The days would not move. They stood like grey stones. Time passed slowly. Two months crawled by.

*   *   *

It was always the park. I read a hundred books. There was Nietzsche and Schopenhauer and Kant and Spengler and Strachey and others. Oh Spengler! What a book! What weight! Like the Los Angeles Telephone Directory. Day after day I read it, never understanding it, never caring either, but reading it because I liked one growling word after another marching across pages with somber mysterious rumblings. And Schopenhauer! What a writer! For days I read him and read him, remembering a bit here and a bit there. And such things about women! I agreed. Exactly my own feelings on the matter. Ah man, what a writer!

Once I was reading in the park. I lay on the lawn. There were little black ants among the blades of grass. They looked at me, crawling over the pages, some wondering what I was doing, others not interested and passing by. They crawled up my leg, baffled in a jungle of brown hairs, and I lifted my trousers and killed them with my thumb. They did their best to escape, diving frantically in and out of the brambles, sometimes pausing as if to trick me by their immobility, but never, for all their trickery, did they escape the menace of my thumb. What stupid ants! Bourgeois ants! That they should try to dupe one whose mind lived on the meat of Spengler and Schopenhauer and the great ones! It was their doom – the Decline of Ant Civilization. And so I read and killed ants.

It was a book called *Jews Without Money*. What a book that was! What a mother in that book! I looked from the woman on the pages and there before me on the lawn in crazy old shoes was a woman with a basket in her arms.

She was a hunchback with a sweet smile. She smiled sweetly at anything; she couldn't help it; the trees, me, the grass, anything. The basket pulled her down, dragging her toward the ground. She was such a tiny woman, with a hurt face, as if slapped forever. She wore a funny old hat, an absurd hat, a maddening hat, a hat to make me cry, a hat with faded red berries on the brim. And there she was, smiling at everything, struggling across the carpet with a heavy basket containing Lord knew what, wearing a plumed hat with red berries.

I got up. It was so mysterious. There I was, like magic, standing up, my two feet on the ground, my eyes drenched.

I said, 'Let me help.'

She smiled again and gave me the basket. We began to walk. She led the way. Beyond the trees it was stifling. And she smiled. It was so sweet it nearly tore my head off. She talked, she told me things I never remembered. It didn't matter. In a dream she held me, in a dream I followed under the blinding sun. For blocks we went forward. I hoped it would never end. Always she talked in a low voice made of human music. What words! What she said! I remembered nothing. I was only happy. But in my heart I was dying. It should have been so. We stepped from so many curbs, I wondered why she did not sit upon one and hold my head while I drifted away. It was the chance that never came again.

That old woman with the bent back! Old woman, I feel so joyfully your pain. Ask me a favor, you old woman you! Anything. To die is easy. Make it that. To cry is easy, lift your skirt and let me cry and let my tears wash your feet to let you know I know what life has been for you, because my back is bent too, but my heart is whole, my tears are delicious, my love is yours, to give you joy where God has failed. To die is so easy and you may have my life if you wish it, you old woman, you hurt me so, you did, I will do anything for you, to die for you, the blood of my eighteen years flowing in the gutters of Wilmington and down to the sea for you, for you that you might find such joy as is now mine and stand erect without the horror of that twist.

I left the old woman at her door.

The trees shimmered. The clouds laughed. The blue sky took me up. Where am I? Is this Wilmington, California? Haven't I been here before? A melody moved my feet. The air soared with Arturo in it, puffing him in and out and making him something and nothing. My heart laughed and laughed. Goodbye to Nietzsche and Schopenhauer and all of you, you fools, I am much greater than all of you! Through my veins ran music of blood. Would it last? It could not last. I must hurry. But where? And I ran toward home. Now I am home. I left the book in the park. To hell with it. No more books for me. I kissed my mother. I clung to her passionately. On my knees I fell at her feet to kiss her feet and cling to her ankles until it must have hurt her and amazed her that it was I.

'Forgive me,' I said. 'Forgive me, forgive me.'

'You?' she said. 'Certainly. But why?'

Ach! What a foolish woman! How did I know why? Ach! What a mother. The strangeness was gone. I got to my feet. I felt like a fool. I blushed in a bath of cold blood. What was this? I didn't know. The chair. I found it at the end of the room and sat down. My hands. They were in the way; stupid hands! Damned hands! I did something with them, got them out of the way somewhere. My breath. It hissed for horror and fear of something. My heart. It no longer tore at my chest, but dwindled, crawling deep into the darkness within me. My mother. She watched me in a panic, afraid to speak, thinking me mad.

'What is it? Arturo! What's the matter?'
'None of your business.'
'Shall I get a doctor?'
'Never.'
'You act so strange. Are you hurt?'
'Don't talk to me. I'm thinking.'
'But what is it?'
'You wouldn't know. You're a woman.'

Chapter Eight

The days went on. A week passed. Miss Hopkins was in the library every afternoon, floating on white legs in the folds of her loose dresses in an atmosphere of books and cool thoughts. I watched. I was like a hawk. Nothing she did escaped me.

Then came a great day. What a day that was!

I was watching her from the shadows of the dark shelves. She held a book, standing behind her desk like a soldier, shoulders back, reading the book, her face so serious and so soft, her grey eyes following the beaten path of line under line. My eyes – they were so eager and so hungry they startled her. With a suddenness she looked up and her face was white with the shock of something dreadful near her. I saw her wet her lips, and then I turned away. In a while I looked again. It was like magic. Again she twitched, glanced around uneasily, put her long fingers to her throat, sighed, and commenced to read. A few moments, and once more I looked. She still held that book. But what was that book? I didn't know, but I must have it for my eyes to follow the path her eyes had followed before me.

Outside it was the evening, the sun spangling the floor in gold. With white legs as silent as ghosts she crossed the library to the windows and raised the shades. In her right hand swung that book, brushing against her dress as she walked, in her very hands, the immortal white hands of Miss Hopkins, pressed against the warm white softness of her clinging fingers.

What a book! I've got to have that book! Lord, I wanted it, to hold it, to kiss it, to crush it to my chest, that book fresh from her fingers, the very imprint of her warm fingers still upon it perhaps. Who knows? Perhaps she perspires through her fingers as she reads it. Wonderful! Then her imprint is surely upon it. I must have it. I will wait forever for it. And so I waited until seven o'clock, seeing how she held the book, the exact position of her wonderful fingers that were so slim and white, just off the back binding, no more than an inch from the bottom, the perfume of her perhaps entering those very pages and perfuming them for me.

Until at last she was finished with it. She carried it to the shelves and slipped it into a slot marked biography. I ambled by, seeking a book to read, something to stimulate my mind, something in the line of biography today, the life of some great figure, to inspire me, to make my life sublime.

Ha, there it was! The most beautiful book I ever saw, larger than the others on that shelf, a book among books, the very queen of biography, the princess of literature – that book with the blue binding. *Catherine of Aragon*. So that was it! A queen reads of another queen – most natural. And her grey eyes had followed the path of those lines – then so would mine.

I must have it – but not today. Tomorrow I will come, tomorrow. Then the other librarian, that fat and ugly one, will be on duty. Then it shall be mine, all mine. And so, until the next day, I hid the book behind others so no one could take it away while I was gone.

I was there early next day – at nine o'clock to the

second. Catherine of Aragon: wonderful woman, the Queen of England, the bedmate of Henry VIII – that much I knew already. Undoubtedly Miss Hopkins had read of the intimacy of Catherine and Henry in this book. Those sections dealing with love – did they delight Miss Hopkins? Did shivers run down her back? Did she breathe hard, her bosom swelling, and a mysterious tingling enter her fingers? Yes, and who knew? Perhaps she even screamed for joy and felt a mysterious stirring somewhere within her, the call of womanhood. Yes indeed, no doubt about it at all. And wonderful too. A thing of great beauty, a thought to ponder over. And so I got the book, and there it was, in my own two hands. To think of it! Yesterday she had held it with her fingers warm and close, and today it was mine. Marvelous. An act of destiny. A miracle of succession. When we married I would tell Miss Hopkins about it. We would be lying stark naked in bed and I would kiss her on the lips and laugh softly and triumphantly and tell her that the real beginning of my love was on a day I saw her reading a certain book. And I would laugh again, my white teeth flashing, my dark romantic eyes aglow as I told her at last the real truth of my provocative and eternal love. Then she would crush herself to me, her beautiful white breasts full against me, and tears would stream down her face as I carried her away on wave after wave of ecstasy. What a day!

I held the book close to my eyes, searching for some trace of white fingers no more than an inch from the bottom. There were finger-prints all right. No matter if they belonged to so many others, they nevertheless belonged to Miss Hopkins alone. Walking toward the park I kissed them, and I kissed them so much that finally they were gone altogether, and only a blue wet spot remained on the book, while on my mouth I tasted the sweet taste of blue dye. In the park I found my favorite spot and began to read.

Near the bridge it was, and I made a shrine from twigs and blades of grass. It was the throne of Miss Hopkins. Ah, if she but knew it! But at that moment she was at home in Los Angeles, far away from the scene of her devotions, and not thinking of them at all.

I crawled on all fours to the place at the edge of the lily pond where roamed bugs and crickets, and I caught a cricket. A black cricket, fat and well-built, with electric energy in his body. And there he lay in my hand, that cricket, and he was I, the cricket that was, he was I, Arturo Bandini, black and undeserving of the fair white princess, and I lay on my belly and watched him crawl over the places her sacred white fingers had touched, he too enjoying as he passed the sweet taste of blue dye. Then he tried to escape. With a jump he was on his way. I was forced to break his legs. There was absolutely no alternative.

I said to him, 'Bandini, I am sorry. But duty compels me. The Queen wishes it – the beloved Queen.'

Now he crawled painfully, in wonder at what had taken place. Oh fair white Miss Hopkins, observe! Oh queen of all the heavens and the earth. Observe! I crawl at thy feet, a mere black cricket, a scoundrel, unworthy to be called human. Here I lie with broken legs, a paltry black cricket, ready to die for thee; aye, already nearing death. Ah! Reduce me to ashes! Give me a new form! Make me a man! Snuff out my life for the glory of love everlasting and the loveliness of your white legs!

And I killed the black cricket, crushing him to death after

proper farewells between the pages of *Catherine of Aragon*, his poor miserable unworthy black body crackling and popping in ecstasy and love there at that sacred little shrine of Miss Hopkins.

And behold! A miracle: out of death came life everlasting. The resurrection of life. The cricket was no more, but the power of love had found its way, and I was again myself and no longer a cricket, I was Arturo Bandini, and the elm tree yonder was Miss Hopkins, and I got to my knees and put my arms around the tree, kissing it for love everlasting, tearing the bark with my teeth and spitting it on the lawn.

I turned around and bowed to the bushes at the edge of the pond. They applauded gloriously, swaying together, hissing their delight and satisfaction at the scene, even demanding that I carry Miss Hopkins away on my shoulders. This I refused to do, and with sly winks and suggestive movements I told them why, because the fair white queen didn't want to be carried, if you please, she wanted instead to be laid flat, and at this they all laughed and thought me the greatest lover and hero to ever visit their fair country.

'You understand, fellows. We prefer to be alone, the queen and I. There is much unfinished business between us – if you get what I mean.'

Laughter, and wild applauding from the bushes.

Chapter Nine

One night my uncle dropped in. He gave my mother some money. He could only stay a moment. He said he had good news for me. I wanted to know what he meant. A job, he said. At last he had found me a job. I told him this was not good news, necessarily, because I didn't know what kind of a job he got me. To this he told me to shut up, and then he told me about the job.

He said, 'Take this down and tell him I sent you.'

He handed me the note he had already written.

'I talked to him today,' he said. 'Everything is set. Do what you're told, keep your fool mouth shut, and he'll keep you on steady.'

'He ought to,' I said. 'Any paranoiac can do cannery work.'

'We'll see about that,' my uncle said.

Next morning I took the bus for the harbor. It was only seven blocks from our house, but since I was going to work I thought it best not to tire myself by walking too much. The Soyo Fish Company bulged from the channel like a black dead whale. Steam spouted from pipes and windows.

At the front office sat a girl. This was a strange office. At a desk with no papers or pencils upon it, sat this girl. She was an ugly girl with a hooknose who wore glasses and a yellow skirt. She sat at the desk doing absolutely nothing, no telephone, not even a pencil before her.

'Hello,' I said.

'That's not necessary,' she said. 'Who do you want?'

I told her I wanted to see a man named Shorty Naylor. I had a note for him. She wanted to know what the note was about. I gave it to her and she read it. 'For pity's sakes,' she said. Then she told me to wait a minute. She got up and went out. At the door she turned around and said, 'Don't touch anything, please.' I told her I wouldn't. But when I looked about I saw nothing to touch. In the corner on the floor was a full tin of sardines, unopened. It was all I could see in the room, except for the desk and chair. She's a maniac, I thought; she's dementia praecox.

As I waited I could feel something. A stench in the air all at once began to suck at my stomach. It pulled my stomach toward my throat. Leaning back, I felt the sucking. I began to feel afraid. It was like an elevator going down too fast.

Then the girl returned. She was alone. But no – she wasn't alone. Behind her, and unseen until she stepped out of the way, was a little man. This man was Shorty Naylor. He was much smaller than I was. He was very thin. His collarbones stuck out. He had no teeth worth mentioning in his mouth, only one or two which were worse than nothing. His eyes were like aged oysters on a sheet of newspaper. Tobacco juice caked the corners of his mouth like dry chocolate. His was the look of a rat in waiting. It seemed he had never been out in the sun, his face was so grey. He didn't look at my face but at my belly. I wondered what he saw there. I looked down. There was nothing, merely a belly, no larger than ever and not worth observation. He took the note from my hands. His fingernails were gnawed to stumps. He read the note bitterly, much annoyed, crushed it, and stuck it in his pocket.

'The pay is twenty-five cents an hour,' he said.

'That's preposterous and nefarious.'

'Anyway, that's what it is.'

The girl was sitting on the desk watching us. She was smiling at Shorty. It was as if there was some joke. I couldn't see anything funny. I lifted my shoulders. Shorty was ready to go back through the door from which he had come.

'The pay is of little consequence,' I said. 'The facts in the case make the matter different. I am a writer. I interpret the American scene. My purpose here is not the gathering of money but the gathering of material for my forthcoming book on California fisheries. My income of course is much larger than what I shall make here. But that, I suppose, is a matter of no great consequence at the moment, none at all.'

'No,' he said. 'The pay is twenty-five cents an hour.'

'It doesn't matter. Five cents or twenty-five. Under the circumstances, it doesn't matter in the least. Not at all. I am, as I say, a writer. I interpret the American scene. I am here to gather material for my new work.'

'Oh for Christ's sake!' the girl said, turning her back. 'For the love of God get him out of here.'

'I don't like Americans in my crew,' Shorty said. 'They don't work hard like the other boys.'

'Ah,' I said. 'That's where you're wrong, sir. My patriotism is universal. I swear allegiance to no flag.'

'Jesus,' the girl said.

But she was ugly. Nothing she could possibly say would ever disturb me. She was too ugly.

'Americans can's stand the pace,' Shorty said. 'Soon as they get a bellyful they quit.'

'Interesting, Mr Naylor.' I folded my arms and settled back on my heels. 'Extremely interesting what you say there. A fascinating sociological aspect of the canning situation. My book will go into that with great detail and footnotes. I'll quote you there. Yes, indeed.'

The girl said something unprintable. Shorty scraped a bit of pocket sediment from a plug of tobacco and bit off a hunk. It was a large bite, filling his mouth. He was scarcely listening to me, I could tell by the scrupulous way he chewed the tobacco. The girl had seated herself at the desk, her hands folded before her. We both turned and looked at one another. She put her fingers to her nose and pressed them. But the gesture didn't disturb me. She was far too ugly.

'Do you want the job?' Shorty said.

'Yes, under the circumstances. Yes.'

'Remember: the work is hard, and don't expect no favors from me either. If it wasn't for your uncle I wouldn't hire you, but that's as far as it goes. I don't like you Americans. You're lazy. When you get tired you quit. You fool around too much.'

'I agree with you perfectly, Mr Naylor. I agree with you thoroughly. Laziness, if I may be permitted to make an aside, laziness is the outstanding characteristic of the American scene. Do you follow me?'

'You don't have to call me Mister. Call me Shorty. That's my name.'

'Certainly, sir! But by all means, certainly! And Shorty, I would say, is a most colourful sobriquet − a typical Americanism. We writers are constantly coming upon it.'

This failed to please him or impress him. His lip curled. At the desk the girl was mumbling. 'Don't call me sir, neither,' Shorty said. 'I don't like none of that high-toned crap.'

'Take him out of here,' the girl said.

But I was not in the least disturbed by the remarks from one so ugly. It amused me. What an ugly face she had! It was too amusing for words. I laughed and patted Shorty on the back. I was short, but I towered over this small man. I felt great – like a giant.

'Very amusing, Shorty. I love your native sense of humor. Very amusing. Very amusing indeed.' And I laughed again. 'Very amusing. Ho, ho, ho. How very amusing.'

'I don't see nothing funny,' he said.

'But it is! If you follow me.'

'The hell with it. You follow me.'

'Oh, I follow you, all right. I follow.'

'No,' he said. 'I mean, you follow me now. I'll put you in the labeling crew.'

As we walked through the back door the girl turned to watch us go. 'And stay out of here!' she said. But I paid no attention at all. She was far too ugly.

We were inside the cannery works. The corrugated iron building was like a dark hot dungeon. Water dripped from the girders. Lumps of brown and white steam hung bloated in the air. The green floor was slippery from fish oil. We walked across a long room where Mexican and Japanese women stood before tables gutting mackerel with fish knives. The women were wrapped in heavy oil-skins, their feet cased in rubber boots ankle-deep in fish guts.

The stench was too much. All at once I was sick like the sickness from hot water and mustard. Another ten steps across the room and I felt it coming up, my breakfast, and I bent over to let it go. My insides rushed out in a chunk. Shorty laughed. He pounded my back and roared. Then the others started. The boss was laughing at something, and so did they. I hated it. The women looked up from their work to see, and they laughed. What fun! On company time, too! See the boss laughing! Something must be taking place. Then we will laugh too. Work was stopped in the cutting room. Everybody was laughing. Everybody but Arturo Bandini.

Arturo Bandini was not laughing. He was puking his guts out on the floor. I hated every one of them, and I vowed revenge, staggering away, wanting to be out of sight somewhere. Shorty took me by the arm and led me toward another door. I leaned against the wall and got my breath. But the stench charged again. The walls spun, the women laughed, and Shorty laughed, and Arturo Bandini the great writer was heaving again. How he heaved! The women would go home tonight and talk about it at their houses. That new fellow! You should have seen him! And I hated them and even stopped heaving for a moment to pause and delight over the fact that this was the greatest hatred of all my life.

'Feel better?' Shorty said.

'Of course,' I said. 'It was nothing. The idiosyncrasies of an artistic stomach. A mere nothing. Something I ate, if you will.'

'That's right!'

We walked into the room beyond. The women were still laughing on company time. At the door Shorty Naylor turned around and put a scowl on his face. Nothing more. He merely scowled. All the women stopped laughing. The show was over. They went back to work.

Now we were in the room where the cans were labeled. The crew was made up of Mexican and Filipino boys. They fed the machines from flat conveyor lines. Twenty or more of them, my age and more, all of them pausing to see who I was and realizing that a new man was about to go to work.

'You stand and watch,' Shorty said. 'Pitch in when you see how they do it.'

'It looks very simple,' I said. 'I'm ready right now.'

'No. Wait a few minutes.'

And he left.

I stood watching. This was very simple. But my stomach would have nothing to do with it. In a moment I was letting go again. Again the laughter. But these boys weren't like the women. They really thought it was funny to see Arturo Bandini having such a time of it.

That first morning had no beginning and no end. Between vomitings I stood at the can dump and convulsed. And I told them who I was. Arturo Bandini, the writer. Haven't you heard of me? You will! Don't worry. You will! My book on California fisheries. It is going to be the standard work on the subject. I spoke fast, between vomitings.

'I'm not here permanently. I'm gathering material for a book on California Fisheries. I'm Bandini, the writer. This isn't essential, this job. I may give my wages to charity: the Salvation Army.'

And I heaved again. Now there was nothing in my stomach except that which never came out. I bent over and choked, a famous writer with my arms around my waist, squirming and choking. But nothing would come. Somebody stopped laughing long enough to yell that I should drink water. Hey writer! Dreenk water! So I found a hydrant and drank water.

It came out in a stream while I raced for the door. And they laughed. Oh that writer! What a writer he was! See him write!

'You get over it,' they laughed.

'Go home,' they said. 'Go write book. You writer. You too good for feesh cannery. Go home and write book about puke.'

Shrieks of laughter.

I walked outside and stretched out on a pile of fish nets hot in the sun between two buildings away from the main road that skirted the channel. Over the hum from the machinery I could hear them laughing. I didn't care, not all. I felt like sleeping. But the fish nets were bad, rich with the smell of mackerel and salt. In a moment the flies discovered me. That made it worse. Soon all the flies in Los Angeles Harbor had got news of men. I crawled off the nets to a patch of sand. It was wonderful. I stretched my arms and let my fingers find cool spots in the sand. Nothing ever felt so good. Even little particles of sand my breath blew were sweet in my nose and mouth. A tiny sandbug stopped on a hill to investigate the commotion. Ordinarily I would have killed him without hesitating. He looked into my eyes, paused, and came forward. He began to climb my chin.

'Go ahead,' I said. 'I don't mind. You can go into my mouth if you want to.'

He passed my chin and I felt him tickle my lips. I had to look at him cross-eyed to see him.

'Come ahead,' I said. 'I'm not going to hurt you. This is a holiday.'

He climbed toward my nostrils. Then I went to sleep.

A whistle woke me up. It was twelve o'clock, noon. The

workers filed out of the buildings, Mexicans, filipinos, and Japanese. The Japanese were too busy to look anywhere other than straight ahead. They hurried by. But the Mexicans and Filipinos saw me stretched out, and they laughed again, for there he was, that great writer, all flattened out like a drunkard.

It had got all over the cannery by this time that a great personality was in their midst, none other than that immortal Arturo Bandini, the writer, and there he lay, no doubt composing something for the ages, this great writer who made fish his specialty, who worked for a mere twenty-five cents an hour because he was so democratic, that great writer. So great he was indeed, that – well, there he sprawled, flat on his belly in the sun, puking his guts out, too sick to stand the smell he was going to write a book about. A book on California fisheries! Oh, what a writer! A book on California puke! Oh, what a writer he is!

Laughter.

Thirty minutes passed. The whistle blew again. They streamed back from the lunch counters. I rolled over and saw them pass, blurred in shape, a bilious dream. The bright sun was sickening. I buried my face in my arm. They were still enjoying it, but not so much as before, because the great writer was beginning to bore them. Lifting my head I saw them out of sticky eyes as the stream moved by. They were munching apples, licking ice-cream bars, eating chocolate covered candy from noisy packages. The nausea returned. My stomach grumbled, kicked, rebelled.

Hey writer! Hey writer! Hey writer!

I heard them gather around me, the laughter and the cackling. Hey writer! The voices were shattered echoes.

The dust from their feet rolled in lazy clouds. Then louder than ever a mouth against my ear, and a shout. Heeey writer! Arms grabbed me, lifted me up and turned me over. Before it happened I knew what they were going to do. This was their idea of a really funny episode. They were going to stick a fish down my waist. I knew it without even seeing the fish. I lay on my back. The mid-day sun smeared my face. I felt fingers at my shirt and the rip of cloth. Of course! Just as I thought! They were going to stick that fish down my waist. But I never even saw the fish. I kept my eyes closed. Then something cold and clammy pressed my chest and was pushed down to my belt: that fish! The fools. I knew it a long time before they did it. I just *knew* they were going to do that. But I didn't feel like caring. One fish more or less didn't matter now.

Chapter Ten

Time passed. Maybe a half hour. I reached into my shirt and felt the fish against my skin. I ran my fingers along the surface, feeling his fins and tail. Now I felt better. I pulled the fish out, held him up, and looked at him. A mackerel, a foot long. I held my breath so I would not smell him. Then I put him in my mouth and bit off his head. I was sorry he was already dead. I threw him aside and got to my feet. There were some big flies making a feast of my face and the wet spot on my shirt where the fish had lain. A bold fly landed on my arm and stubbornly refused to move, even though I warned him by shaking my arm. This made me insanely angry with him. I slapped him, killing him on my arm. But I was still so furious with him that I put him in my mouth and chewed him to bits and spat him out. Then I got the fish again, placed him on a level spot in the sand, and jumped on him until he burst open. The whiteness of my face was a thing I could feel, like plaster. Every time I moved a hundred flies dispersed. The flies were such idiotic fools. I stood still, killing them, but even the dead among them taught the living nothing. They still insisted on annoying me. For some time I stood patiently and quietly, scarcely breathing, watching the flies move into a position where I could kill them.

The nausea was past. I had forgotten that part of it. What

I hated was the laughter, the flies, and the dead fish. Again I wished that fish had been alive. He would have been taught a lesson not soon forgotten. I didn't know what would happen next. I would get even with them. Bandini never forgets. He will find a way. You shall pay for this – all of you.

Just across the way was the lavatory. I started for it. Two impudent flies followed me. I stopped dead in my tracks, fuming, still as a statue, waiting for the flies to land. At last I got one of them. The other escaped. I pulled off the fly's wings and dropped him to the ground. He crawled about in the dirt, darting like a fish, thinking he would escape me in that fashion. It was preposterous. For a while I let him do so to his heart's desire. Then I jumped on him with both feet and crushed him into the ground. I built a mound over the spot, and spat upon it.

In the lavatory I swayed back and forth like a rocking chair, standing and wondering what to do next, trying to get hold of myself. There were too many cannery workers for a fight. I had already settled with the flies and the dead fish, but not the cannery workers. You couldn't kill cannery workers the way you killed flies. It had to be something else, some way of fighting without fists. I washed my face in cold water and thought about it.

In walked a dark Filipino. He was one of the boys from the labeling crew. He stood at the trough along the wall, fighting buttons impatiently and frowning. Then he solved the buttons and was relieved, smiling all the time and shivering a bit for ease. Now he felt a lot better. I leaned over the sink at the opposite wall and let the water run through my hair and over my neck. The Filipino turned around and began again with the buttons. He lit a cigarette and stood against the wall watching me. He did it on purpose, watching me in such a way that I would know he was watching me and nothing else. But I wasn't afraid of him. I was never afraid of him. Nobody in California was ever afraid of a Filipino. He smiled to let me know he didn't think much of me either, or of my weak stomach. I straightened up and let the water drip from my face. It fell to my dusty shoes, making bright dots on them. The Filipino thought less and less of me. Now he was no longer smiling but sneering.

'How you feel?' he said.

'What business is it of yours?'

He was slender and over medium height. I wasn't as large as he, but I was perhaps as heavy. I leered at him from head to foot. I even stuck out my chin and pulled back my lower lip to denote the zenith of contempt. He leered back, but in a different way, not with his chin out. He was not in the least afraid of me. If something didn't happen to interrupt it, his courage would soon be so great that he would insult me.

His skin was a nut brown. I noticed it because his teeth were so white. They were brilliant teeth, like a row of pearls. When I saw how dark he was I suddenly knew what to say to him. I could say it to all of them. It would hurt them every time. I knew because a thing like that had hurt me. In grade school the kids used to hurt me by calling me Wop and Dago. It had hurt every time. It was a miserable feeling. It used to make me feel so pitiful, so unworthy. And I knew it would hurt the Filipino too. It was so easy to do that all at once I was laughing quietly at him, and over me came a cool, confident feeling, at ease with everything. I couldn't fail. I walked close to him and put my face near his, smiling the way he smiled. He could tell something was coming.

Immediately his expression changed. He was waiting for it – whatever it was.

'Give me a cigarette,' I said. 'You nigger.'

That hit him. Ah, but he felt that baby. Instantly there was a change, a shift of feelings, the movement from offense to defense. The smile hardened on his face and his face was frozen: he wanted to keep smiling but he couldn't. Now he hated me. His eyes sharpened. It was a wonderful feeling. He could escape his own squirming. It was open to the whole world. It had been that way with me too. Once in a drug store a girl had called me a Dago. I was only ten years old, but all at once I hated that girl the way the Filipino hated me. I had offered to buy the girl an ice-cream cone. She wouldn't take it, saying, my mother told me not to have anything to do with you because you're a Dago. And I decided I would do it to the Filipino again.

'You're not a nigger at all,' I said. 'You're a damn Filipino, which is worse.'

But now his face was neither brown nor black. It was purple.

'A yellow Filipino. A damn oriental foreigner! Doesn't it make you uncomfortable to be around white people?'

He didn't want to talk about it. He shook his head quickly in denial.

'Christ,' I said. 'Look at your face! You're as yellow as a canary.'

And I laughed. I bent over and shrieked. I pointed my finger at his face and shrieked until I could no longer pretend that the laughter was genuine. His face was tight as ice with pain and humiliation, his mouth lodged in helplessness, like a mouth stuck on a stick, uncertain and aching.

'Boy!' I said. 'You came close to fooling me. All the time I thought you were a nigger. And here you turn out to be yellow.'

Then he softened. His cloggy face loosened. He made a weak smile of jelly and water. Colors moved across his face. He looked down at his shirt front and brushed away a streak of cigarette ash. Then he raised his eyes.

'You feel better now?' he asked.

I said, 'What do you care? You're a Filipino. You Filipinos don't get sick because you're used to this slop. I'm a writer, man! An American writer, man! Not a Filipino writer. I wasn't born in the Philippine Islands. I was born right here in the good old U.S.A. under the stars and stripes.'

Shrugging, he couldn't make much sense out of what I said. 'Me no writer,' he smiled. 'No no no. I born in Honolulu.'

'That's just it!' I said. 'That's the difference. I write books, man! What do you Orientals expect? I write books in the mother tongue, the English language. I'm no slimy Oriental.'

For the third time he said, 'You feel better now?'

'What do you expect!' I said. 'I write books, you fool! Tomes! I wasn't born in Honolulu. I was born right here in good old Southern California.'

He flipped his cigarette across the room to the trough. It hit the wall with sparks flying and then landed not in the trough but on the floor.

'I go now,' he said. 'You come pretty soon, no?'

'Give me a cigarette.'

'No got none.'

He moved toward the door.

'No more. Last one.'

But there was a pack bulging from his shirt pocket.

'You yellow Filipino liar,' I said. 'What're those?'

He grinned and took out the package, offering me one. They were a cheaper brand, a ten cent cigarette. I pushed them away.

'Filipino cigarettes. No thanks. Not for me.'

That was all right with him.

'I see you later,' he said.

'Not if I see you first.'

He went away. I heard his feet moving away on the gravel path. I was alone. His discarded cigarette butt lay on the floor. I tore away the wet and smoked it to my fingertips. When I could no longer hold it I dropped it to the floor and crushed it with my heel. That for you! And I ground it to a brown spot. It had had a different taste than ordinary cigarettes; somehow it tasted more like a Filipino than like tobacco.

It was cool in the room with so much water always running in the trough. I went to the window and relaxed, with my face in my hands, watching the afternoon sun cut a bar of silver through the dust. There was a wire net across the window, with holes an inch square. I thought about the Black Hole of Calcutta. The English soldiers had died in a room no larger than this. But this was an altogether different kind of room. There was more ventilation in it. All of this thinking was only of the moment. It had nothing to do with anything. All little rooms reminded me of the Black Hole of Calcutta, and that made me think of Macaulay. So now I stood at the window thinking of Macaulay. The stench was endurable now; it was unpleasant, but I had got used to it. I was hungry without an appetite, but I couldn't think about food. I still had to face again the boys in the labeling crew. I looked about for another cigarette butt, but could not find any. Then I walked out.

Three Mexican girls walked down the path toward the washroom. They had just come out of the cutting room. I rounded the corner of the building, which was bashed in, as if a truck had smashed it. The girls saw me and I saw them. They were right in the middle of the path. They put their heads together. They were saying that here was that writer again, or something like that.

I drew nearer. The girl in boots nodded toward me. When I came closer they all smiled. I smiled back. We were ten feet apart. I could feel the girl in boots. It was because of her high breasts, they excited me so, all of a sudden, but it was nothing, only a flash, something to think about later on. I stopped in the middle of the path. I spread my legs and barred the path. Frightened, they slowed down; the writer was up to something. The girl in the house cap spoke heatedly to the girl in boots.

'Let's go back,' the girl in boots said.

I could feel her again, and I made up my mind to give her a great deal of thought some other time. Then the third girl, the girl who smoked a cigarette, spoke in quick sharp Spanish. Now the three of them tipped their heads arrogantly and started toward me. I addressed the girl in boots. She was the prettiest. The others were not worth speaking to, being much inferior in looks to the girl in boots.

'Well well well,' I said. 'Greetings to the three pretty Filipino girls!'

They weren't Filipinos at all, not in the least, and I knew it and they knew I knew it. They breezed by snootily, their noses in the air. I had to get out of their way or be bumped off the path. The girl in boots had white arms that curved as easily as a milk bottle. But near her I saw that she was ugly, with tiny purple pimples and a smear of powder on her throat. It was a disappointment. She turned around and made a face at me; she stuck out her pink tongue and puckered her nose.

This was a surprise, and I was glad, because I was expert at making horrible faces. I pulled my eyelids down, showed my teeth, and screwed up my cheeks. The face I made was much more horrible than hers. She walked backward, facing me, her pink tongue out, making all kinds of faces, but all of them variations of the stick-out-your-tongue kind. Each of mine were better than hers. The two other girls walked straight ahead. The boots of the girl-in-boots were too big for her feet; they slushed in the dust as she walked backward. I liked the way the hem of her dress flapped over her legs, the dust coming aburst like a big grey flower all around her.

'That's no way for a Filipino girl to act!' I said.

It infuriated her.

'We're *not* Filipinos!' she screamed. '*You're* the Filipino! Filipino! Filipino!'

Now the other girls turned around. They pitched into the refrain. All three of them walked backward, arm in arm, and shrilled in sing-song.

'Filipino! Filipino! Filipino!'

They made more monkey faces and thumbed their noses at me. The distance between us widened. I raised my arm for them to keep still a minute. They had done most of the talking and shouting. I had scarcely said anything yet. But they kept up the sing-song. I waved my arms and put my finger to my lips for quiet. Finally they consented to stop and listen. At last I had the floor. They were so far away, and there was so much noise coming from the buildings that I had to cup my hands and yell.

'I beg your pardon!' I yelled. 'Excuse me for making a mistake! I'm awfully sorry! I thought you were Filipinos. But you're not. You're a lot worse! You're Mexicans! You're Greasers! You're Spick sluts! Spick sluts! Spick sluts!'

I was a hundred feet away, but I could feel their sudden apathy. It came down upon each of them, jarring them, hurting them silently, each ashamed to admit the pain to the other, yet each giving away the secret hurt by keeping so still. That had happened to me too. Once I licked a boy in a fight. I felt fine until I began to walk away. He got up and ran toward home, shouting that I was a Dago. There were other boys standing around. The shouts of the retreating boy made me feel as the Mexican girls felt. Now I laughed at the Mexican girls. I lifted my mouth to the sky and laughed, not once turning to look back, but laughing so loud I knew they heard me. Then I went inside.

'Nyah nyah nyah!' I said. 'Jabber jabber jabber!'

But I felt crazy for doing it. And they thought I was crazy. They looked dumbfounded at one another and then back at me. They didn't know I was trying to ridicule them. No, the way they shook their heads they were convinced I was a lunatic.

But now for the young fellows in the labeling room. This was going to be the hardest. I walked in with quick meaningful strides, whistling all the time, and taking deep breaths to show them the stench had no effect upon me. I even rubbed my chest and said, ah! The boys were packed around the can dump, directing the flow of cans as they tumbled toward the greasy belt that carried them to the machines. They were crowded shoulder to shoulder around the box-shaped dump that measured ten feet square. The room was as noisy as it was stinking, full of all manner of dead fish odors. There was such noise that they didn't notice me coming. I nudged my shoulder between two big Mexicans who were talking as they worked. I made a big fuss, squirming and prying my way through. Then they looked down and saw me between them. It annoyed them. They couldn't understand what I was trying to do until I spread them apart with my elbows and my arms were finally free.

I yelled, 'One side, you Greasers!'

'Bah!' the largest Mexican said. 'Leave heem alone, Joe. The leetle son of a beetch is crazee.'

I plunged in and worked, straightening cans for their positions on the conveyor belts. They were leaving me alone for sure, with plenty of freedom. Nobody spoke. I felt alone indeed. I felt like a corpse, and that the only reason I was there was because they could do nothing about it.

The afternoon waned.

I stopped work only twice. Once to get a drink of water, and the other time to write something in my little notebook. Every one of them stopped work to watch me when I stepped off the platform to make the notation in my book. This was to prove to them without a doubt that after all I wasn't fooling, that I was a real writer among them, the real thing, and not a fake. I looked scrutinizingly at every face and scratched my ear with a pencil. Then for a second I gazed off into space. Finally I snapped my fingers to show that the thought had come through with flying colors. I put the notebook on my knee and wrote.

I wrote: Friends, Romans, and countrymen! All of Gaul is divided into three parts. Thou goest to woman? Do not forget thy whip. Time and tide wait for no man. Under the spreading chestnut tree the village smithy stands. Then I stopped to sign it with a flourish. Arturo G. Bandini. I couldn't think of anything else. With popping eyes they watched me. I made up my mind that I must think of something else. But that was all. My mind had quit functioning altogether. I could not think of another item, not even a word, not even my own name.

I put the notebook back into my pocket and took my place on the can dump. None of them said a word. Now their doubts were surely shaken. Hadn't I stopped work to do a bit of writing? Perhaps they had judged me too hastily. I hoped someone would ask me what I had written. Quickly I would tell him that it was nothing important, merely a notation concerning the foreign labor conditions in my regular report to the House Ways and Means Committee; nothing you'd understand, old fellow; it's too deep to explain now; some other time; perhaps at lunch some day.

Now they began talking again. Then together they laughed. But it was all Spanish to me, and I understood nothing.

The boy they called Jugo jumped out of line as I had done and pulled a notebook from his pocket too. He ran to where I had stood with my notebook. For a second I thought he must really be a writer who had observed something valuable. He took the same position I had taken. He scratched his ear the way I had scratched mine. He looked off into space the way I had done. Then he wrote. Roars of laughter.

'Me writer too!' he said. 'Look!'

He held the notebook up for all to see. He had drawn a cow. The cow's face was spotted as if with freckles. This was unquestionably ridicule, because I had a face filled with freckles. Under the cow he had written 'Writer.' He carried the notebook around the can dump.

'Very funny,' I said. 'Greaser comedy.'

I hated him so much it nauseated me. I hated every one of them and the clothes they wore and everything about them. We worked until six o'clock. All that afternoon Shorty Naylor did not appear. When the whistle blew the boys dropped everything and rushed from the platform. I stayed on a few minutes, picking up cans that had fallen to the floor. I hoped Shorty would return at that moment. For ten minutes I worked, but not a soul came to watch me, so I quit in disgust, throwing all the cans back on the floor.

Chapter Eleven

At a quarter after six I was on my way home. The sun was slipping behind the big dock warehouses and the long shadows were on the ground. What a day! What a hell of a day! I walked along talking to myself about it, discussing it. I always did that, talking aloud to myself in a heavy whisper. Usually it was fun, because I always had the right answers. But not that night. I hated the mumbling that went on inside my mouth. It was like the drone of a trapped bumblebee. The part of me which supplied answers to my questions kept saying Oh nuts! You crazy liar! You fool! You jack-ass! Why don't you tell the truth once in a while? It's your fault, so quit trying to shift the blame onto somebody else.

I crossed the schoolyard. Near the iron fence was a palm tree growing all by itself. The earth was freshly turned about the roots, a young tree I had never seen before growing in that place. I stopped to look at it. There was a bronze plaque at the foot of the tree. It read: Planted by the children of Banning High in commemoration of Mother's Day.

I took a branch of the tree in my fingers and shook hands with it. 'Hello,' I said. 'You weren't there, but whose fault would you say it was?'

It was a small tree, no taller than myself, and not more than a year old. It answered with a sweet plashing of thick leaves.

'The women,' I said. 'Do you think they had anything to do with it?'

Not a word from the tree.

'Yes. It's the fault of the women. They have enslaved my mind. They alone are responsible for what happened today.'

The tree swayed slightly.

'The women have got to be annihilated. Positively annihilated. I must get them out of my mind forever. They and they alone have made me what I am today.

'Tonight the women die. This is the hour of decision. The time has come. My destiny is clear before me. It is death, death, death for the women tonight. I have spoken.'

I shook hands with the tree again and crossed the street. Traveling with me was the stench of fish, a shadow that could not be seen but smelled. It followed me up the apartment steps. The moment I stepped inside the apartment the smell was everywhere, drifting straight for every corner of the apartment. Like an arrow it traveled to Mona's nostrils. She walked out of the bedroom with a nail file in her hand and a searching look in her eyes.

'Peeeew!' she said. 'What *is* that?'

'It's me. The smell of honest labor. What of it?'

She put a handkerchief to her nose.

I said, 'It's probably too delicate for the nostrils of a sanctified nun.'

My mother was in the kitchen. She heard our voices. The door swung open and she emerged, moving into the room. The stench attacked her. It hit her in the face like a lemon pie in the two-act comedies. She stopped dead in her tracks. A sniff and her face tightened. Then she backed up.

'Smell him!' Mona said.

'I thought I smelt *something*!' my mother said.

'It's me. The smell of honest labor. It's a man's smell. It's not for effetes and dilettantes. It's fish.'

'It's disgusting,' Mona said.

'Bilge,' I said. 'Who are you to criticize a smell? You're a nun. A female. A mere woman. You're not even a woman because you're a nun. You're only half-woman.'

'Arturo,' my mother said. 'Let's not have any talk like that.'

'A nun ought to like the smell of fish.'

'Naturally. That's what I've been telling you for the last half hour.'

My mother's hands rose to the ceiling, her fingers trembling. It was a gesture that always came before tears. Her voice cracked, went out of control, and the tears burst forth.

'Thank God! Oh thank God!'

'A lot he had to do with it. I got this job myself. I'm an atheist. I deny the hypothesis of God.'

Mona sneered.

'How you talk! You couldn't get a job to save your life. Uncle Frank got it for you.'

'That's a lie, a filthy lie. I tore up Uncle Frank's note.'

'I believe that.'

'I don't care what you believe. Anybody who gives credence to the Virgin Birth and the Resurrection is a plain boob whose beliefs are all under suspicion.'

Silence.

'I am now a worker,' I said. 'I belong to the proletariat. I am a writer-worker.'

Mona smiled.

'You'd smell much better if you were only a writer.'

'I love this smell,' I told her. 'I love its every connotation and ramification; every variation and implication fascinates me. I belong to the people.'

Her mouth puckered.

'Mamma, listen to him! Using words without knowing what they mean.'

I could not tolerate a remark like that. It burned me to the core. She could ridicule my beliefs and persecute me for my philosophy and I would not complain. But no one could make fun of my English. I ran across the room.

'Don't insult me! I can endure a lot of your bilge and folderol, but in the name of the Jehovah you worship, don't insult me!'

I shook my fist in her face and butted her with my chest. 'I can stand a lot of your imbecilities, but in the name of your monstrous Yahweh, you sanctimonious, she-nun of a God-worshipping pagan nun of a good-for-nothing scum of the earth, don't insult me! I oppose it. I oppose it emphatically!'

She tilted her chin and pushed me away with her finger-tips.

'Please go away. Take a bath. You smell bad.'

I swung at her, and the tips of my fingers flecked her face. She clenched her teeth and stamped the floor with both feet.

'You fool! You fool!'

My mother was always too late. She got between us.

'Here, here! What's all this about?'

I hitched up my pants and sneered at Mona.

'It's about time I had supper. That's what it's all about.

As long as I'm supporting two parasitical women I guess I'm entitled to something to eat once in a while.'

I peeled off my stinking shirt and threw it on a chair in the corner. Mona got it, carried it to the window, opened the window, and threw it out. Then she swung around and defied me to do something about it. I said nothing, merely staring at her coldly to let her know the depth of my contempt. My mother stood dumbfounded, unable to understand what was going on; not in a million years would she have thought to throw away a shirt simply because it stunk. Without speaking I hurried downstairs and around the house. The shirt hung from a fig tree below our window. I put it on and returned to the apartment. I stood in the exact spot I had stood before. I folded my arms and allowed the contempt to gush from my face.

'Now,' I said. 'Try that again. I dare you!'

'You fool!' Mona said. 'Uncle Frank's right. You're insane.'

'Ho. Him! That boobus Americanus ass.'

My mother was horrified. Every time I said something she did not understand she thought it had something to do with sex or naked women.

'Arturo! To think of it! Your own uncle!'

'Uncle or not. I positively refuse to retract the charge. He's a boobus Americanus now and forever.'

'But your own uncle! Your own flesh and blood!'

'My attitude is unchanged. The charge stands.'

Supper was spread in the breakfast nook. I didn't wash up. I was too hungry. I went in and sat down. My mother came, bringing a fresh towel. She said I should wash. I took the towel from her and put it beside me. Mona came in unwillingly. She sat down and tried to endure me so near.

She spread her napkin and my mother brought in a bowl of soup. But the smell was too much for Mona. The sight of the soup revolted her. She grabbed the pit of her stomach, threw down her napkin and left the table.

'I can't *do* it. I just can't!'

'Haw! Weaklings. Females. Bring on the food!'

Then my mother left. I ate alone. When I was through I lit a cigarette and sat back to give the women some thought. My thought was to find the best possible way to destroy them. There was no doubt of it: they had to be finished. I could burn them, or cut them to pieces, or drown them. At last I decided that drowning would be the best. I could do it in comfort while I took my bath. Then I would toss the remains down the sewer. They would flow down to the sea, where the dead crabs lay. The souls of the dead women would talk to the souls of the dead crabs, and they would talk only of me. My fame would increase. Crabs and women would arrive at one inevitable conclusion: that I was a terror, the Black Killer of the Pacific Coast, yet a terror respected by all, crabs and women alike: a cruel hero, but a hero nevertheless.

Chapter Twelve

After supper I turned on the water for my bath. I was contented from food and in a fine mood for the execution. The warm water would make it even more interesting. While the tub was filling I entered my study, locking the door behind me. Lighting the candle, I lifted the box which concealed my women. There they lay huddled together, all my women, my favorites, thirty women chosen from the pages of art magazines, women not real, but good enough nevertheless, the women who belonged to me more than any real women could ever belong to me. I rolled them up and stuck them under my shirt. I had to do this. Mona and my mother were in the living room and I had to pass them to get into the bathroom.

So this was the end! Destiny had brought this! The very thought of it! I looked around the closet and tried to feel sentimental. But it wasn't very sad: I was too eager to go ahead with the execution to be sad. But just for the sake of formality I stood still and bowed my head as a token of farewell. Then I blew out the candle and stepped into the living room. I left the door open behind me. It was the first time I ever left the door open. In the living room sat Mona, sewing. I crossed the rug, a slight bulge under my waist. Mona looked up and saw the open door. She was greatly surprised.

'You forgot to lock your "study",' she sneered.

'I know what I'm about, if you please. And I'll lock that door whenever I damn well feel like it.'

'But what about Nietzsche, or whatever you call him?'

'Never mind Nietzsche, you Comstock trull.'

The tub was ready. I undressed and sat in it. The pictures lay face down on the bath mat, within range of my hand.

I reached down and picked off the top picture.

For some reason I knew it was going to be Helen. A faint instinct told me so. And Helen it was. Helen, dear Helen! Helen with her light brown hair! I had not seen her for a long time, almost three weeks. A strange thing about Helen, that strangest of women: the only reason I cared for her was because of her long fingernails. They were so pink, such breath-taking fingernails, so sharp and exquisitely alive. But for the rest of her I cared nothing, beautiful though she was throughout. She sat naked in the picture, holding a soft veil about her shoulders, every bit a marvelous sight, yet not interesting to me, except for those beautiful fingernails.

'Goodbye, Helen,' I said. 'Goodbye, dear heart. I shall never forget you. Until the day I die I shall always remember the many times we went to the deep corn-fields of Anderson's book and I went to sleep with your fingers in my mouth. How delicious they were! How sweetly I slept! But now we part, dear Helen, sweet Helen. Goodbye, goodbye.'

I tore the picture to pieces and floated them on the water.

Then I reached down again. It was Hazel. I had named her so because of her eyes in a picture of natural colors. Yet I didn't care for Hazel either. It was her hips I cared about — they were so pillowy and so white. What times we had had,

Hazel and I! How beautiful she really was! Before I destroyed her I lay back in the water and thought of the many times we had met in a mysterious room pierced with dazzling sunlight, a very white room, with only a green carpet on the floor, a room that existed only because of her. In the corner, leaning against the wall, and for no good reason, but always there, a long slender cane with a silver tip, flashing diamonds in the sunlight. And from behind a curtain that I never quite saw because of the mistiness, and yet could never quite deny, Hazel would walk in such a melancholy way to the middle of the room, and I would be there admiring the globed beauty of her hips, on my knees before her, my fingers melting for the touch of her, and yet I never spoke to darling Hazel but to her hips, addressing them as though they were living souls, telling them how wonderful they were, how useless life was without them, the while taking them in my hands and drawing them near me. And I tore that picture to pieces too, and watched the pieces absorb the water. Dear Hazel . . .

Then there was Tanya. I used to meet Tanya at night in a cave we kids built one summer a long time ago along the Palos Verdes Cliffs near San Pedro. It was near the sea, and you could smell the ecstasy of lime trees growing there. The cave was always strewn with old magazines and newspapers. In one corner lay a frying pan I had stolen from my mother's kitchen, and in another corner a candle burned and made hissing noises. It was really a filthy little cave after you had been there a little while, and very cold, for water dripped from the sides. And there I met Tanya. But it was not Tanya I loved. It was the way she wore a black shawl in the picture. And it wasn't the shawl either. One was incomplete without the other, and only Tanya could wear it that way. Always when I met her I found myself crawling through the opening of the cave to the center of the cave and pulling the shawl away as Tanya's long hair fell loosely about her, and then I would hold the shawl to my face and bury my lips in it, admiring its black brilliance, and thanking Tanya over and over for having worn it again for me. And Tanya would always answer, 'But It's nothing, you silly. I do it gladly. You're so silly.' And I would say, 'I love you, Tanya.'

There was Marie. Oh Marie! Oh you Marie! You with your exquisite laughter and deep perfume! I loved her teeth and mouth and the scent of her flesh. We used to meet in a dark room whose walls were covered by cobwebbed books. There was a leather chair near the fireplace, and it must have been a very great house, a castle or a mansion in France, because across the room, big and solid, stood the desk of Emile Zola as I had seen it in a book. I would be sitting there reading the last pages of *Nana*, that passage about the death of Nana, and Marie would rise like a mist from those pages and stand before me naked, laughing and laughing with a beautiful mouth and an intoxicating scent until I had to put the book down, and she walked before me and laid her hands on the book too, and shook her head with a deep smile, so that I could feel her warmth coursing like electricity through my fingers.

'Who are you?'

'I am Nana.'

'Really Nana?'

'Really.'

'The girl who died here?'

'I am not dead. I belong to you.'

And I would take her in my arms.

There was Ruby. She was an erratic woman, so unlike the

others, and so much older too. I always came upon her as she ran across a dry hot plain beyond the Funeral Range in Death Valley, California. That was because I had been there once in the spring, and I never forgot the beauty of that vast plain, and there it was I met the erratic Ruby so often afterward, a woman of thirty-five, running naked across the sand, and I chasing after her and finally catching her beside a pool of blue water which always gave off a red vapor the moment I dragged her into the sand and sank my mouth against her throat, which was so warm and not so lovely, because Ruby was growing old and cords protruded slightly, but I was mad about her throat, and I loved the touch of her cords rising and falling as she panted where I had caught her and brought her to the earth.

And Jean! How I loved Jean's hair! It was as golden as straw, and always I saw her drying the long strands under a banana tree that grew on a knoll among the Palos Verdes Hills. I would be watching her as she combed out the deep strands. Asleep at her feet coiled a snake like the snake under the feet of the Virgin Mary. I always approached Jean on tiptoe, so as not to disturb the snake, who sighed gratefully when my feet sank into him, giving me such an exquisite pleasure everywhere, lighting up the surprised eyes of Jean, and then my hands slipped gently and cautiously into the eerie warmth of the golden hair, and Jean would laugh and tell me she knew it was going to happen this way, and like a falling veil she would droop into my arms.

But what of Nina? Why did I love that girl? And why was she crippled? And what was it within my heart that made me love her so madly simply because she was so hopelessly maimed? Yet it was all so, and my poor Nina was crippled.

Not in the picture, oh she wasn't crippled there, only when I met her, one foot smaller than the other, one foot like that of a doll, the other a proper shape. We met in the Catholic church of my boyhood, St Thomas's in Wilmington, where I, dressed in the robes of a priest, stood with a scepter at the high altar. All around me on their knees were the sinners, weeping after I had castigated them for their sins, and not one of them had the courage to look upon me because my eyes shone with such mad holiness, such a detestation of sin. Then from the back of the church came this girl, this cripple, smiling, knowing she was going to break me from my holy throne and force me to sin with her before the others, so that they could mock me and laugh at me, the holy one, the hypocrite before all the world. Limping she came, disrobing at every painful step, her wet lips a smile of approaching triumph, and I with the voice of a falling king, shouting to her to go away, that she was a devil who bewitched me and made me helpless. But she came forward irresistibly, the crowd horror-stricken, and she put her arms around my knees and hugged me to her, hiding that crippled little foot, until I could endure it no longer, and with a shout I fell upon her and joyfully admitted my weakness while around me rose the rumble of a mob which gradually faded into a bleak oblivion.

And so it was. So it was that one by one I picked them up, remembered them, kissed them good-bye, and tore them to pieces. Some were reluctant to be destroyed, calling in pitiful voices from the misty depths of those vast places where we loved in weird half-dreams, the echoes of their pleas lost in the shadowed darkness of that which was Arturo Bandini as he sat comfortably in a cool bathtub and enjoyed the departure of things which once were, yet never were, really.

But there was one in particular which I was loath to destroy. She alone caused me to hesitate. She it was whom I had named the Little Girl. She it seemed was always that woman of a certain murder case in San Diego; she had killed her husband with a knife and laughingly admitted the crime to the police. I used to meet her in the rough squalor of early Los Angeles before the days of the Gold Rush. She was very cynical for a little girl, and very cruel. The picture I had cut from the detective magazine left nothing to imagine. Yet she wasn't a little girl at all. I merely called her that. She was a woman who hated the sight of me, the touch of me, yet found me irresistible, cursing me, yet loving me fabulously. And I would see her in a dark mud-thatched hut with the windows darkened, the heat of the town driving all the natives to sleep so that not a soul stirred in the streets of that early day of Los Angeles, and lying on a cot she would be, panting and cursing me as my feet sounded upon the deserted street and finally at her door. The knife in her hand would amuse me and make me smile, and so would her hideous screams. I was such a devil. Then my smile would leave her helpless, the hand that held the knife finally growing limp, the knife falling to the floor, and she cringing in horror and hate, yet wild with love. So she was the Little Girl, and of them all she was easily my favorite. I regretted destroying her. For a long time I deliberated, because I knew she would find relief and surcease from me once I destroyed her, because then I could no longer harass her like a devil, and possess her with contemptible laughter. But the Little Girl's destiny was sealed. I could play no favorites. I tore the Little Girl to pieces like the others.

When the last had been destroyed the pieces blanketed the

surface of the water, and the water was invisible beneath. Sadly I stirred it up. The water was a blackish color of fading ink. It was finished. The show was over. I was glad I had made this bold step and put them away all at once. I congratulated myself for having such strength of purpose, such ability to see a job through to the end. In the face of sentimentality I had gone ruthlessly forward. I was a hero, and my deed was not to be sneered at. I stood up and looked at them before I pulled the plug. Little pieces of departed love. Down the sewer with the romances of Arturo Bandini! Go down to the sea! Be off on your dark journey down the drain to the land of dead crabs. Bandini had spoken. Pull the chain!

And it was done. I stood with water dripping from me and saluted.

'Goodbye,' I said. 'Farewell, ye women. They laughed at me down at the cannery today, and it was the fault of ye, for ye hath poisoned my mind and made me helpless against the onslaught of life. Now ye are dead. Goodbye and goodbye forever. He who maketh a sap of Arturo Bandini, be he man or woman, cometh to an untimely end. I have spoken. Amen.'

Chapter Thirteen

Asleep or awake, it did not matter, I hated the cannery, and I always smelled like a basket of mackerel. It never left me, that stench of a dead horse at the edge of the road. It followed me in the streets. It went with me into buildings. When I crawled into bed at night, there it was, like a blanket, all over me. And in my dreams there were fish fish fish, mackerel slithering about in a black pool, with me tied to a limb and being lowered into the pool. It was in my food and clothes, and I even tasted it on my toothbrush. The same thing happened to Mona and my mother. At last it got so bad that when Friday came we had meat for dinner. My mother couldn't bear the idea of fish, even though it was a sin to be without fish.

From boyhood I loathed soap too. I didn't believe I would ever get used to that slimy greasy stuff with its slithering, effeminate smell. But now I used it against the stench of fish. I took more baths than ever before. There was one Saturday when I took two baths – one after work, and another before I went to bed. Every night I stayed in the tub and read books until the water grew cold and looked like old dish water. I rubbed soap into my skin until it shone like an apple. But there was no sense in it all, because it was a waste of time. The only way to get rid of the smell was to quit the cannery. I always left the tub smelling of two mingling stenches – soap and dead mackerel.

Everybody knew who I was and what I did when they smelled me coming. Being a writer was no satisfaction. On the bus I was recognized instantly, and in the theatre too. He's one of those cannery kids. Good Lord, can't you smell him? I had that well-known smell.

One night I went to the theatre to see a picture show. I sat by myself, all alone in the corner, my smell and I. But distance was a ridiculous obstacle to that thing. It left me and went out and around and returned like something dead fastened to a rubber band. In a while heads began to turn. A cannery worker was somewhere in the vicinity, obviously. There were frowns and sniffs. Then mumbling, and the scraping of feet. People all around me got up and moved away. Keep away from him, he's a cannery worker. And so I went to no more picture shows. But I didn't mind. They were for the rabble anyhow.

At night I stayed home and read books.

I didn't dare go to the library.

I said to Mona, 'Bring me books by Nietzsche. Bring me the mighty Spengler. Bring me Auguste Comte and Immanuel Kant. Bring me books the rabble can't read.'

Mona brought them home. I read them all, most of them very hard to understand, some of them so dull I had to pretend they were fascinating, and others so awful I had to read them aloud like an actor to get through them. But usually I was too tired for reading. A little while in the bathtub was enough. The print floated near my eyes like thread in the wind. I fell asleep. Next morning I found myself undressed and in bed, the alarm ringing, wondering how my mother had not waked me up. And as I dressed I thought over the books I had read the night before. I could remember only a sentence here and there, and the fact that I had forgotten everything.

I even read a book of poetry. It made me sick, that book, and I said I would never read another again. I hated that poet. I wished she would spend a few weeks in a cannery. Then her tune would change.

Most of all, I thought about money. I never did have much money. The most I ever had at one time was fifty dollars. I used to roll paper in my hands and pretend it was a wad of thousand dollar bills. I stood in front of a mirror and peeled it off to clothiers, automobile salesmen, and whores. I gave one whore a thousand dollar tip. She offered to spend the next six months with me for nothing. I was so touched I peeled off another thousand and gave it to her for sentiment's sake. At this she promised to give up her bad life. I said tut tut, my dear, and gave her the rest of the roll: seventy thousand dollars.

A block from our apartment was the California Bank. I used to stand at our window at night and see it bulging out so insolently on the corner. I finally thought of a way to rob it without being caught. Next door to the bank was a dry-cleaner establishment. The idea was to dig a tunnel from the dry cleaner's to the bank safe. A getaway car could be waiting in back. It was only a hundred miles to Mexico.

If I didn't dream of fish I dreamed of money. I used to wake up with my fist clenched, thinking there was money in it, a gold piece, and hating to open my hand because I knew my mind was playing a trick, and there was really no money at all in my hand. I made a vow that if I ever got enough money I would buy the Soyo Fish Company, have an all night celebration like the Fourth of July, and burn it to the ground in the morning.

The work was hard. In the afternoons the fog lifted and the sun beat down. The rays lifted themselves from the blue bay inside the saucer formed by the Palos Verdes hills and it was like a furnace. In the cannery it was worse. There was no fresh air, not even enough to fill one nostril. All the windows were nailed down by rusted nails, and the glass was cobwebbed and greasy with age. The sun heated the corrugated iron roof like a torch, forcing the heat downward. Hot steam drifted from the retorts and ovens. More steam came from the big fertilizer vats. These two steams met head on, you could see them meeting, and we were right in the middle of it, sweating in the clamor of the can dump.

My uncle was right about the work, all right. It was work done without thinking. You might just as well have left your brains at home on that job. All we did through the whole day was stand there and move our arms and legs. Once in a while we shifted weight, one foot to the other. If you really wanted to move, you had to leave the platform to go to the water fountain or the lavatory. We had a plan: we took turns: each of us took ten minutes in the lavatory by turn. No boss was necessary with those machines working. When the labeling began in the morning Shorty Naylor threw the switch and left the room. He knew about those machines. We didn't like to see them get ahead of us. When they did it hurt us vaguely. It was not a pain like someone jabbing you in the seat with a pin, but it was a sadness which in the long run was worse. If we escaped there was always someone down the line who didn't. He yelled. Up in front we had to work harder to fill up the space in the conveyor belt so he would feel better. Nobody liked that machine. It didn't matter if you were a Filipino or an Italian or a Mexican. It bothered us all. It needed such care too. It was like a child. Whenever it broke down panic would go through the whole cannery. Everything was done to the minute. When the machines were silenced it was like another place. It was no longer a cannery but a hospital. We waited around, talking in whispers until the mechanics fixed it.

I worked hard because I had to work hard, and I didn't complain much because there wasn't any time to complain. Most of the time I stood feeding the machine and thinking of money and women. Time passed easier with such thoughts. It was the first job I ever had where, the less you thought about your work, the easier it was. I used to get very passionate with my thoughts of women. That was because the platform was in a state of perpetual jerking. One dream of them slipped into another, and the hours passed away as I stood close to the machine and tried to concentrate on my work so the other boys wouldn't know what I was thinking about.

Through the haze of steam I could see across the room to the open door. There lay the blue bay swept by hundreds of dirty lazy gulls. On the other side of the bay was the Catalina Dock. Every few minutes in the morning steamers and airplanes left the dock for Catalina Island, eighteen miles away. Through the hazy door I could see the red pontoons of the planes as they lifted from the water. The steamers left only in the mornings, but all day long the planes soared away to the little island eighteen miles away. The dripping red pontoons flashed in the sunlight, frightening the gulls. But from where I stood I could only see the pontoons. Only the pontoons. Never the wings and fuselage.

This upset me from the first day. I wanted to see the whole plane. Many times I had seen the planes on my way to work. I used to stand on the bridge and watch the pilots tinker with them, and I knew every plane in the fleet. But seeing only the pontoons through the door, it worked on my mind like a bug. I used to think the craziest things. I used to imagine things were happening to the invisible parts of the plane – that stowaways were riding the wings. I wanted to rush to the door to make sure. I was always having hunches. I used to wish for tragedies. I wanted to see the planes blow up and the passengers drown in the bay. Some mornings I would come to work with only one hope in mind – that somebody would be killed in the bay. I used to be convinced of it. The next plane, I would say, the next one will never get to Catalina: it will crash in the take-off; people will scream, women and children will drown in the bay; Shorty Naylor will throw the switch and we will all get to see the rescuers pull the bodies out of the water. It is bound to happen. It is inevitable. And I used to think I was psychic. And so, all day long the planes pulled away. But standing where I was, all I saw was the pontoons. My bones ached to break away. The *next* one would surely crash. I made noises in my throat, biting my lips and waiting feverishly for that next plane. Presently I heard the roar of the motors, faint above the cannery din, and I timed it. Death at last! Now they will die! When the time arrived, I stopped work and stared, hungry for the sight. The planes never varied an inch in the take-off. The perspective through the door never changed. This time, as always, all I saw were the pontoons. I sighed. Ah well, who knows? Maybe it will crash beyond the lighthouse at the end of the breakwater. I will know in a minute. The coast guard sirens will sound. But the sirens didn't sound. Another plane had got through.

Fifteen minutes later I heard the roar of another plane. We were supposed to stay there. But the devil with orders. I jumped from the can dump and ran to the door. The big red plane took off. I saw all of it, every inch of it, and my eyes made a little feast before the tragedy. Out there, anywhere, lurked death. At any moment he would strike. The plane moved across the bay, shot into the air, and moved toward the San Pedro lighthouse. Smaller and smaller. It had escaped too. I shook my fist at it.

'You'll get it yet!' I screamed.

The boys at the can dump watched me in amazement. I felt like a fool. I turned around and returned. Their eyes accused me, as if I had run to the door and tried to kill a beautiful bird.

All at once I had a different view of them. They looked so stupid. They worked so hard. With wives to feed, and a swarm of dirty-faced kids, and worries about the light bill and the grocery bill, they stood so far away, so detached, naked in dirty overalls, with stupid, pock-marked Mexican faces, glutted with stupidity, watching me return, thinking me crazy, making me shiver. They were gobs of something sticky and slow, gobby and glutted and in the way like glue, gluey and stuck and helpless and hopeless, with the whipped sad eyes of old animals from a field. They thought me crazy because I didn't look like an old whipped animal from a field. Let them think me crazy! Of course I'm crazy! You clod-hoppers, you dolts, you fools! I don't care about your thoughts. I was disgusted that I had to be so near them. I wanted to beat them up, one at a time, beat them until they were a mass of wounds and blood. I wanted to yell at them to keep their goddamn mopey melancholy whipped eyes away from me, because they turned a black slab in my heart, an open place, a grave, a hole, a sore, out of which marched in a torturing procession their dead leading other dead after them, parading the bitter suffering of their lives through my heart.

The machine clanged and banged. I took my place beside Eusibio and worked, the same routine, feeding the cans to the machine, resigned to the fact that I was not psychic, that tragedy only struck like a coward in the night. The boys watched me begin again, then they began too, giving me up for a maniac. Nothing was said. The minutes passed. It was an hour later.

Eusibio nudged me.

'For why you run like that?'

'The pilot. An old friend of mine. Colonel Buckingham. I was waving to him.'

Eusibio shook his head.

'Bull, Arturo. You full of bull.'

Chapter Fourteen

From my place on the conveyor I could also see the California Yacht Club. In the background were the first green ripples of the Palos Verdes Hills. It was a scene out of the Italy I knew in books. Bright pennants flapped from the masts of yachts. Farther out were the whitecaps of the big waves that smashed against the jagged breakwater. On the decks of the yachts, lay men and women in careless white suits. These were fabulous people. They were from the movie colony and Los Angeles financial circles. They had great wealth, these boats were their toys. If they felt like it they left their work in the city and came down to the harbor to play with them, and brought along their women.

And such women! It took my breath away to even see them rolling by in big cars, so poised, so beautiful, so easily at home in all that wealth, their cigarettes tipped so elegantly, their teeth so polished and flashing, the clothes they wore so irresistible, covering them with such perfection, concealing every body flaw, and making them so perfect in loveliness. At noon when the big cars roared down the road past the cannery and we were outside for the lunch hour I used to look at them like a thief peeking at jewels. Yet they seemed so far away that I hated them, and hating them made them nearer. Some day they would be mine. I would own them and the cars that carried them. When the revolution came they would be mine, the subjects of Commissar Bandini, right there in the Soviet district of San Pedro.

But I remember a woman on a yacht. She was two hundred yards away. At that distance I could not see her face. Only her movements were plain as she walked the deck like a pirate queen in a brilliant white bathing suit. She walked up and down the deck of a yacht that stretched like a lazy cat in the blue water. It was only a memory, an impression to be got from standing at the can dump and looking out the door. Only a memory, but I fell in love with her, the first real woman I ever loved. Occasionally she paused at the rail to look down into the water. Then she walked again, her luxurious thighs moving up and down. Once she turned and stared at the sprawling cannery. For some minutes she stared. She could not see me, but she looked directly at me. In that instant I fell in love with her. It must have been love, and yet it might have been her white bathing suit. From all angles I considered it, finally admitting that it was love. After looking at me, she turned and paced again. I am in love, I said. So this is love! All day I thought about her. The next day the yacht was gone. I used to wonder about her, and though it never seemed important, I was sure I was in love with her. After a while I ceased to think of her, she became a memory, a mere thought to while away the hours at the can dump. I loved her though; she never saw me, and I never saw her face, but it was love for all that. I couldn't make myself believe I had loved her either, but I decided that for once I was wrong, and that I did love her.

Once a beautiful blonde girl entered the labeling room. She came with a man who had an elegant mustache and wore spats. Later I found out his name was Hugo. He owned the cannery, as well as one on Terminal Island and another in Monterey. Nobody knew who the girl was. She clung to his arm, sickened by the odor. I knew she didn't like the place. She was a girl of not more than twenty. She wore a green coat. Her back was perfectly arched, like a barrel stave, and she wore high white shoes. Hugo was examining the place coldly, appraising it. She whispered to him. He smiled and patted her arm. Together they walked away. At the door the girl turned to look at us. I put my head down, not wanting to be seen by one so lovely among those Mexicans and Filipinos.

Eusibio was next to me on the can dump.

He nudged me and said, 'You like, Arturo?'

'Don't be a fool,' I said. 'She's a slut, pure and simple, a capitalistic slut. Her day is finished when the revolution comes.'

But I never forgot that little girl with her green coat and high white shoes. I was sure I would meet her again some day. Perhaps after I became rich and famous. Even then I wouldn't know her name, but I would hire detectives to shadow Hugo until they came to the apartment where he kept her, a virtual prisoner in his stupid wealth. The detectives would come to me with the address of the place. I would go there and present my card.

'You don't remember me,' I would smile.

'Why no. I'm afraid not.'

Ah. Then I would tell her of that visit she made to the Soyo Fish Company in the years gone by. How I, a poor white lad among that pack of ignorant Mexicans and Filipinos, was so overcome by her beauty that I dared not show my face. Then I would laugh.

'But of course you know who I am now.'

I would lead her to her book shelf, where my own books were to be seen among a few indispensable others, such as the bible and the dictionary, and I would draw out my book *Colossus of Destiny*, the book for which I had been given the Nobel Prize.

'Would you like me to autograph it?'

Then, with a gasp, she would know.

'Why, you're Bandini, the famous Arturo Bandini!'

Haw. And I would laugh again.

'In the flesh!'

What a day! What a triumph!

Chapter Fifteen

A month passed, with four pay checks. Fifteen dollars a week.

I never got used to Shorty Naylor. For that matter, Shorty Naylor never got used to me. I couldn't talk to him, but he couldn't talk to me either. He was not a man to say, Hello, how are you? He merely nodded. And he wasn't a man to discuss the canning situation or world politics. He was too cold. He kept me at a distance. He made me feel as if I were an employee. I already knew I was an employee. I didn't see any need to rub it in.

The end of the mackerel season was in sight. An afternoon came when we finished labeling a two hundred ton batch. Shortly Naylor appeared with a pencil and a checking board. The mackerel were boxed, stenciled, and ready to go. A freighter was moored at the docks, waiting to carry them off to Germany – a wholesale house in Berlin.

Shorty gave the word for us to move the shipment out on the docks. I wiped the sweat from my face as the machine came to a stop, and with easy good-nature and tolerance I walked over to Shorty and slapped him on the back.

'How's the canning situation, Naylor?' I said. 'What sort of competition do we get from those Norwegians?'

He shook the hand from his shoulder.

'Get yourself a hand truck and go to work.'

'A harsh master,' I said. 'You're a harsh master, Naylor.'

I took a dozen steps and he called my name. I returned.

'Do you know how to work a hand truck?'

I had no thought of it. I didn't even know hand trucks went by such a name. Of course I didn't know how to work a hand truck. I was a writer. Of course I didn't know. I laughed and pulled up my dungarees.

'Very funny! Do *I* know how to work a hand truck! And you ask me that! Haw. Do I know how to work a hand truck!'

'If you don't – say so. You don't have to kid me.'

I shook my head and looked at the floor.

'Do *I* know how to work a hand truck! And you ask me that!'

'Well, *do* you?'

'Your question is patently absurd on the face of it. Do I know how to work a hand truck! Of course I know how to work a hand truck. Naturally!'

His lip curled like a rat's tail.

'Where did *you* ever learn to work a hand truck?'

I spoke to the room at large. 'Now he wants to know where I worked a hand truck! Imagine that! He wants to know where I learned to work a hand truck.'

'All right, we're wasting time. Where? I'm asking you where?'

Like a rifle report I responded.

'The docks. The gasoline docks. Stevedoring.'

His eyes crawled over me from head to foot, and his lip took several weary curls, a man utterly nauseated with contempt.

'*You* a stevedore!'

He laughed.

I hated him. The imbecile. The fool, the dog, the rat, the skunk. The skunk-faced rat. What did he know about it. A lie, yes. But what did he know about it? Him – this rat – with not one ounce of culture, who had probably never read a book in his life. My God! What could he ever know about anything? And another thing. He wasn't so big either, with his missing teeth and tobacco-juice mouth and eyes of a boiled rat.

'Well,' I said. 'I've been looking you over, Saylor or Taylor, or Naylor, or whatever the hell they call you down here in this stink-hole, I don't give a damn myself; and unless my perspective is completely awry, you're not so goddamn big yourself, Saylor, or Baylor, or Taylor, or Naylor, or whatever the hell your name is.'

A foul word, too foul to repeat, oozed out of the side of his face. He scratched his checking board, making some sort of pretense not clear to me, but plainly a form of hypocrisy, a ruse from the depths of his brummagem soul, scratching away like a rat, an uncultured rat, and I hated him so much I could have bitten off his finger and spat it in his face. Look at him! That rat, making ratty little scratches on a piece of paper like a piece of cheese with his ratty little paws, the rodent, the pig, the alley rat, the dock rat. But why didn't he say something? Ha. Because at last he had found his match in me, because he was helpless before his betters.

I nodded at the stack of cartoned mackerel.

'I see this stuff is bound for Germany.'

'No fooling?' he said, scratching away.

But I didn't flinch under this plodding effort to be sarcastic.

The witticism found no target upon me. Instead, I lapsed into a serious silence.

'Say Naylor, or Baylor, or whatever it is – what do you think of modern Germany? Do you agree with Hitler's Weltanschauung?'

No response. Not a word, merely a scratching. And why not? Because Weltanschauung was too much for him! Too much for any rat. It baffled, stupefied him. It was the first time and the last he would ever hear the word uttered in his life. He put the pencil in pocket and peered over my shoulder. He had to get up on his tiptoes to do it, he was such a preposterously dwarfed little runt.

'Manuel!' he called. 'Oh Manuel! Come here a minute.'

Manuel came forward, scared, halting, because it was unusual for Shorty to address anybody by name, unless he was going to sack him. Manuel was thirty, with a hungry face and cheek bones protruding like eggs. He worked across from me on the can dump. I used to look at him a lot because of his huge teeth. They were as white as milk, but too big for his face, his upper lip not long enough to cover them. He made me think of teeth, and nothing else.

'Manuel, show this fellow how to work a hand truck.'

I interrupted. 'It's scarcely necessary, Manuel. But under the circumstances, he gives the orders around here and, as they say, an order is an order.'

But Manuel was on Shorty's side.

'Come on,' he said. 'I show you.'

He led me away, the foul words oozing from Shorty's mouth again, easy to hear.

'This amuses me,' I said. 'It's funny, you know. I feel like laughing. That poltroon.'

'I show you. Come on. Boss's orders.'

'The boss is a moron. He's dementia praecox.'

'No no! Boss's orders. Come on.'

'Very amusing in a macabre way – right out of Krafft-Ebing.'

'Boss's orders. Can't help.'

We went to the room where they were kept, and each of us dragged out a hand truck. Manuel pushed his into the clear. I followed. This was easy enough. So they were called hand trucks. When I was a kid we called them pushcarts. Anybody with two hands could work a hand truck. The back of Manuel's head was like the fur of a black cat shaved by a rusty butcher-knife. The growth was like a cliff: it was a home-made hair cut. The seat of his overalls was patched with a hunk of white canvas. It was badly sewed, as if he had used a hair pin and a length of string. His heels were worn down to the wet floor, the soles re-soled with wet fiber, held together by big nails. He looked so poor it made me mad. I knew a lot of poor people, but Manuel didn't have to be *that* poor.

'Say,' I said. 'How much do you make, for God's sake?'

The same as I. Twenty-five cents an hour.

He looked straight into my eyes, a tall lean man looking down, ready to fall apart, with deep dark honest eyes, but very suspicious. They had that whipped, melancholy cast of most all peon eyes.

He said, 'You like cannery work?'

'It amuses me. It has its moments.'

'I like. I like very much.'

'Why don't you get some new shoes?'

'No can afford.'

'You married?'

He nodded fast and hard, tickled to be married.

'Got any kids?'

And he was tickled about that too. He had three kids, because he raised three twisted fingers and grinned.

'How the hell do you live on two bits an hour?'

He didn't know. Lord, he didn't know, but he got by. He put his hand on his forehead and made a hopeless gesture. They lived, it wasn't much, but one day followed another and they were alive to see it.

'Why don't you ask for more money?'

He shook his head violently.

'Maybe get fired.'

'Do you know what you are?' I said.

No. He didn't know.

'You're a fool. A plain, unmitigated, goddamn fool. Look at yourself! You belong to the slave-dynasty. The heel of the ruling classes in your groin. Why don't you be a man and go on strike?'

'No strike. No no. Get fired.'

'You're a fool. A damn fool. Look at yourself! You haven't even got a decent pair of shoes. And look at your overalls! And by God, you even look hungry. Are you hungry?'

He wouldn't talk.

'Answer me, you fool! Are you hungry?'

'No hungry.'

'You dirty liar.'

His eyes dropped to his feet as he shuffled along. He was studying his shoes. Then he glanced at mine, which were better than his in every way. He seemed to be happy because I had the best shoes. He looked at my face and smiled. It made me furious. What was the sense in being glad about it? I wanted to punch him.

'Pretty good,' he said. 'How much you pay?'

'Shut your face.'

We went along, I following him. All at once I got so mad I couldn't keep my mouth shut. 'You fool! You laissez faire fool! Why don't you pull this cannery down and demand your rights? Demand shoes! Demand milk! Look at yourself! Like a boob, a convict! Where's the milk? Why don't you yell for it?'

His arms tensed on the handle-grips. His dark throat cabled with rage. I thought I had gone too far. Maybe there would be a fight. But it wasn't that.

'Keep still!' he hissed. 'Maybe we get fired!'

But the place was too noisy, squealing of wheels and thumping of boxes, with Shorty Naylor a hundred feet away at the door busy checking figures and unable to hear us. And when I saw how safe it was, I decided I wasn't through yet.

'What about your wife and kids? Those dear little babes? Demand milk! Think of them dying of hunger while the babes of the rich swim in gallons of milk! Gallons! And why should it be like that? Aren't you a man like other men? Or are you a fool, a nitwit, a monstrous travesty on the dignity that is man's primordial antecedent? Are you listening to me? Or are you turning your ears because the truth stings them and you are too weak and afraid to be other than an ablative absolute, a dynasty of slaves? Dynasty of slaves! Dynasty of slaves! You want to be a dynasty of slaves! You love the categorical imperative! You don't want milk, you want hypochondria! You're a whore, a slut, a pimp, a whore of modern Capitalism! You make me so sick I feel like puking.'

'Yeah,' he said. 'You puke all right. You no writer. You just puke.'

'I'm writing all the time. My head swims in a transvaluated phantasmagoria of phrases.'

'Bah! You make me puke too.'

'Nuts to you! You Brobdingnagian boor!'

He began stacking boxes for his load. With each he grunted, they were so high and hard to reach. He was supposed to be showing me. Hadn't the boss said to watch? Well, I was watching. Wasn't Shorty the boss? Well, I was carrying out orders. His eyes flashed in anger.

'Come on! Work!'

'Don't talk to me, you capitalistic proletarian bourgeois.'

The boxes weighed fifty pounds apiece. He stacked them ten high, one above the other. Then he eased the nose of his truck under the stack and pinched the bottom box with clamps at the base of the truck. I had never seen that kind of a truck. I had seen hand trucks, but not hand trucks with clamps.

'Again Progress rears its fair head. The new technic asserts itself even in the humble hand truck.'

'Keep still and watch.'

With a jerk he lifted the load from the floor and balanced it on the wheels, the handle-bars at shoulder height. It was a trick. I knew I couldn't do it. He wheeled the load away. And yet, if he could do it, he, a Mexican, a man who without doubt had never read a book in his life, who had never even heard of the transvaluation of values, then so could I. He, this mere peon, had trucked ten boxes.

Then what about you, Arturo? Are you going to be

outdone by him? No – a thousand times no! Ten boxes. Good. I will truck twelve boxes. Then I got my truck. By that time Manuel was back for another load.

'Too many,' he said.

'Shut up.'

I pushed my truck toward the stack and opened the clamps. It had to happen. Too hard. I knew it was going to happen. There was no sense in trying to out-do him, I knew it all the time, yet I did it. There was a splintering and a crash. The tier of boxes tumbled like a tower. They went everywhere. The top box was smashed open. Cans leaped from it, their oval shapes running over the floor like frightened puppies.

'Too many!' Manuel shouted. 'I tell you. Too damn many!'

I turned around and screamed, 'Will you shut your goddamn greaser face, you goddamn Mexican peon of a boot-licking bourgeois proletarian capitalist!'

The fallen stack was in the path of the other truckers. They trucked around it, kicking out of the way the cans that impeded their movement. I knelt down and gathered them up. It was disgusting, with me, a white man, on my knees, picking up cans of fish, while all around me, standing on their feet, were these foreigners.

Soon enough Shorty Naylor saw what happened. He came on the run.

'I thought you knew how to work a hand truck?'

I stood up.

'These aren't hand trucks. These are clamp-trucks.'

'Don't argue. Get that mess cleaned up.'

'Accidents will happen, Naylor. Rome wasn't built in a day. There's an old proverb from *Thus Spake Zarathustra* . . .'

He waved his hands.

'For Christ's sake never mind that! Try again. But this time, don't carry so many. Try five boxes at a time until you get the knack of it.'

I shrugged. Oh well, what could you do amongst that hot-bed of stupidity? The only thing left was to be brave, to have faith in man's intrinsic decency, and to cling to a belief in the reality of progress.

'You're the boss,' I said. 'I'm a writer, you know. Without qualification I . . .'

'Never mind that! I know all about that! Everybody knows you're a writer, everybody. But do me a favor, will you?' He was almost pleading. 'Try carrying five boxes, will you? Just five. Not six or seven. Just five. Will you do that for me? Take it easy. Don't kill yourself. Just five at a time.'

He walked away. The low words rolled under his breath – obscenities meant for me. So that was it! I thumbed my nose at his retreating back. I despised him, a low person, a boob of limited vocabulary, unable to express his own thoughts, however nasty, except through the brummagem medium of foul language. A rat. He was a rat. He was a nasty, evil-tongued rat who knew nothing about Hitler's Weltanschauung.

Pee on him!

I returned to the task of picking up the fallen tins. When they had all been gathered I decided I would get another truck. In the corner I found one unlike the others, a four-wheeler, a sort of wagon with an iron tongue. It was very light with a wide, flat surface. I drew it to where the boys were loading their hand trucks. It created a sensation. They looked at it as though they had never seen it before, exclaiming in Spanish. Manuel scratched his head in disgust.

'What you do now?'

I pulled the truck into place.

'You wouldn't know – you tool of the bourgeoisie.'

Then I loaded it. Not with five boxes. Not with ten. And not with twelve. As I continued to stack them up I realized what possibilities lay in this type of truck. When I finally stopped I had thirty-four aboard.

Thirty-four times fifty? How much was that? I took out my notebook and pencil and figured it. Seventeen hundred pounds. And seventeen hundred times ten were seventeen thousand pounds. Seventeen thousand pounds were eight and one half tons. Eight and one half tons an hour were eighty-five tons a day. Eighty-five tons a day were five hundred and ninety-five tons a week. Five hundred and ninety-five tons a week were thirty thousand nine hundred and forty tons a year. At that rate I would carry three hundred and nine thousand four hundred tons a year. Imagine! And the others carried a mere five hundred pounds per load.

'Gangway!'

They stepped aside and I began to pull. The load moved slowly. I tugged backward, facing the load. My progress was slow because my feet slipped on the wet floor. The load was in the midst of things, directly in the path of the other truckers, which caused a little confusion, but not much, both coming and going. Finally the work stopped. All trucks were glutted in the middle of the room, like a downtown traffic jam. Shorty Naylor hurried in. I was tugging hard, grunting and slipping, losing more ground than I was gaining. But it was no fault of mine. It was the fault of the floor, which was too slippery.

'What the hell's going on here?' Shorty yelled.

I relaxed for a moment's rest. He slapped his hand over his forehead and shook his head.

'What're you doing *now*?'

'Trucking boxes.'

'Get it out of the way! Can't you see you're holding up the job?'

'But look at the size of this load! Seventeen hundred pounds!'

'Get it out of the way!'

'This is more than thre times as many . . .'

'I said, get it out of the way!'

The fool. What could I do against such odds?

The rest of the afternoon I trucked five at a time with a two-wheel truck. It was a very unpleasant task. The only white man, the only American, and he trucking but half as much as the foreigners. I had to do something about it. The boys didn't say anything, but every one of them grinned when they passed me with my measly load of five.

At length I found a way out of it. The worker Orquiza pulled a box from the top of the stack, loosening the whole wall of other boxes. With a yell of warning I ran to the wall and pushed it with my shoulder. It wasn't necessary, but I held the wall against my body, my face purpling, as if the wall was about to collapse upon me. The boys quickly broke down the wall. Afterward I held my shoulder and moaned and clinched my teeth. I staggered away, barely able to walk.

'Are you all right?' they asked.

'It's nothing,' I smiled. 'Don't worry, fellows. I think I

dislocated my shoulder, but it's all right. Don't let it worry you at all.'

So now, with a dislocated shoulder, there was no reason for them to grin at my load of five.

That night we worked until seven o'clock. The fog held us up. I stayed a few minutes overtime. I was stalling. I wanted to see Shorty Naylor alone. I had a few things I wanted to discuss with him. When the others had gone and the cannery was deserted, a strange, pleasant loneliness fell upon it. I went to Shorty Naylor's office. The door was open. He was washing his hands in that strong soap powder which was half lye. I could smell it. He seemed a part of the strange, vast loneliness of the cannery, he belonged to it, like a girder across the roof. For a moment he seemed sad and soft, a man with many worries, a person like me, like anyone else. At that evening hour, with the building exposing him to vast loneliness, it seemed to me he was a pretty good fellow after all. But I had something on my mind. I knocked on the door. He turned around.

'Hello there. What's your trouble?'

'No trouble at all,' I said. 'I merely wanted to get your view on a matter.'

'Well, shoot the works. What is it?'

'A little matter I tried to discuss with you earlier this afternoon.'

He was drying his hands on a black towel.

'I can't remember. What was it about?'

'You were very uncivil about it this afternoon,' I said. 'Maybe you won't want to discuss it.'

'Oh,' he smiled. 'You know how it is when a man's busy. Sure, I'll discuss it. What's the trouble?'

'Hitler's Weltanschauung. What is your opinion of the Führer's Weltanschauung?'

'What's that?'

'Hitler's Weltanschauung.'

'Hitler's what? Weltan – what?'

'Hitler's Weltanschauung?'

'What's that? What's Weltanschauung? You got me there, boy. I don't even know what it means.'

I whistled and backed away.

'My God!' I said. 'Don't tell me you don't even know what it means!'

He shook his head and smiled. It was not very important to him; not as important as drying his hands, for instance. He was not at all ashamed of his ignorance – not in the least shocked. In fact, he seemed rather pleased. I tsk-tsk-tsked with my tongue and backed out of the door, smiling hopelessly. This was almost too much for me. What could I do against an ignoramus like that?

'Well, if you don't know, well, I guess you don't know, and I guess there's no sense in trying to discuss it, if you don't know, and, well, it looks as if you don't know, so, well, goodnight, if you don't know. Goodnight. See you in the morning.'

He stood so surprised he forgot to keep drying his hands. Then he called suddenly. 'Hey!' he called. 'What's this all about?'

But I was gone, hurrying through the darkness of the vast warehouse, only the echo of his voice reaching me. On the way out I passed through the wet clammy room where they dumped mackerel, from the fishing boats. But tonight there were no mackerel, the season had just ended, and instead there were tuna, the first real tuna I ever saw in such numbers, the floor littered with them, thousands of them scattered over a carpet of dirty ice, their white corpse-like bellies blundering through the semi-darkness.

Some of them were still alive. You could hear the sporadic slapping of tails. There in front of me flapped the tail of one who was more alive than dead. I dragged him out of the ice. He was bitter cold and still kicking. I carried him as best I could, dragging him too, until I got him upon the cutting table where the women would dress him tomorrow. He was tremendous, weighing almost a hundred pounds, a monster of a fellow from another world, with great strength still left in his body, and a streak of blood coming from his eye, where he had been hooked. Strong as a man, he hated me and tried to break away from the cutting board. I pulled a gutting knife from the board and held it under his white pulsing gills.

'You monster!' I said. 'You black monster! Spell Weltanschauung! Go on – *spell* it!'

But he was a fish from another world; he couldn't spell anything. The best he could do was fight for his life, and he was already too tired for that. But even so, he almost got away. I slugged him with my fist. Then I slid the knife under his gill, amused at his helpless gasping, and cut off his head.

'When I said spell Weltanschauung, I meant it!'

I pushed him back among his comrades upon the ice.

'Disobedience means death.'

There was no response save the faint flapping of a tail somewhere in the blackness. I wiped my hands on a gunny sack and walked into the street toward home.

Chapter Sixteen

The day after I destroyed the women I wished I had not destroyed them. When I was busy and tired I did not think of them, but Sunday was a day of rest, and I would loaf around with nothing to do, and Helen and Marie and Ruby and the Little Girl would whisper to me frantically, asking me why I had been so hasty to destroy them, asking me if I did not now regret it. And I did regret it.

Now I had to be satisfied with their memories. But their memories were not good enough. They escaped me. They were unlike the reality. I could not hold them and look at them as I did the pictures. Now I went around all the time wishing I had not destroyed them, and I called myself a dirty stinking Christian for having done it. I thought about making another collection, but that was not so easy. It had taken a long time to gather those others. I couldn't at will go about finding women to equal the Little Girl, and probably never again would there ever in my life be another woman like Marie. They could never be duplicated. There was another thing that prevented me from making another collection. I was too tired. I used to sit around with a book of Spengler or Schopenhauer and always as I read I kept calling myself a fake and a fool, because what I really wanted were those women who were no more.

Now the closet was different, filled with Mona's dresses and the disgusting odor of fumigation. Some nights I thought I could not bear it. I walked up and down the grey carpet thinking how horrible grey carpets were, and biting my fingernails. I couldn't read anything. I didn't feel like reading a book by a great man, and I used to wonder if they were so great after all. After all, were they as great as Hazel or Marie, or the Little Girl? Could Nietzsche compare with the golden hair of Jean? Some nights I didn't think so at all. Was Spengler as great as Hazel's fingernails? Sometimes yes, sometimes no. There was a time and place for everything, but as far as I was concerned I would rather have the beauty of Hazel's fingernails to ten million volumes by Oswald Spengler.

I wanted the privacy of my study again. I used to look at that closet door and say it was a tombstone through which I could never enter again. Mona's dresses! It sickened me. And yet I could not tell my mother or Mona to please move the dresses elsewhere. I couldn't walk up to my mother and say, 'Please move those dresses.' The words would not come. I hated it. I thought I was becoming a Babbitt, a moral coward.

One night my mother and Mona were not at home. Just for old time's sake I decided to pay my study a visit. A little sentimental journey into the land of yesterday. I closed the door and stood in the darkness and thought of the many times when this little room was my very own, with no part of my sister disturbing it. But it could never be the same again.

In the darkness I put out my hand and felt her dresses hanging from the clothes-hooks. They were like the shrouds of ghosts, like the robes of millions and millions of dead nuns from the beginning of the world. They seemed to challenge me: they seemed to be there only to harass me and destroy the peaceful fantasy of my women who had never been. A bitterness went through me, and it was painful to even remember the other times. By now I had almost forgotten the features of those others.

I twisted my fist into the folds of a dress to keep from crying out. Now the closet had an unmistakable odor of rosaries and incense, of white lilies at funerals, of carpetry in the churches of my boyhood, of wax and tall, dark windows, of old women in black kneeling at mass.

It was the darkness of the confessional, with a kid of twelve named Arturo Bandini kneeling before a priest and telling him he had done something awful, and the priest telling him nothing was too awful for the confessional, and the kid saying he wasn't sure it was a sin, what he had done, but still he was sure nobody else ever did a thing like that because, father, it's certainly funny, I mean, I don't know how to tell it; and the priest finally wheedling it out of him, that first sin of love, and warning him never to do it again.

I wanted to bump my head against the closet wall and hurt myself so much that I would be senseless. Why didn't I throw those dresses out? Why did they have to remind me of Sister Mary Justin, and Sister Mary Leo, and Sister Mary Corita? I guess I was paying the rent in this apartment; I guess I could throw them out. And I couldn't understand why. Something forbade it.

I felt weaker than ever before, because when I was strong I would not have hesitated a moment; I would have bundled those dresses up and heaved them out the window and spat after them. But the desire was gone. It seemed silly to get angry and start heaving dresses about. It was dead and drifted away.

I stood there, and I found my thumb in my mouth. It seemed amazing that it should be there. Imagine. Me eighteen years old, and still sucking my thumb! Then I said to myself, if you're so brave and fearless, why don't you *bite* your thumb? I dare you to bite it! You're a coward if you don't. And I said, oh! Is that so? Well, I'm not either a coward. And I'll prove it!

I bit my thumb until I tasted blood. I felt my teeth against the pliant skin, refusing to penetrate, and I turned my thumb slowly until the teeth cut through the skin. The pain hesitated, moved to my knuckles, up my arm, then to my shoulder and eyes.

I grabbed the first dress I touched and tore it to pieces. Look how strong you are! Tear it to bits! Rip it until there is nothing left! And I ripped it with my hands and teeth and made grunts like a mad dog, rolling over the floor, pulling the dress across my knees and raging at it, smearing my bloody thumb over it, cursing it and laughing at it as it gave way under my strength and tore apart.

Then I started to cry. The pain in my thumb was nothing. It was a loneliness that really ached. I wanted to pray. I had not said a prayer in two years – not since the day I quit high school and began so much reading. But now I wanted to pray again, I was sure it would help, that it would make me feel better, because when I was a kid prayer used to do that for me.

I got down on my knees, closed my eyes and tried to think of prayer-words. Prayer-words were a different kind of word: I never realized it until that moment. Then I knew the difference.

But there were no words. I had to pray, to say some things; there was a prayer in me like an egg. But there were no words.

Surely not those old prayers!

Not the Lord's Prayer, about Our Father who art in Heaven, hallowed be Thy name, Thy kingdom come . . . I didn't believe that anymore. There wasn't any such thing as heaven; there might be a hell, it seemed very possible, but there wasn't any such thing as heaven.

Not the Act of Contrition, about O my God, I am heartily sorry for having offended Thee, and I detest all my sins . . . Because the only thing I was sorry about was the loss of my women, and that was something which God emphatically opposed. Or did He? Surely, He must be against that. If I were God I would certainly be against it. God could hardly be in favor of my women. No. Then He was against them.

There was Nietzsche, Friedrich Nietzsche.

I tried him.

I prayed, 'Oh dearly beloved Friedrich!'

No good. It sounded like I was a homosexual.

I tried again.

'Oh dear Mr Nietzsche.'

Worse. Because I got to thinking about Nietzsche's pictures in the frontispieces of his books. They made him look like a Forty-niner, with a sloppy mustache, and I detested Forty-niners.

Besides, Nietzsche was dead. He had been dead for years. He was an immortal writer, and his words burned across the pages of his books, and he was a great modern influence, but for all that he was dead and I knew it.

Then I tried Spengler.

I said, 'My dear Spengler.'

Awful.

I said, 'Hello there, Spengler.'

Awful.

I said, 'Listen, Spengler!'

Worse.

I said, 'Well, Oswald, as I was saying . . .'

Brrr. And still worse.

There were my women. They were dead too; maybe I could find something in them. One at a time I tried them out, but it was unsuccessful because as soon as I thought of them it made me wildly passionate. How could a man be passionate and be in prayer? That was scandalous.

After I had thought of so many people without avail I was weary of the whole idea and about to abandon it, when all of a sudden I had a good idea, and the idea was that I should not pray to God or others, but to myself.

'Arturo, my man. My beloved Arturo. It seems you suffer so much, and so unjustly. But you are brave, Arturo. You remind me of a mighty warrior, with the scars of a million conquests. What courage is yours! What nobility! What beauty! Ah, Arturo, how beautiful you really are! I love you so, my Arturo, my great and mighty god. So weep now, Arturo. Let your tears run down, for yours is a life of struggle, a bitter battle to the very end, and nobody knows it but you, no one but you, a beautiful warrior who fights alone, unflinching, a great hero the likes of which the world has never known.'

I sat back on my heels and cried until my sides ached from it. I opened my mouth and wailed, and it felt ah so good, so sweet to cry, so that soon I was laughing with pleasure, laughing and crying, the tears spilling down my face and washing my hands. I could have gone on for hours.

Footsteps in the living room made me stop. The steps were Mona's. I stood up and wiped my eyes, but I knew they were red. Stuffing the torn skirt under my shirt I walked out of the closet. I coughed a little, clearing my throat, to show I was at ease with everything.

Mona didn't know anyone was in the apartment. The lights were out and everything, and she thought the place was deserted. She looked at me in surprise, as if she had never seen me before. I walked a few feet, this way and that, coughing and humming a tune, but still she watched, saying nothing but keeping her eyes glued to me.

'Well,' I said. 'You critic of life – say something.'

Her eyes were on my hand.

'Your finger. It's all . . .'

'It's my finger,' I said. 'You God-intoxicated nun.'

I locked the bathroom door behind me and threw the tattered dress down the air shaft. Then I bandaged my finger. I stood at the mirror and looked at myself. I loved my own face. I thought I was a very handsome person. I had a good straight nose and a wonderful mouth, with lips redder than a woman's, for all her paint and whatnot. My eyes were big and clear, my jaw protruded slightly, a strong jaw, a jaw denoting character and self-discipline. Yes, it was a fine face. A man of judgment would have found much in it to interest him.

In the medicine cabinet I came upon my mother's wedding ring, where she usually left it after washing her hands. I held the ring in the palm of my hand and looked at it in amazement. To think that this ring, this piece of mere metal, had sealed the connubial bond which was to produce me! That was an incredible thing. Little did my father know, when he bought this ring, that it would symbolize the union of man and woman out of which would arrive one of the world's greatest men. How strange it was to be standing in that bathroom and realizing all these things! Little did this piece of stupid metal know its own significance. And yet someday it would become a collector's item of incalculable value. I could see the museum, with people milling about the Bandini heirlooms, the shouting of the auctioneer, and finally a Morgan or a Rockefeller of tomorrow raising his price to twelve million dollars for that ring, simply because it was worn by the mother of Arturo Bandini, the greatest writer the world had ever known.

Chapter Seventeen

A half hour passed. I was reading on the divan. The bandage on my thumb stood out clearly. Mona said no more about it though. She was across the room, reading too, and eating an apple. The front door opened. It was my mother, returning from Uncle Frank's house. The first thing she saw was my bandaged finger.

'My God,' she said. 'What happened?'

'How much money have you got?' I said.

'But your finger! What happened?'

'How much money have you got?'

Her fingers fluttered through her ragged purse as she kept glancing at the bandaged thumb. She was too excited, too frightened to open the purse. It fell on the floor. She picked it up, her knees crackling, her hands going everywhere, groping after the purse lock. Finally Mona got up and took the purse from her. Completely exhausted, and still worried about my thumb, my mother dropped into a chair. I knew her heart was pounding violently. When she got her breath she again asked about the bandage. But I was reading. I didn't answer.

She asked again.

'I hurt it.'

'How?'

'How much money have you got?'

Mona counted it, holding the apple between her teeth.

'Three dollars and a bit of change,' she mumbled.

'How much change?' I said. 'Be specific please. I like precise answers.'

'Arturo!' my mother said. 'What happened? How did you hurt it?'

'Fifteen cents,' Mona answered.

'Your finger!' my mother said.

'Give me the fifteen cents,' I said.

'Come and get it,' Mona said.

'But Arturo!' my mother said.

'Give it to me!' I said.

'You're not crippled,' Mona said.

'Yes he is too crippled!' my mother said. 'Look at his finger!'

'It's *my* finger! And give me that fifteen cents – you!'

'If you want it, come and get it.'

My mother jumped from her chair and sat down beside me. She began stroking the hair from my eyes. Her fingers were hot, and she was so powdered with talcum she smelled like a baby, like an aged baby. I got up at once. She stretched her arm out to me.

'Your poor finger! Let me see it.'

I walked over to Mona.

'Give me that fifteen cents.'

She wouldn't. It lay on the table, but she refused to hand it to me.

'There it is. Pick it up, if you want it.'

'I want you to hand it to me.'

In disgust she snorted.

'You fool!' she said.

I put the coins in my pocket.

'You'll regret this,' I said. 'As God is my judge, you'll rue this impudence.'

'Good,' she said.

'I'm getting tired of being a workhorse for a pair of parasitical females. I tell you I've just about reached the apogee of my fortitude. At any minute now I propose to flee this bondage.'

'Poo poo poo,' Mona sneered. 'Why don't you flee now – tonight? It would make everybody happy.'

My mother was completely out of it. Distraught and rocking to and fro she could learn nothing about my finger. All evening I had heard her voice only vaguely.

'Seven weeks at the cannery. I'm fed up with it.'

'How did you hurt it?' my mother said. 'Maybe it's blood-poisoned.'

Maybe it was! For a moment I thought this possible. Working in the unsanitary conditions at the cannery, anything was possible. Then perhaps it *was* blood-poisoned. Me, a poor kid working down in that sweat hole, and this was my reward: blood-poisoning! Me, a poor kid working to support two women because I had to do it. Me, a poor kid, never complaining; and now to die of blood-poisoning from conditions down there where I earned the bread to feed their mouths. I wanted to burst out crying. I swung around and shouted.

'How did I hurt it? I'll tell you how I hurt it! Now you shall know the truth. Now it can be told. You shall know the demoniacal truth of it. I hurt it in a machine! I hurt it slaving my life away in that carnatic jute-mill! I hurt it because the fungus mouths of two parasitical women depended upon me. I hurt it because of the idiosyncrasies of native intelligence. I hurt it because of incipient martyrdom. I hurt it because my destiny would deny me no dogmatism! I hurt it because the metabolism of my days would deny me no recrudescence! I hurt it because I have a brobdingnagian nobility of purpose!'

My mother sat in shame, understanding nothing I said, but sensing what I was trying to say, her eyes down, her lips pouted, looking innocently into her hands. Mona had gone back to her reading, munching her apple and paying no attention. I turned to her.

'Nobility of purpose!' I screamed. 'Nobility of purpose! Do you hear me, you nun! Nobility of purpose! But now I weary of all nobility. I am in revolt. I see a new day for America, for me and my fellow-workers down in that jute-mill. I see a land of milk and honey. I visualize, and I say, Hail the new America! Hail. Hail! Do you hear me, you nun! I say hail! Hail! Hail!'

'Poo poo poo,' said Mona.

'Don't sneer − you preposterous monster!'

She made a contemptuous noise in her throat, pulled her book about, and now her back was facing me. Then, for the first time, I noticed the book she was reading. It was a brand new library book, with a bright red jacket.

'What's that you're reading?'

No answer.

'I'm feeding your body. I guess I have the right to know who feeds your brains.'

No answer.

'So you won't talk!'

I rushed over and tore the book from her hands. It was a

novel by Kathleen Norris. My mouth flew open with a gasp as the whole shocking situation revealed itself. So this was how matters stood in my own home! While I sweated my blood and bone away at the cannery, feeding her body, this, this, was what she fed her brains! Kathleen Norris. This was modern America! No wonder the decline of the west! No wonder the despair of the modern world. So this was it! With me, a poor kid, working my fingers to the bone, trying my best to give them a decent family-life, and this, this, was my reward! I tottered, measured the distance to the wall, staggered toward it, fell over backward toward the wall, and drooped there, gasping for breath.

'My God,' I moaned. 'My God.'

'What's the matter?' my mother said.

'Matter! Matter! I'll tell you what's the matter. Look what she's reading! Oh God almighty! Oh God have mercy on her soul! And to think that I'm slaving my life away, me, a poor kid, ripping the very flesh from my fingers, while she sits around reading this disgusting pig-vomit. Oh God, give me strength! Increase my fortitude! Spare me from throttling her!'

And I tore the book to shreds. The pieces dropped on the carpet. I ground them with my heels. I spat on them, drooled on them, cleared my throat and exploded at them. Then I gathered them up, carried them into the kitchen, and heaved them into the garbage can.

'Now,' I said. 'Try that again.'

'That's a library book,' Mona smiled. 'You'll have to pay for it.'

'I'll rot in jail first.'

'Here, here!' my mother said. 'What's this all about?'

'Where's that fifteen cents?'
'Let me look at your thumb.'
'I said, where's that fifteen cents.'
'In your pocket,' Mona said. 'You fool.'
And I walked out.

Chapter Eighteen

I crossed the schoolyard toward Jim's Place. In my pocket jingled the fifteen cents. The schoolyard was graveled, and my feet echoed upon it. Here is a good idea, I thought, graveled yards in all prisons, a good idea; something worth remembering; if I were the prisoner of my mother and sister, how futile to escape in this noise; a good idea, something to think about.

Jim was in the back of the store, reading a racing form. He had just put in a new liquor shelf. I stopped in front of it to examine the bottles. Some were very pretty, making their contents appear most palatable.

Jim put down his racing form and walked over. Always impersonal, he waited for the other fellow to speak. He was eating a candy bar. This seemed most unusual. It was the first time I ever saw him with anything in his mouth. I didn't like the looks of him either. I tapped the liquor case.

'I want a bottle of booze.'

'Hello!' he said. 'And how's the cannery job?'

'It's all right, I guess. But tonight I think I'll get drunk. I don't want to talk about the fish cannery.'

I saw a small bottle of whiskey, a five-ounce bottle with contents like liquid gold. He wanted ten cents for that bottle.

It seemed reasonable enough. I asked him if it was good whiskey. He said it was good whiskey.

'The very best,' he said

'Sold. I'll take your word and buy it without further comment.'

I handed him the fifteen cents.

'No,' he said. 'Only a dime.'

'Help yourself to the extra nickel. It's a tip, a gesture of personal goodwill and fellowship.'

With a smile he would not take it. I still held it out, but he put his palm upward and shook his head. I could not understand why he was always refusing my tips. It wasn't that I only offered them rarely; on the contrary, I tried to tip him every time; in fact, he was the only person I ever tipped.

'Let's not start this all over again,' I said. 'I tell you I always tip. It's a matter of principle with me. I'm like Hemingway. I always do it second-nature.'

With a grunt he took it and jabbed it into his jeans.

'Jim, you're a strange man; a quixotic character shot through with excellent qualities. You surpass the best the mob has to offer. I like you because your mind has scope.'

This made him fussy. He would rather talk of other things. He pushed the hair from his forehead and ran his hand over the back of his neck, pulling at it as he tried to think of something to say. I unscrewed the bottle and held it up. 'Saluti!' And took a swig. I didn't know why I had bought the liquor. It was the first time in my life I ever put out money for the stuff. I hated the taste of whiskey. It surprised me to find it in my mouth, but there it was indeed, and before I knew it the stuff was working, gritty against my teeth and halfway down my throat, kicking and tearing like a drowning cat. The taste was awful, like burning hair. I could feel it way down, doing strange things inside my stomach. I licked my lips.

'Marvelous! You were right. It's marvelous!'

It was in the pit of my stomach, rolling over and over, trying to find a place to lie, and I rubbed hard so the burning on the outside would equalize the burning within.

'Wonderful! Superb! Extraordinary!'

A woman entered the store. From the corner of my eye I got a flash of her as she stepped to the cigarette counter. Then I turned around and looked at her. She was a woman of thirty, maybe more. Her age didn't matter: she was there – that was the important thing. There was nothing striking about her. She was very plain to see, and yet I could feel that woman. Her presence jumped across the room and tore my breath from my throat. It was like a deluge of electricity. My flesh trembled in excitement. I could feel my own breathlessness and the rush of red blood. She wore an old faded purple coat with a fur neckpiece attached. She was not aware of me. She didn't seem aware of herself. She glanced in my direction and then turned and faced the counter. For a flash I saw her white face. It disappeared behind the fur neckpiece and I never saw it again.

But one glance was enough for me. I would never forget that face. It was a sickly white, like the police photographs of a criminal female. Her eyes were starved and grey and big and hunted. Her hair was any color at all. Brown and black, light yet dark: I didn't remember. She ordered a pack of cigarettes by tapping the counter with a coin. She didn't speak. Jim handed her the pack. He didn't feel the woman at all. She was just another customer to him.

I was still staring. I knew I shouldn't stare that much. I

didn't care though. I felt that if she would only see my face she would not object. Her furpiece was an imitation squirrel. The coat was old and threadbare at the hem, which reached to her knees. It fit her closely, lifting her figure toward me. Her hose were gun-metal, with streaks where the weave had got loose and run down. Her shoes were blue, with lop-sided heels and frazzled soles. I smiled and stared at her confidently because I was not afraid of her. A woman like Miss Hopkins upset me and made me feel absurd, but not the picture women, for instance, and not a woman like this woman. It was so easy to smile, it was so insolently easy; it was so much fun to feel so obscene. I wanted to say something dirty, something suggestive, like pheew! I can take whatever you've got to offer, you little bitch. But she did not see me. Without turning she paid for her cigarettes, walked out of the store and down Avalon Boulevard toward the sea.

Jim rang up the sale and returned to where I was standing. He started to say something. Without a word to him I walked out. I just walked right out of there and down the street after that woman. She was more than a dozen steps away, hurrying toward the waterfront. I didn't really know I was following her. When I realized it I stopped dead in my tracks and snapped my fingers. Oh! So now you're a pervert! A sex-pervert! Well well well, Bandini, I didn't think it would come to this; I *am* surprised! I hesitated, tearing big slices out of my thumbnail and spitting them out. But I didn't want to think about it. I would rather think about her.

She was not graceful. Her walk was stubborn, brutish; she walked defiantly, as if to say, I dare you to stop me from walking! She walked with a zig-zag too; moving from one side of the wide sidewalk to the other, sometimes at the curbing and sometimes almost bumping the plate glass windows at her left. But no matter how she walked, the figure under the old purple coat rippled and coiled. Her gait was long and heavy. I kept the original distance she maintained between us.

I felt frenzied; deliriously and impossibly happy. There was that smell of the sea, the clean salted sweetness of the air, the cold cynical indifference of the stars, the sudden laughing intimacy of the streets, the brazen opulence of light in darkness, the glowing languor of slitted crescent moon. I loved it all. I felt like squealing, making queer noises, new noises, in my throat. It was like walking naked through a valley of beautiful girls on all sides.

About half a block down the street I suddenly remembered Jim. I turned to see if he had come to his door to learn why I had hurried away. It was a sickly, guilty feeling. But he was not there. The front of his bright little shop was deserted. The length of Avalon Boulevard showed not a sign of life. I looked up at the stars. They seemed so blue, so cold, so insolent, so far away and utterly contemptuous, so conceited. The bright street lamps made the boulevard as light as early twilight.

I crossed the first corner as she reached the front of the theatre in the next block. She was gathering distance, but I allowed it. You shall not escape me, O beautiful lady, I am at your heels and you have no opportunity to elude me. But where are you going, Arturo? Do you realize that you are following a strange woman? You have never done *this* before. What is your motive? Now I was becoming frightened. I thought about those police cruisers. She drew me on. Ah – that was it – I was her prisoner. I felt guilty, but also I felt I was not doing wrong. After all, I am out for a bit of exercise in the night air; I am taking a walk before retiring, Officer. I live over there, Officer. I have lived there over a year, Officer. My Uncle Frank. Do you know him, Officer? Frank Scarpi? Of course, Officer! Everybody knows my Uncle Frank. A fine man. He'll tell you I'm his nephew. No need to book me, under the circumstances.

As I walked along the bandaged thumb slapped against my thigh. I looked down and there it was, that awful white bandage, slapping away with every step, moving with the motion of my arm, a big white ugly lump, so white and glaring, as if every lamp in the street knew of it and why it was there. I was disgusted with it. To think of it! He bit his own thumb until the blood came! Can you imagine a sane man doing that? I tell you he's insane, sir. He's done some strange things, sir. Did I ever tell you about the time he killed those crabs? I think the guy is crazy, sir. I suggest we book him and have his head examined. Then I tore the bandage off and threw it in the gutter and refused to think about it again.

The woman kept widening the distance between us. Now she was a half block away. I couldn't walk faster. I was going along slowly and I told myself to hurry it a bit, but the idea of the police cruisers began to slow me down. The police in the harbor were from the Los Angeles central station; they were very tough cops on a tough beat and they arrested a man first and then told him why he was arrested, and they always appeared from out of the nowhere, never afoot, but in quiet, fast-moving Buicks.

'Arturo,' I said, 'you're certainly walking into trouble. You will be arrested for a degenerate!'

Degenerate? What nonsense! Can't I go for a walk if I feel

like it? That woman up ahead? I don't know a thing about her. This is a free country, by God. Can I help it if she happens to be moving in the same direction as I? If she doesn't like it, let her walk on another street, Officer. This is my favorite street anyhow, Officer. Frank Scarpi is my uncle, Officer. He will testify that I always go for a walk down this street before retiring. After all, this is a free country, Officer.

At the next corner the woman stopped to strike a match against the wall of the bank. Then she lit a cigarette. The smoke hung in the dead air like distorted blue balloons. I sprang to my toes and hurried. When I got to the motionless clouds I lifted myself on tiptoe and drew them down. The smoke from *her* cigarette! Aha.

I knew where her match had fallen. A few steps more and I picked it up. There it lay, in the palm of my hand. An extraordinary match. No perceptible difference from other matches, yet an extraordinary match. It was half burned, a sweet-smelling pine match and very beautiful like a piece of rare gold. I kissed it.

'Match,' I said. 'I love you. Your name is Henrietta. I love you body and soul.'

I put it in my mouth and began to chew it. The carbon tasted of a delicacy, a bitter-sweet pine, brittle and succulent. Delicious, ravishing. The very match she had held in her fingers. Henrietta. The finest match I ever ate, Madam. Let me congratulate you.

She was moving faster now, clots of smoke in her wake. I drew big draughts of them down. Aha. That movement in her hips was like a ball of snakes. I felt it in my chest and finger tips.

Now we were advancing toward the cafes and pool-halls

along the waterfront. The night air plinked with the voices of men and the distant click of pool balls. In front of the Acme stevedores suddenly appeared, pool cues in their hands. They must have heard the click of the woman's heels on the sidewalk, because they came out so suddenly, and now they were out in front, waiting.

She passed along a lane of silent eyes, and they followed her with a slow pivoting of necks, five men lounging in the doorway. I was fifty feet behind. I detested them. One of them, a monster with a bailing hook stuck in his pocket, took the cigar from his mouth and whistled softly. He smiled to the others, cleared his throat, and spat a silver streak across the sidewalk. I detested that ruffian. Did he know there was a city ordinance forbidding expectorating on a sidewalk? Wasn't he aware of the laws of decent society? Or was he merely an illiterate human monster who had to spit and spit and spit for sheer animalism, a loathsome, vicious urge in his body which forced him to blech out his vile spleen whenever he felt like it? If I only knew his name! I would turn him over to the health department and institute suit against him.

Then I reached the front of the Acme. The men watched me pass too, all of them loafing and seeking something to look at. The woman was now in a section where all the buildings were black and vacant, a great lane of black barren depression windows. For a moment she stopped before one of these windows. Then she went on. Something in the window had caught her eyes and detained her.

When I reached the window I saw what it was. It was the window of the only occupied store in the section. A second-hand store, a pawn shop. Now it was long after office hours and the store was closed, the windows piled high with jewelry, tools, typewriters, suitcases and cameras. A sign in the window read: Highest Prices Paid For Old Gold. Because I knew she had read that sign, I read it over and over again. Highest Prices Paid For Old Gold. Highest Prices Paid For Old Gold. Now both of us had read it, she and I – Arturo Bandini and his woman. Wonderful! And had she not peered carefully into the back of the store? Then so would Bandini, for as did Bandini's woman so did Bandini. A small light burned in the back, over a stumpy little safe. The room bulged with second-hand articles. In one corner stood a wire cage behind which was a desk. The eyes of my woman had seen all of this, and I would not forget.

I turned to follow her again. At the next corner she stepped from the curbing just as the stop light signaled green and GO. I came up fast, eager to cross too, but the light changed to red and STOP. The hell with red lights. Love tolerates no barriers. Bandini must get through. On to victory! And I crossed anyhow. She was only twenty feet before me, the curved mystery of her form flooding me. I would soon be upon her. This had not occurred to me.

Well, Bandini; what will you do now?

Bandini does not falter. Bandini knows what to do, don't you Bandini? Of course I do! I am going to speak sweet words to her. I am going to say hello, my beloved! And a beautiful night it is; and would you object if I walked a bit with you? I know some fine poetry, like the Song of Solomon and that long one from Nietzsche about voluptuousness – which do you prefer? Did you know that I was a writer? Yes indeed! I write for Posterity. Let us walk down to the water's edge while I tell you of my work, of the prose for Posterity.

But when I reached her a strange thing took place.

We were abreast of one another. I coughed and cleared my throat. I was about to say, Hello, my good woman. But something jammed in my throat. I could do nothing else. I couldn't even look at her, because my head refused to turn on my neck. My nerve was gone. I thought I was going to faint. I am collapsing, I said; I am in a state of collapse. And then the strange thing happened: I began to run. I picked up my feet, threw back my head, and ran like a fool. With elbows chugging and nostrils meeting the salt air I ran like an Olympic runner, a half-miler sprinting down the home stretch to victory.

What are you doing now, Bandini? Why are you running?

I feel like running. What of it? I guess I can run if I feel like it, can't I?

My feet clacked on the deserted street. I was picking up speed. Doors and windows shot past me in amazing style. I never realized I had such speed. Passing the Longshoremen's Hall at a fast clip, I took a wide turn into Front Street. The long warehouses threw black shadows into the road, and among them was the swift echo of my feet. I was at the docks now, with the sea across the street, beyond the warehouses.

I was none other than Arturo Bandini, the greatest half-miler in the history of the American track and field annals. Gooch, the mighty Dutch champion, Sylvester Gooch, speed demon from the land of windmills and wooden shoes, was fifty feet ahead of me, and the mighty Dutchman was giving me the race of my career. Would I win? The thousands of men and women in the stands wondered — especially the women, for I was known jokingly among the sport scribes as a 'woman's runner,' because I was so tremendously popular among the feminine fans. Now the stands were cheering in a frenzy. Women threw out their arms and begged me to win – for America. Come on, Bandini! Come on Bandini! Oh you Bandini! How we love you! And the women were worried. But there was nothing to worry about. The situation was well in hand, and I knew it. Sylvester Gooch was tiring; he couldn't stand the pace. And I was saving myself for those last fifty yards. I knew I could defeat him. Fear not, my ladies, you who love me, fear not! The American honors depend upon my victory, I know this, and when America needs me you will find me there, in the midst of the fight, eager to give my blood. With proud beautiful strides I opened up at the fifty yard mark. My God, look at that man run! Shrieks of joy from the throats of thousands of women. Ten feet from the tape I lunged forward, snapping it a quarter of a second before the mighty Dutchman. Pandemonium in the stands. Newsreel cameramen gathered around me, begging me for a few words. Please, Bandini, *please*! Leaning against the American-Hawaiian docks I panted for breath and smilingly agreed to give the boys a statement. A nice bunch of fellows.

'I want to say hello to my mother,' I panted. 'Are you there, Mother? Hello! You see, gentlemen, when I was a boy back in California I had a paper route after school. At that time my mother was in the hospital. Every night she was near death. And that's how I learned to run. With the horrible realization that I might lose my mother before finishing with my Wilmington *Gazettes*, I used to run like a madman, finishing my route and then racing five miles to the hospital. And that was my training ground. I want to thank you all, and once more say hello to my mother back in California. Hello, Mother! How's Billy and Ted? And did the dog get well?'

Laughter. Murmurings about my simple native humility. Congratulations.

But after all, there wasn't much satisfaction in defeating Gooch, great victory though it was. Out of breath I was tired of being an Olympic runner.

It was that woman in the purple coat. Where was she now? I hurried back to Avalon Boulevard. She was not in sight. Except for the stevedores in the next block and the circling of moths around street lamps, the boulevard was deserted.

You fool! You've lost her. She is gone forever.

I began a swing around the block in search for her. In the distance I heard the bark of a police dog. That was Herman. I knew all about Herman. He was the mailman's dog. He was a sincere dog; he not only barked, he also bit. Once he had chased me blocks and tore the socks from my ankles. I decided to give up the search. It was growing late anyhow. Some other night I would seek her. I had to be at work early next morning. And so I started for home, walking up Avalon.

I saw the sign again: Highest Prices Paid For Old Gold. It stirred me because she had read it, the woman in the purple coat. She had seen and felt all of this – the store, the glass, the window, the junk inside. She had walked along this very street. This very sidewalk had felt the enchanted burden of her weight. She had breathed this air and smelled that sea. The smoke from her cigarette had mingled with it. Ah, this is too much, too much!

At the bank I touched the place where she had struck a

match. There – on my fingertips. Wonderful. A small black streak. Oh streak, your name is Claudia. Oh Claudia, I love you. I shall kiss you to prove my devotion. I looked about. No one was in sight for two blocks. I reached over and kissed the black streak.

I love you, Claudia. I beg you to marry me. Nothing else in life matters. Even my writings, those volumes for posterity, they mean nothing without you. Marry me or I shall go down to the dock and jump off head first. And I kissed again the black streak.

Then I was horrified to notice that the whole of the bank front was covered with the stripes and streaks of thousands and thousands of matches. I spat in disgust.

Her mark must be a unique mark; something like herself, simple and yet mysterious, a match-streak such as the world had never known before. I shall find it if I have to search forever. Do you hear me? Forever and forever. Until I become an old man I shall stand here, searching and searching for the mysterious mark of my love. Others shall not discourage me. Now I begin: a lifetime or a minute, what does it matter?

After less than two minutes I found it. I was sure of its origin. A small mark so faint that it was almost invisible. Only she could have made it. Wonderful. A tiny little mark with the faintest suggestion of a flair at the tail of it, a bit of artistry to it, a mark like a serpent about to strike.

But someone was coming. I heard footsteps on the sidewalk.

He was a very old man with a white beard. He carried a cane and a book and appeared in deep thought. He limped on his cane. His eyes were very bright and small. I ducked inside the archway until he passed by. Then I emerged and showered savage kisses upon the mark. Again I beseech you to marry me. Greater love than this no man hath. The time and tide wait for no man. A stitch in time saves nine. A rolling stone gathers no moss. Marry me!

Suddenly the night shook with a faint coughing. It was that old man. He had gone down the street about fifty yards and turned around. There he was, leaning on his cane and watching me intently.

Shivering with shame I hurried up the street. At the end of the block I turned around. The old man had now moved back to the wall. He was examining it too. Now he was looking after me. I shuddered at the thought of it. Another block and I turned once more. He was still there, that awful old man. I ran the rest of the way home.

Chapter Nineteen

Mona and my mother were already in bed. My mother snored softly. In the living room the davenport was pulled out, my bed made and the pillow loosened. I undressed and got in. The minutes passed. I couldn't sleep. I tried my back and then my side. Then I tried my stomach. The minutes passed. I could hear them ticking away on the clock in my mother's bedroom. A half hour passed. I was wide awake. I rolled about and felt an ache in my mind. Something was wrong. An hour passed. I began to get angry that I could not sleep, and I started to sweat. I kicked off the covers and lay there, trying to think of something. I had to get up early. I would be no good at the cannery without a lot of rest. But my eyes were sticky and they burned when I tried to close them.

It was that woman. It was the weaving of her form down the street, the flash of her white sickly face. The bed got intolerable. I turned on the light and lit a cigarette. It burned in my throat. I threw it away and resolved to give up smoking forever.

Once more in bed. And I tossed. That woman. How I loved her! The coil of her form, the hunger in her hunted eyes, the fur at her neck, the run in her hose, the feeling in my chest, the color of her coat, the flash of her face, the tingle in my fingers, the floating after her down the street, the coldness of the glittering stars, the dumb slither of a warm crescent moon, the taste of the match, the smell of the sea, the softness of the night, the stevedores, the click of poolballs, the beads of music, the coil of her form, the music of her heels, the stubbornness of her gait, the old man with a book, the woman, the woman, the woman.

I had an idea. I threw the covers off and leaped out of bed. What an idea! It came to me like an avalanche, like a house falling down, like the smash of glass. I felt on fire and crazy. There were papers and pencils in the drawer. I scooped them up and hurried to the kitchen. It was cold in the kitchen. I lit the oven and opened the oven door. Sitting naked I started to write.

Love Everlasting

or

The Woman A Man Loves

or

Omnia Vincit Amor

by

Arturo Gabriel Bandini

Three titles.

Marvelous! A superb start. Three titles, just like that! Amazing! Incredible! A genius! A genius indeed!

And that name. Ah, it looked magnificent.

Arturo Gabriel Bandini.

A name to consider in the long roll of time immortal: A name for endless ages. Arturo Gabriel Bandini. An even better-sounding name than Dante Gabriel Rossetti. And he was an Italian too. He belonged to my race.

I wrote: 'Arthur Banning, the multi-millionaire oil-dealer, tour de force, prima facie, petit maître, table d'hôte, and great lover of ravishing, beautiful, exotic, saccharine, and constellation-like women in all parts of the world, in every corner of the globe, women in Bombay, India, land of the Taj Mahal, of Gandhi and Buddha; women in Naples, land of Italian art and Italian fantasy; women in the Riviera; women at Lake Banff; women at Lake Louise; in the Swiss Alps; at the Ambassador Coconut Grove in Los Angeles, California; women at the famed Pons Asinorum in Europe; this same Arthur Banning, scion of an old Virginia family, land of George Washington and great American traditions; this same Arthur Banning, handsome and tall, six feet four inches in his sox, distingué, with teeth like pearls, and a certain, zippy, nippy, outré quality all women go for in a big way, this Arthur Banning, stood at the rail of his mighty, world-famous, much-loved, American, yacht, the Larchmont VIII, and watched with deleterious eyes, manly, virile, power-ful, eyes, the carmine, red, beautiful, rays of Old Sol, better known as the sun, dip into the gloomy, phantasmagorically, black, waters of the Mediterranean Ocean, somewhere South of Europe, in the year of our Lord, nineteen hundred and thirty-five. And there he was, scion of a wealthy, famous, powerful, magniloquent, family, a gallant homo, with the world at his feet and the great, powerful, amazing, Banning, fortune at his disposal; and yet; as he stood there; something troubled Arthur Banning, tall, darkened, handsome, tanned, by the rays of Old Sol: and, what troubled him, was that, though he had traveled many lands and seas, and, rivers, too, and though he made love, and, had love affairs, the whole world knew about, through the medium of the press, the powerful, grinding press, he, Arthur Banning, this scion, was unhappy, and though rich, famous, powerful, he was lonely and, incastellated for, love. And as he stood so incisively there on the deck of his Larchmont VIII, finest, most beautiful, most powerful, yacht, ever built, he wondered would the girl of his dreams, would he meet her soon, would she, the girl, of his dreams, be anything like the girl, of his boyhood dreams, back there when he was a boy, dreaming on the banks of the Potomac River, on his father's fabulous rich, wealthy, estate, or would she be poor?

'Arthur Banning lit his expensive, handsome, briar, pipe, and called to one of his underlings, a mere second mate, and, asked that underling for a match. That worthy, a famous, well-known, and, expert, character, in the world of ships, and the naval world, a man of international reputation, in the world of ships, and, sealing wax, did not impugn, but pro-offered the match with a respectful bow of obsequiousness, and, young Banning, handsome, tall, thanked him politely, albeit with a bit of gauche, and, then, resumed his quixotic dreaming about the fortunate girl who would some day be his bride and the woman of his wildest dreams.

'At that moment, a hushed moment, there was a sudden, stark, hideous, cry, from the hideous labyrinth of the briny sea, a cry that mingled with the flapping of the frigid waves against the prow of the proud, expensive, famous, Larchmont VIII, a cry of distress, a woman's cry! The cry of a woman! An appealing cry of bitter agony and deathlessness! A cry for help! Help! Help! With a quick glance at the storm-ridden waters, young Arthur Banning, went through an intense photosynthesis of regimentation, his keen, fine, handsome, blue, eyes looked away as he slipped off his costly evening jacket, a jacket which had cost $100, and he stood there in youthful splendor, his young, handsome, athletic, body, that had known gridiron struggles at Yale, and, soccer, at Oxford, in England, and like a Greek god it was silhouetted against the red rays of old sol, as it dipped into the waters of the blue Mediterranean. Help! Help! Help! Came that agonizing cry from a helpless woman, a poor, woman, half-naked, underfed, poverty-stricken, in cheap garments, as she felt that icy grip of stark, tragic, death, around her. Would she die without assistance? It was a crucible, and, sans ceremonie, and, defacto, the handsome Arthur Banning dove in.'

I wrote that much at one fell swoop. It came to me so fast that I didn't get time to cross my t's or dot my i's. Now there was time for a breathing spell, and a chance to read it through. I did so.

Aha!

Wonderful stuff! Superb! I had never read anything like it before in my life. Amazing. I got up, spat on my hands, and rubbed them together.

Come on! Who wants to fight me? I'll fight every damned fool in this room. I can lick the whole world. It was like nothing on earth, that feeling. I was a ghost. I floated and soared and giggled and floated. This was too much. Who would have dreamed of it? That I should be able to write like this. My God! Amazing!

I went to the window and looked out. The fog was descending. Such a beautiful fog. See the beautiful fog. I tossed kisses into it. I stroked it with my hands. Dear Fog, you are a girl in a white dress and I am a spoon on the windowsill. It has been a hot day, and I am hot all over, so please kiss me, dear fog. I wanted to jump, to live, to die, to, to sleep wide awake in a dreamless dream. Such wonderful things. Such wonderful clarity. I was dying and the dead and the ever-living. I was the sky and not the sky. There was too much to say, and no way to say it.

Ah, see the stove. Who would have believed it! A stove. Imagine. Beautiful stove. Oh stove I love you. From now on I shall be faithful, pouring my love upon you every hour. Oh stove, hit me. Hit me in the eye. Oh stove, how beautiful is your hair. Let me pee in it, because I love you so madly, you honey, you immortal stove. And my hand. There it is. My hand. The hand that wrote. Lord, a hand. Such a hand too. The hand that wrote. Me and you and my hand and Keats. John Keats and Arturo Bandini and my hand, the hand of John Keats Bandini. Wonderful. Oh hand land band stand grand land.

Yes, I wrote it.

Ladies and gentlemen of the committee, of the titty committee, ditty, bitty, committee, I wrote it, ladies and gentlemen, I wrote it. Yes indeed. I will not deny it: a poor offering, if I may say so, a mere nothing. But thank you for your kind words. Yes, I love you all. Honestly. I love every one of you, peew, stew, meew, pheew. I love especially the ladies, the women, the womb-men. Let them disrobe and come forward. One at a time please. You there, you gorgeous blonde bitch. I shall have you first. Hurry please, my time is limited. I have much work to do. There is so little time. I am a writer, you know, my books you know, immortality you know, fame you know, you know fame, don't you, fame, you know him, don't you. Fame and all that, tut tut, a mere incident in the time of man. I merely sat down at that little table yonder. With a pencil, yes. A gift of God – no doubt about it. Yes, I believe in God. Of course. God. My dear friend God. Ah, thank you, thank you. The table? Of course. For the museum? Of course. No no. No need to charge admission. The children: admit them free, for nothing. I want all children to touch it. Oh thank you. Thank you. Yes, I accept the gift. Thank you, thank you all. Now I go to Europe and the Soviet Republics. The people of Europe await me. A wonderful people, those Europeans, wonderful. And the Russians, I love them, my friends, the Russians. Goodbye, goodbye. Yes, I love you all. My work, you know. So much of it: my opus, my books, my volumes. Goodbye goodbye.

I sat down and wrote again. The pencil crawled across the page. The page filled. I turned it over. The pencil moved down. Another page. Up one side and down the other. The pages mounted. Through the window came the fog, bashful and cool. Soon the room filled. I wrote on. Page eleven. Page twelve.

I looked up. It was daylight. Fog choked the room. The gas was out. My hands were numb. A blister showed on my pencil finger. My eyes burned. My back ached. I could barely move from the cold. But never in my life had I felt better.

Chapter Twenty

That day at the cannery I was no good. I mashed my finger on the can dump. But thank God no harm was done. The hand that wrote was untouched. It was the other hand, the left hand; my left hand is no good anyway, cut it off if you like. At noon I fell asleep on the docks. When I awoke I was afraid to open my eyes. Was I blind? Had blindness stricken me so early in my career? But I opened my eyes, and thank God I could see. The afternoon moved like lava. Someone dropped a box and it hit me on the knee. It didn't matter. Any part of me gentlemen, but spare my eyes and my right hand.

At quitting time I hurried home. I took the bus. It was my only nickel. On the bus I fell asleep. It was the wrong bus. I had to walk five miles. Eating dinner, I wrote. A very bad dinner: hamburger. It's all right, Mama. Don't you dare fuss about me. I love hamburger. After dinner I wrote. Page twenty-three, page twenty-four. They were piling up. Midnight and I fell asleep in the kitchen. I rolled off the chair and cracked my head against the stove leg. Tut tut, old stove, forget it. My hand is all right, and so are my eyes; nothing else matters. Hit me again, if you like, right in the stomach. My mother pulled off my clothes and put me to bed.

Next night I wrote until dawn again. I got four hours sleep.

That day I brought paper and pencil to work. On the bus going to the cannery a bee stung me on the nape of the neck. How absurd! A bee to sting the genius. You silly bee! Be on your way, if you please. You should be ashamed of yourself. Suppose you had stung me on the left hand? It's ridiculous. I fell asleep again on the bus. When I woke up the bus was at the end of the line, clear over on the San Pedro side of Los Angeles Harbor, six miles from the cannery. I took the ferry back. Then I took another bus. It was ten o'clock when I reached the cannery.

Shorty Naylor stood picking his teeth with a match.

'Well?'

'My mother's sick. They've taken her to the hospital.'

'That's too bad,' was all he said.

That morning I sneaked from work to the lavatory. I wrote in there. The flies were numberless. They hovered over me, crawled on my hands and on the paper. Very intelligent flies. No doubt they were reading what I wrote. Once I stood perfectly still so that they might crawl over the tablet and examine every word thoroughly. They were the loveliest flies I had ever known.

At noon I wrote in the cafe. It was crowded, smelling of grease and strong soup. I hardly noticed it. When the whistle blew I saw my plate before me. It hadn't been touched.

In the afternoon I sneaked back to the lavatory. I wrote in there for half an hour. Then Manuel came. I hid the tablet and pencil.

'The boss wants you.'

I went to see the boss.

'Where the hell you been?'

'My mother. She's worse. I was using the telephone, calling the hospital.'

He rubbed his face.

'That's too bad.'

'It's pretty serious.'

He clucked.

'Too bad. Will she pull through?'

'I doubt it. They say it's only a matter of moments.'

'God. I'm sorry to hear that.'

'She's been a swell mother to me. Perfect. I wouldn't know what to do if she passed on. I think I'd kill myself. She's the only friend I have in the world.'

'What's the trouble?'

'Pulmonary thrombosis.'

He whistled.

'God! That's awful.'

'But that's not all.'

'Not all?'

'Arteriosclerosis, too.'

'Good God Almighty.'

I felt the tears coming and sniffed. All at once I realized that what I had said about my mother being the only friend I had in the world was true. And I was sniffing because the whole thing was possible, with me, a poor kid, slaving my life away in this cannery; and my mother dying, and me, a poor kid without hope or money, slaving away hopelessly while my mother expired, her last thoughts of me, a poor kid, slaving away in a fish cannery. It was a heart-breaking thought. I was gushing tears.

'She's been wonderful,' I said, sobbing. 'Her whole life has been sacrificed for my success. It hurts me to the core.'

'It's tough,' Shorty said. 'I think I know how you feel.'

My head sank. I dragged myself away, tears streaming down my face. I was surprised that such a bare-faced lie could come so near breaking my heart.

'No. You don't understand. You *can't*! No one understands this thing I feel.'

He hurried after me.

'Listen,' he smiled. 'Why don't you be sensible and take the day off? Go to the hospital! Stay with your mother! Cheer her up! Stay a few days – a week! It'll be all right here. I'll give you full time. I know how you feel. Hell, I guess I had a mother once.'

I gritted my teeth and shook my head.

'No. I can't. I won't. My duty is here, with the rest of the fellows. I don't want you to play favorites. My mother would want it this way too. Even if she were drawing her last breath I know she would say so.'

He grabbed my shoulders and shook me.

'No!' I said. 'I won't do it.'

'See here! Who's the boss? Now you do what I tell you. You get out of here and get up to that hospital, and stay there until your mother is better!'

At last I gave in, and reached for his hand.

'God, how wonderful you are! Thanks! God, I'll never forget this.'

He patted my shoulder.

'Forget it. I understand these things. I guess I had a mother once.'

From his wallet he drew a picture.

'Look,' he smiled.

I held the faded photograph to my blurred eyes. She was a

square, bricky woman in a bridal gown that fell like sheets out of the sky, tumbling at her feet. Behind her was an imitation background, trees and bushes, apple blossoms, and roses in full bloom, the canvas scenery slit with holes plain to see.

'My mother,' he said. 'That picture's fifty years old.'

I thought she was the ugliest woman I ever saw. Her jaw was as square as a policeman's. The flowers in her hand, held like a potato-masher, were wilted. Her veil was crooked, like a veil hanging from a broken curtain rod. The edges of her mouth were hooked upward in an unusually cynical smile. She looked as though she despised the idea of being all dressed up to marry one of those damned Naylors.

'It's beautiful – too beautiful for words.'

'She was a wonder all right.'

'She looks it. There's something soft about her – like a hill in the twilight, like a cloud in the distance, something sweet and spiritual; you know what I mean – my metaphors are inadequate.'

'Yeah. She died of pneumonia.'

'God,' I said. 'To think of it! A wonderful woman like that! The limitations of so-called science! And it all started from a common cold, too, didn't it?'

'Yeah. That's what happened all right.'

'We moderns! What fools we are! We forget the unearthly beauty of the old things, the precious things – like that picture. God, she's marvelous.'

'Yeah. God, God.'

Chapter Twenty-one

That afternoon I wrote on a picnic bench in the park. The sun slid away and darkness crept from the east. I wrote in the half-light. When the damp wind rose out of the sea I quit and walked home. Mona and my mother knew nothing, thinking I was arriving from the cannery.

After supper I began again. It wasn't going to be a short story after all. I counted thirty-three thousand, five hundred and sixty words, not including a's and an's. A novel, a full novel. There were two hundred and twenty-four paragraphs, and three thousand five hundred and eighty sentences. One sentence contained four hundred and thirty-eight words, the longest sentence I had ever seen. I was proud of it and I knew it would stupefy the critics. After all, not everybody could get them off at that length.

And I wrote on, whenever I could, a line or two in the mornings, all day at the park for three days, and pages at night. The days and nights passed under the pencil like the running feet of children. Three tablets were packed with writing, and then a fourth. A week later it was finished. Five tablets. 69,009 words.

It was the story of the passionate loves of Arthur Banning. In his yacht he went from country to country seeking the woman of his dreams. He had love affairs with women from every race and country in the world. I went to the dictionary for all my countries, and there was none I missed. There were sixty of them, and a passionate love affair in each.

But Arthur Banning never found the woman of his dreams.

At exactly 3:27 a.m. on Friday, August 7th, I finished the story. The last word of the last page was exactly what I wished.

It was 'Death.'

My hero shot himself through the head.

He held a gun to his temple and spoke.

'I have failed to find the woman of my dreams,' he said. 'Now I am ready for Death. Ah, sweet mystery of Death.'

I didn't exactly write that he pulled the trigger. This was illustrated by suggestion, which proved my ability to use restraint in a smashing climax.

And so it was finished.

Chapter Twenty-two

When I reached home the next evening Mona was reading the manuscript. The tablets were piled on the table, and she was reading the final words on the last page, with its terrific climax. She seemed wild-eyed with intense interest. I pulled off my jacket and rubbed my hands together.

'Ha!' I said 'I see you're absorbed. Gripping, isn't it?'

She looked up with a sickly face.

'It's silly,' she said. 'Plain silly. It doesn't grip me. It gripes me.'

'Oh,' I said. 'Is that so!'

I walked across the room.

'And just who the hell do you think you are?'

'It's silly. I had to laugh. I skipped most of it. I didn't even read three tablets of it.'

I shook my fist in front of her nose.

'And how would you like me to smash your face into a bloody, drooling pulp?'

'It's smart-alecky. All those big words!'

I tore the tablets from her.

'You Catholic ignoramus! You filthy Comstock! You disgusting, nauseating, clod-hopping celibate!'

My spittle sprinkled her face and hair. Her handkerchief

moved across her neck and she pushed me out of the way. She smiled.

'Why didn't your hero kill himself on the first page instead of the last? It would have made a lot better story.'

I got her by the throat.

'Be very careful, what you say, you Roman harlot. I warn you – be very very very careful.'

She tore herself loose, clawing my arm.

'It's the worst book I ever read.'

I grabbed her again. She jumped from the chair and fought wildly, clawing at my face with her nails. I backed away, shouting at every step.

'You sanctimonious, retch-provoking she-nun of a bitch-infested nausea-provoking nun of a vile boobish baboon of a brummagem Catholic heritage.'

On the table was a vase. She spied it, walked to the table and picked it up. She played with it in her hands, stroking it, smiling, feeling its weight, then smiling at me threateningly. Then she poised it at her shoulder, ready to heave it at my head.

'Ha!' I said. 'That's right! Throw it!'

I stripped my shirt open, buttons flying everywhere, and stuck out my bare chest. I jumped down on my knees before her, my chest jutting out. I beat my chest, hammered it with both fists until it turned red and stung.

'Strike!' I shouted. 'Let me have it! Renew the Inquisition. Kill me! Commit fratricide. Let these floors run red with the rich, pure blood of a genius who dared!'

'You fool. You can't write. You can't write at all.'

'You slut! You nunny slutty slut out of the belly of the Roman Harlot.'

She smiled bitterly.

'Call me anything you like. But keep your hands off me.'

'Put that vase down.'

She considered a moment, shrugged, and put it down. I got up from my knees. We ignored one another. It was as if nothing had happened. She went over the rug, picking up the buttons from my shirt. For a while I sat about, doing nothing but sitting and thinking of what she had said about the book. She walked into the bedroom. I could hear the swish of a comb passing through her hair.

'What was the matter with the story?' I asked.

'It's silly. I didn't like it.'

'Why not?'

'Because it was silly.'

'Damn it! Criticize it! Don't say it was silly! Criticize it! What's wrong with it? Why is it silly?'

She came to the door.

'Because it's silly. That's all I can say about it.'

I rushed her ot the wall. I was furious. I pinned her arms against her, locked her firmly with my legs, and glared her in the face. She was speechless with anger. Her teeth chattered helplessly, her face whitened and became blotchy. But now that I had her, I was afraid to let her go. I had not forgotten the butcher-knife.

'It's the craziest book I ever read!' she screamed. 'The awfullest, the vilest, craziest, funniest book in the world! It was so bad I couldn't even read it.'

I decided to be indifferent. I released her and snapped my fingers under her nose.

'Phooey! That for you. Your opinion doesn't bother me in the least.'

I walked to the middle of the room. I stood there and spoke to the walls at large.

'They can't touch us. No – they can't! We have put the Church to rout. Dante, Copernicus, Galileo, and now me – Arturo Bandini, son of a humble carpenter. We go on and on. We are above them. We even transcend their ridiculous heaven.'

She rubbed her bruised arms. I walked over to her and raised my hand to the ceiling.

'They can gibbet us, and burn us, but we go on – we – the yea-sayers; the outcasts; the eternal ones; the yea-sayers to the end of time.'

Before I could duck she picked up the vase and threw it. Her aim was perfect at such close range. The vase hit me just as I turned my head. It struck me behind the ear and smashed to pieces. For a moment I thought my skull was fractured. But it was a small, thin vase. I felt in vain for blood. It had shattered without even scratching me. The tinkling pieces scattered about the room. Not one trace of blood, and scarcely a hair out of place on my head.

A miracle!

Calm and unhurt I turned around. With my finger to the ceiling like one of the Apostles I spoke.

'Even God Almighty is on our side. For amen I say unto you, even when they breaketh vases over our heads, they hurteth us not, neither do our heads cracketh open.'

She was glad I was unhurt. Laughing, she went into the bedroom. She lay on the bed and I heard her laughing and laughing. I stood at the door and watched her twisting a pillow with delight.

'Laugh,' I said. 'Go ahead. For amen I say unto you, he

that laugheth last laugheth best, and ye must say aye, aye again and again, thus spake Zarathustra.'

Chapter Twenty-three

My mother came home, her arms wrapped around packages. I jumped from the divan and followed her into the kitchen. She put the packages down and faced me. She was out of breath, her face red from pounding blood, for the stairs were always too much for her.

'Did you read the story?'

'Yes,' she gasped. 'I certainly did.'

I took her by the shoulders, gripping them hard.

'It was a great story – wasn't it? Answer quick!'

She clasped her hands, swayed, and closed her eyes.

'It certainly was!'

I didn't believe her.

'Don't lie to me, please. You know perfectly well I hate all forms of pretense. I'm not brummagem. I always want the truth.'

Mona got up then, and came and stood inside the door. She leaned with her hands behind her and smiled the smile of Mona Lisa.

'Tell that to Mona,' I said.

My mother turned to Mona.

'I read it – didn't I, Mona?'

Mona's expression was unchanged.

'See!' my mother said in triumph. 'Mona *knows* I read it, don't you Mona?'

She turned to Mona again.

'I said I liked it, didn't I Mona?'

Mona's face was exactly the same.

'See! Mona knows I liked it – don't you Mona?'

I started beating my chest.

'Good God!' I yelled. 'Talk to me! Me! Me! Me! Not Mona! Me! Me! Me!'

My mother's hands went up in despair. She was under some sort of tension. She was not all sure of herself.

'But I just *told* you I thought it was wonderful!'

'Don't lie to me. No chicanery allowed.'

She sighed and resolutely said it again.

'It's wonderful. For the third time I say it's wonderful. Wonderful.'

'Stop lying.'

Her eyes tumbled and tossed. She wanted to scream, to cry. She pressed her temples and tried to think of some other way to say it.

'Then what do you *want* me to say?'

'I want the truth, if you please. Only the truth.'

'All right then. The truth is, it's wonderful.'

'Stop lying. The least I can expect from the woman who gave me life is some semblance of the truth.'

She pressed my hand and put her face next to mine.

'Arturo,' she pleaded. 'I swear I like it. I swear.'

She meant that.

Now here was something at last. Here was a woman who understood me. Here before me, this woman, my mother. She understood me. Blood of my blood, bone of my bone, she could appreciate my prose. She could stand before the world and pronounce it wonderful. Here was a woman for the ages, and a woman who was an aesthete for all her homely ways, a critic by intuition. Something within me softened.

'Little mother,' I whispered. 'Dear little mother. Dear sweet darling mother. I love you so much. Life is so hard for you, my dear darling mother.'

I kissed her, tasting the salty texture of her neck. She seemed so tired, so over-worked. Where was justice in this world, that this woman should suffer without complaint? Was there a God in heaven who judged and found her his own? There should be! There must be!

'Dear little mother. I'm going to dedicate my book to you. To you – my mother. To my mother, in grateful appreciation. To my mother, without whom this great work would have been impossible. To my mother, in grateful appreciation by a son who shall not forget.'

With a shriek Mona turned and went back to the bedroom.

'Laugh!' I yelled. 'Laugh! You jackass!'

'Dear little mother,' I said. 'Dear little mother.'

'Laugh!' I said. 'You intense moron! Laugh!'

'Dear little mother. For you: my mother: a kiss!'

And I kissed her.

'The hero made me think of you,' she smiled.

'Dear little mother.'

She coughed, hesitated. Something was disturbing her. She was trying to say something.

'The only thing is, does your hero have to make love to that Negro woman? That woman in South Africa?'

I laughed and hugged her. This was amusing indeed. I kissed her and patted her cheek. Ho ho, like a little child she was, like a wee bit of a baby.

'Dear little mother. I see the writing made a profound effect upon you. It stirred you to the very brink of your pure soul, dear little mother of mine. Ho, ho.'

'I didn't like that Chinese girl business, either.'

'Dear little mother. My little baby mother.'

'And I didn't like that business with the Eskimo woman. I thought it was awful. It disgusted me.'

I shook my finger at her.

'Now, now. Let us eliminate Puritanism here. Let us have no prudery. Let us try to be logical and philosophical.'

She bit her lip and frowned. There was something else biting inside that head of hers. She thought a moment, then looked simply into my eyes. I knew the trouble: she was afraid to mention it, whatever it was.

'Well,' I said. 'Speak. Out with it. What else?'

'The place he slept with the chorus girls. I didn't like that either. Twenty chorus girls! I thought that was terrible. I didn't like it at all.'

'Why not?'

'I don't think he ought to sleep with so many women.'

'Oh you don't eh? And why not?'

'I just don't – that's all.'

'Why not? Don't beat about the bush. Speak your opinion, if you have any. Otherwise, shut up. You women!'

'He should find a nice clean little Catholic girl, and settle down and marry her.'

So that was it! At last the truth was out. I seized her by the shoulders and spun her around until my face was next to hers, my eyes on a level with hers.

'Look at me,' I said. 'You profess to be my mother. Well, look at me! Do I look like a person who would sell his soul for mere pelf? Do you think I give a hang for mere public opinion? Answer that!'

She backed away.

I pounded my chest.

'Answer me! Don't stand there like a woman, like an idiot, a bourgeois Catholic Comstocking smut-hound. I demand an answer!'

Now she became defiant.

'The hero was nasty. He committed adultery on almost every page. Women, women, women! He was impure from the beginning. He turned my stomach.'

'Ha!' I said. 'At last it is out! At last the awful truth emerges! Papism returns! The Catholic mind again! The Pope of Rome waves his lewd banner.'

I walked into the living room and addressed the door.

'There you have it all. The riddle of the Universe. The transvaluation of values already transvaluated. Romanism. Red Neckery. Papism. The Roman Harlot in all her gaudy horror! Vaticism. Aye – verily I say unto you that unless ye become yeasayers ye shall become one of the damned! Thus spake Zarathustra!'

Chapter Twenty-four

After supper I brought the manuscript into the kitchen. I spread the tablets on the table and lit a cigarette.

'Now we'll see how silly it is.'

As I began to read I heard Mona singing.

'Silence!'

I settled myself and read the first ten lines. When I was finished with that much I dropped the book like a dead snake and got up from the table. I walked around the kitchen. Impossible! It couldn't be true!

'Something's wrong here. It's too hot here. It doesn't suit me. I need room, plenty of fresh air.'

I opened the window and looked out for a moment. Behind me lay the book. Well – go back and read it, Bandini. Don't stand at the window. The book isn't here; it's back there, behind you, on the table. Go back and read it.

Closing my mouth tightly I sat down and read another five lines. The blood rushed to my face. My heart plowed like a wheel.

'This is strange; very strange indeed.'

From the living room came Mona's voice. She was singing. A hymn. Lord, a hymn at a time like this. I opened the door and put out my head.

'Stop that singing or I'll show you something really silly.'

'I'll sing if I feel like it.'

'No hymns. I forbid hymns.'

'And I'll sing hymns too.'

'Sing a hymn – and die. Suit yourself.'

'Who died?' my mother said.

'Nobody,' I said. 'Nobody – yet.'

I returned to the book. Another ten lines. I jumped up and bit my nails. I tore the cuticle loose on my thumb. The pain flashed. Closing my eyes, I seized the loose cuticle between my teeth and ripped it off. A tiny spot of red blood appeared under the nail.

'Bleed! Bleed to death!'

My clothes stuck to me. I hated that kitchen. At the window I watched the stream of traffic down Avalon Boulevard. Never had I heard such noise. Never had I felt such pain as in my thumb. Pain and noise. All the horns in the world were out in that street. The clamor was driving me crazy. I couldn't live in a place like this and write. Downstairs came the zzzzzzzzz of a bath-spigot. Who was taking a bath at this hour? What fiend? Maybe the plumbing was out of order. I ran through the apartment to our bathroom and flushed the water. It worked all right – but it was noisy, so noisy I wondered that I had never noticed it before.

'What's the matter?' my mother said.

'There's too much noise around here. I can't create in this racket. I tell you I'm getting tired of this madhouse.'

'I think it's very quiet tonight.'

'Don't contradict me – you woman.'

I went back to the kitchen. This was an impossible place to write. No wonder. No wonder – what? Well, no wonder it was an impossible place to write. No wonder? What are you talking about? No wonder – *what?* This kitchen was a detriment. This neighborhood was a detriment. This town was a detriment. I sucked the pounding thumb wound. The pain was tearing me to pieces. I heard my mother speak to Mona.

'What's the matter with him now?'

'He's foolish,' Mona said.

I rushed into the room.

'I heard you!' I screamed. 'And I warn you to shut up! I'll show you who's silly around here.'

'I didn't say *you* were silly,' Mona said. 'I said your story was silly. Not you.' She smiled. 'I said *you* were foolish. It was your book that I said was silly.'

'Be careful! As God is my judge, I warn you.'

'What's the matter with you two?' my mother said.

'She knows,' I said. 'Ask her.'

Steeling myself for the ordeal, I gritted my teeth and returned to the book. I held the page before me, and kept my eyes closed. I was afraid to read the lines. No writing could be done in this asylum. No art could come from this chaos of stupidity. Beautiful prose demanded quiet, peaceful surroundings. Perhaps even soft music. No wonder! No wonder!

I opened my eyes and tried to read it. No good. It didn't work. I couldn't read it. I tried it out loud. No good. This book was no good. It was somewhat verbose; there were too many words in it. It was somewhat stodgy. It was a very good book. It missed. It was quite bad. It was worse than that. It was a lousy book. It was a stinking book. It was the goddamnedest book I ever saw. It was ridiculous; it was funny; it was silly; oh it's silly, silly, silly, silly, silly. Shame on you, you silly old thing, for writing a silly thing like this. Mona is right. It's silly.

It's on account of the women. They have poisoned my mind. I can feel it coming – stark madness. The writing of a maniac. Insanity. Ha! Look! He's a madman! Look at him! One of the Jukes! Stark, raving mad. He got that way from too many secret women, sir. I feel awfully sorry for him. A pathetic case, sir. Once he was a good Catholic kid. He went to church and all that sort of thing. Was very devoted, sir. A model boy. Educated by the nuns, a fine young chap once. Now a pathetic case, sir. Very touching. Suddenly he changed. Yeah. Something happened to the guy. He started off on the wrong foot after his old man died, and look what happened.

He got ideas. He had all those phony women. There was always something just a bit screwy about the guy, but it took those phonies to bring it out. I used to see the kid around here, walking around by himself. He lived with his mother and sister in that stucco house across from the school. He used to come into Jim's Place a lot. Ask Jim about him. Jim knew him well. Worked at the cannery. Had a lot of jobs around here. Couldn't keep any though – too erratic. A screw loose, a nut. Nuts, I tell you, plain nuts. Yeah – too many women, the wrong kind. You should have heard the monkey talk. Like a lunatic. Goddamnedest liar in Los Angeles County. Had hallucinations. Delusions of grandeur. Menace to society. Followed women in the streets. Used to get mad at flies and eat them. Women did it. Killed a lot of crabs too. Killed them all afternoon. Just plain screwy. Screwiest guy in Los Angeles County. Glad they locked him up. You say they found him wandering around the docks in a stupor? Well – that's him. Probably looking for more crabs to kill. Dangerous, I tell you. Belongs behind the bars. Ought to look into it very careful. Keep him there the rest of his life. Feel safer with the lunatic in the bug house where he belongs. A sad case though. Awful sorry for his mother and sister. They pray for him every night. Can you imagine that? Yeah! Maybe they're crazy too.

I threw myself across the table and started to cry. I wanted to pray again. Like nothing else in the world I wanted to say prayers.

Ha! The madman wants to pray!

A praying madman! Maybe it's his religious background. Maybe he was too pious when a kid. Funny thing about the guy. Very funny. I bit my knuckles. I clawed the table. My teeth found the flashing thumb cuticle. I gnawed. The tablets lay all about me on the table. What a writer! A book on California Fisheries! A book on California puke!

Laughter.

In the next room I heard them, my mother and Mona. They were talking about money. My mother was complaining bitterly. She was saying that we would never catch up on my salary at the fish-cannery. She was saying we would all go to live at Uncle Frank's house. He would take good care of us. I knew the origin of that kind of talk. Uncle Frank's words. He had been speaking to my mother again. I knew. And I knew she wasn't repeating all he had really said: that I was worthless and couldn't be depended on, that she should always expect the worst from me. And my mother was doing all the talking, with Mona not answering. Why didn't Mona answer her? Why did Mona have to be so rude? So callous?

I jumped up and walked in.

'Answer your mother when she addresses you!'

The instant Mona saw me she was terrified. It was the first time I ever saw that look of fright in her eyes. I sprang into action. It was what I had always wanted. I moved in on her.

She said, 'Be careful!'

She was holding her breath, pressing herself against the chair.

'Arturo!' my mother said.

Mona stepped into the bedroom and slammed the door. She held her weight against the other side. She called to my mother to keep me away. With a lunge I pushed the door open. Mona backed to the bed, tumbled backwards upon it. She was panting.

'Be careful!'

'You nun!'

'Arturo!' my mother said.

'You nun! So it was silly, was it? So it made you laugh, did it? So it was the worst book you ever read, was it?'

I lifted my fist and let fly. It struck her in the mouth. She held her lips and dropped into the pillows. My mother came screaming. Blood oozed through Mona's fingers.

'So you laughed at it, did you? You sneered! At the work of a genius. You! At Arturo Bandini! Now Bandini strikes back. He strikes in the name of liberty!'

My mother covered her with her arms and body. I tried to pull my mother away. She tore at me like a cat.

'Get out!' she said.

I grabbed my jacket and left. Back there my mother was babbling. Mona was moaning. The feeling was that I would never see them again. And I was glad.

Chapter Twenty-five

In the street I didn't know where to go. The town had two
worthwhile directions: East and West. East lay Los Angeles.
West for a half-mile lay the sea. I walked in the direction of
the sea. It was bitterly cold that summer night. The fog had
begun to blow in. A wind pushed it this way and that, great
streaks of crawling white. In the channel I heard foghorns
mooing like a carload of steers. I lit a cigarette. There was
blood on my knuckles – Mona's. I wiped it on the leg of my
pants. It didn't come off. I held up my fist and let the fog wet
it with a cold kiss. Then I wiped it again. But it didn't come
off. Then I rubbed my knuckles in the dirt at the sidewalk's
edge until the blood disappeared, but I tore the skin on my
knuckles doing it, and now my blood was flowing.

'Good. Bleed – you. Bleed!'

I crossed the schoolyard and walked down Avalon, walking
fast. Where are you going, Arturo? The cigarette was hateful,
like a mouthful of hair. I spat it out ahead of me, then crushed
it carefully with my heel. Over my shoulder I looked at it.
I was amazed. It still burned, faint smoke curling in the fog.
I walked a block, thinking about that cigarette. It still lived.
It hurt me that it still burned. Why should it still burn? Why
hadn't it gone out? An evil omen, perhaps. Why should I
deny that cigarette entry into the world of cigarette spirits?

Why let it burn and suffer so miserably? Had I come to this? Was I so terrible a monster as to deny that cigarette its rightful demise?

I hurried back.

There it lay.

I crushed it to a brown mass.

'Goodbye, dear cigarette. We shall meet again in paradise.'

Then I walked on. The fog licked me with its many cold tongues. I buttoned up my leather jacket, all but the last button.

Why not button the last one too?

This annoyed me. Should I button it, or should I leave it unbuttoned, the laughingstock of the button world, a useless button?

I will leave it unbuttoned.

No, I will button it.

Yes, I will unbutton it.

I did neither. Instead I invoked a master decision. I tore the button off my collar and threw it into the street.

'I'm sorry, button. We have been friends a long time. Often I have touched you with my fingers, and you have kept me warm on cold nights. Forgive me for what I have done. We too shall meet in paradise.'

At the bank I stopped and saw the match scratches on the wall. The Limbo of match scratches, their punishing ground for being without souls. Only one match scratch here had a soul – only one, the scratch made by the woman in the purple coat. Should I stop and visit it? Or should I go on?

I will stop.

No, I'll go on.

Yes I will.

No I won't.

Yes and no.

Yes and no.

I stopped.

I found the match scratch she had made, the woman in the purple coat. How beautiful it was! What artistry in that scratch! What expression! I lit a match, a long heavy scratch. Then I forced the burning sulphur tip into the scratch she had made. It clung to the wall, sticking out.

'I am seducing you. I love you, and publicly I am giving you my love. How fortunate you are!'

It clung there, over her artistic mark. Then it fell, the burning sulphur growing cold. I walked on, taking mighty military steps, a conqueror who had ravished the rare soul of a match scratch.

But why had the match grown cold and fallen? It bothered me. I was panic stricken. Why had this happened? What had I done to deserve this? I was Bandini – the writer. Why had the match failed me?

I hurried back in anger. I found the match where it had fallen on the sidewalk, lying there cold and dead for all the world to see. I picked it up.

'Why did you fall? Why do you forsake me in my hour of triumph? I am Arturo Bandini – the mighty writer. What have you done to me?'

No answer.

'Speak! I demand an explanation.'

No answer.

'Very well. I have no other choice. I must destroy you.'

I snapped it in two and dropped it in the gutter. It

landed near another match, one that was unbroken, a very handsome match with a dash of blue sulphur around its neck, a very worldly and sophisticated match. And there lay mine, humiliated, with a broken spine.

'You embarrass me. Now shall you really suffer. I leave you to the laughter of the match kingdom. Now all the matches will see you and make sneering remarks. So be it. Bandini speaks. Bandini, mighty master of the pen.'

But a half block away it seemed terribly unfair. That poor match! That pathetic fellow! This was all so unnecessary. He had done his very best. I knew how badly he felt. I went back and got him. I put him to my mouth and chewed him to a pulp.

Now all the other matches would find him unrecognizable. I spat him out in my hand. There he lay, broken and mashed, already in a state of decomposition. Fine! Wonderful! A miracle of decline. Bandini, I congratulate you! You have performed a miracle here. You have sped up the eternal laws and hurried the return to the source. Good for you, Bandini! Wonderful work. Potent. A veritable god, a mighty superman; a master of life and letters.

I passed the Acme Poolhall, nearing the secondhand store. Tonight the store was open. The window was the same as that night three weeks ago, when she had peered into it, the woman with the purple coat. And there it was, the sign: Highest Prices Paid For Old Gold.

All of this from that night of so long ago, when I'd defeated Gooch in the half-mile and won so gloriously for America. And where was Gooch now, Sylvester Gooch, that mighty Dutchman? Dear old Gooch! Not soon would he forget Bandini. A great runner he was, almost equal to Bandini.

What tales he would have for his grandchildren! When we met again in some other land we would talk of old times, Gooch and I. But where was he now, that streak of Dutch lightning? Doubtless back in Holland, tinkering with his windmills and tulips and wooden shoes, that mighty man, almost the equal of Bandini, waiting for death among sweet memories, waiting for Bandini.

But where was she – my woman of that bright night? Ah fog, lead me to her. I have much to forget. Make me like unto you, floating water, misty as the soul, and carry me to the arms of the woman with the white face. Highest Prices Paid For Old Gold. Those words had gone deep into her eyes, deep into her nerves, deep into her brain, far into the blackness of her brain behind that white face. They had made a gash back there, a match streak of memory, a flare she would carry to the grave, an impression. Wonderful, wonderful, Bandini, how profoundly you see! How mysterious is your nearness to godliness. Such words, lovely words, beauty of language, deep in the temple of her mind.

And I see you now, you woman of that night – I see you in the sanctity of some dirty harbor bedroom flop-joint, with the mist outside, and you lying with legs loose and cold from the fog's lethal kisses, and hair smelling of blood, sweet as blood, your frayed and ripped hose hanging from a rickety chair beneath the cold yellow light of a single, spotted bulb, the odor of dust and wet leather spinning about, your tattered blue shoes tumbled sadly at the bedside, your face lined with the tiring misery of Woolworth defloration and exhausting poverty, your lips slutty, yet soft blue lips of beauty calling me to come come come to that miserable room and feast myself upon the decaying rapture of your form, that I might give you a twisting beauty for misery and a twisting beauty for cheapness, my beauty for yours, the light becoming blackness as we scream, our miserable love and farewell to the tortuous flickering of a grey dawn that refused to really begin and would never really have an ending.

Highest Prices Paid For Old Gold.

An idea! The solution to all my problems. The escape of Arturo Bandini.

I entered.

'How late do you stay open?'

The Jew did not look up from his accounts behind the wire.

'Another hour.'

'I'll be back.'

When I got home they were gone. There was an unsigned note on the table. My mother had written it.

'We have gone to Uncle Frank's for the night. Come right over.'

The bed coverlet had been stripped off, as well as one pillow case. They lay in a heap on the floor, dotted with blood. On the dresser were bandages and a blue bottle of disinfectant. A pan of water tinted red sat on the chair. Beside it lay my mother's ring. I put it in my pocket.

From under the bed I dragged the trunk. It contained many things, souvenirs of our childhood which my mother had carefully saved. One by one I lifted them out. A sentimental farewell, a look at past things before flight by Bandini. The lock of blonde hair in the tiny white prayer book: it was my hair as a child; the prayer book was a gift on the day of my First Communion.

Clippings from the San Pedro paper when I graduated from

grade school; other clippings when I left high school. Clippings about Mona. A newspaper picture of Mona in her First Communion dress. Her picture and mine on Confirmation Day. Our picture on Easter Sunday. Our picture when we both sang in the choir. Our picture together on the Feast of the Immaculate Conception. A sheet of words from a spelling match when I was in grade school; 100% over my name.

Clippings about school plays. All of my report cards from the beginning. All of Mona's. I wasn't smart, but I always passed. Here was one: Arithmetic 70; History 80; Geography 70; Spelling 80; Religion 99; English 97. Never any trouble with religion or English for Arturo Bandini. And here was one of Mona's: Arithmetic 96; History 95; Geography 97; Spelling 94; Religion 90; English 90.

She could beat me at other things, but never at English or religion. Ho! Very amusing, this. A great piece of anecdote for the biographers of Arturo Bandini. God's worst enemy making higher marks in religion than God's best friend, and both in the same family. A great irony. What a biography that would be! Ah Lord, to be alive and read it!

At the bottom of the trunk I found what I wanted. They were family jewels wrapped in a paisley shawl. Two solid gold rings, a solid gold watch and chain, a set of gold cuff links, a set of gold earrings, a gold brooch, a few gold pins, a gold cameo, a gold chain, little odds and ends of gold – jewels my father had bought during his lifetime.

'How much?' I said.

The Jew made a sour face.

'All junk. I can't sell it.'

'How much though? What about that sign: Highest Prices Paid For Old Gold?'

'Maybe a hundred dollars, but I can't use it. Not much gold in it. Mostly plate.'

'Give me two hundred and you can have all of it.'

He smiled bitterly, his black eyes pinched between froggy lids.

'Never. Not in a million years.'

'Make it a hundred and seventy-five.'

He pushed the jewels toward me.

'Take it away. Not a cent more than fifty dollars.'

'Make it a hundred and seventy-five.'

We settled for a hundred and ten. One by one he handed me the bills. It was more money than I ever had in my life. I thought I would collapse from the sight of it. But I didn't let him know.

'It's piracy,' I said. 'You're robbing me.'

'You mean charity. I'm practically giving you fifty dollars.'

'Monstrous,' I said. 'Outrageous.'

Five minutes later I was up the street at Jim's Place. He was polishing glasses behind the counter. His greeting was always the same.

'Hello! And how's the cannery job?'

I seated myself, pulled out the roll of bills, and counted them again.

'Quite a roll you got there,' he smiled.

'How much do I owe you?'

'Why – nothing.'

'Are you sure?'

'But you don't owe me a cent.'

'I'm leaving town,' I said. 'Back to headquarters. I thought I owed you a few dollars. I'm paying off all my debts.'

He grinned at the money.

'I wish you owed me about half of that money.'

'It's not all mine. Some of it belongs to the party. Expense money for traveling.'

'Oh. Having a farewell party, eh?'

'Not that kind of a party. I mean, the Communist Party.'

'You mean Russians?'

'Call it that if you like. Commissar Demetriev sent it. Expense money.'

His eyes got bigger. He whistled and put down his towel.

'You a Communist?' He pronounced it with the wrong accent, so that it rhymed with Tunis.

I got up and went to the door and looked carefully up and down the street. Returning I nodded toward the rear of the store.

I whispered, 'Anybody back there?'

He shook his head. I sat down. We stared at one another in silence. I wet my lips. He looked toward the street and back at me again. His eyes were bugging in and out. I cleared my throat.

'Can you keep your mouth shut? You look like a man I can trust. Can you?'

He swallowed hard, and leaned forward.

'Keep it quiet,' I said. 'Yes. I am a Communist.'

'A Russian?'

'In principle – yes. Give me a chocolate malted.'

It was like a stilet to jabbed in his ribs. He was afraid to take his eyes away. Even when he turned to put the drink in the mixer he looked over his shoulder. I chuckled and lit a cigarette.

'We're quite harmless,' I laughed. 'Yes quite.'

He didn't say a word.

I drank the malt slowly, pausing now and then to chuckle. A gay little fearless laugh floated from my throat.

'But really! We're quite human. Quite!'

He watched me like a bank robber.

I laughed again, gaily, trilling, easily.

'Demetriev shall hear of this. In my next report I shall tell of it. Old Demetriev will roar in his black beard. How he'll roar, that black Russian wolf! But really – we're quite harmless – quite. I assure you, quite. But really, Jim. Didn't you know? But really –'

'No I didn't.'

I trilled again.

'But surely! But certainly you must have known!'

I got up and laughed very humanly.

'Aye – old Demetriev shall hear of this. And how he'll roar in his black beard, that black Russian wolf!'

I stood in front of the magazine stand.

'And what is the bourgeoisie reading tonight?'

He said nothing. His bitter hostility stretched like a taut wire between us, and he polished glasses in a fury, one after another.

'You owe me for the drink,' he said.

I gave him a ten dollar bill.

The cash register clanged. He drew out the change and smashed it down on the counter.

'Here you are! Anything else?'

I took all but a quarter. That was my usual tip.

'You forgot a quarter,' he said.

'Oh no!' I smiled. 'That's for you – a tip.'

'Don't want it. Keep your money.'

Without a word, only smiling confidently, reminiscently, I put it into my pocket.

'Old Demetriev – how he'll roar, that black wolf.'

'Do you want anything else?'

I took all five issues of *Artists and Models* from his shelf. The moment I touched them I knew why I had come to Jim's Place with so much money in my pocket.

'These, I'll take these.'

He leaned over the counter.

'How many have you got there?'

'Five.'

'I can only sell you two. The others are promised to somebody else.'

I knew he was lying.

'Then two it is, Comrade.'

As I stepped into the street his eyes bored into my back. I crossed the schoolyard. The windows in our apartment were unlighted. Ah, the women again. Here comes Bandini with his women. They were to be with me on my very last night in this town. All at once I felt the old hatefulness.

No. Bandini will not succumb. Never again!

I wadded the magazines and threw them away. They landed on the sidewalk, flapping in the fog, the dark photographs standing out like black flowers. I went for them and stopped. No, Bandini! A superman does not weaken. The strong man allows temptation at his elbow so he can resist it. Then I started for them once more. Courage, Bandini! Fight to the last ditch! With all my strength I wheeled away from the magazines and walked straight ahead toward the apartment. At the door I looked back. They were invisible in the fog.

Sad legs lifted me up the creaking stairs. I opened the door and snapped the light on. I was alone. The solitude caressed, inflamed. No. Not this last night. For tonight I depart like a conqueror.

I lay down. Jumped up. Lay down. Jumped up. I walked around, searching. In the kitchen, in the bedroom. The clothes closet. I went to the door and smiled. I walked to the desk, to the window. In the fog the women flapped. In the room I searched. This is your last battle. You're winning. Keep on fighting.

But now I was walking to the door. And down the stairs. You're losing; fight like a superman! The grumbling fog gulped me. Not tonight, Bandini. Be not like dumb, driven cattle. Be a hero in the strife!

And yet I was on my way back, the magazine in my fist. So there he creeps – that weakling. Again he has fallen.

See him slinking through the fog with his bloodless women. Always he will slink through life with the bloodless women of papers and books. When it ends they will find him, as yet in that land of white dreams, groping in the fog of himself.

A tragedy, sir. A great tragedy. A boneless fluid existence, sir. And the body, sir. We found it down by the waterfront. Yes, sir. A bullet through the heart, sir. Yes, a suicide, sir. And what shall we do with the body, sir? For Science – a very good idea, sir. The Rockefeller Institute, no less. He would have wanted it that way, sir. His last earthly wish. A great lover of Science he was, sir – of Science and bloodless women.

I sat on the divan and turned the pages. Ah, the women, the women.

Suddenly I snapped my fingers.

Idea!

I threw down the magazines and raced about looking for a pencil. A novel! A brand new novel! What an idea! Holy God, what an idea! The first one failed, of course. But not this. *Here* was an idea! In this new idea Arthur Banning would not be fabulously wealthy; he would be fabulously poor! He would not be searching the world on an expensive yacht, searching for the woman of his dreams. No! It would be the other way around. The woman would search for him! Wow! What an idea! The woman would represent happiness; she would symbolize it, and Arthur Banning would symbolize all men. What an idea!

I started writing. But in a few minutes I was disgusted. I changed clothes and packed a suitcase. I needed a change in background. A great writer needed variation. When I finished packing I sat down and wrote a farewell note to my mother.

Dear Woman Who Gave Me Life:

The callous vexations and perturbations of this night have subsequently resolved themselves to a state which precipitates me, Arturo Bandini, into a brobdingnagian and gargantuan decision. I inform you of this in no uncertain terms. Ergo, I now leave you and your ever charming daughter (my beloved sister Mona) and seek the fabulous usufructs of my incipient career in profound solitude. Which is to say, tonight I depart for the metropolis to the east – our own Los Angeles, the city of angels. I entrust you to the benign generosity of your brother, Frank Scarpi, who is, as the phrase has it, a good family man (sic!). I am penniless but I urge you in no uncertain terms to cease your cerebral anxiety about my destiny, for truly it lies in the palm of the immortal gods. I have made the lamentable discovery over a period of years that living with you and Mona is deleterious to the high and magnanimous purpose of Art, and I repeat to you in no uncertain terms that I am an artist, a creator beyond question. And, per se, the fumbling fulminations of cerebration and intellect find little fruition in the debauched, distorted hegemony that we poor mortals, for lack of a better and more concise terminology, call home. In no uncertain terms I give you my love and blessing, and I swear to my sincerity, when I say in no uncertain terms that I not only forgive you for what has ruefully transpired this night, but for all other nights. Ergo, I assume in no uncertain terms that you will reciprocate in kindred fashion. May I say in conclusion that I have much to thank you for, O woman who breathed the breath of life into my brain of destiny? Aye, it is, it is.

Signed.

Arturo Gabriel Bandini.

Suitcase in hand, I walked down to the depot. There was a ten minute wait for the midnight train for Los Angeles. I sat down and began to think about the new novel.

Ask the Dust

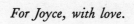

For Joyce, with love.

Chapter One

One night I was sitting on the bed in my hotel room on Bunker Hill, down in the very middle of Los Angeles. It was an important night in my life, because I had to make a decision about the hotel. Either I paid up or I got out: that was what the note said, the note the landlady had put under the door. A great problem, deserving acute attention. I solved it by turning out the lights and going to bed.

In the morning I awoke, decided that I should do more physical exercise, and began at once. I did several bending exercises. Then I washed my teeth, tasted blood, saw pink on the toothbrush, remembered the advertisements, and decided to go out and get some coffee.

I went to the restaurant where I always went to the restaurant and I sat down on the stool before the long counter and ordered coffee. It tasted pretty much like coffee, but it wasn't worth the nickel. Sitting there I smoked a couple of cigarettes, read the box scores of the American League games, scrupulously avoided the box scores of National League games, and noted with satisfaction that Joe DiMaggio was still a credit to the Italian people, because he was leading the league in batting.

A great hitter, that DiMaggio. I walked out of the restaurant, stood before an imaginary pitcher, and swatted a home run over the fence. Then I walked down the street towards Angel's Flight, wondering what I would do that day. But there was nothing to do, and so I decided to walk around the town.

I walked down Olive Street past a dirty yellow apartment house that was still wet like a blotter from last night's fog, and I thought of my friends Ethie and Carl, who were from Detroit and had lived there, and I remembered the night Carl hit Ethie because she was going to have a baby, and he didn't want a baby. But they had the baby and that's all there was to that. And I remembered the inside of that apartment, how it smelled of mice and dust, and the old women who sat in the lobby on hot afternoons, and the old woman with the pretty legs. Then there was the elevator man, a broken man from Milwaukee, who seemed to sneer every time you called your floor, as though you were such a fool for choosing that particular floor, the elevator man who always had a tray of sandwiches in the elevator, and a pulp magazine.

Then I went down the hill on Olive Street, past the horrible frame houses reeking with murder stories, and on down Olive to the Philharmonic Auditorium, and I remembered how I'd gone there with Helen to listen to the Don Cossack Choral Group, and how I got bored and we had a fight because of it, and I remembered what Helen wore that day – a white dress, and how it made me sing at the loins when I touched it. Oh that Helen – but not here.

And so I was down on Fifth and Olive, where the big street cars chewed your ears with their noise, and the smell of gasoline made the sight of the palm trees seem sad, and the black pavement still wet from the fog of the night before.

So now I was in front of the Biltmore Hotel, walking along

the line of yellow cabs, with all the cab drivers asleep except the driver near the main door, and I wondered about these fellows and their fund of information, and I remembered the time Ross and I got an address from one of them, how he leered salaciously and then took us to Temple Street, of all places, and whom did we see but two very unattractive ones, and Ross went all the way, but I sat in the parlour and played the phonograph and was scared and lonely.

I was passing the doorman of the Biltmore, and I hated him at once, with his yellow braids and six feet of height and all that dignity, and now a black automobile drove to the kerb and a man got out. He looked rich; and then a woman got out, and she was beautiful, her fur was silver fox, and she was a song across the sidewalk and inside the swinging doors, and I thought oh boy for a little of that, just a day and a night of that, and she was a dream as I walked along, her perfume still in the wet morning air.

Then a great deal of time passed as I stood in front of a pipe shop and looked, and the whole world faded except that window and I stood and smoked them all, and saw myself a great author with that natty Italian briar, and a cane, stepping out of a big black car, and she was there too, proud as hell of me, the lady in the silver fox fur. We registered and then we had cocktails and then we danced a while, and then we had another cocktail and I recited some lines from Sanskrit, and the world was so wonderful, because every two minutes some gorgeous one gazed at me, the great author, and nothing would do but I had to autograph her menu, and the silver fox girl was very jealous.

Los Angeles, give me some of you! Los Angeles come to me the way I came to you, my feet over your streets, you pretty town I loved you so much, you sad flower in the sand, you pretty town.

A day and another day and the day before, and the library with the big boys in the shelves, old Dreiser, old Mencken, all the boys down there, and I went to see them, Hya Dreiser, Hya Mencken, Hya, hya: there's a place for me, too, and it begins with B, in the B shelf, Arturo Bandini, make way for Arturo Bandini, his slot for his book, and I sat at the table and just looked at the place where my book would be, right there close to Arnold Bennett; not much that Arnold Bennett, but I'd be there to sort of bolster up the B's, old Arturo Bandini, one of the boys, until some girl came along, some scent of perfume through the fiction room, some click of high heels to break up the monotony of my fame. Gala day, gala dream!

But the landlady, the white-haired landlady kept writing those notes: she was from Bridgeport, Connecticut, her husband had died and she was all alone in the world and she didn't trust anybody, she couldn't afford to, she told me so, and she told me I'd have to pay. It was mounting like the national debt, I'd have to pay or leave, every cent of it – five weeks overdue, twenty dollars, and if I didn't she'd hold my trunks; only I didn't have any trunks, I only had a suitcase and it was cardboard without even a strap, because the strap was around my belly holding up my pants, and that wasn't much of a job, because there wasn't much left of my pants.

'I just got a letter from my agent,' I told her. 'My agent in New York. He says I sold another one; he doesn't say where, but he says he's got one sold. So don't worry Mrs Hargraves, don't you fret, I'll have it in a day or so.'

But she couldn't believe a liar like me. It wasn't really a lie; it was a wish, not a lie and maybe it wasn't even a wish, maybe it was a fact, and the only way to find out was watch the mailman, watch him closely, check his mail as he laid it on the desk in the lobby, ask him point blank if he had anything for Bandini. But I didn't have to ask after six months at that hotel. He saw me coming and he always nodded yes or no before I asked: no, three million times; yes, once.

One day a beautiful letter came. Oh, I got a lot of letters, but this was the only beautiful letter, and it came in the morning, and it said (he was talking about *The Little Dog Laughed*) he had read *The Little Dog Laughed* and liked it; he said, Mr Bandini, if ever I saw a genius, you are it. His name was Leonardo, a great Italian critic, only he was not known as a critic, he was just a man in West Virginia, but he was great and he was a critic, and he died. He was dead when my airmail letter got to West Virginia, and his sister sent my letter back. She wrote a beautiful letter, too, she was a pretty good critic too, telling me Leonardo had died of consumption but he was happy to the end, and one of the last things he did was sit up in bed and write me about *The Little Dog Laughed*: a dream out of life, but very important; Leonardo, dead now, a saint in heaven, equal to any apostle of the twelve.

Everybody in the hotel read *The Little Dog Laughed*, everybody: a story to make you die holding the page, and it wasn't about a dog, either: a clever story, screaming poetry. And the great editor, none but J. C. Hackmuth with his name signed like Chinese said in a letter: a great story and I'm proud to print it. Mrs Hargraves read it and I was a different man in her eyes thereafter. I got to stay on in that hotel, not shoved out in the cold, only often it was in the heat, on account of *The Little Dog Laughed*. Mrs Grainger in 345, a Christian

Scientist (wonderful hips, but kinda old) from Battle Creek, Michigan, sitting in the lobby waiting to die, and *The Little Dog Laughed* brought her back to the earth, and that look in her eyes made me know it was right and I was right, but I was hoping she would ask about my finances, how I was getting along, and then I thought why not ask her to lend you a five spot, but I didn't and I walked away snapping my fingers in disgust.

The hotel was called the Alta Loma. It was built on a hillside in reverse, there on the crest of Bunker Hill, built against the decline of the hill, so that the main floor was on the level with the street but the tenth floor was downstairs ten levels. If you had room 862, you got in the elevator and went down eight floors, and if you wanted to go down in the truck room, you didn't go down but up to the attic, one floor above the main floor.

Oh for a Mexican girl! I used to think of her all the time, my Mexican girl. I didn't have one, but the streets were full of them, the Plaza and Chinatown were afire with them, and in my fashion they were mine, this one and that one, and some day when another cheque came it would be a fact. Meanwhile it was free and they were Aztec princesses and Mayan princesses, the peon girls in the Grand Central Market, in the Church of Our Lady, and I even went to Mass to look at them. That was sacrilegious conduct but it was better than not going to Mass at all, so that when I wrote home to Colorado to my mother I could write with truth. Dear Mother: I went to Mass last Sunday. Down in the Grand Central Market I bumped into the princesses accidentally on purpose. It gave me a chance to speak to them, and I smiled and said excuse me. Those beautiful girls, so happy when you acted like a gentleman and all of that, just to touch them and carry the memory of it back to my room, where dust gathered upon my typewriter and Pedro the mouse sat in his hole, his black eyes watching me through that time of dream and reverie.

Pedro the mouse, a good mouse but never domesticated, refusing to be petted or house-broken. I saw him the first time I walked into my room, and that was during my heyday, when *The Little Dog Laughed* was in the current August issue. It was five months ago, the day I got to town by bus from Colorado with a hundred and fifty dollars in my pocket and big plans in my head. I had a philosophy in those days. I was a lover of man and beast alike, and Pedro was no exception; but cheese got expensive, Pedro called all his friends, the room swarmed with them, and I had to quit it and feed them bread. They didn't like bread. I had spoiled them and they went elsewhere, all but Pedro the ascetic who was content to eat the pages of an old Gideon Bible.

Ah, that first day! Mrs Hargraves opened the door to my room, and there it was, with a red carpet on the floor, pictures of the English countryside on the walls, and a shower adjoining. The room was down on the sixth floor, room 678, up near the front of the hill, so that my window was on a level with the green hillside and there was no need for a key, for the window was always open. Through that window I saw my first palm tree, not six feet away, and sure enough I thought of Palm Sunday and Egypt and Cleopatra, but the palm was blackish at its branches, stained by carbon monoxide coming out of the Third Street Tunnel, its crusted trunk choked with dust and sand that blew in from the Mojave and Santa Ana deserts.

Dear Mother, I used to write home to Colorado, Dear Mother, things are definitely looking up. A big editor was in town and I had lunch with him and we have signed a contract for a number of short stories, but I won't try to bore you with all the details, dear mother, because I know you're not interested in writing, and I know Papa isn't, but it levels down to a swell contract, only it doesn't begin for a couple of months. So send me ten dollars, mother, send me five, mother dear, because the editor (I'd tell you his name only I know you're not interested in such things) is all set to start me out on the biggest project he's got.

Dear Mother, and Dear Hackmuth, the great editor — they got most of my mail, practically all of my mail. Old Hackmuth with his scowl and his hair parted in the middle, great Hackmuth with a pen like a sword, his picture was on my wall autographed with his signature that looked Chinese. Hya Hackmuth, I used to say, Jesus how you can write! Then the lean days came, and Hackmuth got big letters from me. My God, Mr Hackmuth, something's wrong with me: the old zip is gone and I can't write anymore. Do you think, Mr Hackmuth, that the climate here has anything to do with it? Please advise. Do you think, Mr Hackmuth, that I write as well as William Faulkner? Please advise. Do you think, Mr Hackmuth, that sex has anything to do with it, because, Mr Hackmuth, because, because, and I told Hackmuth everything. I told him about the blonde girl I met in the park. I told him how I worked it, how the blonde girl tumbled. I told him the whole story, only it wasn't true, it was a crazy lie — but it was something. It was writing, keeping in touch with the great, and he always answered. Oh boy, he was swell! He answered right off, a great man responding to the problems of a man of talent. Nobody got that many letters from Hackmuth, nobody but me, and I used to take them out and read them over, and kiss them. I'd stand before Hackmuth's picture crying out of both eyes, telling him he picked a good one this time, a great one, a Bandini, Arturo Bandini, me.

The lean days of determination. That was the word for it, determination: Arturo Bandini in front of his typewriter two full days in succession, determined to succeed; but it didn't work, the longest siege of hard and fast determination in his life, and not one line done, only two words written over and over across the page, up and down, the same words: palm tree, palm tree, palm tree, a battle to the death between the palm tree and me, and the palm tree won: see it out there swaying in the blue air, creaking sweetly in the blue air. The palm tree won after two fighting days, and I crawled out of the window and sat at the foot of the tree. Time passed, a moment or two, and I slept, little brown ants carousing in the hair on my legs.

Chapter Two

I was twenty then. What the hell, I used to say, take your time, Bandini. You got ten years to write a book, so take it easy, get out and learn about life, walk the streets. That's your trouble: your ignorance of life. Why, my God, man, do you realize you've never had any experience with a woman? Oh yes I have, oh I've had plenty. Oh no you haven't. You need a woman, you need a bath, you need a good swift kick, you need money. They say it's a dollar, they say it's two dollars in the swell places, but down on the Plaza it's a dollar; swell, only you haven't got a dollar, and another thing, you coward, even if you had a dollar you wouldn't go, because you had a chance to go once in Denver and you didn't. No, you coward, you were afraid, and you're still afraid, and you're glad you haven't got a dollar.

Afraid of a woman! Ha, great writer this! How can he write about women, when he's never had a woman? Oh you lousy fake, you phony, no wonder you can't write! No wonder there wasn't a woman in the *The Little Dog Laughed*. No wonder it wasn't a love story, you fool, you dirty little schoolboy.

To write a love story, to learn about life.

Money arrived in the mail. Not a cheque from the mighty Hackmuth, not an acceptance from *The Atlantic Monthly* or *The Saturday Evening Post*. Only ten dollars, only a fortune.

My mother sent it: some dime insurance policies, Arturo, I had them taken up for their cash value, and this is your share. But it was ten dollars; one manuscript or another, at least something had been sold.

Put it in your pocket, Arturo. Wash your face, comb your hair, put some stuff on to make you smell good while you stare into the mirror looking for grey hairs; because you're worried Arturo, you're worried, and that brings grey hair. But there was none, not a strand. Yeah, but what of that left eye? It looked discoloured. Careful, Arturo Bandini: don't strain your eyesight, remember what happened to Tarkington, remember what happened to James Joyce.

Not bad, standing in the middle of the room, talking to Hackmuth's picture, not bad, Hackmuth, you'll get a story out of this. How do I look, Hackmuth? Do you sometimes wonder, Herr Hackmuth, what I look like? Do you sometimes say to yourself, I wonder if he's handsome, that Bandini fellow, author of that brilliant *The Little Dog Laughed*?

Once in Denver there was another night like this, only I was not an author in Denver, but I stood in a room like this and made these plans, and it was disastrous because all the time in that place I thought about the Blessed Virgin and *thou shalt not commit adultery* and the hard-working girl shook her head sadly and had to give it up, but that was a long time ago and tonight it will be changed.

I climbed out the window and scaled the incline to the top of Bunker Hill. A night for my nose, a feast for my nose, smelling the stars, smelling the flowers, smelling the desert, and the dust asleep, across the top of Bunker Hill. The city spread out like a Christmas tree, red and green and blue. Hello, old houses, beautiful hamburgers singing in cheap cafés. Bing Crosby singing too. She'll treat me gently. Not those girls of my childhood, those girls of my boyhood, those girls of my university days. They frightened me, they were diffident, they refused me; but not my princess, because she will understand. She, too, has been scorned.

Bandini, walking along, not tall but solid, proud of his muscles, squeezing his fist to revel in the hard delight of his biceps, absurdly fearless Bandini, fearing nothing but the unknown in a world of mysterious wonder. Are the dead restored? The books say no, the night shouts yes. I am twenty, I have reached the age of reason, I am about to wander the streets below, seeking a woman. Is my soul already smirched, should I turn back, does an angel watch over me, do the prayers of my mother allay my fears, do the prayers of my mother annoy me?

Ten dollars: it will pay the rent for two and a half weeks, it will buy me three pairs of shoes, two pair of pants, or one thousand postage stamps to send material to the editors; indeed! But you haven't any material, your talent is dubious, your talent is pitiful, you haven't any talent, and stop lying to yourself day after day because you know *The Little Dog Laughed* is no good, and it will always be no good.

So you walk along Bunker Hill, and you shake your fist at the sky, and I know what you're thinking, Bandini. The thoughts of your father before you, lash across your back, hot ire in your skull, that you are not to blame: this is your thought, that you were born poor, son of miseried peasants, driven because you were poor, fled from your Colorado town because you are poor, hoping to write a book to get rich, because those who hated you back there in Colorado will not hate you if you write a book. You are a coward, Bandini, a traitor to your soul, a feeble liar before your weeping Christ. This is why you write, this is why it would be better if you died.

Yes, it's true: but I have seen houses in Bel-Air with cool lawns and green swimming pools. I have wanted women whose very shoes are worth all I have ever possessed. I have seen golf clubs on Sixth Street in the Spalding window that make me hungry just to grip them. I have grieved for a necktie like a holy man for indulgences. I have admired hats in Robinson's the way critics gasp at Michelangelo.

I took the steps down Angel's Flight to Hill Street: a hundred and forty steps, with tight fists, frightened of no man, but scared of the Third Street Tunnel, scared to walk through it – claustrophobia. Scared of high places too, and of blood, and of earthquakes; otherwise, quite fearless, excepting death, except the fear I'll scream in a crowd, except the fear of appendicitis, except the fear of heart trouble, even that, sitting in his room holding the clock and pressing his jugular vein, counting out his heartbeats, listening to the weird purr and whirr of his stomach. Otherwise, quite fearless.

Here is an idea with money: these steps, the city below, the stars within throwing distance: boy meets girl idea, good setup, big money idea. Girl lives in that grey apartment house, boy is a wanderer. Boy – he's me. Girl's hungry. Rich Pasadena girl hates money. Deliberately left Pasadena millions 'cause of ennui, weariness with money. Beautiful girl, gorgeous. Great story, pathological conflict. Girl with money phobia: Freudian setup. Another guy loves her, rich guy. I'm poor. I meet rival. Beat him to death with caustic wit and also lick him with fists. Girl impressed, falls for me. Offers me millions. I marry her on condition she'll stay poor. Agrees. But ending happy: girl tricks me with huge trust fund day we get married. I'm indignant but I forgive her 'cause I love her. Good idea, but something missing: Collier's story.

Dearest Mother, thanks for the ten dollar bill. My agent announces the sale of another story, this time to a great magazine in London, but it seems they do not pay until publication, and so your little sum will come in handy for various odds and ends.

I went to the burlesque show. I had the best seat possible, a dollar and ten cents, right under a chorus of forty frayed bottoms: some day all of these will be mine: I will own a yacht and we will go on South Sea Cruises. On warm afternoons they will dance for me on the sun deck. But mine will be beautiful women, selections from the cream of society, rivals for the joys of my stateroom. Well, this is good for me, this is experience, I am here for a reason, these moments run into pages, the seamy side of life.

Then Lola Linton came on, slithering like a satin snake amid the tumult of whistling and pounding feet, Lola Linton lascivious, slithering and looting my body, and when she was through, my teeth ached from my clamped jaws and I hated the dirty lowbrow swine around me, shouting their share of a sick joy that belonged to me.

If Mamma sold the policies things must be tough for the Old Man and I shouldn't be here. When I was a kid pictures of Lola Lintons used to come my way, and I used to get so impatient with the slow crawl of time and boyhood, longing for this very moment, and here I am, and I have not changed nor have the Lola Lintons, but I fashioned myself rich and I am poor.

Main Street after the show, midnight: neon tubes and a light fog, honky tonks and all night picture houses. Second-hand stores and Filipino dance halls, cocktails 15 cents, continuous entertainment, but I had seen them all, so many times, spent so much Colorado money in them. It left me lonely like a thirsty man holding a cup, and I walked towards the Mexican Quarter with a feeling of sickness without pain. Here was the Church of Our Lady, very old, the adobe blackened with age. For sentimental reasons I will go inside. For sentimental reasons only. I have not read Lenin, but I have heard him quoted, religion is the opium of the people. Myself, I am an atheist: I have read *The Anti-Christ* and I regard it as a capital piece of work. I believe in the transvaluation of values, Sir. The Church must go, it is the haven of the booboisie, of boobs and bounders and all Brummagem mountebanks.

I pulled the huge door open and it gave a little cry like weeping. Above the altar sputtered the blood-red eternal light, illuminating in crimson shadow the quiet of almost two thousand years. It was like death, but I could remember screaming infants at baptism too. I knelt. This was habit, this kneeling. I sat down. Better to kneel, for the sharp bite at the knees was a distraction from the awful quiet. A prayer. Sure, one prayer: for sentimental reasons. Almighty God, I am sorry I am now an atheist, but have You read Nietzche? Ah, such a book! Almighty God, I will play fair in this. I will make You a proposition. Make a great writer out of me, and I will return to the Church. And please, dear God, one more favour: make my mother happy. I don't care about the Old Man; he's got his wine and his health, but my mother worries so. Amen.

I closed the weeping door and stood on the steps, the

fog like a huge white animal everywhere, the Plaza like our courthouse back home, snowbound in white silence. But all sounds travelled swift and sure through the heaviness, and the sound I heard was the click of high heels. A girl appeared. She wore an old green coat, her face moulded in a green scarf tied under the chin. On the stairs stood Bandini.

'Hello, honey,' she said, smiling, as though Bandini were her husband, or her lover. Then she came to the first step and looked up at him. 'How about it, honey? Want me to show you a good time?'

Bold lover, bold and brazen Bandini.

'Nah,' he said. 'No thanks. Not tonight.'

He hurried away, leaving her looking after him, speaking words he lost in flight. He walked half a block. He was pleased. At least she had asked him. At least she had identified him as a man. He whistled a tune from sheer pleasure. Man about town has universal experience. Noted writer tells of night with woman of the streets. Arturo Bandini, famous writer, reveals experience with Los Angeles prostitute. Critics acclaim book finest written.

Bandini (being interviewed prior to departure for Sweden): 'My advice to all young writers is quite simple. I would caution them never to evade a new experience. I would urge them to live life in the raw, to grapple with it bravely, to attack it with naked fists.'

Reporter: 'Mr Bandini, how did you come to write this book which won you the Nobel Award?'

Bandini: 'The book is based on a true experience which happened to me one night in Los Angeles. Every word of that book is true. I lived that book, I experienced it.'

Enough. I saw it all. I turned and walked back towards

the church. The fog was impenetrable. The girl was gone. I walked on: perhaps I could catch up with her. At the corner I saw her again. She stood talking to a tall Mexican. They walked, crossed the street and entered the Plaza. I followed. My God, a Mexican! Women like that should draw the colour line. I hated him, the Spick, the Greaser. They walked under the banana trees in the Plaza, their feet echoing in the fog. I heard the Mexican laugh. Then the girl laughed. They crossed the street and walked down an alley that was the entrance to Chinatown. The oriental neon signs made the fog pinkish. At a rooming house next door to a chop suey restaurant they turned and climbed the stairs. Across the street upstairs a dance was in progress. Along the little street on both sides yellow cabs were parked. I leaned against the front fender of the cab in front of the rooming house and waited. I lit a cigarette and waited. Until hell freezes over, I will wait. Until God strikes me dead, I will wait.

A half hour passed. There were sounds on the steps. The door opened. The Mexican appeared. He stood in the fog, lit a cigarette, and yawned. Then he smiled absently, shrugged, and walked away, the fog swooping upon him. Go ahead and smile. You stinking Greaser – what have you got to smile about? You come from a bashed and busted race, and just because you went to the room with one of our white girls, you smile. Do you think you would have had a chance, had I accepted on the church steps?

A moment later the steps sounded to the click of her heels, and the girl stepped into the fog. The same girl, the same green coat, the same scarf. She saw me and smiled. 'Hello, honey. Wanna have a good time?'

Easy now, Bandini.

'Oh,' I said. 'Maybe. And maybe not. Whatcha got?'

'Come up and see, honey.'

Stop sniggering, Arturo. Be suave.

'I might come up,' I said. 'And then, I might not.'

'Aw honey, come on.' The thin bones of her face, the odour of sour wine from her mouth, the awful hypocrisy of her sweetness, the hunger for money in her eyes.

Bandini speaking: 'What's the price these days?'

She took my arm, pulled me towards the door, but gently.

'You come on up, honey. We'll talk about it up there.'

'I'm really not very hot,' said Bandini. 'I – I just came from a wild party.'

Hail Mary full of grace, walking up the stairs, I can't go through with it. I've got to get out of it. The halls smelling of cockroaches, a yellow light at the ceiling, you're too aesthetic for all this, the girl holding my arm, there's something wrong with you, Arturo Bandini, you're a misanthrope, your whole life is doomed to celibacy, you should have been a priest, Father O'Leary talking that afternoon, telling us the joys of denial, and my own mother's money too, Oh Mary conceived without sin, pray for us who have recourse to thee – until we got to the top of the stairs and walked down a dusty dark hall to a room at the end, where she turned out the light and we were inside.

A room smaller than mine, carpetless, without pictures, a bed, a table, a wash-stand. She took off her coat. There was a blue print dress underneath. She was bare-legged. She took off the scarf. She was not a real blonde. Black hair grew at the roots. Her nose was crooked slightly. Bandini on the bed, put himself there with an air of casualness, like a man who knew how to sit on a bed.

Bandini: 'Nice place you got here.'

My God I got to get out of here, this is terrible.

The girl sat beside me, put her arms around me, pushed her breasts against me, kissed me, flecked my teeth with a cold tongue. I jumped to my feet. Oh think fast, my mind, dear mind of mine please get me out of this and it will never happen again. From now on I will return to my Church. Beginning this day my life shall run like sweet water.

The girl lay back, her hands behind her neck, her legs over the bed. I shall smell lilacs in Connecticut, no doubt, before I die, and see the clean white small reticent churches of my youth, the pasture bars I broke to run away.

'Look,' I said. 'I want to talk to you.'

She crossed her legs.

'I'm a writer,' I said. 'I'm gathering material for a book.'

'I knew you were a writer,' she said. 'Or a business man, or something. You look spiritual, honey.'

'I'm a writer, see. I like you and all that. You're okay, I like you. But I want to talk to you, first.'

She sat up.

'Haven't you any money, honey?'

Money – ho. And I pulled it out, a small thick roll of dollar bills. Sure I got money, plenty of money, this is a drop in the bucket, money is no object, money means nothing to me.

'What do you charge?'

'It's two dollars, honey.'

Then give her three, peel it off easily, like it was nothing at all, smile and hand it to her because money is no object, there's more where this came from, at this moment Mamma sits by the window holding her rosary, waiting for the Old Man to come home, but there's money, there's always money.

She took the money and slipped it under the pillow. She was grateful and her smile was different now. The writer wanted to talk. How were conditions these days? How did she like this kind of life? Oh, come on honey, let's not talk, let's get down to business. No, I want to talk to you, this is important, new book, material. I do this often. How did you ever get into this racket. Oh honey, Chrissakes, you going to ask me that too? But money is no object, I tell you. But my time is valuable, honey. Then here's a couple more bucks. That makes five, my God, five bucks and I'm not out of here yet, how I hate you, you filthy. But you're cleaner than me because you've got no mind to sell, just that poor flesh.

She was overwhelmed, she would do anything. I could have it any way I wanted it, and she tried to pull me to her, but no, let's wait a while. I tell you I want to talk to you, I tell you money is no object, here's three more, that makes eight dollars, but it doesn't matter. You just keep that eight bucks and buy yourself something nice. And then I snapped my fingers like a man remembering something, something important, an engagement.

'Say!' I said. 'That reminds me. What time is it?'

Her chin was at my neck, stroking it. 'Don't you worry about the time, honey. You can stay all night.'

A man of importance, ah yes, now I remembered, my publisher, he was getting in tonight by plane. Out at Burbank, away out in Burbank. Have to grab a cab and taxi out there, have to hurry. Goodbye, goodbye, you keep that eight bucks, you buy yourself something nice, goodbye, goodbye, running down the stairs, running away, the welcome fog in the doorway below, you keep that eight bucks, oh sweet fog I see you and I'm coming, you clean air, you wonderful world,

I'm coming to you, goodbye, yelling up the stairs, I'll see you again, you keep that eight dollars and buy yourself something nice. Eight dollars pouring out of my eyes. Oh Jesus kill me dead and ship my body home, kill me dead and make me die like a pagan fool with no priest to absolve me, no extreme unction, eight dollars, eight dollars . . .

Chapter Three

The lean days, blue skies with never a cloud, a sea of blue day after day, the sun floating through it. The days of plenty – plenty of worries, plenty of oranges. Eat them in bed, eat them for lunch, push them down for dinner. Oranges, five cents a dozen. Sunshine in the sky, sun juice in my stomach. Down at the Japanese market he saw me coming, that bullet-faced smiling Japanese, and he reached for a paper sack. A generous man, he gave me fifteen, sometimes twenty for a nickel.

'You like banana?' Sure, so he gave me a couple of bananas. A pleasant innovation, orange juice and bananas. 'You like apple?' Sure, so he gave me some apples. Here was something new: oranges and apples. 'You like peaches?' Indeed, and I carried the brown sack back to my room. An interesting innovation, peaches and oranges. My teeth tore them to pulp, the juices skewering and whimpering at the bottom of my stomach. It was so sad down there in my stomach. There was much weeping, and little gloomy clouds of gas pinched my heart.

My plight drove me to the typewriter. I sat before it, overwhelmed with grief for Arturo Bandini. Sometimes an idea floated harmlessly through the room. It was like a small white bird. It meant no ill-will. It only wanted to help me, dear little bird. But I would strike at it, hammer it out across the keyboard, and it would die on my hands.

What could be the matter with me? When I was a boy I had prayed to St Teresa for a new fountain pen. My prayer was answered. Anyway, I did get a new fountain pen. Now I prayed to St Teresa again. Please, sweet and lovely saint, gimme an idea. But she has deserted me, all the gods have deserted me, and like Huysmans I stand alone, my fists clenched, tears in my eyes. If someone only loved me, even a bug, even a mouse, but that too belonged to the past; even Pedro had forsaken me now that the best I could offer him was orange peel.

I thought of home, of spaghetti swimming in rich tomato sauce, smothered in Parmesan cheese, of Mamma's lemon pies, of lamb roasts and hot bread, and I was so miserable that I deliberately sank my fingernails into the flesh of my arm until a spot of blood appeared. It gave me great satisfaction. I was God's most miserable creature, forced even to torturing myself. Surely upon this earth no grief was greater than mine.

Hackmuth must hear of this, mighty Hackmuth, who fostered genius in the pages of his magazine. Dear Mr Hackmuth, I wrote, describing the glorious past, dear Hackmuth, page upon page, the sun a ball of fire in the West, slowly strangling in a fog bank rising off the coast.

There was a knock on my door, but I remained quiet because it might be that woman after her lousy rent. Now the door opened and a bald, bony, bearded face appeared. It was Mr Hellfrick, who lived next door. Mr Hellfrick was an atheist, retired from the army, living on a meagre pension, scarcely enough to pay his liquor bills, even though he purchased the cheapest gin on the market. He lived perpetually in a grey bathrobe without a cord or button, and though he made a pretence at modesty he really didn't care, so that his bathrobe was always open and you saw much hair and bones underneath. Mr Hellfrick had red eyes because every afternoon when the sun hit the west side of the hotel, he slept with his head out the window, his body and legs inside. He had owed me fifteen cents since my first day at the hotel, but after many futile attempts to collect it, I had given up hope of ever possessing the money again. This had caused a breach between us, so I was surprised when his head appeared inside my door.

He squinted secretively, pressed a finger to his lips, and shhhhhhhhhed me to be quiet, even though I hadn't said a word. I wanted him to know my hostility, to remind him that I had no respect for a man who failed to meet his obligations. Now he closed the door quietly and tiptoed across the room on his bony toes, his bathrobe wide open.

'Do you like milk?' he whispered.

I certainly did, and I told him so. Then he revealed his plan. The man who drove the Alden milk route on Bunker Hill was a friend of his. Every morning at four this man parked his milk truck behind the hotel and came up the back stairs to Hellfrick's room for a drink of gin. 'And so,' he said, 'if you like milk, all you have to do is help yourself.'

I shook my head.

'That's pretty contemptible, Hellfrick,' and I wondered at the friendship between Hellfrick and the milkman. 'If he's your friend, who do you have to steal the milk? He drinks your gin. Why don't you ask him for milk?'

'But I don't drink milk,' Hellfrick said. 'I'm doing this for you.'

This looked like an attempt to squirm out of the debt he

owed me. I shook my head. 'No thanks, Hellfrick. I like to consider myself an honest man.'

He shrugged, pulled the bathrobe around him.

'Okay, kid. I was only trying to do you a favour.'

I continued my letter to Hackmuth, but I began to taste milk almost immediately. After a while I could not bear it. I lay on the bed in the semi-darkness, allowing myself to be tempted. In a little while all resistance was gone, and I knocked on Hellfrick's door. His room was madness, pulp western magazines over the floor, a bed with sheets blackened, clothes strewn everywhere, and clothes-hooks on the wall conspicuously naked, like broken teeth in a skull. There were dishes on the chairs, cigarette butts pressed out on the window sills. His room was like mine except that he had a small gas stove in one corner and shelves for pots and pans. He got a special rate from the landlady, so that he did his own cleaning and made his own bed, except that he did neither. Hellfrick sat in a rocking chair in his bathrobe, gin bottles around his feet. He was drinking from a bottle in his hand. He was always drinking, day and night, but he never got drunk

'I've changed my mind,' I told him.

He filled his mouth with gin, rolled the liquor around in his cheeks, and swallowed ecstatically. 'It's a cinch,' he said. Then he got to his feet and crossed the room towards his pants, which lay sprawled out. For a moment I thought he was going to pay back the money he owed me, but he did no more than fumble mysteriously through the pockets, and then he returned empty handed to the chair. I stood there.

'That reminds me,' I said. 'I wonder if you could pay the money I loaned you.'

'Haven't got it,' he said.

'Could you pay me a portion of it – say ten cents?'

He shook his head.

'A nickel?'

'I'm broke, kid.'

Then he took another swig. It was a fresh bottle, almost full.

'I can't give you any hard cash, kid. But I'll see that you get all the milk you need.' Then he explained. The milkman would arrive around four. I was to stay awake and listen for his knock. Hellfrick would keep the milkman occupied for at least twenty minutes. It was a bribe, a means of escaping payment of the debt, but I was hungry.

'But you ought to pay your debts, Hellfrick. You'd be in a bad spot if I was charging you interest.'

'I'll pay you, kid,' he said. 'I'll pay every last penny, just as soon as I can.'

I walked back to my room, slamming Hellfrick's door angrily. I didn't wish to seem cruel about the matter, but this was going too far. I knew the gin he drank cost him at least thirty cents a pint. Surely he could control his craving for alcohol long enough to pay his just debts.

The night came reluctantly. I sat at the window, rolling some cigarettes with rough cut tobacco and squares of toilet paper. This tobacco had been a whim of mine in more prosperous times. I had bought a can of it, and the pipe for smoking it had been free, attached to the can by a rubber band. But I had lost the pipe. The tobacco was so coarse it made a poor smoke in regular cigarette papers, but wrapped twice in toilet tissue it was powerful and compact, sometimes bursting into flames.

The night came slowly, first the cool odour of it, and then the darkness. Beyond my window spread the great city, the street lamps, the red and blue and green neon tubes bursting to life like bright night flowers. I was not hungry, there were plenty of oranges under the bed, and that mysterious chortling in the pit of my stomach was nothing more than great clouds of tobacco smoke marooned there, trying frantically to find a way out.

So it had happened at last: I was about to become a thief, a cheap milk-stealer. Here was your flash-in-the-pan genius, your one-story-writer: a thief. I held my head in my hands and rocked back and forth. Mother of God. Headlines in the papers, promising writer caught stealing milk, famous protégé of J. C. Hackmuth hauled into court on petty thief charge, reporters swarming around me, flashlights popping, give us a statement, Bandini, how did it happen? Well, fellows, it was like this: you see, I've really got plenty of money, big sales of manuscripts and all that, but I was doing a yarn about a fellow who steals a quart of milk, and I wanted to write from experience, so that's what happened, fellows. Watch for the story in the *Post*, I'm calling it 'Milk Thief'. Leave me your address and I'll send you all free copies.

But it would not happen that way, because nobody knows Arturo Bandini, and you'll get six months, they'll take you to the city jail and you'll be a criminal, and what'll your mother say? and what'll your father say? and can't you hear those fellows around the filling station in Boulder, Colorado, can't you hear them snickering about the great writer caught stealing a quart of milk? Don't do it, Arturo! If you've got an ounce of decency in you, don't do it!

I rose from the chair and paced up and down. Almighty

God, give me strength! Hold back this criminal urge! Then, all at once, the whole plan seemed cheap and silly, for at that moment I thought of something else to write in my letter to the great Hackmuth, and for two hours I wrote, until my back ached. When I looked out of my window to the big clock on the St Paul Hotel, it was almost eleven. The letter to Hackmuth was a very long one – already I had twenty pages. I read the letter. It seemed silly. I felt the blood in my face from blushes. Hackmuth would think me an idiot for writing such puerile nonsense. Gathering the pages, I tossed them into the wastebasket. Tomorrow was another day, and tomorrow I might get an idea for a short story. Meanwhile I would eat a couple of oranges and go to bed.

They were miserable oranges. Sitting on the bed I dug my nails into their thin skins. My own flesh puckered, my mouth was filled with saliva, and I squinted at the thought of them. When I bit into the yellow pulp it shocked me like a cold shower. Oh Bandini, talking to the reflection in the dresser mirror, what sacrifices you make for your art! You might have been a captain of industry, a merchant prince, a big league ball player, leading hitter in the American League, with an average of .415; but no! Here you are, crawling through the days, a starved genius, faithful to your sacred calling. What courage you possess!

I lay in bed, sleepless in the darkness. Mighty Hackmuth, what would he say to all this! He would applaud, his powerful pen would eulogize me in well-turned phrases. And after all, that letter to Hackmuth wasn't such a bad letter. I got up, dug it from the wastebasket, and re-read it. A remarkable letter, cautiously humoured. Hackmuth would find it very amusing. It would impress upon him the fact that I was the selfsame author of *The Little Dog Laughed*. There was a story for you! And I opened a drawer filled with copies of the magazine that contained the story. Lying on the bed I read it again, laughing and laughing at the wit of it, murmuring in amazement that I had written it. Then I took to reading it aloud, with gestures, before the mirror. When I was finished there were tears of delight in my eyes and I stood before the picture of Hackmuth, thanking him for recognizing my genius.

I sat before the typewriter and continued the letter. The night deepened, the pages mounted. Ah, if all writing were as easy as a letter to Hackmuth! The pages piled up, twenty-five, thirty, until I looked down to my navel, where I detected a fleshy ring. The irony of it! I was gaining weight: oranges were filling me out! At once I jumped up and did a number of setting-up exercises. I twisted and writhed and rolled. Sweat flowed and breathing came hard. Thirsty and exhausted, I threw myself on the bed. A glass of cool milk would be fine now.

At that moment I heard a knock on Hellfrick's door. Then Hellfrick's grunt as someone entered. It could be no one but the milkman. I looked at the clock: it was almost four. I dressed quickly: pants, shoes, no socks, and a sweater. The hallway was deserted, sinister in the red light of an old electric bulb. I walked deliberately, without stealth, like a man going to the lavatory down the hall. Two flights of whining, irritable stairs and I was on the ground floor. The red and white Alden milk-truck was parked close to the hotel wall in the moon-drenched alley. I reached into the truck and got two full quart bottles firmly by their necks. They felt cool and delicious in my fist. A moment later I was back in my room, the bottles of milk on the dresser table. They seemed to fill the room. They were like human things. They were so beautiful, so fat and prosperous.

You Arturo! I said, you lucky one! It may be the prayers of your mother, and it may be that God still loves you, in spite of your tampering with atheists, but whatever it is, you're lucky.

For old times' sake, I thought, and for old times' sake I knelt down and said grace, the way we used to do it in grade school, the way my mother taught us back home: Bless us, Oh Lord, and these Thy gifts, which we are about to receive from Thy most bountiful hands, through the same Christ, Our Lord, Amen. And I added another prayer for good measure. Long after the milkman left Hellfrick's room I was still on my knees, a full half hour of prayers, until I was ravenous for the taste of milk, until my knees ached and a dull pain throbbed in my shoulder blades.

When I got up I staggered from cramped muscles, but it was going to be worthwhile. I took the toothbrush from my glass, opened one of the bottles, and poured a full glass. I turned and faced the picture of J. C. Hackmuth on the wall.

'To you, Hackmuth! Hurray for you!'

And I drank, greedily, until my throat suddenly choked and contracted and a horrible taste shook me. It was the kind of milk I hated. It was buttermilk. I spat it out, washed my mouth with water, and hurried to look at the other bottle. It was buttermilk, too.

Chapter Four

Down on Spring Street, in a bar across the street from the secondhand store. With my last nickel I went there for a cup of coffee. An old style place, sawdust on the floor, crudely drawn nudes smeared across the walls. It was a saloon where old men gathered, where the beer was cheap and smelled sour, where the past remained unaltered.

I sat at one of the tables against the wall. I remember that I sat with my head in my hands. I heard her voice without looking up. I remember that she said, 'Can I get you something?' and I said something about coffee with cream. I sat there until the cup was before me, a long time I sat like that, thinking of the hopelessness of my fate.

It was very bad coffee. When the cream mixed with it I realized it was not cream at all, for it turned a greyish colour, and the taste was that of boiled rags. This was my last nickel, and it made me angry. I looked around for the girl who had waited on me. She was five or six tables away, serving beers from a tray. Her back was to me, and I saw the tight smoothness of her shoulders under a white smock, the faint trace of muscle in her arms, and the black hair so thick and glossy, falling to her shoulders.

At last she turned around and I waved to her. She was only faintly attentive, widening her eyes in an expression of bored aloofness. Except for the contour of her face and the brilliance of her teeth, she was not beautiful. But at that moment she turned to smile at one of her old customers, and I saw a streak of white under her lips. Her nose was Mayan, flat, with large nostrils. Her lips were heavily rouged, with the thickness of a negress's lips. She was a racial type, and as such she was beautiful, but she was too strange for me. Her eyes were at a high slant, her skin was dark but not black, and as she walked her breasts moved in a way that showed their firmness.

She ignored me after that first glance. She went on to the bar, where she ordered more beer and waited for the thin bartender to draw it. As she waited she whistled, looked at me vaguely and went on whistling. I had stopped waving, but I made it plain I wanted her to come to my table. Suddenly she opened her mouth to the ceiling and laughed in a most mysterious fashion, so that even the bartender wondered at her laughter. Then she danced away, swinging the tray gracefully, picking her way through the tables to a group far down in the rear of the saloon. The bartender followed her with his eyes, still confused at her laughter. But I understood her laughter. It was for me. She was laughing at me. There was something about my appearance, my face, my posture, something about me sitting there that had amused her, and as I thought of it I clenched my fists and considered myself with angry humiliation. I touched my hair: it was combed. I fumbled with my collar and tie: they were clean and in place. I stretched myself to the range of the bar mirror, where I saw what was certainly a worried and sallow face, but not a funny face, and I was very angry.

I began to sneer, watched her closely and sneered. She did

not approach my table. She moved near it, even to the table adjacent, but she did not venture beyond that. Each time I saw the dark face, the black large eyes flashing their laughter, I set my lips to a curl that meant I was sneering. It became a game. The coffee cooled, grew cold, a scum of milk gathered over the surface, but I did not touch it. The girl moved like a dancer, her strong silk legs gathering bits of sawdust as her tattered shoes glided over the marble floor.

Those shoes, they were huaraches, the leather thongs wrapped several times around her ankles. They were desperately ragged huaraches; the woven leather had become unravelled. When I saw them I was very grateful, for it was a defect about her that deserved criticism. She was tall and straight-shouldered, a girl of perhaps twenty, faultless in her way, except for her tattered huaraches. And so I fastened my stare on them, watched them intently and deliberately, even turning in my chair and twisting my neck to glare at them, sneering and chuckling to myself. Plainly I was getting as much enjoyment out of this as she got from my face, or whatever it was that amused her. This had a powerful effect upon her. Gradually her pirouetting and dancing subsided and she merely hurried back and forth, and at length she was making her way stealthily. She was embarrassed, and once I saw her glance down quickly and examine her feet, so that in a few minutes she no longer laughed; instead, there was a grimness in her face, and finally she was glancing at me with bitter hatred.

Now I was exultant, strangely happy. I felt relaxed. The world was full of uproariously amusing people. Now the thin bartender looked in my direction and I winked a comradely greeting. He tossed his head in an acknowledging nod. I sighed and sat back, at ease with life.

She had not collected the nickel for the coffee. She would have to do so, unless I left it on the table and walked out. But I wasn't going to walk out. I waited. A half hour passed. When she hurried to the bar for more beer, she no longer waited on the rail in plain sight. She walked around to the back of the bar. She didn't look at me anymore, but I knew she knew I watched her.

Finally she walked straight for my table. She walked proudly, her chin tilted, her hands hanging at her sides. I wanted to stare, but I couldn't keep it up. I looked away, smiling all the while.

'Do you want anything else?' she asked.

Her white smock smelled of starch.

'You call this stuff coffee?' I said.

Suddenly she laughed again. It was a shriek, a mad laugh like the clatter of dishes and it was over as quickly as it began. I looked at her feet again. I could feel something inside her retreating. I wanted to hurt her.

'Maybe this isn't coffee at all,' I said. 'Maybe it's just water after they boiled your filthy shoes in it.' I looked up to her black blazing eyes. 'Maybe you don't know any better. Maybe you're just naturally careless. But if I were a girl I wouldn't be seen in a Main Street alley with those shoes.'

I was panting when I finished. Her thick lips trembled and the fists in her pocket were writhing under the starched stiffness.

'I hate you,' she said.

I felt her hatred. I could smell it, even hear it coming out of her, but I sneered again. 'I hope so,' I said. 'Because there must be something pretty fine about a guy who rates your hatred.'

Then she said a strange thing; I remember it clearly. 'I hope you die of heart failure,' she said. 'Right there in that chair.'

It gave her keen satisfaction, even though I laughed. She walked away smiling. She stood at the bar again, waiting for more beer, and her eyes were fastened on me, brilliant with her strange wish, and I was uncomfortable but still laughing. Now she was dancing again, gliding from table to table with her tray, and every time I looked at her she smiled her wish, until it had a mysterious effect on me, and I became conscious of my inner organism, of the beat of my heart and the flutter of my stomach. I felt that she would not come back to my table again, and I remember that I was glad of it, and that a strange restlessness came over me, so that I was anxious to get away from that place, and away from the range of her persistent smile. Before I left I did something that pleased me very much. I took the five cents from my pocket and placed it on the table. Then I spilled half the coffee over it. She would have to mop up the mess with her towel. The brown ugliness spread everywhere over the table, and as I got up to leave it was trickling to the floor. At the door I paused to look at her once more. She smiled the same smile. I nodded at the spilled coffee. Then I tossed my fingers in a salute farewell and walked into the street. Once more I had a good feeling. Once more it was as before, the world was full of amusing things.

I don't remember what I did after I left her. Maybe I went up to Benny Cohen's room over the Grand Central Market. He had a wooden leg with a little door in it. Inside the door were marijuana cigarettes. He sold them for fifteen cents apiece. He also sold newspapers, the *Examiner* and the *Times*. He had a room piled high with copies of *The New Masses*. Maybe he saddened me as always with his grim horrible vision of the world tomorrow. Maybe he poked his stained fingers under my nose and cursed me for betraying the proletariat from which I came. Maybe, as always, he sent me trembling out of his room and down the dusty stairs to the fog-dimmed street, my fingers itching for the throat of an imperialist. Maybe, and maybe not; I don't remember.

But I remember that night in my room, the lights of the St Paul Hotel throwing red and green blobs across my bed as I lay and shuddered and dreamed of the anger of that girl, of the way she danced from table to table, and the black glance of her eyes. That I remember, even to forgetting I was poor and without an idea for a story.

I looked for her early the next morning. Eight o'clock, and I was down on Spring Street. I had a copy of *The Little Dog Laughed* in my pocket. She would think differently about me if she read that story. I had it autographed, right there in my back pocket, ready to present at the slightest notice. But the place was closed at that early hour. It was called the Columbia Buffet. I pushed my nose against the window and looked inside. The chairs were piled upon the tables, and an old man in rubber boots was swabbing the floor. I walked down the street a block or two, the wet air already bluish from monoxide gas. A fine idea came into my head. I took out the magazine and erased the autograph. In its place I wrote, 'To a Mayan Princess, from a worthless Gringo.' This seemed right, exactly the correct spirit. I walked back to the Columbia Buffet and pounded the front window. The old man opened the door with wet hands, sweat seeping from his hair.

I said, 'What's the name of that girl who works here?'

'You mean Camilla?'

'The one who worked here last night.'

'That's her,' he said. 'Camilla Lopez.'

'Will you give this to her?' I said. 'Just give it to her. Tell her a fellow came by and said for you to give it to her.'

He wiped his dripping hands on his apron and took the magazine. 'Take good care of it,' I said. 'It's valuable.'

The old man closed the door. Through the glass I saw him limp back to his mop and bucket. He placed the magazine on the bar and resumed his work. A little breeze flipped the pages of the magazine. As I walked away I was afraid he would forget all about it. When I reached the Civic Centre I realized I had made a bad mistake: the inscription on the story would never impress that kind of a girl. I hurried back to the Columbia Buffet and banged the window with my knuckles. I heard the old man grumbling and swearing as he fumbled with the lock. He wiped the sweat from his old eyes and saw me again.

'Could I have that magazine?' I said. 'I want to write something in it.'

The old man couldn't understand any of this. He shook his head with a sigh and told me to come inside. 'Go get it yourself, goddamnit,' he said. 'I got work to do.'

I flattened the magazine on the bar and erased the inscription to the Mayan Princess. In place of it I wrote:

Dear Ragged Shoes,

You may not know it, but last night you insulted the author of this story. Can you read? If so, invest fifteen minutes of your time and treat yourself to a masterpiece. And next time, be careful. Not everyone who comes into this dive is a bum.

Arturo Bandini

I handed the magazine to the old man, but he did not lift his eyes from his work. 'Give this to Miss Lopez,' I said. 'And see to it that she gets it personally.'

The old man dropped the mop handle, smeared the sweat from his wrinkled face, and pointed at the front door. 'You get out of here!' he said.

I laid the magazine on the bar again and strolled away leisurely. At the door I turned and waved.

Chapter Five

I wasn't starving. I still had some old oranges under the bed. That night I ate three or four and with the darkness I walked down Bunker Hill to the downtown district. Across the street from the Columbia Buffet I stood in a shadowed doorway and watched Camilla Lopez. She was the same, dressed in the same white smock. I trembled when I saw her and a strange hot feeling was in my throat. But after a few minutes the strangeness was gone and I stood in the darkness until my feet ached.

When I saw a policeman strolling towards me I walked away. It was a hot night. Sand from the Mojave had blown across the city. Tiny brown grains of sand clung to my fingertips whenever I touched anything, and when I got back to my room I found the mechanism of my new typewriter glutted with sand. It was in my ears and in my hair. When I took off my clothes it fell like powder to the floor. It was even between the sheets of my bed. Lying in the darkness, the red light from the St Paul Hotel flashing on and off across my bed was bluish now, a ghastly colour jumping into the room and out again.

I couldn't eat any oranges the next morning. The thought of them made me wince. By noon, after an aimless walk downtown, I was sick with self-pity, unable to control my grief. When I got back to my room I threw myself on the bed and wept from deep inside my chest. I let it flow from every part of me, and after I could not cry anymore I felt fine again. I felt truthful and clean. I sat down and wrote my mother an honest letter. I told her I had been lying to her for weeks; and please send some money, because I wanted to come home.

As I wrote Hellfrick entered. He was wearing pants and no bathrobe, and at first I didn't recognize him. Without a word he put fifteen cents on the table. 'I'm an honest man, kid,' he said, 'I'm as honest as the day is long.' And he walked out.

I brushed the coins into my hand, jumped out the window and ran down the street to the grocery store. The little Japanese had his sack ready at the orange bin. He was amazed to see me pass him by and enter the staples department. I bought two dozen cookies. Sitting on the bed I swallowed them as fast as I could, washing them down with gulps of water. I felt fine again. My stomach was full, and I still had a nickel left. I tore up the letter to my mother and lay down to wait for the night. That nickel meant I could go back to the Columbia Buffet. I waited, heavy with food, heavy with desire.

She saw me as I entered. She was glad to see me; I knew she was, because I could tell by the way her eyes widened. Her face brightened and that tight feeling caught my throat. All at once I was so happy, sure of myself, clean and conscious of my youth. I sat at that same first table. Tonight there was music in the saloon, a piano and a violin; two fat women with hard masculine faces and short haircuts. Their song was *Over the Waves*. Ta de da da, and I watched Camilla dancing with her beer tray. Her hair was so black, so deep and clustered, like grapes hiding her neck. This was a sacred place, this saloon. Everything here was holy, the chairs, the tables, that rag in her hand, that sawdust under her feet. She was a Mayan princess and this was her castle. I watched the tattered huaraches glide across the floor, and I wanted those huaraches. I would like them to hold in my hands against my chest when I fell asleep. I would like to hold them and breathe the odour of them.

She did not venture near my table, but I was glad. Don't come right away, Camilla; let me sit here a while and accustom myself to this rare excitement; leave me alone while my mind travels the infinite loveliness of your splendid glory; just leave a while to myself, to hunger and dream with eyes awake.

She came finally, carrying a cup of coffee in her tray. The same coffee, the same chipped, brownish mug. She came with her eyes blacker and wider than ever, walking towards me on soft feet, smiling mysteriously, until I thought I would faint from the pounding of my heart. As she stood beside me, I sensed the slight odour of her perspiration mingled with the tart cleanliness of her starched smock. It overwhelmed me, made me stupid, and I breathed through my lips to avoid it. She smiled to let me know she did not object to the spilled coffee of the other evening; more than that, I seemed to feel she had rather liked the whole thing, she was glad about it, grateful for it.

'I didn't know you had freckles,' she said.

'They don't mean anything,' I said.

'I'm sorry about the coffee,' she said. 'Everybody orders beer. We don't get many calls for coffee.'

'That's exactly why you don't get many calls for it.

Because it's so lousy. I'd drink beer too, if I could afford it.'

She pointed at my hand with a pencil. 'You bite your fingernails,' she said. 'You shouldn't do that.'

I shoved my hands in my pockets.

'Who are you to tell me what to do?'

'Do you want some beer?' she said. 'I'll get you some. You don't have to pay for it.'

'You don't have to get me anything. I'll drink this alleged coffee and get out of here.'

She walked to the bar and ordered a beer. I watched her pay for it from a handful of coins she dug out of her smock. She carried the beer to me and placed it under my nose. It hurt me.

'Take it away,' I said. 'Get it out of here. I want coffee, not beer.'

Someone in the rear called her name and she hurried away. The backs of her knees appeared as she bent over the table and gathered empty beer mugs. I moved in my chair, my feet kicking something under the table. It was a spittoon. She was at the bar again, nodding at me, smiling, making a motion indicating I should drink the beer. I felt devilish, vicious. I got her attention and poured the beer into the spittoon. Her white teeth took hold of her lower lip and her face lost blood. Her eyes blazed. A pleasantness pervaded me, a satisfaction. I sat back and smiled to the ceiling.

She disappeared behind a thin partition which served as a kitchen. She reappeared, smiling. Her hands were behind her back, concealing something. Now the old man I had seen that morning stepped from behind the partition. He grinned expectantly. Camilla waved to me. The worst was about to happen: I could feel it coming. From behind her back she revealed the little magazine containing *The Little Dog Laughed*. She waved it in the air, but she was out of view, and her performance was only for the old man and myself. He watched with big eyes. My mouth went dry as I saw her wet her fingers and flip the pages to the place where the story was printed. Her lips twisted as she clamped the magazine between her knees and ripped away the pages. She held them over her head, waving them and smiling. The old man shook his head approvingly. The smile on her face changed to determination as she tore the pages into little pieces, and these into smaller pieces. With a gesture of finality, she let the pieces fall through her fingers and trickle to the spittoon at her feet. I tried to smile. She slapped her hands together with an air of boredom, like one slapping the dust from her palms. Then she put one hand on her hip, tilted her shoulder, and swaggered away. The old man stood there for some time. Only he had seen her. Now that the show was over, he disappeared behind the partition.

I sat smiling wretchedly, my heart weeping for *The Little Dog Laughed*, for every well-turned phrase, for the little flecks of poetry through it, my first story, the best thing I could show for my whole life. It was the record of all that was good in me, approved and printed by the great J. C. Hackmuth, and she had torn it up and thrown it into a spittoon.

After a while I pushed back my chair and got up to leave. Standing at the bar, she watched me go. There was pity for me upon her face, a tiny smile of regret for what she had done, but I kept my eyes away from her and walked into the street, glad for the hideous din of street cars and the queer noises of the city pounding my ears and burying me in an avalanche of banging and screeching. I put my hands in my pockets and slumped away.

Fifty feet from the saloon I heard someone calling. I turned around. It was she, running on soft feet, coins jingling in her pockets. 'Young fellow!' she called. 'Oh kid!'

I waited and she came out of breath, speaking quickly and softly. 'I'm sorry,' she said. 'I didn't mean anything – honest.'

'It's okay,' I said. 'I didn't mind.'

She kept glancing towards the saloon. 'I have to get back,' she said. 'They'll miss me. Come back tomorrow night, will you? Please! I can be nice. I'm awfully sorry about tonight. Please come, please!' She squeezed my arm. 'Will you come?'

'Maybe.'

She smiled. 'Forgive me?'

'Sure.'

I stood in the middle of the sidewalk and watched her hurry back. After a few steps she turned, blew a kiss and called, 'Tomorrow night. Don't forget!'

'Camilla!' I said. 'Wait. Just a minute!'

We ran towards each other, meeting halfway.

'Hurry!' she said. 'They fire me.'

I glanced at her feet. She sensed it coming and I felt her recoiling from me. Now a good feeling rushed through me, a coolness, a newness like new skin. I spoke slowly.

'Those huaraches – do you have to wear them, Camilla? Do you have to emphasize the fact that you always were and always will be a filthy little Greaser?'

She looked at me in horror, her lips open. Clasping both hands against her mouth, she rushed inside the saloon. I heard her moaning. 'Oh, oh, oh.'

I tossed my shoulders and swaggered away, whistling with pleasure. In the gutter I saw a long cigarette butt. I picked it up without shame, lit it as I stood with one foot in the gutter, puffed it and exhaled towards the stars. I was an American, and goddamn proud of it. This great city, these mighty pavements and proud buildings, they were the voice of my America. From sand and cactus we Americans had carved an empire. Camilla's people had had their chance. They had failed. We Americans had turned the trick. Thank God for my country. Thank God I had been born an American!

Chapter Six

I went up to my room, up the dusty stairs of Bunker Hill, past the soot-covered frame buildings along that dark street, sand and oil and grease choking the futile palm trees standing like dying prisoners, chained to a little plot of ground with black pavement hiding their feet. Dust and old buildings and old people sitting at windows, old people tottering out of doors, old people moving painfully along the dark street. The old folk from Indiana and Iowa and Illinois, from Boston and Kansas City and Des Moines, they sold their homes and their stores, and they came here by train and by automobile to the land of sunshine, to die in the sun, with just enough money to live until the sun killed them, tore themselves out by the roots in their last days, deserted the smug prosperity of Kansas City and Chicago and Peoria to find a place in the sun. And when they got here they found that other and greater thieves had already taken possession, that even the sun belonged to the others; Smith and Jones and Parker, druggist, banker, baker, dust of Chicago and Cincinnati and Cleveland on their shoes, doomed to die in the sun, a few dollars in the bank, enough to subscribe to the *Los Angeles Times*, enough to keep alive the illusion that this was paradise, that their little papier-mâché homes were castles. The uprooted ones, the empty sad folks, the old and the young folks, the folks from back home. These were my countrymen, these were the new Californians. With their bright polo shirts and sunglasses, they were in paradise, they belonged.

But down on Main Street, down on Towne and San Pedro, and for a mile on lower Fifth Street were the tens of thousands of others; they couldn't afford sunglasses or a four-bit polo shirt and they hid in the alleys by day and slunk off to flop houses by night. A cop won't pick you up for vagrancy in Los Angeles if you wear a fancy polo shirt and a pair of sunglasses. But if there is dust on your shoes and that sweater you wear is thick like the sweaters they wear in the snow countries, he'll grab you. So get yourselves a polo shirt boys, and a pair of sunglasses, and white shoes, if you can. Be collegiate. It'll get you anyway. After a while, after big doses of the *Times* and the *Examiner*, you too will whoop it up for the sunny south. You'll eat hamburgers year after year and live in dusty, vermin-infested apartments and hotels, but every morning you'll see the mighty sun, the eternal blue of the sky, and the streets will be full of sleek women you never will possess, and the hot semi-tropical nights will reek of romance you'll never have, but you'll still be in paradise, boys, in the land of sunshine.

As for the folks back home, you can lie to them, because they hate the truth anyway, they won't have it, because soon or late they want to come out to paradise, too. You can't fool the folks back home, boys. They know what Southern California's like. After all they read the papers, they look at the picture magazine glutting the newsstands of every corner in America. They've seen pictures of the movie stars' homes. You can't tell them anything about California.

Lying in my bed I thought about them, watched the blobs

of red light from the St Paul Hotel jump in and out of my room, and I was miserable, for tonight I had acted like them. Smith and Parker and Jones, I had never been one of them. Ah, Camilla! When I was a kid back home in Colorado it was Smith and Parker and Jones who hurt me with their hideous names, called me Wop and Dago and Greaser, and their children hurt me, just as I hurt you tonight. They hurt me so much I could never become one of them, drove me to books, drove me within myself, drove me to run away from that Colorado town, and sometimes, Camilla, when I see their faces I feel the hurt all over again, the old ache there, and sometimes their heartlessness, the same faces, the same set, hard mouths, faces from my home town, fulfilling the emptiness of their lives under a blazing sun.

I see them in the lobbies of hotels, I see them sunning in the parks, and limping out of ugly little churches, their faces bleak from proximity with their strange gods, out of Aimee's Temple, out of the Church of the Great I Am.

I have seen them stagger out of their movie palaces and blink their empty eyes in the face of reality once more, and stagger home, to read the *Times*, to find out what's going on in the world. I have vomited at their newspapers, read their literature, observed their customs, eaten their food, desired their women, gaped at their art. But I am poor, and my name ends with a soft vowel, and they hate me and my father, and my father's father, and they would have my blood and put me down, but they are old now, dying in the sun and in the hot dust of the road, and I am young and full of hope and love for my country and my times, and when I say Greaser to you it is not my heart that speaks, but the quivering of an old wound, and I am ashamed of the terrible thing I have done.

Chapter Seven

I am thinking of the Alta Loma Hotel, remembering the people who lived there. I remember my first day there. I remember that I walked into the dark lobby carrying two suitcases, one of them filled with copies of *The Little Dog Laughed*. It was a long time ago, but I remember it well. I had come by bus, dusty to the skin, the dust of Wyoming and Utah and Nevada in my hair and in my ears.

'I want a cheap room,' I said.

The landlady had white hair. Around her neck was a high net collar fitting tightly like a corset. She was in her seventies, a tall woman who increased her height by rising on tiptoe and peering at me over her glasses.

'Do you have a job?' she said.

'I'm a writer,' I said. 'Look, I'll show you.'

I opened my suitcase and got out a copy. 'I wrote that,' I told her. I was eager in those days, very proud. 'I'll give you a copy,' I said. 'I'll autograph it for you.'

I took a fountain pen from the desk, it was dry and I had to dip it, and I rolled my tongue around thinking of something nice to say. 'What's your name?' I asked her. She told me unwillingly. 'Mrs Hargraves,' she said. 'Why?' But I was honouring her, and I had no time to answer questions, and I wrote above the story, 'For a woman of ineffable charm, with lovely blue eyes and a generous smile, from the author, Arturo Bandini.'

She smiled with a smile that seemed to hurt her face, cracking it open with old lines that broke up the dry flesh around her mouth and cheeks. 'I hate dog stories,' she said, putting the magazine out of sight. She looked at me from an even higher view over her glasses. 'Young man,' she said, 'are you a Mexican?'

I pointed at myself and laughed.

'Me, a Mexican?' I shook my head. 'I'm an American, Mrs Hargraves. And that isn't a dog story, either. It's about a man, it's pretty good. There isn't a dog in the whole story.'

'We don't allow Mexicans in this hotel,' she said.

'I'm not a Mexican. I got that title after the fable. You know: "And the little dog laughed to see such sport."'

'Nor Jews,' she said.

I registered. I had a beautiful signature in those days, intricate, oriental, illegible, with a mighty slashing underscore, a signature more complex than that of the great Hackmuth. And after the signature I wrote, 'Boulder, Colorado.'

She examined the script, word for word.

Coldly: 'What's your name, young man?'

And I was disappointed, for already she had forgotten the author of *The Little Dog Laughed* and his name printed in large type on the magazine. I told her my name. She printed it carefully over the signature. Then she crossed the page to the other writing.

'Mr Bandini,' she said, looking at me coldly, 'Boulder is *not* in Colorado.'

'It is too!' I said. 'I just came from there. It was there two days ago.'

She was firm, determined. 'Boulder is in Nebraska. My husband and I went through Boulder, Nebraska, thirty years ago, on our way out here. You will kindly change that, if you please.'

'But it *is* in Colorado! My mother lives there, my father. I went to school there!'

She reached under the desk and drew out the magazine. She handed it to me. 'This hotel is no place for you, young man. We have fine people here, honest people.'

I didn't accept the magazine. I was so tired, hammered to bits by the long bus ride. 'All right,' I said. 'It's in Nebraska.' And I wrote it down, scratched out the Colorado and wrote Nebraska over it. She was satisfied, very pleased with me, smiled and examined the magazine. 'So you're an author!' she said. 'How nice!' Then she put the magazine out of sight again. 'Welcome to California!' she said. 'You'll love it here!'

That Mrs Hargraves! She was lonely, and so lost and still proud. One afternoon she took me to her apartment on the top floor. It was like walking into a well-dusted tomb. Her husband was dead now, but thirty years ago he had owned a tool shop in Bridgeport, Connecticut. His picture was on the wall. A splendid man, who neither smoked nor drank, dead of a heart attack; a thin, severe face out of a heavy framed picture, still contemptuous of smoking and drinking. Here was the bed in which he died, a high mahogany four-poster; here were his clothes in the closet and his shoes on the floor, the toes turned upwards from age. Here on the mantel was his shaving mug, he always shaved himself, and his name was Bert. That Bert! Bert, she used to say, why don't you go to the barber, and Bert would laugh, because he knew he was a better barber than the regular barbers.

Bert always got up at five in the morning. He came from a family of fifteen children. He was handy with tools. He had done all the repair work around the hotel for years. It had taken him three weeks to paint the outside of the building. He used to say he was a better painter than the regular painters. For two hours she talked of Bert, and Lord! how she loved that man, even in death, but he was not dead at all; he was in that apartment, watching over her, protecting her, daring me to hurt her. He frightened me, and made me want to rush away. We had tea. The tea was old. The sugar was old and lumpish. The tea cups were dusty, and somehow the tea tasted old and the little dried up cookies tasted of death. When I got up to leave, Bert followed me through the door and down the hall, daring me to think cynically of him. For two nights he hounded me, threatened me, even cajoled me in the matter of cigarettes.

I am remembering that kid from Memphis. I never asked his name and he never asked mine. We said 'Hi' to one another. He was not there long, a few weeks. His pimpled face was always covered by his long hands when he sat on the front porch of the hotel: every night late he was there; twelve and one and two o'clock, and coming home I would find him rocking back and forth in the wicker chair, his nervous fingers picking at his face, searching his uncut black hair. 'Hi,' I would say, and 'Hi' he would answer.

The restless dust of Los Angeles fevered him. He was a greater wanderer than myself, and all day long he sought out perverse loves in the parks. But he was so ugly he never found his desire, and the warm nights with low stars and yellow moon tortured him away from his room until the dawn arrived. But one night he talked to me, left me nauseated and unhappy as he revelled in memories of Memphis, Tennessee, where the real people came from, where there were friends and friends. Some day he would leave this hated city, some day he would go back where friendship meant something, and sure enough, he went away and I got a postcard signed 'Memphis Kid' from Fort Worth, Texas.

There was Heilman, who belonged to the Book of the Month Club. A huge man with arms like logs and legs tight in his pants. He was a bank teller. He had a wife in Moline, Illinois and a son at the University of Chicago. He hated the southwest, his hatred bulging from his big face, but his health was bad, and he was doomed to stay here or die. He sneered at everything western. He was sick after every intersectional football game that saw the east defeated. He spat when you mentioned the Trojans. He hated the sun, cursed the fog, denounced the rain, dreamed always of the snows of the middle-west. Once a month his letter box had a big package. I saw him in the lobby, always reading. He wouldn't lend me his books.

'A matter of principle,' Heilman said.

But he gave me the *Book of the Month Club News*, a little magazine about new books. Every month he left it in my letter box.

And the redheaded girl from St Louis who always asked about the Filipinos. Where did they live? How many were there? Did I know any of them? A gaunt redheaded girl, with brown freckles below the neckline of her dress, out here from St Louis. She wore green all the time, her copper head too startling for her beauty, her eyes too grey for her face. She got a job in a laundry, but the pay was too little, so she quit. She too wandered the warm streets. Once she lent me a quarter, another time, postage stamps. Endlessly she spoke of the Filipinos, pitied them, thought them so brave in the face of prejudice. One day she was gone, and another day I saw her again, walking the streets, her copper hair catching sunbeams, a short Filipino holding her arm. He was very proud of her. His padded shoulders and tight waisted suit were the ultimate of tenderloin fashion, but even with the high leather heels he was a foot shorter than she.

Of them all, only one read *The Little Dog Laughed*. Those first days I autographed a great number of copies, brought them upstairs to the waiting room. Five or six copies, and I placed them conspicuously everywhere, on the library table, on the divan, even in the deep leather chairs so that to sit down you had to pick them up. Nobody read them, not a soul, except one. For a week they were spread about, but they were hardly touched. Even when the Japanese boy dusted that room he never so much as lifted them from where they lay. In the evenings people played bridge in there, and a group of the old guests gathered to talk and relax. I slipped in, found a chair, and watched. It was disheartening. A big woman in one of the deep chairs had even seated herself upon a copy, not bothering to remove it. A day came when the Japanese boy piled the copies neatly together on the library table. They gathered dust. Once in a while, every few days, I rubbed my handkerchief over them and scattered them about. They always returned untouched to the neat stack on the library table. Maybe they knew I had written it, and deliberately avoided it. Maybe they simply didn't care. Not even Heilman, with all his reading. Not even the landlady. I shook my head: they were very foolish, all of them. It was a story about their own middle-west, about Colorado and a snowstorm, and there they were with their uprooted souls and sun-burned faces, dying in a blazing desert, and the cool homelands from whence they came were so near at hand, right there in the pages of that little magazine. And I thought, ah well, it was ever thus – Poe, Whitman, Heine, Dreiser, and now Bandini; thinking that, I was not so hurt, not so lonely.

The name of the person who read my story was Judy, and her last name was Palmer. She knocked on my door that afternoon, and opening it, I saw her. She was holding a copy of the magazine in her hand. She was only fourteen, with curls of brown hair, and a red ribbon tied in a bow above her forehead.

'Are you Mr Bandini?' she said.

I could tell from her eyes she had read *The Little Dog Laughed*. I could tell instantly. 'You read my story, didn't you?' I said. 'How did you like it?'

She clutched it close to her chest and smiled. 'I think it's wonderful,' she said. 'Oh, so wonderful! Mrs Hargraves told me you wrote it. She told me you might give me a copy.'

My heart fluttered in my throat.

'Come in!' I said. 'Welcome! Have a chair! What's your name? Of course you can have a copy. Of course! But please come in!'

I ran across the room and got the best chair. She sat down so delicately, the child's dress she wore even concealing her knees. 'Do you want a glass of water?' I said. 'It's a hot day. Maybe you're thirsty.'

But she wasn't. She was only nervous. I could see I frightened her. I tried to be nicer, for I didn't want to scare her away. It was in those early days when I still had a bit of money. 'Do you like ice cream?' I said. 'Would you like me to get you a milk nickel or something?'

'I can't stay,' she said. 'Mother will get angry.'

'Do you live here?' I said. 'Did your mother read the story too? What's your name?' I smiled proudly. 'Of course you already know my name,' I said. 'I'm Arturo Bandini.'

'Oh, yes!' she breathed, and her eyes widened with such admiration I wanted to throw myself at her feet and weep. I could feel it in my throat, the ticklish impulse to start sobbing.

'Are you sure you won't have some ice cream?'

She had such beautiful manners, sitting there with her pink chin tilted, her tiny hands clinging to the magazine. 'No thank you, Mr Bandini.'

'How about a Coke?' I said.

'Thank you,' she smiled. 'No.'

'Root beer?'

'No, if you please. Thank you.'

'What's your name?' I said. 'Mine's –' but I stopped in time.

'Judy,' she said.

'Judy!' I said, over and over. 'Judy, Judy! It's wonderful!' I said. 'It's like the name of a star. It's the most beautiful name I ever heard!'

'Thank you!' she said.

I opened the dresser drawer containing copies of my story. It was still well stocked, some fifteen remaining. 'I'm going to autograph it. Something nice, something extra special!'

Her face coloured with delight. This little girl was not joking; she was really thrilled, and her joy was like cool water running down my face. 'I'm going to give you two copies,' I said. 'And I'm going to autograph both of them!'

'You're such a nice man,' she said. She was studying me as I opened an ink bottle. 'I could tell by your story.'

'I'm not a man,' I said. 'I'm not much older than you, Judy.' I didn't want to be old before her. I wanted to cut it down as much as possible. 'I'm only eighteen,' I lied.

'Is that all?' She was astonished.

'Be nineteen in a couple of months.'

I wrote something special in both the magazines. I don't remember the words but it was good, what I wrote, it came from my heart because I was so grateful. But I wanted more, to hear her voice that was so small and breathless, to keep her there in my room as long as I could.

'You would do me a great honour,' I said. 'You would make me terribly happy, Judy, if you'd read my story out loud to me. It's never happened, and I'd like to hear it.'

'I'd love to read it!' she said, and she sat erect, rigid with eagerness. I threw myself on the bed, buried my face in the pillow, and the little girl read my story with a soft sweet voice that had me weeping at the first hundred words. It was like a dream, the voice of an angel filling the room, and in a little while she was sobbing too, interrupting her reading now and then with gulps and chokes, and protesting. 'I can't read anymore,' she would say, 'I can't.' And I would turn over and beseech her: 'But you've got to, Judy. Oh, you got to!'

As we reached the high point of our emotion, a tall, bitter-mouthed woman suddenly entered the room without knocking. I knew it was Judy's mother. Her fierce eyes studied me, and then Judy. Without a word she took Judy's hand and led her away. The little girl clutched the magazines to her thin breast, and over her shoulder she blinked a tearful goodbye. She had come and gone as quickly as that, and I never saw her again. It was a mystery to the landlady too, for they had arrived and departed that very day, not even staying overnight.

Chapter Eight

There was a letter from Hackmuth in my box. I knew it was from Hackmuth. I could tell a Hackmuth letter a mile away. I could feel a Hackmuth letter, and it felt like an icicle sliding down my spine. Mrs Hargraves handed the letter to me. I grabbed it out of her hand.

'Good news?' she said, because I owed her so much rent. 'You never can tell,' I said. 'But it's from a great man. He could send blank pages, and it would be good news to me.'

But I knew it wasn't good news in that sense that Mrs Hargraves meant it, for I hadn't sent mighty Hackmuth a story. This was merely the answer to my long letter of a few days ago. He was very prompt, that Hackmuth. He dazzled you with his speed. You no sooner dropped a letter in the mail box down on the corner, and when you got back to the hotel, there was an answer. Ah me, but his letters were so brief. A forty page letter, and he replied in one small paragraph. But that was fine in its way, because his replies were easier to memorize and know by heart. He had a way, that Hackmuth; he had a style; he had so much to give, even his commas and semi-colons had a way of dancing up and down. I used to tear the stamps off his envelopes, peel them off gently, to see what was under them.

I sat on the bed and opened the letter. It was another brief message, no more than fifty words. It said:

Dear Mr Bandini,

With your permission I shall remove the salutation and ending of your long letter and print it as a short story for my magazine. It seems to me you have done a fine job here. I think 'The Long Lost Hills' would serve as an excellent title. My cheque is enclosed.

Sincerely yours,

J. C. Hackmuth.

The letter slipped from my fingers and zigzagged to the floor. I stood up and looked in the mirror. My mouth was wide open. I walked to Hackmuth's picture on the opposite wall and put my fingers on the firm face that looked out at me. I picked the letter up and read it again. I opened the window, climbed out, and lay in the bright hillside grass. My fingers clawed the grass. I rolled upon my stomach, sank my mouth into the earth, and pulled the grass roots with my teeth. Then I started to cry. Oh God, Hackmuth! How can you be such a wonderful man? How is it possible? I climbed back to my room and found the cheque inside the envelope. It was $175. I was a rich man once more. $175! Arturo Bandini, author of *The Little Dog Laughed* and *The Long Lost Hills*.

I stood before the mirror once more, shaking my fist defiantly. Here I am, folks. Take a look at a great writer! Notice my eyes, folks. The eyes of a great writer. Notice my jaw, folks. The jaw of a great writer. Look at those hands, folks. The hands that created *The Little Dog Laughed* and *The Long Lost Hills*. I pointed my index finger savagely. And as for you, Camilla Lopez, I want to see you tonight. I want to talk to you, Camilla Lopez. And I warn you, Camilla Lopez, remember that you stand before none other than Arturo Bandini, the writer. Remember that, if you please.

Mrs Hargraves cashed the cheque. I paid my back rent and two months' rent in advance. She wrote out a receipt for the full amount. I waved it aside. 'Please,' I said. 'Don't bother, Mrs Hargraves. I trust you completely.' She insisted. I put the receipt in my pocket. Then I laid an extra five dollars on the desk. 'For you, Mrs Hargraves. Because you've been so nice.' She refused it. She pushed it back. 'Ridiculous!' she said. But I wouldn't take it. I walked out and she hurried after me, chased me into the street.

'Mr Bandini, I insist you take this money.'

Pooh, a mere five dollars, a trifle. I shook my head. 'Mrs Hargraves, I absolutely refuse to take it.' We haggled, stood in the middle of the sidewalk under the hot sun and argued. She was adamant. She begged me to take it back. I smiled quietly. 'No, Mrs Hargraves, I'm sorry. I never change my mind.'

She walked away, pale with anger, holding the five dollar bill between her fingers as though she were carrying a dead mouse. I shook my head. Five dollars! A pittance as far as Arturo Bandini, author of numerous stories for J. C. Hackmuth, was concerned.

I walked downtown, fought my way through the hot cramped streets to The May Company basement. It was the finest suit of clothes I ever bought, a brown pin-stripe with two pairs of pants. Now I could be well dressed at all times. I bought two-tone brown and white shoes, a lot of shirts and a lot of socks, and a hat. My first hat, dark brown, real felt with a white silk lining. The pants had to be altered. I told them to hurry. It was done in a little while. I changed behind a curtain stall, put on everything new, with the hat to top it off. The clerk wrapped my old clothes in a box. I didn't want them. I told him to call up the Salvation Army, to give them away, and to deliver the other purchases to my hotel. On the way out I bought a pair of sunglasses. I spent the rest of the afternoon buying things, killing time. I bought cigarettes, candy and candied fruit. I bought two reams of expensive paper, rubber bands, paper clips, note pads, a small filing cabinet, and a gadget for punching holes in paper. I also bought a cheap watch, a bed lamp, a comb, toothbrushes, tooth paste, hair lotion, shaving cream, skin lotion, and a first aid kit. I stopped at a tie shop and bought ties, a new belt, a watch chain, handkerchiefs, bathrobe and bedroom slippers. Evening came, and I couldn't carry any more. I called a taxi and rode home.

I was very tired. Sweat soaked through my new suit, and crawled down my leg to my ankles. But this was fun. I took a bath, rubbed the lotion into my skin, and washed my teeth with the new brush and paste. Then I shaved with the new cream and doused my hair with the lotion. For a while I sat around in my bedroom slippers and bathrobe, put away my new paper and gadgets, smoked good, fresh cigarettes and ate candy.

The delivery man from The May Company brought the rest of my purchases in a big box. I opened it and found not only the new stuff but also my old clothes. These I tossed into the wastebasket. Now it was time to dress again. I got into a pair of new shorts, a brand new shirt, socks, and the other pair of pants. Then I put on a tie and my new shoes. Standing at the mirror, I tilted my hat over one eye, and examined myself. The image in the glass seemed only vaguely familiar. I didn't like my new tie, so I took off my coat and tried another. I didn't like the change either. All at once everything began to irritate me. The stiff collar was strangling me. The shoes pinched my feet. The pants smelled like a clothing store basement and were too tight in the crotch. Sweat broke out at my temples where the hat band squeezed my skull. Suddenly I began to itch, and when I moved everything crackled like a paper sack. My nostrils picked up the powerful stench of lotions, and I grimaced. Mother in Heaven, what had happened to the old Bandini, author of *The Little Dog Laughed*? Could this hog-tied strangling buffoon be the creator of *The Long Lost Hills*? I pulled everything off, washed the smells out of my hair, and climbed into my old clothes. They were very glad to have me again; they clung to me with cool delight, and my tormented feet slipped into the old shoes as into the softness of spring grass.

Chapter Nine

I rode down to the Columbia Buffet in a taxi. The driver wheeled to the kerb directly in front of the open door. I got out and handed him a twenty dollar bill. He didn't have the change. I was glad because when I finally found a smaller bill and paid him off, there was Camilla standing in the door. Very few taxis stopped before the Columbia Buffet. I nodded casually to Camilla and walked in and sat at the first table. I was reading Hackmuth's letter when she spoke.

'Are you mad at me?' she said.

'Not that I know of,' I said.

She put her hands behind her and looked down at her feet. 'Don't I look different?'

She was wearing new white pumps, with high heels.

'They're very nice,' I said, turning to Hackmuth's letter once more. She watched me with a pout. I glanced up and winked. 'Excuse me,' I said. 'Business.'

'You want to order anything?'

'A cigar,' I said. 'Something expensive from Havana.'

She brought the box. She said, 'A quarter.'

I smiled and gave her a dollar.

'Keep the change.'

She refused the tip.

'Not from you,' she said. 'You're poor.'

'I used to be,' I said. I lit the cigar, let the smoke tumble out of my mouth as I leaned far back and stared at the ceiling. 'Not a bad cigar for the money,' I said.

The female musicians in the rear were hacking out *Over the Waves*. I made a face and pushed the change from the cigar towards Camilla. 'Tell them to play Strauss,' I said. 'Something Viennese.'

She picked up a quarter, but I made her take it all. The musicians were aghast. Camilla pointed at me. They waved and beamed. I nodded with dignity. They plunged into *Tales from the Vienna Woods*. The new shoes were hurting Camilla's feet. She didn't have her old sparkle. She winced as she walked, gritted her teeth.

'You want a beer?' she asked.

'I want a Scotch highball,' I said. 'St James.'

She discussed it with the bartender, then came back. 'We don't have St James. We have Ballantine's, though. It's expensive. Forty cents.'

I ordered one for myself and one each for the two bartenders. 'You shouldn't spend your money like that,' she said. I acknowledged the toast from the two bartenders, and then I sipped my highball. I screwed up my face.

'Rotgut,' I said.

She stood with her hands stuffed inside her pockets.

'I thought you'd like my new shoes,' she said.

I had resumed the reading of Hackmuth's letter.

'They seem all right,' I said.

She limped away to a table just vacated and began picking up empty beer mugs. She was hurt, her face long and sad. I sipped the highball and went on reading and rereading Hackmuth's letter. In a little while she returned to my table.

'You've changed,' she said. 'You're different. I like you better the other way.'

I smiled and patted her hand. It was warm, sleek, brown, with long fingers. 'Little Mexican princess,' I said. 'You're so charming, so innocent.'

She jerked her hand away and her face lost colour.

'I'm *not* a Mexican!' she said. 'I'm an American.'

I shook my head.

'No,' I said. 'To me you'll always be a sweet little peon. A flower girl from old Mexico.'

'You dago sonofabitch!' she said.

It blinded me, but I went on smiling. She stomped away, the shoes hurting her, restraining her angry legs. I was sick inside, and my smile felt as though tacks held it there. She was at a table near the musicians, wiping it off, her arm churning furiously, her face like a dark flame. When she looked at me the hatred out of her eyes bolted across the room. Hackmuth's letter no longer interested me. I stuffed it into my pocket and sat with my head down. It was an old feeling, and I traced it back and remembered that it was a feeling I had the first time I sat in the place. She disappeared behind the partition. When she returned she moved gracefully, her feet quick and sure. She had taken off the white shoes and put on the old huaraches.

'I'm sorry,' she said.

'No,' I said. 'It's my fault, Camilla.'

'I didn't mean what I said.'

'You were alright. It was my fault.'

I looked down at her feet.

'Those white shoes were beautiful. You have such lovely legs and they fitted so perfectly.

She put her fingers through my hair, and the warmth of her pleasure poured through them, and through me, and my throat was hot, and a deep happiness seeped through my flesh. She went behind the partition and emerged wearing the white shoes. The little muscles in her jaws contracted as she walked, but she smiled bravely. I watched her at work, and the sight of her lifted me, a buoyancy like oil upon water. After a while she asked me if I had a car. I told her I didn't. She said she had one, it was in the parking lot next door, and she described her car, and we arranged to meet in the parking lot and then drive out to the beach. As I got up to leave the tall bartender with the white face looked at me with what seemed the faintest trace of a leer. I walked out, ignoring it.

Her car was a 1929 Ford roadster with horsehair bursting from upholstery, battered fenders and no top. I sat in it and fooled with the gadgets. I looked at the owner's certificate. It was made out to Camilla Lombard, not Camilla Lopez.

She was with somebody when she entered the lot, but I couldn't see who it was because it was so dark, no moonlight and a thin web of fog. Then they came closer, and it was the tall bartender. She introduced him, his name was Sammy, and he was quiet and not interested. We drove him home, down Spring Street to First and over the railroad tracks to a black neighbourhood that picked up the sounds of the rattling Ford and threw the echoes over an area of dirty frame houses and tired picket fences. He got out at a place where a dying pepper tree had spilled its brown leaves over the ground, and when he walked to the porch you could hear his feet wading through the hissing dead leaves.

'Who is he?' I said.

He was just a friend, she said, and she didn't want to talk

about him, but she was worried about him; her face assumed that solicitous cast one gets from concern over a sick friend. This worried me, made me jealous all at once, and I kept after her with little questions, and the drawling way she answered made it worse. We went back over the tracks and through the downtown section. She would go right through a stop signal if no cars were around, and when anyone got in her way she would smash her palm on the squealing horn and hold it there. The sound rose like a cry of help through the canyons of buildings. She kept doing this, no matter whether she needed it or not. I cautioned her once, but she ignored it.

'I'm driving this car,' she said.

We got to Wilshire where the traffic was regulated to a minimum of thirty-five. The Ford couldn't travel that fast, but she clung to the middle lane and big fast cars shot around us. They infuriated her and she shook her fist at them. After a mile she complained about her feet and asked me to hold the wheel. As I did it she reached down and took off her shoes. Then she took the wheel again and threw one foot over the side of the Ford. At once her dress ballooned out, spanked her face. She tucked it under herself, but even so her brown thighs were exposed even to a pinkish underthing. It drew a lot of attention. Motorists shot by, pulled up short, and heads came out of windows to observe her brown naked leg. It made her angry. She took to shouting at the spectators, yelling that they ought to mind their own business. I sat at her side, slouched down, trying to enjoy a cigarette that burned too hotly in the rush of wind.

Then we got to a major stop-signal at Western and Wilshire. It was a busy corner, a movie palace and night clubs and drug stores pouring pedestrians into the street.

She couldn't go through that signal because so many other cars were in front of us, waiting the change of light. She sat back, impatient, nervous, swinging her leg. Faces began to turn our way, horns tooted gaily, and behind us a fancy roadster with an impish klaxon sent out an insistent yoohoo. She turned around, her eyes ablaze, and shook her fist at the collegians in the roadster. By now every eye was on us, and everyone smiled. I nudged her.

'Pull it in at stop signals, at least.'

'Oh shut up!' she said.

I reached for Hackmuth's letter and sought refuge in it. The boulevard was well-lighted, I could read the words, but the Ford kicked like a mule, rattled and jerked and broke wind. She was proud of that car.

'It's got a wonderful engine,' she said.

'It sounds good,' I said, hanging on.

'You ought to have a car of your own,' she said.

I asked her about the Camilla Lombard written on her owner's certificate. I asked her if she was married.

'No,' she said.

'What's the Lombard for?'

'For fun,' she said. 'Sometimes I use it professionally.

I didn't understand.

'Do you like your name?' she asked. 'Don't you wish it was Johnson, or Williams, or something?'

I said no, that I was satisfied.

'No you're not,' she said. 'I know.'

'But I am!' I said.

'No you're not.'

After Beverly Hills there was no fog. The palms along the road stood out green in the bluish darkness, and the white line in the pavement leaped ahead of us like a burning fuse. A few clouds tumbled and tossed, but there were no stars. We passed through low hills. On both sides of the road were high hedges and lush vines with wild palms and cypress trees scattered everywhere.

In silence we reached the Palisades, driving along the crest of the high cliffs overlooking the sea. A cold wind sideswiped us. The jalopy teetered. From below rose the roar of the sea. Far out fogbanks crept towards the land, an army of ghosts crawling on their bellies. Below us the breakers flayed the land with white fists. They retreated and came back to flay it again. As each breaker retreated, the shoreline broke into an ever-widening grin. We coasted in second down the spiral road, the black pavement perspiring, fog tongues licking it. The air was so clean. We breathed it gratefully. There was no dust here.

She drove the car into an endless stretch of white sand. We sat and watched the sea. It was warm below the cliffs. She touched my hand. 'Why don't you teach me to swim?' she said.

'Not out there,' I said.

The breakers were tall. The tide was high and they came in fast. A hundred yards out they formed and came in all the way. We watched them burst against the shore, foamy lace exploding like thunder.

'You learn to swim in still water,' I said.

She laughed and began undressing. She was brown underneath, but it was natural brown and not a tan. I was white and ghostlike. There was a blob of heaviness at my stomach. I pulled it in to hide it. She looked at the whiteness, at my loins and legs, and smiled. I was glad when she walked towards the water.

The sand was soft and warm. We sat facing the sea and talked of swimming. I showed her the first principles. She lay on her stomach, paddled her hands and kicked her feet. Sand sprinkled her face and she imitated me without enthusiasm. She sat up.

'I don't like learning to swim,' she said.

We waded hand in hand into the water, our fronts caked with sand. it was cold, then just right. It was my first time in the ocean. I breasted the waves until my shoulders were under water, then I tried to swim. The waves lifted me. I began diving under oncoming breakers. They poured over me harmlessly. I was learning. When the big breakers appeared, I threw myself at their crests and they coasted me to the beach.

I kept my eye on Camilla. She waded to her knees, saw a breaker coming, and ran towards the shore. Then she came back. She shouted with delight. A breaker struck her and she squealed and disappeared. A moment later she reappeared, laughing and shouting. I yelled at her not to take such chances, but she staggered out to meet a white crest that rose up and tumbled her out of sight. I watched her roll like a hamper of bananas. She waded to the shore, her body glistening, her hands in her hair. I swam until I was tired, then I waded out of the water. My eyes stung from salt water. I lay on my back and panted. After a few minutes my strength returned and I sat up and felt like smoking a cigarette. Camilla was not in sight. I walked to the car, thinking she was there. But she wasn't. I ran down to the edge of the water and searched the foamy confusion. I called her name.

Then I heard her scream. It came from far out, beyond the surge of breakers and into the fog bank over choppy water. It seemed a good hundred yards. She screamed again; 'Help!' I waded in, hit the first breakers with my shoulders, and started swimming. Then I lost the sound of her voice in the roar. 'I'm coming!' I yelled, and I yelled again and again, until I had to stop to save my strength. The big breakers were easy, I dived under them, but the small waves confused me, slapped my face and choked me. Finally I was in choppy water. The little waves leaped for my mouth. Her cries had stopped. I churned water with my hands, waiting for another cry. It did not come. I shouted. My voice was weak, like a voice under water.

Suddenly I was exhausted. The little waves leaped over me. I swallowed water, I was sinking. I prayed, I groaned and fought the water, and I knew I should not fight it. The sea was quiet out here. Far inland I heard the roar of the breakers. I called, waited, called again. No answer save the slush of my arms and the sound of the little choppy waves. Then something happened to my right leg, to the toes of the foot. They seemed lodged. When I kicked the pain shot to the thigh. I wanted to live. God, don't take me now! I swam blindly towards the shore.

Then I felt myself in the big breakers once more, heard them booming louder. It seemed too late. I couldn't swim, my arms were so tired, my right leg ached so much. To breathe was all that mattered. Under water the current rushed, rolling and dragging me. So this was the end of Camilla, and this was the end of Arturo Bandini – but even then I was writing it all down, seeing it across a page in a typewriter, writing it out and coasting along the sharp sand, so sure I would never come out alive. Then I was in water to my waist, limp and too far gone to do anything about it, floundering helplessly with my mind clear, composing the whole thing, worrying about excessive adjectives. The next breaker smashed me under once more, dragged me to water a foot deep, and I crawled on my hands and knees out of water a foot deep, wondering if I could perhaps make a poem out of it. I thought of Camilla out there and I sobbed and noticed my tears were saltier than the sea water. But I couldn't lie there, I had to get help somewhere, and I got to my feet and staggered towards the car. I was so cold and my jaws chattered.

I turned and looked at the sea. Not fifty feet away Camilla waded towards the land in water to her waist. She was laughing, choking from it, this supreme joke she had played, and when I saw her dive ahead of the next breaker with all the grace and perfection of a seal, I didn't think it was funny at all. I walked out to her, felt my strength returning with every step, and when I got to her I picked her up bodily, over my shoulders, and I didn't mind her screaming, her fingers scratching my scalp and tearing my hair. I lifted her as high as my arms and threw her in a pool of water a few feet deep. She landed with a thud that knocked the breath out of her. I waded out, took her hair in both my hands, and rubbed her face and mouth in the muddy sand. I left her there, crawling on her hands and knees, crying and moaning, and I walked back to the car. She had mentioned blankets in the rumble seat. I pulled them out, wrapped myself up, and lay down on the warm sand.

In a little while she made her way through the deep sand and found me sitting under the blankets. Dripping and clean she stood before me, showing herself, proud of her nakedness, turning round and round.

'You still like me?'

I stole glances at her. I was speechless, and I nodded and grinned. She stepped upon the blankets and asked me to move over. I made a place and she slipped under, her body sleek and cold. She asked me to hold her, and I held her, and she kissed me, her lips wet and cool. We lay a long time, and I was worried and afraid and without passion. Something like a grey flower grew between us, a thought that took shape and spoke of the chasm that separated us. I didn't know what it was. I felt her waiting. I drew my hands over her belly and legs, felt my own desire, searched foolishly for my passion, strained for it while she waited, rolled and tore my hair and begged for it, but there was none, there was none at all, only the retreat to Hackmuth's letter and thoughts that remained to be written, but no lust, only fear of her, and shame and humiliation. Then I was blaming and cursing myself and I wanted to get up and walk into the sea. She felt my retreat. With a sneer she sat up and began drying her hair on the blanket.

'I thought you liked me,' she said.

I couldn't answer. I shrugged and stood up. We dressed and drove back to Los Angeles. We didn't speak. She lit a cigarette and looked at me strangely, lips pursed. She blew smoke from her cigarette into my face. I took the cigarette out of her mouth and threw it into the street. She lit another and inhaled languidly, amused and contemptuous. I hated her then.

Dawn climbed the mountains in the east, gold bars of light cutting the sky like searchlights. I took out Hackmuth's letter and read it again. Back East in New York Hackmuth would just now be entering his office. Somewhere in that office was my manuscript *The Long Lost Hills*. Love wasn't everything.

Women weren't everything. A writer had to conserve his energies.

We reached the city. I told her where I lived.

'Bunker Hill?' She laughed. 'It's a good place for you.'

'It's perfect,' I said. 'In my hotel they don't allow Mexicans.'

It sickened both of us. She drove to the hotel and killed the engine. I sat wondering if there was anything more to say, but there was nothing. I got out, nodded, and walked towards the hotel. Between my shoulder blades I felt her eyes like knives. As I got to the door she called me. I walked back to the car.

'Aren't you going to kiss me goodnight?'

I kissed her.

'Not that way.'

Her arms slipped around my neck. She pulled my face down and sank her teeth into my lower lip. It stung and I fought her until I was free. She sat with one arm over the seat, smiling and watching me enter the hotel. I took out my handkerchief and dabbed my lips. The handkerchief had a spot of blood on it. I walked down the grey hall to my room. As I closed the door all the desire that had not come a while before seized me. It pounded my skull and tingled in my fingers. I threw myself on the bed and tore the pillow with my hands.

Chapter Ten

All that day it was on my mind. I remembered her brown nakedness and her kiss, the flavour of her mouth as it came cold from the sea, and I saw myself white and virginal, pulling in the pudgy line of my stomach, standing in the sand and holding my hands over my loins. I walked up and down the room. Late in the afternoon I was exhausted and the sight of myself in the mirror was unbearable. I sat at the typewriter and wrote about it, poured it out the way it should have happened, hammered it out with such violence that the portable typewriter kept moving away from me and across the table. On paper I stalked her like a tiger and beat her to the earth and overpowered her with my invincible strength. It ended with her creeping after me, in the sand, tears streaming from her eyes, beseeching me to have mercy upon her. Fine. Excellent. But when I read it over it was ugly and dull. I tore the pages and threw them away.

Hellfrick knocked on the door. He was pale and trembling, his skin like wet paper. He was off the booze; never would he touch another drop. He sat on the edge of my bed and wrung his bony fingers. Nostalgically he talked of meat, of the good old steaks you got back in Kansas City, of the wonderful T-bones and tender lamb chops. But not out here in this land of the eternal sun, where the cattle ate nothing but dead weeds and sunshine, where the meat was full of worms and they had to paint it to make it look bloody and red. And would I lend him fifty cents? I gave him the money and he went down to the butcher shop on Olive Street. In a little while he was back in his room and the lower floor of the hotel was fragrant with the tangy aroma of liver and onions. I walked into his room. He sat before a plate of the food, his mouth bloated, his thin jaws working hard. He shook his fork at me. 'I'll make it good with you, kid. I'll pay you back a thousand times.'

It made me hungry. I walked down to the restaurant near Angel's Flight and ordered the same thing. I took my time having dinner. But no matter how long I loitered over coffee I knew I would eventually walk down the Flight to the Columbia Buffet. I had only to touch the lump on my lip to grow angry, and then to feel passion.

When I got down to the buffet I was afraid to enter. I crossed the street and watched her through the windows. She was not wearing her white shoes, and she seemed the same, happy and busy with her beer tray.

I got an idea. I walked quickly, two blocks, to the telegraph office. I sat down before the telegraph blank, my heart pounding. The words writhed across the page. I love you Camilla I want to marry you Arturo Bandini. When I paid for it the clerk looked at the address and said it would be delivered in ten minutes. I hurried back to Spring Street and stood in the shadowed doorway waiting for the telegraph boy to appear.

The moment I saw him coming around the corner I knew the telegram was a blunder. I ran into the street and stopped him. I told him I wrote the telegram and didn't want it delivered. 'A mistake,' I said. He wouldn't listen. He was tall with a pimply face. I offered him ten dollars. He shook his head and smiled emphatically. Twenty dollars, thirty.

'Not for ten million,' he said.

I walked back to the shadows and watched him deliver the telegram. She was amazed to get it. I saw her finger point at herself, her face dubious. Even after she signed for it she stood holding it in her hand, watching the telegraph boy disappear. As she tore it open I locked my eyes shut. When I opened them she was reading the telegram and laughing. She walked to the bar and handed the wire to the sallow-faced bartender, the one we had driven home the night before. He read it without expression. Then he handed it to the other bartender. He, too, was unimpressed. I felt a deep gratitude for them. When Camilla read it again, I was grateful for that, too, but when she took it to a table where a group of men sat drinking my mouth opened slowly and I was sick. The laughter of the men floated across the street. I shuddered and walked away quickly.

At Sixth I turned the corner and walked down to Main. I wandered through the crowds of seedy, hungry derelicts without destination. At Second I stopped before a Filipino taxi-dancehall. The literature on the walls spoke eloquently of forty beautiful girls and the dreamy music of Lonny Killula and his Melodic Hawaiians. I climbed one flight of echoing stairs to a booth and bought a ticket. Inside were the forty women, lined against the opposite wall, sleek in tight evening dresses, most of them blondes. Nobody was dancing, not a soul. On the platform the five-piece orchestra banged out a tune with fury. A few customers like myself stood behind a short wicker fence, opposite the girls. They beckoned to us. I surveyed the group, found a blonde whose gown I liked, and bought a few dance tickets. Then I waved at the blonde. She fell into my arms like an old lover and we beat the oak for two dances.

She talked soothingly and called me honey, but I thought only of that girl two streets away, of myself lying with her in the sand and making a fool of myself. It was useless. I gave the cloying blonde my handful of tickets and walked out of the hall and into the streets again. I could feel myself waiting, and when I kept looking at street clocks I knew what was wrong with myself. I was waiting for eleven o'clock when the Columbia closed.

I was there at a quarter to eleven. I was there in the parking lot, walking towards her car. I sat on the burst upholstery and waited. Off in one corner of the parking lot was a shed where the attendant kept his accounts. Over the shed was a neon clock in red. I kept my eye on the clock, watched the minute hand rush towards eleven. Then I was afraid to see her again and as I squirmed and writhed in the seat my hand touched something soft. It was a cap of hers, a tam-o-shanter, it was black with a tiny fluffy knob on the crown. I felt it with my fingers and smelled it with my nose. Its powder was like herself. It was what I wanted. I stuffed it into my pocket and walked out of the parking lot. Then I climbed the stairs of Angel's Flight to my hotel. When I got to my room I took it out and threw it on the bed. I undressed, turned out the light, and held her hat in my arms.

Another day, poetry! Write her a poem, spill your heart to her in sweet cadences; but I didn't know how to write poetry. It was love and dove with me, bad rhymes, blundering sentiment. Oh Christ in Heaven, I'm no writer: I can't even put down a little quatrain, I'm no good in this world. I stood at the window and waved my hands at the sky; no good at all, just a cheap fake; neither writer nor lover; neither fish nor fowl.

Then what was the matter?

I had breakfast and went to a little Catholic Church at the edge of Bunker Hill. The rectory was in back of the frame church. I rang the bell and a woman in a nurse's apron answered. Her hands were covered with flour and dough.

'I want to see the pastor,' I said.

The woman had a square jaw and a hostile pair of sharp grey eyes. 'Father Abbot is busy,' she said. 'What do you want?'

'I have to see him,' I said.

'I tell you he's busy.'

The priest came to the door. He was stocky, powerful, smoking a cigar, a man in his fifties. 'What is it?' he asked.

I told him I wanted to see him alone. I had some trouble on my mind. The woman sniffed contemptuously and disappeared through a hall. The priest opened the door and led me to his study. It was a small room crammed with books and magazines. My eyes bulged. There in one corner was a huge stack of Hackmuth's magazine. I walked to it at once, and pulled out the issue containing *The Little Dog Laughed*. The priest had seated himself. 'This is a great magazine,' I said. 'The greatest of them all.'

The priest crossed his legs, shifted his cigar.

'It's rotten,' he said. 'Rotten to the core.'

'I disagree,' I said. 'I happen to be one of its leading contributors.'

'You?' the priest asked. 'And what did you contribute?'

I spread *The Little Dog Laughed* before him on the desk. He glanced at it, pushed it aside. 'I read that story,' he said. 'It's a piece of hogwash. And your reference to the Blessed Sacrament was a vile and contemptible lie. You ought to be ashamed of yourself.'

Leaning back in his chair, he made it very plain that he didn't like me, his angry eyes centred on my forehead, his cigar rolling from one side of his mouth to the other.

'Now,' he said. 'What is it you wish to see me about?'

I didn't sit down. He made it very clear in his own way that I wasn't to use any of the furniture in the room. 'It's about a girl,' I said.

'What have you done to her?' he said.

'Nothing,' I said. But I could speak no more. He had plucked out my heart. Hogwash! All those nuances, that superb dialogue, that brilliant lyricism – and he had called it hogwash. Better to close my ears and go away to some far off place where no words were spoken. Hogwash!

'I changed my mind,' I said. 'I don't want to talk about it now.'

He stood up and walked towards the door.

'Very well,' he said. 'Good day.'

I walked out, the hot sun blinding me. The finest short story in American Literature, and this person, this priest, had called it hogwash. Maybe that business about the Blessed Sacrament *wasn't* exactly true; maybe it didn't really happen. But my God, what psychological values! What prose! What sheer beauty!

As soon as I got to my room I sat down before my typewriter and planned my revenge. An article, a scathing attack upon the stupidity of the Church. I pecked out the title:

The Catholic Church Is Doomed. I hammered it out furiously, one page after another, until there were six. Then I paused to read it. The stuff was awful, ludicrous. I tore it up and threw myself on the bed. I still hadn't written a poem to Camilla. As I lay there, inspiration came. I wrote it out from memory:

> I have forgot much, Camilla! gone with the wind,
> Flung roses, roses riotously with the throng,
> Dancing, to put the pale, lost lilies out of mind;
> But I was desolate and sick with an old passion,
> yes, all the time, because the dance was long;
> I have been faithful to thee, Camilla, in my fashion.
>
> Arturo Bandini

I sent it by telegraph, proud of it, watched the telegraph clerk read it, beautiful poem, my poem to Camilla, a bit of immortality from Arturo to Camilla, and I paid the telegraph man and walked down to my place in the dark doorway, and there I waited. The same boy floated by on his bicycle. I watched him deliver it, watched Camilla read it in the middle of the floor, watched her shrug and rip it to pieces, saw the pieces floating to the sawdust on the floor. I shook my head and walked away. Even the poetry of Ernest Dowson had no effect upon her, not even Dowson.

Ah well, the hell with you Camilla. I can forget you. I have money. These streets are full of things you cannot give me. So down to Main Street and to Fifth Street, to the long dark bars, to the King Edward Cellar, and there a girl with yellow hair and sickness in her smile. Her name was Jean, she was thin and tubercular, but she was hard too, so anxious to get my money, her languid mouth for my lips, her long fingers at my trousers, her sickly lovely eyes watching every dollar bill.

'So your name is Jean,' I said. 'Well, well, well, a pretty name.' We'll dance, Jean. We'll swing around, and you don't know it, you beauty in a blue gown, but you're dancing with a freak, an outcast from the world of man, neither fish, fowl, nor good red herring. And we drank and we danced and we drank again. Good fellow Bandini, so Jean called the boss. 'This is Mr Bandini. This is Mr Schwartz.' Very good, shake hands. 'Nice place you got, Schwartz, nice girls.'

One drink, two drinks, three drinks. What's that you're drinking, Jean? I tasted it, that brownish stuff, looked like whiskey, must have been whiskey, such a face she made, her sweet face so contorted. But it wasn't whiskey, it was tea, plain tea, forty cents a slug. Jean, a little liar, trying to fool a great author. Don't fool me, Jean. Not Bandini, lover of man and beast alike. So take this, five dollars, put it away, don't drink, Jean, just sit here, only sit and let my eyes search your face because your hair is blonde and not dark, you are not like her, you are sick and you are from down there in Texas and you have a crippled mother to support, and you don't make very much money, only twenty cents a drink, you've only made ten dollars from Arturo Bandini tonight, you poor little girl, poor little starving girl with the sweet eyes of a baby and the soul of a thief. Go to your sailor boys, honey. They don't have the ten dollars but they've got what I haven't got, me, Bandini, neither fish, fowl nor good red herring, goodnight, Jean, goodnight.

And here was another place and another girl. Oh, how lonely she was, from away back in Minnesota. A good family too. Sure, honey. Tell my tired ears about your good family.

They owned a lot of property, and then the depression came. Well, how sad, how tragic. And now you work down here in a Fifth Street dive, and your name is Evelyn, poor Evelyn, and the folks are out here too, and you have the cutest sister, not like the tramps you meet down here, a swell girl, and you ask me if I want to meet your sister. Why not? She got her sister. Innocent little Evelyn went across the room and dragged poor little sister Vivian away from those lousy sailors and brought her to our table. Hello Vivian, this is Arturo. Hello Arturo, this is Vivian. But what happened to your mouth, Vivian, who dug it out with a knife? And what happened to your bloodshot eyes, and your sweet breath smelling like a sewer, poor kids, all the way from glorious Minnesota. Oh no, they're not Swedish, where did I get that idea? Their last name was Mortensen, but it wasn't Swedish, why their family had been Americans for generations. To be sure. Just a couple of home girls.

Do you know something? – Evelyn talking – Poor little Vivian had worked down here for almost six months and not once had any of these bastards ever ordered her a bottle of champagne, and I there, Bandini, I looked like such a swell guy, and wasn't Vivian cute, and wasn't it a shame, she so innocent, and would I buy her a bottle of champagne? Dear little Vivian, all the way from the clean fields of Minnesota, and not a Swede either, and almost a virgin too, just a few men short of being a virgin. Who could resist this tribute? So bring on the champagne, cheap champagne, just a pint size, we can all drink it, only eight dollars a bottle, and gee wasn't wine cheap out here? Why back in Duluth the champagne was twelve bucks a bottle.

Ah, Evelyn and Vivian, I love you both, I love you for

your sad lives, the empty misery of your coming home at dawn. You too are alone, but you are not like Arturo Bandini, who is neither fish, fowl nor good red herring. So have your champagne, because I love you both, and you too, Vivian, even if your mouth looks like it had been dug out with raw fingernails and your old child's eyes swim in blood written like mad sonnets.

Chapter Eleven

But this was expensive. Take it easy, Arturo; have you forgotten those oranges? I counted what was left. It was twenty dollars and some cents. I was scared. I racked my brains over figures, added everything I had spent. Twenty dollars left – impossible! I had been robbed, I had misplaced the money, there was a mistake somewhere. I looked over the room, burrowed into pockets and drawers, but that was all, and I was scared and worried and determined to go to work, write another one quick, something written so fast it had to be good. I sat before my typewriter and the great awful void descended, and I beat my head with my fists, put a pillow under my aching buttocks and made little noises of agony. It was useless. I had to see her, and I didn't care how I did it.

I waited for her in the parking lot. At eleven she came around the corner, and Sammy the bartender was with her. They both saw me from the distance and she lowered her voice, and when she got to the car Sammy said, 'Hi there,' but she said, 'What do you want?'

'I want to see you,' I said.

'I can't see you tonight,' she said.

'Make it later on tonight.'

'I can't. I'm busy.'

'You're not that busy. You can see me.'

She opened the car door for me to get out, but I did not move, and she said, 'Please get out.'

'Nothing doing,' I said.

Sammy smiled. Her face flared.

'Get out, goddamnit!'

'I'm staying,' I said.

'Come on, Camilla,' Sammy said.

She tried to pull me out of the car, seized my sweater and jerked and tugged. 'Why do you act like this?' she said. 'Why can't you see I don't want to have anything to do with you?'

'I'm staying,' I said.

'You fool!' she said.

Sammy had walked towards the street. She caught up with him and they walked away, and I was there alone, horrified, and smiling weakly at what I had done. As soon as they were out of sight I got out and walked up the stairs of the Flight and down to my room. I couldn't understand why I had done that. I sat on the bed and tried to push the episode out of my mind.

Then I heard a knock on my door. I didn't get a chance to say come in, because the door opened then and I turned around and there was a woman standing in the doorway, looking at me with a peculiar smile. She was not a large woman and she was not beautiful, but she seemed attractive and mature, and she had nervous black eyes. They were brilliant, the sort of eyes a woman gets from too much bourbon, very bright and glassy and extremely insolent. She stood in the door without moving or speaking. She was dressed intelligently: black coat with a furpiece, black shoes, black skirt, a white blouse and a small purse.

'Hello,' I said.

'What are you doing?' she said.

'Just sitting here.'

I was scared. The sight and nearness of that woman rather paralysed me; maybe it was the shock of seeing her so suddenly, maybe it was my own misery at that moment, but the nearness of her and that crazy, glassy glitter of her eyes made me want to jump up and beat her, and I had to steady myself. The feeling lasted for only a moment, and then it was gone. She started across the room with those dark eyes insolently watching me, and I turned my face towards the window, not worried by her insolence but about that feeling which had gone through me like a bullet. Now there was the scent of perfume in the room, the perfume that floats after women in luxurious hotel lobbies, and the whole thing made me nervous and uncertain.

When she got close to me I didn't get up but sat still, took a long breath, and finally looked at her again. Her nose was pudgy at the end but it was not ugly and she had rather heavy lips without rouge, so that they were pinkish; but what got me were her eyes: their brilliance, their animalism and their recklessness.

She walked over to my desk and pulled a page out of the typewriter. I didn't know what was happening. I still said nothing, but I could smell liquor on her breath, and then the very peculiar but distinctive odour of decay, sweetish and cloying, the odour of oldness, the odour of this woman in the process of growing old.

She merely glanced at the script; it annoyed her and

she flipped it over her shoulder and it zigzagged to the floor.

'It's no good,' she said. 'You can't write. You can't write at all.'

'Thanks very much,' I said.

I started to ask her what she wanted, but she did not seem the kind who accepts questions. I jumped off the bed and offered her the only chair in the room. She didn't want it. She looked at the chair and then at me, thoughtfully, smiling her disinterestedness in merely sitting down. Then she went around the room reading some stuff I had pasted on the walls. They were some excerpts I had typed from Mencken and from Emerson and Whitman. She sneered at them all. Poof, poof, poof! Making gestures with her fingers, curling her lips. She sat on the bed, pulled off her coat jacket to the elbows, and put her hands on her hips and looked at me with insufferable contempt.

Slowly and dramatically she began to recite:

What should I be but a prophet and a liar,
Whose mother was a leprechaun, whose father was a friar?
Teethed on a crucifix and cradled under water,
What should I be but the fiend's god-daughter?

It was Millay, I recognized it at once, and she went on and on; she knew more Millay than Millay herself, and when she finally finished she lifted her face and looked at me and said, 'That's *literature!* You don't know anything about literature. You're a fool!' I had fallen into the spirit of the lines and when she broke off so suddenly to denounce me I was at sea again.

I tried to answer but she interrupted and went off in a Barrymore manner, speaking deeply and tragically; murmuring of the pity of it all, the stupidity of it all, the absurdity of a hopelessly bad writer like myself buried in a cheap hotel in Los Angeles, California, of all places, writing banal things the world would never read and never get a chance to forget.

She lay back, laced her fingers under her head, and spoke dreamily to the ceiling: 'You will love me tonight, you fool of a writer; yes, tonight you will love me.'

I said, 'Say, what *is* this, anyway?'

She smiled.

'Does it matter? You are nobody, and I might have been somebody, and the road to each of us is love.'

The scent of her was pretty strong now, impregnating the whole room so that the room seemed to be hers and not mine, and I was a stranger in it, and I thought we had better go outside so she could get some of the night air. I asked her if she would like to walk around the block.

She sat up quickly. 'Look! I have money, money! We will go somewhere and drink!'

'Sure thing!' I said. 'A good idea.'

I pulled on my sweater. When I turned around she was standing beside me, and she put the tips of her fingers on my mouth. That mysterious saccharine odour was so strong on her fingers that I walked towards the door and held it open and waited for her to pass through.

We walked upstairs and through the lobby. When we reached the front desk I was glad the landlady was gone to bed; there was no reason for it, but I didn't want Mrs Hargraves to see me with this woman. I told her to tiptoe

across the lobby, and she did it; she enjoyed it terribly, like
an adventure in little things; it thrilled her and she tightened
her fingers around my arm.

It was foggy on Bunker Hill, but not downtown. The
streets were deserted, and the sound of her heels on the
sidewalk echoed among the old buildings. She tugged my
arm and I bent down to hear what she wanted to whisper.

'You're going to be so marvellous!' she said. 'So wonderful!'

I said, 'Let's forget it now. Let's just walk.'

She wanted a drink. She insisted upon it. She opened her
purse and waved a ten dollar bill. 'Look. Money! I have lots
of money!'

We walked down to Solomon's Bar on the corner, where I
played the pin games. Nobody was there but Solomon, who
stood with his chin in his hands, worried about business. We
walked to a booth facing the front window, and I waited for
her to sit down, but she insisted I get in first. Solomon walked
over for our order.

'Whiskey!' she said. 'Lots of whiskey.'

Solomon frowned.

'A short beer for me,' I said.

Solomon was watching her sternly, searchingly, his bald
spot crinkling from a frown. I could sense the consanguinity,
and I knew then that she was Jewish too. Solomon went back
for the drinks and she sat there with her eyes blazing, her
hands folded on the table, her fingers twining and untwining.
I sat trying to think of some way of dodging her.

'A drink'll fix you up fine,' I said.

Before I knew it she was at my throat, but not roughly,
her long fingernails and short fingers against my flesh as she

talked about my mouth, my wonderful mouth; oh God, what a mouth I had.

'Kiss me!' she said.

'Sure,' I said. 'Let's have a drink first.'

She clenched her teeth.

'Then you too know about me!' she said. 'You're like the rest of them. You know about my wounds, and that's why you won't kiss me. Because I disgust you!'

I thought, she *is* crazy; I've got to get out of here. She kissed me, her mouth tasting of liverwurst on rye. She sat back, breathing with relief. I took out my handkerchief and wiped the sweat from my forehead. Solomon returned with the drinks. I reached for some money, but she paid quickly. Solomon went back for the change, but I called him back and handed him a bill. She fussed and protested, pounding her heels and fists. Solomon lifted his hands in a gesture of hopelessness and took her money. The moment his back was turned I said, 'Lady, this is your party. I've got to go.' She pulled me down and her arms went around me and we fought until I thought it was absurd. I sat back and tried to think of another escape.

Solomon brought back the change. I took a nickel from it and told her I'd like to play the pin game. Without a word she let me pass and I got up and walked over to the machine. She watched me like a prize dog, and Solomon watched her like a criminal. Then I won on the machine, and I called Solomon to come over and check the score.

I whispered, 'Who is that woman, Solomon?'

He didn't know. She had been there earlier in the evening, drinking a great deal. I told him I wanted to go out the back way. 'It's the door on the right,' he said.

She finished her whiskey and hammered the table with the empty glass. I walked over, took a sip of beer, and told her to excuse me a minute. I jerked my thumb towards the men's room. She patted my arm. Solomon was watching me as I took the door opposite the men's room. It led to the storeroom, and the door to the alley was a few feet beyond. As soon as the fog smothered my face I felt better. I wanted to be as far away as possible. I wasn't hungry but I walked a mile to a hotdog stand on Eighth Street and had a cup of coffee to kill time. I knew she would go back to my room after she missed me. Something told me she was insane, it could have been that she had too much liquor, but it didn't matter, I didn't want to see her again.

I got back to my room at two in the morning. Her personality and that mysterious smell of old age still possessed it, and it was not my room at all. For the first time its wonderful solitude was spoiled. Every secret of that room seemed laid open. I threw open the two windows and watched the fog float through in sad tumbling lumps. When it got too cold I closed the windows and, though the room was wet from the fog and my papers and books were filmed with dampness, the perfume was still there unmistakably. I had Camilla's tam-o-shanter under my pillow. It too seemed drenched with the odour, and when I pressed it to my mouth it was like my mouth in that woman's black hair. I sat in front of the typewriter, idly tapping the keys.

As soon as I got started I heard steps in the hall and I knew she was coming back. I turned off the lights quickly and sat in the darkness, but I was too late, for she must have seen the light under the door. She knocked and I did not answer.

She knocked again, but I sat still and puffed on a cigarette. Then she began to beat the door with her fists and she called out that she would start kicking it, and that she would kick it all night long, unless I opened it. Then she started kicking it, and it made a terrible noise through that rickety hotel, and I rushed over and opened the door.

'Darling!' she said, and she held out her arms.

'My God,' I said. 'Don't you think this has gone far enough? Can't you see I'm fed up?'

'Why did you leave me?' she asked. 'Why did you do that?'

'I had another engagement.'

'Darling,' she said. 'Why do you lie to me like that?'

'Oh nuts.'

She walked across the room and pulled the page from my typewriter again. It was full of all manner of nonsense, a few odd phrases, my name written many times, bits of poetry. But this time her face broke into a smile.

'How wonderful!' she said. 'You're a genius! My darling is so talented.'

'I'm awfully busy,' I said. 'Will you please get out?'

It was as though she hadn't heard me. She sat on the bed, unbuttoned her jacket, and dangled her feet. 'I love you,' she said. 'You're my darling, and you're going to love me.'

I said, 'Some other time. Not tonight. I'm tired.'

That saccharine odour came through.

'I'm not kidding,' I said. 'I think you'd better go. I don't want to throw you out.'

'I'm so lonely,' she said.

She meant that. Something was wrong with her, twisted,

gushing from her with those words, and I felt ashamed for being so harsh.

'Alright,' I said. 'We'll just sit here and talk for a while.'

I pulled up the chair and straddled it, with my chin on the back, looking at her as she snuggled on the bed. She wasn't as drunk as I thought. Something was wrong with her and it was not alcohol and I wanted to find out what it was.

Her talk was madness. She told me her name, and it was Vera. She was a housekeeper for a rich Jewish family in Long Beach. But she was tired of being a housekeeper. She had come from Pennsylvania, fled across the country because her husband had been unfaithful to her. That day she had come down to Los Angeles from Long Beach. She had seen me in the restaurant on the corner of Olive Street and Second. She had followed me back to the hotel because my eyes 'had pierced her soul'. But I couldn't remember seeing her there. I was sure I had never seen her before. Having found out where I lived, she had gone to Solomon's and got drunk. All day she had been drinking, but it was only that she might become reckless and go to my room.

'I know how I revolt you,' she said. 'And that you know about my wounds and the horror my clothes conceal. But you must try to forget my ugly body, because I'm really good at heart, I'm so good, and I deserve more than your disgust.'

I was speechless.

'Forgive my body!' she said. She put her arms out to me, the tears flowing down her cheeks. 'Think of my soul!' she said. 'My soul is so beautiful, it can bring you so much! It is not ugly like my flesh!'

She was crying hysterically, lying on her face, her hands groping through her dark hair, and I was helpless, I didn't know what she was talking about; ah, dear lady, don't cry like that, you mustn't cry like that, and I took her hot hand and tried to tell her she was talking in circles; it was all so silly, her talk, it was self-persecution, it was a lot of silly things, and I talked like that, gesturing with my hands, pleading with my voice.

'Because you're such a fine woman, and your body is so beautiful, and all this talk is an obsession, a childish phobia, a hangover from the mumps. So you mustn't worry and you mustn't cry, because you'll get over it. I know you will.'

But I was clumsy, and making her suffer even more, because she was down in an inferno of her own creation, so far away from me that the sound of my voice made the hiatus seem worse. Then I tried to talk to her of other things, and I tried to make her laugh at my obsessions. Look lady, Arturo Bandini, he's got a few himself! And from under the pillow I drew out Camilla's tam-o-shanter with the little tassle on it.

'Look lady! I've got them too. Do you know what I do, lady? I take this little black cap to bed with me, and I hold it close to me, and I say: "Oh I love you, I love you, beautiful princess!"' And then I told her some more; oh, I was no angel; my soul had a few twists and bends all its own; so don't you feel so lonely, lady; because you've got lots of company; you've got Arturo Bandini, and he's got lots to tell you. And listen to this: Do you know what I did one night? Arturo, confessing it all: do you know the terrible thing I did? One night a woman too beautiful for this world came along on wings of perfume, and I could not bear it, and who she was I never knew, a woman in a red fox and a pert little hat, and Bandini trailing after her because she was better than dreams, watching her enter Bernstein's Fish Grotto, watching her in a trance through a window swimming with frogs and trout, watching her as she ate alone; and when she was through, do you know what I did, lady? So don't you cry, because you haven't heard anything yet, because I'm awful, lady, and my heart is full of black ink; me, Arturo Bandini, I walked right into Bernstein's Fish Grotto and I sat upon the very chair that she sat upon, and I shuddered with joy, and I fingered the napkin she had used, and there was a cigarette butt with a stain of lipstick upon it, and do you know what I did, lady? You with your funny little troubles, I ate the cigarette butt, chewed it up, tobacco and paper and all, swallowed it, and I thought it tasted fine, because she was so beautiful, and there was a spoon beside the plate, and I put it in my pocket, and every once in a while I'd take the spoon out of my pocket and taste it, because she was so beautiful. Love on a budget, a heroine free and for nothing, all for the black heart of Arturo Bandini, to be remembered through a window swimming with trout and frog legs. Don't you cry, lady; save your tears for Arturo Bandini, because he has his troubles, and they are great troubles, and I haven't even begun to talk, but I could say something to you about a night on the beach with a brown princess, and her flesh without meaning, her kisses like dead flowers, odourless in the garden of my passion.

But she was not listening, and she staggered off the bed, and she fell on her knees before me and begged me to tell her she was not disgusting.

'Tell me!' she sobbed. 'Tell me I am beautiful like other women.'

'Of course you are! You're really very beautiful!'

I tried to lift her, but she clung to me frantically, and I couldn't do anything but try to soothe her, but I was so clumsy, so inadequate, and she was so far down in the depths beyond me, but I kept trying.

Then she started again about her wounds, those ghastly wounds, they had wrecked her life, they had destroyed love before it came, driven a husband from her and into another woman's arms, and all of this was fantastic to me and incomprehensible because she was really handsome in her own way, she was not crippled and she was not disfigured, and there were plenty of men who would give her love.

She staggered to her feet and her hair had fallen on her face, the strands of hair pasted against her tear-soaked cheeks; her eyes were blotchy and she looked like a maniac, sodden with bitterness.

'I'll show you!' she screamed. 'You'll see for yourself, you liar! liar!'

With both hands she jerked loose her dark skirt and it fell into a nest at her ankles. She stepped out of it and she was really beautiful in a white slip and I said it. I said, 'But you're lovely! I told you you were lovely!'

She kept sobbing as she worked at the clasps of her blouse, and I told her it wasn't necessary to take off any more; she had convinced me beyond a doubt and there was no need for hurting herself further.

'No,' she said. 'You're going to see for yourself.'

She couldn't release the clasps at the back of the blouse, and she backed towards me and told me to unclasp them. I waved my hand. 'For God's sake, forget about it,' I said. 'You've convinced me. You don't have to do a strip act.' She sobbed desperately and seized the thin blouse with her two hands and ripped it from her with one jerk.

When she began to lift her slip I turned my back and

walked to the window, because I knew then she was going to show me something unpleasant, and she began to laugh at me and shriek at me and point her tongue at my worried face. 'Ya, ya! See! You know already! You know all about them!'

I had to go through with it, and I turned around and she was nude except for hose and shoes, and then I saw the wounds. It was at the loins; it was a birthmark or something, a burn, a seared place, a pitiful, dry, vacant place where flesh was gone, where the thighs suddenly became small and shrivelled and the flesh seemed dead. I closed my jaws and then I said, 'What – that? Is that all, just that? It's nothing, a mere trifle.' But I was losing the words, I had to say them quickly or they would never form. 'It's ridiculous,' I said. 'I hardly noticed it. You're lovely; you're wonderful!'

She studied herself curiously, not believing me, and then she looked at me again, but I kept my eyes on her face, felt the floating nausea of my stomach, breathed the sweetish thickish odour of her presence, and I said again that she was beautiful, and the world slipped out like a whimper, so beautiful she was, a small girl, a virgin child, so beautiful and rare to behold, and without a word, and blushing, she picked up her slip and drew it over her head, a crooning and mysterious satisfaction in her throat.

She was so shy all at once, so delighted, and I laughed to find the words coming easier now, and I told her again and again of her loveliness, of how silly she had been. But say it fast, Arturo, say it quickly, because something was coming up in me, and I had to get out, so I told her I had to go down the hall a minute and for her to dress while I was gone. She covered herself and her eyes were swimming in joy as she watched me leave. I went down to the end of the hall to the landing of the fire-escape, and there I let go, crying and unable to stop because God was such a dirty crook, such a contemptible skunk, that's what he was for doing that thing to that woman. Come down out of the skies, you God, come on down and I'll hammer your face all over the city of Los Angeles, you miserable unpardonable prankster. If it wasn't for you, this woman would not be so maimed, and neither would the world, and if it wasn't for you I could have had Camilla Lopez down at the beach, but no! You have to play your tricks: see what you have done to this woman, and to the love of Arturo Bandini for Camilla Lopez. And then my tragedy seemed greater than the woman's, and I forgot her.

When I got back she was dressed and combing her hair in front of the little mirror. The torn blouse was stuffed inside her coat pocket. She seemed so exhausted and yet so serenely happy, and I told her I would walk downtown with her to the Electric Depot, where she would catch a train for Long Beach. She told me no, I wouldn't have to do that. She wrote out her address on a piece of paper.

'Some day you'll come to Long Beach,' she said. 'I will wait a long time, but you'll come.'

At the door we said goodbye. She held out her hand, it was so warm and alive. 'Goodbye,' she said. 'Take care of yourself.'

'Good bye, Vera.'

There was no solitude after she left, there was no escape from that strange scent. I lay down and even Camilla who was a pillow with a tam-o-shanter for a head seemed so far away and I could not bring her back. Slowly I felt myself filling with desire and sadness; you could have had her, you fool, you could have done what you pleased, just like Camilla, and you didn't do anything. All through the night she mangled my sleep. I would wake up to breathe the sweet heaviness she had left behind, and touch the furniture she had touched, and think of the poetry she had recited. When I fell asleep I had no recollection of it, for when I awoke it was ten in the morning and I was still tired, sniffing the air and thinking restlessly of what had happened. I could have said so much to her, and she would have been so kind. I could have said, look Vera, such and such is the situation, and such and such happened, and if you could do such and such, perhaps it would not happen again, because such and such a person thinks such and such about me, and it's got to stop; I shall die trying, but it's got to stop.

So I sit around all day thinking about it; and I think about a few other Italians, Casanova and Cellini, and then I think about Arturo Bandini, and I have to punch myself in the head. I begin to wonder about Long Beach, and I say to myself that perhaps I should at least visit the place, and maybe Vera, to have a talk with her concerning a great problem. I think of that cadaverous place, the wound on her body, and try to find words for it, to fit it across the page of a manuscript. Then I say to myself that Vera, for all her flaws, might perform a miracle, and after the miracle is performed a new Arturo Bandini will face the world and Camilla Lopez, a Bandini with dynamite in his body and volcanic fire in his eyes, who goes to this Camilla Lopez and says: see here, young woman, I have been very patient with you, but now I have had enough of your impudence, and you will kindly oblige me by removing your clothes. These vagaries please me as I lie there and watch them unfold across the ceiling.

One afternoon I tell Mrs Hargraves that I shall be gone for

a day or so, Long Beach, some business, and I start out. I have Vera's address in my pocket, and I say to myself, Bandini, prepare yourself for the great adventure; let the conquering spirit possess you. On the corner I meet Hellfrick, whose mouth is watering for more meat. I give him some money and he dashes into a butcher's shop. Then I go down to the Electric Station and catch a Red Car for Long Beach.

Chapter Twelve

The name on the mailbox was Vera Rivken, and that was her full name. It was down on the Long Beach Pike, across the street from the Ferris Wheel and the Roller Coaster. Downstairs a poolhall, upstairs a few single apartments. No mistaking that flight of stairs; it possessed her odour. The banister was warped and bent, and the grey wallpaint was swollen, with puffed places that cracked open when I pushed them with my thumb.

When I knocked, she opened the door.

'So soon?' she said.

Take her in your arms, Bandini. Don't grimace at her kiss, break away gently, with a smile, say something. 'You look wonderful,' I said. No chance to speak, she was over me again, clinging like a wet vine, her tongue, like a frightened snake's head, searching my mouth. Oh great Italian Lover Bandini, reciprocate! Oh Jewish girl, if you would be so kind, if you would approach these matters more slowly! So I was free again, wandering to the window, saying something about the sea and the view beyond. 'Nice view,' I said. But she was taking off my coat, leading me to a chair in the corner, taking off my shoes. 'Be comfortable,' she said. Then she was gone, and I sat with my teeth gritted, looking at a room like ten million California rooms, a bit of wood here and a bit of rag there, the furniture, with cobwebs in the ceiling and dust in the corners, her room, and everybody's room, Los Angeles, Long Beach, San Diego, a few boards of plaster and stucco to keep the sun out.

She was in a little white hole called the kitchen, scattering pans and rattling glasses, and I sat and wondered why she could be one thing when I was alone in my room and something else the moment I was with her. I looked for incense, that saccharine smell, it had to come from somewhere, but there was no incense burner in the room, nothing in the room but dirty blue overstuffed furniture, a table with a few books scattered over it, and a mirror over the panelling of a Murphy bed. Then she came out of the kitchen with a glass of milk in her hand. 'Here,' she offered. 'A cool drink.'

But it wasn't cool at all, it was almost hot, and there was a yellowish scum on top, and sipping it I tasted her lips and the strong food she ate, a taste of rye bread and Camembert cheese. 'It's good,' I said, 'delicious.'

She was sitting at my feet, her hands on my knees, staring at me with the eyes of hunger, tremendous eyes so large I might have lost myself in them. She was dressed as I saw her the first time, the same clothes, and the place was so desolate I knew she had no others, but I had come before she had had a chance to powder or rouge and now I saw the sculpture of age under her eyes and through her cheeks. I wondered that I had missed these things that night, and then I remembered that I had not missed them at all, I had seen them even through rouge and powder, but in the two days of reverie and dream about her they had concealed themselves, and now I was here, and I knew I should not have come.

We talked, she and I. She asked about my work and it was a pretence, she was not interested in my work. And when I answered it was a pretence. I was not interested in my work either. There was only one thing that interested us, and she knew it, for I had made it plain by my coming.

But where were all the words, and where were all the little lusts I had brought with me? And where were those reveries, and where was my desire, and what had happened to my courage, and why did I sit and laugh so loudly at things not amusing? So come, Bandini – find your heart's desire, take your passion the way it says in the books. Two people in a room; one of them a woman; the other, Arturo Bandini, who is neither fish, fowl, nor good red herring.

Another long silence, the woman's head on my lap, my fingers playing in the dark nest, sorting out strands of grey hair. Awake, Arturo! Camilla Lopez should see you now, she with the big black eyes, your true love, your Mayan princess. Oh Jesus, Arturo, you're marvellous! Maybe you did write *The Little Dog Laughed*, but you'll never write Casanova's Memoirs. What are you doing, sitting here? Dreaming of some great masterpiece? Oh you fool, Bandini!

She looked up at me, saw me there with eyes closed, and she didn't know my thoughts. But maybe she did. Maybe that was why she said, 'You're tired. You must take a nap.' Maybe that was why she pulled down the Murphy bed and insisted that I lie upon it, she beside me, her head in my arms. Maybe, studying my face, that was why she asked, 'You love somebody else?'

I said, 'Yes. I'm in love with a girl in Los Angeles.'

She touched my face.

'I know,' she said. 'I understand.'

'No you don't.'

Then I wanted to tell her why I had come, it was right there at the tip of my tongue, springing to be told, but I knew I would never speak of that now. She lay beside me and we watched the emptiness of the ceiling, and I played with the idea of telling her. I said, 'There's something I want to tell you. Maybe you can help me out.' But I got no farther than that. No, I could not say it to her; but I lay there hoping she would somehow find out for herself, and when she kept asking me what it was that bothered me I knew she was handling it wrong, and I shook my head and made impatient faces. 'Don't talk about it,' I said. 'It's something I can't tell you.'

'Tell me about her,' she said.

I couldn't do that, be with one woman and speak of the wonders of another. Maybe that was why she asked, 'Is she beautiful?' I answered that she was. Maybe that was why she asked, 'Does she love you?' I said she didn't love me. Then my heart pounded in my throat, because she was coming nearer and nearer to what I wanted her to ask, and I waited while she stroked my forehead.

'And why doesn't she love you?'

There it was. I could have answered and it would have been in the clear, but I said, 'She just doesn't love me, that's all.'

'Is it because she loves somebody else?'

'I don't know. Maybe.'

Maybe this and maybe that, questions, questions, wise, wounded woman, groping in the dark, searching for the passion of Arturo Bandini, a game of hot and cold, with Bandini eager to give it away. 'What is her name?'

'Camilla,' I said.

She sat up, touched my mouth.

'I'm so lonely,' she said. 'Pretend that I am she.'

'Yes,' I said. 'That's it. That's your name. It's Camilla.'

I opened my arms and she sank against my chest.

'My name is Camilla,' she said.

'You're beautiful,' I said. 'You're a Mayan princess.'

'I am Princess Camilla.'

'All of this land and this sea belongs to you. All of California. There is no California, no Los Angeles, no dusty streets, no cheap hotels, no stinking newspapers, no broken, uprooted people from the East, no fancy boulevards. This is your beautiful land with the desert and the mountains and the sea. You're a princess, and you reign over it all.'

'I am Princess Camilla,' she sobbed. 'There are no Americans, and no California. Only deserts and mountains and the sea, and I reign over it all.'

'Then I come.'

'Then you come.'

'I'm myself. I'm Arturo Bandini. I'm the greatest writer the world ever had.'

'Ah yes,' she choked. 'Of course! Arturo Bandini, the genius of the earth.' She buried her face in my shoulder and her warm tears fell on my throat. I held her closer. 'Kiss me, Arturo.'

But I didn't kiss her. I wasn't through. It had to be my way or nothing. 'I'm a conqueror,' I said. 'I'm like Cortés, only I'm an Italian.'

I felt it now. It was real and satisfying, and joy broke through me, the blue sky through the window was a ceiling, and the whole living world was a small thing in the palm of my hand. I shivered with delight.

'Camilla, I love you so much!'

There were no scars, and no desiccated place. She was Camilla, complete and lovely. She belonged to me, and so did the world. And I was glad for her tears, they thrilled me and lifted me, and I possessed her. Then I slept, serenely weary, remembering vaguely through the mist of drowsiness that she was sobbing, but I didn't care. She wasn't Camilla anymore. She was Vera Rivken, and I was in her apartment and I would get up and leave just as soon as I had had some sleep.

She was gone when I woke up. The room was eloquent with her departure. A window open, curtains blowing gently. A closet door ajar, a coat-hanger on the knob. The half-empty glass of milk where I had left it on the arm of the chair. Little things accusing Arturo Bandini, but my eyes felt cool after sleep and I was anxious to go and never come back. Down in the street there was music from a merry-go-round. I stood at the window. Below two women passed, and I looked down upon their heads.

Before leaving I stood at the door and took one last look around the room. Mark it well, for this was the place. Here too history was made. I laughed. Arturo Bandini, suave fellow, sophisticated; you should hear him on the subject of women. But the room seemed so poor, pleading for warmth and joy. Vera Rivken's room. She had been nice to Arturo Bandini, and she was poor. I took the small roll from my pocket, peeled off two one dollar bills, and laid them on the table. Then I walked down the stairs, my lungs full of air, elated, my muscles so much stronger than ever before.

But there was a tinge of darkness in the back of my mind. I walked down the street, past the Ferris Wheel and canvassed concessions, and it seemed to come stronger; some disturbance of peace, something vague and nameless seeping into my mind. At a hamburger stand I stopped and ordered coffee. It crept upon me – restlessness, the loneliness. What was the matter? I felt my pulse. It was good. I blew on the coffee and drank it: good coffee. I searched, felt the fingers of my mind reaching out but not quite touching whatever it was back there that bothered me. Then it came to me like crashing thunder, like death and destruction. I got up from the counter and walked away in fear, walking fast down the boardwalk, passing people who seemed strange and ghostly: the world seemed a myth, a transparent plane, and all things upon it were here for only a little while; all of us, Bandini, and Hackmuth and Camilla and Vera, all of us were here for a little while, and then we were somewhere else; we were not alive at all; we approached living, but we never achieved it. We are going to die. Everybody was going to die. Even you, Arturo, even you must die.

I knew what it was that swept over me. It was a great white cross pointing into my brain and telling me I was a stupid man, because I was going to die, and there was nothing I could do about it. *Mea culpa, mea culpa, mea maxima culpa*. A mortal sin, Arturo. Thou shalt not commit adultery. There it was, persistent to the end, assuring me that there was no escape from what I had done. I was a Catholic. This was a mortal sin against Vera Rivken.

At the end of the row of concessions the sand beach began. Beyond were dunes. I waded through the sand to a place where the dunes hid the boardwalk. This needed thinking out. I didn't kneel; I sat down and watched the breakers eating the shore. This is bad, Arturo. You have read Nietzsche, you have read Voltaire, you should know better. But reasoning wouldn't help. I could reason myself out of it, but that was not my blood. It was my blood that kept me alive, it was my blood pouring through me, telling me it was wrong. I sat there and gave myself over to my blood, let it carry me swimming back to the deep sea of my beginnings. Vera Rivken, Arturo Bandini. It was not meant that way: it was never meant that way. I was wrong. I had committed a mortal sin. I could figure it mathematically, philosophically, psychologically: I could prove it a dozen ways, but I was wrong, for there was no denying the warm even rhythm of my guilt.

Sick in my soul I tried to face the ordeal of seeking forgiveness. From whom? What God, what Christ? They were myths I once believed, and now they were beliefs I felt were myths. This is the sea, and this is Arturo, and the sea is real, and Arturo believes it real. Then I turn from the sea, and everywhere I look there is land; I walk on and on, and still the land goes stretching away to the horizons. A year, five years, ten years, and I have not seen the sea. I say unto myself, but what has happened to the sea? And I answer, the sea is back there, back in the reservoir of memory. The sea is a myth. There never was a sea. But there *was* a sea! I tell you I was born on the seashore! I bathed in the waters of the sea! It gave me food and it gave me peace, and its fascinating distances fed my dreams! No Arturo, there never was a sea. You dream and you wish, but you go on through the wasteland. You will never see the sea again. It was a myth you once believed. But, I have to smile, for the salt of the sea is in my blood, and there may be ten thousand roads over the land, but they shall never confuse me, for my heart's blood will ever return to its beautiful source.

Then what shall I do? Shall I lift my mouth to the sky,

stumbling and burbling with a tongue that is afraid? Shall I open my chest and beat it like a loud drum, seeking the attention of my Christ? Or is it not better and more reasonable that I cover myself and go on? There will be confusions, and there will be hunger; there will be loneliness with only my tears like wet consoling little birds, tumbling to sweeten my dry lips. But there shall be consolation, and there shall be beauty like the love of some dead girl. There shall be some laughter, a restrained laughter, and quiet waiting in the night, a soft fear of the night like the lavish, taunting kiss of death. Then it will be night, and the sweet oils from the shores of my sea, poured upon my senses by the captains I deserted in the dreamy impetuousness of my youth. But I shall be forgiven for that, and for other things, for Vera Rivken, and for the ceaseless flapping of the wings of Voltaire, for pausing to listen and watch that fascinating bird, for all things there shall be forgiveness when I return to my homeland by the sea.

I got up and plodded through the deep sand towards the boardwalk. It was the full ripeness of evening, with the sun a defiant red ball as it sank beyond the sea. There was something breathless about the sky, a strange tension. Far to the south sea gulls in a black mass roved the coast. I stopped to pour sand from my shoes, balanced on one leg as I leaned against a stone bench.

Suddenly I felt a rumble, then a roar.

The stone bench fell away from me and thumped into the sand. I looked beyond to the Long Beach skyline; the tall buildings were swaying. Under me the sand gave way; I staggered, found safer footing. It happened again.

It was an earthquake.

Now there were screams. Then dust. Then crumbling and roaring. I turned round and round in a circle. I had done this. I had done this. I stood with my mouth open, paralysed, looking about me. I ran a few steps towards the sea. Then I ran back.

You did it, Arturo. This is the wrath of God. You did it.

The rumbling continued. Like a carpet over oil, the sea and land heaved. Dust rose. Somewhere I heard a booming of debris. I heard screams and then a siren. People running out of doors. Great clouds of dust.

You did it, Arturo. Up in that room on that bed you did it.

Now the lamp posts were falling. Buildings cracked like crushed crackers. Screams, men shouting, women screaming. Hundreds of people rushing from buildings, hurrying out of danger. A woman lying on the sidewalk, beating it. A little boy crying. Glass splintering and shattering. Fire bells. Sirens. Horns. Madness.

Now the big shake was over. Now there were tremors. Deep in the earth the rumbling continued. Chimneys toppled, bricks fell and a grey dust settled over all. Still the tremblors. Men and women running towards an empty lot away from buildings.

I hurried to the lot. An old woman wept among the white faces. Two men carrying a body. An old dog crawling on his belly, dragging his hind legs. Several bodies in the corner of the lot, beside a shed, blood-soaked sheets covering them. An ambulance. Two high school girls, arms locked, laughing. I looked down the street. The building fronts were down. Beds hung from the walls. Bathrooms were exposed. The street was piled with three feet of debris. Men were shouting orders.

Each tremblor brought more tumbling debris. They stepped aside, waited, then plunged in again.

I had to go. I walked to the shed, the earth quivering under me. I opened the shed door, felt like fainting. Inside were bodies in a row, sheets over them, blood oozing through. Blood and death. I walked off and sat down. Still the temblors, one after another.

Where was Vera Rivken? I got up and walked to the street. It had been roped off. Marines with bayonets patrolled the roped area. Far down the street I saw the building where Vera lived. Hanging from the wall, like a man crucified, was the bed. The floor was gone and only one wall stood erect. I walked back to the lot. Somebody had built a bonfire in the middle of the lot. Faces reddened in the blaze. I studied them, found nobody I knew. I didn't find Vera Rivken. A group of old men were talking. The tall one with the beard said it was the end of the world; he had predicted it a week before. A woman with dirt smeared over her hair broke into the group. 'Charlie's dead,' she said. Then she wailed. 'Poor Charlie's dead. We shouldn't have to come! I told him we shouldn't a come!' An old man seized her by the shoulders, swung her around. 'What the hell you sayin'?' he said. She fainted in his arms.

I went off and sat on the kerb. Repent, repent before it's too late. I said a prayer but it was dust in my mouth. No prayers. But there would be some changes made in my life. There would be decency and gentleness from now on. This was the turning point. This was for me, a warning to Arturo Bandini.

Around the bonfire the people were singing hymns. They were in a circle, a huge woman leading them. Lift up thine eyes to Jesus, for Jesus is coming soon. Everybody was singing. A kid with a monogram on his sweater handed me a hymn book. I walked over. The woman in the circle swung her arms with wild fervour, and the song tumbled with the smoke towards the sky. The temblors kept coming. I turned away. Jesus, these Protestants! In my church we didn't sing cheap hymns. With us it was Handel and Palestrina.

It was dark now. A few stars appeared. The temblors were ceaseless, coming every few seconds. A wind rose from the sea and it grew cold. People huddled in groups. From everywhere sirens sounded. Above, aeroplanes droned, and detachments of sailors and marines poured through the streets. Stretcher-bearers dashed into ruined buildings. Two ambulances backed towards the shed. I got up and walked away. The Red Cross had moved in. There was an emergency headquarters at one corner of the lot. They were handing out big tins of coffee. I stood in line. The man ahead of me was talking.

'It's worse in Los Angeles,' he said. 'Thousands dead.'

Thousands. That meant Camilla. The Columbia Buffet would be the first to tumble. It was so old, the brick walls so cracked and feeble. Sure, she was dead. She worked from four until eleven. She had been caught in the midst of it. She was dead and I was alive. Good. I pictured her dead: she would lie still in this manner; her eyes closed like this, her hands clasped like that. She was dead and I was alive. We didn't understand one another, but she had been good to me, in her fashion. I would remember her a long time. I was probably the only man on earth who would remember her. I could think of so many charming things about her; her huaraches, her shame for her people, her absurd little Ford.

All sorts of rumours circulated through the lot. A tidal wave was coming. A tidal wave wasn't coming. All of California had been struck. Only Long Beach had been struck. Los Angeles was a mass of ruins. They hadn't felt it in Los Angeles. Some said the dead numbered fifty thousand. This was the worst quake since San Francisco. This was much worse than the San Francisco quake. But in spite of it all, everybody was orderly. Everybody was frightened, but it was not a panic. Here and there people smiled: they were brave people. They were a long way from home, but they brought their bravery with them. They were tough people. They weren't afraid of anything.

The marines set up a radio in the middle of the lot, with big loudspeakers yawning into the crowd. The reports came through constantly, outlining the catastrophe. The deep voice bellowed instructions. It was the law and everybody accepted it gladly: Nobody was to enter or leave Long Beach until further notice. The city was under martial law. There wasn't going to be a tidal wave. The danger was definitely over. The people were not to be alarmed by the temblors, which were to be expected, now that the earth was settling once more.

The Red Cross passed out blankets, food, and lots of coffee. All night we sat around the loudspeaker, listening to developments. Then the report came that the damage in Los Angeles was negligible. A long list of the dead was broadcast. But there was no Camilla Lopez on the list. All night I swallowed coffee and smoked cigarettes, listening to the names of the dead. There was no Camilla; not even a Lopez.

Chapter Thirteen

I got back to Los Angeles the next day. The city was the same, but I was afraid. The streets lurked with danger. The tall buildings forming black canyons were traps to kill you when the earth shook. The pavement might open. The street cars might topple. Something had happened to Arturo Bandini. He walked the streets of one-storey buildings. He clung to the kerbstone, away from the overhanging neon signs. It was inside me, deeply. I could not shake it. I saw men walking through deep, dark alleys. I marvelled at their madness. I crossed Hill Street and breathed easier when I entered Pershing Square. No tall buildings in the Square. The earth could shake, but no debris could crush you.

I sat in the Square, smoked cigarettes and felt sweat oozing from my palms. The Columbia Buffet was five blocks away. I knew I would not go down there. Somewhere within me was a change. I was a coward. I said it aloud to myself: you are a coward. I didn't care. It was better to be a live coward than a dead madman. These people walking in and out of huge concrete buildings – someone should warn them. It would come again; it had to come again, another earthquake to level the city and destroy it forever. It would happen any minute. It would kill a lot of people, but not me. Because I was going to keep out of these streets, and away from falling debris.

I walked up Bunker Hill to my hotel. I considered every building. The frame buildings could stand a quake. They merely shook and writhed, but they did not come down. But look out for the brick places. Here and there were evidences of the quake; a tumbled brick wall, a fallen chimney. Los Angeles was doomed. It was a city with a curse upon it. This particular earthquake had not destroyed it, but any day now another would raze it to the ground. They wouldn't get me, they'd never catch me inside a brick building. I was a coward, but that was my business. Sure I'm a coward, talking to myself, sure I'm a coward, but you be brave, you lunatic, go ahead and be brave and walk around under those big buildings. They'll kill you. Today, tomorrow, next week, next year, but they'll kill you and they won't kill me.

And now listen to the man who was in the earthquake. I sat on the porch of the Alta Loma Hotel and told them about it. I saw it happen. I saw the dead carried out. I saw the blood and the wounded. I was in a six-storey building, fast asleep when it happened. I ran down the corridor to the elevator. It was jammed. A woman rushed out of one of the offices and was struck on the head by a steel girder. I fought my way back through the ruins and got to her. I slung her over my shoulders, it was six floors to the ground, but I made it. All night I was with the rescuers, knee deep in blood and misery. I pulled an old woman out whose hand stuck through the debris like a piece of statue. I flung myself through a smoking doorway to rescue a girl unconscious in her bathtub. I dressed the wounded, led battalions of rescuers into the ruins, hacked and fought my way to the dead and dying. Sure I was scared, but it had to be done. It was a crisis, calling for action and not words. I saw the earth open like a huge mouth, then close again over the paved street. An old man was trapped by the foot. I ran to him, told him to be brave while I hacked the pavement with a fireman's axe. But I was too late. The vice tightened, bit his leg off at the knee. I carried him away. His knee is still there, a bloody souvenir sticking out of the earth. I saw it happen, and it was awful. Maybe they believed me, maybe they didn't. It was all the same to me.

I went down to my room and looked for cracks in the wall. I inspected Hellfrick's room. He was stooped over his stove, frying a pan of hamburger. I saw it happen, Hellfrick. I was atop the highest point of the Roller Coaster when the quake hit. The Coaster jammed in its tracks. We had to climb down. A girl and myself. A hundred and fifty feet to the ground, with a girl on my back and the structure shaking like St Vitus Dance. I made it though. I saw a little girl buried feet first in debris. I saw an old woman pinned under her car, dead and crushed, but holding her hand out to signal for a right hand turn. I saw three men dead at a poker table. Hellfrick whistled: is that so? Is that so: Too bad, too bad. And would I lend him fifty cents? I gave it to him and inspected his walls for cracks. I went down the halls, into the garage and laundry room. There were evidences of the shock, not serious, but indicative of the calamity that would inevitably destroy Los Angeles. I didn't sleep in my room that night. Not with the earth still trembling. Not me, Hellfrick. And Hellfrick looked out the window to where I lay on the hillside, wrapped in blankets. I was crazy Hellfrick said. But Hellfrick remembered that I had been lending him money, so maybe I wasn't crazy. Maybe you're right, Hellfrick said. He turned out his light and I heard his thin body settle upon the bed.

*   *   *

The world was dust, and dust it would become. I began going to Mass in the mornings. I went to Confession. I received Holy Communion. I picked out a little frame church, squat and solid, down near the Mexican quarter. Here I prayed. The new Bandini. Ah life! Thou sweet bitter tragedy, thou dazzling whore that leadeth me to destruction! I gave up cigarettes for a few days. I bought a new rosary. I poured nickels and dimes into the Poor Box. I pitied the world.

Dear Mother back home in Colorado. Ah, beloved character, so like the Virgin Mary. I only had ten dollars left, but I sent her five of it, the first money I ever sent home. Pray for me, Mother dear. The vigil of your rosaries is all that keeps my blood astir. These are dark days, Mother. The world is so full of ugliness. But I have changed, and life has begun anew. Long hours I spend glorying thee before God. Ah mother, be with me in these miseries! But I must hasten to close this epistle, Oh beloved Mother Darling, for I am making a *novena* these days, and each afternoon at five I am to be found prostrate before the figure of Our Blessed Saviour as I offer prayers for His sweet Mercy. Farewell, O Mother! Heed my plea for your aspirations. Remember me to Him that giveth all and shineth in the skies.

So off to mail the letter to my mother, to drop it in the box and walk down Olive Street, where there were no brick buildings, and then across an empty lot and down another street that was barren of buildings to a street where only a low fence marked the spot, and then a block to a section of town where high buildings rose to the sky; but there was no escaping that block, save to walk across the street from the high buildings, walk very fast, sometimes run. And at the end of the street was the little church, and here I prayed, making my *novena*.

An hour later I come out, refreshed, soothed, spirits high. I take the same route home, hurry past the high buildings, stroll along the fence, dawdle through the empty lot, taking note of God's handiwork in a line of palm trees near the alley. And so up to Olive Street, past the drab frame houses. What doth it profit a man if he gain the whole world and suffer the loss of his own soul? And then that little poem: Take all the pleasures of all the spheres, multiply them by endless years, one minute of heaven is worth them all. How true! How true! I thank thee, Oh heavenly light, for showing the way.

A knock on the window. Someone was knocking on the window of that house obscured by heavy vines. I turned and found the window, saw a head; the flash of teeth, the black hair, the leer, the gesturing long fingers. What was that thunder in my belly? And how shall I prevent that paralysis of thought, and that inundation of blood making my senses reel? But I want this! I shall die without it! So I'm coming you woman in the window; you fascinate me, you kill me dead with delight and shudder and joy, and here I come, up these rickety stairs.

So what's the use of repentance, and what do you care for goodness, and what if you *should* die in a quake, so who the hell cares? So I walked downtown, so these were the high buildings, so let the earthquake come, let it bury me and my sins, so who the hell cares? No good to God or man, die one way or another, a quake or a hanging, it didn't matter why or when or how.

And then, like a dream it came. Out of my desperation it came — an idea, my first sound idea, the first in my entire life, full-bodied and clean and strong, line after line, page after page. A story about Vera Rivken.

I tried it and it moved easily. But it was not thinking, not cogitation. It simply moved of its own accord, spurted out like blood. This was it. I had it at last. Here I go, leave me be, oh boy do I love it, Oh God do I love you, and you Camilla and you and you. Here I go and it feels so good, so sweet and warm and soft, delicious, delirious. Up the river and over the sea, this is you and this is me, big fat words, little fat words, big thin words, whee whee whee.

Breathless, frantic, endless thing, going to be something big, going on and on, I hammered away for hours, until gradually it came upon me in the flesh, stole over me, haunted my bones, dripped from me, weakened me, blinded me. Camilla! I had to have that Camilla! I got up and walked out of the hotel and down Bunker Hill to the Columbia Buffet.

'Back again?'

Like film over my eyes, like a spider web over me.

'Why not?'

Arturo Bandini, author of *The Little Dog Laughed* and a certain plagiarization from Ernest Dowson, and a certain telegram proposing marriage. Could that be laughter in her eyes? But forget it, and remember the dark flesh under her smock. I drank beer and watched her at work. I sneered when she laughed with those men near the piano. I cackled when one of them put his hand on her hip. This Mexican! Trash, I tell you! I signalled her. She came at her leisure, fifteen minutes later. Be nice to her, Arturo. Fake it.

'You want something else?'

'How are you, Camilla?'

'Alright, I guess.'

'I'd like to see you after work.'

'I have another engagement.'

Gently: 'Could you postpone it, Camilla? It's very important that I see you.'

'I'm sorry.'

'Please Camilla. Just tonight. It's so important.'

'I can't, Arturo. Really, I can't.'

'You'll see me,' I said.

She walked away. I pushed back my chair. I pointed my finger at her, yelled it out: 'You'll see me! You little insolent beerhall twirp! You'll see me!'

You're goddamn right she'd see me. Because I was going to wait. Because I walked out to the parking lot and sat on the running board of her car and waited. Because she wasn't so good that she could excuse herself from a date with Arturo Bandini. Because, by God, I hated her guts.

Then she came into the lot, and Sammy the bartender was with her. She paused when she saw me get to my feet. She put her hand on Sammy's arm, restraining him. They whispered. Then it was going to be a fight. Fine. Come you, you stupid scarecrow of a bartender, just you make a pass at me and I'll break you in half. And I stood there with both fists hard and waiting. They approached. Sammy didn't speak. He walked around me and got into the car. I stood beside the driver's seat. Camilla looked straight ahead, opened the car door. I shook my head.

'You're going with me, Mexican.'

I seized her wrist.

'Let go!' she said. 'Get your filthy hands off!'

'You're going with me.'

Sammy leaned over.

'Maybe she doesn't feel like it, kid.'

I had her with my right hand. I raised my left fist and shoved it against Sammy's face. 'Listen,' I said. 'I don't like you. So keep that lousy trap shut.'

'Be sensible,' he said. 'What for you want to get all burned up about a dame?'

'She's going with me.'

'I'm *not* going with you!'

She tried to pass. I grabbed her arms and flung her like a dancer. She went spinning across the lot, but she did not fall. She screamed, charged me. I caught her in my arms and pinned her elbows down. She kicked and tried to scratch my legs. Sammy watched with disgust. Sure I was disgusting, but that was my affair. She cried and fought, but she was helpless, her legs dangling, her arms held tight. Then she tired a little, and I released her. She straightened her dress, her teeth chattering her hatred.

'You're going with me,' I said.

Sammy got out of the car.

'This is terrible,' he said. He took Camilla's arm and led her towards the street. 'Let's get out of here.'

I watched them go. He was right. Bandini, the idiot, the dog, the skunk, the fool. But I couldn't help it. I looked at the car certificate and found her address. It was a place near 24th and Alameda. I couldn't help it. I walked to Hill Street and got aboard an Alameda trolley. This interested me. A new side to my character, the bestial, the darkness, the unplumbed depth of a new Bandini. But after a few blocks the mood evaporated. I got off the car near the freight yards. Bunker Hill was two miles away, but I walked back. When I got home I said I was through with Camilla Lopez forever. And you'll regret it, you little fool, because I'm going to be famous. I sat before my typewriter and worked most of the night.

I worked hard. It was supposed to be autumn, but I couldn't tell the difference. We had sun every day, blue skies every night. Sometimes there was fog. I was eating fruit again. The Japanese gave me credit and I had the pick of their stalls. Bananas, oranges, pears, plums. Once in a while I ate celery. I had a full can of tobacco and a new pipe. There wasn't any coffee, but I didn't mind. Then my new story hit the magazine stands. *The Long Lost Hills!* It was not as exciting as *The Little Dog Laughed*. I scarcely looked at the free copy Hackmuth sent me. This pleased me nevertheless. Some day I would have so many stories written I wouldn't remember where they appeared. 'Hi there, Bandini! Nice story you had in *The Atlantic Monthly* this month.' Bandini puzzled. 'Did I have one in the *Atlantic*? Well, well.'

Hellfrick the meat-eater, the man who never paid his just debts. So much I had lent him during that lush period, but now that I was poor again he tried to barter with me. An old raincoat, a pair of slippers, a box of fancy soap – these he offered me for payment. I refused them. 'My God, Hellfrick. I need money, not secondhand goods.' His meat craze had got out of hand. All day I heard him frying cheap steaks, the odour creeping under my door. It gave me a mad desire for meat. I would go to Hellfrick. 'Hellfrick,' I would say. 'How about sharing that steak with me?' The steak would be so large it filled the skillet. But Hellfrick would lie brazenly. 'I haven't had a thing for two days.' I would call him violent names, soon I lost all respect for him. He would shake his red, bloated face, big eyes staring pitifully. But he never offered me so much as the scraps from his plate. Day after day I worked, writhing from the tantalizing odour of fried pork chops, grilled steaks, fried steaks, breaded steaks, liver and onions, and all manner of meats.

One day his craze for meat was gone, and the craze for gin returned. He was steadily drunk for two nights. I could hear him stumbling about, kicking bottles and talking to himself. Then he went away. He was gone another night. When he returned, his pension cheque was spent, and he had somehow, somewhere, he did not remember it, bought a car. We went behind the hotel and looked at this car. It was a huge Packard, more than twenty years old. It stood there like a hearse, the tyres worn, the cheap black paint bubbling in the hot sun. Somebody down on Main Street had sold it to him. Now he was broke, with a big Packard on his hands.

'You want to buy it?' he said.

'Hell, no.'

He was dejected, his head bursting from a hangover.

That night he walked into my room. He sat on the bed, his long arms dangling to the floor. He was homesick for the middle-west. He talked of rabbit-hunting, of fishing, of the good old days when he was a kid. Then he began on the subject of meat. 'How would you like a big thick steak?' he said, his lips loose. He opened two fingers. 'Thick as that. Broiled. Lots of butter over it. Burned just enough to give it a tang. How would you like it?'

'I'd love it.'

He got up.

'Then come on, and we'll get one.'

'You got money?'

'We don't need any money. I'm hungry.'

I grabbed my sweater and followed him down the hall to the alley. He got into his car. I hesitated. 'Where you going, Hellfrick?'

'Come on,' he said. 'Leave it to me.'

I got in beside him.

'No trouble,' I said.

'Trouble!' he sneered. 'I tell you I know where to get us a steak.'

We drove in moonlight out Wilshire to Highland, then out Highland over Cahuenga Pass. On the other side lay the flat plain of the San Fernando Valley. We found a lonely road off the pavement and followed it through tall eucalyptus trees to scattered farmhouses and pasture lands. After a mile the road ended. Barbed wire and fence posts appeared in the glare of headlights. Hellfrick laboriously turned the car around, faced it towards the pavement from which we had detoured. He got out of the front seat, opened the rear door, and fumbled with car tools under the rear cushion.

I leaned over and watched him.

'What's up, Hellfrick?'

He stood up, a jackhammer in his hand.

'You wait here.'

He stopped under a loop in the barbed wire and crossed the pasture. A hundred yards away a barn loomed in the moonlight. Then I knew what he was after. I jumped out of the car and called to him. He shushed me angrily. I watched him tiptoe towards the barn door. I cursed him and waited tensely. In a little while I heard the mooing of a cow. It was a piteous cry. Then I heard a thud and a scuffle of hoofs. Out of the barn door came Hellfrick. Across his shoulder lay a dark mass, weighing him down. Behind him, mooing continually, a cow followed. Hellfrick tried to run, but the dark mass beat him down to a fast walk. Still the cow pursued, pushing her nose into his back. He turned around, kicked wildly. The cow stopped, looked towards the barn, and mooed again.

'You fool, Hellfrick. You goddamn fool!'

'Help me,' he said.

I raised the loose barbed wire to a width that would permit him and his burden to pass under. It was a calf, blood spurting from a gash between the ears. The calf's eyes were wide open. I could see the moon reflected in them. It was coldblooded murder. I was sick and horrified. My stomach twisted when Hellfrick dumped the calf into the back seat. I heard the body thump, and then the head. I was sick, very sick. It was plain murder.

All the way home Hellfrick was exultant, but the steering wheel was sticky with blood, and once or twice I thought I heard the calf kicking in the back seat. I held my face in my hands and tried to forget the melancholy call of the calf's mother, the sweet face of the dead calf. Hellfrick drove very fast. On Beverly we shot by a black car moving slowly. It was a police cruiser. I gritted my teeth and waited for the worst. But the police did not follow us. I was too sick to be relieved. One thing was certain: Hellfrick was a murderer, he and I were through. On Bunker Hill we turned down our alley and pulled up at the parking space adjacent the hotel wall. Hellfrick got out.

'Now I'm going to give you a lesson in butchering.'

'You are like hell,' I said.

I acted as lookout for him as he wrapped the calf's head in newspapers, slung it over his shoulder, and hurried down the dim hallway to his room. I spread newspapers over his dirty floor, and he lowered the calf upon them. He grinned at his bloody trousers and his bloody shirt, his bloody arms.

I looked down at the poor calf. Its hide was spotted black and white and it had the most delicate ankles. From the slightly open mouth there appeared a pink tongue. I closed my eyes and ran out Hellfrick's room and threw myself on the floor in my room. I lay there and shuddered, thinking of the old cow alone in the field in the moonlight, old cow mooing for her calf. Murder! Hellfrick and I were through. He didn't have to pay back the debt. It was blood money – not for me.

After that night I was very cold towards Hellfrick. I never visited his room again. A couple of times I recognized his knock, but I kept the door bolted so he couldn't barge in. Meeting in the hall, we merely grunted. He owed me almost three dollars, but I never did collect it.

Chapter Fourteen

Good news from Hackmuth. Another magazine wanted *The Long Lost Hills* in digest form. A hundred dollars. I was rich again. A time for amends, for righting the past. I sent my mother five dollars. I cried when she sent me a letter of thanks. The tears rolled down my eyes as I quickly replied. And sent five more. I was pleased with myself. I had a few good qualities. I could see them, my biographers, talking to my mother, a very old lady in a wheel chair: he was a good son, my Arturo, a good provider.

Arturo Bandini, the novelist. Income of his own, made it writing short stories. Writing a book now. Tremendous book. Advance notices terrific. Remarkable prose. Nothing like it since Joyce. Standing before Hackmuth's picture, I read the work of each day. I spent whole hours writing a dedication: To J. C. Hackmuth, for discovering me. To J. C. Hackmuth, in admiration. To Hackmuth, a man of genius. I could see them, those New York critics, crowding Hackmuth at his club. You certainly found a winner in that Bandini kid on the coast. A smile from Hackmuth, his eyes twinkling.

Six weeks, a few sweet hours every day, three and four and sometimes five delicious hours, with the pages piling up and all other desires asleep. I felt like a ghost walking the earth, a lover of man and beast alike, and wonderful waves of tenderness flooded me when I talked to people and mingled with them in the streets. God Almighty, dear God, good to me, gave me a sweet tongue, and these sad and lonely folk will hear me and they shall be happy. Thus the days passed. Dreamy, luminous days, and sometimes such great quiet joy came to me that I would turn out my lights and cry, and a strange desire to die would come to me.

Thus Bandini, writing a novel.

One night I answered a knock on my door, and there she stood.

'Camilla!'

She came in and sat down on the bed, something under her arm, a bundle of papers. She looked at my room: so this was where I lived. She had wondered about the place I lived. She got up and walked around, peering out of the window, walking around the room, beautiful girl, tall Camilla, warm dark hair, and I stood and watched her. But why had she come? She felt my question, and she sat on the bed and smiled at me.

'Arturo,' she said. 'Why do we fight all the time?'

I didn't know. I said something about temperaments, but she shook her head and crossed her knees, and a sense of her fine thighs being lifted lay heavily in my mind, thick suffocating sensation, warm lush desire to take them in my hands. Every move she made, the soft turn of her neck, the large breasts swelling under the smock, her fine hands upon the bed, the fingers spread out, these things disturbed me, a sweet painful heaviness dragging me into stupor. Then the sound of her voice, restrained, hinting of mockery, a voice that talked to my blood and bones. I remembered the peace of those past weeks, it seemed so unreal, it had been a hypnotism of my own creation, because this was being alive, this looking into the black eyes of Camilla, matching her scorn with hope and a brazen gloating.

She had come for something else beside a mere visit. Then I found out what it was.

'You remember Sammy?'

Of course.

'You didn't like him.'

'He was alright.'

'He's good, Arturo. You'd like him if you knew him better.'

'I suppose.'

'He liked you.'

I doubted that, after the scuffle in the parking lot. I remembered certain things about her relationship with Sammy, her smiles for him during work, her concern the night we took him home. 'You love that guy, don't you?'

'Not exactly.'

She took her eyes off my face and let them travel around the room.

'Yes you do.'

All at once I loathed her, because she had hurt me. This girl! She had torn up my sonnet by Dowson, she had shown my telegram to everybody in the Columbia Buffet. She had made a fool of me at the beach. She suspected my virility, and her suspicion was the same as the scorn in her eyes. I watched her face and lips and thought how it would be a pleasure to strike her, send my fist with all force against her nose and lips.

She spoke of Sammy again. Sammy had had all the rotten

breaks in life. He might have been somebody, except that his
health had always been poor.

'What's the matter with him?'

'T. B.,' she said.

'Tough.'

'He won't live long.'

I didn't give a damn.

'We all have to die some day.'

I thought of throwing her out, saying to her: if you've
come here to talk about that guy, you can get the hell out
because I'm not interested. I thought that would be delightful:
order her out, she so wonderfully beautiful in her own way,
and forced to leave because I ordered her out.

'Sammy's not here any more. He's gone.'

If she thought I was curious about his whereabouts, she
was badly mistaken. I put my feet on the desk and lit a
cigarette.

'How are all your other boy friends?' I said. It had bolted
out of me. I was sorry at once. I softened it with a smile. The
corners of her lips responded, but with an effort.

'I haven't any boy friends,' she said.

'Sure,' I said, touching it slightly with sarcasm. 'Sure, I
understand. Forgive an incautious remark.'

She was silent for a while. I made a pretence at whistling.
Then she spoke: 'Why are you so mean?' she said.

'Mean?' I said. 'My dear girl. I am equally fond of man
and beast alike. There is not the slightest drop of enmity
in my system. After all, you can't be mean and still be a
great writer.'

Her eyes mocked me. 'Are you a great writer?'

'That's something you'll never know.'

She bit her lower lip, pinched it between two white sharp teeth, looking towards the window and the door like a trapped animal, then smiled again. 'That's why I came to see you.'

She fumbled with the big envelopes on her lap, and it excited me, her own fingers touching her lap, lying there and moving against her own flesh. There were two envelopes. She opened one of them. It was a manuscript of some sort. I took it from her hands. It was a short story by Samuel Wiggins, General Delivery, San Juan, California. It was called 'Coldwater Gatling', and it began like this: 'Coldwater Gatling wasn't looking for trouble but you never can tell about those Arizona rustlers. Pack your cannon high on the hip and lay low when you seen one of them babies. The trouble with trouble was that trouble was looking for Coldwater Gatling. They don't like Texas Rangers down in Arizona, consequently Coldwater Gatling figured shoot first and find out who you killed afterwards. That's how they did it in the Lone Star State where men were men and women didn't mind cooking for hard-riding straight-shooting people like Coldwater Gatling, the toughest man in leather they had down there.'

That was the first paragraph.

'Hogwash,' I said.

'Please help him.'

He was going to die in a year, she said. He had left Los Angeles and gone to the edge of the Santa Ana desert. There he lived in a shack, writing feverishly. All his life he had wanted to write. Now, with such little time remaining, his chance had come.

'What's in it for me?' I said.

'But he's dying.'

'Who isn't?'

I opened the second manuscript. It was the same sort of stuff. I shook my head. 'It stinks.'

'I know,' she said. 'But couldn't you do something to it? He'll give you half the money.'

'I don't need money. I have an income of my own.'

She rose and stood before me, her hands on my shoulders. She lowered her face, her warm breath sweet in my nostrils, her eyes so large they reflected my head in them and I felt delirious and sick with desire. 'Would you do it for me?'

'For you?' I said. 'Well, for you – yes.'

She kissed me. Bandini, the stooge. Thick, warm kiss, for services about to be rendered. I pushed her away carefully. 'You don't have to kiss me. I'll do what I can.' But I had an idea or two of my own on the subject, and while she stood at the mirror and rouged her lips I looked at the address on the manuscripts. San Juan, California. 'I'll write him a letter about this stuff,' I said. She watched me through the mirror, paused with the lipstick in her hand. Her smile was mocking me. 'You don't have to do that,' she said. 'I could come back and pick them up and mail them myself.'

That was what she said, but you can't fool me, Camilla, because I can see your memories of that night at the beach written upon your scornful face, and do I hate you, oh God how I loathe you!

'Okay,' I said. 'I guess that would be best. You come back tomorrow night.'

She was sneering at me. Not her face, her lips, but from within her. 'What time shall I come?'

'What time are you through work?'

She turned around, snapped her purse shut, and looked at me. 'You know what time I'm through work,' she said.

I'll get you, Camilla. I'll get you yet.

'Come then,' I said.

She walked to the door, put her hands on the knob.

'Goodnight, Arturo.'

'I'll walk up to the lobby with you.'

'Don't be silly,' she said.

The door closed. I stood in the middle of the room and listened to her footsteps on the stairs. I could feel the whiteness of my face, the awful humiliation, and I got mad and I reached my hair with my fingers and howled out of my throat as I pulled at my hair, loathing her, beating my fists together, lurching around the room with arms clasped against myself, struggling with the hideous memory of her, choking her out of my consciousness, gasping with hatred.

But there were ways and means, and that sick man out in the desert was going to get his too. I'll get you, Sammy. I'll cut you to pieces, I'll make you wish you were dead and buried a long time ago. The pen is mightier than the sword, Sammy boy, but the pen of Arturo Bandini is mightier still. Because my time has come, Sir. And now you get yours.

I sat down and read his stories. I made notes on every line and sentence and paragraph of it. The writing was pretty terrible, a first effort, clumsy stuff, vague, jerky, absurd. Hour after hour I sat there consuming cigarettes and laughing wildly at Sammy's efforts, gloating over them, rubbing my hands together gleefully. Oh boy, would I lay him low! I jumped up and strutted around the room, shadow-boxing: take that, Sammy boy, and that, and how do you like this left hook, and how do you like this right cross, zingo, bingo, bang, biff, blooey!

I turned around and saw the crease on the bed where Camilla had been seated, the sensuous contour where her thighs and hips had sunk beneath the softness of the blue chenille bedspread. Then I forgot Sammy, and wild with longing I threw myself upon my knees before the spot and kissed it reverently.

'Camilla, I love you!'

And when I had worn the sensation to vaporous nothingness, I got up, disgusted with myself, black awful Arturo Bandini, black vile dog.

I sat down and grimly went to work on my letter of criticism to Sammy.

Dear Sammy,

That little whore was here tonight; you know, Sammy, the little Greaser dame with a wonderful figure and a mind for a moron. She presented me with certain alleged writings purportedly written by yourself. Furthermore she stated the man with the scythe is about to mow you under. Under ordinary circumstances I would call this a tragic situation. But having read the bile your manuscripts contain, let me speak for the world at large and say at once that your departure is everybody's good fortune. You can't write, Sammy. I suggest you concentrate on the business of putting your idiotic soul in order these last days before you leave a world that sighs with relief at your departure. I wish I could honestly say that I hate to see you go. I wish too that, like myself, you could endow posterity with something like a monument to your days upon this earth. But since this is so obviously impossible, let me urge you to be without bitterness in your final days. Destiny has indeed been unkind to you. Like the rest of the world, I suppose you too are glad that in a short time all will be finished, and the ink spot you have splattered will never be examined from a larger view. I speak for all sensible, civilized men when I urge you to burn this mass of literary manure and thereafter stay away from pen and ink. If you have a typewriter, the same holds true; because even the typing in this manuscript is a disgrace. If, however, you persist in your pitiful desire to write, by all means send me the pap you compose. I found at least you are amusing. Not deliberately, of course.

There it was, finished, devastating. I folded the manuscripts, placed the note with them inside a big envelope, sealed it, addressed it to Samuel Wiggins, General Delivery, San Juan, California, stamped it, and shoved it into my back pocket. Then I went upstairs and out of the lobby to the mailbox on the corner. It was a little after three o'clock of an incomparable morning. The blue and white of stars and sky were like desert colours, a gentleness so stirring I had to pause and wonder that it could be so lovely. Not a blade of the dirty palms stirred. Not a sound was to be heard.

All that was good in me thrilled in my heart at that moment, all that I hoped for in the profound, obscure meaning of my existence. Here was the endlessly mute placidity of nature, indifferent to the great city; here was the desert beneath these streets, around these streets, waiting for the city to die, to cover it with timeless sand once more. There came over me a terrifying sense of understanding about the meaning and the pathetic destiny of men. The desert was always there, a patient white animal, waiting for men to die, for civilizations to flicker and pass into the darkness. Then men seemed brave to me, and I was proud to be numbered among them. All the evil of the world seemed not evil at all, but inevitable and good and part of that endless struggle to keep the desert down.

I looked southward in the direction of the big stars, and I knew that in that direction lay the Santa Ana desert, that under the big stars in a shack lay a man like myself, who would probably be swallowed by the desert sooner than I, and in my hand I held an effort of his, an expression of his struggle against the implacable silence towards which he was being hurled. Murderer or bartender or writer, it didn't matter: his fate was the common fate of all, his finish my finish; and here tonight in this city of darkened windows were other millions like him and like me: as indistinguishable as dying blades of grass. Living was hard enough. Dying was a supreme task. And Sammy was soon to die.

I stood at the mailbox, my head against it, and grieved for Sammy, and for myself, and for all the living and the dead. Forgive me, Sammy! Forgive a fool! I walked back to my room and spent three hours writing the best criticism of his work I could possibly write. I didn't say that this was wrong or that was wrong. I kept saying, in my opinion this would be better if, and so forth, and so forth. I got to sleep about six o'clock, but it was a grateful, happy sleep. How wonderful I really was! A great, soft-spoken, gentle man, a lover of all things, man and beast alike.

Chapter Fifteen

I didn't see her again for a week. In the meantime I got a letter from Sammy, thanking me for the corrections. Sammy, her true love. He also sent some advice: how was I getting along with the Little Spick? She wasn't a bad dame, not bad at all when the lights were out, but the trouble with you, Mr Bandini, is that you don't know how to handle her. You're too nice to that girl. You don't understand Mexican women. They don't like to be treated like human beings. If you're nice to them, they walk all over you.

I worked on the book, pausing now and then to re-read his letter. I was reading it the night she came again. It was about midnight, and she walked in without knocking.

'Hello,' she said.

I said, 'Hello, Stupid.'

'Working?' she said.

'What does it look like?' I said.

'Mad?' she said.

'No,' I said. 'Just disgusted.'

'With me?'

'Naturally,' I said. 'Look at yourself.'

Under her jacket was the white smock. It was spotted, stained. One of her stockings was loose, wrinkled at the ankles. Her face seemed tired, some of the lip rouge having vanished. The coat she wore was dotted with lint and dust. She was perched on cheap high heels.

'You try so hard to be an American,' I said. 'Why do you do that? Take a look at yourself.'

She went to the mirror, studied herself gravely. 'I'm tired,' she said. 'We were busy tonight.'

'It's those shoes,' I said. 'You ought to wear what your feet were meant to wear – huaraches. And all that paint on your face. You look awful – a cheap imitation of an American. You look frowsy. If I were a Mexican I'd knock your head off. You're a disgrace to your people.'

'Who are you to talk like that?' she said. 'I'm just as much an American as you are. Why, you're not an American at all. Look at your skin. You're dark like Eyetalians. And your eyes, they're black.'

'Brown,' I said.

'They're not either. They're black. Look at your hair. Black.'

'Brown,' I said.

She took off her coat, threw herself on the bed and stuck a cigarette in her mouth. She began to fumble and search for a match. There was a pack beside me on the desk. She waited for me to hand them to her.

'You're not crippled,' I said. 'Get them yourself.'

She lit a cigarette and smoked in silence, her stare at the ceiling, smoke tumbling from her nostrils in quiet agitation. It was foggy outside. Far away came the sound of a police siren.

'Thinking of Sammy?' I said.

'Maybe.'

'You don't have to think of him here. You can always leave, you know.'

She snubbed out the cigarette, twisted and gutted it and her words had the same effect. 'Jesus, you're nasty,' she said. 'You must be awfully unhappy.'

'You're crazy.'

She lay with her legs crossed. The tops of her rolled stockings and an inch or two of dark flesh showed where the white smock ended. Her hair spilled over the pillow like a bottle of overturned ink. She lay on her side, watching me out of the depth of the pillow. She smiled. She lifted her hand and wagged her finger at me.

'Come here, Arturo,' she said. It was a warm voice.

I waved my hand.

'No thanks. I'm comfortable.'

For five minutes she watched me stare through the window. I might have touched her, held her in my arms; yes, Arturo, it was only a matter of getting out of the chair and stretching out beside her, but there was the night at the beach and the sonnet on the floor and the telegram of love and I remembered them like nightmares filling the room.

'Scared?' she said.

'Of you?' I laughed.

'You are,' she said.

'No I'm not.'

She opened her arms and all of her seemed to open to me, but it only closed me deeper into myself, carrying with me the image of her at that time, how lush and soft she was.

'Look,' I said. 'I'm busy. Look.' I patted the pile of manuscript beside the typewriter.

'You're afraid, too.'

'Of what?'

'Me.'

'Pooh.'

Silence.

'There's something wrong with you,' she said.

'What?'

'You're queer.'

I got up and stood over her.

'That's a lie,' I said.

We lay there. She was forcing it with her scorn, the kiss she gave me, the hard curl of her lips, the mockery of her eyes, until I was like a man made of wood and there was no feeling within me except terror and a fear of her, a sense that her beauty was too much, that she was so much more beautiful than I, deeper rooted than I. She made me a stranger unto myself, she was all of those calm nights and tall eucalyptus trees, the desert stars, that land and sky, that fog outside, and I had come there with no purpose save to be a mere writer, to get money, to make a name for myself and all that piffle. She was so much finer than I, so much more honest, that I was sick of myself and I could not look at her warm eyes, I suppressed the shiver brought on by her brown arms around my neck and the long fingers in my hair. I did not kiss her. She kissed me, author of *The Little Dog Laughed*. Then she took my wrist with her two hands. She pressed her lips into the palm of my hand. She placed my hand upon her bosom between her breasts. She turned her lips towards my face and waited. And Arturo Bandini, the great author dipped deep into his colourful imagination, romantic Arturo Bandini, just chock-full of clever phrases, and he said, weakly, kittenishly, 'Hello.'

'Hello?' she answered, making a question of it. 'Hello?' And she laughed. 'Well, how are you?'

Oh that Arturo! That spinner of tales.

'Swell,' he said.

And now what? Where was the desire and the passion? She would go away in a little while and then it would come. But my God, Arturo. You can't *do* that! Recall your marvellous predecessors! Measure to your standards. I felt her groping hands, and I groped to discourage them, to hold them in passionate fear. Once more she kissed me. She might have given her lips to a cold boiled ham. I was miserable.

She pushed me away.

'Get away,' she said. 'Let me go.'

The disgust, the terror and humiliation burned in me, and I would not let go. I clung to her, forced the cold of my mouth against her warmth, and she fought with me to break away, and I lay there holding her, my face in her shoulder, ashamed to show it. Then I felt her scorn grow to hatred as she struggled, and it was then that I wanted her, held her and pleaded with her, and with each wrench of her black rage my desire mounted and I was happy, saying hooray for Arturo, joy and strength, strength through joy, the delicious sense of it, the rapturous self-satisfaction, the delight to know that I could possess her now if I wished. But I did not wish it, for I had had my love. Dazzled I had been by the power and joy of Arturo Bandini. I released her, took my hand from her mouth, and jumped off the bed.

She sat there, the white of saliva at the ends of her mouth, her teeth gritted, her hands pulling at her long hair, her face fighting off a scream, but it didn't matter; she could scream if she liked, for Arturo Bandini wasn't queer, there was nothing at all wrong with Arturo Bandini; why, he had a passion like six men, that boy, he had felt it coming to the surface: some guy, mighty writer, mighty lover; right with the world, right with his prose.

I watched her straighten her dress, watched her stand up, panting and frightened, and go to the mirror and look at herself, as though to make sure it was really herself.

'You're no good,' she said.

I sat down and chewed on a fingernail.

'I thought you were something else,' she said. 'I hate rough stuff.'

Rough stuff: pooh. What did it matter what she thought? The big thing was proved: I could have had her, and whatever she thought was not important. I was something else besides a great writer: I was no longer afraid of her: I could look into her face as a man should look into the face of a woman. She left without speaking again. I sat in a dream of delight, an orgy of comfortable confidence: the world was so big, so full of things I could master. Ah, Los Angeles! Dust and fog of your lonely streets, I am no longer lonely. Just you wait, all of you ghosts of this room, just you wait, because it will happen yet, and that Camilla, she can have her Sammy in the desert, with his cheap short stories and stinking prose, but wait until she has a taste of me, because it will happen, as sure as there's a God in heaven.

I don't remember. Maybe a week passed, maybe two weeks. I knew she would return. I did not wait. I lived my life. I wrote a few pages. I read a few books. I was serene: she would come back. It would be at night. I never thought of her as a thing to be considered by daylight. The many times I had seen her, none had been in the day. I expected her like I expected the moon.

She did come. This time I heard pebbles plinking off my windowpane. I opened the window wide, and there she stood on the hillside, a sweater over her white apron. Her mouth was open slightly as she gazed up at me.

'What you doing?' she said.

'Just sitting here.'

'You mad at me?'

'No. You mad at me?'

She laughed. 'A little.'

'Why?'

'You're mean.'

We went for a ride. She asked if I knew anything about guns. I didn't. We drove to a shooting gallery on Main Street. She was an expert shot. She knew the proprietor, a kid in a leather jacket. I couldn't hit anything, not even the target in the middle. It was her money, and she was disgusted with me. She could hold a revolver under her armpit and hit the bull's eye of the big target. I took about fifty shots, and missed every time. Then she tried to show me how to hold the gun. I jerked it away from her, flung the barrel recklessly in all directions. The kid in the leather jacket ducked under the counter. 'Be careful!' he yelled. 'Look out!'

Her disgust became humiliation. She dug a fifty cent piece out of her pocketful of tips. 'Try again,' she said. 'And this time, don't miss, or I won't pay for it.' I didn't have any money with me. I put the gun down on the counter and refused to shoot again. 'To hell with it,' I said.

'He's a sissy, Tim,' she said. 'All he can do is write poetry.'

Tim obviously liked only people who knew how to shoot a gun. He looked at me with distaste, saying nothing. I picked up a repeating Winchester rifle, took aim, and started pumping lead. The big target sixty feet away, three feet above the ground on a post, showed no sign of being hit. A bell was supposed to ring when the bull's eye was hit. Not a sound. I emptied the gun, sniffed the tart stench of powder, and made a face. Tim and Camilla laughed at the sissy. By now a crowd had gathered on the sidewalk. They all shared Camilla's disgust, for it was a contagious thing, and I felt it too. She turned, saw the crowd, and blushed. She was ashamed of me, annoyed and mortified. Out of the side of her mouth she whispered to me that we should leave. She broke through the crowd, walking fast, six feet ahead of me. I followed leisurely. Ho ho, and what did I care if I couldn't shoot a damned gun, and what did I care if those mugs had laughed, and that she had laughed, for which one of them, the boobish swine, the lousy grinning Main Street dopes, which one of them could compose a story like *The Long Lost Hills*? Not a one of them! And so to hell with their scorn.

The car was parked in front of a café. When I reached it she had already started the engine. I got in but she did not wait for me to get seated. Still sneering, she looked at me quickly, and let out the clutch. I was thrown against the seat, then against the windshield. We were jammed between two other cars. She banged into one, and then into the other, her way of letting me know what a fool I had been. When we finally broke from the kerb and swung into the street, I sighed and sat back.

'Thank God for that,' I said.

'You dry up!' she said.

'Look,' I said. 'If you have to feel this way, why don't you just let me out. I can walk.'

She immediately put her foot on the throttle. We raced through the downtown streets. I sat hanging on and thought of jumping. Then we reached a section where the traffic was sparse. We were two miles from Bunker Hill, in the east part of town, in the section of factories and breweries. She slowed the car down and pulled up to the kerb. We were alongside of a low black fence. Beyond it were stacks of steel pipe.

'Why here?' I said.

'You wanted to walk,' she said. 'Get out and walk.'

'I feel like riding again.'

'Get out,' she said. 'I mean it, too. Anybody that can't shoot any better than that! Go on, get out!'

I reached for my cigarettes, offered her one.

'Let's talk this over,' I said.

She slapped the pack of cigarettes out of my hand, knocked them to the floor, and glared at me defiantly. 'I hate you,' she said. 'God, how I hate you!'

As I picked up the cigarettes the night and the deserted factory district quivered with her loathing. I understood it. She did not hate Arturo Bandini, not really. She hated the fact that he did not meet her standard. She wanted to love him, but she couldn't. She wanted him like Sammy: quiet, taciturn, grim, a good shot with a rifle, a good bartender who accepted her as a waitress and nothing else. I got out of the car, grinning, because I knew that would hurt her.

'Good night,' I said. 'It's a fine night. I don't mind walking.'

'I hope you never make it,' she said. 'I hope they find you dead in the gutter in the morning.'

'I'll see what I can do,' I said.

As she drove away a sob came from her throat, a cry of pain. One thing was certain: Arturo Bandini was not good for Camilla Lopez.

Chapter Sixteen

The good days, the fat days, page upon page of manuscript; prosperous days, something to say, the story of Vera Rivken, and the pages mounted and I was happy. Fabulous days, the rent paid, still fifty dollars in my wallet, nothing to do all day and night but write and think of writing: ah, such sweet days, to see it grow, to worry for it, myself, my book, my words, maybe important, maybe timeless, but mine nevertheless, the indomitable Arturo Bandini, already deep into his first novel.

So an evening comes, and what to do with it, my soul so cool from the bath of words, my feet so solid upon the earth, and what are the others doing, the rest of the people of the world? I will go sit and look at her, Camilla Lopez.

It was done. It was like old times, our eyes springing at one another. But she was changed, she was thinner, and her face was unhealthy, with two eruptions at each end of her mouth. Polite smiles. I tipped her and she thanked me. I fed the phonograph nickels, playing her favourite tunes. She wasn't dancing at her work, and she didn't look at me often the way she used to. Maybe it was Sammy: maybe she missed the guy.

I asked her, 'How is he?'

A shrug: 'Alright, I guess.'

'Don't you see him?'

'Oh, sure.'

'You don't look well.'

'I feel alright.'

I got up. 'Well, I gotta go. Just dropped in to see how you were getting along.'

'It was nice of you.'

'Not at all. Why don't you come and see me?'

She smiled. 'I might, some night.'

Dear Camilla, you did come finally. You threw pebbles at the window, and I pulled you into the room, smelled the whiskey on your breath, and puzzled while you sat slightly drunk at my typewriter, giggling while you played with the keyboard. Then you turned to look at me, and I saw your face clearly under the light, the swollen lower lip, the purple and black smudge around your left eye.

'Who hit you?' I said. And you answered, 'Automobile accident.' And I said, 'Was Sammy driving the other car?' And you wept, drunk and heartbroken. I could touch you then and not fuss with desire. I could lie beside you on the bed and hold you in my arms and hear you say that Sammy hated you, that you drove out to the desert after work, and that he slugged you twice for waking him up at three in the morning.

I said. 'But why see him?'

'Because I'm in love with him.'

You got a bottle from your purse and we drank it up; first your turn, then mine. When the bottle was empty I went down to the drugstore and bought another, a big bottle. All night we wept and we drank, and drunk I could say the things bubbling in my heart, all those swell words, all the clever similes, because you were crying for the other guy and you didn't hear a word I said, but I heard them myself, and Arturo Bandini was pretty good that night, because he was talking to his true love, and it wasn't you, and it wasn't Vera Rivken either, it was just his true love. But I said some swell things that night, Camilla. Kneeling beside you on the bed, I held your hand and I said, 'Ah Camilla, you lost girl! Open your long fingers and give me back my tired soul! Kiss me with your mouth because I hunger for the bread of a Mexican hill. Breathe the fragrance of lost cities into fevered nostrils, and let me die here, my hand upon the soft contour of your throat, so like the whiteness of some half-forgotten southern shore. Take the longing in these restless eyes and feed it to lonely swallows cruising an autumn cornfield, because I love you Camilla, and your name is sacred like that of some brave princess who died with a smile for a love that was never returned.'

I was drunk that night, Camilla, drunk on seventy-eight cent whiskey, and you were drunk on whiskey and grief. I remember that after turning off the lights, naked except for one shoe that baffled me, I held you in my arms and slept, at peace in the midst of your sobs, yet annoyed when the hot tears from your eyes dripped upon my lips and I tasted their saltiness and thought about that Sammy and his hideous manuscript. That *he* should strike you! That fool. Even his punctuation was bad.

When we woke up it was morning and we were both nauseated, and your swollen lip was more grotesque than ever, and your black eye was now green. You got up, staggered to the wash-stand and washed your face. I heard you groan. I watched you dress. I felt your kiss on my forehead as you said goodbye, and that nauseated me too. Then you climbed out the window and I heard you stagger up the hillside, the grass swishing and the little twigs breaking under your uncertain feet.

I am trying to remember it chronologically. Winter or spring or summer, they were days without change. Good for the night, thanks for the darkness, otherwise we would not have known that one day ended and another began. I had 240 pages done and the end was in sight. The rest was a cruise on smooth water. Then off to Hackmuth it would go, tra la, and the agony would begin.

It was about that time that we went to Terminal Island, Camilla and I. A man-made island, that place, a long finger of earth pointing at Catalina. Earth and canneries and the smell of fish, brown houses full of Japanese children, stretches of white sand with wide black pavements running up and down, and the Japanese kids playing football in the streets. She was irritable, she had been drinking too much, and her eyes had that stark old woman's look of a chicken. We parked the car in the broad street and walked a hundred yards to the beach. There were rocks at the water's edge, jagged stones swarming with crabs. The crabs were having a tough time of it, because the sea gulls were after them, and the sea gulls screeched and clawed and fought among themselves. We sat on the sand and watched them, and Camilla said they were so beautiful, those gulls.

'I hate them,' I said.

'You!' she said. 'You hate everything.'

'Look at them,' I said. 'Why do they pick on those poor crabs? The crabs ain't doing anything. Then why in the hell do they mob them like that?'

'Crabs,' she said. 'Ugh.'

'I hate a sea gull,' I said. 'They'll eat anything, the deader the better.'

'For God's sake shut up for a change. You always spoil everything. What do I care what they eat?'

In the street the little Japanese kids were having a big football game. They were all youngsters under twelve. One of them was a pretty good passer. I turned my back on the sea and watched the game. The good passer had flung another into the arms of one of his teammates. I got interested and sat up.

'Watch the sea,' Camilla said. 'You're supposed to admire beautiful things, you writer.'

'He throws a beautiful pass,' I said.

The swelling had gone from her lips, but her eye was still discoloured. 'I used to come here all the time,' she said. 'Almost every night.'

'With that other writer,' I said. 'That really great writer, that Sammy the genius.'

'He liked it here.'

'He's a great writer, alright. That story he wrote over your left eye is a masterpiece.'

'He doesn't talk his guts out like you. He knows when to be quiet.'

'The stupe.'

A fight was brewing between us. I decided to avoid it. I got up and walked towards the kids in the street. She asked where I was going. 'I'm going to get in the game,' I said.

She was outraged. 'With them?' she said. 'Those Japs?' I ploughed through the sand.

'Remember what happened the other night!' she said.

I turned around. 'What?'

'Remember how you walked home?'

'That suits me,' I said. 'The bus is safer.'

The kids wouldn't let me play because the sides were evenly numbered, but they let me referee for a while. Then the good passer's team got so far ahead that a change was necessary, so I played on the opposite team. Everybody on our team wanted to be quarterback, and great confusion resulted. They made me play centre, and I hated it because I was ineligible to receive passes. Finally the captain of our team asked me if I knew how to pass, and he gave me a chance in the tailback spot. I completed the pass. It was fun after that. Camilla left almost immediately. We played until darkness, and they beat us, but it was close. I took the bus back to Los Angeles.

Making resolutions not to see her again was useless. I didn't know from one day to the next. There was the night two days after she left me stranded at Terminal Island. I had been to a picture show. It was after midnight when I went down the old stairway to my room. The door was locked, and from the inside. As I turned the knob I heard her call. 'Just a minute. It's me, Arturo.'

It was a long minute, five times as long as usual. I could hear her scurrying about within the room. I heard the closet door slam, heard the window being thrown open. I fumbled with the doorknob once more. She opened the door and stood there, breathless, her bosom rising and falling. Her eyes were points of black flame, her cheeks were full of blood, and she seemed alive with intense joy. I stood in a kind of fear at the change, the sudden widening and closing of her lashes, the quick wet smile, the teeth so alive and stringy with bubbled saliva.

I said, 'What's the idea?'

She threw her arms around me. She kissed me with a passion I knew was not genuine. She barred my entrance by a flourish of affection. She was hiding something from me, keeping me out of my own room as long as she could. Over her shoulder I looked around. I saw the bed with the mark of a head's indentation upon the pillow. Her coat was flung over the chair, and the dresser was strewn with small combs and bobby pins. That was alright. Everything seemed in order except the two small red mats at the bedside. They had been moved, that was plain to me, because I liked them in their regular place, where my feet could touch them when I got out of bed in the morning.

I pulled her arms away and looked towards the closet door. Suddenly she began to pant excitedly as she backed to the door, standing against it, her arms spread to protect it. 'Don't open it, Arturo,' she pleaded. 'Please!'

'What the hell is all this?' I said.

She shivered. She wet her lips and swallowed, her eyes filled with tears and she both smiled and wept. 'I'll tell you sometime,' she said. 'But please don't go in there now, Arturo. You mustn't. Oh, you mustn't. Please!'

'Who's in there?'

'Nobody,' she almost shouted. 'Not a soul. That isn't it, Arturo. Nobody's been here. But please! Please don't open it now. Oh please!'

She came towards me, almost stalking, her arms out in an embrace that was yet a protection against my attack on the closet door. She opened her lips and kissed me with peculiar fervour, a passionate coldness, a voluptuous indifference. I didn't like it. Some part of her was betraying some other part, but I could not find it. I sat on the bed and watched her as she stood between me and that closet door. She was trying so hard to conceal a cynical elation. She was like one who is forced to hide his drunkenness, but the elation was there, impossible to conceal.

'You're drunk, Camilla. You shouldn't drink so much.'

The eagerness with which she acknowledged that indeed she was drunk made me immediately suspicious. There she stood, nodding her head like a spoiled child, a coy smiling admission, the pouted lips, the look out of downcast eyes. I got up and kissed her. She was drunk, but she was not drunk on whiskey or alcohol because her breath was too sweet for that. I pulled her down on the bed beside me. Her ecstasy swept across her eyes, wave after wave of it, the passionate languor of her arms and fingers searched my throat. She crooned into my hair, her lips against my head.

'If you were only him,' she whispered. Suddenly she screamed, a piercing shriek that clawed the walls of the room. 'Why can't you be him! Oh Jesus Christ, why can't you?' She began to beat me with her fists, pounding my head with rights and lefts, screaming and scratching in an outburst of madness against the destiny that did not make me her Sammy. I grabbed her wrists, yelled at her to be quiet. I pinned her arms and clamped my hand over her shrieking mouth. She looked out at me with bloated, protruding eyes, struggling for breath. 'Not until you promise to keep quiet,'

I said. She nodded and I let go. I went to the door and listened for footsteps. She lay on the bed, face down, weeping. I tiptoed towards the closet door. Instinct must have warned her. She swung around on the bed, her face soggy with tears, her eyes like crushed grapes.

'You open that door and I'll scream,' she said. 'I'll scream and scream.'

I didn't want that. I shrugged. She resumed her face down position and wept again. In a little while she would cry it off; then I could send her home. But it didn't happen that way. After a half hour she was still crying. I bent over and touched her hair. 'What is it you want, Camilla?'

'Him,' she sobbed. 'I want to go see him.'

'Tonight?' I said. 'My God, it's a hundred and fifty miles.'

She didn't care if it was a thousand miles, a million, she wanted to see him tonight. I told her to go ahead; that was her affair; she had a car, she could drive there in five hours.

'I want you to come with me,' she sobbed. 'He doesn't like me. He likes you, though.'

'Not me,' I said. 'I'm going to bed.'

She pleaded with me. She fell on her knees before me, clung to my legs and looked up at me. She loved him so much, surely a great writer like myself understood what it was to love like that; surely I knew why she couldn't go out there alone; and she touched the injured eye. Sammy wouldn't drive her off if I were to come with her. He'd be grateful that she had brought me, and then Sammy and I could talk, because there was so much I could show him about writing, and he would be so grateful to me, and to her. I looked down at her, gritted my teeth, and tried to resist her arguments; but when she put it that way it was too much for me, and when I agreed to go I was crying with her. I helped her to her feet, dried her eyes, smoothed the hair from her face, and felt responsible for her. We tiptoed up the stairs and through the lobby to the street, where her car was parked.

We drove south and slightly east, each of us taking a turn at the wheel. By dawn we were in a land of grey desolation, of cactus and sagebrush and Joshua trees, a desert where the sand was scarce and the whole vast plain was pimpled with tumbled rocks and scarred by stumpy little hills. Then we turned off the main highway and entered a wagon trail clogged with boulders and rarely used. The road rose and fell to the rhythm of the listless hills. It was daylight when we came to a region of canyons and steep gulches, twenty miles in the interior of the Mojave Desert. There below us was where Sammy lived, and Camilla pointed to a squat adobe shack planted at the bottom of three sharp hills. It was at the very edge of a sandy plain. To the east the plain spread away infinitely.

We were both tired, hammered to exhaustion by the bouncing Ford. It was very cold at that hour. We had to park two hundred yards from the house and take a stony path to its door. I led the way. At the door I paused. Inside I could hear a man snoring heavily. Camilla hung back, her arms folded against the sharp cold. I knocked and got a groan in response. I knocked again, and then I heard Sammy's voice. 'If that's you, you little Spick, I'll kick your goddamn teeth out.'

He opened the door and I saw a face clutched in the persistent fingers of sleep, the eyes grey and dazed, the hair in ruins across his forehead. 'Hello, Sammy.'

'Oh,' he said. 'I thought it was her.'

'She's here,' I said.

'Tell her to screw outa' here. I don't want her around.'

She had retreated to a place against the wall of the hut, and I looked at her and saw her smiling away her embarrassment. The three of us were very cold, our jaws chattering. Sammy opened the door wider. 'You can come in,' he said. 'But not her.'

I stepped inside. It was almost pitch dark, smelling of old underwear and the sleep of a sick body. A feeble light came from a crack in the window covered by a slice of sacking. Before I could stop him, Sammy had bolted the door.

He stood in long underwear. The floor was of dirt, dry and sandy and cold. He yanked the sacking from the window and the early light tumbled through. Vapors spilled from our mouths in the cold air. 'Let her in, Sammy,' I said. 'What the hell.'

'Not that bitch,' he said.

He stood in long underwear, the knees and elbows capped with the blackness of dirt. He was tall, gaunt, a cadaver of a man, tanned almost to blackness. He padded across the hut to a coal stove and began making a fire. His voice changed and became soft when he spoke. 'Wrote another story last week,' he said. 'Think I got a good one this time. Like you to see it.'

'Sure,' I said. 'But hell, Sammy. She's a friend of mine.'

'Bah,' he said. 'She's no good. Crazy as hell. Cause you nothing but trouble.'

'Let her in anyway. It's cold out there.'

He opened the door and pushed his head out.

'Hey, you!'

I heard the girl sob, heard her try to compose herself. 'Yes, Sammy.'

'Don't stand out there like a fool,' he said. 'You coming in or ain't you?'

She entered like a frightened deer while he went back to the stove. 'Thought I told you I didn't want you hanging around here no more,' he said.

'I brought him,' she said. 'Arturo. He wanted to talk to you about writing. Didn't you, Arturo?'

'That's right.'

She was like a stranger to me. All the fight and glory of her was drained like blood from her veins. She stood off by herself, a creature without spirit or will, her shoulder blades humped, her head drooping as though too heavy for her neck.

'You,' Sammy said to her. 'Go get some wood, you.'

'I'll go,' I said.

'Let her go,' he said. 'She knows where it is.'

I watched her slink out the door. In a while she came back, her arms loaded. She dumped the sticks into a box beside the stove, and without speaking she fed the flames, a stick at a time. Sammy sat on a box across the room, pulling on his socks. He talked incessantly about his stories, a continuous flow of chatter. Camilla stood dismally beside the stove.

'You,' he said. 'Make some coffee.'

She did as she was told, serving us coffee out of tin cups. Sammy, fresh from sleep, was full of enthusiasm and curiosity. We sat at the fire, and I was tired and sleepy, and the hot fire toyed with my heavy lids. Behind us and all around us, Camilla worked. She swept the place out, made up the bed, washed dishes, hung up stray garments and kept up an incessant activity. The more Sammy talked, the more cordial and personal he became. He was interested in the financial side of writing more than in writing itself. How much did this magazine pay, and how much did that one pay, and he was convinced that only by favouritism were stories sold. You had to have a cousin or a brother or somebody like that in an editor's office before they took one of your stories. It was useless to try to dissuade him, and I didn't try, because I knew that his kind of rationalizing was necessary in view of his sheer inability to write well.

Camilla cooked breakfast for us, and we ate from plates on our laps. The fare was fried corn meal and bacon and eggs. Sammy ate with the peculiar robustness of unhealthy people. After the meal, Camilla gathered the tin plates and washed them. Then she had her own breakfast, seated in a far corner, quiet except for the sound of her fork against the tin plate. All that long morning Sammy talked. Sammy really didn't need any advice about writing. Vaguely through the fog of semi-slumber I heard him telling me how it should and shouldn't be done. But I was so tired. I begged to be excused. He led me outside to an arbour of palm branches. Now the air was warm and the sun was high. I lay in the hammock and fell asleep, and the last thing I remember was the sight of Camilla bent over a wash tub filled with dark water and several pairs of underwear and overalls.

Six hours later she woke me to tell me that it was two o'clock, and that we had to start back. She was due at the Columbia Buffet at seven. I asked her if she had slept. She shook her head negatively. Her face was a manuscript of misery and exhaustion. I got off the hammock and stood up in the hot desert air. My clothes were soaked in perspiration, but I was rested and refreshed.

'Where's the genius?' I said.

She nodded towards the hut. I walked towards the door, ducking under a long heavy clothesline sagging with clean, dry garments. 'You did all of that?' I asked. She smiled. 'It was fun.'

Deep snores came from the hut. I peeked inside. On the bunk lay Sammy, half naked, his mouth wide open, his arms and legs spread apart. I tiptoed away. 'Now's our chance,' I said. 'Let's go.'

She entered the hut and quietly walked to where Sammy lay. From the door I watched her lean over him, study his face and body. Then she bent down, her face near his, as if to kiss him. At that moment he awoke and their eyes met. He said: 'Get out of here.'

She turned and walked out. We drove back to Los Angeles in complete silence. Even when she let me out at the Alta Loma Hotel, even then we did not speak, but she smiled her thanks and I smiled my sympathy, and she drove away. Already it was dark, a smudge of the pink sunset fading in the west. I went down to my room, yawned, and threw myself on the bed. Lying there I suddenly remembered the clothes closet. I got up and opened the closet door. Everything seemed as it should, my suits hanging from hooks, my suitcases on the top shelf. But there was no light in the closet. I struck a match and looked down at the floor. In the corner was a burned matchstick and a score of grains of brown stuff, like coarsely ground coffee. I pressed my finger into the stuff and then tasted it on the end of my tongue. I knew what that was: it was marijuana. I was sure of it, because Benny Cohen had once showed me the stuff to warn me against it. So that was why she had been in here. You had to have an air-tight room to smoke marijuana. That explained why the two rugs had been moved: she had used them to cover the crack under the door.

Camilla was a hophead. I sniffed the closet air, put my nostrils against the garments hanging there. The smell was that of burned cornsilk. Camilla, the hophead.

It was none of my business, but she was Camilla; she had tricked me and scorned me, and she loved somebody else, but she *was* so beautiful and I needed her so, and I decided to make it my business. I was waiting in her car at eleven that night.

'So you're a hophead,' I said.

'Once in a while,' she said. 'When I'm tired.'

'You cut it out,' I said.

'It's not a habit,' she said.

'Cut it out anyway.'

She shrugged. 'It doesn't bother me.'

'Promise me you'll quit.'

She made a cross over her heart. 'Cross my heart and hope to die,' but she was talking to Arturo now, and not to Sammy. I knew she would not keep the promise. She started the car and drove down Broadway to Eighth, then south towards Central Avenue. 'Where we going?' I said.

'Wait and see.'

We drove into the Los Angeles Black Belt, Central Avenue, night clubs, abandoned apartment houses, broken-down business houses, the forlorn street of poverty for the Negro and swank for the whites. We stopped under the marquee of a night spot called the Club Cuba. Camilla knew the doorman, a giant in a blue uniform with gold buttons. 'Business,' she said. He grinned, signalled someone to take his place, and jumped on the running board. It was done like a routine procedure, as though it had been done before.

She drove around the corner and continued for two streets, until we came to an alley. She turned down the alley, switched off the lights and steered carefully into pitch blackness. We came to some kind of opening and killed the engine. The big Negro jumped off the running board and snapped on a flashlight, motioning us to follow. 'May I ask just what the hell this is all about?' I said.

We entered a door. The Negro took the lead. He held Camilla's hand, and she held mine. We walked down a long corridor. It was carpetless, a hardwood floor. Far away like frightened birds, the echo of our feet floated through the upper floors. We climbed three flights of stairs and proceeded the length of another hall. At the end was a door. The Negro opened it. Inside was complete darkness. We entered. The room reeked with smoke that could not be seen, and yet it burned like an eyewash. The smoke choked my throat, leaped for my nostrils. In the darkness I swallowed for breath. Then the Negro flashed on his light.

The beam travelled around the room, a small room. Everywhere were bodies, the bodies of Negroes, men and women, perhaps a score of them, lying on the floor and across a bed that was only a mattress on springs. I could see their eyes, wide and grey and oyster-like as the flashlight hit them, and gradually I accustomed myself to the burning smoke and saw tiny red points of light everywhere, for they were all smoking marijuana, quietly in the darkness, and the pungency stabbed my lungs. The big Negro cleared the bed of its occupants, flung them like so many sacks of grain to the floor, and the flash spot revealed him digging something from a slot in the mattress. It was a Prince Albert tobacco can. He opened the door, and we followed him down the stairs and through the same darkness to the car. He handed the can to Camilla, and she gave him two dollars. We drove him back to his doorman's job, and then we continued down Central Avenue to metropolitan Los Angeles.

I was speechless. We drove to her place on Temple Street. It was a sick building, a frame place diseased and dying from the sun. She lived in an apartment. There was a Murphy bed, a radio, and dirty blue overstuffed furniture. The carpeted floor was littered with crumbs and dirt, and in the corner, sprawled out like one naked, lay a movie magazine. There were kewpie dolls standing about, souvenirs of gaudy nights at beach resorts. There was a bicycle in the corner, the flat tyres attesting to long disuse. There was a fishing pole in one corner with tangled hooks and line, and there was a shotgun in the other corner, dusty. There was a baseball bat under the divan, and there was a bible lodged between the cushions of the overstuffed chair. The bed was down, and the sheets were not clean. There was a reproduction of the Blue Boy on one wall and a print of an Indian Brave saluting the sky on another.

I walked into the kitchen, smelled the garbage in the sink, saw the greasy frying pans on the stove. I opened the Frigidaire and it was empty save for a can of condensed milk and a cube of butter. The icebox door would not close, and that seemed as it should be. I looked into the closet behind the Murphy bed and there were lots of clothes and lots of clothes-hooks, but all the clothes were on the floor, except a straw hat, and that hung alone, ridiculous up there by itself.

So this is where she lived! I smelled it, touched it with my fingers, walked through it with my feet. It was as I had imagined. This was her home. Blindfolded I could have acknowledged the place, for her odour possessed it, her fevered, lost existence proclaimed it as part of a hopeless scheme. An apartment on Temple Street, an apartment in Los Angeles. She belonged to the rolling hills, the wide deserts, the high mountains, she would ruin any apartment, she would lay havoc upon any such little prison as this. It was so, ever in my imagination, ever a part of my scheming and thinking about her. This was her home, her ruin, her scattered dream.

She threw off her coat and flung herself on the divan. I watched her stare dismally at the ugly carpet. Sitting in the overstuffed chair, I puffed a cigarette and let my eyes wander the profile of her curved back and hips. The dark corridor of that Central Avenue Hotel, the sinister Negro, the black room and the hopheads, and now the girl who loved a man who hated her. It was all of the same cloth, perverse, drugged in fascinating ugliness. Midnight on Temple Street, a can of marijuana between us. She lay there, her long fingers dangling to the carpet, waiting, listless, tired.

'Have you ever tried it?' she asked.

'Not me,' I said.

'Once won't hurt you.'

'Not me.'

She sat up, fumbled for the can of marijuana in her purse. She drew out a packet of cigarette papers. She poured a paperful, rolled it, licked it, pinched the ends, and handed it to me. I took it, and yet I said, 'Not me.'

She rolled one for herself. Then she arose and closed the windows, clamped them tightly by their latches. She dragged a blanket off the bed and laid it against the crack of the door. She looked around carefully. She looked at me. She smiled. 'Everybody acts different,' she said. 'Maybe you'll feel sad, and cry.'

'Not me,' I said.

She lit hers, held the match for mine.

'I shouldn't be doing this,' I said.

'Inhale,' she said. 'Then hold it. Hold it a long time. Until it hurts. Then let it out.'

'This is bad business,' I said.

I inhaled it. I held it. I held it a long time, until it hurt. Then I let it out. She lay back against the divan and did the same thing. 'Sometimes it takes two of them,' she said.

'It won't affect me,' I said.

We smoked them down until they burned our fingertips. Then I rolled two more. In the middle of the second it began to come, the floating, the wafting away from the earth, the joy and triumph of a man over space, the extraordinary sense of power. I laughed and inhaled again. She lay there, the cold languor of the night before upon her face, the cynical passion. But I was beyond the room, beyond the limits of my flesh, floating in a land of bright moons and blinking stars. I was invincible. I was not myself, I had never been that fellow with his grim happiness, his strange bravery. A lamp on the table beside me, and I picked it up and looked at it, and dropped it to the floor. It broke into many pieces. I laughed. She heard the noise, saw the ruin, and laughed too.

'What's funny?' I said.

She laughed again. I got up, crossed the room, and took

her in my arms. They felt terribly strong and she panted at their crush and desire.

I watched her stand and take off her clothes, and somewhere out of an earthly past I remembered having seen that face of hers before, that obedience and fear, and I remembered a hut and Sammy telling her to go out and get some wood. It was as I knew it was bound to be sooner or later. She crept into my arms and I laughed at her tears.

When it was all gone, the dream of floating towards bursting stars, and the flesh returned to hold my blood in its prosaic channels, when the room returned, the dirty sordid room, the vacant meaningless ceiling, the weary wasted world, I felt nothing but the old sense of guilt, the sense of crime and violation, the sin of destruction. I sat beside her as she lay on the divan. I stared at the carpet. I saw the pieces of glass from the broken lamp. And when I got up to walk across the room, I felt pain, the sharp agony of the flesh of my feet torn by my own weight. It hurt with a deserving pain. My feet were cut when I put on my shoes and walked out of that apartment and into the bright astonishment of the night. Limping, I walked the long road to my room. I thought I would never see Camilla Lopez again.

Chapter Seventeen

But big events were coming, and I had no one to whom I could speak of them. There was the day I finished the story of Vera Rivken, the breezy days of rewriting it, just coasting along, Hackmuth, a few more days now and you'll see something great. Then the revision was finished and I sent it away, and then the waiting, the hoping. I prayed once more. I went to mass and Holy Communion. I made a *novena*. I lit candles at the Blessed Virgin's altar. I prayed for a miracle.

The miracle happened. It happened like this: I was standing at the window in my room, watching a bug crawling along the sill. It was three-fifteen on a Thursday afternoon. There was a knock on my door. I opened the door, and there he stood, a telegraph boy. I signed for the telegram, sat on the bed, and wondered if the wine had finally got the Old Man's heart. The telegram said: your book accepted mailing contract today. Hackmuth. That was all. I let the paper float to the carpet. I just sat there. Then I got down on the floor and began kissing the telegram. I crawled under the bed and just lay there. I did not need the sunshine anymore. Nor the earth, nor heaven. I just lay there, happy to die. Nothing else could happen to me. My life was over.

Was the contract coming via air mail? I paced the floor

those next days. I read the papers. Air mail was too impractical, too dangerous. Down with the air mail. Every day planes were falling, covering the earth with wreckage, killing pilots: it was too damned unsafe, a pioneering venture, and where the hell was my contract? I called the post office. How were flying conditions over the Sierras? Good. All planes accounted for? Good. No wrecks? Then where was my contract? I spent a long time practising my signature. I decided to use my middle name, the whole thing Arturo Dominic Bandini, A. D. Bandini, Arturo D. Bandini, A. Dominic Bandini. The contract came Monday morning, first class mail. With it was a cheque for five hundred dollars. My God, five hundred dollars! I was one of the Morgans. I could retire for life.

War in Europe, a speech by Hitler, trouble in Poland, these were the topics of the day. What piffle! You warmongers, you old folks in the lobby of the Alta Loma Hotel, here is the news, here: this little paper with all the fancy legal writing, my book! To hell with that Hitler, this is more important than Hitler, this is about my book. It won't shake the world, it won't kill a soul, it won't fire a gun, ah, but you'll remember it to the day you die, you'll lie there breathing your last, and you'll smile as you remember the book. The story of Vera Rivken, a slice out of life.

They weren't interested. They preferred the war in Europe, the funny pictures, and Louella Parsons, the tragic people, the poor people. I just sat in that hotel lobby and shook my head sadly.

Someone had to know, and that was Camilla. For three weeks I had not seen her, not since the marijuana on Temple Street. But she was not at the saloon. Another girl had her place. I asked for Camilla. The other girl wouldn't talk.

Suddenly the Columbia Buffet was like a tomb. I asked the fat bartender. Camilla had not been there for two weeks. Was she fired? He couldn't say. Was she sick? He didn't know. He wouldn't talk either.

I could afford a taxicab. I could afford twenty cabs, riding them day and night. I took one cab and rode to Camilla's place on Temple Street. I knocked on her door and got no answer. I tried the door. It opened, darkness inside, and I switched on the light. She lay there in the Murphy bed. Her face was the face of an old rose pressed and dried in a book, yellowish, with only the eyes to prove there was life in it. The room stank. The blinds were down, the door opened with difficulty until I kicked away the rug against the crack. She gasped when she saw me. She was happy to see me. 'Arturo,' she said. 'Oh, Arturo!'

I didn't speak of the book or the contract. Who cares about a novel, another goddamn novel? That sting in my eyes, it was for her, it was my eyes remembering a wild lean girl running in the moonlight on the beach, a beautiful girl who danced with a beertray in her round arms. She lay there now, broken, brown cigarette butts overflowing a saucer beside her. She had quit. She wanted to die. Those were her words. 'I don't care,' she said.

'You gotta eat,' I said, because her face was only a skull with yellow skin stretched tightly over it. I sat on the bed and held her fingers, conscious of bones, surprised that they were such small bones, she who had been so straight and round and tall. 'You're hungry,' I said. But she didn't want food. 'Eat anyway,' I said.

I went out and started buying. It was a few doors down the street, a small grocery store. I ordered whole sections of the place. Gimme all of those, and all of these, gimme this and gimme that. Milk, bread, canned juices, fruit, butter, vegetables, meat, potatoes. It took three trips to carry it all up to her place. When it was all piled there in the kitchen I looked at the stuff and scratched my head, wondering what to feed her.

'I don't want anything,' she said.

Milk. I washed a glass and poured it full. She sat up, her pink nightgown torn at the shoulder, ripping all the more as she moved to sit up. She held her nose and drank it, three swallows, and she gasped and lay back, horrified, nauseated.

'Fruit juice,' I said. 'Grape juice. It's sweeter, tastes better.' I opened a bottle, poured a glassful, and held it out to her. She gulped it down, lay back and panted. Then she put her head over the side of the bed and vomited. I cleaned it up. I cleaned the apartment. I washed the dishes and scrubbed the sink. I washed her face. I hurried downstairs, grabbed a cab, and rode all over town looking for a place to buy her a clean nightgown. I bought some candy too, and a stack of picture magazines, *Look*, *Pic*, *See*, *Sic*, *Sac*, *Whack*, and all of them – something to distract her, to put her at ease.

When I got back the door was locked. I knew what that meant. I hammered it with my fists and kicked it with my heels. The din filled the whole building. The doors of other apartments opened in the hall, and heads came out. From downstairs a woman came in an old bathrobe. She was the landlady; I could spot a landlady instantly. She stood at the head of the stairs, afraid to come closer.

'What do you want?' she said.

'It's locked,' I said. 'I have to get inside.'

'You leave that girl alone,' she said. 'I know your kind. You leave that poor girl alone or I'll call the police.'

'I'm her friend,' I said.

From inside came the elated, hysterical laughter of Camilla, the giddy shriek of denial. 'He's not my friend! I don't want him around!' Then her laughter once more, high and frightened and birdlike, trapped in the room. The atmosphere was nasty, ominous. Two men in shirt sleeves appeared at the other end of the hall. The big one with a cigar hitched up his pants and said, 'Let's throw the guy out of here.' I started moving then, retreating from them walking fast, past the despicable sneer of the landlady and down the stairs to the lower hall. Once in the street I started running. On the corner of Broadway and Temple I saw a cab parked. I got in and told the driver to just keep moving.

No, it was none of my business. But I could remember, the black cluster of hair, the wild depth of her eyes, the jolt in the pit of my stomach in the first days I knew her. I stayed away from the place for two days, and then I couldn't bear it; I wanted to help her. I wanted to get her away from that curtained trap, send her somewhere to the south, down by the sea. I could do it. I had a pile of money. I thought of Sammy, but he loathed her too deeply. If she could only get out of town, that would help a lot. I decided to try once more.

It was about noon. It was very hot, too hot in the hotel room. It was the heat that made me do it, the sticky ennui, the dust over the earth, the hot blasts from the Mojave. I went to the rear of the Temple Street apartment. There was a wooden stairway leading to the second floor. On such a day as this, her door would be open, to cool the place by cross ventilation from the window.

I was right. The door was open, but she was not there. Her stuff was piled in the middle of the room, boxes and suitcases with garments squirming from them. The bed was down, the naked mattress showing the sheets gone. The place was stripped of life. Then I caught the odour of disinfectant. The room had been fumigated. I took the stairs three at a time to the landlady's door.

'You!' she said, opening the door. 'You!' and she slammed it shut. I stood outside and pleaded with her. 'I'm her friend,' I said. 'I swear to God. I want to help her. You got to believe me.'

'Go away or I'll call the police.'

'She was sick,' I said. 'She needed help. I want to do something for her. You've got to believe me.'

The door opened. The woman stood looking straight into my eyes. She was of medium height, stout, her face hardened and without emotion. She said: 'Come in.'

I stepped into a drab room, ornate and weird, cluttered with fantastic gadgets, a piano littered with heavy photographs, wild-coloured shawls, fancy lamps and vases. She asked me to sit down, but I didn't.

'That girl's gone,' she said. 'She's gone crazy. I had to do it.'

'Where is she? What happened?'

'I had to do it. She was a nice girl too.'

She had been forced to call the police – that was her story. That had happened the night after I was there. Camilla had gone wild, throwing dishes, dumping furniture out of the window, screaming and kicking the walls, slashing the curtains with a knife. The landlady had called the police. The police had come, broken down the door, and seized her. But the police had refused to take her away. They had held her, quieted her, until an ambulance arrived. Wailing and struggling, she had been led away. That was all, except that Camilla owed three weeks' rent and had done irreparable damage to the furniture and apartment. The landlady mentioned a figure, and I paid her the money. She handed me a receipt and smiled her greasy hypocrisy. 'I knew you were a good boy,' she said. 'I knew it from the moment I first laid eyes on you. But you just can't trust strangers in this town.'

I took the street car to the County Hospital. The nurse in the reception room checked a card file when I mentioned the name of Camilla Lopez. 'She's here,' the nurse said. 'But she can't have visitors.'

'How is she?'

'I can't answer that.'

'When can I see her?'

Visiting day was Wednesday. I had to wait four more days. I walked out of the huge hospital and around the grounds. I looked up at the windows and wandered through the grounds. Then I took the street car back to Hill Street and Bunker Hill. Four days to wait. I exhausted them playing pin games and slot machines. Luck was against me. I lost a lot of money, but I killed a lot of time. Tuesday afternoon I walked downtown and started buying things for Camilla. I bought a portable radio, a box of candy, a dressing gown, and a lot of face creams and such things. Then I went to a flower shop and ordered two dozen camellias. I was loaded down when I got to the hospital Wednesday afternoon. The camellias had wilted overnight because I didn't think about putting them in water. Sweat poured from my face as I climbed the hospital steps. I knew my freckles were in bloom, I could almost feel them popping out of my face.

The same nurse was at the reception desk. I unloaded the gifts into a chair and asked to see Camilla Lopez. The nurse checked the file card. 'Miss Lopez isn't here anymore,' she said. 'She's been transferred.' I was so hot and so tired. 'Where is she?' I said. I groaned when she said she couldn't answer that. 'I'm her friend,' I told the nurse. 'I want to help her.'

'I'm sorry,' the nurse said.

'Who'll tell me?'

Yes, who'll tell me? I went all over the hospital, up one floor and down the other. I saw doctors and assistant doctors, I saw nurses, and assistant nurses, I waited in lobbies and halls, but nobody would tell me anything. They all reached for the little card file, and they all said the same thing: she had been transferred. But she wasn't dead. They all denied that, coming quickly to the point; no, she wasn't dead: they had taken her elsewhere. It was useless. I walked out the front door and into the blinding sunlight to the street car line. Boarding the car, I remembered the gifts. They were back there somewhere; I couldn't even remember which waiting room. I didn't care. Disconsolate, I rode back to Bunker Hill.

If she had been transferred, it meant another State or County institution, because she had no money. Money. I had the money. I had three pocketfuls of money, and more at home in my other pants. I could get it all together and bring it to them, but they wouldn't even tell me what had happened to her. What was money for? I was going to spend it anyway, and those halls, those etherized halls, those low-voiced enigmatic doctors, those quiet, reticent nurses, they baffled me. I got off the street car in a daze. Halfway up the stairs of Bunker Hill I sat down in a doorway and looked down at the city below me in the nebulous, dusty haze of the late afternoon. The heat rose out of the haze and my nostrils breathed it. Over the city spread a white murkiness like fog. But it was not the fog: it was the desert heat, the great blasts from the Mojave and Santa Ana, the pale white fingers of the wasteland, ever reaching out to claim its captured child.

The next day I found out what they had done to Camilla. From a drugstore downtown I called long distance and got the switchboard at County Institute for the Insane at Del Maria. I asked the switchboard girl for the name of the doctor in charge there. 'Doctor Danielson,' she said.

'Give me his office.'

She plugged the board and another woman's voice came through the wire. 'Dr Danielson's office.'

'This is Dr Jones,' I said. 'Let me speak to Dr Danielson. This is urgent.'

'One moment please.'

Then a man's voice. 'Danielson speaking.'

'Hello, Doctor,' I said. 'This is Dr Jones, Edmond Jones, Los Angeles. You have a transfer there from the County Hospital, a Miss Camilla Lopez. How is she?'

'We can't say,' Danielson said. 'She's still under observation. Did you say Edmond Jones?'

I hung up. At least I knew where she was. Knowing that was one thing; trying to see her was another. It was out of the question. I talked to people who knew. You had to be a relative of an inmate, and you had to prove it. You had to write for an appointment, and you came after they had investigated. You couldn't write the inmates a letter, and you couldn't send gifts. I didn't go out to Del Maria. I was satisfied that I had done my best. She was insane, and it was none of my business. Besides, she loved Sammy.

The days passed, the winter rains began. Late October, and the proofs of my book arrived. I bought a car, a 1929 Ford. It had no top, but it sped like the wind, and with the coming of dry days I took long rides along the blue coastline, up to Ventura, up to Santa Barbara, down to San Clemente, down to San Diego, following the white line of the pavement, under the staring stars, my feet on the dashboard, my head full of plans for another book, one night and then another, all of them together spelling dream days I had never known, serene days I feared to question. I prowled the city with my Ford: I found mysterious alleys, lonely trees, rotting old houses out of a vanished past. Day and night I lived in my Ford, pausing only long enough to order a hamburger and a cup of coffee at strange roadside cafés. This was the life for a man, to wander and stop and then go on, ever following the white line along the rambling coast, a time to relax at the wheel, light another cigarette, and grope stupidly for the meanings in that perplexing desert sky.

One night I came upon the place at Santa Monica where Camilla and I had gone swimming in those first days. I stopped and watched the foamy breakers and the mysterious mist. I remembered the girl running through the foaming thunder, revelling in the wild freedom of that night. Oh, that Camilla, that girl!

There was that night in the middle of November, when I was walking down Spring Street, poking around in the secondhand bookstores. The Columbia Buffet was only a block away. Just for the devil of it, I said, for old time's sake, and I walked up to the bar and ordered a beer. I was an old-timer now. I could look around sneeringly and remember when this was really a wonderful place. But not any more. Nobody knew me, neither the new barmaid with her jaw full of gum, nor the two female musicians still grinding out *Tales from the Vienna Woods* on a violin and a piano.

And yet the fat bartender did remember me. Steve, or Vince, or Vinnie, or whatever his name. 'Ain't seen you in a long time,' he said.

'Not since Camilla,' I said.

He clucked his tongue. 'Too bad,' he said. 'Nice kid too.' That was all. I drank another beer, then a third. He gave me the fourth, and then I bought for the two of us on the next round. An hour passed in that fashion. He stood before me, reached into his pocket, and drew out a newspaper clipping. 'I suppose you already seen this,' he said. I picked it up. It was no more than six lines, and a two line headline from the bottom of an inside page:

Local police today were on the lookout for Camilla Lopez, 22, of Los Angeles, whose disappearance from the Del Maria institution was discovered by authorities last night.

The clipping was a week old. I left my beer and hurried out of there and up the hill to my room. Something told me she was coming there. I could feel her desire to return to my room. Pulling up a chair, I sat with my feet in the window, the lights on, smoking and waiting. Deeply I felt she would come, convinced there was no one else to whom she could turn. But she did not come. I went to bed, leaving the lights on. Most of the next day and all through the following night I stayed in my room, waiting for the plink of pebbles against my window. After the third night the conviction that she was coming began to wane. No, she would not come here. She would flee to Sammy, to her true love. The last person of whom she would think would be Arturo Bandini. That suited me just fine. After all, I was a novelist now, and something of a short story writer too, even if I did say so myself.

The next morning I got the first of her collect telegrams. It was a request for money to be wired to Rita Gomez, care of Western Union, San Francisco. She had signed the wire 'Rita' but the identity was obvious. I wired her twenty and told her to come south as far as Santa Barbara, where I would meet her. She wired this answer: 'Would rather go north thanks sorry Rita.'

The second wire came from Fresno. It was another request for money, to be sent to Rita Gomez, care of Postal Telegraph. That was two days after the first wire. I walked downtown and wired her fifteen. For a long time I sat in the telegraph office composing a message to go with the money, but I couldn't make up my mind. I finally gave up and sent the money alone. Nothing I said made any difference to Camilla Lopez. But one thing was certain. I vowed it on the way back to the hotel: she would get no more money out of me. I had to be careful from now on.

Her third wire arrived Sunday night, the same kind of message, this time from Bakersfield. I clung to my resolution for two hours. Then I pictured her wandering around, penniless, probably caught in the rain. I sent her fifty, with a message to buy some clothes and keep out of the rain.

Chapter Eighteen

Three nights later I came home from a ride to find my hotel door locked from the inside. I knew what that meant. I knocked but got no answer. I called her name. I hurried down the hall to the back door and ran up the hillside to the level of my window. I wanted to catch her redhanded. The window was down and so was the curtain on the inside, but there was an opening in the curtain and I could see into the room. It was lighted by a desk lamp and I could see all of it, but I couldn't see her anywhere. The clothes closet door was locked, and I knew she was in there. I prised the window open. I pushed the glass quietly and slipped inside. The bed rugs were not on the floor. On tiptoe I walked towards the closet door. I could hear her moving inside the closet, as though she were sitting on the floor. Faintly I caught the cubeb-like smell of marijuana.

I reached for the knob of the closet door, and all at once I didn't want to catch her at it. The shock would be as bad for me as for her. Then I remembered something that had happened to me when I was a little boy. It was a closet like that one, and my mother had opened it suddenly. I remembered that terror of being discovered, and I tiptoed from the closet door and sat in the chair at my desk. After five minutes I couldn't stay in the room. I didn't want her to know. I crept out of the window, closed it, and returned to the back door of the hotel. I took my time. When I thought it must be over, I walked loudly and briskly towards the door of my room and barged in.

She lay on the bed, a thin hand shielding her eyes. 'Camilla!' I said. 'You here!' She rose and looked at me with delirious black eyes, black and wanton and in a dream, her neck stretched and defining the bulging cords at her throat. She had nothing to say with her lips, but the ghastly cast of her face, the teeth too white and too big now, the frightened smile, these spoke too loudly of the horror shrouding her days and nights. I bit into my jaws to keep from crying. As I walked towards the bed, she pulled up her knees, slipping into a crouched frightened position, as though she expected me to strike her.

'Take it easy,' I said. 'You'll be alright. You look swell.'

'Thanks for the money,' she said, and it was the same voice, deep, yet nasal. She had bought new clothes. They were cheap and garish: an imitation silk dress of bright yellow with a black velvet belt; blue and yellow shoes and ankle-length stockings with greens and reds forming the tops. Her nails were manicured, polished a blood red, and around her wrists were green and yellow beads. All of this was set against the ash-yellow of her bloodless face and throat. She had always looked at her best in the plain white smock she wore at work. I didn't ask any questions. Everything I wanted to know was written in tortured phrases across the desolation of her face. It didn't look like insanity to me. It looked like fear, the terrible fear screaming from her big hungered eyes, alert now from the drug.

She couldn't stay in Los Angeles. She needed rest, a chance

to eat and sleep, drink a lot of milk and take long walks. All at once I was full of plans. Laguna Beach! That was the place for her. It was winter now, and we could get a place cheap. I could take care of her and get started on another book. I had an idea for a new book. We didn't have to be married, brother and sister was alright with me. We could go swimming and take long walks along the Balboa shore. We could sit by the fireplace when the fog was heavy. We could sleep under deep blankets when the wind roared off the sea. That was the basic idea: but I elaborated, I poured it into her ears like words from a dream book, and her face brightened, and she cried.

'And a dog!' I said. 'I'll get you a little dog. A little pup. A Scottie. And we'll call him Willie.'

She clapped her hands. 'Oh Willie!' she said. 'Here, Willie! Here, Willie!'

'And a cat,' I said. 'A Siamese cat. We'll call him Chang. A big cat with golden eyes.'

She shivered and covered her face with her hands. 'No,' she said. 'I hate cats.'

'Okay. No cats. I hate them too.'

She was dreaming it all, filling in a picture with her own brush, the elation like bright glass in her eyes. 'A horse too,' she said. 'After you make a lot of money we'll both have a horse.'

'I'll make millions,' I said.

I undressed and got into bed. She slept badly, jerking awake suddenly, moaning and mumbling in her sleep. Sometime during the night she sat up, turned on the light, and smoked a cigarette. I lay with my eyes closed, trying to sleep. Soon she got up, pulled my bathrobe around her, and found her purse on the desk. It was a white oil-cloth purse, bulging with stuff. I heard her shuffle down the hall to the lavatory in my slippers. She was gone ten minutes. When she returned a calm had come over her. She believed me asleep, kissed me on the temple. I caught the smell of the marijuana. The rest of the night she slept heavily, her face bathed in peace.

At eight the next morning we climbed out the hotel window and went down the hillside to the back of the hotel, where my Ford was parked. She was wretched, her face bitter and sleepless. I drove through town and out Crenshaw, and from there to Long Beach Boulevard. She sat scowling, her head down, the cold wind of the morning combing her hair. In Maywood we stopped at a roadside café for breakfast. I had sausage and eggs, fruit juice and coffee. She refused everything but black coffee. After the first swallow she lit a cigarette. I wanted to examine her purse, for I knew it contained marijuana, but she clung to it like life itself. We each had another cup of coffee, and then we drove on. She felt better, but her mood was still dark. I didn't talk.

A couple of miles outside of Long Beach we came upon a dog farm. I drove in and we got out. We were in a yard of palm and eucalyptus trees. From all points a dozen dogs charged us, barking joyously. The dogs loved her, sensed her instantly as their friend, and for the first time that morning she smiled. They were collies, police dogs, and terriers. She dropped to her knees to embrace them, and they overwhelmed her with their yelps and their big pink tongues. She took a terrier in her arms and swayed him like an infant, crooning her affection. Her face was bright again, full of colour, the face of the old Camilla.

The kennel owner emerged from his back porch. He was an old man with a short white beard, and he limped and carried a cane. The dogs paid little attention to me. They came up, sniffed my shoes and legs, and turned away sharply, with considerable contempt. It was not that they disliked me; they preferred Camilla with her lavishing emotion and her strange dog-talk. I told the old man we wanted some kind of a pup, and he asked what kind. It was up to Camilla, but she couldn't make up her mind. We saw several litters. They were all touchingly infantile, furry little balls of irresistible tenderness. Finally we came upon the dog she wanted: he was pure white, a collie. He was not quite six weeks old, and he was so fat he could scarcely walk. Camilla put him down, and he staggered through her legs, walked a few feet, sat down, and promptly fell asleep. More than any other, she wanted that pup.

I swallowed when the old man said, 'Twenty-five dollars,' but we took the pup along, with his papers, with his pure white mother following us to the car, barking as if to tell us to be very careful how we raised him. As we drove away I looked over my shoulder. In the driveway sat the white mother, her beautiful ears perked, her head cocked sideways, watching us as we disappeared into the main highway.

'Willie,' I said. 'His name's Willie.'

The dog lay in her lap, whimpering.

'No,' she said. 'It's Snow White.'

'That's a girl's name,' I said.

'I don't care.'

I pulled over to the side of the road. 'I care,' I said. 'Either you change his name to something else, or he goes back.'

'Alright,' she admitted. 'His name's Willie.'

I felt better. We had not fought about it. Willie was already helping her. She was almost docile, ready to be reasonable.

Her restlessness was gone, and a softness curved her lips. Willie was sound asleep in her lap, but he sucked her little finger. South of Long Beach we stopped at a drugstore and bought a bottle with a nipple, and a bottle of milk. Willie's eyes opened when she put the nipple to his mouth. He fell to his task like a fiend. Camilla lifted her arms high, ran her fingers through her hair, and yawned with pleasure. She was very happy.

Ever south, we followed the beautiful white line. I drove slowly. A tender day, a sky like the sea, the sea like the sky. On the left the golden hills, the gold of winter. A day for saying nothing, for admiring lonely trees, sand dunes, and piles of white stones along the road. Camilla's land, Camilla's home, the sea and the desert, the beautiful earth, the immense sky, and far to the north, the moon, still there from the night before.

We reached Laguna before noon. It took me two hours, running in and out of real estate offices and inspecting houses, to find the place we wanted. Anything suited Camilla. Willie now possessed her completely. She didn't care where she lived, so long as she had him. The house I liked was a twin-gabled place, with a white picket fence around it, not fifty yards from the shore. The backyard was a bed of white sand. It was well furnished, full of bright curtains and water-colours. I liked it best because of that one room upstairs. It faced the sea. I could put my typewriter at the window, and I could work. Ah man, I could do a lot of work at that window. I could just look out beyond that window and it would come, and merely looking at that room I was restless, and I saw sentence after sentence marching across the page.

When I came downstairs, Camilla had taken Willie for a walk along the shore. I stood at the back door and watched them, a quarter of a mile away. I could see Camilla bent over, clapping her hands, and then running, with Willie tumbling after her. But I couldn't actually see Willie, he was so small and he blended so perfectly with the white sand. I went inside. On the kitchen table lay Camilla's purse. I opened it, dumped the contents on the table. Two Prince Albert cans of marijuana fell out. I emptied them into the toilet, and threw the cans into the trash box.

Then I went out and sat on the porch steps in the warm sun, watching Camilla and the dog as they made their way back to the house. It was about two o'clock. I had to go back to Los Angeles, pack my stuff, and check out of the hotel. It would take five hours. I gave Camilla money to buy food and the house things we needed. When I left she was lying on her back, her face to the sun. Curled up on her stomach was Willie, sound asleep. I shouted goodbye, let the clutch out, and swung into the main coast highway.

On the way back, loaded down with typewriter, books, and suitcases, I had a flat tyre. Darkness came quickly. It was almost nine o'clock when I pulled into the yard of the beach house. The lights were out. I opened the front door with my key and shouted her name. There was no answer. I turned on all the lights and searched every room, every closet. She was gone. There was no sign of her, or of Willie. I unloaded my things. Perhaps she had taken the dog for another walk. But I was deceiving myself. She was gone. By midnight I doubted that she would return, and by one o'clock I was convinced she wouldn't. I looked again for some note, some message.

There was no trace of her. It was as though she had not so much as set foot in that house.

I decided to stay on. The rent was paid for a month, and I wanted to try the room upstairs. That night I slept there, but the next morning I began to hate the place. With her there it was part of a dream; without her, it was a house. I packed my things into the rumble seat and drove back to Los Angeles. When I got back to the hotel, someone had taken my old room during the night. Everything was awry now. I took another room on the main floor, but I didn't like it. Everything was going to pieces. The new room was so strange, so cold, without one memory. When I looked out the window the ground was twenty feet away. No more climbing out the window, no more pebbles against the glass. I set my typewriter in one place and then another. It didn't seem to fit anywhere. Something was wrong, everything was wrong.

I went for a walk through the streets. My God, here I was again, roaming the town. I looked at the faces around me and I knew mine was like theirs. Faces with the blood drained away, tight faces, worried, lost. Faces like flowers torn from their roots and stuffed into a pretty vase, the colours draining fast. I had to get away from that town.

Chapter Nineteen

My book came out a week later. For a while it was fun. I could walk into department stores and see it among thousands of others, my book, my words, my name, the reason why I was alive. But it was not the kind of fun I got from seeing *The Little Dog Laughed* in Hackmuth's magazine.

That was all gone too. And no word from Camilla, no telegram. I had left her fifteen dollars. I knew it couldn't last more than ten days. I felt she would wire as soon as she was penniless. Camilla and Willie – what had happened to them?

A postcard from Sammy. It was in my box when I got home that afternoon. It read:

Dear Mr Bandini: That Mexican girl is here, and you know how I feel about having women around. If she's your girl you better come and get her because I won't have her hanging around here. Sammy

The postcard was two days old. I filled the tank with gasoline, threw a copy of my book in the front seat, and started for Sammy's abode in the Mojave Desert.

I got there after midnight. A light shone in the single window of his hut. I knocked and he opened the door. Before speaking, I looked around. He went back to a chair beside a coal-oil lamp, where he picked up a pulp western magazine and went on reading. He did not speak. There was no sign of Camilla.

'Where is she?' I said.

'Damned if I know. She left.'

'You mean you kicked her out.'

'I can't have her around here. I'm a sick man.'

'Where'd she go?'

He jerked his thumb towards the southeast.

'That way, somewhere.'

'You mean out in the desert?'

He shook his head. 'With the pup,' he said. 'A little dog. Cute as hell.'

'When did she leave?'

'Sunday night,' he said.

'Sunday!' I said. 'Jesus Christ, man! That was three days ago! Did she have anything to eat with her? Anything to drink.'

'Milk,' he said. 'She had a bottle of milk for the dog.'

I went out beyond the clearing of his hut and looked towards the southwest. It was very cold and the moon was high, the stars in lush clusters across the blue dome of the sky. West and south and east spread a desolation of brush, sombre Joshua trees, and stumpy hills. I hurried back to the hut. 'Come out and show me which way she went,' I said. He put down his magazine and pointed to the southeast. 'That way,' he said.

I tore the magazine out of his hand, grabbed him by the neck and pushed him outside into the night. He was thin and light, and he stumbled about before balancing himself.

'Show me,' I said. We went to the edge of the clearing and he grumbled that he was a sick man, and that I had no right to push him around. He stood there, straightening his shirt, tugging at his belt. 'Show me where she was when you saw her last,' I said. He pointed.

'She was just going over that ridge.'

I left him standing there and walked out a quarter of a mile to the top of the ridge. It was so cold I pulled my coat around my throat. Under my feet the earth was churning of coarse dark sand and little stones, the basin of some prehistoric sea. Beyond the ridge were other ridges like it, hundreds of them stretching infinitely away. The sandy earth revealed no footstep, no sign that it had ever been trod. I walked on, struggling through the miserable soil that gave slightly and then covered itself with crumbs of grey sand.

After what seemed two miles, I sat on a round white stone and rested. I was perspiring, and yet it was bitterly cold. The moon was dipping towards the north. It must have been after three. I had been walking steadily but slowly in a rambling fashion, still the ridges and mounds continued, stretching away without end, with only cactus and sage and ugly plants I didn't know marking it from the dark horizon.

I remembered road maps of the district. There were no roads, no towns, no human life between here and the other side of the desert, nothing but wasteland for almost a hundred miles. I got up and walked on. I was numb with cold, and yet the sweat poured from me. The greying east brightened, metamorphosed to pink, then red, and then the giant ball of fire rose out of the blackened hills. Across the desolation lay a supreme indifference, the casualness of night and another day, and yet the secret intimacy of those hills, their silent consoling wonder, made death a thing of no great importance. You could die, but the desert would hide the secret of your death, it would remain after you, to cover your memory with ageless wind and heat and cold.

It was no use. How could I search for her? Why should I search for her? What could I bring her but a return to the brutal wilderness that had broken her? I walked back in the dawn, sadly in the dawn. The hills had her now. Let these hills hide her! Let her go back to the loneliness of the intimate hills. Let her live with stones and sky, with the wind blowing her hair to the end. Let her go that way.

The sun was high when I got back to the clearing. Already it was hot. In the doorway of his hut stood Sammy. 'Find her?' he asked.

I didn't answer him. I was tired. He watched me a moment, and then he disappeared into the shack. I heard the door being bolted. Far out across the Mojave there arose the shimmer of heat. I made my way up the path to the Ford. In the seat was a copy of my book, my first book. I found a pencil, opened the book to the fly leaf, and wrote:

To Camilla, with love,
Arturo

I carried the book a hundred yards into the desolation, towards the southeast. With all my might I threw it far out in the direction she had gone. Then I got into the car, started the engine, and drove back to Los Angeles.

Dreams From Bunker Hill

Also for Joyce

Chapter One

My first collision with fame was hardly memorable. I was a busboy at Marx's Deli. The year was 1934. The place was Third and Hill, Los Angeles. I was twenty-one years old, living in a world bounded on the west by Bunker Hill, on the east by Los Angeles Street, on the south by Pershing Square, and on the north by Civic Center. I was a busboy nonpareil, with great verve and style for the profession, and though I was dreadfully underpaid (one dollar a day plus meals) I attracted considerable attention as I whirled from table to table, balancing a tray on one hand, and eliciting smiles from my customers. I had something else beside a waiter's skill to offer my patrons, for I was also a writer. This phenomenon became known one day after a drunken photographer from the *Los Angeles Times* sat at the bar, snapped several pictures of me serving a customer as she looked up at me with admiring eyes. Next day there was a feature story attached to the *Times* photograph. It told of the struggle and success of young Arturo Bandini, an ambitious, hard-working kid from Colorado, who had crashed through the difficult magazine world with the sale of his first story to *The American Phoenix*, edited, of course, by the most renowned personage in American literature, none other than Heinrich Muller. Good old Muller! How I loved that man!

Indeed, my first literary efforts were letters to him, asking his advice, sending him suggestions for stories I might write, and finally sending him stories too, many stories, a story a week, until even Heinrich Muller, curmudgeon of the literary world, the tiger in his lair, seemed to give up the struggle and condescended to drop me a letter with two lines in it, and then a second letter with four lines, and finally a two-page letter of twenty-four lines and then, wonder of wonders, a check for $150, payment in full for my first acceptance.

I was in rags the day that check arrived. My nondescript Colorado clothes hung from me in shreds, and my first thought was a new wardrobe. I had to be frugal but in good taste, and so I descended Bunker Hill to Second and Broadway, and the Goodwill store. I made my way to the better quality section and found an excellent blue business suit with a white pinstripe. The pants were too long and so were the sleeves, and the whole thing was ten dollars. For another dollar I had the suit altered, and while this was being taken care of, I buzzed around in the shirt department. Shirts were fifty cents apiece, of excellent quality and all manner of styles. Next I purchased a pair of shoes – fine thick-soled oxfords of pure leather, shoes that would carry me over the streets of Los Angeles for months to come. I bought other things too, several pairs of shorts and T-shirts, a dozen pairs of socks, a few neckties and finally an irresistible glorious fedora. I set it jauntily at the side of my head and walked out of the dressing room and paid my bill. Twenty bucks. It was the first time in my life that I had bought clothing for myself. As I studied my reflection in a long mirror I could not help remembering that in all my Colorado years my people had been too poor to buy me a suit of clothes, even for the graduation exercises in high school. Well, I was on my way now, nothing could stop me. Heinrich Muller, the roaring tiger of the literary world, would lead me to the top of the heap. I walked out of the Goodwill and up Third Street, a new man. My boss, Abe Marx, was standing in front of the deli as I approached.

'Good God, Bandini!' he exclaimed. 'You've been to the Goodwill or something?'

'Goodwill, my ass,' I snorted. 'This is straight from Bullock's, you boob.'

A couple of days later Abe Marx handed me a business card. It read:

Gustave Du Mont, PhD
Literary Agent
Preparation and Editing
of books, plays, scenarios, and stories
Expert editorial supervision
513 Third Street, Los Angeles
No triflers

I slipped the card into the pocket of my new suit. I took the elevator to the fifth floor. Du Mont's office was down the corridor. I entered.

The reception room lurched like an earthquake. I caught my breath and looked around. The place was full of cats. Cats on the chairs, on the valances, on the typewriter. Cats on the bookcases, in the bookcases. The stench was over-powering. The cats came to their feet and swirled around me, pressing my legs, rolling playfully over my shoes. On the floor and on the surface of the furniture a film of cat fur heaved and eddied like a pool of water. I crossed to an open window and looked down the fire escape. Cats were ascending and descending. A huge grey creature climbed toward me, the head of a salmon in his mouth. He brushed past me and leaped into the room.

By now the whir of cat fur enveloped the air. An inner office door opened. Standing there was Gustave Du Mont, a small aged man with eyes like cherries. He waved his arms and rushed among the cats shrieking,

'Out! Out! Go, everybody! Time to go home!'

The cats simply glided off at their leisure, some ending up at his feet, some playfully pawing his pants. They were his masters. Du Mont sighed, threw up his hands, and said,

'What can I do for you?'

'I'm from the deli downstairs. You left your card.'

'Enter.'

I stepped into his office and he closed the door. We were in a small room in the presence of three cats lolling atop a bookcase. They were elite felines, huge Persians, licking their paws with regal aplomb. I stared at them. Du Mont seemed to understand.

'My favorites,' he smiled. He opened a desk drawer and drew out a fifth of Scotch.

'How about some lunch, young man?'

'No thanks, Dr Du Mont. What did you want to see me about?'

Du Mont uncorked the bottle, took a swig from it and gasped.

'I read your story. You're a good writer. You shouldn't be slinging hash. You belong in more amenable surroundings.' Du Mont took another swig. 'You want a job?'

I looked at all those cats. 'Maybe. What you got in mind?'

'I need an editor.'

I smelled the pungency of all those cats. 'I'm not sure I could take it.'

'You mean the cats? I'll take care of that.'

I thought a minute. 'Well ... what is it you want me to edit?'

He hit the bottle again. 'Novels, short stories, whatever comes in.'

I hesitated. 'Can I see the stuff?'

His fist came down on a pile of manuscripts. 'Help yourself.'

I lifted off the top manuscript. It was a short story, written by a certain Jennifer Lovelace, entitled *Passion at Dawn*. I groaned.

Du Mont took another swig. 'It's awful,' he said. 'They're all awful. I can't read them anymore. It's the worst writing I ever saw. But there's money in it if you've got the stomach. The worse they are the more you charge.'

By now the whole front of my new suit was coated with cat fur. My nose itched and I felt a sneeze coming. I choked it back.

'What's the job pay?'

'Five dollars a week.'

'Hell, that's only a dollar a day.'

'Nothin' to it.'

I snatched the bottle and took a swig. It scorched my throat. It tasted like cat piss.

'Ten dollars a week or no deal.'

Du Mont shoved out his fist. 'Shake,' he said. 'You start Monday.'

Monday morning I reported for work at nine o'clock.

The cats were gone. The window was closed. The reception room had been refurbished. There was a desk for me beside the window. Everything was clean and dusted. Not a single strand of cat fur clung to my finger when I rubbed it against the window sill. I sniffed the air. The urine was still potent but masked by a powerful fumigant. There was another odor too – cat repellent. I sat down at the desk and pulled out the typewriter. It was an ancient Underwood. I rolled a sheet of paper under the platen and experimented with the keyboard. The machine functioned like a rusty lawnmower. Suddenly I was dissatisfied. There was something about this job that made me apprehensive. Why should I work on somebody else's product? Why wasn't I in my room writing my own stuff? What would Heinrich Muller do in a case like this? Surely I was a fool.

The door opened and there was Du Mont. I was surprised to see him in a bowler hat, a gray vest under his frock coat, spats, and sporting a walking stick. I had never been in Paris but the sight of the natty little man made me think of the place. Was he crazy? Suddenly I thought he was.

'Good morning,' he said. 'How do you like your quarters?'

'What happened to the cats?'

'The fumigant,' he said. 'It drives them off. Don't worry. I know cats. They won't be back.' He hung his hat and cane on a couple of door hooks. Then he pulled up a chair and we sat side by side at the desk. He picked up the top manuscript, *Passion at Dawn* by Jennifer Lovelace, and began to teach me the art of literary revision. He did it brutally, because in truth it was a brutal job. A black crayon in his hand, he marked and slashed and obliterated sentences, paragraphs, and whole pages. The manuscript fairly bled from the mutilation. I soon got the idea, and by the end of the day I was hacking away.

Late in the afternoon I heard a thump at my window. It was a cat, an old codger with a bruised forlorn face. He peered at me through the glass, rubbing his nose against it, then licking it expectantly. I ignored him for a few moments, and when I looked again two more cats were with him on the window sill, staring at me in orphaned alms-seeking. I couldn't take it. I went down the elevator to the deli and found some slices of pastrami in the garbage can. I wrapped them in a napkin and brought them back to the cats. When I opened the window they burst into the room and ate ravenously from my hand.

I heard Du Mont laughing. He was in the doorway of his office, one of his three Persians in his arms.

'I knew you were a cat man,' he said. 'I could tell from your eyes.'

Chapter Two

It took me three days to revise Jennifer Lovelace's story. Her version had been thirty pages long. Mine reduced the manuscript down to half of that. It really wasn't a bad story; it was simply bad construction and phrasing, the story of six school teachers riding in a covered wagon across the plains, having skirmishes with Indians and outlaws, and finally arriving in Stockton. I was pleased with what I had done and took the manuscript to Du Mont. He hefted it and frowned.

'Couldn't you add another ten pages?' he asked.

'It's long enough,' I insisted. 'I won't add another line. I think Jennifer Lovelace is going to like it.'

He reached for the telephone. 'I'll tell her the script is ready.'

I was feeding the cats next afternoon when Jennifer arrived. Her beauty was staggering. She was in a white linen suit with sheer black stockings and black pumps, a black purse hanging from her arm. Her hair was a froth of shimmering black, her face exquisite, illumined by black eyes. There was so much to see as I looked at her, and my eyes fell upon the contour of her body, the sensuality of her waist and hips, tantalizing, challenging, unbelievable. I had looked at thousands of beautiful women since arriving in Los Angeles but Jennifer Lovelace's beauty had me by the throat.

'Hi,' I said, and stumbled to my feet.

'Good afternoon,' she smiled. 'I'm Jennifer Lovelace. Is Dr Du Mont here?'

'I'll see. Please sit down.'

She floated down into a chair like a lovely satin pillow and I watched the mechanics of her knees, her thighs, her hips. She folded her exquisite hands in her lap and I felt a gloat of pleasure. I tapped Du Mont's door and he called to me to enter. I went in, carefully closed the door and whispered, 'She's here!'

'Shh!' Du Mont said, pressing his lips. 'Let her wait awhile. She's rich.'

'She *looks* rich.'

Du Mont pulled a gold watch from his vest pocket and stared at it for what seemed a long time. Then he snapped, 'Now! Show her in!'

I opened the door and found her sitting there in patient aplomb, like a queen.

'Please come in,' I said.

'Thank you,' she said, rising. As she stepped toward Du Mont's office I saw the back of her suit covered with cat fur.

'Wait!' I said. She paused and looked at me puzzled. Here was my chance. I dropped to my knees behind her and began brushing away the cat fur from her glorious buttocks, feeling the taut muscled thighs, the roundness of her effulgent rear. She whirled away from me.

'What are you doing?' she demanded. 'What on earth?'

'The cats,' I said, holding out my two hands covered with cat fur.

She twisted her torso to look at the clinging fur, and began to brush it away with one hand. I crawled to her assistance and she pushed me away.

'Please!' she implored. 'Leave me alone.' By now Du Mont was at her side, gallant, collected.

'Come, my dear,' he soothed, leading her through the door, then closing it behind her. I knelt on the floor, confused and embarrassed, as the cats swirled around me, whining to be fed.

There was a silence in Du Mont's office. On my knees I peered through the keyhole at Jennifer seated across the desk from Du Mont. Her face was a furious frown as she read the revised version of her story.

'My manuscript!' she gasped. 'What happened to it?' She groped through her purse. 'Give me a cigarette, please.'

Du Mont proffered one.

'What have you done to my story, Dr Du Mont? You've destroyed it – my beautiful story! How could you do this to me?'

Du Mont lifted his palms placatingly. 'I did nothing, my dear,' he lied. 'I had no idea that he was doing it.'

Jennifer Lovelace stiffened. 'He? Who's he?'

Du Mont didn't say a word. He merely nodded guiltily at the reception room door. As Jennifer Lovelace leaped to her feet I took off – into the hall, down the stairs, through the deli, and out the back way to the alley. There I found a packing box and sat upon it and smoked a cigarette, my hands trembling. About me I noticed the cats, the same old gang who visited my office. They looked at me curiously, wondering what I was doing in their territory.

I looked up at the window of my office. I couldn't go

back there. I wouldn't. I felt betrayed. Du Mont had tricked me. The savage editing of Jennifer's script filled me with shame now. If someone had hacked up my work like that I would have punched him. I wondered what Heinrich Muller would say about my integrity. Integrity! I laughed. Integrity – balls. I was a nothing, a zero. To hell with it. I decided to go shopping for a pair of pants. I still had over a hundred dollars. I would splurge and forget my troubles in profligate spending. What was money anyway?

At the Goodwill I selected and tried on three pairs of pants. Somehow they did very little for me. I looked at myself in the long, mirror, and there I was – the cipher, the zero. Shameful in the presence of Heinrich Muller, the lion of literature.

Walking across Third and Hill to Angel's Flight, I climbed aboard the trolley and sat down. The only other passenger was a girl across the aisle reading a book. She was in a plain dress and without stockings. She was rather attractive but not my style. As the trolley lurched into motion she moved to another seat. No ass at all, I thought. An ass, yes, but without the splendor of Jennifer Lovelace's. Without nobility, without the grandeur of a thing of beauty. Just an ass, a plain common ass. It was not my day.

I got off the cablecar at the top of Angel's Flight and started down Third Street toward my hotel. Then I decided on a cup of coffee and a cigarette in the small Japanese restaurant a few doors ahead. The coffee erased my gloom and I walked on to my hotel. The landlady sat behind the desk in the lobby. The first thing I noticed was a copy of *The American Phoenix*. It was exactly where I had placed it three weeks ago. Annoyed, I walked boldly to the desk and picked it up.

'You haven't read it, have you?'

She smiled, hostile. 'No, I haven't.'

'Why not?' I said.

'It bored me. I read the first paragraph and that was enough for me.'

I put the magazine under my arm.

'I'm moving out,' I said. 'Real soon.'

'Suit yourself.'

I walked away and down the hall. As I turned the key in my door I heard the click of a lock across the hall. The door opened and the girl from the trolley stepped out. She still carried the book. It was Zola's *Nana*. She smiled in greeting.

'Hi!' I said. 'I didn't know you lived here.'

'I just moved in.'

'You work around here?'

'I suppose you'd call it that.' She made a sensual glance. 'Would you like to see me?'

'When?'

'How about right now?'

I didn't want her. Nothing of her lured me, but I had to be manly. These situations could only be resolved in one way.

'Sure,' I said.

She turned on the tiny flame of sensuality in her eyes and pushed open her door.

'What are we waiting for?' she said.

I hesitated. Lord help me, I thought, as I crossed the hall and entered her room.

She followed me inside and closed the door.

'What's your name, honey?'

'Arturo,' I said. 'Arturo Bandini.'

She held out her hands and removed my coat.

'How much?' I asked.

'A fin.'

She guided me around to face her and began unbuttoning my shirt. Hanging it over a chair she crossed to the bathroom.

'See you in a minute.'

She entered the bathroom and closed the door. I sat on the bed and pulled off my clothes. I was naked when she emerged. I tried to hide my disappointment. She was clean and bathed but somehow impure. Her bottom hung there like an orphan child. We would never make it together. My presence there was insanity. She grasped my rod and led me to the bathroom. She washed and soaped my loins and her fingers kneaded my joint determinedly, but there was no response. I could only think of Jennifer Lovelace and the gallantry of her flanks. Then she towelled me off and we went back to the bedroom and lay on the bed. She spread herself out naked and I lay beside her.

'Go ahead,' she said. I traced one finger through her pubic hair.

'Do you mind if I read?' she said. 'Hand me my book.'

I gave her the book and she opened it to her place and began to read. I lay there and wondered. Good God, what if my mother were to walk in? Or my father? Or Heinrich Muller? Where would it all end? She nodded toward a bowl of apples at the bedside.

'Want an apple?' she asked.

'No thanks.'

'Give me one please.'

I handed her an apple. And so she read and ate.

'Come on, honey,' she coaxed. 'Enjoy yourself.'

I swung my legs out of bed and stood up.

'What's the matter?' she asked, her voice hostile.

'Don't worry. I'll pay you off.'

'Would you like me to suck you?'

'No,' I said.

She slammed the book shut.

'Do you know what's the matter with you, sonny? You're queer. That's what's the matter with you. You're a fag. I know your kind.'

She grabbed my coat, pants, underwear, shoes and socks, raced to the door and threw it all in the hall. I stepped out and began gathering my things.

'I owe you five bucks,' I said.

'No, you don't. You don't owe me a thing.'

I groped through my coat pocket for the door key. Down the hall, watching me with her arms folded, was Mrs Brownell, the landlady. I turned the key and jumped into my room.

I felt relieved, saved, rescued. I went to the window to look at all of the great city spread below me. It was like a view of the whole world. Far to the southwest the sun struck the ocean in bars of heavenly light. A message from God. A sign. The Infant Jesus in the manager, the light from the Star of Bethlehem. I fell on my knees.

'Oh blessed Infant Jesus,' I prayed. 'Thank you for saving me this day. Bless you for the surge of God's goodness that moved me from that room of sin. I swear it now – I will never sin again. For the rest of my life I will remember your glorious intercession. Thank you, little Son of God. I am your devoted servant forever henceforth.'

I made the sign of the cross and got to my feet. How good I felt. How recharged with the feelings of my early boyhood.

I had to get in touch with Jennifer Lovelace. I dressed and went out to the lobby. At the pay station I dialed Du Mont's number.

'What happened to you?' he asked.

'I'm at my hotel. What's Jennifer Lovelace's phone number?'

He gave it to me and I wrote it down.

I went back to my room and sat at the typewriter. I typed for fifteen minutes – two pages of heartbreak. I folded the paper and walked out of the hotel to the pay station across the street and telephoned Jennifer. Unfolding my notes, I heard the telephone ringing.

'Hello.' It was she.

'Jennifer, this is Arturo Bandini.'

There was a silence. The sweat popped from my skin. My voice quivered.

'Jennifer, I want you to forgive me. I don't know why I destroyed your beautiful manuscript. It was simply a matter of inexperience. I'm a good writer, Jennifer. I can prove that. I'll bring you some of my work. You'll see what a superb writer I am. I didn't mean to ruin your manuscript. I'm not a critic, Jennifer. I only followed Du Mont's instruction. I made a terrible mistake. Won't you let me see you and explain? I'd like to tell you what a wonderful talent I am. Please, Jennifer. Give me the chance to explain . . .'

There was more to say, but she cut in.

'How about Sunday?'

'Any day, any time. You name it.'

She gave me her address in Santa Monica and I wrote it down.

'Thank you, Jennifer. You won't regret this.'
She hung up.

Chapter Three

The sun hit my face like big golden eye, wakening me. It was
Sunday morning and it promised a bright and glorious day. I
shot out of bed, opened the window wide and called out to
the world, hello everybody! Good luck to all! A good day, a
fresh day. I remembered my father in Colorado at the kitchen
sink on a bright spring morning, singing with happiness as he
shaved. *O Sole Mio*. I stood before my bathroom mirror and
sang it too. Oh God, how good I felt! How was it possible?
For breakfast I peeled and ate two oranges.

In my fine Goodwill pinstripe suit and my rakish fedora,
I tucked a copy of *The American Phoenix* under my arm
and strode out to conquer a woman. Down Olive Street
I marched on the clear Sunday morning. The city seemed
deserted, the street was quiet. I paused and listened. I heard
something. It was the sound of happiness. It was my own
heart beating softly, rhythmically. A clock, that's what I
was, a little happiness machine. I crossed Fifth Street to
the Biltmore Hotel. Well-dressed folk moved in and out
through the revolving doors. They were people like myself,
neatly attired, the better class. At the main entrance stood a
uniformed doorman. He looked ten feet tall as he saluted me.
I returned the salute.

'Do you have the time, sir?' I asked.

'Yes, sir.' He glanced at his wristwatch. 'It's eleven o'clock, sir.'

'Thank you, sir.'

I walked to the curbing and looked at a long line of taxi cabs, a waiting driver in each. Suddenly an idea exploded in my head. I would take a taxi to Jennifer's. All my life I had wanted to take a taxi, but for a number of reasons, all financial, I had never done so. Now I could do it. I could arrive in style. I could sweep up to her house, wait for the driver to open the door, then leap out like a prince. The doorman came to my side.

'Taxi, sir?'

'Yes, sir.' He opened the door of the nearest taxi and I got inside. The driver swung around and looked at me.

'Where to, sir?'

'1724 Eighteenth Street, Santa Monica.'

'Pretty long fare,' he said.

'It's of no consequence,' I answered. 'No consequence at all.'

The cab drew away from the curb, turned right on Seventh Street, then right on Hope Street to Wilshire Boulevard. I watched the street and the shops and felt a lump in my throat. What a wonderful city! Look at all those beautiful people walking in their fine garments as they came from churches and window shopped along the bright boulevard. No doubt about it, this was my day, my city.

The cab driver was right. It was a long fare – seven dollars and twenty cents worth. He punched the meter and I studied the final figure. I stepped out of the cab and handed the driver a ten-dollar bill. He dug out the exact change, which I counted. Then it occurred to me that tipping was also the custom. He was watching me. I handed him a dime.

His lip curled. 'Gee, thanks.'

I turned away and looked at Jennifer's house. It was out of Mother Goose, a yellow and white Victorian fantasy with cupolas at both corners of the second story. The cupolas were adorned with wood panels of carved spools and intricate patterns of scrolls and twirling figures. It was a wedding cake, complete in every detail except the bride and groom. It sat there proudly in an enclosure of huge fir trees, strangely out of place, belonging instead to the Land of Oz. Jennifer's house! I saw the big comfortable chairs on the veranda and smiled at the thought that her marvellous bottom had graced them all.

She came to the door as I mounted the porch stairs.

'Hello!' she smiled. 'I'm glad you came. Please come in.'

She pushed open the screen door and I walked inside. The room was dazzling. A grand piano, luxurious chairs, gigantic Boston ferns, Tiffany lamps, and a large painting in oils above the fireplace – of a child with long curls. She permitted me enough time to study the portrait as she explained that it was a painting of herself.

'Do sit down,' she said. 'Mother and Dad are at mass. They should be back soon.'

'Did you go to mass this morning?' I asked.

'Oh, yes. Are you a Catholic?'

'What else?' I smiled. 'The church has been part of my family for generations.'

'Then you went to mass this morning?'

'Naturally. Missing mass is a mortal sin. Surely you know that.'

She smiled. 'Of course.'

I sat down. 'As a matter of fact I had something of a theological dispute with my confessor this morning.'

She smoothed out the seat of her yellow sun suit as she sat down. Her bottom filled the chair like a lovely egg in a nest.

'Where's your parish?' she asked.

I knew that somewhere in Los Angeles there had to be a St Mary's Church, and I answered, 'Saint Mary of Guadalupe.'

'Isn't it gorgeous?' she exclaimed. 'I love that church.'

'I often pray there.'

'You were saying something about a dispute with your confessor. What did you mean?'

'I'll tell you, but only in strictest confidence. The sacred seal of the confessional.'

She gasped and her hand touched her bosom. 'Should you?' she asked.

'I must,' I said. I wrung my hands in my lap for a moment or two and then I continued.

'You remember the debauchery of your manuscript? Have you forgotten how I destroyed it in wanton disregard for your feelings? Have you forgotten your anger at the outrage?'

She nodded solemnly.

'When I entered the confessional and faced the priest my one question was – had I committed a mortal sin in ruining your work? Was it an extreme offense against the law of God? Would he forgive me for it? The priest looked at me through the screen and thought a moment, and then he said, "The desecration of any artistic achievement is one of the great sins against the law of God."'

She seemed terribly impressed and stood up.

'Would you like a coke, Mr Bandini?'

'Yes, thank you.'

She walked quickly toward the kitchen, her glorious ass following her in ritualistic cadence.

I went after her and she took a couple of cokes from the refrigerator and handed one to me. We opened the bottles and drank. There was a covered picnic basket on the table. I lifted the lid and peeked inside.

'That's for us,' she said.

'We're going someplace?'

'The beach.'

'The ocean?'

'Naturally.'

'Can we swim?'

'That's what it's for.'

'I don't have any swimming trunks.'

'You can borrow a pair of my brother's.'

We finished our cokes.

'Let's go,' she said.

Carrying the picnic basket, I followed her down the back stairs to the garage where a two-door Chevy was parked. I put the basket in the back seat and slid in beside her. She started the engine and drove down the alley to the cross street and turned into traffic.

A mile north of the Santa Monica pier on the Pacific Coast Highway was a cluster of beach bungalows, weather beaten and very old. We drew to the curb and got out. A wooden path led us through a high fence to one of a dozen cottages built on the sand. She turned a key in the door of the first cottage and we went inside. The bungalow belonged to her family. It was not pretentious – a stove, a refrigerator, table and chairs. Off the kitchen were two bedrooms. She went into one and emerged in a black bathing suit, tossing me a pair of trunks. While I undressed she went outside and ran toward the surf. I stripped off my clothes and frowned at my lily-white body. It reminded me of a pink pig, and I dreaded the shock in her face when I made my appearance. But she wasn't shocked at all as she lay on the warm sand and read *The American Phoenix* through dark horn-rimmed glasses.

The ocean was staggering. I forgot my pale, sunless body and stared in wonder. The beach was almost deserted. A group of children came trotting past, stopping to stare at me; then giggling, they trotted on. Carefully I permitted the small waves to cover my toes as I splashed along in pleasure. Gradually I moved into deeper water and began to swim, invigorated by the cool tangy surf. Colorado seemed an eternity away. I told myself that at this moment my mother had arrived home from mass and was preparing lunch. She was probably thinking of me even as I thought of her.

I kept glancing at Jennifer. She was absorbed in the magazine and paid no attention to me. I stood before her and caught her attention.

'Watch!'

I did a handspring, then another, and a third. She smiled vaguely and turned back to the magazine. I had other tricks, for I had been a member of the trumbling team at Colorado University.

'Watch this one!'

I did a number of cartwheels. She looked up and gave me a distracted smile.

'Watch this!'

I got up on my hands and walked out into the water until

my hands and shoulders were submerged. Then I tumbled off my balance. I looked toward the beach. Jennifer was gone. I saw her wade through the sand and enter the cottage. I went after her.

She was taking things from the picnic basket – lettuce, onions, tomatoes – washing them in the sink, then cutting them up in a wooden bowl. She had put on a cocktail apron over her sleek black bathing suit. It made me gape. Her figure was voluptuous, tantalizing, irresistible. I lit a cigarette and my hand shook, and I thought the moment has come. It's now or never. Don't be a dummy. Act. This time will never come again. Be brave. You've got nothing to lose. Everything to gain. I stood up and flung myself at her, falling to my knees and throwing my arms around her waist.

'I love you,' I said. 'I want you.'

She twisted her superb hips to escape my grip. I clung like a tiger. She lifted the salad bowl and brought it down on my head. I felt the inundation of mayonnaise, olive oil and vegetables as I sprawled on the floor, dragging her down upon me.

'You fool!' she screamed. 'Let me go! You crazy fool!'

We were caught up in some sort of inexplicable violence, wrestling with one another, sliding across the floor, fighting a meaningless combat. She screamed when I bit her ass. She got to her hands and knees and crawled out of my grasp and into the bedroom, kicking the door closed.

I sat panting in the quagmire of salad dressing. What had I done? On the messy floor was my copy of *The American Phoenix*, smeared with oil and mayonnaise. What now, I asked. Go, I said. Take flight. Get out of here. I crawled into a chair and saw scratch marks on my chest and legs.

The end of the world. The end of me. The end of my love. The bedroom door opened and she stepped out. She was towelling off her body, smearing away the salad dressing. She didn't say a word.

'I'm sorry,' I said.

'You sonofabitch!' she said. She picked up her keys from the table and went to the door. 'And another thing,' she snapped, 'there's no such church as St Mary's of Guadalupe!'

She went out. I followed her through the front gate to the highway. She entered her car and drove away.

I wanted to cry, but my stupidity overwhelmed me. I went back to the bungalow, took off the bathing trunks and got under a cold shower. I towelled myself off, dressed, closed the cottage doors, and stepped out beside the highway. Across the street bathers were climbing down the steep path from the top of the palisades. I crossed the highway and started up the path. It took me to Ocean Avenue and a street car depot. I took the next car and rode back to my hotel.

As I turned the key in my door I heard a radio playing across the hall. The song was *Begin the Beguine*. I entered my room, took off my clothes, and put on a bathrobe. It was almost dark now, dark, lonely and erotic. I left my room, crossed the hall, and knocked on her door. The radio went off and she called,

'Come in.'

I opened the door.

She was stretched out on the bed dressed in a pink slip, still reading *Nana*. She frowned.

'What do *you* want?'

'Let's fuck,' I said.

Chapter Four

The days stumbled past. August came, hot and sticky. One evening it rained. People streamed out of the hotel and stood in the street catching the rain in their hands. A sweet smell came over Bunker Hill. The rain splashed our faces. Then it was gone. I worked hard, pecking away on a short story. I took the work with me to Du Mont's office. Several times during the day he drifted over and studied what I was writing. Suddenly he tore the page from my typewriter.

'You're fired,' he said. He was trembling. 'Take your story and get out.'

I left. I went to a movie. I loafed down Main Street to the Follies, the marquee lit with the name of Ginger Britton. She was in the midst of her strip, swinging from the drapes, her ass a perfect Rubens. I found a seat in the first row and watched her ravenously. She was magnificent, with the ass of a young colt, stomping the stage in high heels, turning her back on the audience, bending down to look at us between her legs. An absolutely world-champion ass, incomparable, her skin glowing like the meat of a honeydew melon. Her long red hair hung to her hips, her Valkyrie breasts flying about in wild circles. The audience cheered and whistled. They angered me. Why were they so fucking vulgar? They were watching a work of art with the same acclaim as a boxing match. It was sacrilegious. As she left the stage the applause was raucous, impossible. I couldn't bear it, and stomped out of the theater. In a rage I returned to my hotel. I sat at the typewriter and wrote a letter to Ginger Britton:

Dear Ginger Britton:
   I love you. I saw you today and I love you madly. I reverence you. I long to know you, to talk to you, to hold your hand, to take you in my arms and smother you with kisses. The sight of you dancing was like a flame through my body. What I would give to take you to dinner in some quiet supper club, your red hair in my face, your lips wet with wine, kissing mine! Be kind to me, dear lady of the Follies, and invite me to visit you some evening after the show. I tremble with love.
                                                      Arturo Bandini

I signed the letter, put it in an envelope and took it to the lobby. Mrs Brownell was behind the desk. I asked her for a stamp. Then I smelled an intoxicating odor wafted from the door of her living quarters behind the desk.

'What's that?' I asked, sniffing.

'Mince pie,' she said. 'I just took it out of the oven.'

'Smells wonderful.'

'Would you like a piece?'

It was the first firendly remark I ever heard from her. I looked at her clear blue eyes and wondered at the change. She was actually hospitable and not the bitch I had gotten used to.

'Thank you, Mrs Brownell. I'd love a piece.'

She invited me into her room. I stood there looking

around. It was a housekeeping room – a stove, a refrigerator, a breakfast table, a couple of chairs, and a studio couch.

'Sit down, Mr Bandini.'

I sat at the table and watched her cut a wedge from a large mince pie. She wasn't young. Maybe fifty-five. If you looked closely you saw that her figure was trim and well formed. There was even a hint of a nice ass. She placed the wedge of pie in a deep plate and poured brandy over it.

'It's funny,' she said. 'All this hot day I've been thinking of mince pie. Now I know why.' She smiled, her perfect dentures showing, and put the pie before me. She handed me a spoon, and I tasted the pie. I must have eaten very quickly, for she soon served me a second piece. It was very powerful pie, but I loved it, and sipped the brandy like soup, and felt great heat in my stomach. Then everything was vague and I was drunk. I heard Mrs Brownell talking of Kansas and Thanksgiving dinner on a farm outside of Topeka, an account of her brothers and sisters and how her father ran away with a woman from Wichita.

I woke up in bed. Not my bed, but Mrs Brownell's. I lay on my back next to the wall. The person asleep at my side was Mrs Brownell. She was in a white nightgown and nightcap. She lay facing me, her two hands clutching my arm as she snored musically. The bedside clock showed three A.M. I closed my eyes and went back to sleep.

We were good for each other, Helen Brownell and I. Every night I found the passage to her room an easy journey. She sometimes smiled as I sat down and removed my shoes. Other times she paid no attention, as if expecting me. I was her little champion, she said, for I was a small man, no larger than her husband, an accountant who had died five years before. When it was time to close up shop she disappeared into the bathroom to undress, then emerging in her muslin nightie and nightcap. She snapped off the bathroom light and slipped into bed beside me. We shared the darkness together, sometimes, that is. Sometimes I groped a little and she responded. Mostly she was like a relative in the night, a maiden aunt, my Aunt Cornelia who lived with us when I was a boy and who hated children. In the morning I awoke to the hiss of bacon, and saw her over the stove, cooking my breakfast.

'Good morning,' I'd say, and she'd answer,

'Time for breakfast, little champ.'

Sometimes she bent over and kissed me on the forehead. She must have known that I was broke for every day or two I found a couple of dollars in my pocket. I tried to do the dishes, but she wouldn't have it. Well fed and rested I went down to my room and faced the black monster typewriter glaring at me with gaping white teeth. Sometimes I wrote ten pages. I didn't like that, for I knew that whenever I was prolific I also stank. I stank most of the time. I had to be patient. I knew it would come. Patience! It was the least of my virtues.

One day there was a surprise in my mail. The letter sparkled in my hand. I recognized it instantly. It was a letter from Ginger Britton, scented with the fragrance of gardenias. I took it to my room and sat on the bed and opened it, a letter in a stately hand of elegant penmanship. Ginger Britton thanked me for my letter. She appreciated all that I had written and she was delighted. Unfortunately she could not meet me for a supper date because she was certain her husband would never permit it, but she urged me to come often to the Follies to watch her perform. She loved my letter. She was deeply moved by it. She would treasure it always.

I unfolded the letter and pressed it to my face, breathing the fragrance of her gardenias. I pressed my lips into it and gurgled gratefully. Da, da, da I murmured. Oh Ginger Britton, how I love you! Da da da.

I was in the first row of the Follies Theater when the curtain rose for the burlesque show. She entered the stage with the full cast and I sank gratefully into my seat. I had come with plans: to whisper to her, to wave, to toss her a kiss, but as I looked around, every face was the face of her husband, and I lost courage. Then I looked up at her face. She was smiling down at me. She recognized me. I *knew* that she recognized me, and there was an intimacy about her smile that thrilled me, and I waved two or three fingers in a cowardly acknowledgment. Then she entered her specialty routine, twirling midstage, then bending backward to look at the audience between her legs, and from that position she turned her face to me and smiled emphatically. I looked about nervously. The customers ignored me except a man two aisles back, a black man, rugged, tough, unsmiling, staring straight at me. I sensed trouble, got up and walked out. The black man was either her husband or another fan who had written her.

Chapter Five

On the way back to Bunker Hill I went through Pershing Square. It was a warm night and the park was brilliant beneath the street lamps. People sat on park benches enjoying the cool tranquillity after a hot day. In the center of the square was a park bench occupied by chess players. There were four players on either side of the long table, each with a chessboard in front of him. They were playing rapid transit chess – eight players matching their skills against one man, an old man, a raucous, insolent, brilliant man in shirt sleeves, dancing about as he moved from player to player, making a chess move, delivering an insult, then moving on to the next player. In a matter of minutes he had checkmated all eight of his opponents and snatched up a bet of twenty-five cents for his victory. As the disgruntled players moved away, the old man, whose name was Mose Moss, shouted out,

'Who's next? Who thinks he's a great chess player? I'll beat any man here, any two men, any ten men.' He whirled and looked at me.

'What are you standing there for?' he shouted. 'Who the hell do you think you are? You got two bits? Sit down, and put it up, you smart-ass kid. I'll beat your britches off!'

I turned away.

'That's it!' he sneered. 'You fucking coward! I knew you was yellow the minute I laid eyes on you!'

By now another group of chess players had taken seats around the long table. There were seven of them. I had not played chess in two years, but I had been a good chess player at Colorado, and had even won a tournament at the chess club. I knew I could hold my own against this garrulous, insulting old bastard, but I didn't know if I could win against his scatological attack. He slapped me on the back.

'Sit down, sonny. Learn something about chess.'

That did it. I dug a quarter from my pocket, slapped it on the table, and sat down.

He beat me and the others in ten moves. We, the victims, rose from the table as he gathered up the quarters and jingled them in his pocket.

'Is it over?' he asked. 'Have I won again?'

I dug out another quarter, but the other players had had enough. Mose Moss sat across from me and we began to play. He lit a cigarette.

'Who taught you this game, kid? Your mother?'

'Your move,' I said. 'You sonofabitch!'

'Now you're sounding like real chess player,' he said, moving a pawn. He beat me in twelve moves. I plumped down another quarter. He beat me again quickly, decisively. There was no way I could defeat this old man. Then he began to toy with me. It was cruel. It was brutal. It was sadistic. He offered to engage me without his queen, and I lost. Next he removed his queen, his two bishops, and his two knights, and I lost again. Finally he stripped his forces down to just pawns. By now a crowd three deep was gathered about us, howling with laughter as his pawns mowed my pieces down and he worked another checkmate. I had one quarter left. I placed it on the table. Mose Moss rubbed his hands together and smiled with benign triumph.

'Tell you what I'm going to do now, kid. I'm going to let you win. You're going to checkmate me.'

The audience applauded, moved closer. Forty people crowded about. He needed about twenty moves to finish me off, maneuvering his pieces in such a way that I could not avoid checkmating him. I was tired, frustrated, and sick of soul. My stomach ached, my eyes burned.

'I'm through, Mose,' I said. 'That was my last quarter.'

'Your credit is good,' he said. 'You look like an honest kid. You're a goddamn fool, but you look honest.'

Numbly I began to play, too confused to walk away, too ashamed to get to my feet and move off. Suddenly there was a commotion. The bystanders fled. The police were on the scene. They grabbed a couple of people and Mose and I were hustled off to the paddy wagon. We were taken to the city jail, six of us, and lined up at the sergeant's desk, each accused of loitering. After the booking, we were taken to the drunk tank. I followed Mose around, for he seemed to know the routine. We sat on a bench and I asked Mose what happened next.

'Ten dollars or five days,' he said. 'Fuck 'em. Let's play chess.' To my horror he pulled a miniature chess game from his back pocket, and we put the chess men into place and began to play. He was indefatigable. My eyes would not open. I slept with my chin on my chest. He shook me awake and I moved a player. We were playing for astronomical sums now. I owed him fifteen thousand dollars. We doubled it. I lost again, and as Mose tried to awaken me, I slipped off the bench and fell asleep on the floor. I heard his last words:

'You bastard, you owe me thirty thousand dollars.'

'Put it on my bill,' I said.

I slept. Vaguely I heard the night sounds around me – the snores, the farts, the moans, the puking, the mumbling in sleep. It was cold in the big cell. The gray dawn crept through the window. Daylight gradually came. At six o'clock the jailer rattled the cell bars with a riot stick.

'Everybody get ready for Sunrise Court,' he shouted. 'You have five minutes to make a phone call.'

I followed Mose down the hall to a waiting room with telephones on the wall. They were pay phones. I searched my pockets for a dime. I had nothing. Mose was in front of me, talking to someone by phone. As he hung up I crowded him.

'Loan me a dime,' I said.

He frowned. 'Jesus, kid,' he said. 'You already owe me thirty grand.'

'I'll pay you back, Mose,' I implored. 'Every cent. Believe me.'

He dug into his pocket and pulled out a handful of silver coins. 'Take one.'

I selected a dime and stepped up to the telephone. I dialled my hotel. Mrs Brownell answered.

'I'm in Sunrise Court,' I told her. 'Can you bail me out? It's ten dollars.'

There was a silence. 'Are you in trouble?'

'No, but I'm broke.'

'I'll be right there.' She hung up.

She was in the courtroom when the prisoners were brought in. My name was called and I approached the bench. The judge never saw me, never even looked at me.

'You are charged with loitering. Ten dollars or five days. How do you plead?'

'Guilty,' I said.

'Pay the bailiff,' he said. 'Next.'

As I moved to the bailiff's desk Mrs Brownell arose and came to my side. She opened her purse and gave the bailiff a ten-dollar bill. I bent over the desk and signed a bail receipt. Mrs Brownell sped down the hall, moving fast. I ran to catch her.

'Thanks,' I said. She raced ahead, out the front door, down the steps to the street, where her car was parked. I got in beside her, and the car lurched as she threw it into gear.

'I appreciate what you did,' I said. She flung me a bitter glance.

'Jailbird!' she said. We did not speak as she drove up Temple Street and turned onto Bunker Hill. She parked the car in the empty lot next to the hotel.

'I didn't commit a crime,' I explained. 'I was booked for playing chess, that's all.'

She looked sullen. 'And now you have a prison record.'

'Oh shit,' I said.

We got out and crossed to the hotel. We went through the office into her living quarters. She stepped into the bathroom and turned on the hot water. Clouds of steam rose and drifted into the living room.

'You're going to take a bath,' she said. 'You're going to cleanse yourself of all that jailhouse scruff and dirt and filth, the lice and fleas and bedbugs.'

I dropped my clothes around my feet and she gathered them like dead animals and tossed them into the laundry hamper. The water was warm and soapy, and I sank to my neck and let the goodness of heat sink in. Mrs Brownell bent over me with a washcloth and a lump of fels naphtha soap. She lathered the washcloth and began to scrub me. The washcloth ground into my ears until I screamed.

'Dirt,' she said. 'Look at the dirt! Aren't you ashamed?'

She plunged the washcloth into my crotch and I screamed again.

'Get out,' I said. 'Leave me alone.'

She flung the washcloth into my face. 'Jailbird!' she said. 'Convict!'

She turned and left me alone. I dried myself off, got into my shorts and walked into the kitchen. She was at the stove, cooking my breakfast, her back to me. Skilled ass man that I was, I quickly detected the contraction of her buttocks – a sure sign of rage in a woman. Experience had taught me great caution in the face of such dramatic change in the derrière and I was quiet as I sat down. It was like being in the presence of a coiled snake. She brought ham and eggs to the table and slammed the dish in front of me. The telephone rang. I heard her answer it.

'For you,' she said.

I picked up the phone. The caller was Harry Schindler, the movie director. He was an old friend of H. L. Muller. He had obtained my address from Muller, and was anxious to talk to me.

'What about?'

'Have you ever written for pictures?'

'No.'

'That's fine,' Schindler said. 'Would you like a job?'

'Doing what?'

'Writing a screenplay.'

'I don't know how.'

'Nothing to it,' Schindler said. 'I'll show you. Meet me at Columbia Pictures tomorrow morning at ten o'clock.'

I went back to Mrs Brownell's living room and sat down. She had obviously overheard the telephone conversation.

'I may have a job in the movies.'

'At least you'll be clean,' she said. I noticed her derrière. It was still contracted. I ate quickly and went back to my room.

Chapter Six

Next morning Mrs Brownell gave me directions and I took the Sunset bus to Gower Avenue. The studio was down the street half a block. I took the elevator to the fourth floor and found Schindler's office. His secretary sat at her desk reading a novel. She was blonde, with her hair severely coiffured, drawn back to a knot at the nape of her neck. She had golden eyebrows and her eyes were pure topaz, hostile, not friendly.

'Yes?' she said.

I told her my name. She rose and moved to Schindler's office door. Her dress was green velvet. Instantly I was aware of her sensational ass, a Hollywood perfecto. She moved like a snake, a large snake, a lustful boa constrictor. I was very pleased. She knocked on Schindler's door and opened it.

'Mr Bandini,' she announced.

Schindler rose from his desk and we shook hands.

'Sit down,' he said. 'Make yourself at home.'

He was a short, bullet-shaped man with a crew cut, an unlit cigar in his mouth.

'I've read all of your published stories,' he said. 'You've got lots of style, kid. You're just what I need. H. L. Muller strikes again!' he laughed. 'We're old friends, H. L. Muller and I. We worked on the *Baltimore Sun* together. I've known him for twenty years.'

'I told you I've never written for pictures. Don't expect too much.'

'Leave that to me,' Schindler said.

'Just what did you have in mind?'

'Nothing, for the time being. First, get used to the place. Get acclimated. Get oriented. Read some of my screenplays, look at some of my films. Meet the other writers on this floor – Benchley, Ben Hecht, Dalton Trumbo, Nat West. You're in good company, kid.'

'Does Sinclair Lewis work here?' I asked.

'I wish he did. Why? Do you know Lewis?'

'He's my favorite American writer.'

'And a good friend of H. L. Muller,' Schindler smiled. He pushed a buzzer and the secretary came in.

'Set Mr Bandini up in the other office,' Schindler told her. 'Arrange for him to look at some of my films, and see that he gets some of my screenplays.'

We shook hands.

'Good luck, Bandini. We're going to do great things together.'

'I hope so.'

I turned to leave.

'By the way,' he said, 'do you two know one another?'

I said no, and the girl said nothing.

'Arturo,' Schindler said, 'meet your secretary, Thelma Farber.'

I smiled at her. 'Hi.'

I wasn't sure, but I thought I saw her lip curl. She turned and walked out, and I followed the undulations of the boa constrictor in the green velvet dress. We crossed the reception room to an adjoining office. I looked around. A desk, a couple of chairs, a couch, a typewriter, some empty bookshelves.

'Fine,' I said. 'What do I do now?'

'Suit yourself,' she said, and promptly walked out and closed the door. I wondered about her, puzzled. Then I opened the door. She was at her desk reading her novel.

'Hey,' I said. She looked up. 'Are you this friendly with everybody?'

She smiled sweetly. 'Not everybody.'

Chapter Seven

My assignment from Harry Schindler was an unfathomable mystery. I spent the days reading his screenplays, a dozen of them, one a day, none of which I cared for. He was a specialist in gangster films and if you looked closely you discovered that all of his scripts were essentially the same, the same plot, the same characters, the same morality. I read them and set them aside. Sometimes I left the office and wandered down the halls. On each office door I saw the nameplate of the famous – Ben Hecht, Tess Slessinger, Dalton Trumbo, Nat West, Horace McCoy, Abem Candel, Frank Edgington. Sometimes I saw these writers entering or leaving their offices. They all looked alike to me. I didn't know them, and they didn't know me. At lunch time one day I went upstairs to the private dining room of the elite, where writers and directors gathered. I took a seat at a long table, and found myself between John Garfield and Rowland Brown, the director. To break the ice I said to Garfield, 'Please pass the salt.'

He passed it without saying a word. I turned to Brown and asked, 'You been here long?'

'Christ, yes,' he said, and that was all. It wasn't their fault, I decided. It was I, a social misfit, intimidated, lacking confidence. I never went back there again.

One day walking down the fourth floor corridor I saw a

man sitting behind a typewriter in Frank Edgington's office. He was a tall Englishman, smoking a pipe.

I said, 'Are you Frank Edgington?'

'That's me.'

I crossed to his desk and offered my hand.

'I'm Arturo Bandini. I'm a writer too. I work for Harry Schindler.'

'Welcome to the madhouse,' Edgington said.

'What are you working on?' I asked.

'A piece of crap. Do you know how to play pick-up-sticks?'

'Sure,' I said.

'Want to play a game?'

'Sure.'

He took a box of pick-up-stick pieces from his desk and we started to play. Edgington's big bony hands were ill suited for such delicate play. I wasn't any good either. We spent the afternoon at the game, just killing time. Edgington was an Eastern writer. He had contributed to the *New Yorker* and *Scribner's*. He hated Hollywood. He had been in pictures for five years, loathing every moment of it.

'Why don't you leave here?' I asked. 'If you hate it so much why don't you go back to New York?'

'Money. I love money.'

We went downstairs to the drugstore and ordered cokes.

'Are you married, Edgington?'

'Three times,' he said.

'You must like women very much.'

'Not anymore. You married?'

'No.'

'You're smart. Let's get back to the game.'

We returned to his office and played pick-up-sticks until five o'clock.

'Let's have dinner,' he said. 'Be my guest.'

Edgington drove a long black Cadillac. We went to Musso-Frank's. He knew a lot of people, mostly writers. We drank a lot, Edgington putting down scotch, while I drank wine. After dinner and another two hours of liquor we were both pretty drunk. His gray eyes looked at me unsteadily.

'Let's get laid,' he said.

'No, I don't need it.'

He was suddenly angry, and hammered the table in a drunken stupor.

'Everybody needs it,' he shouted, turning to address people sitting at the surrounding tables. 'Let's all get fucked,' he shouted.

Three waiters suddenly surrounded our table and hustled us out the back way and into the parking lot. Edgington dropped wearily onto a concrete slab and I sat beside him and lit a cigarette. His face twisted in a sneer.

'God, I hate this town,' he said. 'Let's get out of here. Let's go to New York.'

'I don't want to go to New York, Frank. Take me home.'

He staggered to his feet and stumbled toward the car. I didn't like the looks of it.

'Are you sober enough to drive?'

'Get in,' he said, 'trust me.'

He climbed in behind the steering wheel and I circled around to the other door and got in beside him. He bent forward, his face against the steering wheel. I waited a moment, studying him. He began to snore. He was sound asleep. I left him there, quietly slipped out, walked to Hollywood Boulevard, and took a red car to Bunker Hill.

Frank Edgington and I became buddies. He loved the flip side of Hollywood, the bars, the mean streets angling off Hollywood Boulevard to the south. I was glad to tag along as he took in the saloons along El Centro, McCadden Place, Wilcox, and Las Palmas. We drank beer and played the pinball games. Edgington was a pinball addict, a tireless devotee, drinking beer and popping the pinballs. Sometimes we went to the movies. He knew all the fine restaurants, and we ate and drank well. On weekends we toured the Los Angeles basin, the deserts, the foothills, the outlying towns, the harbor. One Saturday we drove to Terminal Island, a strip of white sand in the harbor. The canneries were there and we saw the weatherbeaten beach houses where Filipinos and Japanese lived. It was an enchanting place, lonely, decrepit, picturesque. I saw myself in one of the shacks with my typewriter. I longed for the chance to work there, to write in that lonely, forsaken place, where the sand half covered the streets, and the porches and fences hung limp in the wind. I told Frank I wanted to live there and write there.

'You're crazy,' he said. 'This is a slum.'

'It's beautiful,' I said. 'It gives me a warm feeling.'

At the studio we indulged another of Frank Edgington's obsessions – child games. We played pitch, old maid, Parcheesi, and Chinese checkers. We played for small stakes – five cents a game. When Frank was alone he worked on a short story for the *New Yorker*. When I was alone I sat in my office hungering for Thelma Farber. She was impregnable. Sometimes she even denied me a hello, and I was thoroughly squelched and breathing hard. Harry Schindler ordered his old films and Thelma and I sat in the projection room watching them unroll. I tried to sit next to her and she promptly moved two seats away. She was a bitch, unreasonably hostile. I felt like vermin.

After two weeks I picked up my first paycheck, $600. It was a staggering sum. Three hundred dollars a week for doing nothing! I knocked on Schindler's door and thanked him for the check.

'It's okay,' he grinned. 'We want you happy. That's the whole idea.'

'But I'm not doing anything. I'm going crazy. Give me something to write.'

'You're doing fine. I need you in case of emergency. I got to have a backup man, someone with talent. Don't worry about it. You're doing a great job. Keep up the good work. Cash the check and have fun.'

'Let me write you a western.'

'Not yet,' Schindler said. 'Just do what you're doing and leave the rest to me.'

Suddenly I choked up. I wanted to cry. I turned and walked out, brushed past Thelma and into my office. I sat at my desk crying. I didn't want charity. I wanted to be brilliant on paper, to turn fine phrases and dig up emotional gems for Schindler to see. Choking back my sobs I hurried down the hall to Edgington's office, and flung myself into a chair.

'What the hell's the matter?' Edgington asked.

I told him. 'They won't let me write,' I said. 'Schindler won't assign me anything. I'm going crazy.'

Edgington threw his pencil across the room in disgust.

'What the hell's the matter with you? There are writers in this studio who go months without scratching out a line. They earn ten times as much as you do, and they laugh all the way to the bank. Your trouble is that you're a fucking peasant. If there's so much you don't like about this town, stop jerking off and go back to that dago village your people came from. You make my ass tired!'

I stared at him gratefully. Then I began to laugh.

'Frank,' I said. 'You're a wonderful person.'

'Go and sin no more.'

I went downstairs to Gower Street, up to Sunset, and across Sunset to the Bank of America, where I cashed my check. I walked out with a new sensation, a feeling of bitter joy. Down Sunset half a block was a used car lot. I found a second-hand Plymouth for $300 and drove away. I was a new person, a successful Hollywood writer, without even writing a line. The future was limitless.

Chapter Eight

A few nights later Edgington invited me to dinner. 'Best restaurant in town,' he said. We left my car in the studio parking lot and drove off in Frank's Cadillac. He went up Beverly Boulevard to Doheny and pulled into the parking lot of an adjacent restaurant. It was Chasen's. Before we entered Frank straightened my tie.

'This is a high-class joint,' he said. 'I don't want you to embarrass me.'

We walked inside. There was a small outer bar, and beyond that the main dining room. We straddled bar stools and ordered drinks. As usual Frank knew everybody. He shook hands with Dave Chasen and introduced me.

'Nice to know you,' Chasen grinned, then turned hastily to welcome a man and two women entering from the street. They stood talking a moment.

Frank nudged me. 'Guess who's here,' he said.

I turned and studied the man and his two feminine companions.

'Who's he?' I whispered, as the trio moved past and entered the dining room.

'Sinclair Lewis,' Frank said.

Startled, I coughed in my drink.

'Are you sure?' I asked.

'Sure I'm sure.' He beckoned to Chasen, who joined us again. 'Who was the guy with the two women?' Frank asked.

'Sinclair Lewis,' Chasen said.

'Good God,' I said, 'the greatest writer in America!' I leaped off the bar stool and crossed to the curtained door leading to the dining room. Pulling the curtain aside, I saw a waiter ushering Lewis and his friends into a booth.

I couldn't stop myself. All at once I was threading my way between tables toward the greatest author in America. It was a blind, crazy impulse. Suddenly I stood before Lewis's booth. Absorbed in conversation with the women, he did not see me. I smiled at his thinning red hair, his rather freckled face, and his long delicate hands.

'Sinclair Lewis,' I said.

He and his friends looked up at me.

'You're the greatest novelist this country ever produced,' I spluttered. 'All I want is to shake your hand. My name is Arturo Bandini. I write for H. L. Muller, your best friend.' I thrust out my hand. 'I'm glad to know you, Mr Lewis.'

He fixed me with a bewildered stare, his eyes blue and cold. My hand was out there across the table between us. He did not take it. He only stared, and the women stared too. Slowly I drew my hand away.

'It's nice to know you, Mr Lewis. Sorry I bothered you.' I turned in horror, my guts falling out, as I hurried between the tables and back to the bar, and joined Frank Edgington. I was raging, sick, mortified, humiliated. I snatched Frank's Scotch and soda and gulped it down. The bartender and Frank exchanged glances.

'Give me a pencil and paper, please.'

The bartender put a notepad and a pencil before me. Breathing hard, the pencil trembling, I wrote:

Dear Sinclair Lewis:

You were once a god, but now you are a swine. I once reverenced you, admired you, and now you are nothing. I came to shake your hand in adoration, you, Lewis, a giant among American writers, and you rejected it. I swear I shall never read another line of yours again. You are an ill-mannered boor. You have betrayed me. I shall tell H. L. Muller about you, and how you have shamed me. I shall tell the world.

Arturo Bandini

P.S. I hope you choke on your steak.

I folded the paper and signalled a waiter. He walked over. I handed him the note.

'Would you please give this to Sinclair Lewis.'

He took it and I gave him some money. He entered the dining room. I stood in the doorway watching him approach Lewis's table. He handed Lewis the note. Lewis held it before him for some moments, then leaped to his feet, looking around, calling the waiter back. He stepped out of the booth and the waiter pointed in my direction. Carrying his napkin, Lewis took big strides as he came toward me. I shot out of there, out the front door, and down the street to the parking lot, to Frank's Cadillac, and leaped into the back seat. I could see the street from where I sat, and in a moment Lewis appeared nervously on the sidewalk, still clutching his napkin. He glanced about, agitated.

'Bandini,' he called. 'Where are you? I'm Sinclair Lewis. Where are you, Bandini?'

I sat motionless. A few moments, and he walked back toward the restaurant. I sat back, exhausted, bewildered, not knowing myself, or my capabilities. I sat with doubts, with shame, with torment, with regret. I lit a cigarette and sucked it greedily. In a little while Frank Edgington walked out of the restaurant and came to the car. He leaned inside and looked at me.

'You okay?'

'Okay,' I said.

'What happened?'

'I don't know.'

'What was that note you wrote?'

'I don't know.'

'You're crazy. You want to eat?'

'Not here. Let's go someplace else.'

'It's up to you.' He got behind the wheel and started the engine.

Chapter Nine

I was born in a basement apartment of a macaroni factory in North Denver. When my father learned that his third child was also a son he reacted in the same fashion as when my two brothers came into the world – he got drunk for three days. My mother found him in the back room of a saloon down the street from our apartment and dragged him home. Beyond that my father paid little attention to me.

One day in my infancy I stood outside the bathroom window of my aunt's house and watched my cousin Catherine standing before the dresser mirror combing out her long red hair. She was stark naked except for her mother's high-heeled shoes, a full-fledged woman of eight years. I did not understand the ecstasy that boiled up in me, the confusion of my cousin's electric beauty pouring into me. I stood there and masturbated. I was five years old and the world had a new and staggering dimension.

I was also a criminal. I felt like a criminal, a skulking, snot-nosed, freckle-faced, inscrutable criminal for four years thereafter, until sagging beneath the weight of my cross, I dragged myself into my first confession and told the priest the truth of my bestial life. He gave me absolution and I flung away the heavy cross and walked out into the sunlight, a free soul again.

Our family moved to Boulder when I was seven and my two brothers and I attended Sacred Heart School. During the ensuing eight years I achieved high marks in baseball, basketball and football, and my life was not cluttered with books or scholarship.

My father, a building contractor, prospered for a while in Boulder and sent me to a Jesuit high school. Most of the time I was miserable there. I got fair marks but chafed at the discipline. I hated boarding school and longed to be home, but my marks were fair and after four years I enrolled in the University of Colorado. During my second year at the university I fell in love with a girl who worked in a clothing store. Her name was Agnes, and I wanted to marry her. She moved to North Platte, Nebraska, for a better job, and I quit the university to be near her. I hitchhiked from Boulder to North Platte and arrived dusty and broke and triumphant at the rooming house where Agnes lived. We sat on the porch swing and she was not glad to see me.

'I don't want to marry you,' she said. 'I don't want to see you any more. That's why I'm here, so we don't see each other.'

'I'll get a job,' I insisted. 'We'll have a family.'

'Oh for Christ's sake.'

'Don't you want a family? Don't you like kids?'

She got quickly to her feet. 'Go home, Arturo. Please go home. Don't think about me any more. Go back to school. Learn something.' She was crying.

'I can lay brick,' I said, moving to her. She threw her arms around me, and planted a wet kiss on my cheek, then pushed me away.

'Go home, Arturo. Please.' She went inside and closed the door.

I walked down to the railroad tracks and swung aboard a freight train bound for Denver. From there I took another freight to Boulder and home. The next day I went to the job where my father was laying brick.

'I want to talk to you,' I said. He came down from the scaffold and we walked to a pile of lumber.

'What's the matter?' he said.

'I quit school.'

'Why?'

'I'm not cut out for it.'

His face twisted bitterly. 'What are you going to do now?'

'I don't know. I haven't figured it out.'

'Jesus, you're crazy.'

I became a bum in my home town. I loafed around. I took a job pulling weeds, but it was hard and I quit. Another job, washing windows. I barely got through it. I looked all over Boulder for work, but the streets were full of young, unemployed men. The only job in town was delivering newspapers. It paid fifty cents a day. I turned it down. I leaned against walls in the pool halls. I stayed away from home. I was ashamed to eat the food my father and mother provided. I always waited until my father walked out. My mother tried to cheer me. She made me pecan pie and ravioli.

'Don't worry,' she said. 'You wait and see. Something will happen. It's in my prayers.'

I went to the library. I looked at the magazines, at the

pictures in them. One day I went to the bookshelves, and pulled out a book. It was *Winesburg, Ohio*. I sat at a long mahogany table and began to read. All at once my world turned over. The sky fell in. The book held me. The tears came. My heart beat fast. I read until my eyes burned. I took the book home. I read another Anderson. I read and I read, and I was heartsick and lonely and in love with a book, many books, until it came naturally, and I sat there with a pencil and a long tablet, and tried to write, until I felt I could not go on because the words would not come as they did in Anderson, they only came like drops of blood from my heart.

Chapter Ten

Not a week passed without a letter from my mother. Written on lined grade-school paper they reflected her fears, her hopes, her anxiety, and her curious view of what went on in the world. They bothered me, those letters. Their phrasing fluttered in my head like trapped birds, flapping about at the most inopportune times. Often I simply laughed at them, other times they angered and frustrated me and I pitied my poor innocent mother:

> Be careful, Arturo. Say your prayers. Remember that one Hail Mary to the Virgin Mary will get you any-thing. Wear your scapular medal. It was blessed by Father Agatha, a very holy man. Thank God you all have one . . .

Joe Santucci, my high school buddy next door, had completed a tour in the navy and was now back in Boulder again. My mother wrote:

> Poor Mrs Santucci. Her boy is back after three years and he is a communist. She asked me to pray for him. Such a nice boy. I talked to him this morning and I

couldn't believe he was a communist. He seems just the same . . .

Please send us some money when you can. Our grocery bill is $390. I pay cash now, but there isn't enough and your father hasn't worked for two weeks . . .

I miss you all the time. I found a pair of your socks with holes in them, and darned them and started to cry. Say your prayers. I went to mass this morning and offered communion for your good luck . . .

Joe Santucci told Papa about Los Angeles. He says the women are bad and all over and there are saloons every place. Wear your scapular medal for protection. Go to mass, try to meet some nice Catholic girls . . .

I am glad you are working in the restaurant, and the other job with the writer. Send me some money if you can. Your father hurt his hand and can't work for a while. We miss you. Try a novena. Nobody ever said a novena without getting help . . .

I sent her $200 from my first studio paycheck and eventually paid off the grocery bill.

Chapter Eleven

Mrs Brownell and I were experiencing some turbulence. She had doubts about my working in the studio, and was careful not to question me about it. We were silent together during long periods, and it was difficult to invent small talk. Sitting before the radio we listened to Jack Benny and Bob Hope and Fred Allen until it was time to go to bed. We lay in the darkness and stared at the ceiling until sleep came. I felt far away from her, a drifting away as the strangeness developed. She was cold and silent in the morning, the gap widening. It was coming, and I knew it, a separation, a break. I told myself I didn't care. I was working, I had money. I didn't have to stay in that ancient hotel. I could move to Hollywood now, into the Hollywood hills. I could rent my own house and even hire a cleaning woman. Bunker Hill was not forever. A man had to move on.

Thinking of her depressed me. I sat in my office and squirmed, thinking how old she was, five years older than my own mother, and I gagged, and tried to cough away the unpleasantness. I thought of her face, the little lines around her eyes, the cables in her neck, the crinkled skin of her arms, her old body, the buttocks too small, her dresses too long, the crack of her knees when she sat down, her sunken cheeks when she removed her dentures, her cold feet, her old Kansas ways. I didn't need it, I told myself. I had only to turn my back to make it go away. I could have any girl in town, any starlet, maybe even a star. All I had to do was apply myself. It was wrong to spend my best years with an old woman who gave me only old thoughts in return. I needed a bright and lovely creature familiar with the arts, steeped in literature, someone who loved Keats and Rupert Brooke and Ernest Dowson. Not a woman who got her literary inspiration from her hometown Kansas newspaper. She had befriended me, yes, she had been kind to me, yes, but I had been kind to her too. I had given my juices to her, served as her friend and companion. Now it was time to move on.

I looked around my office and sighed. I loved it all. I was born to it. Maybe I wasn't writing a line, but I had found my station. I was making good money and the future was limitless. I had to get away from that woman.

All morning I sat brooding in gloom, for it was ever thus with me, probing the ashes, searching for blemishes, overwhelmed in despair. At noon she telephoned, and my heart leaped and I was glad.

'Still mad?' she asked.

'No. And you?'

'No,' she said, 'I'm so sorry. I don't know what got into me.'

'It wasn't your fault. I did it. I don't know why. I never know why. It's for you to forgive me.'

'I do, I do. You're a sweet boy. You're good for me. We mustn't quarrel.'

'Never again. Let's have some fun. Let's celebrate.'

'I'd love that. Let's do something crazy.'

'How about a good dinner first?'

'I'll wear my new suit.'

'I've got a new suit too.'

'Wear it.'

'I love you,' I said. 'You're the dearest woman in the world. We'll have a party.'

She wasn't there when I returned to the hotel at six o'clock. There was a note for me on the desk. Back in a moment, it said. I walked back to my room, showered, and got into my new suit. I had never worn it before. A fine, hand-tailored $200 job. I studied myself in the mirror. The reflection was perfect: a high-priced writer. The shoulders were padded a little more than I wanted, but it was a pleasant garment. We belonged together. I walked down the hall to the lobby and she was there behind the desk, beaming as I kissed her. There was a scarf over her hair. She withdrew it and primped.

'Like it?' she asked. 'It's a pageboy.'

Her graying hair had been turned under at the ends in a sleek roll. It was stiff from the beauty parlor. I studied it but could not conjure up an opinion.

'Great,' I said. 'Fine.'

I noticed a touch of rouge on her cheeks. It seemed superfluous.

'Where are we going?' she asked.

'First we're going to Rene and Jean's.'

'Lovely,' she said. 'Let's have a cocktail.'

We walked into her apartment, and there were two martinis on the table. I lifted one and toasted her:

'To the kindest, sweetest girl in all the world.'

She smiled and sipped her drink. It made her cough and she laughed. While she dressed I sat down and had a couple more. She was in the bathroom for a long time. When she emerged, playfully stilted as if modelling, she showed off her Joan Crawford suit with wide shoulders and narrow skirt. She was taller, in high-heeled ankle-strap shoes. I felt a shudder of lust and kissed her. There was a thin film of scarlet lip rouge on her mouth. Perhaps it was too much. I didn't know. It made me wonder.

We took my car and drove out Wilshire to Vermont and parked in Rene and Jean's lot. We had been to the restaurant frequently and it was a pleasure to be greeted by old Jean and the waiters. We drank wine and ate too much. When it was time to leave she asked, 'Where to now?'

I was ready for it. 'Leave that to me.'

We drove back to Wilshire and turned toward the Ambassador Hotel. She was quiet and smiling and a little frowsy. Leaning back against the seat, the wide shoulders of her tailored suit had lost their elegance and seemed to overdress her. At the Ambassador I turned into the driverway, and parked the car and got out. She stepped from the car and looked about mystified. I took her arm.

'Let's go,' I said, leading her toward the hotel.

'Where are we going?' she asked.

'To the Coconut Grove and the music of Anson Weeks.'

She squealed and hugged my arm in delight. 'It's so nice to be with a famous writer!'

'Not famous, but working.'

We walked to the hotel entrance.

'My feet hurt,' she whispered.

The strains of Anson Weeks' music wafted from the ballroom as we entered the lobby. The song was 'Where the Blue of the Night Meets the Gold of the Day.' I held her arm and could feel the beat of her heart.

'I'm so happy,' she said. 'I always wanted to come to the Coconut Grove and here I am.'

The headwaiter greeted us and bowed, 'Good evening.'

I nodded. 'We'd like a table.'

He led us into the big resplendent room with its colored lights and coconut trees. On the dance floor couples glided to the music, and spotlights played colored beams over the walls and ceiling. Our table was on the second tier. We sat down.

'Would you like a cocktail now?' the waiter asked.

Mrs Brownell was so breathless that she could only nod in assent.

'I'll have a brandy,' I said.

She put her hand on mine across the table. 'I'll have one too,' she said.

The waiter disappeared. We watched the dancers.

'I can't dance,' I said. 'At least, not very well.'

She squeezed my hand again. 'I'll teach you.'

I started to rise. 'Let's try it.'

'Not now,' she breathed. 'Let's wait a dance or two.'

Then the waiter returned with our drinks. He put my brandy before me and smiled as he served Mrs Brownell.

'Here you are, mother,' he said.

It cut her like a knife. Her startled eyes fixed me. They seemed guilt stricken, embarrassed, intimidated. She lowered her head and I thought she was going to cry. But she did not cry. She lifted her face and smiled bravely. The embarrassed waiter moved off.

'Drink your brandy,' I urged.

She sipped carefully and our attention went back to the dancers.

What happened thereafter was my effort to make a joke, to cheer her, to make light of the waiter's gaffe. The band began to play a Strauss waltz. Then I said it.

'Shall we dance, mother dear?'

She looked frightened, biting her lip and staring helplessly at me, her eyes suddenly awash with tears. Crying uncontrollably, she shook the table as she groped to her feet and rushed away toward the lobby. I downed my brandy and hurried after her. She was not in the lobby nor on the staircase, and I stepped outside in time to see a cab pulling out of the driveway with Mrs Brownell in the back seat. I ran after her calling, but the cab sped away. I walked back to the Grove, paid my bill, and went out to my car.

What a mess. I drove back to the hotel reluctantly. I hated facing her, her tears, but it had to be. I turned the key in her apartment door and walked inside. There was a hiss of water from the shower in the bathroom. Sprawled on the floor, wantonly discarded, was her Joan Crawford suit, as if dropped from her body and kicked aside. Her blouse hung over a chair, her shoes and stockings carelessly discarded.

I undressed down to my shorts, and slipped between the covers of the studio couch, folding my arms behind my head, waiting for her to appear. I had nothing to say. I decided to leave it up to her. She emerged finally, dressed in her nightie, my unexpected presence irritating her. She had washed her hair, washed out her coiffure, and her hair hung in moist strands. Her face was scrubbed and plain and wrinkled.

'Please go,' she said.

'I'm sorry.'

She crossed to the window and flung it open. The cool of the night wafted in from the hillside. Without a word she gathered up my clothes, my coat and pants, my shirt, my shoes. At first I thought she was tidying up. Instead she turned to the window and flung everything out into the night. I leaped out of bed and rushed to the window. Below I saw my clothes flung about on the weed-clogged terrain. It was a steep incline. My scattered garments looked like dead bodies. My pants hung from the branch of a tree. I glared at her.

'Satisfied?'

'Not until you leave.'

I started to gather up her garments – the Crawford suit, the blouse, the underskirt. She rushed to stop me, and we struggled, pushing and pulling, but I was the stronger, and broke her grasp, and flung her things through the window. With a smile I said, 'I'll go now.'

'And don't come back,' she panted. I walked down the hall to my room, put on a robe and slippers and moved down to a door at the rear of the hotel, which opened on the yard area. As I scrambled up the hillside to my clothes I saw Mrs Brownell making her way down the hillside. We glared at one another and began gathering our things. I had to climb the tree to reach my pants. When I dropped to the ground she was crawling back toward the hotel front. At my feet was one of her shoes. I picked it up and threw it. The shoe hit her in the ass. Enraged, she picked it up and hurled it down at me. It sailed over my head.

I was very sad when I got back to my room. Women! I knew nothing about women. There was no understanding them. I opened a suitcase and dumped my things into it. The room spoke to me, and implored me to stay – the Maxfield Parrish picture on the wall, the typewriter on the table, my bed, my marvellous bed, the window overlooking the hill, the source of so many dreams, so many thoughts, so many words, a part of myself, the echo of myself pleading with me to stay. I didn't want to go but there was no denying it, I had somehow blundered and kicked myself out, and there was no turning back. Goodbye to Bunker Hill.

Chapter Twelve

When Frank Edgington learned that I was homeless he invited me to his house in the hills above Beechwood Drive. It was a two-bedroom place in a thicket of eucalyptus. He showed me to my bedroom, and I put my suitcase on the bare floor. There was no bed in the room – except for a double mattress pushed against the wall.

Living with Edgington was a strange experience. His style emerged out of his childhood, and the games we played in his office were as nothing compared to the games scattered about in his living room. We plunged into the glamorous, romantic, enthralling life in Hollywood, beginning with a game of ping pong in the garage. Then we moved to the kitchen and filled our tumblers with table wine. On to the living room, throwing ourselves on the parquet floor, and thrilling to a game of tiddlywinks. The more we drank the wilder we played. We battled one another at the dart board. Sometimes we fell asleep playing bingo. It was pure and it was clean and when it rained and water thundered on the roof we turned on the gaslight in the fireplace and it was like turning back to a boyhood time beside a campfire in the mountains.

I rarely saw my boss Harry Schindler. When I ran into

him in the elevator or down the hall he grabbed my arm affectionately and steered me along.

'How's it going?'

'Okay,' I'd answer, 'just fine.'

'You're doing a hell of a job. Keep it up.'

'I'm not writing, Harry. I want to write.'

'Hang in there. Take your time. Let me worry about your writing.'

Every day the reception room we shared was full of mysterious people waiting to see him. They must have been writers, directors, production people. When I asked my secretary who they were she wouldn't tell me. As time went by I felt like an orphan, a pariah, non-productive, unknown and exiled. The money kept me there, the absence of poverty, the fear of its return. The thought of being a busboy again made me shiver. I took out my little savings account passbook and studied the figures. I was up to $1,800, and still sending money home. I had no cause for complaint.

One morning Thelma knocked on my door and opened it.

'Harry wants to see you.'

I found Schindler lighting a fresh cigar.

'I may have something for you pretty soon,' he said. I got excited.

'You mean an assignment?'

'Maybe. We're negotiating.'

'What is it?'

'A novel, *The Genius*, by Theodore Dreiser.'

'Oh my God! When will you know?'

'A couple of weeks.'

I left his office in a dream. Thelma studied my face. I bent down and kissed her on the mouth.

'Get me a copy of *The Genius* by Theodore Dreiser.' The novel came up from the studio library within the hour, and I began to read. It was a very long novel and by the end of the week I had read it twice and collected a notebook of ideas on how to convert it into a picture.

Two months later I read *The Genius* for what must have been the tenth time and I had four notebooks filled with observations, stacked on my desk. I jumped whenever the phone rang, thinking it was Schindler. I kept my door open watching the reception room for his appearance. His office had another door leading to the hall. Whenever I heard it open I jumped up and rushed outside. A couple of times I stood waiting as he appeared. It was as if he did not see me at all as he walked by. I slunk back to my office and sat brooding.

Why was he doing this? What was happening to me? Was there some conspiracy against me in the world? Had I offended him? Hadn't he offered me this job? Was I accursed by Almighty God? Perhaps my mother was right. Lose your faith and you lose all. Was she better informed than I on the ways of the Lord? Was I too late to make amends? I walked down to the parking lot, got in my car, and drove up Sunset to the Catholic church. Kneeling in the front pew, I prayed:

'Please, God, do something about that assignment. I haven't asked anything of you for years. Do this for me and I will come back into the arms of Mother Church for the rest of my days.'

After a while a priest appeared and moved into the confessional. A few old women knelt in the vicinity. I went to kneel with them. Then it was my turn and I entered the confessional. Through the wooden grillwork I saw the priest's white face. I had nothing to say. The guilt for past sins had left me. I knelt there in embarrassment. The moments passed. The priest stirred. His eyes sought mine through the grill.

'Yes?' he asked.

'I'm sorry,' I whispered, 'I haven't prepared myself.' I rose and walked out, down the aisle and through the heavy front doors to the street. I was more despondent than ever, for somewhere in my heart there had always been a conviction that the church was my ace in the hole. I had always believed this without articulating it. Now the conviction was gone and I was lost, and facing a hostile world. I walked down to my car and got in. Suddenly, desperately, I got out again and hurried back into the church and knelt down and tried to pray.

I murmured a Hail Mary and found it interrupted by Thelma Farber. Hail Mary full of grace and Thelma Farber naked in my arms. Holy Mary, Mother of God, kissing Thelma Farber's breasts, groping at her body and running my hands along her thighs. Pray for us sinners now and at the hour of our death and my lips moved to Thelma's loins and I kissed her ecstatically. I was lost, writhing. I felt my body kneeling there, the hardness in my loins, the fullness of an erection, the absurdity of it, the maddening dichotomy. I arose and dashed out of there, down to my car, and drove off, frightened, shaking, absurd.

I was glad when I got back to my office. It was like a nest that comforted me. Thelma was not there. I closed the door, sat at my desk and lit a cigarette. Mysterious unsettling things were happening to me. I had stepped out of the world and now it was hard to find my way back. I thought of Frank Edgington down the hall. Perhaps I could tell him my problem. But that was no good. Edgington was too sardonic, too impatient. He would merely laugh and blame it on my peasant origin.

There was a knock on the door. It was Thelma. A few minutes ago I had knelt in the church and kissed her loins and there she was again. She sensed something.

'You okay?' she asked.

'Sure.'

'Harry wants to see you.'

'What about?'

'How should I know?'

I crossed the reception room to Schindler's door and knocked.

'Come in.'

I opened the door and found him sitting there.

'You wanted to see me?'

'Bad news.'

I moved closer.

'We can't buy the Dreiser book,' he said.

'Why not?'

'It's not for sale.' Somehow it didn't seem important.

'What now?' I asked.

'Continue what you're doing.'

'I have pages and pages of notes on Dreiser's book. Do you want to see them?'

'No,' he said, 'forget it.'

'Give me something to write.'

'I don't have anything.'

I felt rage. 'Think of something, you bastard!'

He looked at me with a tight jaw, and got slowly to his feet.

'Get out of here.'

I turned and walked out, back to my office. I felt it then, my grief, the rim of the world, the loneliness of being far away and lost, and I was crying. I threw myself on the studio couch and let myself go, sobbing. Thelma came to the door. She spoke softly.

'Arturo, what is it?'

I sat up and told her what Schindler had said, and started crying again.

'You poor thing!' She moved to the couch and sat down. I felt the weight of her body sinking upon the couch. It felt good. Encouraged, I sobbed again. She put her long soft arm around my shoulder and dabbed my eyes with her handkerchief. It was scented with her fragrance. I turned toward her and put my head on her shoulder. She hugged me gently.

'Help me, Thelma,' I said. 'I'm so unhappy.'

She dabbed my wet eyes and pulled me closer, her bosom pressed against mine.

'Oh, Thelma, help me!'

'There, there,' she soothed, stroking my hair.

'Oh, Thelma, kiss me!'

She rose, went to the door and closed it, then returned to sit beside me again.

'Oh, Thelma. If you only knew how I've hungered for you, how I've wanted to hold you in my arms, to kiss you.'

'I've guessed it,' she said. 'The way you've looked at me, I've known all the time.'

I lay back on the couch and pulled her toward me, her mouth settled on mine, soft and cool and full. Suddenly I groped at my fly, and tugged at the zipper, while she stood up and lifted her skirt and pulled down her white panties. She sank to the floor and spread her limbs.

'Hurry,' she breathed.

I rolled off the couch and positioned myself between her long smooth stockinged legs, but the zipper gave me trouble still, and I fought it desperately. Her hands probed at my belt and in one violent jerk my pants were down. I bent over her, my shooter at the ready as I sought to spear her, but I missed, and missed again, and with a little cry of annoyance she grabbed the thing and tried to insert it, and at that moment I heard the click of the doorknob and the sound of the door opening, and I rolled my eyes toward the door and saw Harry Schindler looking down at us. The life went out of the shooter, and I could do no more than lie there stupified while Thelma lay shocked, holding the limp thing in one hand.

'All right, Thelma,' Schindler said quietly. 'Put that mushroom down, and get the hell out of here.'

She arose, straightened her dress, and looked at him in contempt and defiance, striding past him and out of the room, her panties in one hand.

'I'll see you later!' he threatened. She tossed her head defiantly.

I got to my feet and pulled up my trousers.

'Let's talk,' Schindler said. He turned and walked out.

I found him waiting for me, his feet on the desk, a new cigar in his mouth. He looked at me with a smirk.

'I can't believe it,' he said. 'It's not possible.'

'I'm sorry, Harry.'

'Sorry for what? It wasn't your fault. It never is.'

'But it was. I seduced her.'

He dropped his feet to the floor and leaned forward.

'Listen, kid. She eats writers alive. I mean big writers, Pulitzer prize winners, academy award writers, $3,000-a-week writers. That's what I don't understand. You! You don't even have a screen credit!'

I didn't know whether he was complimenting me or not.

'It just happened,' I said. 'I hardly expected it. But don't hold it against her. I mean don't fire her.'

'I'm firing you,' Schindler said. 'As of now, you're through.'

'What about Thelma? Is she fired too?'

'I can't fire her. I'll never fire her. I want her around so I can keep an eye on her, but I'll tell you this – if it happens again I'll divorce her.'

I said, 'Oh God, Schindler,' and walked out in a daze.

Chapter Thirteen

You had to have an agent. Without one you were an outcast, an unknown. Having an agent gave you status, even if he never delivered. When one writer said to another, 'Who's your agent?' and you answered, 'I don't have any,' he immediately surmised that you lacked talent. Edgington's agent was Cyril Korn.

'You won't like him,' Edgington warned, 'but he's good.'

I sent three magazine stories to Korn's office in Beverly Hills, and waited for his telephone call.

It never came. Finally, Edgington phoned him and made an appointment for me. His office was in a new building on Beverly Drive. His secretary announced me and I sat down to wait. After two hours I was admitted to the great man's office.

He stood in the middle of his carpeted room, tapping golf balls into a glass. He didn't even say hello. Finally, stroking his putter with great concentration, he spoke without looking at me.

'I read your short stories,' he said.

'Did you like them?'

'Hated them. You got no chance trying to peddle that kind of trash in pictures.'

'I'm not trying to peddle them in pictures. I just wanted to prove that I can write.'

He put away the putter, and looked at me for the first time. 'I don't think you can.'

'You mean you don't want to handle me?'

'Have you written any screenplays?'

'No, but I've written a treatment for Harry Schindler. I did Dreiser's *The Genius*.'

'And he fired you. Have you ever collaborated with anybody?'

'No.'

'I have a client who needs a collaborator – somebody who's young and unsophisticated and unspoiled. My client's name is Velda van der Zee. Ever heard of her?'

'Never have.'

'Where you been all these years? Velda van der Zee has written more screenplays than you'll ever write in three life times.'

'You think we'd work well together?'

'It's a big opportunity for you. Maybe you'll get a screen credit.'

'I'd like to try.'

'I'll let you know.' The phone rang. Korn picked it up and gestured to me with a wave of his hand. It meant: get out. I left in disgust. He had put me down and insulted me and filled me with misery, and I wanted no part of him. All the way home I ground my teeth when I thought of him standing there in a red velvet vest putting golf balls. I would rather get out of the business than have him for my agent. I would rather sling hash in Abe Marx's deli than have him represent me. When I told Edgington about our meeting he smiled quietly.

'He's peculiar, but he's a good agent. Wait and see what happens.'

'I won't even talk to the sonofabitch.'

Next morning the Cyril Korn office telephoned. It was the secretary: 'Mr Korn would like to see you at two o'clock this afternoon.' She hung up.

At two o'clock I sat in Korn's office waiting. At four, after one pack of cigarettes, I was admitted.

There was Cyril Korn behind his desk, red vest and all, talking to a woman seated across from him. She was a large, florid woman, with melonlike breasts, wearing a big hat and bouncing earrings. Her makeup was heavy, her lips too red. She smiled at me.

'Velda,' Korn said, 'I want you to meet Arturo Bandini. He says he's a writer.'

Velda held out her jewelled hand and I shook it. 'It's nice to know you,' I said.

'A pleasure,' she answered.

Korn rose. 'I'll leave you two for a while,' he said. 'I want you to read something. He lifted a couple of manuscripts from his desk and handed one to each of us. 'Read this and tell me what you think. I'll be back in an hour.' He left the office and closed the door.

'You *are* young, aren't you?' Velda said.

'I may be young but I'm a hell of a writer.'

She laughed. Her teeth were false. 'You know something?' she said. 'You look like Spencer Tracy. I saw Spence this morning at Musso-Frank's. We had breakfast together. He was telling me about working with Loretta Young – how he loved it. She's really gorgeous, don't you think? I know Loretta and Sally and their mother. Such a lovely family. She was under contract at Metro when I was out there. We used to have lunch together, Loretta and I and Carole

Lombard and Joan Crawford. You'd love Joan. Such a fine figure of a woman. And Robert Taylor! I swear he's the handsomest man in Hollywood, excluding Clark Gable, of course. Clark and I are old friends. I knew him when he first started in the business. I've seen him scale the heights, and look at him now! They say he's in love with Claudette Colbert, but I don't believe it. I saw him at the tennis club the other day and asked him if it was true. He laughed that merry masculine laugh of his, and kissed me on the cheek and said, "You want the truth, Velda? I'm in love with you." Wasn't that priceless? John Barrymore always said the same thing to me. Such a tease! Not at all like Lionel or Ethel, but a free spirit, a romantic poem of a man. Some people say that Errol Flynn is more handsome, but I can't believe it. Ronald Coleman, though, he's something else – so dashing, with sparkling eyes, and princely manners. He gave a party a couple of weeks ago in Santa Barbara. It had to be the most wonderful soirée in Hollywood history. Norma Shearer was there, and Tallulah Bankhead and Alice Faye and Jean Harlow and Wallace Beery and Richard Barthelmess and Harold Lloyd and Douglas Fairbanks, Jr. Oh, it was fabulous – a night I'll never forget!'

She paused for breath. 'But here I am talking about myself as usual. Tell me, do you like Hollywood?'

'Sometimes yes,' I said, 'and sometimes no.'

'Isn't that funny!' she exclaimed. 'Pat O'Brien said the same thing to me last week at Warner Brothers. We were having lunch in the Green Room at Warner Brothers – Pat and I and Bette Davis and Glenda Farrell. I don't know why we got on the subject of Hollywood, but Pat looked very reflective and said exactly what you've just said.'

The door opened and Cyril Korn returned. 'How are you two getting along?' he asked.

'Just fine,' Velda van der Zee said. 'We're going to make a great team.'

He turned to me. 'You like the story?' he asked.

'Of course he does,' Velda said. 'He's in love with it, aren't you, Arturo?'

'I guess so.'

Korn clapped his hands. 'Then it's settled. I'll call Jack Arthur and tell him it's a deal.'

'Who's Jack Arthur?' I asked. Before he could answer Velda said:

'Jack Arthur happens to be one of the most delightful producers in Hollywood. He's been my close friend for ten years. I was a bridesmaid at his wedding, and the godmother of his two children. Need I say more?'

'No,' I said. 'That's fine, fine.'

One thing about Cyril Korn: When he wanted you to leave he almost threw you out. He returned to his desk and sat down. 'That's it, kids. I'll be in touch.'

I walked out with Velda. We descended the elevator to the street floor and walked out on the parking lot.

'Do you know anything about Indian wrestling?' she asked.

'Not much,' I said.

'Last night at Jeannette McDonald's house, Lewis Stone and Frank Morgan tried their hands at Indian wrestling. It was a scream. They tugged and pushed until the sweat broke out on their faces. And do you know who won?'

'Who?'

'Lewis Stone!' she exclaimed. 'That fine elderly gentleman defeated Frank Morgan at Indian wrestling. Everybody screamed with laughter and applauded.'

I glanced at her. Her round face was flushed with excitement. Words tumbled from her lips, unstoppable. No doubt about it, she was a dingbat. She lived in a world of names, not bodies, not human beings, but famous names. Nothing she said could possibly be true. She simply invented as she prattled on. She was a liar, a lovable liar, her mind bubbling with preposterous tales.

She led me to her car – a bronze-colored Bentley.

'Wow!' I said. She beamed at her sleek car.

'It looks expensive,' I said. That pleased her.

'I bought it from Wallace Beery,' she said. 'Wally decided on a Rolls Royce, and I got it for a bargain.'

She threw open the rear door and I peered inside. The seat was green velour. There was a stain in the middle, a brown stain. She smiled.

'You're looking at that brown spot, aren't you? Claire Dodd did it. I took her home from a party at Jeannettte McDonald's and she spilled a glass of wine on it. Poor Claire! So humiliated! She wanted to pay for getting it cleaned, but I wouldn't have it. After all, what are friends for?'

'Do you want me to call you?' I asked. She gave me her telephone number, and we shook hands.

'Can I give you a ride?'

'I have a car,' I said, nodding toward my Plymouth.

'Isn't that a Ford?' she asked.

'Almost,' I said. 'It's a Plymouth.'

'I used to own one. They're very uncomfortable.'

We said goodbye and I walked to my uncomfortable car.

The script Cyril Korn had given us was by Harry Browne. It was the story of a range war – the struggle between cattle men and sheep men. The cattle men were the bad guys and the sheep men the good guys. Also featured was a tribe of hostile Indians who captured Julia, the heroine, and imprisoned her in the Indian village. When the sheep men and the cattle men learn of her capture they join forces and ride off to rescue Julia. After the battle in which Julia is saved, the cattle men and sheep men shake hands and the range war is brought to a peaceful solution.

A couple of days later Velda van der Zee and I drove the Bentley out Ventura to Liberty Studios to meet the producer, Jack Arthur. I sat beside her as she handled the quiet magnificent machine. She liked the story, she said. It was a classic, a sure nominee for the academy awards. She visualized Gary Cooper and Claire Trevor in the leading roles, with Jack La Rue playing the part of Magua, the Indian chief.

'Gary Cooper's a friend of mine,' she said. 'I'll give him the screenplay. He has a high regard for my opinion.'

'Sounds good,' I said.

We pulled into the parking lot at Liberty Studios and walked down the hall to Jack Arthur's office. Jack Arthur was a pipe smoker. He kissed Velda on the cheek and shook my hand.

'Well,' he said, 'what do you think of the story?'

'Priceless,' Velda said. 'We love it.'

'It has possibilities,' Arthur said. 'Are you ready to go to work?'

'Of course,' Velda said. 'How are the children?'

'They're fine, fine.'

'You must meet Jack's children, Arturo. They're the most delightful creatures in the world.'

Jack Arthur beamed. 'You'll need an office,' he said, reaching for the telephone.

Quickly Velda said, 'That won't be necessary. We'll work at my house.' She turned to me and smiled. 'Is that all right with you, Arturo?'

'Fine, fine,' I said.

'Okay, then,' Arthur said. 'I'll get in touch with Cyril Korn and we'll draw up the contracts. You people need anything, just holler.' He shook my hand. 'Good luck, Bandini. Write me a smash hit.'

'I'll try.' Velda and I said goodbye and left.

On the way back to town I said, 'I didn't know we were going to work at your place.'

'I always work there.'

'Where do you live?'

'In Benedict Canyon. William Powell's old house. You'll love it.' She began to speak of Irene Dunne and Myrna Loy, but I was used to it by now and scarcely heard her as she moved on to Lew Ayres, Frederic March, Jean Harlow and Mary Astor. When she pulled up in front of Frank Edgington's house she was well into a reminiscence of Franchot Tone, and I had to sit there patiently until the tale was told. Then I stepped out and she drove away.

The next day I drove out Benedict Canyon to Velda van der Zee's French chateau. It was nestled in a grove of birch trees, white and serene and aristocratic. Twin towers with slate roofs guarded the front entrance, and a great oak door stood between Doric columns. A housekeeper answered the summons of the lion's-head knocker. She was a middle-aged black woman in a maid's costume.

'I'm Arturo Bandini.'

'I know,' she smiled. 'Please come in.'

I followed her through an entry hall and into the living room. The place was awesome, intimidating, crowded with Louis Quinze furniture and huge beaded lamps. Over the mantel hung the large oil portrait of an elderly man with a white beard and mustache.

'Who's that?' I asked.

'Mr van der Zee,' the maid said.

'I guess I've never met him.'

'You can't,' the maid said. 'He's dead.'

'He must have been very rich,' I said.

She laughed. 'You'd be rich too if you owned half of Signal Hill.'

'Oh.'

Down the grand staircase came Velda van der Zee, afloat in a diaphanous hostess gown. Silken panels floated behind her like attendant cherubs, and a cloud of exotic perfume enveloped me as she offered her hand.

'Good morning, Arturo. Shall we go to work, or would you like to see the rest of the house?'

'Let's work,' I said.

She took my arm. 'That's what I like about you, young man, your dedication.' She guided me into an eerie room.

'This is my den,' she said.

I looked around. It was indeed a den. Every inch of wallspace was crowded with autographed photos of film stars. The beautiful people. So handsome, so full of buoyant smiles and glittering teeth and graceful hands and beautiful skins. But it was a sad room too, a kind of mausoleum, a display of the living and the dead. Velda looked at them reverently.

'My beloved friends,' she sighed.

I wanted to ask about her husband, but it seemed inappropriate. She crossed to an elaborate French provincial desk, a typewriter upon it.

'My favorite desk,' she said. 'A Christmas present from Maurice Chevalier.'

'It's a beauty,' I said.

Velda pulled a red bellcord beside the doorway. A bell rang and the maid appeared. Velda ordered coffee. I went to the desk and sat before the typewriter.

'Have you read the script?' I asked.

'Not yet. I plan to do it this morning.'

She crossed to a divan and sat down.

'Shall I tell you something very interesting about this room?'

'Please do.'

'This is where I signed my first contract with Louis B. Mayer. He sat exactly where you are and signed the papers. That was ten years ago. He's a wonderful man. One of these days we'll have a party and you can meet him. If he likes you your future is assured.'

'I'd love to meet him.' I pulled the script from my coat pocket. 'Let's get started.'

The maid entered with a coffee tray. Velda talked as she poured. 'Lots of famous people have graced this room throughout the years. Do you remember Vilma Banky and Rod La Roque?'

That started her off. Vilma Banky, Rod La Roque, Clara Bow, Lillian Gish, Marian Davies, John Gilbert, Colleen Moore, Clive Brooke, Buster Keaton, Harold Lloyd, Wesley Barry, Billie Dove, Corinne Griffith, Claire Windsor. On and on she sailed through clouds of reverie, sipping coffee, lighting cigarettes, dreaming the absurd, invoking the glamour of enchanting lies and impossible worlds she had made for herself.

I sat listening in quiet despair, thinking of ways to escape, to run out of there, to leap into my car and drive back to the reality of Bunker Hill, to scream, to jump up and scream, to beg her to shut up, and then finally to give in and sink mortally wounded into the big chair that once held Louis B.'s ass.

We got nothing done, nothing at all, and when she grew sleepy and exhausted and switched from coffee to martinis, I could stand no more. Her eyes were barely open when I stood over her and took her hand.

'Goodbye, Velda. We'll try again tomorrow.' I left.

Next day everything was exactly the same except that the characters were changed, and so was the location. We sat in the gazebo out on the lawn, under the pepper tree. This time there was no coffee either, but there was a pitcher of martinis, and the sonorous, slumberous voice of Velda talking of Jean Arthur, Gary Cooper, Tyrone Power, Errol Flynn, Lily Damita, Lupe Velez, Dolores del Rio, Merle Oberon, Claude Rains, Leslie Howard, Basil Rathbone, Nigel Bruce, Cesar Romero, George Arliss, Henry Armetta, Gregory La Cava, Paulette Goddard, Walter Wanger, Norma Talmadge, Constance Talmadge, Janet Gaynor, Frederic March, Nils Asther, Norman Foster, Ann Harding, and Kay Francis.

Chapter Fourteen

We were supposed to meet the following day, but I gagged at it. It was like suffering from a hangover, and all I saw were her wet eyes in that soft face, and all I heard was the sound of her babbling voice. I knew I could never work with her, that she would drive me crazy. I telephoned her around ten o'clock the next morning and of course the line was busy. It was busy at eleven o'clock and at noon and all that afternoon until evening. Finally I gave up and went to my typewriter and wrote her a note:

Dear Velda:
  I must be honest with you. We will never be able to work as a team. I'm not blaming you, I blame myself. Starting tomorrow I plan to write the screenplay. When I finish I will deliver it to you, and you can edit it and improve it in any way you like. I hope this plan meets with your approval.
                                    Sincerely yours,
                                    Arturo Bandini

Two days later she telephoned.
'Are you sure you know what you're doing, Arturo?'
'Absolutely.'

'Very well. You write the first draft and I'll follow with the final. Call me if you run into trouble.'

'I will.'

I began writing immediately, but the more I wrote the less I liked it. I started another draft. And another. Then a fresh full-blown idea came to me. A new story. No more cattle men and sheep men, but something more conventional, made up of film fragments I remembered from boyhood. It moved right along. The pages piled up. It was fun. I got hot. In one sitting I wrote twenty pages.

Next day I still had a head of steam. Twenty more pages. That night I wrote until one in the morning, another fifteen pages. I loved it. I marvelled at it. How fast I was! What acuity! What dialogue! I was on to something touched with greatness. It could not fail. I saw myself a hero, an overnight sensation. And away I went: up canyons and down ravines, horse careening, six-guns blazing, Indians falling, blood in the dust, screams of women, the burning buildings, the menace of evil, the triumph of good, the victory of love. Bang bang bang a thrill a minute, the greatest goddam western story ever written. Finally, drugged on coffee, a bellyache from cigarettes, eyes burning, back aching, I finished it. Proudly I folded it into a big envelope and mailed it to Velda van der Zee. Then I took it easy and waited, knowing that there was hardly a word she could change, that she was dealing with perfection.

I spent the days on Hollywood Boulevard, in Stanley Rose's bookshop, in the off-boulevard saloons, playing the pinball games, going to movies. Then I could wait no longer, and I phoned Velda van der Zee. The line was busy. An hour later it was busy again. All day it was busy. Far into the night it was busy. In the morning I could not bear it any longer. I got into my Plymouth and shot up Benedict Canyon. The engine pinged. It needed a ring job. I pulled into Velda's driveway and knocked on the door. It was twelve o'clock. The maid greeted me.

'I came to see Velda.'

'You can't,' she said. 'She's still asleep.'

'I'll wait.'

She watched me return to the car and sit behind the wheel. I was there at one o'clock, at two o'clock, at three o'clock, and at four I drove away. I drove as far as the hotel on Sunset. I went to the pay phone in the lobby, and dialled Velda's number. Even as I stood there I knew it would happen, and I was right. The line was busy. I was shaking when I stumbled toward home. I walked two blocks before I realized that I was not in my car.

The best thing about my collaboration with Velda was the money. After fifteen weeks, a three-hundred-dollar check each week, she telephoned. She had finished the script. She was sending it special delivery. It should arrive the next day. She was very proud of her work. She knew I would like it, that we had achieved a masterpiece.

'Did you change it much?' I asked.

'Here and there. Small changes. But the essence of your version, the main thrust, is still there.'

'I'm glad, Velda. Frankly, I was worried.'

'You're going to be very pleased, Arturo. There was so little for me to do. I hardly deserve any credit at all.'

Next day I sat on the porch of Edgington's house and waited for the mailman. At noon a postal truck drove up and the driver put the large envelope in my hands. I signed the receipt, sat on the porch step, and opened the manuscript.

The title page read *Sin City*, screenplay by Velda van der Zee and Arturo Bandini, from a story by Harry Browne. I was down the first page halfway when my hair began to stiffen. In the middle of the second page I was forced to put the script aside and hang on to the porch banister. My breathing was uneven and there were mysterious shooting pains in my legs and across my stomach. I staggered to my feet and went inside to the kitchen and drank a glass of water. Edgington was sitting at the table eating breakfast. He saw my face and stood up.

'Good God, what's wrong?'

I could not speak. I could only point in the direction of the manuscript. Edgington walked to the front door and looked around.

'What's up?' he said. 'Who's out there?'

I came through the house to the porch and pointed at the manuscript. He picked it up.

'What's this?' He looked at the title page. 'What's wrong with it?'

'Read it.'

He took it to the porch swing and sat down.

'I've been had,' I said. 'I didn't write it. My name's on it, but I didn't write it.'

He began to read. Suddenly he laughed, a short barking laugh. 'It's funny,' he said. 'It's a very funny script.'

'You mean it's a comedy?'

'That's what's funny. It's not a comedy.' He went back to the script and read in silence, another ten pages. Then, deliberately, he folded the manuscript shut and looked at me.

'Is it still funny?'

He rolled up the script and threw it into an ivy patch beyond the porch.

'It's ghastly,' he said.

I rescued the script from the ivy bed. He had read my version more than fifteen weeks ago. He had liked it, praised it.

'What should I do?' I asked.

'How about going back to Colorado and learning to lay brick with your old man?'

'That's no solution.'

'The only solution is to get your name off this script. Disown it. Don't be associated with it.'

'Maybe I can save it.'

'Save it from what? It's dead, man. It's been murdered. Call your agent and tell him to remove your name. Either that or get out of town.' He rose and walked back into the kitchen. I opened the screenplay and started to read again. What I read was as follows:

A stagecoach rolls across the Wyoming plain pursued by band of Indians. Stagecoach brought to halt. Indians swarm over it. Two passengers: Reverend Ezra Drew and daughter Priscilla. Indian chief drags Priscilla out, throws her on his horse. Priscilla struggles. Chief mounts, rides off with her. Indians follow.

Indian village. Chief rides up with Priscilla, shoves her into teepee, then enters. Indian chief is Magua, enemy of white man. He seizes girl, handles her roughly, kissing her as she struggles.

Over the hill comes posse, led by Sheriff Lawson. He

dismounts, hears girl scream, enters teepee, struggles with Magua, knocks him down, helps girl outside, puts her in saddle of his horse, mounts, and rides off. Posse follows.

Sin City. Posse arrives, Sheriff puts Priscilla down. Posse brings up Reverend Drew. Priscilla runs into his arms. Townspeople gather. Sheriff Lawson leads Priscilla into Sin City Hotel.

That night townfolk gather at hotel. Sheriff comes out with Priscilla and Reverend Drew. Townfolk beg them to stay. Local church recently burned out by hostile Indians of Chief Magua. People urge Reverend Drew to rebuild church. He promises to consider it. Playing banjo, Reverend Drew accompanies daughter in singing of 'I Love You, Jesus.' Great applause. Holding tambourine, Priscilla moves among townfolk and they drop coins into tambourine. Reverend Drew mounts hotel porch and delivers speech. He and daughter promise to remain and rebuild Sin City church. Citizens repair to big saloon. Once more the Reverend strums banjo and Priscilla sings 'Lord Welcome Me.' Again she passes tambourine and makes generous collection.

Church being rebuilt. Townspeople help, carrying lumber and building material. Sheriff rides up and puts Priscilla in his buckboard. They ride off. In lovely pine grove Sheriff embraces Priscilla and they kiss.

Evening. Sin City saloon. Priscilla sings 'The Lord Is My Shepherd,' while saloon patrons listen and admire the lovely young woman. She passes tambourine. A drunk at bar seizes her, tries to kiss her. Sheriff Lawson intervenes, fight develops. Lawson knocks intruder down. Priscilla looks to Sheriff gratefully.

On hillside overlooking town sits the sinister Magua on his horse, watching. He dismounts and slinks to window of saloon as Priscilla addresses bar patrons in little speech. She wants townsfolk to form a church choir where hymns can be sung and offerings made for new church. Townspeople agree and applaud. Outside at window the evil Magua smirks as he listens.

Change comes over Sin City. No more liquor in town saloon. No more gambling. Group of women under Priscilla's direction sing spirited hymns. Work on church proceeds. Day arrives when church is complete, and townfolk gather for first service. Watching from above, Magua observes the happenings below and rides off.

Evening. Women of Sin City prepare barbecue outside church. A square dance in progress, led by Reverend Drew and his banjo. Priscilla whirls to music, her partner the Sheriff. Meanwhile at Indian village Magua gathers his forces. Indians with painted bodies mount their horses and Magua leads them away.

Square dance. Sheriff leads Priscilla into woods. She lifts face for his kiss. He asks her to marry him. She consents. Suddenly the sound of pounding hoofs and Indian yells. Down the hill come Magua and his bloodthirsty Arapahoes. Riding furiously, they ring the church and townspeople with bloodcurdling shouts and thundering hoofs. Shrieking townfolk retreat to church as Indians continue to circle and fire their rifles. Sheriff and Priscilla rush to safety of new church. Round and round the Indians tighten their noose about the church. Gunfire. Cries of wounded. Indians hurl torches upon church roof. Townsfolk mount gun positions at church windows. Battle rages. Women reload rifles. Priscilla reloads her father's rifle. At that moment he is shot. Priscilla shoots Indian who felled her father. Then she turns and gathers fallen parent in her arms and cries.

Meanwhile the treacherous Magua has dismounted and comes slithering toward church door. He enters unseen and swoops down on Priscilla, cups hand over her mouth, and drags her outside. Throwing her upon back of his horse, he mounts behind her and rides off just as Sheriff Lawson appears in doorway. Taking dead aim, Magua fires rifle at Sheriff and bullet strikes him in shoulder. Lawson staggers but does not go down. Instead he lurches toward Magua, who rides off with the struggling Priscilla.

Wounded but undaunted, Sheriff gropes to his horse, mounts, and rides in pursuit. Over hill and dale he follows fleeing Indian and girl. They come to a creek in the foothills and stop. Bleeding and weak, Lawson rides up, then falls to the ground. Eagerly Magua dismounts with menacing tomahawk. Fierce battle, men rolling and twisting, Priscilla watching in horror. They fall into creek. Magua leaps upon weakened Sheriff and tries to drown him, but Sheriff frees himself.

Too weak to resist further, Sheriff collapses in water. With yell of triumph Magua raises tomahawk to strike. Suddenly the crack of a rifle breaks the stillness. Magua falls into the water. Priscilla, smoking rifle in her hands, dismounts and rushes to Sheriff. She drags him from creek. Weakened but defiant, Sheriff throws arms around her. They rise and stagger away. In the water Magua lies dead.

Back in Sin City church siege goes on. Whites slowly gain upper hand. Launch counter attack. Hand to hand combat. Many Indians retreat. Others captured by townsfolk. A dozen savages being led to city jail. In the distance come Priscilla and Sheriff Lawson. Strapped across their horse is body of dead Magua. Great cheer from townsfolk. Priscilla runs into father's arms.

Epilogue. Bright Sunday morning. Songfest comes from church. Inside Priscilla leads choir in 'Oh Gentle Jesus.' Church packed with townsfolk listening reverently. In back pews, segregated from others, are a dozen captive Indians, penitent, heads bowed. Sheriff comes to Priscilla's side. She looks up adoringly. Fade out.

So there it was, the whole dirty business. My screenplay, without a line of my work in it, in fact an altogether different story, impossible for me to have concocted. I laughed. It was a joke. Somebody was playing around. It was impossible. I went into the house and sat there smoking cigarettes, suddenly aware of the falling rain, the sweet sound of it on the shingle roof, the sweet smell of it coming through the front door. No question about it, Edgington was right. My only course was to have my name removed from the title. I picked up the telephone and dialled Cyril Korn.

'Yeah?' he barked.

'Hello, Korn. This is me. Have you read the story?'

'I liked it.'

'You're crazy.'

'It's a great western.'

'Take my name off.'

'What?'

'Remove my name from this monstrosity. You hear me?
I want no part of it.'

There was a long silence before Korn spoke again. Then
he said:

'Suit yourself, kid. This is good news for Velda. She'll get
a solo credit now.'

'She can have it.' I hung up.

The rain came down in sheets, whipping the leaves from
the eucalyptus trees, digging little rivers across the yard and
into the gutter. I drank a glass of wine. Edgington stepped out
of the kitchen. He had heard my conversation with Korn.

'You did right,' he said. 'It was self preservation. You
had no choice. If you'd listened to me this wouldn't have
happened.'

'What do you mean?'

'You should have joined the Guild. I've been telling you
for three months.'

The cold rainy wind swept in through the front door,
chilling the room. Edgington went to the fireplace and lit
the gas logs. He took a tobacco sack from his pocket.

'Here,' he said, tossing it to me.

It was marijuana. There were cigarette papers in the sack.
I had smoked marijuana only once before, in Boulder, and
it made me sick. It was time to get sick again. I rolled a
cigarette. We sat looking at one another, drawing down the
weed into our lungs. Edgington laughed. I laughed too.

'You're a rotten no-good sonofabitchin English limey
toad,' I said.

He nodded agreement. 'And you, sir, are a miserable, disagreeable dago dog.'

We lapsed into silence, smoking the grass. I picked up the manuscript.

'Let's do something to it,' I said.

'Let's burn it.'

I took it to the fireplace and dropped it on the flames. The pot was taking over. I took off my shirt.

'Let's be Indians,' I said. 'Let's burn her at the stake.'

'Great,' Edington said, pulling off his shirt.

'Let's take off our pants,' I said. We laughed and kicked off our pants. In a moment we were naked, dancing in a circle, making what we thought were Indian cries. From the clouds came a clap of thunder. We laughed and rolled on the floor. Edgington had a beer. I drank a glass of wine. The downpour was earshattering. I rushed out and we held hands and danced round and round laughing. I ran into the house, sipped on my wine and ran outside again. Edgington rushed in, took a swig of his beer, and joined me in the rain. We lay on the grass, rolling in the rain, shouting at the thunder. A woman's voice pierced the storm. It was from next door.

'Shame on you, Frank Edgington,' she screamed. 'Put on some clothes before I call the police.'

Frank got to his feet and shoved his bare bottom toward her.

'That for you, Martha!'

We ran into the house. Standing before the fireplace, dripping wet, we watched the sparks from Velda's screenplay dancing up the chimney. We looked at one another and smiled. Then we performed a fitting climax to the whole crazy ritual. We pissed on the fire.

Now a curious thing happened. I looked at Edgington's sopping hair and rain-soaked body and I did not like him. I did not like him at all. There was something obscene about our nakedness, and the burning screenplay, and the floor wet from rain, and our bodies shivering in the cold, and the insolent smile from Edgington's lips, and I recoiled from him, and blamed him for everything. After all, hadn't he sent me to Cyril Korn, and hadn't Cyril Korn brought me together with Velda van der Zee, and hadn't Edgington sneered and scoffed all the weeks that I had been writing the screenplay? I no longer liked this man. He disgusted me. Similar thoughts must have boiled up in his brain for I noticed the hostile sharpness of his glance. We did not speak. We stood there hating one another. We were on the verge of fighting. I picked up my clothes, walked into the bedroom and slammed the door.

Chapter Fifteen

After that it was a feud. When he was at work in the studio I loafed about, drinking wine and playing the radio. Day after day the rain beat down. I sat at my desk in the bedroom and tried to write. Nothing came. It was the house, Edgington's house. I had to get away from him. Whenever he returned from the studio I pretended to be busy at the desk pecking at the typewriter. He stayed only a short while, then he was gone again. One day I found an old *New Yorker* in a stack of magazines. It contained a story Edgington had written. I tore it up. I began going out, getting into my car and driving off in the rain. The storm was exasperating. The streets were like rivers. Manhole covers popped from storm drains. Trees fell. Wilshire was a barricade of sandbags. The streets were deserted. I drove into Hollywood and sat in a saloon on Wilcox, drinking wine and playing the pinball games. Sometimes I parked at Musso-Frank's and sloshed through the rain to the restaurant. I knew no one. I ate alone and felt my hatred for the town. I went next door to Stanley Rose's bookshop. Nobody knew me. I hung around like a bird seeking crumbs. I missed Mrs Brownell and Abe Marx and Du Mont. My memory of Jennifer Lovelace almost broke my heart. Knowing those few had made me feel as if I knew thousands in the city.

I drove to Bunker Hill and parked in front of the hotel, but I could not bring myself to go inside. Suddenly I had a dream, a beautiful dream of a novel. It was about Helen Brownell and myself. I could taste it. I could embrace it. All at once the self pity drained from me. There was life still, there was a typewriter and paper and eyes to see them, and thoughts to keep them alive. I sat in my car at the top of Bunker Hill in the rain and the dream enfolded me, and I knew what I would do. I would go to Terminal Island and find myself a fisherman's shack on the sandy beach and sit there and write a novel about Helen Brownell and myself. I would spend months in that shack, piling up the pages while I smoked a Meerschaum pipe and became a writer once more in the world.

I hoped to pack my stuff and get out of there before Edgington returned, but as I drove up to his bungalow I saw his car in the driveway. I got out and ran through the rain to the house. Frank lay on the couch reading a book. He said 'Hi.' I walked past him into my room and began to pack. After a while he arose and stood in the bedroom door with a magazine in his hand.

'I bring you good tidings of great joy,' he smiled, holding out the magazine. It was a copy of *Daily Variety*. I spread it open and saw red pencil markings around a front page story. It read:

Velda van der Zee, who screenplayed *Sin City* for Liberty Films, will also direct opus, according to producer Jack Arthur. Film casting will terminate this week and shooting will commence in Arizona.

I was in shock, but hid it from Edgington, and tossed him the magazine. 'This makes you very happy, doesn't it?' I said. He smiled and shrugged.

'C'est la vie.'

I went back to my packing, filled a suitcase and carried it out to the car, where the rest of my things – typewriter, books, clothing – were piled up in the back seat. Now that I was ready to leave for the last time there was one matter not concluded. I stood beside the car and gathered resolve. I would probably never encounter Edgington again. How could I impress upon him the memory of this departure on this rainy day? At last I resolved the matter and walked back to the house. He was on the couch.

'I'm leaving now,' I said.

He stood up and offered his hand. 'Good luck, dago.'

I hit him in the face and knocked him down on the couch. He sat there nursing a nosebleed. I walked back to the car and drove away. I shouldn't have struck Edgington. He had been hospitable and friendly and generous and kind. But I couldn't bear his arrogance. He was too successful for me. He had it coming. I had no regrets. That was life. I was sorry for his nosebleed, but he deserved it. As for Velda van der Zee, fuck her. What was another director? The town was crawling with them.

Chapter Sixteen

I drove to Avalon Boulevard and south to Wilmington. It was almost sunset as I passed over the bridge onto the big sandbar known as Terminal Island. The rain had washed the sand from the road and I drove on pavement to the little fishing settlement a mile or so from the canneries. There were six rustic bungalows, all in a row facing the channel waters a hundred yards down the beach. None of the bungalows appeared to be occupied. I drove slowly past them. Each showed a 'For Rent' sign on the front porch. Then I noticed a light in the last house. Exactly like the others, the house was dark green and rainsoaked. The light shone through the open front door. I pulled to a stop and ran through the rain to the porch.

In ten minutes I had rented one of the cottages and moved in. It was the center cottage, combination bedroom, living room, and a kitchen and bath. Twenty-five dollars a month. I did some quick calculations and realized that I had enough money to live there for ten years. I had it made.

The place was paradise, the South Pacific, Bora Bora. I could hear the sea. It came whispering, saying shshsh, for it was always low tide, the island protected by a breakwater. The nights were wondrous. I lay on my small cot and felt the memory of Velda van der Zee slipping from me. In a few days it had vanished. I listened to the sea and felt my heart restored. Sometimes I heard the bark of seals. I stood in the door and watched them in the shallow water, three or four big fellows playing in the soft tide, barking as if to laugh. The city was far away. I had no thought of writing. My mind was barren as the long shore. I was Robinson Crusoe, lost in a distant world, at peace, breathing good air, salty, satisfying.

When day broke I walked barefoot in the water, in the moist sand, a mile to the cannery settlement, teeming with workers, men and women, emptying the fishing boats, dressing and canning the fish in big corrugated buildings. They were mostly Japanese and Mexican folk from San Pedro. There were two restaurants. The food was good and cheap. Sometimes I walked to the end of the pier, to the ferryboat landing, where the boats took off across the channel to San Pedro. It was twenty-five cents round trip. I felt like a millionaire whenever I plunked down my quarter and sailed for Pedro. I rented a bike and toured the Palos Verdes hills. I found the public library and loaded up on books. Back at my shack I built a fire in the woodstove and sat in the warmth and read Dostoevsky and Flaubert and Dickens and all those famous people. I lacked for nothing. My life was a prayer, a thanksgiving. My loneliness was an enrichment. I found myself bearable, tolerable, even good. Sometimes I wondered what had happened to the writer who had come there. Had I written something and left the place? I touched my typewriter and mused at the action of the keys. It was another life. I had never been here before. I would never leave it.

My landlady was a Japanese woman. She was pregnant.

She had a noble kind of walk, small steps, very quiet, her black hair in braids. I learned from her how to bow. We were always bowing. Sometimes we walked on the beach too. We stopped, folded our hands and bowed. Then she went her way and I went mine. One day I found a rowboat flopping along the shore. I got in and rowed away, doing poorly, for I could not manage the oars. But I learned how, and pulled the skiff all the way across the channel to the rocks on the San Pedro side. I bought fishing equipment and bait, and rowed out a hundred yards beyond my house and caught corbina and mackerel, and once a halibut. I brought them home and cooked them and they were ghastly, and I threw them out upon the sand, and watchful seagulls swooped down and carried them away. One day I said, I must write something. I wrote a letter to my mother, but I could not date the letter. I had no memory of time. I went to see the Japanese lady and asked her the date of the month.

'January fourth,' she said.

I smiled. I had been there two months, and thought it no more than two weeks.

Chapter Seventeen

One afternoon as I dozed, I heard a car outside. I went to the door and watched a long red Marmon touring car pull up to the house next door. The car had a royal insignia painted on the hood – a crown with crouching lions in red and gold. Beneath was the inscription: Duke of Sardinia. The driver of the car shut off the engine and stepped down. He was short and powerful, his black hair in a crew cut. He was so muscular he seemed made of rubber, his arms like red sewer pipe, his legs so thick a space separated them. He saw me and smiled.

'How you say?' he asked.

'Fine, fine. How you?'

'Purty good. You live here?'

'Yep.'

'We neighbors.' He crossed to me and shook my hand. I nodded at his Marmon.

'Duke of Sardinia, what's that mean?'

'I am son of the prince of Sardinia. Also champion of the world.'

'You a weight lifter?'

'Rassler. World champion. I come here to train.'

He moved to the wagon hitched to the back of the car. It was a two-wheeled vehicle with enormous spokes, a big cart.

The bed of the vehicle was piled with gym mats, weight-lifting paraphernalia, and sports equipment. He began unloading the cart.

'Who you?' he asked.

I told him.

'Italiano?'

'Sure.'

He smiled. 'That's good.'

I watched him unload the cart for a while. Then I went inside. It had been weeks since I sat down before the typewriter. I began a letter to my mother. After a while I felt a pair of intense eyes drilling the back of my neck. I turned. The Duke stood in the doorway watching me.

'Come in,' I said.

He entered and carefully inspected the room, the walls, the sink, and finally the typewriter.

'Write some more,' he said, gesturing. 'Don't stop.' He sat across from me and I pecked away at the letter.

'What you write?' he asked.

'Stories. Movies. Sometimes poetry.'

'You make money?'

I laughed. 'Naturally. Big money.'

He grinned doubtfully and stood up. 'I go now. Time to work out.'

Half an hour later I heard the cluck and clatter of cartwheels as the Duke of Sardinia pulled the empty cart out upon the beach. He was in wrestler's tights and barefooted, hitched to the tongue of the cart by a strap about his waist and another strap from his forehead down to the front of the cart. He pulled the cart without effort, the big wheels crunching in the soft sand. After he had gone a few yards he snatched a shovel from the cart and began filling the vehicle with sand. I walked out and watched him. Sweat was popping from his back and down his neck. He worked furiously.

'What are you doing?' I asked.

'Workout,' he panted, continuing to shovel. It wasn't long before the cart was full. He threw the shovel atop the load, adjusted the harness around his waist, fixed the strap about his forehead, grunted mightily and began to pull. The wheels dug into the sand, but there was no progress. He struggled, his feet gave way, he fell, he struggled and tried again. I pitied him. I leaped to help him, butting my shoulder against the back of the cart. It began to move. The Duke turned in shock and saw me. Enraged, he grabbed me under the armpits and threw me across the sand. I landed on my back with a thud that took my breath away.

'No,' he said, shaking his fist. 'Go away. I train myself.'

I sat there gasping, watching him get into his harness and try again. The Duke of Sardinia! He had to be crazy. I turned my back and went into the house. An hour later I stepped out on the porch and saw him far down the beach. He seemed barely to move, like a distant turtle. It was two hours before he pulled the cart up to his house. His body was awash with sweat. Sand clung to the sweat, and he looked frosted, and very tired. I watched him trot to the edge of the water, then fling himself into the depths. He played in the water like a short, stumpy fish. It was dark when he dragged himself out and came back to his porch. I watched him towel off.

'You like spaghett'?' he asked.

'Yeah.'

'I fix.'

* * *

Next day he heard my typewriter and came inside again. He sat there watching me rattle the keys.

'What you write now?'

'Letter.'

'You write poetry?'

'Any time.'

'How much for one poetry?'

I looked at him. I really didn't like him very much. He had handled me badly the day before. And there was this insolent smile, and his preposterous title. He was stupid and I would use it against him.

'Ten dollars,' I said. 'Ten dollars for ten lines. What do you want me to write about?'

'I have woman in Lompoc. She like poetry.'

'Love?' I said.

'Yeah.'

I turned to the typewriter, wrenched myself into a poetic mood, and began to peck away:

O paramour of New Hebrides
Beseech me not to deride thy trust.
Love's a strophe amid the bloom of lost heavens.
Bring me the weal and woe of scattered dreams.
My heart lusts for fin de siècle,
That vision of beleaguered days.
Want not, oh love! Look to the bastions!
Flee the scoundrel, grant mercy only to love,
And when the bounty is sated in reparation
Believe what is in my heart.

I cleared my throat and read it to the Duke.

'She'sa beautiful,' he said. 'I take. Give me pencil.'

I handed him a pencil. He spread out the page of poetry and signed it below the bottom line. It read: 'Mario, Duke of Sardinia.'

'You have envelope?' he asked.

I took one from the desk and rolled it into the typewriter. 'Send to Jenny Palladino, 121 Celery Avenue, Lompoc.'

I typed it out and he went away.

At supper time he returned with a tureen of cooked white spaghetti. I rolled a forkful of the pasta and put it in my mouth. It was terrifying – a sauce of garlic, onions, and hot peppers. It simply would not go down. I leaped for a bottle of wine. The Duke laughed.

'Make you strong,' he said, 'be a man.'

But I couldn't eat it. He took the plate from me and ate methodically, down to the last white strand. I poured us glasses of wine, and lit a cigarette.

'How about some more poetry?'

He shrugged. 'One more – maybe.'

I turned to my typewriter and wrote effortlessly, ten lines. The Duke watched with folded arms.

'Want to hear it?' I asked.

'Sure – I listen.'

I read:

O tumbrels in the night past the lugubrious sea,
Mute birds ride they salt-soaked wheels.
Heaviness brings the clouds down to earth,
Seeking the tracks of the wheels.
Gulls cry, fish leap, the moon appears.
Where are the children?

What happened to the children?
My love is away, and the children are gone.
A dark boat passes on the horizon.
What has happened here?

The Duke lifted the poem from my hand and curled his lip dubiously.

'You don't like it?' I asked.

'I give you seven dollars.'

I snatched the poem from his hand. 'No deal. It's a good poem. One of my best. Don't chisel me. If you don't like it, say so.'

He sighed. 'Putum in the mailbox.' He meant the envelope.

He dug a roll of bills from his pocket and peeled off a ten spot. I thanked him for it and put it away. Turning to the typewriter I said:

'Now I'm going to give you a little bonus, Duke. Something you'll really appreciate.' I began to type out my favorite sonnet from Rupert Brooke, *The Hill*:

Breathless, we flung us on the windy hill,
Laughed in the sun, and kissed the lovely grass.
You said, 'Through glory and ecstasy we pass;
Wind, sun, and earth remain, the birds sing still,
When we are old, are old . . .' 'And when we die
All's over that is ours; and life burns on
Through other lovers, other lips,' said I,
'Heart of my heart, our heaven is now, is won!'
'We are Earth's best, that learnt her lesson here.
Life is our cry. We have kept the faith!' we said;

'We shall go down with unreluctant tread
Rose-crowned into the darkness! . . .' Proud we were,
And laughed, that had such brave true things to say.
And then you suddenly cried, and turned away.

As I finished reading it, his mouth was curled in annoyance,
and he snatched the paper from my hand, studying it, glaring
at it, half crumpled in his fist.

'Steenk!' he exclaimed, crushing the page into a ball, and
throwing it on the floor. He was a very short man, but as
he got to his feet he took on the enormity of a great turtle.
Suddenly his hands were under my armpits and I was lifted
toward the ceiling, and shaken violently. His livid face and
smoldering dark eyes looked up at me.

'Nobody cheat Duke of Sardinia. *Capeesh?*' His fingers
opened and I dropped heavily into my chair. As he left, the
crushed ball of paper lay in his way. He gave it a violent kick
and walked out.

Chapter Eighteen

Every day the Duke pulled his wagon of sand a mile up the beach to the cannery and back. One afternoon I timed him. It took two hours. He always returned in the same state of exhaustion, falling flat on his face in the sand. I wanted to be friends. I smiled, said 'Hi,' but he was still offended, until one afternoon, sweat pouring from him, he said:

'Tomorrow I fight. Olympic Auditorium. You come.' I was startled, about to say something, but he grabbed my jaw. 'Tomorrow! Understand?'

I shook my head. 'Who you fighting, Duke?'

'Animal,' he said. 'Name of Richard Lionheart.'

'Is he good?'

'He'sa good. I kill him anyway.'

He trudged toward the water and dove in, happy as a porpoise. I had no desire to go to his wrestling match. The more I thought of it the more I resented him, but there was a simple way out of the matter. I would get into my car and drive into Wilmington and go to a movie. He came dripping out of the water and towelled himself on the porch.

'We take my car tomorrow,' he said. 'Leave six o'clock. Be ready.' He went into his house.

I didn't want any part of his goddamned fight, and I resolved not to go. All that day I sat about nurturing my resolve not to go with him, and by bedtime I had worked myself into such a frenzied protest that sleep was impossible. All night I rolled and tossed. At two in the morning I could stand it no more, and I got up and dressed quietly. On tiptoe I walked to the door and went outside, careful not to produce a loud squeal in the screendoor. Quietly I crossed to my car and slipped behind the wheel. As I turned the starter key a hand clutched me by the throat. There stood the Duke.

'Where you go?' he asked.

'To get a candy bar,' I improvised.

'Too late for candy bar,' he said. 'Go to bed.'

I got out of the car and walked back to the house. He followed me like a tireless cop. I slammed the front door and locked it. I was so mad I wanted to kill him. I threw open the front door and yelled at him:

'Fuck you, you no good peasant wop! I hate your guts! I'm not coming to your fight tomorrow – not even to see your head knocked off! You're scum! You're a fake and a farce and a scum! You know how dumb you are? You're so dumb you didn't even like a Rupert Brooke poem. I fooled you, you ignoramus. Pure Brooke, and you didn't like it!'

I slammed the door, locked it, and went to bed.

Next morning I found him sitting on my front porch. He stared at me with contrite eyes.

'You mad?' he asked.

'No.'

'You are my friend. I like you.'

'I like you too.'

'I go alone to fight.'

'Is it so important?'

'The fans don't like me. I need someone in my corner.'

I sighed. 'Okay, Duke. I'll go with you.'

He crossed to me and put his hand over the back of my neck and shook me gently. '*Grazie*,' he smiled.

The papers said the wrestling matches that Thursday night attracted five thousand people. The Duke of Sardinia was right – everyone in the place with the exception of myself hated him. From the moment we got out of his car in the parking lot and walked toward the Olympic Auditorium, he gathered an increasingly hostile crowd. They were Mexicans, blacks, and gringos, heckling him, throwing things at him, calling him obscene names. I walked beside him and felt the breaking waves of hate.

As we entered a side door reserved for fighters, a huge black man loomed before us and flung a lemon pie in the Duke's face. It did not shame the Duke at all. Instead he charged like a terrier, throwing a scissors hold around the black man's legs, and toppling him. Then the Duke sat on him and smeared the lemon pie from his own face to that of the black man. Instantly a crowd boiled up, tearing the two men apart. The police arrived, and whisked the Duke down the hall to the dressing room. The Duke was invigorated now, full of fight, ready for Richard Lionheart.

At fight time I followed my gladiator into the arena and down the aisle to the ring. The hatred he generated entered my bones. I could not understand why the crowd disliked him so. Still, he need not have sneered so blatantly, or gestured back so obscenely. A woman leaped from her seat and slapped him in the face. The Duke sneered and spat at her. Several ushers gathered below ringside and protected him as he climbed into the ring. He walked about, shaking his fist, the crowd shrieked in rage, and again the onslaught of debris flung at him. The referee entered the ring and asked him to sit down. The duke did so, and the scene quieted.

After a moment or two a roar of approval rose from the throats of the crowd. There were whistles and cheers as Richard Lionheart appeared. He was garbed in a white silk robe. His shoes were a soft blue, and his lovely blond hair, carefully coiffured, hung down to his shoulders. He was beautiful, and the crowd adored him. He removed his white robe and revealed powder blue trunks. He bowed grandly to one and all. Then, quite ostentatiously, he knelt in the center of the ring, made the sign of the cross, bowed his head, closed his eyes, and prayed. Suddenly the Duke leaped from his corner and kicked out with both feet, knocking Richard flat on the canvas. The crowd was like a pack of lions. Things were hurled – things like chairs and bottles, fruit and tomatoes, and now I knew why everybody hated this man. He was the enemy.

The drama was clear. The Duke could not win in this ring. He would dish out a lot of punishment, for he was the devil, but Richard Lionheart, blessed with purity, would conquer him in the end. It was what the crowd came to see and paid its money for.

Chapter Nineteen

The fight began with the two wrestlers facing one another in the center of the ring. The Duke was five feet two and weighed 235. Richard Lionheart was six feet eight and weighed 235. They moved about, sparring for a grip. Quickly, the Duke slipped between Lionheart's legs and grasped the big man's flowing coiffure. He went down like a ton of coal. The Duke leaped upon him, and managed a scissor hold around his neck. Lionheart kicked helplessly, his face turning blue. The crowd was on its feet, shrieking in rage. A woman climbed through the ropes and smacked the Duke in the face several times with her purse. The crowd cheered. Two other women scrambled into the ring, removed their shoes, and delivered a terrible pasting to the rugged Italiano, forcing him to break his scissor hold on Lionheart's neck.

The referee cleared the ring and the two wrestlers confronted one another again. This time Lionheart got the advantage, hoisting the Duke above his head and whirling him round and round, then hurling him violently to the canvas. The crowd shrieked with joy. The Duke lay still, seemingly unconscious. Lionheart picked him up, carried him to the edge of the ring and dropped him over the ropes and into the laps of three women. He seemed senseless, motionless. The women dumped him on the floor and stomped him. He rolled away from them, staggered to his feet, and climbed painfully back into the ring, his face covered with blood.

The referee blew his whistle and helped the Duke into his corner. A doctor was called. He wiped the blood away, pronounced the Duke in good shape, and ordered the fight to continue. The Duke lumbered to his feet, but so stunned was he that he wandered about the ring in a daze. From across the ring Lionheart took dead aim and butted the Duke in the stomach. Down went the Duke again. Lionheart hurled himself on the prone body, seized the Duke's foot and bent it backward in a frightening toehold. The crowd, fascinated, seemed to croon with pleasure. The referee bent down to determine if the Duke's shoulders had touched the canvas. The triumphant Lionheart, still bending the Duke's foot deep into the small of his back, waved at the crowd, and the crowd waved back. I was not worried about the Duke's defeat so much as his death, for he was motionless, eyes closed, panting heavily.

Suddenly he made his move, and his short thick arms thrust out toward Lionheart's flowing locks. Horror transfixed the crowd. A roar of agony filled the auditorium, as the Duke's hands formed two fistfuls of golden hair, and flung Lionheart aside. Grotesquely, like a crab righting himself, the Duke clung to the hair as he struggled to his feet. Women shrieked. Some wept as he pulled Lionheart about the ring by the hair.

He varied his attack. Now he kicked Lionheart in the jaw. Now he sat on his face and bounced his body mercilessly, laughing at the crowd, jeering at their protests. Then he had Lionheart on his back, his shoulders perilously close to the canvas. Suddenly the beautiful man collapsed, his shoulders touching. The Duke sat on him and tweaked his nose. It was an unbearable insult. The referee pronounced the Duke winner of the first fall.

The crowd could not bear it. All five thousand crowded the ring and a dozen fans descended on the Duke of Sardinia. They would have rent his body to shreds had not the police intervened. He was escorted from the ring and down the aisle to his dressing room.

Lionheart's handlers lifted him to his stool in the corner. His right leg stood out stiffly. A doctor entered the ring and examined him. Lionheart was in tears. The doctor and the referee spoke together quietly. A judge at ringside rang the bell. In the quiet that followed the referee declared the fight a draw, and since Lionheart could not continue, the match was terminated. Bedlam followed. Lionheart's followers poured into the ring and attacked the referee, tearing off his shirt and beating him to the canvas. Police leaped to his rescue as I scurried down the aisle to the rear of the auditorium.

The Duke lay on a rubbing table in his dressing room, a trainer massaging his muscles. He smiled as I walked over.

'Purty good, no?' he asked.

'It was a draw, Duke.'

'Draw?' He leaped off the rubbing table. 'Who say so?'

'The referee.'

The Duke shot out of the dressing room and down the hall. I watched him fight his way through a crowd thronging the aisle. The police were on him instantly, carrying him struggling and screaming back to the dressing room, and shutting the door behind him. I stood in the hall for ten minutes, wondering what to do. Inside the dressing room the Duke screamed and threw furniture.

I walked back to the arena and watched two wrestlers grappling in the ring. It bored me. I walked out to the car and lit a cigarette. For an hour I awaited the Duke's appearance. The final match ended and the crowd poured out to the parking lot. One by one the cars drove away until only the Duke's Marmon remained.

It was an hour later, at midnight, when he strode to the car. He got in beside me and I saw that his face was badly cut, his nose bleeding, his knuckles and his trousers splattered with blood. He reached into the glove compartment and took out a packet of paper towels. He dabbed his broken and bleeding face. I saw a water hydrant at the corner of the building, and told him. He stepped from the car and walked to the hydrant and turned it on. He rubbed his hands into the flowing water, then cupping them he flushed his face. I felt sorrow for him. Someone had beaten him up, and he was angry and stoical and brooding. We went back to the car and got in. I held the roll of paper towels. Every now and then he held out his hand and I gave him a fresh batch of towels. We drove to Avalon and turned right toward the harbor. He drove in silence except that now and then he sobbed.

Chapter Twenty

All the next day the Duke lay in bed, his face to the wall. Whenever I knocked on the door and entered he did not move.

'Are you okay?' I asked.

'Thank you. Go away.'

The next day it was the same. I could not detect any movement in his body at all.

'Can I get you anything?'

'No. Go away.'

'You have to eat something, Duke.'

'Please. Leave me alone.'

The morning of the third day I was asleep when I heard his Marmon revving up outside. I went to the door and watched him back the car out. He saw me and pressed the brakes. I went down to the car. He looked refreshed and smiling.

'Feeling okay?'

'Feeling good. I go to Los Angeles for a fight.'

'Who you fighting?'

'I fight Lionheart again. I go for rematch. This time I kill him.' He shifted gears, waved, and drove off. He was gone all day and far into the night. Around midnight I heard him drive in.

In the morning I heard the big cart being moved, the

wheels clucking in the sand. The Duke was back in business. I watched him harness his body to the wagon and push off in the soft white sand. I went out on the porch and called out:

'When do you fight?'

'Two weeks. Olympic Auditorium.'

'It's bad, Duke. The fans hate you over there.'

He grinned.

'No, no. They love me. Everybody love the Duke of Sardinia.'

I was sitting on the porch reading Melville when the car drove up. It was a model-A Ford, and the driver was a girl. She shut the engine and stepped out. I looked up the beach. The Duke was not in sight. The girl crossed to his front porch and knocked on the door. She was gorgeous in a blue polka dot skirt and a blue sweater. Her ass was from heaven. Her face was exquisitely refined in the frame of her dark hair and sparkling eyes.

'He's not here,' I said. 'He's working out on the beach.'

She looked up and down the sand. 'Which way did he go?'

I nodded. 'He's pulling a big red cart.'

'Thank you,' she said. 'Will he be long?'

'Maybe an hour. The Duke and I are friends. Why don't you sit down and wait?'

She glanced about for a chair.

'I'm sorry,' I said. 'Would you like to come inside?'

'No, thank you.' She leaned against the post and lapsed into silence. I stood up. 'Can I get you something? How about some coffee? I just made it.'

'No thank you.'

'I'm Arturo Bandini.'

She smiled. 'How do you do? I'm Jenny Palladino.'

'From Lompoc,' I smiled.

Startled, she asked, 'How did you know?'

'The Duke mentioned it.' I held open the screendoor. 'Please come in. I make wonderful coffee.'

'No thanks.'

'Don't be afraid. If you're a friend of the Duke's, you're perfectly safe here. Do I look like someone who'd make a pass at the girlfriend of the Duke of Sardinia?'

Her face studied me seriously, then she smiled. 'I guess not.'

'Come in,' I urged. 'Be my guest.'

'Well . . .' she hesitated.

'Please don't worry. I'm deathly afraid of the Duke.'

She entered. I led her to the best chair and she sat down. All at once a sense of frivolity overcame me. There was something disapproving in her eyes and the jut of her lower lip. I had no thought of making a pass. I merely wanted to play, to enter into some sort of game with her. I poured her a cup of coffee and she thanked me and sipped it. She was beautiful and sensuous and wonderfully formed, yet I had no desire for her, only a wish to tumble about with her in the manner of kittens. I dropped to one knee before her, and she quickly pulled her feet up on the chair.

'Oh thou loveliest of the children of Eve,' I intoned, 'sweet are thy eyes, and the wonderment of their arch. Bless you, lovely maiden, in the curvature of your sculptured neck. Seek not to banish me, for I long to bask in the glow of thy wondrous eyes.'

Her lips turned in a frown. 'So you're the one!' she said. 'I knew it wasn't the Duke. It couldn't be.'

I'm not going to hurt her, I said to myself. I'm not going to seduce her. I only want to make her smile.

'Listen, oh love! to the flight of the partridge, winging through the open barn, seeking his love in the fresh-mown hay. Bring her to me, oh wandering birds, suffer her not to flee in fear.'

She jumped to her feet, and pushed me aside. 'Leave me alone,' she said. Then she screamed:

'Duke! Duke!'

She paused to remove her shoes, and then she was off like a terrified deer. In the distance, appearing now, I saw the cumbersome figure of the Duke at the helm of his red wagon. I stood there in terror for a moment. Then I did what had to be done.

I flung my clothes into the suitcases, gathered up my typewriter, and ran to my car, tossing everything into the back seat. I rushed into the house again for another load. On the way out I saw Jenny Palladino confronting the Duke, and gesticulating with both hands. He unharnessed himself and broke into a run toward me. I gathered the books and a raincoat, ran to the car, and started the engine. The Duke was fifty feet away when I shot out of the yard and down the road. Through the rearview mirror I saw him shaking his fist at me and cursing. I got to the highway, and swung the car toward the bridge back to Los Angeles.

Chapter Twenty-one

Like a homing bird I flew to Bunker Hill, to my old hotel, to the kindest woman I had ever known. I parked the car in front of the hotel, pulled out two suitcases, and carried them inside. The lobby was vacant. I stood there a moment, breathing the fragrance of the place, the tender reminiscent scent of Helen Brownell's incense. I looked around lovingly. What solidarity. What permanence. It was as if that lobby would last forever, as if always waiting for me. I crossed to the desk, set down my suitcases, and rang the bell. The door behind the desk opened cautiously and I saw her peering at me uncertainly, as if not quite seeing.

'Hello, Helen,' I smiled.

She kept looking at me. Then she closed the door. I waited a moment. When she did not reappear I rang the bell again. The door opened. She looked at me sternly. I noticed her hair. It was pure white now, white as lamb's wool.

'Helen,' I said, and moved around to her side of the desk. 'Oh, Helen, I'm so glad to see you again.' I put my hands on her shoulders and bent to kiss her.

'Don't,' she said. 'Please don't.'

'I love you.'

She turned her back to me. 'Go away,' she implored. 'I don't want you here. I can't do it any more.'

'Please let me stay. Let me have my old room back.'

'Impossible. It's rented. Please leave.'

'Let's talk awhile,' I coaxed. 'Make me a cup of coffee, please.'

'Why are you so stubborn? Can't you see that I don't want you here?' She spun around and hurried to the door behind the desk. 'Go away, Arturo. Find somebody your own age. I'm not for you. I never was.' She closed the door.

It hurt very much. I sat down on a divan and tried to think it out. How could I entice her back? What could I say to her? Suddenly I was very tired. What had I done to her? Why couldn't we carry on as usual? We had had a little tiff, that was all. Why couldn't we be friends, just talking to one another, sitting on the veranda in the evening, watching the city light up below, and talking like old friends? Why was she cutting me off? I didn't care that she was so much older. I would love her forever. When she was ninety I would still love her, like the woman in Yeats's poem:

> When you are old and grey and full of sleep,
> And nodding by the fire, take down this book,
> And slowly read, and dream of the soft look
> Your eyes had once, and of their shadows deep;
>
> How many loved your moments of glad grace,
> And loved your beauty with love false or true,
> But one man loved the pilgrim soul in you,
> And loved the sorrows of your changing face.

Chapter Twenty-two

I found a room on Temple Street, above a Filipino restaurant. It was two dollars a week without towels, sheets, or pillow cases. I took it, sat on the bed and brooded about my life on the earth. Why was I here? What now? Who did I know? Not even myself. I looked at my hands. They were soft writer's hands, the hands of a writer peasant, not suited for hard work, not equal to making phrases. What could I do? I looked around the room, the wine-stained walls, the carpetless floor, the little window looking out on Figueroa Street. I smelled the cooking from the Filipino restaurant below. Was this the end of Arturo Bandini? Would this be the place where I was to die, on this gray mattress? I could lie here for weeks before anyone discovered me. I got to my knees and prayed:

'What have I done to you, Lord? Why do you punish me? All I ask is the chance to write, to have a friend or two, to cease my running. Bring me peace, oh Lord. Shape me into something worthwhile. Make the typewriter sing. Find the song within me. Be good to me, for I am lonely.'

It seemed to hearten me. I went to the typewriter and sat before it. A gray wall loomed up. I pushed back my chair and walked down into the street. I got into my car and drove around.

* * *

I had trouble sleeping in the little room, even though I bought sheets and blankets. The trouble was, the misery of the day, the fruitlessness of working remained in the room during the night. In the morning it was still there, and I went to the street again. Then I remembered one of Edgington's axioms: 'When stuck, hit the road.' At sunset I wheeled my car out of the parking lot and hit the streets. Hour after hour I drove around. The city was like a tremendous park, from the foothills ot the sea, beautiful in the night, the lamps glowing like white balloons, the streets wide and plentiful and moving off in all directions. It did not matter which way you went, the road always stretched ahead, and you found yourself in strange little towns and neighborhoods, and it was soothing and refreshing, but it did not bring story ideas. Moving with the traffic, I wondered how many like myself took to the road merely to escape the city. Day and night the city teemed with traffic and it was impossible to believe that all those people had any rhyme or reason for driving.

In February Liberty Films released Velda van der Zee's picture, *Sin City*. I caught it at the Wiltern, on Wilshire, the early evening show. I went prepared to loathe it, and I was pleased to find the theater less than half full. I bought a sack of popcorn and found a seat in the loges. I sat there pleased that my name had been scrubbed from the film, and as the lights darkened, I felt very pleased and relieved that my name would not be among the credits. I laughed loudly when Velda's name appeared, and as the picture unreeled and the stagecoach bounded over the terrain, I laughed again loudly. A hand touched my shoulder. I turned to see a woman frowning.

'You're disturbing me,' she said.

'I can't help it,' I answered. 'It's a very funny picture.'

Now the hostile band of Indians appeared, and I guffawed. Several people in the vicinity got up and scattered to different seats.

And so it went. All of my work, all of my thinking, was so remote from the picture, that it was stunning, unbelievable. In only two places did I come upon lines that I might possibly have written, that the director did not delete. The first was in an early scene when the sheriff rode into Sin City at full gallop and brought his horse to a halt at the saloon, shouting 'Whoa!' Now I remembered that line: 'Whoa!' My line. A little further on the sheriff stalked out of the saloon, mounted his horse, and shouted 'Giddyup!' That was my line too: 'Giddyup.' Whoa and giddyup – my fulfillment as a screenwriter.

It was not a good picture, or an exciting picture, or a mature picture, and as it came to an end and the house lights went on, I saw the weary patrons half asleep in their seats, showing no pleasure at all. I was glad. It proved my integrity. I was a better man for having refused the credit, a better writer. Time would prove it. When Velda van der Zee was a forgotten name in tinsel town, the world would still reckon with Arturo Bandini. I walked out into the night, and God, I felt good and refreshed and restored! Whoa and giddyup! Here we go again. I got into my car and took off in the traffic along Wilshire Boulevard, hell bent for my hotel.

I went up to my room and fell on the bed exhausted. I had been deluding myself. There was no pleasure in seeing *Sin City*. I was really not pleased at Velda's failure. In truth I felt sorry for her, for all writers, for the misery of the craft. I lay in that tiny room and it engulfed me like a tomb.

I got up and went down into the street. Half a block away was a Filipino saloon. I sat at the bar and ordered a glass of Filipino wine. The Filipinos around me laughed and played the dart game. I drank more wine. It was sweet and tinged with peppermint, warm in the stomach, tingling. I drank five more glasses, and stood up to leave. I felt nausea, and my stomach seemed to float into my chest. I got out on the sidewalk, leaned against the lamppost and felt the strength ooze from my knees.

Then everything vanished, and I was in a bed somewhere. It was a white room with big windows and it was daylight. There were tubes in my nose and down my throat and I felt the pain of vomiting. A nurse stood at the bedside and watched me gag and writhe until there was no more of it, only the terrible pain in my stomach and throat. The nurse removed the tubes.

'Where am I' I asked.

'Georgia Street Hospital,' she said.

'What's the matter with me?'

'Poison,' she said. 'Your friend is here.'

I looked toward the door. There stood Helen Brownell. She came quietly to the bedside and sat down. I took her hand and began to sob.

'There now,' she soothed. 'Everything's all right.'

'What's the matter with me?' I choked. 'What's going on?'

'Don't you remember?'

'I drank some wine – that's all.'

'You drank too much,' she said. 'You passed out, and the wine made you very ill.'

'Who brought me here?'

'The police ambulance.'

'How did you find out?'

'My address was in your wallet.'

'How long have you been here?'

'Since midnight,' she said.

'Can I leave now?'

The nurse stepped up. 'Not for a while,' she said. 'The doctor has to look at you first.'

Mrs Brownell stood up and squeezed my hand. 'I must go now.'

'I'll see you at the hotel.'

She bit her lip. 'Perhaps you shouldn't.'

'Why not? I love you.'

'Don't say that,' she answered.

'It's true,' I insisted. 'I love you more than anybody in the world. I always have. I always will.'

Without answering, she turned with a wisp of a smile, and walked out of the room. I felt my stomach heaving, and the nurse held my head as I vomited into a basin.

It was late afternoon when the doctor checked me out and permitted me to leave. When I asked about the charges for my stay he answered that they had been paid.

'By whom?' I said.

'Mrs Brownell.'

I got dressed and walked down the hall to the front door, where I took a trolley to Hill Street. At Third I got off and rode the cablecar to the top of Bunker Hill.

Chapter Twenty-three

A man stood behind the desk in the hotel lobby. He was thin and tall with a halo of gray hair. I asked to see Mrs Brownell.

'She ain't here,' he said.

'When are you expecting her?'

'Can't say. She went to San Francisco.'

There was something familiar about him. 'Are you a relative?' I asked.

'I'm her brother,' he said. 'Is your name Bandini?'

'That's right.'

He lifted the desk blotter, and removed an envelope and handed it to me. My name was on it. I tore open the envelope. Inside was a statement from the Georgia Street Hospital, marked paid, a bill for twelve dollars. I looked inside the envelope for an explanation. There was none. The man watched me.

'Did she leave any message beside this?'

'That's all.'

I took out my wallet and paid him the twelve dollars. Without thanking me he put it into the cash drawer. I nodded at the door to Mrs Brownell's apartment, and stared sternly.

'Are you sure she's not in there?'

He pushed the door open and folded his arms. 'See for yourself.'

I shook my head. 'It's not like her to do a thing like this.'

The old man smiled. 'That's what you think, sonny.'

I walked out into the street. The sun was tumbling into the ocean thirty miles west, and the city was in a tumult of radiant sunset colors, shards of clouds gathering on the far horizon, a touch of rain in the air. From beneath Bunker Hill I heard the uproar of the city, the clanging of trolley bells, the roar of cars, the lower depths. Beneath my feet was the Third Street tunnel, the sudden hush of traffic entering, and the roar of traffic emerging.

What am I doing here, I asked. I hate this place, this friendless city. Why was it always thrusting me away like an unwanted orphan? Had I not paid my dues? Had I not worked hard, tried hard? What did it have against me? Was it the incessant sense of my peasantry, the old conviction that somehow I did not belong?

If not Los Angeles, then what? Where could I find welcome, where could I sit among people who loved me and cared for me and took pride in me? Then it came to me. There *was* a place, and there were people who loved me, and I would go to them. So fuck you, Los Angeles, fuck your palm trees, and your highassed women, and your fancy streets, for I am going home, back to Colorado, back to the best damned town in the USA – Boulder, Colorado.

Chapter Twenty-four

I put my car in storage and got aboard a Greyhound bus with two suitcases. The bus pulled out of Los Angeles at seven in the evening of a very hot day. In fact, it was the last hot day I would experience for a month. The interior of the bus was even hotter than the day, the leather seats heaving with heat when one sat down, and the passengers sprawled in exhaustion and discomfort by the time we reached the city limits. They looked as if they had been aboard for days, billows of cigarette smoke filling the air.

When we crossed into Nevada, the first snowflakes began to fall. Through Nevada we drove in the gathering storm, the snow piling up, the bus slowing down in a blinding storm. When we reached Utah and made a stop the snow was above the wheels. We rushed into the depot, drank cups of revolting coffee, and got aboard again. The hours passed, the snow fell with insidious determination, as if to bury us on the plain. In Wyoming snowplows came out of Rock Springs to rescue us, and the journey was slowed to a crawl. By the time we pulled in at the Boulder depot I had to struggle to my feet as I staggered out.

The snow was terrifying, the flakes as big as dollars, wafting slowly toward earth, and lying there, not melting. I stood in front of the bus depot shivering in a light sweater, blinking at my home town. Where the hell was it? The snow played tricks with the scene. I knew there was a bridge half a block away, but now it was invisible. I knew there was a lumberyard across the street, but it had vanished. I shivered, and lit a cigarette, and pounded my feet to keep them warm. Suddenly a figure stood before me. I thought I knew his face, but I wasn't sure until he said:

'What are you doing here?'

That could only be my father.

'I've come home.'

His breath burst like steam.

'You're cold,' he said. 'Where's your overcoat?'

'You're wearing it,' I said. He unbuttoned the heavy sheepskin coat, and peeled it off.

'Put it on,' he said, holding it out for me.

'What about you?'

'Never mind me. Put it on.'

He helped me get into it. He was in shirtsleeves now, the snowflakes banging him.

'Let's go,' he said. We quickly walked away. The overcoat felt warm from the heat of his body. It was all of a piece, a part of my life, like an old chair, or a worn fork, or my mother's shawl, the things of my life, the precious worthless treasured things.

'What'd you come home for?'

'I wanted to. I had to. I got lonesome.'

'You leave your job in the pitchers?'

'For a while – until later, maybe.'

'There's nothing for you here,' my father said, his breath steaming. 'What are you going to do now?'

'I'll think of something,' I said.

'You won't listen to me,' he half groaned. 'You never did listen to your father.'

'I had to do it my own way.'

He cursed. 'And what's it got you?'

The storm heaved and sighed. I looked at Arapahoe Street. The big elms seemed so much bigger in the snow light. The houses huddled like animals in the storm. A car clattered by, its chains clanging. A mile away were the first tall hills of the Rocky Mountains, but the snow hid them away in a white veil. Across the street in the Delaney yard stood old Elsie, their cow, patiently in the storm, watching us pass by.

What a wonderful street! How much of my life I had spent here, under the quiet elms, our house a block away — Christmases and baseball and first communion and Hallowe'en, and kites and sleigh rides, and ballgames and Easter and graduation and all of my life evoked by this wondrous street of old houses, with dim lights in windows, and home at the end of the block.

We reached the house, and there it was, parked in the street, my brother's decrepit Overland touring car, the top down, the inside overflowing with new snow. No matter. It had a life of its own. Once the snow melted, it would start up and merrily chug away. My father and I mounted the porch steps and pounded the snow from our shoes before entering. Opening the door, my father shouted:

'Here he is!'

In the kitchen I saw my mother at the stove, a ladling spoon in her hand. She turned and saw me. With a cry to God, she flung out her arms and sent the ladling spoon flying, and came running toward me.

'I knew it,' she said. 'I've been saying it all day.'

We met and embraced in the dining room, hugging and kissing, as she sobbed and her tears splashed my face. My brother Mario stood aside, embarrassed. He had grown a great deal since I last saw him, a bashful, inarticulate kid of nineteen. My sister Stella slipped into my arms. She was sixteen, very beautiful and very shy, but not ashamed of her tears. Over her shoulder I saw my little brother Tom, a seventh grader at Sacred Heart School. We embraced, and he said:

'You're littler than I thought.'

My mother took me by the hand and led me into the kitchen.

'You think I didn't know?' she said. 'You think I'd go to all this trouble if I didn't know you were coming?' She gestured at the cast iron baking dish on the stove. 'Look!'

It was lasagne, red tomato sauce bubbling in an ocean of pasta.

'How could you know I was coming?' I asked. 'I didn't know myself until the last minute.'

'I prayed. How else?'

My brother Tom took my hand and pulled me into the dining room, and through to the bedroom. In a whisper he asked, 'Did you ever see Hedy Lamarr?'

'All the time,' I said.

'You're a liar.' Then, 'What's she like?'

'Unbelievable. When she walks into a room the whole building shakes.'

'I wrote her a letter. She didn't even answer it.'

'Before I leave you write her again. I'll take it to her house.'

He grinned, and then, 'You're a liar.'

I put my hand over my heart. 'I swear to God.'

We were poor, but as always we ate very well, the table overflowing with salad and homemade bread and lasagne, and my father's dandelion wine. When we were finished it was time to talk, to question the prodigal son. They did not regard me as a failure. I was a hero, a conqueror back from distant battlefields. They even gave me a sense of my importance in the world.

'Now then,' my father said, finishing his wine, 'what'd you come home for?'

'To see my family, got any objections?'

He looked right at me. 'Got any money?'

'Some.'

'We need it. Give it to your mother.'

I pulled out my wallet and removed two one-hundred-dollar bills, and pushed them toward my mother. She began to cry.

'It's too much,' she said.

My father flared. 'Shut up and take it.'

My mother pushed the bills into her apron pocket.

'Arturo,' Stella said, 'do you know Clark Gable?'

'Very well – a good friend of mine.'

'Is he really that nice? Is he stuck up?'

'He's as shy as a bird.'

My father filled his glass again. 'How about Tom Mix? You ever see him?'

'At the studio every day. Him and Tony.'

My father smiled, remembering. 'Tony. Great horse.'

My brother Tom looked sheepish and asked, 'How tall is Hedy Lamarr?'

'A lot taller than you.'

'Smart ass,' Tom said.

My father whacked the table. 'Don't use that kind of language in this house.' There was a respectful silence. Then Mario spoke:

'You ever run into James Cagney?'

'Frequently.'

'What kind of a car does he drive?'

'Duesenberg.'

'Figures,' Mario said.

Chapter Twenty-five

Home was a good place. I slept well. I ate well. The first few days I lounged about the house, showing off my wardrobe. The stuff in my bulging suitcases fascinated my mother – my suits, my sportscoats, my slacks. She sewed buttons and darned socks, pressed and cleaned my suits, and hung them up. With every change of wardrobe my mother was awed. She touched the fabrics, she gloated over me. I was two characters. When I wore corduroys and a T-shirt I was her boy, but when I put on my splendidly draped suits I was a prince.

'God has been good to me,' she would sigh. 'You look so important.'

As time passed I tired of loafing about the house, and began to spend my days in town, visiting old haunts: Benny's poolhall on Pearl Street, the bowling alley on Walnut. I went to the library and found again the books that had changed my life: Sherwood Anderson, Jack London, Knut Hamsun, Dostoevsky, D'Annunzio, Pirandello, Flaubert, de Maupassant. The welcome they gave me was much warmer than the cold curiosity of old friends I met in the town.

One day I ran into Joe Kelly, the reporter for the *Boulder Times*. We shook hands and were glad to see one another. In high school Kelly and I used to hitchhike to Denver to watch Western League baseball. Joe took me to the office of the *Times*, had my picture taken, and interviewed me. It was not a flattering interview, nor was it unkind, but there was a challenging quality to it, as if many questions about myself and my work needed more answers. My father bought twenty-five copies of the interview when it appeared, and everyone in the family sat at the dining-room table reading his copy.

The next day Agnes Lawson telephoned. We were old members of the Red Pencil, a literary society sponsored by the church. I had not seen her in two years. She was a haughty, spoiled girl with wealthy parents, and when she invited me to a party at her house, my first impulse was to refuse. The same nasal twang was in her voice, the same snobbish reserve.

'A lot of Red Pencil alumni are coming,' she said. 'We want to see you now that you're famous.'

'I'll try to make it,' I said. 'I'm supposed to go to another party, but I can drop in at your place for a while.'

The invitation thrilled my mother, for Agnes was the daughter of one of Boulder's leading citizens, as well as owner of its best known clothing store.

The next night I dressed carefully for Agnes's party. Gray tweed suit, red necktie, gray shirt. My mother beamed.

'What an honor!' she said. 'Isn't it nice, going into those lovely houses! I'm so proud of you.'

My brother Mario swept the snow from his Overland, covered the front seat with a tarp, and drove me to the three-story Lawson house on University Hill. I looked at that house with unpleasant memories, a house that had been forbidden before. I remembered many summers when Agnes threw parties that always excluded me, nor could I forget the large clothing bill my family owed the Lawson store. Mr Lawson never spoke of the bill, but he always managed a look of annoyance whenever he saw me.

I rang the doorbell, and Agnes answered. Standing beside her, his arm around her waist, was Biff Newhouse, a star fullback on the Colorado University football team. Biff sported a letterman's sweater, with a gold 'C' across his chest. Agnes held out her hand and said 'Hi.'

'Hello, Agnes.'

She was a small girl, with bobbed hair, fashionably dressed in a black frock.

'This is Biff Newhouse.'

Biff and I shook hands. His grip was unnecessarily harsh.

'What do you say?' he grinned.

'Hello, Biff,' I said.

There were a dozen people gathered in the living room. I had known all of them through grade school and high school. They looked at me without expression, as if to deny me even the slightest hint of warmth or reunion. Only Joe Kelly stepped up and shook my hand.

'I liked what you wrote about me,' I said.

'Good. I was afraid you wouldn't.'

'What about a drink?' Agnes said.

'Fine. I'll have a Scotch and soda.'

She moved to the bar and mixed the drink. A tall girl wearing glasses walked up.

'I hear you're a screenwriter,' she said.

'Best in Hollywood.'

She smiled faintly. 'I knew you'd say something like that. Are you still writing that miserable poetry?'

'What's miserable about it? I sold one to the *New Yorker*.'

Agnes brought my drink. I gulped it down quickly. We sat on divans and big chairs in front of the fireplace. Agnes mixed another drink for me.

'How are things in tinsel town?' she asked.

'Fabulous,' I said. 'You should come out some time.'

She laughed. 'Me in Hollywood? That's funny.'

'What kinda money you screenwriters make?' Biff asked.

'I started modestly,' I said. 'Three hundred a week. My current salary is a thousand a week.'

Biff smiled doubtfully. 'Bullshit,' he said.

'Maybe bullshit to you, but it's good money to me.'

'Do you know Joel McCrea?' the tall poetess asked.

'I not only know him, he happens to be one of my best friends.'

Agnes gave me another drink, and I sipped it.

'How about Ginger Rogers?' Agnes coaxed. 'Tell us about Ginger Rogers, Arturo.'

I looked into her mocking eyes.

'Ginger Rogers is a superior person. She has charm and beauty and talent. I regard her as one of the great artists of our time. However, my favorite star is Norma Shearer. Her beauty is breathtaking. Her eyes are marvellous, and she has a figure that's ravishing. I know lots of actresses with ravishing figures – Bette Davis, Hedy Lamarr, Claudette Colbert, Jean Harlow, Katharine Hepburn, Carole Lombard, Maureen O'Sullivan, Myrna Loy, Janet Gaynor, Alice Faye, Irene Dunne, Mary Astor, Gloria Swanson, Margaret Lindsay, Dolores del Rio. I know them all. They're part of my life. I've dined with them, danced with them, made love with them, and I'll tell you this – I never disappointed any of them. You go among them, ask them questions about Arturo Bandini, ask them if they were ever turned away in disappointment.'

I paused and drained off another Scotch highball. Then I stood up.

'What's the matter with you people?' I crossed to the bar and leaned against it. 'How can you live such dull lives? Is there no romance? Is there no beauty among you?' I looked straight at Biff Newhouse. 'Can't you think of anything else but football? Not me, buster. I live a different life. And without your fucking snow. I play in the sun. I play golf with Bing Crosby and Warner Baxter and Edmund Lowe. I play tennis with Nils Asther and George Brent and William Powell and Pat O'Brien and Paul Muni. I play by day, I fuck in the twilight, and I work by night. I swim with Johnny Weismuller and Esther Williams and Buster Crabbe. Everybody loves me. Understand? Everybody.'

I swung around in a grand gesture, and my heels slipped out from under me, and I sat on the floor, my glass splattering. I heard their laughter, and tried to get to my feet, but I slipped again and fell. Biff Newhouse lifted me to a standing position. Suddenly I loathed him, and swung at him, and hit him in the jaw. His eyes boiled in fury and he let me have it – one short punch, squarely in the nose, and I was down on the floor again, blood coursing from my nose, down my chest, on to my pants, the sleeve of my coat. In a daze I saw the others swirling, walking around me, walking out of the house. Then Joe Kelly hoisted me to my feet, pushed a bar towel under my nose and steadied me as I wiped the blood away.

'I'll take you home,' he said. He held me up as we walked outside and down the porch steps. Cars were starting up and leaving. Joe helped me to his Ford. The blood was still pouring. I pressed the towel into my nose as we drove away.

We got to my house and I stepped out, careful not to slam the car door. Kelly drove off and I stopped to gather snow in my two hands and press it against my nose until the bleeding stopped. Quietly I walked through the snow to my brother's window and tapped on the glass. He came to the side door. Choking in alarm, he looked at my bloody face.

'What happened?' he said.

'I fell down and cracked my nose. Be quiet. I don't want Mama to hear. Is the old man home?'

'He's in bed.'

'I'm leaving here,' I whispered. 'I'm getting out – tonight, right now. Be quiet.'

We entered the side door. I opened my suitcases on the bed and quietly transferred my clothes from the dresser and closet to the luggage. Mario dressed and watched me wash the blood from my face and hands. I changed clothes, and bundled my bloodstained suit and shirt and put them in the suitcase.

'Let's go,' I whispered. He hefted one suitcase and I took the other. Without a sound we stepped out into the snow, and walked to his old car. Mario's voice trembled.

'What'll I tell Mama?' he asked.

'Nothing,' I said.

'Are you sure you fell down?' he asked. 'Are you sure somebody didn't pop you?'

'Absolutely.'

We threw the luggage into the car and drove to the bus depot. The Denver bus was parked in front, panting like an animal. I bought a ticket to Los Angeles and climbed aboard. Mario stood beneath my window, looking up at me with tears in his eyes. I rushed out of the bus and stepped down and threw my arms around him.

'Thanks, Mario. I won't forget this.'

He sobbed and put his head on my shoulder. 'Be careful,' he said. 'Don't fight, Arturo.'

'I can take care of myself.'

I turned and got aboard the bus. That was Wednesday night. We drove through snow most of the way and arrived in Los Angeles on a sunburst Saturday morning.

Chapter Twenty-six

So I was back again, back to LA, with two suitcases and seventeen dollars. I liked it, the sweep of blue skies, the sun in my face, the endearing streets, tempting, beckoning, the concrete and cobblestones, soft and comforting as old shoes. I picked up my grips and walked along Fifth Street. Purposefully I walked, wondering why I could almost never bring myself to call her Helen. I had to break the habit. I would walk to the top of Bunker Hill and open my arms to her and say, 'Helen, I love you.'

We would start over again. Maybe we'd buy a little house in Woodland Hills, the Kansas type, with a chickenyard and a dog. Oh, Helen, I've missed you so, and now I know what I want. Maybe she wouldn't like Woodland Hills. Maybe she preferred the hotel. It had aged so well, like an aristocrat, like Helen herself. I would choose a room for writing and we would complete our days together. Oh, Helen. Forgive me for ever leaving you. It will never happen again.

I rode on the trolley to the crest of Bunker Hill, and looked at the hotel in the distance. It was magic, like a castle in a book of fairy tales. I knew she would have me this time. I felt the strength of my years, and I knew I was stronger than she, and that she would melt in my arms. I entered the hotel and lowered my suitcases against the wall. She was not behind the desk. I had to smile as I crossed to the desk and rang the bell. When there was no answer I struck the bell again, harder. The door opened slightly. There stood the man I had seen before, the man who said he was her brother. He did not come forward, and spoke in a whisper.

'Yes?'

'I'm looking for Helen.'

'She's not here,' he said, and closed the door. I walked around the desk and knocked. He opened the door and stood there crying.

'She's gone. She's dead.'

'How?' I said. 'When?'

'A week ago. She died of a stroke.'

I felt myself weakening, as I staggered toward an armchair at the window. I didn't want to cry. Something deep and abiding had caved in, swallowing me up. I felt my chest heaving. The brother came over and stood beside me, crying.

'I'm sorry,' he said.

I got up, hefted my suitcase, and walked out. At the little depot on Angel's Flight I saw on a park bench and let my grief have its way. For two hours I was there, griefstricken and bewildered. I had thought of many things since knowing her, but never her death. For all her years, she nourished a love in me. Now it was gone. Now that she was dead I could think of her no longer. I had sobbed and whimpered and wept until it was all gone, all of it, and as always I found myself alone in the world.

The manager of the Filipino hotel was glad to see me. It was no surprise when he said that my room was unoccupied. It was my kind of room. I deserved it – the smallest, most uninviting room in Los Angeles. I started up the stairs and pushed opened the door to the dreadful hole.

'You forgot something,' the manager said. He stood in the doorway holding my portable typewriter. It startled me, not because it was there, but because I had completely forgotten it. He placed it on the table and I thanked him. Closing the door, I opened a suitcase and took out a copy of Knut Hamsun's *Hunger*. It was a treasured piece, constantly with me since the day I stole it from the Boulder library. I had read it so many times that I could recite it. But it did not matter now. Nothing mattered.

I stretched out on the bed and slept. It was twilight when I awakened and turned on the light. I felt better, no longer tired. I went to the typewriter and sat before it. My thought was to write a sentence, a single perfect sentence. If I could write one good sentence I could write two and if I could write two I could write three, and if I could write three I could write forever. But suppose I failed? Suppose I had lost all of my beautiful talent? Suppose it had burned up in the fire of Biff Newhouse smashing my nose or Helen Brownell dead forever? What would happen to me? Would I go to Abe Marx and become a busboy again? I had seventeen dollars in my wallet. Seventeen dollars and the fear of writing. I sat erect before the typewriter and blew on my fingers. Please God, please Knut Hamsun, don't desert me now. I started to write and I wrote:

'The time has come,' the Walrus said,
    'To talk of many things:
Of shoes – and ships – and sealing wax –
    Of cabbages – and kings –'

I looked at it and wet my lips. It wasn't mine, but what the hell, a man had to start someplace.